Maxim Jakubowski is a London-based novelist and editor. He was born in the UK and educated in France. Following a career in book publishing, he opened the world-famous Murder One bookshop in London. He now writes full-time. He has edited over thirty bestselling erotic anthologies and books on erotic photography, as well as many acclaimed crime collections. His novels include *It's You That I Want to Kiss*, *Because She Thought She Loved Me* and *On Tenderness Express*, all three collected and reprinted in the USA as *Skin in Darkness*. Other books include *Life in the World of Women*, *The State of Montana*, *Kiss Me Sadly*, *Confessions of a Romantic Pornographer*, *I Was Waiting For You* and *Ekaterina and the Night*. In 2006 he published *American Casanova*, a major erotic novel, which he edited and on which fifteen of the top erotic writers in the world collaborated, and his collected erotic short stories as *Fools For Lust*. He compiles two annual acclaimed series for the Mammoth list: *Best New Erotica* and *Best British Crime*. He is a winner of the Anthony and the Karel Awards, a frequent TV and radio broadcaster, a past crime columnist for the *Guardian* newspaper and Literary Director of London's Crime Scene Festival. Over the past years, he has authored under a pen name a series of *Sunday Times* bestselling erotic romance novels which have sold over two million copies and been sold to twenty-two countries, and translated the acclaimed French erotic novel *Monsieur* by Emma Becker. His monthly review column appears at www.lovereading.co.uk.

THE MAMMOTH BOOK OF

Best
New Erotica

Volume 13

Edited by Maxim Jakubowski

ROBINSON

RUNNING PRESS
PHILADELPHIA · LONDON

ROBINSON

First published in Great Britain in 2014 by Robinson

1 3 5 7 9 10 8 6 4 2

A CIP catalogue record for this book is available from the British Library.

ISBN: 978-1-47211-086-2 (paperback)
ISBN: 978-1-47211-623-9 (ebook)

Typeset in Plantin by Hewer Text UK Ltd, Edinburgh
Printed and bound by CPI Group (UK) Ltd, Croydon, CR0 4YY

Robinson
is an imprint of
Constable & Robinson Ltd
100 Victoria Embankment
London EC4Y 0DY

An Hachette UK Company
www.hachette.co.uk

www.constablerobinson.com

First published in the United States in 2014 by Running Press Book Publishers,
A Member of the Perseus Books Group

Books published by Running Press are available at special discounts for bulk
purchases in the United States by corporations, institutions, and other organizations.
For more information, please contact the Special Markets Department at the Perseus
Books Group, 2300 Chestnut Street, Suite 200, Philadelphia, PA 19103, or call
(800) 810-4145, ext. 5000, or e-mail special.markets@perseusbooks.com.

US ISBN: 978-0-7624-5471-6
US Library of Congress Control Number: 2014937947

9 8 7 6 5 4 3 2 1
Digit on the right indicates the number of this printing

Running Press Book Publishers
2300 Chestnut Street
Philadelphia, PA 19103-4371

Visit us on the web!
www.runningpress.com

Printed and bound in the UK

Contents

Acknowledgements

"Invisible Lines" by Raziel Moore, © 2013. First appeared on the Erotica Readers and Writers Association website. Reprinted by permission of the author.

"A Problem with Authority" by Lucy Felthouse, © 2013. First appeared in COMING TOGETHER:IN THE TRENCHES, edited by Lady Grey. Reprinted by permission of the author.

"Limits: A Love Story" by Lisabet Sarai, © 2012. First appeared in the author's collection SPANK ME AGAIN, STRANGER. Reprinted by permission of the author.

"The Purpose of Tongues" by Kirsty Logan, © 2013. First appeared in GEEK LOVE, edited by Shanna Germain and Janine Ashbless. Reprinted by permission of the author.

"The Cock Killers" by Ian Mason, © 2013. First appeared in GROUPIES, edited by N.T. Morley. Reprinted by permission of the author.

"Marylou" by Lucy Debussy, © 2013. First appeared in BEST WOMEN'S EROTICA 2014, edited by Violet Blue. Reprinted by permission of the author.

"Moving" by M. Christian, © 2013. First appeared in the author's collection IN CONTROL. Reprinted by permission of the author.

"The Mattress" by Kay Jaybee, ©c 2013. First appeared in SMUT ALFRESCO, edited by Lucy Felthouse and Victoria Blisse. Reprinted by permission of the author.

"The Naughty Chair" by Donna George Storey, © 2013.

First appeared in THE BIG BOOK OF BONDAGE, edited by Alison Tyler. Reprinted by permission of the author.

"Endangered" by Michael Crawley, © 2014 by Estate of Michael Crawley. Original publication. Reprinted by permission of the author's executor, Laurie Clayton.

"The Bondage Pig" by Kristina Lloyd, © 2013. First appeared in THE BIG BOOK OF BONDAGE, edited by Alison Tyler. Reprinted by permission of the author.

"Slowhand" by Isabella Johns, © 2013. First appeared as MY HOT MENAGE in E-book format. Reprinted by permission of the author.

"The Nude, Stripped Naked" by Jeremy Edwards, © 2013. First appeared in ONLY YOU, edited by Rachel Kramer Bussel. Reprinted by permission of the author.

"Cancer" by Anna Lidia Vega Serova, © 2013. First appeared in WORDS WITHOUT BORDERS. Reprinted by permission of the author and the translator, Lawrence Schimel.

"The Beautiful Boy" by Shaun Levin, © 2013. First appeared in WITH, edited by Jameson Currier. Reprinted by permission of the author.

"Eighty Days of Christmas" by Vina Jackson, © 2012. First appeared in THE EIGHTY DAYS COLLECTION eBook. Reprinted by permission of the author and Sarah Such Literary Agency.

"Fluffed" by Mathew Klickstein, ©2014. Original publication. Reprinted by permission of the author.

"Beating the Gothic Out of Her" by Amanda Earl, © 2013. First appeared on the Erotica Readers and Writers Association website. Reprinted by permission of the author.

"Madame Chocolat" by Vanessa Clark, © 2013. First appeared in a different version as "La Femme Chocolat" by V. C. in FEMME FATALE, edited by Lana Fox. Reprinted by permission of the author.

"Federico" by Michèle Larue, © 2013. First appeared in

OSEZ: 20 HISTOIRES DE SEXE AVEC DES POMPIERS. Reprinted by permission of the author.

"The Corruption of the Innocent Pornographer" by Destiny Moon, © 2013. First appeared in WILD GIRLS, WILD NIGHTS edited by Sacchi Green. Reprinted by permission of the author.

"Man of Marble" by N. J. Streitberger, © 2014. Original publication. Reprinted by permission of the author.

"Atrocity Ballet" by Remittance Girl, © 2013. First appeared on the Burning Books Press website. Reprinted by permission of the author.

"Pity Fuck" by Lawrence Schimel, © 2013. First appeared in ANYTHING FOR A DOLLAR, edited by Todd Gregory. Reprinted by permission of the author.

"Layover" by Lisabet Sarai, © 2013. First appeared in UNDER HER THUMB, edited by D. L. King. Reprinted by permission of the author.

"Does Immortality Come with a Pension?" by Robert Buckley, © 2013. First appeared on the Erotica Readers and Writers Association website. Reprinted by permission of the author.

"Subbing" by Rachel Kramer Bussel, © 2013. First appeared in SERVING HIM, edited by Rachel Kramer Bussel. Reprinted by permission of the author.

"Burned" by Alison Tyler, © 2013. First appeared in THE BIG BOOK OF BONDAGE, edited by Alison Tyler. Reprinted by permission of the author.

"The Saturday Pet" by N. T. Morley, © 2013. First appeared in TWISTED, edited by Alison Tyler. Reprinted by permission of the author.

"Stolen Hours" by Madeline Moore, © 2013. First appeared on the author's blog. Reprinted by permission of the author.

"In Control" by M. Christian, © 2013. First appeared in the author's collection IN CONTROL. Reprinted by permission of the author.

"Of Canes and Men" by Sacha Lasalle © 2013. First appeared

on the Erotica Readers and Writers Association website. Reprinted by permission of the author.

"Escape" by Mitzi Szereto, © 2013. First appeared in THRONES OF DESIRE, edited by Mitzi Szereto. Reprinted by permission of the author.

"Business Managing" by Teresa Noelle Roberts, © 2013. First appeared in UNDER HER THUMB, edited by D. L. King. Reprinted by permission of the author.

"Pages and Play Things" by Haralambi Markov, © 2013. First appeared as by Harry Markov, in GEEK LOVE, edited by Shanna Germain and Janine Ashbless. Reprinted by permission of the author.

"Thumbelina" by Vanessa de Sade, © 2013. First appeared in the author's collection IN THE FORESTS OF THE NIGHT. Reprinted by permission of the author and Sweetmeats Press.

"The Love We Make" by Kristina Wright, © 2013. First appeared in ONLY YOU, edited by Rachel Kramer Bussel. Reprinted by permission of the author.

"Soul Naked" by Chris Garcia, © 2014. Original publication. Reprinted by permission of the author.

"Three Nights Before the Wedding" by Catherine Paulssen, © 2013. First appeared in BEST EROTIC ROMANCE 2013, edited by Kristina Wright. Reprinted by permission of the author.

"Double-Cross" by Salome Wilde, © 2013. First appeared in LEGAL BRIEFS, edited by S. L. Armstrong. Reprinted by permission of the author.

"Sudden Showers" by Thomas S. Roche, © 2013. First appeared in LET 'EM LOOK, edited by N. T. Morley. Reprinted by permission of the author.

"Becoming Alice" by Jean Roberta, © 2013. First appeared in the author's collection THE PRINCESS AND THE OUTLAW. Reprinted by permission of the author.

"The Too Beautiful Boy" by Arthur Chappell, © 2013. First appeared on the Erotica Readers and Writers Association website. Reprinted by permission of the author.

"Peek Hour" by Adrea Kore, © 2013. First appeared on the Erotica Readers and Writers Association website. Reprinted by permission of the author.

"Porn Enough at Last" by Jesse Bullington, © 2013. First appeared in GEEK LOVE, edited by Shanna Germain and Janine Ashbless. Reprinted by permission of the author.

Introduction

Maxim Jakubowski

As we stealthily approach our second decade of annual explorations of the world of literary erotica (even though this is volume 13 of the series, our initial five years were not numbered . . .), we contemplate a brand-new landscape.

The tide that came in fifty shades of grey and thanks to unimaginative publishers a whole assortment of other colours and numbers has begun to seriously ebb, and we are left with a book world in turmoil. In the wake of the E. L. James tsunami a rare few fortunes have been made, careers briefly boosted then deflated and, sadly, the majority of good erotic writers generally unaffected, with the spoils of war appropriated by authors from the romantic field and Elysian fields of happy endings, and many are now finding prospects for publication even more difficult than before, what with the avalanche of generally dismal material available for free or thereabouts on the internet and digitally.

As someone, as both writer and editor, who has been toiling in the galleys of erotica for so many years, I tend to be philosophical about this state of affairs, having witnessed so many cycles in the life and popularity of popular genre fiction. We have found ourselves briefly in fashion, only to be overcome by the lemmings and a publishing industry that will never learn its lessons properly, but we're still alive and kicking and, I would venture to say, the general level of quality now to be found in erotica writing is higher than ever. Also, to my great pleasure – a bee that's been flying in my bonnet for ages – more male writers have grown attracted to the genre, giving lie to the common wisdom that writing about sex is mostly done and appreciated by women. After all, it takes two (or more, I know . . .) to have sex . . .

So, here we are again with a selection of the best sensual writing of the year. Popular authors return, new ones make their first appearance in the series, as do writers sometimes previously known in other areas, like the wonderful Jesse Bullington, whose three splendidly imaginative SF and fantasy novels are well worth the detour. In another first, we also welcome new talents from Bulgaria and Cuba, and a handful of sexy Australians alongside our bevvy of Brits, Yanks and French talent. No Italians this year, not for want of quality but because I've been too busy on the writing front to find time to translate anything!

It's been a sad year for other reasons. Nick Robinson of Constable & Robinson, who first gave this series the go-ahead many years back, against the advice of his then staff, and has been both a friend and a great publisher all along, died at a tragically early age, as well as two of our best writers: Michael Hemmingson and Michael Crawley. Both had featured regularly in the series ever since it began and will be sorely missed. Michael Crawley's partner has generously allowed me to feature what will be his final story to be published for which many thanks. Alas, Michael Hemmingson's estate is still in a state of disarray due to the suddenness and circumstances of his passing and I was unable to obtain any unpublished material.

At any rate, this volume is dedicated to these three great friends.

Enjoy another sterling celebration of joy and the senses!

Invisible Lines

Raziel Moore

1

Big Lou, of Big Lou's Tattoos, scowled.

"Let me get this straight," he said, "You want that tattoo."

Sima looked again at the full color lotus blossom design, bit her lip and nodded.

"With no ink."

The artist, his sleeveless T revealing an Illustrated Man's worth of his own ink, stood in front of a wall covered with sketches and photographs; Big Lou's catalog and oeuvre.

"Get out of my shop."

"I'll pay full pri—"

"Out. I've heard about you, girly. You've got a rep, you know? Think this is some kind of a joke? Some kind of rich-girl's joke?" His voice rose as he spoke, bald head shading redder. "This is my art. My religion. This is my life. You respect the ink or get the fuck out of my face!"

The last words were yelled. Lou didn't move from his place behind the counter, but suddenly he seemed larger, menacing. The twinned dragons on his biceps looked like they were going to leap for her. Sima fled.

She blinked away the tears as she walked down the dirty street and scanned for a cab. It was still early afternoon. She'd given herself plenty of time to get out of the District before dark, but hadn't counted on so many defeats. Now she felt like everyone she saw knew she didn't belong there. She'd tried to prepare well enough, a dark worn coat over old jeans and flats. A loose blouse that was easy to lift or take off. She ignored the flip of her stomach and the ache between her legs as she walked, not meeting anyone's gaze.

Afraid, angry, ashamed, Sima slammed the door of the taxi hard enough to draw an admonishing look from the cabby. Why did this have to be so hard? What was wrong with her?

"Hey! Lady. I said where to?" The driver's accent was like Daadaagee's.

Sima mumbled her street and turned to look sullenly out the window. The interior of the cab smelled of masala spices. The scent both made her feel safe, and intensified the gnawing of need in her bones. Outside, the street slipped by, the doorways and shopfronts losing their angles as the light failed.

"Wait. Stop. Stop here!" She peered at a little shopfront through the gloom. The name rang a bell. She fumbled in her coat pocket, pulled out a tattered little notebook and flipped through the pages.

It'd only been two blocks, right at Old Market, where Midtown's gentrification was waging a pitched battle with the District's decay.

She could practically hear the driver roll his eyes, but stop he did. Sima overpaid him and stepped out without a word. She stood in front of Chrysalis Tattoo. It was on her dwindling list of places she hadn't tried and been turned away from.

She had a reputation now? Like just finding willing tattooists wasn't enough trouble? But dammit, it was almost like claws inside her now. One more try.

The bell on the door tinkled as she went in. This parlor looked like half a dozen others. The small, brightly lit front space, showcased walls covered with art. The front room was scrupulously clean, and smelled of antiseptic, indigo and electricity. Behind the counter, a tall, lean man reclined, reading an electronic book. He had close-cut black hair and a pointed beard, and unlike most tattooists she'd seen she didn't notice any tattoos on him right away, though he was wearing a buttoned-up long-sleeved shirt. Without moving his head he looked over his half-glasses and raised an eyebrow.

"Can I help you today, miss?"

No games, now, Sima told herself. "I want to get a tattoo."

The man looked around the store. "Looks like you've come to the right place."

"I don't know. Maybe. It's . . . Look. I want the tattoo. But I don't want any ink."

"Say again?"

"I want a tattoo—" and she had already spotted exactly which, as well "—without ink." She finished through nearly gritted teeth, bracing for an explosion.

"Why?"

She'd been asked this before, of course; she forged on, determined. "Because that's what I want."

"Come on now." He'd laid his book on the counter and taken off his glasses. His eyes were light brown, practically copper, and their gaze somehow destroyed her resolve.

This is useless. She'd been through this conversation so many times. And no matter how she phrased it, the outcome was almost always the same. She pulled herself deeper into her coat and began to turn away.

He leaned his elbows on the thick counter glass, and inter-laced the fingers of his hands. "I didn't say no. I asked why."

"Because . . ." She could feel herself blushing, but she couldn't get herself to say anything more. "Because!"

He looked at her until she met his eyes, and then until she had to look away, ready again to turn and leave. He tipped his chin at her.

"You've done this before." It wasn't a question.

"Yes."

"How many times?"

". . . Eight."

His eyebrow rose. "When was the last time?"

"Three months ago."

"Show me."

"Excuse me?"

"Show me the work."

"It's my left shoulder blade—"

"OK, let me see."

"But there was no—"

"You can show me or you can argue with someone else."

He didn't sound angry. But he wasn't joking around.

Sima stepped up to the counter and shrugged out of her coat. She looked over at the door as she opened the top two buttons of her blouse and pulled it down over her shoulder, turning so the man could see her.

He grabbed his glasses and leaned further over the counter to see. She stiffened as he slid her bra strap off her shoulder. His fingers were smooth, cool against her skin.

"Butterfly," he said. "Monarch."

She craned her neck around to look at him. She'd examined that shoulder in the mirror just the other day, and seen no sign.

"How?!"

"Trace scarring. The fluorescent lights make it easier to see."

"Scarring?! Oh, no!"

Sima jerked away from the man's hand and dropped to kneel on the floor, yanking at the cuff of her pant leg. Fuck these jeans!

Then she froze, and looked up in near panic. Over his glasses and his counter, the man peered down at her. And her open blouse. Sima felt the color rising in her cheeks, jerked her shirt closed and then hid her head from him as a sob shook her.

2

Not the usual kind of tears we get here, Paul thought.

The girl, curled up in her crouch on his white tile floor, looked like she was trying to disappear within herself.

"Are you all right?" he asked, knowing the answer, but not why.

"Yes." Her hands muffled her answer. "No."

She took a deep breath and looked up at him with visible effort.

"I can't see my calf. That's where the next to last one was. I thought there'd be no . . ."

She didn't look like she was on anything; no smell of alcohol. Just distraught. Jeans too slim to let her pull them up.

"Look, miss, that shoulder isn't so bad. It'd take someone who knows to see anything. And if you're a good healer, I'll bet even that will fade in time."

She grabbed at that. "Can you look – at the calf one?"

It's not like tonight's terribly busy or anything, he thought.

"Sure. You'll probably need to get your leg out of those pants. I have robes," he added before she could say anything.

She wiped her eyes and nodded.

As he waited for her to change, Paul wondered what this girl—young woman's story was. He'd done inkless tattoos before. On himself, for practice, sure, but the others he'd done were usually test lines or little circles for skittish customers; to show them what it would be like. Paul knew plenty of artists who wouldn't do that, but he would because he had little interest in anyone who didn't really want the ink. Which made him wonder in turn why he was even thinking about saying yes to this frightened girl.

She emerged from the change room clad in one of the robes he kept on hand, her black hair and cinnamon skin, where exposed, showed stark contrasts to the white terrycloth. She perched on the edge of the client's chair, as if ready to bolt.

The studio lights were plenty bright, but Paul turned his work light on as he motioned her to sit back.

"Relax a little. It's all right." It looked like she didn't believe him, but wanted to. "Right leg?"

She nodded, and he raised the right side split leg of the chair and aimed the light, pulling the robe just high enough to expose the shin.

"Turn."

He guided her to turn her leg out so he could see her calf. Smooth, cinnamon skin moved under his fingers.

Ah, yes. This is why you didn't say no. This skin would take the needle very nicely indeed, ink or no.

Paul looked carefully. The faintest trace of a line here, a swept curve there. Barely anything. *Some kind of bird?*

"What was it?"

Her skin smelled a bit like ginger, with other spices he couldn't place. Not at all unpleasant.

"A flying robin. Can you see it?"

"No. I can barely see anything. You got it six months ago?"

"Five."

He set her leg back down and re-covered it.

"Well. It looks like you heal quite well. The shoulder should go the same way."

She exhaled the breath she'd been holding and sank back into the chair. Then pulled the left robe sleeve up to expose her forearm to him.

"Anything there?"

Paul turned the light, took her arm in his hands and examined.

"No. Not a thing."

"It was a Gothic letter 'S'."

"Not any more."

She smiled for the first time. That was good.

"I got that nine months ago."

He chuckled. "No, you *didn't* get it nine months ago."

She made as if to argue with him, but then realized what he meant, and nodded, though her smile faded as she did.

"So, will you do one for me?"

"I don't know yet. I still want to know why. I have a guess."

She waited, expression neutral.

"You get off on it. Either the pain, or the blood. Or both."

Her breath caught for a moment. Found out. He watched her war with herself. Her body tensed to jump from the chair. On her face, a look of anguish he usually saw only from the needle. It wasn't unattractive. She sat that way for only a few panicked breaths, but he couldn't guess how long it felt for her. In the end, she stayed where she was, and nodded. So did he.

"You know, that's not really too unusual. A lot of people get a rush from the pain. Endorphins, adrenaline, all that, and for some it's quite a bit more. Though usually they want something to show at the end of it."

Her expression said she *hadn't* known that.

"But that's the whole deal for you, eh? Just pain? Blood?"

She slowly shook her head no. That made some sense. The three places she'd shown him weren't particularly high-pain areas on most people, after all.

"Then what?"

She didn't answer, and Paul shrugged. It was enough for now, anyway. To himself he'd already admitted he'd do it. Once he'd had a feel of her skin. Some skin was easier, and far more pleasant to work with, after all. But that wasn't really why.

"All right," he said, earning a beaming smile. "On one condition."

The smile closed up to caution almost instantly. Paul wondered what her . . . obsession? fetish? – had cost her besides money.

"What?" Warily.

"That you never ask for something like this again without establishing the cred of who you're asking. This is my shop, and I'm going to show you everything whether you want to see it or not. But if you ask the wrong person, you *could* get scarred for life. Or an infection, or worse. So, deal?"

"Deal. And thank you."

"What and where?"

"I want . . . that stalking Chinese tiger. Here." She brushed her hand over the left side of her ribcage.

Paul gave a low whistle.

"Well. That's a big design and a tough place. You look like you don't have much fat to protect you there. But then, you're looking for that, yeah? How about something smaller, though?

After a few tens of minutes, you're going to be largely numb to the pain anyway – unless we were going to go for an all-day session which—" he looked at his watch "—would have to be another time."

She thought for a moment, then said, "How about just the line drawing, no shading or colors. I'll still pay for the whole thing." Her voice had some of its confidence back. Bargaining instead of confessional. She also must have known full well that the single needle outliner was going to be a rougher ride than the multi-point coloring needles. *Does Dad know what you spend his money on? Or is it your money, after all?* Paul wondered.

"All right. I'm game. I'm Paul, by the way. This is my shop."

He extended his hand, and she took it, gingerly.

"I'm Sima."

The look she gave him was full of gratitude and, he thought, hunger.

This'll be interesting, at least.

3

Sima knew not to hold her breath, or grit her teeth, or clench her muscles. She lay on her back on the tattooist's – Paul's – chair, opened up to something like a recliner-qua-bed, with her left arm stretched over her head. She'd changed back out of the robe, and now had her blouse rolled up to just under her bra. Her ribcage clean and cool in the studio air; sprayed with alcohol, cleaned with green soap, swabbed with ointment.

It's all foreplay, isn't it? she thought.

Paul had partly rolled up his sleeves, revealing some of his own tattoos at last. The one that held Sima's attention most was the rattlesnake coiled around his right arm. There, just above the wrist of the hand that held the needled instrument, open, fanged jaws dripped a black drop of venom – or ink.

The fact Paul saw part-way through her so quickly made her wonder how many of the others had known. How much she'd given away before or on the table. It's not like she could be much *more* mortified or exposed than she already had been, in front of others, and now this one. It mattered less and less as the preparation continued, too. This was where she wanted to go, and she found embarrassment and caring, and caution, fading. Like always.

"Try to keep your breathing steady as possible," Paul said from far away. "A rising and falling chest is fine, but tell me if you need to do much more."

She nodded, and her skin tingled with anticipation, not just where Paul's black-gloved hands touched it, or where the lowering needle pointed, but lower down. The ache between her legs liquefied.

The machine buzzed, and she watched, exhaling a meas-ured breath as it first kissed her. Bit her. Pierced her. The sensation shot from her rib and bloomed. Pain, more than any of her recent experiences. But more. Her cunt spasmed, and she had to fight not to jerk her body and shove her hand between her legs. Her exhalation turned to a moan.

Paul lifted the needle. "Are you ok, Sima?"

"Yesss," she hissed. "Go."

And he did. One long, curving line of fire on her skin. In her skin. Another. The needle broke occasional capillaries as it dove into her flesh. Not many, but a fresh antiseptic cloth wiped away each red welling of blood. She twinged with them, going molten. Being able to watch was *different* than not being able to see. She wasn't sure which was better, but seeing the lines grow . . . She forced herself not to grit her teeth, but didn't try to stop her thighs from squeezing together. Paul was talking.

"I'm not using a stencil, because I don't want to chance any of its line getting driven in by the needle. It may make the design less than perfect, I'm afraid. Though I did draw the one you picked freehand."

"It's . . . OK. Not like it . . . matters." It was hard to speak. For several reasons.

"Well, it matters to me. Art is art, even inkless. But try not to talk. It's all right. Let me know if you need a rest or a drink . . ."

He continued talking, about how long he'd had his own studio (seven years), about learning the art and trade in Los Angeles, and more that Sima didn't retain. Each stroke, hundreds, thousands of stabs of steel, irritated and violated her outer layer, and brought the red outline of the tiger to life, and made her want to buck her hips.

Her first orgasm hit when he drew the circles in circles of the tiger's eye. Sima closed her eyes, breathed raggedly, and rode it, trying to keep as still as possible, give as little away as possible while the pain-transmuted-to-pleasure wracked her.

Paul didn't stop. Sliding up and around the cat's face, cleaning, stretching, needling.

The second eye was right over one of her ribs. The circles there were both ticklish and – *fuck* – the most painful yet, like razor scraping bone, and Sima sobbed. And came again, this time without the ability, or desire, to hide. She wanted to cry. She held her chest as still as she could, knowing she was failing. She wanted to plead, shout, *Don't stop!* She heard herself make a nonsensical sound.

Paul continued, one hand pressing down steady on her, as if holding her in place, the other holding the damnable machine. Smooth, efficient, professional, implacable, merciless. She knew he'd stop if she told him to, but even though part of her wanted to scream for it to end, Sima said nothing, and thanked him silently for not trying to spare her or go easy. As the needle broke her skin, and opened her, and spilled her, and flooded her.

4

Spine line. Haunches.

Time lost its meaning for Paul when he worked. One part of his brain was always on alert for signals from his client. That part bantered and talked, gauging response and attention. Most of the rest of him was in a complex fugue of skin, fingers, swab, needle and ink. Entire designs could take shape under his fingers in the seeming space of a breath, while

sometimes it seemed he could witness every individual penetration of the needle and deposition of ink. Those experiences
often occurred together in a paradox of causality.

Forepaw. Claw.

Working on this woman, Sima, was different. Lack of ink
was the obvious, but with it came a heightened attention to the
other components. As if he'd been deprived of one sense, and
all the others had become stronger. Over and over, Paul
jabbed, broke this clean pristine skin, to do . . . *nothing*. It felt
so gratuitous. Enraging and intriguing at the same time.

Head. Jaw.

Sima had stopped listening to him. Her sighs, and increasingly obvious arousal, didn't faze him much, though. He'd
seen that before, albeit not as intensely. He'd had his share of
couples using tattoos as a form of foreplay or mating ritual –
one or two even consummating in his washroom because they
just couldn't wait.

Whiskers. Teeth.

He could understand. Looked at a certain way, the tattoo
needle *was* a sexual instrument. A tiny sharp cock that didn't
need a pre-existing hole to penetrate you. It made its own,
every single time. And its ejaculate, dark or vibrant, left you
impregnated with color, marked forever by its intrusion. Paul
had, in this way, pierced, inseminated, left a piece of himself
indelibly in thousands of people – men and women – through
his career. He also inflicted pain, every time. And to a one,
everyone he'd hurt this way had thanked him for doing it. He
didn't get a sexual thrill out of it *per se*, but this wasn't a
platonic thing.

Rear Leg. Belly.

And now Sima. Here she was, writhing under his needle, in
pain and pleasure. And he marked her, yes. But only for now.
These bites would fade. Like the eight before, his lines would
go invisible, and perhaps even be forgotten one day. Paul
thought of his tattoos as art, yes, but it was permanence, a
form of procreation. But this . . . this was just fucking.

He disapproved.

But.

Eyes.

But Sima was coming, under his touch and his needle, and doing so, well, *beautifully*. Not from the creation of art or the act of change of one's body, but from the pure destructive acts of the needle. It was moving, in a way, and disturbing. This was his quiet enjoyment of the artful pain he inflicted reflected back at him, but purified and magnified. Pain – and this specific kind – exposed as the end itself rather than the means. And this was the thing she'd craved. The obsession that had driven her to potentially dangerous decisions and situations. And here he was feeding it exactly. True she was a paying, if eccentric, client, but was this *right*? And why was he even asking himself these questions?

His needle, a single round, in one sense the purest form, lanced at her, several times a second, dimpling and piercing her skin, faithfully, linearly, obediently creating the pattern he chose. Her chest rose and fell with her breathing, but not steadily any more; she shook, gasped, shuddered. Paul rode it out with her, pressing, massaging, stretching skin with his left hand, steadying the work area, and drawing, sweeping, lining with his right. She didn't tell him to stop, so he didn't stop.

Expression. Stripes.

He counted three orgasms of increasing intensity before Sima descended into a glassy-eyed detachment, conscious, but almost entranced. This was familiar territory for Paul. Lots of his return customers, especially the ones embarking on big, multi-session pieces, strove for a Zen-like state very much like this. None of them got there the same way, though.

Tail. Last stripes.

The tiger's tail swept around, halfway between ribs and navel, and Paul was done. Lifting and turning off the needle, he leaned back, and stretched his neck and his fingers. Sima breathed slow and deep, eyes moving slowly between her own red, lined skin, the iron now resting on the work tray, and Paul's face.

"Thank you."

"You're welcome."

She smiled dreamily, beatific, and his cock lurched.

Why wouldn't it? She fucking climaxed under your needle, because *of it.*

Still, the bare red lines on her skin, without pigment, were an affront. *No. They're the absence of illusion.*

Paul began the after-care work, pants tented and straining. Green soap, antibacterial ointment, plastic wrap and medical tape. She watched him quietly the whole time, eyes half closed, looking so . . . fucked.

As soon as he'd carefully laid the last strip of tape, he ripped off a glove so he could adjust himself. It was almost uncomfortable by now. Sima's eyes followed his hand.

The progression from shifting, to unzipping, to freeing his cock from pants and boxers seemed so logical, under her gaze. She'd shown him what he'd done to her, beyond the tattoo, it was fair to show what she'd done to him. He might have turned away after that, gone to the restroom and taken care of his own business, if she hadn't, just then, licked her lips.

Maybe it was late. Maybe it was fatigue or comedown from finishing a job. Maybe . . . he couldn't be *finished* if he didn't leave some mark. Paul stepped closer to Sima, reached for the chair control and reclined the backrest. She didn't move away as he brought his ungloved hand to her head, weaving his fingers in her hair and pulling her to him. Her lips closing around his cock were so soft, her mouth wet-hot.

5

Sima floated; relaxed, exhausted, unspeakably satisfied.

God, that hurt, but the only ache left was that of well-used muscles. Paul had soothed and cooled lines of fire on her torso into the kind of stings that reminded her she was alive. Tomorrow, everything would be tender and sore, which was good in its own way, too. But, for the moment, she was just happy, relieved, and, looking at Paul, simply grateful. He'd been cool, almost serene, as she'd gone to pieces under him. None of her previous sojourns under the needle had been quite like this, given and taken so much. Her fourth tattoo had actually never been finished because she'd freaked out the artist with her imperfectly hidden climax. But Paul kept on – almost as solid and steady as the machine itself.

But he was human, after all. The bulge in his pants, and then the erect cock he'd freed to the air, demonstrated that. The move had surprised her, but it was flattering in its way, and, well, it was a natural reaction. It was also a lot better than it could have been. Sima could now face the memory of her third tattooist, though she'd succeeded in blotting out his name and face. "Pre-payment" the guy had called it, and it had tainted almost the whole experience.

This was different. Sima wanted it. Or at least, she was more than OK with it when he laid her back and took hold of her head in one strong hand. His cock fit her lips well, tasting . . . *male* against her tongue. She knew she was no expert fellator, but old boyfriends had never complained. Paul didn't complain. He just held her with strong fingers as she sucked him. She brought her hands to his hips, not so much to resist as to hold on to him. The rhythm lasted a short while, as her tongue teased, cheeks hollowed, lips slid along the shaft, until he felt his muscles tensing. His cock swelled one last fraction as he let out a low, breaking sigh and pushed almost to the back of her throat, nearly causing her to gag. She relaxed herself as best she could when his come erupted into her.

Paul held her there until his cock began softening and subsiding in her mouth, then relaxed his fingers and released her. He finally pulled the glove off the other hand, and stroked her cheek with its warm fingers. His thumb collected an errant drop of come, and brought it back to her lips; she licked the salty-sweet stuff from it as she looked up at his face. Then, they both took a deep breath almost together, and something, maybe the very air itself, sighed in release. Paul half turned to put himself away and set his pants in order.

"Thank you," he said, and then almost audibly shifting gears, went into care and healing instructions for the tattoo. Of course she'd heard them many times before, but she listened dutifully, in case his methods were different.

"Take the bandage off between six and eight hours, OK? Even if it means waking up early."

She nodded.

"I'd recommend loose clothing for a few days, too."

He helped her sit up, then busied himself cleaning his work area, keeping an eye on her as she gingerly stretched her limbs and back. He insisted she drink water, and watched her as she stood up. She waved that she felt fine, and he finished putting things away, opening the glass studio door to the front of the shop. Sima felt the presence of her new lines as she moved. She felt warm and damp between her legs, and decided not to look too carefully at her jeans.

"It's dark out now. You shouldn't walk alone."

Was that some kind of offer?

"I live uptown. I'll catch a taxi."

"No, I'll call one to come pick you up right here."

"All right."

He went over to the computer/register at the counter and rang her up while he dialed the cab company on his cell phone. Full price, which Sima paid with her credit card.

"Yellow has somebody a couple blocks away. Just a few minutes."

"Thanks."

She still glowed, embers inside still hot. Yet there was something missing in how she was feeling, and Sima couldn't quite place it at first, but then realized that missing thing wasn't a bad thing at all. For the first time since she'd started doing this, she felt unashamed.

"Um, Paul?"

"Yes?"

"If I come back here, next time . . ."

"Yes?"

"Would you do another one?" This was the first time she'd

asked *before* she'd left. The first time she'd been emboldened to think of it.

Paul regarded her for a moment, eyes shifting to where her blouse covered the inkless tattoo he'd just given her. Sima guessed he was in his late thirties. And his hair wasn't all black – there were a handful of grey hairs at his temples.

"Maybe. I have to think about it. I can't say yes right now. But I won't say no."

"All right." It was not the answer she'd hoped for, but better than the one she'd made herself expect.

The cab ride home was a blur of city lights. This one smelled of cigar smoke, which made her realize that Chrysalis Tattoo, unlike most of the parlors she'd been to, hadn't had a hint of smoke smell at all. The dreadlocked cabby talked non-stop in a thick Jamaican accent on a hands-free phone about some soccer game the whole way home.

Back in her apartment, Sima moved quietly so as not to awaken sleeping roommates. In the privacy of her room, she forewent her usual nightshirt, opting for only a fresh pair of panties before carefully laying down in her bed. She closed her eyes and thought of the needle and what it did to her: the lines, Paul's hands, Paul's . . . She slept like the dead until her alarm woke her to change her dressing.

6

Spring was almost done being just a tease, and really starting to show some warmth. Paul truly appreciated the season. The human harbingers of spring were the first to start wearing short sleeves and pants, and that population logically included a disproportionate number of the illustrated, and otherwise modified, revealing art-covered skin like plumage.

Moreover, a Thursday evening was a good time to walk the Downtown Mall for people watching. It was also a decent evening for business, but Eejay was in today, holding down the fort at the shop, and he'd call if there was a sudden rush. Paul had finished a grueling trompe l'oeil cuneiform tablet back piece that afternoon and was happy to be out and about, stretching legs, back and fingers. And doing a little research.

Paul leaned against a lamppost on the brick-finished street, penciling in his pocket sketchbook the sharp profile of the woman with the vintage eighties Mohawk smoking with her goth and emo friends outside Mata Hari's Vintage Clothes. This was his third sketch of the night, which reminded him that his book had only a few pages left. Fortunately, Amsterdam Art Supply was a block and a half away, and Paul let that become his primary destination.

Inside Amsterdam was glaring white compared to the darkened blues and browns of the street. The color of potential, of canvas, though not his chosen one. Picking out a new book was a quick affair, and Paul tended not to linger in stores. It was late enough that only one register remained open, with a queue a few people deep. It took a moment to recognize Sima in this different context, as she took her place in line behind him with an armful of watercolor supplies. Eyes down, mentally counting off items in her bundle, she hadn't noticed him. And, unlike two Saturdays ago, those eyes, and the rest of her posture were neutral; calmly between the wire-tense and blissed-to-laxity he'd seen. However free of decoration her bare arms and shoulders were, she was very attractive.

Paul had pretty much put Sima and her strange non-tattoo out of his mind, but now the odd, disquieting experience returned. It still bothered him, and only partly because of its conclusion. He'd pretty much decided he'd decline, politely, to do another inkless job for the girl. If she ever came through his door again.

And yet.

Paul was used to his own secret pleasure with every wince and gasp of his clients. It aroused him deep in his core, no matter whether he worked on men or women, and he owned it as his own twisted soul, his own private kink. He never – ever – caused more pain than necessary to make the design, but he didn't shy from giving it. And here was confronted by someone who sought it out. Who took the pain given and converted it so obviously and purely into pleasure. Wanting literally nothing other than that. It was something he'd not even realized was possible – to manipulate someone's pain *and pleasure* with his needle. Tantalizing, and he realized, arousing in a way different from, and beyond, his private sadism; what unique power this combination of twists held. Unflappable as he liked to think of himself, it freaked him; Sima took his secret pleasure and turned it into something different, bigger, open. And on top of that, not to leave his mark . . .

The line moved forward. As she stepped up, Sima looked up and saw him, and gave a little start. She smiled, much more shyly than the first time he'd seen her.

"Hello, Sima."

"Hi," she said, quickly, shyly. Her expression changed as he watched, shifting away from calm to something more nervous.

"How are you?" Pleasantries, reintroductions.

"Good. I'm good." And antsy, now, Paul noted.

"How is everything healing up?" Paul stopped himself from asking how the tattoo looked, since that was immaterial.

"Um . . . really well! It's doing fine." She passed her free hand over her ribcage. Paul wasn't sure if she was conscious of tracing the hidden path of the tiger's tail with a finger as she looked over her shoulder. *How hidden is it now? Not completely gone yet*, Paul wagered, and then, the odd thought, *I want to see it anyway*.

"I'm glad. Look, I might as well say now and save—"

"Seem! They're opening another line – c'mere! I got a place!"The voice cut in from the register a lane over. Another woman, younger than, but looking very much like Sima, was beckoning to her with exaggerated urgency, waving a package of feathered paintbrushes.

Sima turned to Paul briefly, apologetically, but the relief in her voice was plain to hear.

"I . . . gotta go."

Well, Paul thought, *Sister, or whoever she is, probably doesn't know, then.* Paul conceptually understood body shame, and other kinds. He'd had enough clients who got inked precisely to face down and overcome those issues. But he knew he'd likely never get it on the visceral level. And whatever Sima felt, it probably wasn't exactly the same either. *And do I really want to know what she feels about it?* Paul couldn't, or wouldn't answer himself.

"Who was *that* guy talking to you?" Sima's companion had a "city whisper", meaning her voice was simply below a shout. "Did you see his *arms*? Was that a snake? And a scorpion? Brrr! But scary hot for an old—" Sima shushed her quietly, fiercely. Paul smiled to himself, and let the smile stay on his face as he caught the sister's stare. She colored visibly. She turned away, and Paul met Sima's somewhat pained eyes for a moment before her attention shifted to the cashier.

By the time Paul paid and exited the store, Sima and companion were nowhere to be seen.

Well, that's probably that.

Paul walked and sketched some more, then dropped in to Royal Blues for some music and beer. Only Venus and a couple of her cohorts were there from the inker crowd tonight – Saturdays, and later at night, were much more of a thing for them. It was decent music, but Paul didn't stay long. He found himself thinking of the shudder of Sima's skin under his fingers as he'd drawn stripe after stripe on her.

On the bus home, he filled the last page of his old sketchbook from memory with a study of a pair of lips encircling a cock.

7

"Chrysalis Tattoos" glowed in blue neon above her as the cab departed. Unlike her week, the sign was clear and clean, with easily interpretable meaning. *Why are you here?* bubbled in Sima's head, but she refused to actually ask it of herself. She'd done that many times already over the last couple of days, as the need grew in her.

The outline of the tiger was still clear on her skin. She traced it regularly, ritualistically, as part of her own pleasure foreplay, just like she had with the others. It wouldn't disappear for a while yet, and, as it had gone in the past, she should be fine for months, tracing the ghosts of lines, before she felt it again. But she wasn't fine, and didn't know why.

Actually, that wasn't true. She knew the proximate cause: Paul at the art store. "Scary hot" Paul. Lavani's description made her shake her head, again, in part because she was right. Sima had dodged her sister's questions about him and diverted her to other topics, but the whole encounter had left her feeling odd. Exposed. All that night out she felt as if Paul's tattoo showed through her shirt to whoever was looking her way, and especially to Van. Her sister, much less family, didn't know. Neither did her roommates, who thought Sima's occasional periods of super-modesty were some Hindu religious thing.

This whole thing was supposed to be simple, contained, intimate, personal. Well, mostly personal. And that was the problem. Paul's tattoo had been the best/worst yet. Something about his quiet intensity had been different. Like he wasn't just tolerating her obscene reaction, and something else she couldn't place, but wanted to figure out, and experience again. And so here she was, feeling the ache too soon, because of him.

Stepping into the shop, Sima was brought up short by the woman behind the counter. This woman, not too much older than herself, was *festooned*. Chains and garlands of vari-colored and shaped flowers wound around the pale skin of her arms and neck and disappeared under her halter-top. An assortment of piercings adorned her ears and eyebrows, and Sima thought the woman would jingle as she nodded a greeting.

"Evenin'." She had a Southern drawl, seemingly way out of place.

"Hi. Is, um, is Paul here?"

"Sure thing, did you have an appointment?" she asked, stepping over to the computer/register.

"Oh, no. I just . . . came by."

The woman stopped and looked back to Sima, eyebrow raised.

"Well, he's with a client at the moment. I'll guess another half an hour to forty-five." Her eyes surveyed Sima, "You lookin' for something new?"

Sima nodded.

"Something in particular?" The woman turned her head to indicate the samples and designs decorating the walls.

"Yes, I know what I want." *Was that true?* Sima asked herself.

"Well, I can do it if y'all like. I'm Eejay, and that's my work over on that wall."

Sima looked for what she hoped was a polite amount of time. The designs and photos of finished work showed skill, no question.

"If it's OK, I'd like to wait for Paul?" Sima wasn't sure if she could stay, though. Not if there were going to be other people around. She realized, too late, that she'd made the silly assumption that Paul would be alone. It hadn't mattered much before, when she could conceal her reactions better. But after last time . . .

Eejay seemed to take her hesitation for concern about offense.

"Hey, sure thing, sugar. Don't worry, if you've found the right hand, it makes perfect sense to go back to it. Hell—" she leaned in conspiratorially "—I take part of my salary in ink from Paul."

She traced a woven wisteria pattern up her left arm with the fingers of her right. Sima was tempted to lean in for a sniff. Eejay smiled and looked back at the screen.

"He doesn't have anything scheduled next. Have a seat. I'll ask."

A trio of distressed, comfortable chairs lined one wall, behind a coffee table with a small pile of magazines. Sima sat, and fidgeted, and leafed through a three-month-old issue of *Skin Art*.

Eejay re-emerged from the back. "Lucky night. They're finishing up early." Eejay's look had changed, more distracted, glancing back behind her.

"Everything OK?"

"Oh, yes. Sometimes on the big pieces you can only get so far in one session."

Eejay didn't elaborate, and Sima contented herself with the answer until a tall, lanky man emerged from the back. His left arm bore bold, curving black tribal patterns, which still managed to stand out on his dark-brown skin. He walked gingerly, stiff-backed, and Eejay smiled when she saw him.

"You okay, darlin?"

"I'll live. Managed to hit a spot I just couldn't take much of tonight."

"Well, you show me when I get home and I'll make it all better."

He smiled broadly. "You know I will."

"You can take off, Eej. Go take care of your man." Paul had come in while they were talking. Sima had been tracking the man's ink pattern with her eyes and hadn't noticed. Paul's white button-down – collarless this time – had sleeves rolled up almost to his biceps, showing the wicked menagerie on both his arms. *Scary hot indeed.*

"You sure?" Eejay looked surprised and hopeful.

"Yeah. I'll close up. Give it two weeks unless you're really feeling up for it, all right, Xav?"

Paul busied himself at the computer/register as Eejay carefully ushered her beau out of the shop. Sima tried to read an article on feathering techniques.

"Sima, I was going to tell you at Amsterdam's the other day I don't think I can do another inkless tattoo."

"What?" She stood up too quickly, spilling the magazine to the floor. "Why?" It was happening again, like all the other times. Sima felt stricken. She'd thought ... "I thought it worked out OK, after—"

"That wasn't part of the transaction, Sima. That was ...

something else. I don't want to do work that isn't really wanted or won't be enjoyed in the long term. That won't be seen."

At least he didn't call her names. Out loud. But she'd heard this excuse before, or ones like it. Usually the voice speaking them wasn't as kind, but the meaning was the same. Before, she'd hang her head and leave, holding tears until she was clear of the place that no longer welcomed her.

"No! I . . . I *do* want it. And I see them. I see them all! I feel them all. It doesn't matter that they're gone from the skin. They're . . . they're all still here."

And before she knew it, she was showing Paul every location she'd had done, telling him each design, tracing it with her finger, reliving a shadow of each needle as she traced, ending with the tiger, its fading lines still red on her skin. She didn't repress the shiver that came with it.

"This is permanence for me. I remember them. I use them. I . . . need them. And I want more."

8

But what is it you really want more of, Sima? Paul thought.

"So it's *not* getting off on the needle?"

"No!" She was blushing deeply. "I mean I do. Of course I do. There. I said it. But it's not just that. It's more. You have to believe me."

"I could believe you, Sima. But I have to know what it is to you. Because what it is to me is incompleteness. I don't just stick people for money." *I stick them because I like to, also. And because they get something from it. But you, you could be more.*

Sima nodded, seeing she had a chance to seize. She took a breath.

"Everything about the tattoo . . . except this part. This fucking begging part, makes me feel alive, and in control." She looked surprised to be saying it. "I decide to get it, I pick the design, I permit the tattooist to damage me, hurt me, and I heal. My body absorbs, erases the damage. I'm powerful."

Paul had to wonder at how near a counterpart that was to

his own feelings. He'd never thought that this particular power exchange could run both ways. At the same time.

"It makes everything, even the pain, even the memory of the pain, feel so good. But . . . I don't know why it feels *that* good, when it's happening. It just does, and it's also something I want. I could just be a freak. Other tattooists have called me that."

She was so turned inward. Focused on her side of the equation. Paul realized this was another way she was like a converse of himself. It made him want to cross that divide.

"Whether 'freak' is a badge of honor or shame depends on us, not someone else. There are those who call anyone who has ink a freak, or worse. But tell me. Why so soon? It's been, what, three weeks? You said you usually went three months or more, at least until the last one had faded."

"It was . . . It was seeing you at the art store. I don't know."

Paul pursed his lips in thought. He wasn't sure if she was withholding from him. *Is it because you want* my *needle? I can give you what you want, and take what I want quietly, like I always do. But that's not enough. I want more from . . . with you.* He decided.

"All right, Sima. One more. But I don't know about any more after that."

"Thank you, Paul." Her tone conveyed true gratitude.

"So. What and where?"

After another deep breath, she pulled a slip of watercolor paper out of her back pocket, and unfolded it to show him three tightly coiled spirals radiating from a single point.

"Triskelion," she said. "Sort of. Here, about this big." She passed her hand down to her skirt – over the front inside of her right thigh.

Paul raised his eyebrow. She was going for the gusto. The tight spirals were going to maximize continuous needle contact. The place . . .

"The inside part is going to go harder, depending on how sensitive the skin there is. Is yours?"

"Very."

"I can spray the area with lidocaine before starting, that would—"

"No, thank you."

Paul nodded. He'd expected that answer. He liked that answer. "Will you be able to hold still?"

"I think so."

"OK. Let's head on back."

Sima smiled and followed him.

He set the chair on slight recline, and to raise her right leg only, and pulled his stool and tools close on the left side. She pulled her skirt up almost to her hip, revealing a truly lovely canvas of flesh. He prepped quickly, efficiently. With machine in hand, he laid a glove on her thigh. For the first time in a very long while, he pushed away professional detachment and let himself really feel the softness under his touch.

With his eyes, Paul marked out the center of the design as a whole, and the center of each spiral. He lowered his hand and drew with the needle a tiny trefoil at the center, and small circles where each spiral center would be. He saved the innermost spot for last, and was rewarded by a little gasp. He looked up at her flushed face, slowly inhaling her scent: soap, spice and, yes, sex.

"Because I don't have to watch the ink, I can maintain the cleanest line if I stop as few times as possible. You tell me if you need a rest." Then he added, "But I hope you don't."

Her eyes widened, as he smiled and turned toward his work.

9

The circling, buzzing path of the needle felt like Paul was auguring into her leg. The spiral pattern passed the same spots again and again, coiling ever tighter. It was maddening, excruciating, and made her entire body sing. Her cunt twitched each time the arc of the needle swept up towards it, and made her want to arch her back. And this was only the first of the spirals.

Sima hardly ever asked for a break. Usually it was because most of the tattoos never came that close to her pain threshold, but sometimes it was because she didn't want to give the artist a chance to end the session out of pity or disgust. This, however, was everything Paul had warned her about and more. She *did* want to make him stop, just for a moment. Just to catch her breath, from both the sharp bite of the needle and what her body was doing to her in reaction. It was almost overwhelming.

But I hope you won't. He was telling her something she needed to understand. And then he took away her ability to think cogently as he went to work. It was almost cruel of him. A challenge. And a revelation.

"You," she gasped, not used to trying to talk under the needle, "you like that it hurts me."

The sweeping curve didn't slow. Only a few tiny beads of blood welled in the needle's wake.

"Yes. Yes I do. Does that matter?"

The coiling line was almost at the center now, feeling like he was nearing bone, though she could still see it just sweeping her skin.

"I . . . don't . . . know."

She was on the brink, breathless, as he finished and lifted his hand. He carefully cleaned and wiped the area.

"I think, Sima," he said, " it matters to me."

He brought the needle to the center-point and began the second spiral, this one lower on her thigh, but more inside. Sima moaned loud, the fading almost-peak screaming back into that wonderful agony that only that infernal machine could bring. Sima knew she couldn't move her leg, knew she shouldn't clench her muscles. She channeled everything into a wail as the outermost turn of the spiral finished.

Paul didn't stop, and as the needle bit its way into the next coil in, and then the next, Sima came. The climax was dizzying, disorienting, riding the needle tighter and tighter into her flesh, piercing as deep as any cock ever had, and more. It went on and on, winding tighter and flooding loose all at once, until Paul finally lifted his hand, the second spiral done.

Sima hadn't seen him complete it; her eyes had been open but staring blind. She'd broken out in sweat, and her eyes had teared. She wiped the blur away with a shaky hand.

Paul was looking at her, one hand holding the cleaning swab. But before he wiped her raw skin with it, he bent forward and kissed her, right in the center of the spiral he'd just completed. His lips, soft and hot, touched and smeared the small beads of blood, and stung her in a way entirely unlike the needle when they pressed against her. A shudder shook her, and she sighed as he lifted his head and carefully, thoroughly cleaned her, wiping his lips on the back of the folded pad after he was done. She stared at him the whole time.

"Are you ready for the last part?" he asked. His voice was different, professional detachment missing.

Sima nodded.

"I didn't think I would like this, Sima. But I do. I do very much."

He lowered the needle.

"You take pleasure in what gives me pleasure. I never knew. But it's beautiful," he said.

He began the third spiral, highest, farthest inside her thigh, the most sensitive part. It was by far the worst pain of the night. It may or may not have been the most pain from a needle, but this needle, in Paul's hand, was suddenly laden with much more. It wasn't just metal sticking her skin, she realized. It was *Paul*. On top of the excruciation, and even without the ink, Sima felt it now – really felt being marked. She lay limp as a rag doll, and screamed. And came. And couldn't stop. Didn't care to stop, as Paul seemed to tear a hole right through her . . .

Lips on her skin. Colors swam back into her vision and she felt burning lips in the center of the last torturous spiral. Paul was kissing her again, and though she felt fluid, flooded, drained, something melted in her. She reached, gripped his short hair as best she could in a trembling hand and pulled at his head. She wanted that kiss on *her* lips.

Paul obliged, letting her guide his mouth to hers. The tattoo machine clanked on its tray, latex snapped as he tore his gloves off. Then his warm hands slid up and down her sides. His lips tasted coppery with the smear of her blood, but his tongue, when she licked at it, was just Paul.

He was a good kisser, which was a good thing, because she didn't have the energy to do much work. Endorphins, or whatever they were, permeated her. It was all so lovely. Paul's hands moved lower, to her waist, her legs (carefully on the outside of the tattoo), sliding her skirt higher. *Yes*, she thought, kissing her permission.

Sima had worn bathing suit bottoms, for a semblance of modesty, but at this point they couldn't have been more damp if she'd actually been swimming. She'd anticipated having to deal with a just-tattooed leg and had the foresight to wear her string bottoms.

His hands found the bows. And pulled. She exhaled into his mouth as they came loose, and let go every last bit of tension left in her.

10

The professional instinct in Paul scolded, then yelled at him to take care of his client: hygiene, proper care, responsibility. He wasn't listening. He'd broken that rationality with his first kiss, and had finished the tattoo with no detachment whatsoever. His line had been just as clean, just as perfect as the first two spirals, but his hand hadn't moved in service of the design. He'd guided the needle out of his need and hers, seeking the perfect match of giving and taking. And if he hadn't found it, he'd come so close as for it not to matter.

The line – the empty line curving away from the needle – was only the trail of interface. The real line, he saw it now, was from him to Sima, *through* the needle. It was almost frightening to see it that way, but Paul couldn't deny how it felt. And when the pattern was finished, he couldn't deny what he wanted.

Kissing her blood-beaded thigh, he inhaled her scent,

visualizing the heat radiating from her sex. Just a turn of his head and he could devour her. *Later*.

Kissing her lips – soft, languorous, sated – stirred him further. He'd done that to her, for her. Sima's kiss back, the tease of her tongue, her finger on his beard, her breath as he found and pulled the strings that opened her to him, all drew new lines between them. She went limp under him. Not in surrender, not mere exhaustion, but, it felt like, offering. Oblation.

He moved her carefully, draping her untouched leg over the armrest, pulling her hips to the edge of the chair, opening and pulling down his jeans in a quick moment. He'd ignored the ache of his confined cock until it was freed, and then could think of nothing else until he was buried in her cunt.

Paul held her hips as they connected and watched as he entered her in one smooth breathtaking motion. The small sound she made as he filled her seemed as loud to him as her cries under the needle. She squeezed him tight as he hilted in her, gasping as his hip brushed her red-weeping thigh. He didn't spare the time or attention to curse, but shifted his hand to the crook of her knee, to move her leg away from the contact. This opened her to him even more, and he used that space to fuck deeper into her.

Her head lolled as he thrust into her, relaxed as a veteran under the needle. Sima's only movements were inside, where she milked and coaxed his cock, and her eyes, shifting slowly over his sweating, rutting body. He fucked her like a rag doll, unable, or unwilling by the end to temper the thrust of his hips. Fucking was a sloppy, imprecise parody of the needle's precision. But really, the machine was the parody. This was the fundamental, primal piercing, creation of symbols, drawing of the true line.

Paul yanked Sima's hips to him as he arched into her and came, chin thrust up and exhaling a sharp exuberant sound. His cock pulsed inside her clutching cunt, and filled her. Needle, ink, mark. When he became aware again, he found himself kissing her, and her kissing weakly back.

"Sima." Paul didn't really have anything to say just then. Just the name.

She stretched under him, like a cat readying to nap. It felt good. Her thigh brushed him, and she mumbled and moved it away, the lethargic equivalent of a gasp and a jerk.

Sense clacked inside his skull, and Paul galvanized into action. He withdrew, not without a last shudder of pleasure, and systematically, extremely thoroughly, cleaned, disinfected, soothed and bandaged Sima's thigh. He didn't let himself be distracted by the beads of come on the lips of her cunt, until he was completely finished with the after-care of the tattoo. Then, he gently tended to the other, lovely mess he'd made with a soft towel. By the time he was done, with cleaning, gear stowage and waste disposal, Sima looked to be asleep, or so zoned as to make no difference. *Not a good time to talk, and probably just as well.*

Paul had locked the shop door and set the sign to "Closed" as he was setting up earlier, an even wiser precaution than he'd originally thought.

"I'm not going to pour you into a cab like that," he said aloud, and set to closing the front end of the shop; lights and alarm system, shut most of the studio lights as well. Then, gently, mindful of her leg, Paul bent to the chair and picked Sima up. She was solid, with a nice heft in his arms. It felt good. She curled into him as he held her. That felt good, too. Paul carried her to the back of the shop, through the door labeled "Private" in Art Nouveau lettering, and up the stairs to his apartment over the shop.

He brought her to his bed, pulled the covers aside and laid her down, arranging her carefully, giving the thigh some room. He slipped off her short boots one at a time, and paused, looking at her foot in his hands a moment, before setting the boots by the bed. A designer logo glinted at him in the bed-table light as he tucked her under the sheet and blanket. She murmured, non-words of drowsiness and breathed deep. Paul fetched a glass of water from the kitchen sink and set it on the bed table.

"What now, Sima?" he asked her sleeping form. He hadn't stopped thinking of the evening and its events, but he didn't know what more to think *about* them. And now . . .

Paul returned to the kitchen, and set his kettle on for tea. Then turned the stove off, poured himself a generous brandy instead, and got out his sketchbook. He started with the small lotus tattoo he'd found just above Sima's left ankle.

11

Sima woke from a dreamless sleep in a strange bed. *No, Paul's bed.* She'd been drowsy, even sort of stoned on the aftermath of the tattoo and what followed, but that wasn't the same thing as inebriated or drugged. She remembered everything: Paul's kiss, his hands, his cock, his *presence.* She remembered him picking her up and carrying her up the stairs, and tucking her in. It had been . . . very nice. Every bit of it.

She sat up in the bed, carefully avoiding touching or moving her raw leg. A clock by the bedside told her in red LED that it wasn't even midnight yet. The bedroom was dark, but light spilled in from a door open to an adjacent room where muted sounds of scratchy, ancient blues music played. The room itself was spare, and seemed well kept in the dim light. Dark furniture, and a handful of framed pictures she couldn't make out, nothing remarkable or odd. Another door, on the opposite wall, led to a bathroom. Which was good, because she really needed to pee.

Her bottoms were still absent under her skirt, which made it easier, and she was rather messy and a bit achy, which made it less easy. She found she really didn't mind. She hadn't gotten laid in longer than she cared to think about, but it hadn't been just "getting laid". Paul knew something about her none of her lovers ever had, and it was the strangest thing to feel acceptance for it – and more than that – when she'd been so certain the opposite was the only possible thing.

Paul was sprawled on a very comfortable-looking scuffed-leather couch, reading in the living/dining room. He'd changed clothes, wearing a faded concert T-shirt of a band Sima didn't know, and black skater shorts. They revealed his legs were tattooed as well, but she couldn't make out what the designs were from her angle.

He looked up as she emerged, and smiled a small smile. "Hi, Sima. How do you feel?"

"Hi, Paul. I feel . . ." Her thigh throbbed with familiar pain. "Good. Really good."

"You should drink some water, but do you want tea also? Something to eat?"

"No, thank you. Wait." Suddenly she was starving. "Yes!"

Paul nodded, put his reader down on a scarred-wood coffee table, next to an empty tumbler and sketchbook. He got up and turned to the kitchen alcove at the far corner of the room. The place was immaculately clean, though every piece of furniture was old and spoke of a past functional life before arriving in Paul's apartment. The coffee table had wheels – it used to be a factory loading pallet. The couch itself looked like it could have once adorned the office of an eighties fat-cat CEO. And so on through an eclectic mix of styles. Nothing antique, but everything weathered and well used, and yet well cared for.

"How do you feel about turkey sandwiches?" he asked, peering into his open fridge door.

"I'm in favor of them," she said, smiling.

Paul nodded, reaching for ingredients. Sima stepped to the kitchen area and took a seat on one of the rickety-looking, solid-feeling stools fronting the counter/table. As he extracted food and implements, and poured water, Sima tried to read him, and couldn't. She watched his creature-covered arms as he worked.

"Thank you," she said, wondering if she could actually name the things she was thanking him for.

Paul smiled thinly, opening a deli package, and then putting it down and looking up at her.

"Tell me about the lotus."

Her breath caught for a moment, the chain of thoughts

flashing from *How did he see?* to *Of course he saw*, to *What does he think?* to *Nothing good, he thinks I'm a hypocrite or game player*. But if Paul did think that, it wasn't apparent on his face, which was almost maddeningly neutral. She let out a breath and dove in, words rushing.

"I hate it. It's how I discovered I don't want . . . can't have real tattoos. The others, I know they're all there, but . . . they're *mine*. I own them. I just can't stand something so visibly permanent talking to other people. I don't even have pierced ears. I usually cover it with make-up if I'm going to be bare-footed."

"Then why did you get it?" he asked.

"Because of the needle. You probably saw, *you* would be able to, the bottom of it covers a scar. That I gave it to myself. Because I was playing with needles. No, not playing. You know what I was doing."

"No. Tell me."

Paul's attention was on her, still neutral, but hyper-focused. Now the words came harder.

"I was trying to find that feeling. To make it. I'd been doing it for years, one little stick at a time. Well, it started with one at a time . . ."

"How. How did it start?"

She felt a flash of rage at him for pushing, for digging at her like this, for needling. But as soon as she thought of the meta-phor, the anger dissipated. He wanted to see what was under her skin. Of course he did. She took a deep breath.

"My parents took me to India when I was eleven, to visit extended family. We went for two months and travelled all over. My father loved the old, crowded marketplaces, and took us to more than I can remember, though he never let my sister or me out of his sight. There was one, I think in Surat. Almost in the middle of the street there was this really old, really skinny, almost naked yogi, lying on a bed of nails. I didn't believe it, because, at eleven, I knew everything and was certain that had just been a story for children – and tourists. But there he was, and he got up as I watched him while my father was haggling for something. His back and legs . . . they were smooth. No pinpricks, no indents from the nails, no nothing. I was *sure* then it was fake, and just for show, and to prove it to myself, walked over to the board with all the nails and poked it with my finger.

"I was wrong. The nails weren't just sharp, they were *very* sharp. I'd just stuck two fingers in four places and they bled. And they hurt! The shock of it . . .I kind of shrieked, which alerted my dad that I had snuck from his side, and then there was a huge to-do. My father angry and scared, the yogi annoyed and bemused, the people crowding around . . . It all kind of focused the pricks in my fingers. The feeling went right down my spine. I didn't realize it was basically indistinguishable from . . . arousal until a little later. But once I made the connection, I stole some of my mother's sewing needles.

"The ankle was stupid. About four years ago, I neglected to clean everything properly, got an infection and was left with a visible scar. It felt a lot bigger than it was, but I thought it was like a spotlight. I convinced myself that covering it up was better than having it there . . . and, well, I was living on my own for the first time. I could make my own decisions. Even bad ones."

"So, the tattoo was bad, but getting that tattoo . . ."

"Yeah. It felt like that day. Like what I'd been looking for, but *more*. And so . . . I'm a . . .I don't know. Freak. Addict. Per—"

"Names don't matter, Sima. You are what you are."

12

Sima looked startled at his interruption. Paul had the feeling she'd gone through this little spiral of review and recrimination more than once before.

"You've never told anyone about this, have you?"

Sima gave a short, humorless laugh. "No! My father still tells the story as 'the time Sima almost got kidnapped in the market', though there had never been anything like that."

Paul reached across the counter and took her hand in his; she let him.

"Thank you for telling me. No matter whether we wear them inside or out, the marks of our history are always on us, and the oddest small things can leave the biggest marks."

Paul turned his left arm, showing her the underside of his forearm. The legs of the black scorpion design that seemed perched on the top of the arm wrapped most of the way around his wrist, but didn't close. In that gap, artfully framed by arthropod legs was a rather sloppy-looking, and faded, "REBEL" with cartoony flames coming off the letters.

"That was my first tattoo. I did it myself when I was thirteen, and had no idea what I was doing."

Sima's eyes went wide.

"It hurt, and it changed things. The trade of pain for something. It was powerful, even though the *art* was crude and poor. I expended a lot of teen angst trying to figure out whether I'd ruined my life, or opened an amazing new door. I didn't get another for a long time, but I studied them – and the people that got them. And then the people who gave them. When I decided on more, I still wanted to do it myself. And when I decided I wanted to do it for a living, I promised myself I wouldn't use any technique on a client that I hadn't tried on myself first."

"So all of your tattoos . . . ?"

"Most. Not all of them. Some areas are harder to reach." He smiled. "My main mentor, and one more, are the only two others who've inked me."

Sima looked thoughtful. "You're . . . very careful with who you let under your skin."

Paul nodded, smiling wryly. "It is indeed that literal."

"Kind of like wearing your heart on your sleeve."

Paul made a show of checking the bestiary on his arms. There were no hearts of any kind on display. "Yes, but *not* literally,"

Sima laughed.

"But here's the point," Paul continued. "While our whole

past builds us, key events draw outsized, unexpected patterns in us. So in the end, we are the canvases we are, whether or not you can see the designs clearly. And . . . I like what you are. The histories that marked us, I think they made us, in this one maybe unique way, matched opposites."

Sima nodded, slowly.

"You took me by surprise that way. But I like that I found you. That you found me. I like it a lot. And there's a part of me that'd be quite content for us to simply use each other to scratch our respective itches. I think you know by now you can come back to me again for that. I want to take my needle to you again."

Sima shivered visibly at that. Maybe she hadn't known.

"But I have one condition," he said. "Your lotus tattoo. Let me color it. I want one mark that shows. I . . . need that much. I can make it something you'll like. Or at least hate less."

Sima sat quietly for a long moment, eyes searching his face, then tracing his arms to where he still held her hands. She disengaged one and drank most of her water in one go. She nodded slowly. "Okay."

Paul smiled, part exultant, but then went serious again, and considerably less certain. "But, I really want more still than that. Or rather, I want to know if there's more to be had."

A range of expressions played across her face, culminating in an almost bashful smile. "Are you . . . asking me out?"

"Yes. I suppose I am." Paul broke eye contact, and set to the organizing and assembling of snacks. "But not tonight. Sandwiches in tonight. And tea – unless you want something stronger. "

"Paul." Sima's hand was on his, index finger caressing the fang of the snake.

"Yes?"

"I want to see your tattoos. And hear their stories. All of them."

The first part, Paul had heard a number of times before, but the second, only once, and when he had far less ink than now. Sima was asking for a not-small thing. *And,* Paul thought, *she knows it.* Which was why he agreed.

13

"Nine years ago, hiking the Rockies with May, before we'd gotten serious."

May, Paul's last long-term relationship, had been the inspiration or impetus for two other of Paul's tattoos, though nothing so banal as a name.

"We were almost at our campsite of the day, off on a spur trail by ourselves. She spotted it first lying in the sun on an overhanging rock and I almost crashed into her. We took off our packs and stood there, watching it together for almost half an hour, until it got up, stretched, gave us a thorough look-over, and disappeared into the rocks."

Paul stood in his bedroom, in nothing but a pair of boxers, facing Sima sitting on the edge of his bed. The tattoo of the mountain lion, the last of his bestiary, curved down his left leg, looking like it was about to step down onto his foot.

"That night was the night we *got* serious."

"Can I ask, how did things end with her?"

"Yeah. Part of the story, after all. We were together about three years. Lived together for half that. When I started Chrysalis things were pretty hand to mouth for a while, and she missed LA, and we as a couple weren't strong enough to handle both those things."

"I'm sorry, Paul." Sima meant it, just as she felt a tiny, ridiculous tinge of jealousy for a woman she'd never known.

"Nah. She's happier now. Married, too."

"What about you?"

"Me? Not married."

Sima rolled her eyes and poked his shoulder. "No. You know what I mean. Are you happier?"

"Than I was at the end there? Yes. Than I would have been had we toughed it out? I have no idea. But, I'm not much for regrets and what-ifs."

Sima nodded. She now knew there had been at least two other serious lovers since May, but only one had associated ink, the thunderbird on his right thigh. He'd let her touch them as he told her about each one. They'd forgone the tea altogether, and washed their sandwiches down with brandy, a drink Sima wasn't very familiar with. It had emboldened her to ask questions during the show and tell. She liked the feel of his skin, and the contrast of its smoothness and warmth under the fierce images.

All Paul's tattoos were animals of one sort or another, though some – like the thunderbird – were highly stylized. They covered his arms to his shoulders, and his legs to his upper thighs, but his chest and back were bare, save for a modest pattern of hair as black as that on his head. She planned on asking about that, later.

"Have I missed any?" she asked.

"No. That's the last of them."

"Are you sure? You're not hiding anything under there?" She hooked the waistband of his boxers and snapped it playfully, feeling bold.

Paul chuckled. "I may be hiding something, but not a tattoo."

"Show me?" She used the voice that used to get her (almost) anything she wanted from her father. She probably wasted it, because he smiled instead of scowled.

"Trade. You show me, too. I want to check your bandage, anyway."

She had to admit it was fair, and it was kind of what she'd had in mind anyway. But being asked to get undressed made it a *thing*. Still, Paul went first, and pulled off his last piece of clothing to stand naked before her. Van was right. Even after the full tour, Paul, with his feral menagerie of ink, was scary hot. His cock, the first time she really had a chance to see it, was not-quite soft. And, as he watched her pull her shirt over her head and undo her bra, she saw it harden.

She stood to unfasten her skirt and let it drop to the floor, and then Paul was there, one hand at her hip, the other lifting her chin so her lips could meet his. He kissed her once, gently, then again, like kissing her was saving one of their lives. His beard was half soft, half wiry. She liked it. The head of his cock, fully hard now, nudged her stomach and Sima couldn't help but giggle at the fleshy poke. She feared she'd ruined the moment when Paul disengaged from that wonderful kiss. But he was smiling. "Devilishly" would have been the right adverb, too.

"Bandage check. Stay there," he said, and sank down, kissing her every couple of inches as he knelt. He placed a last, slow kiss halfway between her bellybutton and her vulva. It made her catch her breath.

"Open," he said, tapping her left foot. Sima shifted it away, standing now with her feet a bit more than shoulder width apart. It was plenty for Paul to check the wrap, and it seemed to meet his approval. Sima was going to ask to be sure, but only a gasp came out. In one slight, quick motion, Paul had turned his head and pressed his mouth against her cunt. His tongue was wet, and hot, and ... *Oh God.* Sima's fingers threaded and gripped his hair as Paul pulled her to him, and she moaned aloud as they pressed into each other.

Paul knew what to do with lips and tongue, and made Sima shudder as he discovered each new nuance of her pleasure. But right now, she wanted something else. She pulled on his hair until he came away and looked up at her, lips and beard soaked with her. She pulled up, to get him to stand, and then released him to step back and sit on the bed, legs parting in invitation.

Paul smiled hungrily, wiping his lips on his forearm and eyed her bandage. "I don't want to aggravate that. Turn around."

After a tiny hesitation, Sima turned. She kept her eyes on Paul's face the best she could, as she turned to hands and knees on the mattress. The touch of his hands on the curve of her waist was electric. The nestling of his cock into her open cunt was lightning. He gripped her and pushed inside. All the way.

"Ooh. God. It hurts." It *had* been a long time for Sima. She was sore from before. Paul's filling of her made her taxed, stretched inner muscles protest.

"Does it, Sima?" Paul's voice lower, growling. The hands on her hips dug into her flesh as he pulled part-way out and thrust back in, hard enough to make her gasp.

"Yes," she breathed, half whining. Then she looked over her shoulder at him. "Please don't stop."

Paul didn't stop. He didn't stop as her bruised-feeling insides screamed at her and brought tears to her eyes. He didn't stop when the pain seared its way into something so much more. He didn't even stop when she screamed and came, her thoroughly fucked passage squeezing him in agonized, delicious overuse. He didn't stop when her arms gave out and her front half sank limply to the bed; he held her hips up to his fuck and only drove harder. Until he yanked her back to him with a brutal finality and came.

14

It had been a long, sweltering summer, and the bones of the city still radiated warmth even as the night air finally began to cool. The low clouds this Friday night reflected the orange urban light back down, and promised welcome rain, at long last.

The vacant shopfront to the left of Chrysalis now housed an upstart Chai-bar, a sign that the battlefront between Midtown and District may have moved to the next block. The bell on Paul's door was the same, though, as was the smile on Eejay's face when Sima stepped in.

"Hi, mystery girl," Eejay said, "Paul said you were coming. Hot date?" Sima had gotten to know Eejay, and Xavier, a bit over the summer, as she became something of a fixture at Chrysalis in the late week and weekends. They'd even all four gone out a couple of times. Eejay seemed convinced that aside from "seeing" Paul, Sima was getting secret, intimately located tattoos she wouldn't show anyone. And she was right, in a way.

"Something like." Sima smiled.

"That you, Sima?" came Paul's voice from the studio. "Come on back."

"Listen to the man, sugar. I've got some supplies to put away, then it's me and *my* man all . . . weekend . . . long." She said each of the last three words with a sway of her hips.

Sima was still laughing as she passed through to the studio. Paul was working. The client was an older man, in his sixties at least, eyes closed, breathing slow and steady as Paul worked on his back. As Sima approached, he opened his eyes and winked at her.

"Tell me what you think, missy."

She walked around to see Paul's work. He was refreshing an old, faded tattoo of a fighter jet, weapons blazing across his shoulder.

"A6-Intruder, meanest thing in the sky when I flew. And the chicks so dug it."

"Please do not flirt with my girlfriend, Mr Randall." Paul's voice scolded, but he was smiling.

"Only because you know I can steal her." Mr Randall turned to wink at Sima again, and continued to flirt light-heartedly and unashamedly as Paul finished.

"What a nice, dirty old man, Paul," Sima said, as he returned from seeing the client out and locking the shop.

Paul smiled. "And devotedly married, too. For forty years. He has his aircraft carrier on his chest, but with his wife's name on it." He made as if to lead her toward the back door. "I know the guys playing at Royal Blues tonight, they're really good."

"I don't feel like going out tonight," Sima said, smile slipping as she stepped over to the client's chair. Her voice changed. Needful. Paul heard it.

"Ah. Well. Tell me, love."

"I want your thunderbird. Here." Sima pulled the bottom of her sweater up, and the waist of her skirt down, baring the skin of her lower abdomen, to just above her mound. Bare skin.

"My thunderb—You've shaved!" Paul remarked.

"I needed room for the talons."

"Mmm. It's going to be tricky. You're going to have to be very still."

"I'll try."

"It's going to hurt."

He said it almost like a ritual incantation. Like he had with the other two inkless tattoos he'd given her over the spring and summer. The anatomic heart on her sternum was a faint trace now even he barely could see, and the multiple star pattern across the small of her back was nearly as gone. The lotus blossom on her ankle, however, was now a vibrant, gorgeous red.

"I know."

Paul smiled that smile, *her* smile, then leaned in and kissed her.

As she scooted back onto the seat, Sima's leg brushed Paul. He was already hard.

Which was just as well. Sima was soaked as she pulled her skirt and panties low enough to expose the work area, but no lower. Not yet.

Equal, opposed anticipation buzzed between them.

They both watched the needle descend to her skin.

A Problem with Authority

Lucy Felthouse

Private Jesse Bagnall glowered and muttered to himself all the way to the mess. He'd just been bawled out by Corporal Roxanne Grey – yet again – and he was getting seriously fed up of it. He knew he wasn't perfect in the drill exercises, but then nor were any of the other guys. It was like she was singling him out and aiming all her abuse in his direction. Being shouted at was to be expected in the Army – it was almost part of the job description – but Corporal Grey's attitude was bordering on discriminatory, and he didn't know what to do about it. Especially without looking like a total pussy.

Spotting some of his closest friends at a table towards the back of the mess, he caught the eye of one of them – Matt Kay – raised a hand in greeting, then got in line for his food.

Several minutes later, he loaded his cup of tea onto his tray along with everything else and headed over to where he'd seen Matt and the boys. Hopefully they'd take his mind off the Queen Bitch. They were always game for a laugh.

"All right, lads?" he said, sliding his tray onto the table and taking a seat.

There were mumbles of assent.

"Yeah," replied Ed Patterson. "You?"

"Yeah, I suppose."

Ed raised an eyebrow, and the other men turned their attention to Jesse, too. "Well," Ed said, "that wasn't very convincing. What's up, mate?"

Jesse sighed, ran a hand through his hair. "It's the drill instructor."

His friends exchanged confused looks. "Care to elaborate?" Matt said.

Not wanting to look a wimp in front of his mates, Jesse changed his tone. But once he had, the anger took over him. "She's a fucking bitch, that's what!"

The confused expressions turned to surprised ones.

"I'm fed up with her treating me like a twat. I know it's her job to bawl us out, but she takes it too far. I do my fucking best, work my arse off, and it's still not good enough for her."

He barely noticed the gazes of his friends shifting slightly, carried on regardless. "She definitely picks on me more than everyone else. As though I've been sitting on my arse when everyone else is killing themselves to get it right. She's just being a complete and utter bitch. Bitch face fucking Grey!"

Matt cleared his throat, to no avail.

"You know what her problem is? She needs a fucking good shag, she does. That might cheer the miserable cow up. Mind you, Christ knows what man would be brave enough to go there. She'd probably bite your cock off as soon as suck it."

As the red mist of his anger dissipated, Jesse finally clocked the reactions of the other men around his table. They weren't at all what he'd expect. Ed and Matt looked mighty chagrined, staring at a point over his left shoulder. Private Graham Pilgrim had actually put his head down and begun to bang it on the table.

A cold trickle of dread ran down his back, and he turned, wondering which of his superiors had heard his rant.

Fuck. It was none other than the target of his diatribe. Corporal Roxanne Grey stood, her arms crossed, one high-heeled foot tapping on the floor. Her facial expression was as far from impressed as it was possible to be.

Coolly, she said, "Guard room, now."

Jesse's heart sunk into his heavy-duty boots, and he had to resist the temptation to drop his gaze to the floor. His buddies would never let him live it down. He had to do as the woman said otherwise he'd be guilty of insubordination, but he was going to do it in the manliest way possible.

Turning back to the table, he sneaked a quick glance at each of his friends in turn, hoping his expression looked irritated, not shit scared, which was what he really was. Standing, he left his lunch where it was and followed Corporal Grey out of the mess, across the yard and into the scruffy-looking building that was the guard room. God, the government really needed to put some money into this place – it certainly didn't give off the air of tough professionalism that the personnel were expected to show.

After opening the door, Corporal Grey stood aside and ushered him in. She then followed him, shutting the door behind them and twisting the lock. The room was empty. She moved to sit in a chair, and motioned him to take another one.

"I suppose you know why you're here?"

"Yes, ma'am. My unforgivable words and actions back in the mess." Now it was just the two of them, he could grovel as much as he felt necessary without worrying about losing face.

"Hmm. Yes. But actually, it's more the reason behind the words I'm interested in."

"W—what do you mean?"

"You mentioned that you feel like I pick on you, more than I do anyone else during drill instruction. As though you're sitting on your arse, I do believe were your words."

Jesse fought the colour coming to his face, and failed miserably. "Y—yes, ma'am."

"Do I really make you feel that way? Or were you just having a whinge to your mates? Tell me honestly, please."

The anger had gone from her tone, and her expression was open, expectant. She really and truly wanted him to be honest. He opened and closed his mouth, not unlike a fish, a couple of times, before clearing his throat and attempting to form an answer. It didn't help that, now she'd stopped screaming at him and was actually being quite pleasant, he'd come to the conclusion that she was hot. Even in her army uniform, she looked feminine, as though she was hiding a delicious body underneath all that olive green.

"O—okay then. Yes, you do. Ever since you turned up to drill us in preparation for the parade, you've made me feel like a useless sack of shit. I know it's important, God, do I know, and I want to get it right, but I really am trying my best. I'm giving this my all, and it seems as though it's just not good enough for you. Some of the other guys are worse than me, and you don't come down on them like a ton of bricks. Maybe just half a ton." He smiled weakly, hoping she'd realize he was joking.

A tiny smile played at the corners of the corporal's lips. "Would it make you feel any better if I told you why I'm doing it? Shouting at you more than the others, I mean."

"Um, I guess it depends on what you're going to say. I'm really not as shit as some of the other guys."

"I know. But . . ." She got to her feet and moved to stand in front of Jesse. Leaning down and placing her hands on the arms of his chair, she continued. "Let's just say I'm trying not to let my true feelings show. If people found out how much I want you, I don't think it would go down too well."

"W—want me? *You* want *me*?" His heart pounded, and his brain raced to keep up with what she was saying. Did she really mean what he thought she meant? Was there a way he could have misunderstood her words? He didn't think so. "You mean, like, want me in the sex way?" He knew his phrasing was ridiculous, but he couldn't think of anything better right at that moment. His brain was too fried.

Corporal Grey laughed, her blue eyes sparkling as crinkles appeared in their corners. It was adorable and sexy all at once, and his cock surprised him by hardening.

"Yes," she said, "I mean in the sex way. But I guess you know now why I've been behaving the way I have. Can you forgive me? I didn't mean to make you feel like a useless sack of shit. I'm sorry."

"Yeah, I can forgive you. But only if you make it up to me." It seemed his cock had taken over control of his mouth and voice box now, because as the words floated into the air, he realized he had no idea what he actually meant.

"Oh yeah?" Moving her hands to her hips, Corporal Grey adopted a saucy stance. "And how am I supposed to do that?"

Jesse cast his gaze about the room rapidly, hoping for inspiration. Thankfully, he spotted something that would serve his purpose perfectly. He stood, gently pushed past her and retrieved the pace stick that was propped up in the corner. Designed for marking time in parades and similar when it was open in a 'V' shape, closed it was just a wooden stick. One he could use to get his own back on Corporal Grey. And he really had to stop thinking of her as Corporal Grey, especially considering what he was about to do. She was Roxanne.

Turning back to her, he stifled a grin when he saw the look on her face. She obviously hadn't been expecting that. Pointing to a nearby table, he commanded, "Pull your skirt up to your waist and bend over that table."

"O—okay."

She sounded nervous, and he didn't blame her. Frankly, he was surprised she'd agreed. He was wielding quite an interesting weapon, and she was going to allow him to use it on her. Perhaps she was into a bit of pain. He'd soon find out.

Following her to the table, he waited while she summoned her courage, then lifted her skirt. His eyebrows nearly disappeared into his close-cropped hairline when he saw the skimpy black thong that had been hidden beneath her dull skirt. It bisected lovely pale, round bum cheeks, and suddenly he wanted nothing more than to pull the material aside and bury his cock in her warm depths.

First, though, Roxanne had some making up to do. "Ready?"

Pressing her hands to the surface of the table, she nodded quickly.

Jesse moved into the position he thought best and waved the pace stick around a little, to get used to the way it moved and balanced. He'd never spanked a woman before, never mind with one of these things. God knows why he'd even suggested it. She probably thought he was some kind of kinky bastard, now. Never mind, it was just a bit of fun.

Fun that was already making his cock throb and press insistently at the inside of his combats, he realized. Sucking in a deep breath, he drew his arm back and forth a couple of times, practising the correct angle to strike Roxanne's delectable bottom. He didn't want to accidentally whack the back of her legs, or miss utterly and hit the table.

Coming to the conclusion he could do this all day and not feel any more confident, he figured he should just go for it. Shifting his arm back once more, he then swung it all the way forward until the pace stick hit her naked skin. There was an interesting slapping sound, followed by a yelp from Roxanne. Milliseconds later, a red stripe decorated her skin. It looked kinda sexy, and as she hadn't screamed blue murder and run away or tried to kill him, he decided she could take it.

After lining up carefully once more, he laid another stripe on her arse. It bobbed enticingly with the impact, and another red mark appeared next to the first. His cock was fit to burst. God, he hoped she'd be up for sex after this. Perhaps he oughtn't push her too far, just in case. He definitely didn't want to go and have to rub one out in his bunk.

Two more swings later and Jesse decided to change his tactics. The stick was fun and it probably hurt like hell, but it was damn unwieldy and he wanted to lay strikes on her faster and with more precision. There was only one thing for it – he'd have to use his hand.

Discarding the stick with more eagerness than he'd admit to, he reached out and stroked Roxanne's burning cheeks. "OK for a few with my hand?" he asked.

"Yes." She was breathless, sounded as though she was on the verge of tears, but if she wanted him to stop, she'd have said so. Corporal Roxanne Grey was no pushover.

Shrugging, he altered his position once more and whacked her right cheek. Then the left. If her skin hadn't already been red, he was sure he'd have left handprints. Growing more confident, he slapped her harder, experimenting with a flattened hand, a cupped hand, to see which made the best sounds or caused her to gasp more loudly.

Soon, he could take no more. His hand stung like fuck, and if he didn't do something with his cock soon he was probably going to come in his underwear. He rained a few more blows down on her for good measure, then grabbed her by the shoulders, pulled her upright and spun her round.

Her face was red, her eyes wide. But she hadn't been crying, and she didn't look angry. In fact, she looked as horny as he felt, her lips parted enticingly. Taking advantage, he slanted his mouth over hers and kissed her with all the need and arousal he was experiencing, hoping like hell she wouldn't decide he'd gone a step too far.

Thankfully, she didn't. She returned the embrace, slipping her arms around his neck and kissing him back with a bruising ferocity. So it seemed she *did* like the pain. That was something clearly worth knowing. Their tongues brushed together, explored, tickled and fought until Jesse was dizzy with need. Pulling away, he gasped for air, then said, "Roxanne, I really need to fuck you, but I don't have a condom."

A coquettish smile taking over her lips, she replied, "It's OK, I do." She moved away from him, over to a bank of lockers, opened one of the doors and pulled out a handbag. She dipped her hand inside, rummaged around a little and emerged with a foil packet.

"Wow, you're prepared." He couldn't hide his surprise.

"Wouldn't you be if you were one of the few women on an army base?"

"Touché. Now, shall we make use of it?"

"Abso-fucking-lutely. Get your cock out."

The woman really was full of surprises. Doing as he was told, he undid his combats and pulled his cock out, stroking it up and down a couple of times while she ripped open the packet. He took the protection from her and rolled it down his shaft carefully, then pushed on the base to make sure it was secure.

Shuffling towards the table, where Roxanne had now

perched, skirt still up, legs akimbo and the gusset of her panties pulled to one side, Jesse was slammed with another massive wave of arousal. Her cunt was gorgeous. Hairless, swollen, pink and slick, he wanted to taste it. But that would have to wait for another time – if he was lucky enough to get one. For now, he'd give her the most memorable fuck he possibly could.

"Ready?" he said, gripping his shaft with one hand and moving the other around her back.

"Yes, Private, I'm ready. Just get on with it, will you?" Her words were harsh, but the look in her eyes told him that she was feeling as horny, as playful as he, and she really wanted to fuck.

Not wanting to disappoint, he positioned himself between her thighs, aimed his cockhead at her entrance and pushed home. She was tight, yet incredibly wet, so he didn't meet much resistance as he penetrated her. And yet, she felt like a warm, slick glove around him. If he wasn't careful, he was going to be in danger of premature ejaculation.

Slipping a hand between their bodies, he sought her clit, which was not difficult considering how large it was, distended with arousal. God, could this woman get any damn sexier? Stroking, pinching and rolling the flesh as he rocked in and out of her, he was determined to find out exactly what pushed her buttons so her climax would wring his own out of him. He'd come then, but not before.

Capturing her lips once more, he poured everything he had into pleasuring her. A long, hard, sensual kiss. Varying movements on her bud, and alternate fast and shallow, then slow and deep pumps of his cock. He'd find out what worked for her and exploit it to the extreme. In the meantime, he had to hang on to his own orgasm. He would not come until she did. Absolutely not.

Soon, he found the perfect formula. Suckling on her bottom lip, he pressed hard on her clit and fucked her fast and furiously. Her moans grew louder, then quieter as she remembered where she was. It wouldn't do either of them any good to get caught.

Suddenly, Roxanne's internal walls gripped him so hard he

thought she'd pull his cock off. The pressure was intense, constant. Then she pulled her face away from his, yanked the collar of her shirt into her mouth and bit down as she tumbled into bliss.

Amazed, he watched her face go through a number of changes as her cunt gripped harder still, then released and went into a series of spasms, milking his cock. Shunting into her a couple more times, he let himself go with a sense of relief. The tingle shot from the base of his spine, leaving a line of fire running up his shaft and out of the tip as he came. He gritted his teeth to keep himself quiet, enjoying the immense sensations of his own climax and Roxanne's combined. He wouldn't have been able to hang on much longer, she was just too good.

They held on to one another as they rode out their respective orgasms, and Jesse found himself hoping against all hope that this wasn't a one-off.

"Hey," he said gently, when he finally regained his voice. "You all right?"

Looking every inch as though she'd just floated down to Earth, she nodded, and grinned dopily. "Yeah. You? We all square? Have I made it up to you sufficiently?"

"Hell yeah." He pressed a kiss to her forehead. "So does this mean you're gonna be nicer to me now?"

"Uh, no. People will notice. I'd rather carry on being a total bitch to you, then I can keep fucking you in private and no one will suspect a thing."

"Oh, well, when you put it like that . . . be as bitchy as you like."

"I thought you might say that."

Grinning, Jesse voiced his next thought. "So, you got another condom?"

Limits: A Love Story

Lisabet Sarai

He's the sadist in our relationship. But I'm the one who's more extreme.

He wanted to strap a butterfly vibe to my clit, to ramp up my arousal so I could better bear the pain. Does he really believe I could be more aroused than I already am?

I'm immobilized in one of our dinette chairs. Leather cuffs secure my wrists and ankles. Woven straps encircle my thighs, my upper arms, my waist and torso. The first rasp of separating Velcro liquefied me. No, that's not right. I've been soaked since I served him dinner and he informed me, ever so casually, that tonight was the night.

He putters around the kitchen, drawing out the preparations, making me wait. My Master possesses an instinctive sense of timing – an asset for any Dom. He plays every action for greatest effect. The goose-necked lamp from my desk has already been plugged in, ready to dispel any shadows. After spreading a clean towel on the breakfast bar beside my chair, he lays out his materials and implements, one at a time: latex gloves, a cigarette lighter, rubbing alcohol, cotton balls, Betadine, gauze, surgical tape, and, finally, two gleaming, silvery scalpels. The steel flashes under the fluorescent lights, impossibly sharp. A shudder ripples through my bound body, half terror, half lust. My juices pool under my bare ass.

He cups my chin in his palm and raises my face to his. His lips curve into a half-smile. I know from his eager inhalation that he's caught my pussy scent. My cheeks burn, but he won't let me look away.

"Are you all right, Becca?" His voice makes me think of polished mahogany and warm honey, dark, rich and sweet beyond measure. He could order me to do anything in that voice and I'd rush to obey. "Still want to go ahead?"

Shame and desire battle inside me. No matter how many scenes we play, I'm always appalled by my own perversity. I swallow hard, unable to force the words out. How can I want this? How can I admit that I do?

"Answer me, slut!" With his free hand he gives a vicious twist to my right nipple. It's still swollen and tender from the clamps he made me wear through dinner. A bolt of pain arcs from the abused nub down to my engorged clit, transmuting to electric pleasure along the way.

"Ow! Oh!" He slides a finger along the wet slit between my splayed thighs, then snatches it away. I jerk against the straps, trying to follow his retreat. "Oh, please . . ." When he licks off my juices, I nearly come at the sight of his tongue, nimble and delicate as a cat's.

"You're certainly wet enough to make me believe this is what you want. But you know the rules, Becca. You've got to ask for it."

He's almost a foot taller than I am. Normally he looms over me, his massive physicality reinforcing his psychological power, but now he sinks into a crouch, his gaze level with mine. "You can still call this off," he tells me, his voice deep and calm as a waveless lake. "I won't punish you. I won't think less of you. You'll still belong to me."

Something flickers in his chocolate-brown eyes, the merest hint of doubt. I notice a faint sheen of perspiration on his forehead, below the tangled black curls. He's wearing a rubberized apron – the implications making me shiver – so I can't see his crotch. Is he as turned on as I am? And as fright-ened?

"Do *you* want to do it?" I whisper, forgetting to add an honorific, breaking out of the scene in my concern for him.

There's an ache in my chest, a low-frequency, bitter-edged pain quite unlike the bite of his clamps or the sting of his lash. If he's not sure, how can I be? Have I forced this on him? Long ago he seduced me with his tales of handcuffs and spankings. Now I realize he created a monster.

All our firsts parade through my imagination, an escalating frenzy of sadomasochist indulgence. The first time he fucked my ass (during our very first sexual encounter, but after a long and filthy epistolary courtship). The first time he whipped me. The first caning, first fisting, fire play, golden shower. In our years together, we've demolished one limit after another, only to move on to the next.

I know he cherishes me, that my willingness to explore and experiment delights him. When I surrender, the assurance that I've pleased him brings me far more fulfillment than any physical release he might graciously provide. Now I wonder though, whether I've been topping from below all along.

Perusing his serious face, noting the way his lips press together and his brows knit in tension, I'm suddenly convinced that this is all wrong. I'm pushing him way beyond his comfort zone with my implicit demands for ever more extreme submission.

"I'm sorry," I mutter. "Forgive me, Master."

"What? What are you talking about?" He grips my shoulder, leaning forward, cruel fingers digging into my naked flesh. The slight pain does not distract me from my misery. "I told you, Becca, it's your choice. You can stop this now. You don't have to apologize."

"No, no, you don't understand." My eyes itch as tears well up. Trussed up as I am, I can't stop one from spilling down the side of my nose. "I don't want to stop. But I think you do."

He stares at me for a long instant, confused, before bursting into laughter. "You think I want to stop this?"

I nod, swallowing a sob.

"You believe I don't want to carve my initials into your flesh? Mark you permanently, so that everyone will know you're mine? You think I don't have the guts?" He rises to his feet, towering above me. For a moment I expect a slap in the face. A wave of lust crests and drowns me. I squirm in my chair, struggling for control, feeling the straps tighten around my limbs.

"No, no, it's not like that, Master . . . I'm sorry . . . but I've been the one . . . I'm never satisfied, it seems, always wanting to go one step further, to try something more . . . ."

"More intense." He finishes my sentence for me. "More dangerous. Something that requires even more trust."

"I shouldn't be so greedy, so selfish. You're my Master. You should decide how far we go, and how fast. What I want – it shouldn't matter."

"Ah, but it does matter to me, little one." He strokes my hair, working out the tangles. His gentle touch floods me with a sense of well-being. "I love your kinky mind, Becca, as much as your lush body. I love pushing you – seeing how far you'll go for me. Discovering the depths to which you'll sink if I ask."

He seizes a handful of hair and drags my mouth to his. His tug on my scalp turns me molten. New flows of searing liquid leak from between my legs. I relax into his brutal embrace, letting the heat rise.

His kiss sucks the breath from my lungs and the last shreds of doubt from my mind. I open, deliciously helpless to resist or even reciprocate. While he devours me, his fingers roam and hover, tracing phantom paths down my throat, circling my navel, brushing across my damp pussy fur to send reverberations through my cunt. I imagine my aching nipples, flashing bright red like landing beacons to beckon him closer. He ignores my breasts, though, as well as my desperate clit, teasing me with barely there caresses while his fierce kiss continues.

Finally, he releases me, leaving my lips bruised and my cheeks smeared with saliva. He stands back, surveying my bound and naked form with obvious satisfaction. My skin radiates energy; I feel as though I'm glowing. His face is flushed, too, and his eyes glitter like diamonds, brilliant and unrelenting. He crosses his arms over his massive chest and favors me with a mocking grin.

"Speak up, Becca. Tell me. What do you want?"

I must be brave. He expects that of me, and I can't bear to disappoint him. Still, it's difficult to actually say the words.

"I want . . . I want you to cut me, sir. To leave your mark on me. Please, sir."

"Good girl." His palm cradles my cheek for an instant. Then he's gone, over at the sink, washing his hands with anti-bacterial soap. As he worms his hands into the gloves, he murmurs, almost too soft for me to hear, "That's what I want, too."

He's silent and focused as he begins the procedure. Time expands. My pulse slows to synchronize with the Tangerine Dream album he put on after securing me to the chair. The hypnotic music holds me in a trance of arousal. I let my fear drain away with the fluid notes from the synthesizer. I'm in his hands now, his thing, his creation. The realization, as always, brings acute pleasure.

He swabs my left breast with alcohol, leaving icy tracks on my sensitized skin. The hospital scent pricks my nostrils, cold and pitiless. He flicks the lighter and holds one of the blades in the orange fire for what seems like an endless time, twisting and turning it. I'm transfixed by the shiny steel dancing in the flame, falling deeper into the moment. I forget to breathe. Then he raises the tiny knife in front of my face.

"See how sharp it is, Becca. We want clean cuts, no jagged edges. Deep. Perfect. Beautiful." A manic glee illumines his face now. The tender lover has vanished. The sadist has come out to play. A frisson of terror crawls up my spine. I remind myself of all the other times this man has dangled me over the edge of the precipice and still kept me safe. My fear trans-mutes into searing lust.

The tip of the blade is still hot from the flame. My Master presses it against my breast, just hard enough to indent the skin but not to break it. Our eyes lock. He has not asked if I want a blindfold. He knows that I'd refuse.

"Breathe, Rebecca," he instructs. I barely have time to fill my lungs before he increases the force. There's a tangible pop as the blade pierces the top layer of skin. My Master makes a tiny gesture, slicing into me.

I watch the blade part my flesh as though my body were nothing but mist and cloud. The pain is like a falling star streaking across the sky, like sunrise exploding over the ocean, like glass shattering – too high and bright to bear. I suck in my breath and bite my lip. My Master does not look up from his work, but I know he hears me.

A shimmering ruby droplet oozes up around the silver metal. My skin is snowy in contrast. The jewel-like orb swells as more blood feeds it, until it bursts. A scarlet rivulet meanders down over the side of my breast and onto my belly, steaming, it seems, like molten lava. My clit feels ready to burst as well. The sting of the wound is all but erased by a clenching surge of pleasure.

"Be still," my lover commands, sensing my need to writhe almost before I do. "It would be a shame if I made a mistake."

He moves the scalpel with infinite care, tracing a graceful curve just above my nipple. A crimson trail follows his progress. I watch in fascination as he turns me into a bloody canvas for his twisted art.

We'd agreed he'd carve his initials, signing his name to his property. We'd debated about the location. He'd suggested somewhere less visible – my inner thigh or my ass. I'd insisted that my breasts were most appropriate, given his fondness for that area of my anatomy. I wanted him to sign over my heart. Plus, I told him, I wanted to watch.

Now, though, I can scarcely endure it. It's simply too much sensation. The blade rips through me like fire. My breast is being consumed. A lingering, throbbing agony plays counterpoint to the initial bite when the blade breaks the skin. I struggle to inhale and exhale, slowly and deeply, the way I've been taught, as my Master continues.

His entire being is focused on his work. My left breast is smeared with gore, as are his gloves. I can't make out the design; I wonder that he can. A twinge of horror creeps into my soul. It's too extreme, too cruel. Who would choose such madness? I can't believe I'm doing this.

And yet, I am – no, we are, he and I, so perfectly matched that he intuits my desires almost before I'm aware of them. He glances up from my torn flesh, his face luminous with power and lust. "Mine," he murmurs, or perhaps I just imagine this, my mind hazed by the heady mix of pain and pleasure. "Mine, forever."

I'm sunk too far into my submissive fugue to speak. All I can do is open to him, heart, mind, body, spirit, trusting that he'll read my answer.

How long has he been cutting me? I don't know. I don't care, not really. I float in a rosy fog where love and surrender are the only realities. Not until he begins to loosen my bonds do I return to my body.

"Little one," he's saying, chafing my wrists. "Are you OK?"

I nod, warmed by his smile, soothed by his voice. I feel vague, intoxicated, boneless. When he unfastens the strap around my waist, I slump forward. He captures me in his arms and carries me to the bedroom, where he stretches out beside me and peppers my face with kisses.

"Oh, Becca! The things you make me do!" He cups my unmarked breast and suckles the tip. Pleasure emanates from that taut nub to suffuse my whole body.

His tenderness focuses my thoughts and my lust. I grope downward, seeking his cock. He's already swollen; he hardens further at my touch. "Please . . . Master . . ."

He lifts his head from my breast and arches one eyebrow. "Yes? What do you want now, my little slut?"

"Take off your clothes. Please? And fuck me."

"You're weak. You've lost blood. You need to rest." He's trying to be the sane, responsible Dom, but I know him too well.

I try to pull his shirt out from his trousers. "I need you inside me. More than anything else."

He doesn't resist, not really. He knows how stubborn I can

be, and of course he's dying to take me, too, to finish the job of claiming me.

I lie on my back, arms spread wide and thighs even wider, as though I were cuffed. We both like to pretend I'm power-less. He kneels between my legs, huge and fearsome in his nakedness, his massive erection arrowing toward the ceiling. Ocean-musk rises from my cunt to fill the room. He rubs the fat bulb of his cock back and forth over my lower lips, care-fully avoiding my clit.

"Don't tease," I beg. "I can't take it."

"You can take more than you realize," he replies with an evil laugh. "And I'm the one to give it you." Aligning his cock with my slick opening, he impales me with a single jerk of his hips.

After the eternity of the cutting, the pain-tinged pleasure and pleasure-muted pain, his cock is pure delight. He belongs right here, buried in my pussy, filling and stretching me, sparking every nerve. We both know it. A climax shimmers like heat lightning in the distance. He shifts, slides out, drives back in with thrilling force.

"Oh, yes," I moan.

"Yes!" he agrees, lifting my legs to his shoulders so he can plunge deeper still.

We climb together, in near silence save for grunts of effort and exhalations of ecstasy. There's no need for speech; we have years of practice reading each other's body. His fierce thrusts shake me, waking echoes of pain under the white gauze swathing my chest. He senses the change and slows down.

"No, no . . . never mind! Fuck me hard!" I love his concern, but I love his ferocious, possessive energy even more.

I remember him bending over my breast, concentrating on his bloody handiwork, lost in our joint obsession. That's what makes me come, writhing and jerking and yelling his name.

He's still hammering me when the sweet convulsions subside. I try to stay focused on his face, though I feel another climax building already. My pussy will be sore tomorrow but, right now, I want nothing but this: my Master hovering over me, grinning with mad lust, pounding me with his cock, proving I'm his.

The flood of his come erupting inside sweeps me away, too. We clutch each other, both helpless, both slaves to pleasure.

We fall asleep, tangled together as if bound.

A relentless ache from my gauze-covered breast wakes me before dawn. I try to get up without disturbing my Master, but don't succeed.

"What's going on, Becca?"

"Um, thought I'd get some aspirin."

"Your breast hurting?"

I don't want to admit the fact, but it's more painful now than when he actually did the cutting, perhaps because I'm not as aroused. Still, every twinge makes me proud.

When I get back into bed, he gathers me into his arms. "Thank you," he says. "I love you." His kiss makes the pain vanish, at least for the duration.

"You know I love you, too." I snuggle against him. "I'm worried, though. If we keep doing this – pushing limits, going to extremes – what if we go too far?"

He tweaks my right nipple, making me yelp. "What's the meaning of 'too far'?"

"I don't know."

"Guess we haven't gotten there yet." He swirls his tongue in the hollow under my ear, making me shiver with delight. "Don't worry, Becca. I'll know when to say no to you. Trust me."

"I do, Master. I trust you with my life."

"I promise I'll take care of you, Becca. I own you. Now more than ever. I've marked you."

Hearing him say that almost makes me come. It has nothing to do with his fingers dabbling in my pussy.

As he slides into me, uncharacteristically gentle, I start to fantasize about branding.

The Purpose of Tongues

Kirsty Logan

In the electric city of Akihabara, nothing has a taste. There are endless promises: girls dressed as maids offering tea and cream cakes, girls done up like cats offering bowls of flavoured milk, girls plastic-wrapped and LED-eyed with lips shaped like strawberries.

Girls, girls. All delicious. All tasteless.

I steer my feet past the escalators and the temples, the moon-high hotels and boxes spread into the street. Everything here is wrapped in plastic. Everything is stacked in vending machines. Everything is stickered and reduced and piled in bins, designed to entice the senses. Music pulses at the back of my throat and lights blur into the sky. The air smells of nothing.

The light turns and I'm in the street, shouldering along with the crowd. A diamond of schoolgirls, all pleats and bunches, giggle at me as they pass. The girls here like me because they think I'm a boy. Tokyo women are dolls: petite and preened, thin as magazine models in their knee-skirts and bow-peppered blouses. Back home in Manchester I'm a femme in my skinny jeans and pixie crop, but here I'm a stone-cold butch.

One of the schoolgirls calls out to me, but they're already across the street and I don't understand anyway. I'm third-generation Japanese so I blend into the crowd, but I'm England born and monolingual. Six months here, and I still don't know much more than *konnichiwa*, *domo arigato* and *su nomimasen*

– I use that last one most, as I haven't mastered the art of not bumping into people on the chopstick-thin streets. Greeting, thanking and apologizing seem to be enough to get by.

I don't want to go home yet. Home still holds the scent of Lilia and the shape of her body in the sheets. Right after she taught me the purpose of tongues, she left. Food still has texture and weight and colour and temperature, but that's it. When it's in my mouth it could be sashimi or sheets of sugar paper for all I can tell. Now all of Akihabara is just my toes bumping the kerb and lights catching the corners of my eyes.

I go into the coffee shop and let the escalator carry me skywards. The girl behind the counter has hair bleached white with forest-green tips, and she wears a skirt that sticks out all round like a toadstool. I take a long time to figure out which drink has been designed to have the strongest flavour. It's pointless as I won't be able to taste it, but I have to try. I order a peppermint-chilli latte and lean against the counter as the girl froths milk and tips syrup into my cup. No actual peppermint or chilli, obviously, just chemicals of flavour; no one eats plants in Akihabara. Aside from our polite exchange of mug for coins, we don't speak.

I take my coffee over to the window and sit for a while, warming my hands on the mug. The Starbucks is one floor up at a busy intersection, and out of the window I see the crowd of people below surge and pulse like insects. It's better to look out of the window than around me, though; everyone in this bloody coffee shop is lost in their own personal orgasm of taste and smell. I feel like my tongue has been freeze-dried.

I dip my head over my mug and then – there! – a scent nudges into my nostrils. It's nutmeg, cinnamon, a breeze straight from the tops of trees. Not what I ordered, but still – this is the best bloody coffee I've ever had. My heart starts to thud at the realization that the problem is not me. It's just that all the food in Akihabara is bland as fuck. It's been so long since I've smelled or tasted that I forgot how sensual it is; I am filled by the scent, caressed by it, willingly overtaken.

I close my eyes and lift the mug to my mouth, ready for the taste to spread across my tongue. I taste . . .

Nothing.

The milk slips down my throat, warm and smooth, and my lips tingle from the chilli. But I can't taste anything at all.

Then I realize: that delicious smell isn't coming from the coffee. I glance around, but there are no obvious candidates. I don't know where that delicious smell is coming from, but for now it's enough to know it's there. To know that I am not broken, that the inside of my mouth has not been worn smooth. That my tongue still has a purpose.

The train home is busy, and I stand as close as I can to the people beside me, trying to sear away the blankness of all that plastic and metal. That spicy-foresty taste from the coffee shop is still faintly there on the back of my tongue, but it's fading. I stand so close to the other travellers that our shoes touch and the waves of our coat-hems interlock and my breath mists their glasses. But the people – all of them, every one – smell of nothing.

I stop at the *conbini* on the way home and buy my dinner from the vending machines. It's not like I can taste it anyway, so I might as well go for the cheap option. In this city it's so easy to go days without speaking to anyone or even looking them in the eye. In England it would be rude not to thank the shop-keeper handing you your change, but here there are little metal dishes by the checkouts for the exchange of money, so you and the checkout operator don't even have to graze skin. In Tokyo, every man is an island. Every woman. Whatever.

I swallow a seafood miso Cup Noodle – which tastes of neither seafood nor miso – and some royal milk tea, then sort the containers into the recycling bins behind my apartment. That spicy, outdoor scent has entirely faded from my mouth, and I can barely remember it. When I get back inside, the room seems even smaller than before. The evening stretches out ahead of me, silent and cold. I browse X-Tube's girl-on-girl category, masturbate efficiently, then stare at the TV for a while. Fuck this shit.

I get on the Metro, riding shapes on the map – four stops on Hibiya, three on Chiyoda, on to Shinjuku, then back. Every ad-poster shouts about flavour – so salty! so buttery! so unnaturally, impossibly delicious! – but I don't bother to note the names of the products. I've tried them all. The trains are quiet now, and I can't get so close to the other people.

The man three seats over is asleep. A salaryman, suit jacket crumpled and hands gone slack on his briefcase. I move one seat over, then another. He's within arm's reach. I lean in closer, trying to smell him without making it obvious what I'm doing. He's so crumpled and damp; he must smell of something. It's only logical, and it frustrates me that reality is eluding me. All the adverts tell me that smelling bad is the worst possible sin, but at this point I don't care what this guy smells of as long as it's something. I breathe in, deep and slow, but there's nothing; it's like the inside of my mouth and nose are numb. Without scent, without taste, the world is just surface. Nothing can get inside me. And it's not that I want to fuck this guy – I'm not even attracted to him – but I'd do anything to feel connected to the world again. Maybe if I got closer . . .

I must be tired, or confused, or temporarily insane because without even thinking I lean over towards the man and lick his fleshy cheek, from jaw to eyebrow. His eyelids flicker, and he starts to wake. I scrabble back to my seat and stare pointedly in the other direction. When I'm sure that the man isn't looking at me, I press my tongue to the roof of my mouth, trying to squeeze out a taste. Nothing.

I collapse back into my seat, peering into the next carriage to make sure no one has seen. I can't shake the feeling that I must be asleep. I'm pretty sure I've never tasted in my dreams.

For the rest of the night, I ride the Metro so that I don't have to go home to that empty bed. I keep my tongue to myself.

* * *

Over the next few weeks, I ride the subway every night. Sometimes I ride it all the way out of the city, until the train sways up out of the ground and I'm crossing fields and mountains and rivers. That's when I get off the train and catch one going back again. I don't want the daylight; the night bleaches everything into neon on black, and that suits me better.

My night-time subway adventures are turning me increasingly nocturnal. It doesn't really matter: my job is online so my bosses don't care when I work as long as I rack up enough hours, and it's not like my friends will miss me. A couple of social media updates, and they'll feel like I'm around, even though I haven't seen them face to face in months.

I taste a lot of people. Or at least, I try to. It starts small – just an experiment, you understand – but I don't get caught, so I carry on. Everything in this city seems geared towards taste, so is it really so strange? OK, yes, it is strange; but I still do it. Mostly I taste sleeping salarymen, and there are a couple of tourists and some motherly types too. I don't know if they notice, but they don't say anything. They all taste of nothing, but they keep me hoping. At least I'm doing something, moving closer to a solution – or that's what I tell myself. Because there has to be a reason that I'm doing this, and it has to be more than just the empty space that Lilia left in my bed.

Sometimes I'm sure I catch a faint tendril of that smell, that cinnamon, nutmeg, breeze-from-the-trees smell, but it's always gone before I can catch hold of it. Even the memory of the smell sends all my senses into overdrive: my clit tingling, my throat constricting, my nipples ultra-sensitive as I brush past the endless commuters.

Once, as the train doors sigh open, the smell is so strong it makes me dizzy. I'm immediately on high alert, breathing to the bottom of my lungs to try to figure out where it's coming from. I'm too slow, there are too many people, but as the doors shut and the train pulls out of the station I swear I see a flash of white-blonde hair with green tips. The sight catches on something in my memory, and I feel a sudden need for caffeine. I get off at the next stop and walk back to the

Starbucks at Akihabara, riding the glass-walled escalator up above the heads of the crowd.

Behind the counter is the blonde girl with the toadstool skirt. I order a triple-shot peanut-pumpkin latte – that repulsive mix of flavours has to trigger something in my mouth – and lean on the counter while she froths milk. My head is still full of that fresh green smell, and it's making me dizzy.

I don't know whether I've become suddenly impulsive or the lack of sleep is making me crazy, but when she puts my coffee down on the counter I reach for the handle before she lets go. The tips of my fingers stroke along her knuckles.

The moment stretches out in slow motion, and when she lets go of the cup, my heart is thudding so hard I can't speak. I nod at her and carry my mug away, the skin of my fingertips tingling. As I walk away I realize that the scent is fading, and it all clicks into place. It's her, the girl behind the counter. She was there, every time I smelled that scent – in the café, on the train – but there were so many other people there that I didn't know it was her. That she was the only one who mattered. I don't know why, but it's clear now that she's the only thing in all of Tokyo that I'll be able to taste.

I spend the next few days hatching plans to get the forest-girl to notice me: going in every day to order increasingly elaborate cups of coffee; dressing up in biker boots or ballet pumps or penny loafers to see which she prefers; sneaking glances at her nametag ("MORIKO"); trying to eavesdrop on her conversations with colleagues, which are, of course, all in Japanese so I can barely understand a word. It doesn't seem like any of it is getting me closer to Moriko, but I don't care because every time I go near her I can smell that forest-breeze scent of her. It makes me dizzy.

"You are coming here a lot," she says one day – the first non-coffee related exchange we've had.

"Yes," I say, "it's just that I really like—"and then, because I suck, I chicken out "—I really like the vanilla syrup. It's sweet."

"Sweet," she says, and I swear she knows exactly what I'm up to, because I think I've ordered just about every flavour except the vanilla. But she just smiles and hands me my coffee, and I don't even dare to accidentally-on-purpose touch her hand.

I keep going back, and I keep chickening out of telling her that I don't just like the damn vanilla syrup. Just when I start to despair at my crappy powers of seduction, Moriko asks me out.

Well, to be accurate, she asks me whether I want to meet her after her shift to get "a real drink". I mumble a yes, then go home to shower and change and generally kill time until it's dark. I decide that if Moriko takes me to one of Tokyo's few gay bars, that means she's into me. Then I decide that if she puts her hand on my leg, she's into me. Then I decide that if she takes me into the bathroom and unzips my jeans and shoves her hand down my underwear and finger-fucks me until I scream, she's into me. I'm hopeless at this; I'm better sticking to X-Tube, efficient masturbation and eyeing Moriko creepily from across a café.

As it turns out, Moriko does take me to a gay bar and does put her hand on my leg and – later, after several drinks that taste of nothing but make the world spin – does take me into the bathroom and unzips my jeans and finger-fucks me. Although I don't scream, I do come so hard that it feels like my heart has come unmoored and is throbbing its way through my entire body. In the darkness of the bathroom stall, Moriko's white-blonde hair seems to glow as bright as the moon.

I take her back to my apartment to return the favour – I'm English, after all, so I have to be polite. On the way back to mine we're all manners, not catching one another's eye on the subway and walking down the street with a few inches of space between us. We pass through eye-watering clouds: steam from the streetside noodle bars, smoke from a stranger's cigarette, exhaust fumes from a hundred thousand cars. It numbs me until I can't even smell Moriko any more.

In the door, shoes off, door locked.

"I'll put the kettle on," I say. "Would you like—"

Mid-sentence I look over at Moriko, and her expression pushes all my bullshit niceties back down my throat. I breathe out the remnants of the city and step closer to her, splaying out her fingers, interlocking them with my own. Her skin is warm and, as I press kisses along the side of her neck, I fill myself up on her smell. Between kisses I dart out my tongue: her skin tastes slightly salty, and I can smell the laundry powder from her clothes.

Two steps and we're on my bed. I unbutton Moriko's blouse slowly, peppering kisses on each patch of newly revealed skin. She's as soft as a cat's nose, and I investigate her by all the tiny pockets of scent caught in her skin: coffee grounds from the café, chlorine from the swimming pool, soap from the shower. I feel connected to everywhere she's been.

I tug off her skirt and she leans back on the bed, spreadeagled, ready for me. She doesn't need to direct me; even in silence she's still in charge here. I bend down and press my mouth between her legs, exhaling into the thin layer of cotton over her cunt. She smells musky, like a garden after the rain, and already my mouth is watering.

I pull aside the fabric and bury my nose in her cunt, flattening my tongue against her clit. She bucks her hips up to me and I press them back down, my palms cupping her hips as I slide my tongue in and out of her. I close my eyes and pull her legs over my shoulders, pressing her thighs against my ears. No sight, no sound: all my attention is concentrated on my tongue.

I tiptoe my hands up from her hips, feeling her body curve inwards at her waist and then outwards at her breasts. My fingers find her nipples and I tug on them gently, matching the rhythm of my tongue in her cunt sliding faster, faster, until I'm tongue-fucking her and squeezing her nipples and pressing my top lip to her slippery clit and she's bucking against my face, her thighs tensing to push me closer into her, and her whole body tenses and she comes in one almighty throb, her wetness all down my face, her cunt clenching tight around my tongue, and it's the most delicious thing I've ever tasted.

Afterwards, we curl close on my single bed in a tangle of limbs. I think I'm being subtle, but I can't help drawing every breath to the bottom of my lungs, just to get more of her smell.

"You like me, huh?" she whispers into my ear, her English clipped. "You stay so close."

"I do," I whisper back. "I really do."

"Then I will see you soon, at the café. Maybe you can take me out again."

My apartment smells of sex and heat and, nudging through it all, that scent like a breeze straight off the tops of the trees. I breathe deep and lean in for another kiss.

The Cock Killers

Ian Mason

Some people might say if you go to see a band called the Cock Killers, you deserve what you get. But it still came as a surprise when she picked me out of the crowd and hauled me up on stage to be permanently damaged in front of everyone.

You know the band? They're brutal. I mean, their music is brutal. Six guys who look like they could be murderous bikers lay down an avalanche of screaming noise that is guaranteed to turn your nuts to jelly if you're not built hard enough to take it. And right up there at the top, spewing the hardest and nastiest energy of all, is the lead singer, Killita, five foot ten in bare feet, gorgeous and blonde, a former female competitive weightlifter. She wears heels on stage; she towers over even me. And yeah, I've mixed it up in my day, but the day I had to take on Killita? I was left bent over and helpless, and that's how she liked me.

As to whether *I* liked it? I'm still working that out.

I'm not a pervert, you see. I'm just a big fan of rock 'n' roll. I won't go so far as to say I'm a he-man, but once upon a time I liked to think even a girl like Killita would have her hands full with me. Now I'm not so sure.

Though nowadays I work in an office, I've also been an occasional fill-in bouncer at the club, Consumption, where the Cock Killers were playing that night. I'm a big fan of their hard-driving music – have been since the beginning. So I cashed in my favor to the manager, Davo, and scored myself a couple of tickets. I went with Sarah, this hot piece of ass I'd been planning on screwing, since she was a fan. She was the ex of a friend of mine, but I'd already checked it out with him and he was cool if she and I fucked. She was putting out signals, and I already got the impression that if I pulled this concert off, my dick was going to get wet. Little did I know.

Cashing in more favors got us jumped ahead in line to the VIP entrance – so we were right up there against the stage before the mad crush started. There was no chance for conversation over the scream of the opening band, but Sarah seemed to be pretty into them, so that was OK. She snuggled back against me and even let me put my arms around her once she started dancing, her perfect little bubble ass against my cock. Yeah, things were going well. They were going fuckin' perfect.

Sarah and I made out right up there against the stage when the opening act was finished. I was getting the message loud and clear that Sarah was one of those girls who gets turned on by music – no surprise there. I pushed my luck a little, and right there in public, I got a taste. She let me finger her. Nothing too big . . . just a quick dip down in her tight leather pants while I ground against her ass. I'd already gotten my hand up this little tube top she was wearing, and let me tell you, she didn't mind at all when I fingered her nips. They were hard. No one around us seemed to notice. Everyone was fucked-up beyond all recognition, anyway; the reputation of the Cock Killers is as tied to alcohol and drugs as it is to reckless perversion and lyrics about dick torture.

Sarah and I made out until the lights went down again and the screaming started. That was the cue for the Cock Killers to take the stage and start doing crimes.

Oh, man. You have not fuckin' seen a band until you see these motherfuckers tear into the sound barrier. We're talking about guitars that sound just like chainsaws, bass that throbs right through your breastbone into your balls. It throbbed into Sarah, too; she danced and ground and rubbed against me as she sang along with the lyrics, hanging on Killita's every move, every word, every quiver. I danced along with her, working up a sweat. I got a taste again about halfway through the Cock

Killers' set – just a quick dip down into Sarah's leather pants. It wouldn't have been possible if they weren't so low-cut and tight. I mean, they were so low there had to be like an inch, maybe two, between the top of Sarah's sweet wet pussy and the waistband of her leather pants. And they looked like they were painted on, and they felt it, too, when she rubbed against my cock – that cute little ass of hers felt like it was naked against the front of my pants. But then, leather's always felt like flesh to me. Funny thing, though, as tight as Sarah's pants were, they seemed to stretch open real easy when I slid my hand down there. She didn't mind the occasional rub and, let me tell you . . . that taste was sweet.

It was fuckin' weird, though, to be making out and rubbing all over this sweet, warm, compliant and gorgeous blonde piece of ass who was singing along with screamed-out lyrics like: "Fuckin' cut his dick off/Teach him what it means to crawl/Make his nuts your bitches/Show him how low he can fall!"

It got more explicit from there. Killita was a former dominatrix as well as a former weightlifter, and she had a serious thing for lyrics about hurting men's cocks and balls. I'm not really a lyrics guy, but that probably should have tipped me off to the fact that Killita was a dangerous bitch.

But how could I care? Killita was hot as fuck. And Sarah was getting as turned on by Killita as she was by me. I couldn't decide if I liked that or not. But yeah, as soon as I realized how horny Sarah seemed to get, leaning there up against the edge of the stage hero-worshipping Killita, I had a serious jones for a threesome. I mean, I already knew from my buddy that Sarah was pretty easy and that she was great in bed. And here she was rubbing all over me, horny to fuck, almost ready to do it right here in the middle of the crowd. Wouldn't be much of a stretch to think the girl might be bi, right?

Right. But I had bigger problems in my future. That Killita cunt was about to make my life very interesting.

Don't get me wrong, Killita is hotter than hot. She's built out of muscle, but proportioned like the most perfect woman you ever wanted to run your tongue over. And Killita wasn't wearing leather pants. On most of her body, she had nothing but a black leather bikini, and in back it was just a thong. But then, she was wearing these *boots*, man, these heavy fuckin' boots, and as she stomped around the stage, those boots made an impact. They were supple black leather, not all that different from the knee-high boots that Sarah happened to be wearing. Of course, where Sarah's hot skinny legs were poured into those leather pants, Killita's were bare from the top of her boots to her skimpy leather bikini bottoms. Put either of those bitches on a buffet and I'd have a hell of a time deciding.

But it was Sarah who had me for the night.

Too bad for me, it was Killita who grabbed me.

Sarah had started gyrating with one particularly nasty song, "Worship". The lyrics were all about guys serving women, and Sarah seemed to know every word. She sang along and danced away from me, pressing into the crowd. Her hips were really moving and, much as I wanted to dance along with her, I couldn't keep up, so I let go and she spun away a little bit, just a few feet into the crowd. I was soaked in sweat, my T-shirt soggy and clinging to my body. I was charged up and horny, all right, after all that teasing Sarah had done. But then the last thing I expected happened, just seconds after "Worship" screamed to a dead stop.

Killita pointed at me from the stage and said: "Him!"

I looked dumbly up at her. She grinned wolfishly at me and said, "Wanna play?"

I don't know what the fuck I was thinking. I just yelled it out: "Yeah!"

Killita pointed again, jabbing her finger at me. "Him!"

Then she gestured at me to come around to the side of the stage, and I started over tentatively – not knowing what was happening. I was a little drunk from Sarah's and my pre-show lubrication, which I had thought would help me get some mileage – and so far, I'd been right. But I was also a little uninhibited, so when the roadies grabbed me and wrestled me onto the stage, I just went with it.

I'm not a small guy. I'm six foot two in socks and I work out regularly. But these guys were built like brick shithouses. They tossed me at Killita's feet. I went down on all fours like I'd never stood before.

That's when I saw the whip.

"Get your shirt off!" she screamed.

I don't know why I did it. I can only tell you that there's no way you can ever be prepared for having Killita scream orders at you.

I took off the soggy mess that was my T-shirt. Killita snatched it out of my hand and threw it into the crowd.

The crowd cheered.

"Tell me your name, slave!" Killita ordered me. She shoved the microphone into my face.

I said it – my whole name. The crowd applauded.

"Do you know how to worship?" she asked.

I looked at her like a deer in the headlights.

The whip was a big heavy black leather number, and Killita barely even had to spin it to bring it down on my naked, sweaty back with a hiss.

I howled into the microphone. To my horror and humiliation, I sounded just like a girl. Pain arced across my back. Killita flicked her hand again and I screamed.

She laughed. So did the crowd.

Killita said: "Don't give me that, slave. I barely even touched you! If you want to feel real pain, I can give you some of—"

She gave it to me, hard, in a hot white stripe of screaming agony, right across the meaty part of my shoulders. I swear, I don't think I've ever felt such pain. I screamed again – even girlier this time, and Killita dangled the whip in my face.

"I asked you a question, slave! Do you know how to worship?"

Another slash of the whip, and I was whimpering into the microphone. "No," I said.

"No, what?"

Another slash of fucking agony, and I dropped to my belly

and writhed. Killita laughed at me, and I felt roadies' hands on me, pulling me up to all fours again.

"No," I said. "Just, no."

Killita slashed me with the whip. This time I managed to bear up without squealing like a pig, but it hurt like hell. The microphone was right in my face, and I made a surprisingly pathetic sound. It echoed through the club. The crowd rippled with laughter and applause.

The guitarist was tuning. This was nothing but them killing time.

Killita said, "The correct form of address for all men to all women is, 'Yes, Mistress.' Say it!"

My back exploded in pain again.

"Yes, Mistress!"

"And it's easy to learn how to worship, slave. Here's how you start."

Killita had the grace of a gymnast. I felt the sole of her huge boot on the back of my head. She pushed me down. With one boot, she forced my head down until my face was pressed to her other boot.

"Kiss it, slave. And not the way you kiss your fucking mother. Kiss it the way you eat out that hot little blonde piece of ass you were fingering in the front of the crowd. You do eat her out, don't you?"

My face burned. The whole world was spinning. She pushed the microphone in my face, and I whimpered, "Yes."

"You'd better," she said. "Now, I gave you an order."

Another slash from the whip.

I started kissing. I tasted the leather of her boots. The smooth, supple texture made my cock start to swell. I realized with horror that my legs were spread, and my crotch was aimed right at the crowd. They could probably see me getting hard.

"That's good, slave. Why don't you kiss a little higher?"

I did. I let Killita guide me up her legs, gradually, kissing her calves, her knees, her inner thighs. Before I knew it, she had my face shoved between her legs, and I was tonguing that skimpy leather bikini.

A hot slash of agony across my back put an end to my "worship", as I howled in pain.

My eyes were watering. It was the lights – it was the lights, not the pain. My vision was blurry as I looked into the crowd.

I saw Sarah, looking up at me, looking like she was ready to rip me to shreds. I've never seen a girl look so angry.

Then, with a sneer of contempt, she turned her eyes from me to Killita, as she started to sing in earnest, the music rising in waves as she screamed.

And Sarah sang along, watching Killita's every move.

I don't know what happened next. It's sort of a blur. What I know is, the music flowed over me, and I just knelt there on all fours, my face lowered almost to the ground. I should have crawled away, but I was too afraid. Killita came back to me three or four times through the song, making me "worship" her boots during the first bridge, shoving her boot in between my legs and toeing my balls during the second, then shoving my face in her crotch again for all of the guitar solo. She whipped me as the bass went crazy in the song's final, brutal transition. Then, while the crowd went apeshit, Killita grabbed my hair, hauled my face up . . .

. . . and spat three times in my face.

She planted her boot on my shoulder and shoved. I went spilling over, sprawled at the edge of the stage. The roadies grabbed me and hauled me down the stairs.

Then they shoved me out into the crowd that had just cheered my utter and total degradation.

Sarah didn't come back to me for the rest of the show. She danced on her own – and, yeah, I saw her rubbing up against other guys. She seemed drunker as the evening wore on; I was sobering up. I caught glimpses of her with drinks; she'd given me her wallet to stash in my pocket, so I knew she didn't have any money. Guys were buying drinks. I saw her rubbing ass-against-crotch, and my dick throbbed hard in my pants. I looked up at Killita, hating her like I've never hated any woman on earth.

Shirtless and covered in sweat.

Desperately wanting my face back between her legs. I relived the moment a thousand times during those last few songs.

Killita never even noticed me.

I was right against the stage, but she never looked down.

Until the very end of the concert – after the second encore – when she pointed at me, then at the roadies.

I never saw the T-shirt coming. It hit me in the face and fell to the beery floor. I bent down and picked it up.

It was a Cock Killers T-shirt – the one with Killita bending down to reach for the wearer's junk . . . with a big pair of pliers. In her other hand was a vise grip.

I put it on. Sarah migrated back to me, looking at me sternly.

"Let's go," she said.

Sarah was blasted by then. I was sober. I could smell all the drinks that other guys had bought her. I drove. She told me to take her home.

I wanted to explain, but I didn't have anything worth saying. I didn't know what happened. I didn't know what to do.

"Listen," I finally began.

"Don't," she said harshly. "Just don't."

I said, "I didn't mean to—"

"Don't!" she hissed.

I shut up after that, and took her home.

As we drove, I brushed my fingers against my nose. I could still smell Sarah's pussy. It made me go blurry.

That's why I said what I said, when I pulled up to her apartment complex, but before I stopped the car.

I said, "Mistress?"

"What?" she hissed angrily.

I looked at her shyly. I let my eyes drop. "I called you Mistress," I said. "I . . . I know it was bad what I did. What I let happen."

She sneered at me.

"Mistress," I repeated. I gulped. "If you ask me in," I said softly, my face reddening, "I could give you a goodnight kiss . . ." I looked at her boots.

Then I glanced up; her eyes were hard. When I dropped my own gaze again, I looked at her thighs.

I said, "If it pleases you, Mistress."

I could see the wheels turning in the very drunk Sarah's head.

She thought about it for a long time.

She finally said, "What would please me is to pay you back for having humiliated me."

Humiliated *her*? That's rich. I was the one who was humiliated . . . in front of everyone.

But I didn't tell her that.

What I said is, "However you wish, Mistress."

Her slim hand went out and touched my back. I gasped as she fingered the welts.

"I'll think of something," she said without smiling.

She got out of the car. I followed three steps behind her up the stairs and to her front door. I followed her in.

In the living room, she glared at me furiously.

I dropped to all fours.

Sarah put Cock Killers on the stereo.

Marylou

Lucy Debussy

There were eight sailors who worked in the stokehold. Four ordinary stokers, one chief stoker, one checkman and a petty stokers officer. Marylou was one of the stokers but she called herself Max when she was on-board. She strapped her breasts down with cotton bandages and worked her biceps every evening to keep them hard. She wore short-sleeved shirts to bulk out her form and sometimes she stuffed a single folded sock down the front of her panties. She had dodged her way through the sign-up by pretending she had a testosterone deficiency that had kept her voice high.

When it came time to go to the bathroom, she would make sure the coast was clear and use the cubicle. Sometimes she had to be patient, and if they were drinking beer in the crew mess her discomfort could last for hours. She regretted slightly that she could not stand next to her co-workers at the urinals because she had great curiosity about their penises. Marylou had always had great curiosity about sailors' bodies. Her father had owned a small, shabby tattoo parlour in a small shabby port town in the west of Oahu, and she had grown up watching men with chests far too bronzed and big and hard for their faces, clenching their jaws while the needle buzzed over their perspiring skin.

Sometimes when she was folding her uniform at the foot of her bunk, she would catch a glimpse of one of them; a thigh covered in wiry hair, a bellybutton, a brown flank, a smooth lazy cock. If they were in warmer waters, the men would sleep topless and Marylou would admire the different bronzes and peaches and browns of their skin on their shoulders and chests.

There was one in particular she liked to look at. He was Romanian and had hair the colour of treacle and skin so white it shone like a pebble even in the dark. He spoke perfect English with a perfect English accent. Not like the Dutch sailors who had learned to talk American, or the Indians who spoke with their own inflections. He had impeccable manners. He tipped his hat to ladies in port. He always made sure he was immaculately turned out. She loved, when she had the chance, to watch the attention and care he took when grooming himself, combing his parting or cleaning his teeth. His clothes were always folded and pressed as if he had ironed them onto the contours of his body. Marylou imagined that his skin underneath the thick blue twill would be just as immaculate, just as smooth and creamy. She thought up close his body must smell of the same warm cotton soap as his fresh clothing.

The sailors all had a favourite. Marylou would watch in the bar each night as pairs formed off, two by two, as they sipped beer and cracked the shells off monkey nuts. When they got into port they would go in twos and threes to the brothels.

She often wondered what it must be like to be one of the dockside prostitutes, to take so many men at once, men who had so much excitement in them. It would be impossible, she thought, not to be aroused by that quantity of excitement, not to feel it slipping through the red-raw flesh and into the blood, a nourishing pain that had so much promise in it.

They lived in cabins with bunks of four. Marylou slept on the bottom. When it came time to disrobe for bed she usually waited until the men were all asleep or distracted and in she went to the little bathroom. There she would unthread the straps on her breasts, ease them from their bandages, rub the soreness out of them, and dress herself in a loose pyjama top. Sometimes she found her nipples extra-sensitive from the pressure of being bound down all day and the light feel of the loose cotton brushing them would be almost unbearable in its delicacy.

The men were all on varying contracts, which meant that the bunk formation was liable to change without notice. Marylou came back from the bathroom one day to find the Romanian boy sitting up in bed, his back to her. She knew it was him because she had looked so many times at the back of his neck. She knew intimately the line where his shoulders centred, where his hair faded into his skin. His back was the colour of fresh cream, the disc on the top of a bottle of milk.

Desire shivered like a fish down her body. She felt it low in her belly, the nerves waking up below.

From then on she slept in the bunk underneath him. Every night she would lie, looking up, imagining the shape of his body imprinting on the mattress, trying to see where his weight was falling and the lines of his arms, his back, his thighs, his head. She would close her eyes and picture the way he was reclining with his hand under his cheek, sleep floating the tension away from his body; his muscles, still hurting from lifting and hauling, relaxing slowly.

She would feel a telltale wetness begin to moisten the very soft tops of her inner thighs. And she would squeeze her legs together, squeezing as much pleasure as she could out of the moment. Then he would turn or shift in his sleep or clear his throat and it would trigger a whole new wave of pleasure in her, like he was moving for her, to make her more comfortable. The other sailors snored on during these silent encounters. She didn't mind their noises, she found them comforting, and she would know then that the way was clear for her to slide her hand down to where the wetness was slowly growing, and gently stroke its barrier along the sensitive lips of her sex. Underneath the seal of liquid they would feel plump and inviting – the warmth of him pressing down from above, the sound of his breathing. She would dip her finger in the wetness like it was an inkwell and gently coax out her bud between two fingers, rubbing it and teasing it and pressing it.

These episodes could last for hours. If she had caught sight of him, fresh from the shower that day, she would have fuel for her imagination, until in silent tight closed ecstasy she would finally come, squeezing her eyes shut, holding on to the rush of breath lest it wake up one of the sleeping men and give her away.

And so Marylou settled into this new rhythm, accepting what she could not have and making the most of what she could.

She was pleasuring herself in this way one night, when she heard a sound, a drawing of breath. She opened her eyes.

From the parallel bunk, a big bronze-armed man called Rafe was staring at her. Rafe was an Englishman, rough-tongued with a brittle London accent and a gold earring in his ear. He had cropped blond hair and skin so much darker than its natural colour from the deck sun that the contrast where the shirtsleeves and the collar ended made him look dipped.

His grizzled chin was propped up on a hand, his eyes were open but langorously relaxed. He had green irises and pig-pink lids; he closed one of them in a slow wink. She looked down, and saw that the covers were off, her trimmed mound was on display, her belly curving down to it, her hand still glistening.

That look haunted her all day in the stokehold. She worked extra hard to tire herself. She shovelled coal that wasn't from her pile and when her oven was full she helped the boy next to her. She ran round the deck six times after her shift, and felt as if the sting in her lungs was punishment for her careless-ness. Later on in the crew mess, when all hands were occupied with their bowls of corned beef hash, Marylou looked up, and there it came again, Rafe's languorous wink, promising some-thing, conspiring over some shared secret.

She was careful that night to make sure the cabin was empty before she went into the little bathroom to change for bed. She took her bandages off and slipped on her loose pyjama bottoms. When she came out into the cabin, Rafe was couched on her bunk, his shoulders hunched into the low space. He too had changed into his sleepwear, drawstring cotton trousers. His chest was bare and Marylou could see the white where the sun hadn't hit, his bulky pectorals, the huge tattoo of the Virgin Mary across his sternum, the dragon on his bicep. He had taken his penis out from his pyjama bottoms and was squeezing it at the base. It was huge, shockingly huge, ripe and smooth and crimson at the head, plump as a damson, a wet pearl shining on its tip. He glanced at Marylou. She stood frozen. Then he dropped it so it bounced a couple of times before hanging firm.

Eight weeks of hunger rushed to her sex and Marylou suddenly found herself wanting him more than she had wanted anything before or ever would again.

He climbed out from the bunk, his flushed cock still twanging in front of him, and reached behind her back. He pushed his hand down her pyjamas, carelessly gripping the flesh of her buttocks. The startle of his touch, his undisguised bestiality, stirred her. She caught her breath as he turned her round by the hips.

He pulled her pyjama bottoms down to the ankles and groped until he found the parting underneath her buttocks. His smell came over her shoulder: seawater and an aquatic aftershave. She let him separate the folds of her labia, hold them open with two of his big muscled fingers and slide a third inside her hard enough that she could just feel a strain, a sting and an ache. A second finger joined it. His thumb grazed her clitoris. Pleasure spread down all the way to her toes. He was comfortable playing with a woman.

She forgot the Romanian as he caressed her, one hand in the hair on the back of her head, two of his fingers inside her, rutting back and forth in her slippery juice. Aware of the urgency of time, he brought his penis close and took her without ceremony against the wall of the cabin. His forearms braced the wall in front of them and she took great pleasure in digging her nails into the tattoos on them, and thought about all the different women he had brought to orgasm in all the different ports, and it began to excite her, the thought of a promiscuous lover, the cursory animal need of both of them, to rub each other to pleasure, no matter whether she liked him or not. His climax was great and hulking, as rough as the stubble on his face. She felt her cheeks grow very hot and came in rocking waves while he was still inside her.

After that, the arrangement had to be maintained. She let him take her whenever he could: on the floor of the shower room, in the cupboard where the engineers' boiler suits were hanging, on quiet corners of the deck at night. She played with herself less and less, but sometimes she would catch sight of the Romanian boy – his shoulders bent over his breakfast, his hands tightening a knot – and when she fucked Rafe later that day she would imagine Rafe's huge scarred arms were the Romanian's soft milky ones, his drooping eyelids the Romanian's liquid brown irises.

They were anchored off an island near Fiji when the captain called a day's shore leave. The sun was hot as a griddle, and they paddled ashore in tenders. Marylou's boat was the last and as she approached she could already see that the men had all taken their shirts off and were spread out on the sand like crabs drying for market. Some of them were burnt already.

She found some shade under a tree and looked out at the water, foamy peaks fizzing into hot brown sand leaving tangles of seaweed and crumbs of shell in its wake. From her pocket she took a penknife, found a piece of wood and began to carve idly.

After she had sat for a while, a deep New York accent made her jump. "Now, Max, what's a guy like you doing on a day like this with his shirt on. Sun's hot as a pancake, don't you want to get some colour?" She looked up to see one of the deckhands, a huge handsome blond man with cruel green eyes, standing above her.

Marylou kept carving away at the little stick of wood. "Don't like the heat."

"You're in the wrong job then, ain't you?" He dropped to

his haunches. She smelled beer and manly sweet pomade on him. He wiped his sweaty brow with a palm and looked at it.

"You try working the stoke room. Get enough heat in a day. Besides I'm fair, I burn."

"Come on." He had a look in his eye. "What are you hiding under there?"

She could feel the blood creeping up to her face, the neckline of her T-shirt gathering moisture.

"All I'm sayin'." He stood up and moved off back down to the shore, shooting her a look over his shoulder.

Marylou looked further up the beach and saw that three of the bosun's men were kneeling down. The bosun flung a pebble to the ground and the men dropped to their flanks, wrestled their cocks out of their shorts and pushed them into holes dug where the sand met the waterline. They fucked furiously, cursing and swearing at the friction, the grit. The bosun on the starting post laughed hysterically. Marylou watched as each sailor grew red, then beet, then panted wildly. The man in the middle came in a raw fierce voice, raised both his stocky arms in triumph and collapsed onto the sand. The other men fell head first too and they all laughed and wiped the grit out of their eyes.

The sun moved higher in the sky before it began its blinding descent. Some of the sailors looked painfully burnt and took to the sea to cool themselves. Marylou watched the Romanian stand up and walk down to the waterline, and wished she had some salve or ointment she could rub on her palms and smooth across his back. He took off his shorts and tossed them back up where he had left his duffel bag and for the first time Marylou saw his dimpled buttocks, the swing of his slender cock hanging perfectly between his hipbones. It was pink compared to the rest of him, striking against the shiny black curls of hair that ran down all the way from the base of his belly. She felt her blood drop, her nether lips wake up just looking at him. He turned and she coloured, then looked quickly back down at the carving in her hand, a piece of nothing she was whittling down to the green wood.

They swam and swam, while the sun tilted sideways and made crystal the tips on the waves. She saw Rafe looking at her from where he was drinking beer on the sand, and looked around for a patch of trees or shrubbery where they could go.

"Say, Max, you don't swim?" The blond New Yorker had appeared again.

"Nope."

"Come on, perfect way to cool off."

Marylou flashed a look at Rafe. His lips spread into a great lupine smile and he rubbed beer foam off his mouth.

"Say, Max," said the New Yorker, "we all think you got something to hide. Bosun's boy says it's a third nipple." He had a raucous look in his eyes that made her uncomfortable. "What about it? Want to play tattoo snap? You've been to Henry's on Oahu, haven't you?"

"Got none."

"I don't believe you."

Marylou scratched the back of her neck. "True."

"You need one then. Dimitri—" he waved his arm at a big Russian man playing cards near the shore "—he can give 'em. Gives the best. Come on, boys, hold him down, let's give him a tattoo." A few of the men began to stir. Marylou shifted. She held tighter onto the knife and spear of carved wood in her hand.

"Just take your shirt off, man, you're the only one on the beach who hasn't."

A shadow cut the sun off her legs and she looked up to see Rafe standing over her, rolling a cigarette, a damp swelling pressing against the inside of his cotton shorts. She noticed that two of the bosun's men who had been competing in the sand had drawn closer too, and now their shadows loomed long in front of her, darkening the piece of wood in her hands.

She looked at the four faces – all copper-skinned; all sweating like the men in her father's tattoo parlour. The heat had made them mad and she suddenly realized exactly why a boy like her would be prime flesh on a day like today.

Marylou felt then not a sense of threat but a sharp

anticipation. That something was going to happen now that she had spent long teenage summer nights wishing and willing for, but which she never really believed could come true, so hadn't bothered to think much about whether she wanted it to or not. She placed her knife and her sharpened stick carefully down on the earth beside her, remembering the day she had first set foot on the ship and how pleased with her reflection in the mirror she had been, starched and proud in her man's uniform.

She sat up and took her burly arms across her chest, and while the four men looked on, peeled her damp white T-shirt off over her head. A big laugh lit up the New Yorker's mouth as he saw the bandages. "What's up with that? Got a tattoo after all, Max?"

Marylou breathed in and her torso swelled until it was plain to see the shape of her breasts, even with the hard supporting muscle giving definition to her abdomen below; the gentler curve on top was unmistakably sensuous, unmistakably feminine.

The bosun's men fell silent. The New Yorker took a couple of sarcastic breaths, barely concealing his shock. Marylou felt the perception of her slowly alter. The New Yorker, who was an able-bodied seaman and accustomed to hoiking barrels and ropes and anchors, dropped his neck delicately, as if he was nervous or embarrassed.

Almost shaking, barely controlling her own nerves and excitement, she reached her hand behind her back and began to unfurl her bandages. She unwound herself until her breasts were hanging full and fine, the nipples visibly relaxing and swelling beneath the pattern the cloth had left on them.

For a moment, it didn't seem real. She felt as if she was watching it happen to someone else. Until one of the New Yorker's hands reached tentatively for her breast; the heat and the damp of it radiating towards her skin. It hovered for a measure of time, then cupped her, tracing the mound with a flat palm, catching her nipple between two fingers, triggering its sensitive release.

His coarse dirty fingers roamed her flesh, prised apart the skin that stretched across her cleavage. Carefully, he tossed the rest of her bandages into the sand. She kept very still while the New Yorker knelt beside her, then ran his hand down her hard flat belly and pushed the waistband of her loose trousers lower and lower, until one finger slipped into the curls of her mound and she heard him gasp, almost a sob, so excited, so pleased he was with what he found.

It was not so much that she knew then that her fate was sealed as that the infectiousness of their starvation moved her, aroused in her something between maternity – poor bestial slaves to their urges – and vanity. She saw herself reflected in the shine of their eyes, changed at that moment from Max, the runt of the litter, to Marylou, a moon around which planets fed. Her spine burned. Her flesh shivered under their touches, the hesitant rub of their sandy fingers, as now all four men knelt down to explore each of her limbs, stroking her breasts, tangling her hair, touching her face, her toes, as if they had never seen a woman before; now took a digit into their mouths, now took a lobe of ear or mouthful of neck or inhaled her like she was new-found flowers or clean salt air.

She felt the heat of the whole day seeping out of them. She smelled rum, brandy, beer, soap, linen and seaweed.

She closed her eyes and stopped thinking of them stoking, showering, shovelling fish and potatoes into their mouths, and instead stretched in the hot sand, felt the coolness of the palm shade above her and the drift of seashore wind, felt now a thick finger stirring her juice, whose she didn't care, and now another, pushing her wider. And now her trousers and shorts had been slipped down her legs and off by two or more hands, and soon her own hands were reaching out, finding coarse resistance in patches of curled hair, soft wet skin, scents from different parts of them – sweet shampoo, cool soap, warm breath, cigarettes. She felt fingers massage the sand from between her toes, hot tongues clean her stomach and shoulders. She reached out and probed a navel, kissed a sweet stubbly moving mouth, she revelled in being the well from which thirsty sailors drank like madmen, stroking her, pushing her, stretching, aching her.

She opened her eyes to see the New Yorker had slipped between her legs. His hot brown nipples were grazing her breasts; his cock drove hard inside her. From down the beach, other sailors had drifted closer, curious, and now the orgy was spreading, trousers were being lowered, penises dug out and fondled and shared, open mouths touching. She saw from under the hoods of her lids two of the other stokers grab each other with such fervour it sent a fresh shock of pleasure down her. She arched her back, prising her limbs into the ground like a sea creature, opening her lips, her mouth, her sex, making herself available, pushing her left nipple closer to a man's tongue, hearing the scale of pleasure trickle up his voice as she took his balls between her fingers, poked ass cheeks open with her toes, rocked in the rhythm the blond New Yorker fucked her with.

She heard Scandinavian accents, French accents, Russian curses, American shouts. Her eyes closed, her mind travelled their faces, journeyed their excitement, their fevered desires. She thought of their fetishes, the places they had sailed to, their first kisses, tender and tentative, repressed under years of thickened personality and sea work.

Marylou thought that now she must know what it felt like to be one of the dockside whores confronted with such depraved lust, such swollen, bursting mouths that could bruise with their impatience. She opened her eyes.

Her beautiful Romanian was lifting one of her feet, kissing the ball of her ankle. His brown eyes were closed, his lashes long and black, his hands as reverent as they were when he prepared a knot, or carried letters he had written home to the purser's office, or ran along the surface of the mouth organ he sometimes played. His cock was darker now, long and engorged and pointing skywards.

Now, she thought, watching him, now as they take their pleasure, I will take mine.

Moving

M. Christian

"Don't move," she said.

"That's it?" I said.

"That's it. That's it, exactly. Don't move."

"Right now?" Smiling.

She returned my smile. "Right now. But get comfortable first."

"Isn't that sort of counterproductive?"

She tapped the tip of my nose. "Comedian. Don't worry, you'll get an experience."

"But not a moving one, eh?"

The smile stayed, but her words were serious: "Great experiences are always moving – but not vice versa. Not at all."

At least Sylvia's basement was warm . . . no, not basement. Dungeon: that was it, though I still couldn't think of it that way. "Dungeon" – that was bricks, rats, iron bars, and *The Man in the Iron Mask*. Who was in that, anyway? Lon Chaney? Errol Flynn? José Ferrer? I'll have to look it up later.

"Dungeon" certainly wasn't a basement rec room in the Avenues, the perpetually foggy ocean side of San Francisco. No bricks, no iron bars, no rats, at least not as far as I could see. But that's what Sylvia called it, so that's what I should probably call it, too.

Golden-yellow, close-cropped, shag carpeting. A heavy table covered in black leather. A pine chest with a latch and padlock – closed and locked. It certainly wasn't anything Lon Chaney, Errol Flynn or José Ferrer would have been scared of.

But I wasn't Lon or Errol or José, or even Brendan Fraser, and I'd be lying if I said I wasn't at least nervous. It wasn't that I didn't trust Sylvia, but this was more than a bit new to me. For me, sex had always been about a cock (mine), tits and pussies. Not whips, chains and "Yes, Mistress." But that's what it was for Sylvia. At least she understood my trepidation, thus the padlock on her war chest.

What am I doing here? It wasn't the first time I thought that, walking in the door to her place. The response was the same as it had always been: because this was part of her life, and I wanted to be part of her life, too.

But there was something else – bing! – right in front of my face. Sure I wanted to stay in good graces with Sylvia, but there was something else as well. Face it, I told myself, you just want to see why this isn't a rec room but a dungeon. You want to get it.

"Ready?" she asked.

"Rip roarin' – to do absolutely nothing that is," I said, smiling as always.

"Get comfy – you don't want to cramp up," she said. In a bow to my nervousness she wasn't wearing any of her S and M gear, the leather and latex she'd shown me in the dark depths of her closet, but rather a comfy yellow bathrobe. She still was damned sexy – a beautifully full, round woman with deep night hair and flickering amber eyes – and, looking at her, the last thing I wanted to do was play her game. It took a huge effort not to just part that robe, cup her breasts, run a thumb over her nipples. But a promise was a promise.

It was also hard – or rather I should say *I* was also hard, because I definitely was that – because she'd asked me to strip down, and I had. I hopped up onto the table, my cock slapping back and forth against my thighs, and tried to work myself into a comfortable position.

After a few minutes I thought I'd found it. "OK," I said. "I'm all set – to do nothing."

"You said that," she said, tightening the flannel sash around her waist. "Now, look me in the eyes."

"Yes, Mistress," I said, curbing the mischief I felt tickling my voice.

She frowned, and I felt suddenly, deeply sad. "Don't say that unless you mean it. I'm serious."

"Sorry," I said, opening my hands in supplication.

She looked at me for a moment. "OK." She took a deep breath. "You do the same, a couple of deep slow breaths: in, out, in, out. Think about your body, the position you're sitting in. If it doesn't feel good then move."

I breathed in time with her, feeling my chest rise and fall. I moved my leg a bit, then my right arm.

"When it feels good, when it feels right, then nod and we'll start. It's a really simple game: just don't move. Try to keep the same position as long as you can."

"Hum . . . how do I win?"

"Win? Sweetie, this isn't a win/lose kind of game." She kissed the tip of my nose and I smiled, despite myself. Then she looked thoughtful for a long minute. "But you know, there might very well be a way to win, but I'm not going to tell you. You've got to figure that out for yourself. Now, you ready?"

What the hell was that about? I thought. "Ready as I'll ever be."

"Good. Now start: don't say anything, don't nod – don't move."

I didn't say anything, I didn't nod, and I didn't move. We started.

There were rules. For something that wasn't a game, it seemed to have a lot of them: breathing was OK, blinking was OK, involuntary movement was OK, but anything like a conscious twitch or jerk was right out – game over, thank you for playing, here's your complimentary Turtle Wax and a copy of the home game. Thinking of that, the game almost ended before it began: an image dancing through my mind of a 2.5 kid nuclear family sitting down around a Parker Brothers game of S & M, spinning the punishment wheel. "Oh, oh, Bobby, you drew the golden showers card . . ." But I fought down a smirk, locking down my face.

Sylvia, meanwhile, sat down on the chest and watched me. She was quite simply exquisite, old bathrobe and all. Looking at her, watching her watch me, a thought flickered through my mind. With a view like this, who cares about moving? Distantly, I was aware that my cock still hadn't gone down. It was still gently throbbing, and the sight of Sylvia seemed to increase its tempo.

I blinked.

Then I wondered, still looking at my lover, what am I supposed to do now? The rules of the game were easy enough, but what was the damned point? Was I supposed to make her feel good, by obeying her? "Yes, Mistress"; "No, Mistress"; 'Right away, Mistress." That could make anyone feel good, having a humble little slave – but what the hell do I get out of it, aside from a nasty cramp?

When I agreed to play Sylvia's game I knew it could be weird, but, hell, I loved her – or at least I thought I did. But this part of her life was something that baffled me, and after a minute of immobility, it still did. But something was also niggling at the back of my stock-still noggin. I didn't want to be a pet, a slave, a subservient little twit who'd follow her around, wipe her ass, or who knew what. That pissed me off.

I wanted to move, to say, "Fuck this," and get up and walk away. I wanted to break her spell, smash it up and get the hell out of there. It wasn't something I'd thought of when I'd agreed to play Sylvia's game, but sitting there, frozen, it made my face burn: I'm not one of those "top dog" kind of guys, but I sure as shit didn't want to be a whipped one.

Then I thought of something else and I fought to keep a sneer down again: one finger. I wanted to lift just one finger on the hand she couldn't see. She wouldn't know, but I would. There was something juicy in that: a little victory in our battle of "play". When the game was over she'd think she'd had a victory when I'd really won, and I'd get to smile my secret little smile as she came out the big, bad, Mistress.

I felt my hand, behind me on the warm leather. I was sitting on the edge of the table, one hand at my side, where she could see it, the other behind me. That one. The one behind. My left. Maybe the first finger, perhaps the second? The birdie digit I decided was too rude, too harsh for my subtle little gesture of defiance.

Have you ever thought about moving a part of your body before you actually move it? It's weird, putting consciousness into something you don't often even think about. I felt a tension in my hand, my finger (the first one, if you're curious), the muscles, tendons, tissues and all that wet, squishy stuff changing from not moving to start-to-move. The will was there, definitely, and my body was prepared, absolutely, but then something really interesting happened.

Nothing – that's what happened. Or didn't happen. I didn't know. But I do know that I didn't move, not at all, not even my finger. The room, which previously felt warm if not hot, was suddenly chilly and a parade of goosebumps ran up and down my spine, arms and thighs. I remained frozen, still, immobile.

Why? Thoughts in my head, thumping around together like idea bumper cars, weird feelings, odd impressions – and something else. Have you ever suddenly realized that your body was doing something you *didn't* ask it to do – some part of yourself that normally you have to tell to perform, all of a sudden acts on its own? Because that's what happened.

My cock, you see, was still hard – rock hard, steel hard, very damned hard. I was angry, or had just been angry, and the one thing that doesn't happen to me when I get angry is to get hard. I shrink, shrivel, deflate – you name it, that's what normally happens, or doesn't happen. Negative erection. But then, frozen for Sylvia, my cock was still hard – no that's not quite right. I'd been hard before (my dick pulsed against my thigh) but, still not moving, I was incredibly hard. My whole groin ached, swollen, tingling, huge. The one thing I wanted more than anything in the world was to sink my wonderfully hard dick deep into Sylvia. I didn't move though, didn't let the slightest grimace of pain or desire show on my face.

Sylvia, watching, smiled and winked at me.

I don't think I'd ever been as hard as that, but I certainly hoped I'd be again. It felt like a deep part of myself, somewhere down below my belly button, my guts, my soul even, was happy at this situation. Very, very happy.

But that was deep down, cock-response deep, but at the top of it all, in my brain, something else was ringing loud and long: why?

I still didn't know Sylvia's "why"– not really – I'd guessed but I didn't know, but that wasn't what was bugging me. Why didn't I move? Why didn't I get up and leave?

Because that's what you've always done, I heard a voice say, clear in my mind, down there in my guts, somewhere near my soul.

Goosebumps. Big, obvious, goosebumps. I didn't care so much that I was thinking to myself in a new voice, that I'd possibly had a psychotic break, or that I'd been telepathically contacted by beings Not of This Earth but rather that what that voice said was right. It wasn't something I'd considered before, but hearing it said as I tried to stay as still as possible, it was frightening.

Because it was true.

I liked to laugh. Not because I was jolly, or good spirited, but because everything to me seemed laughable. I giggled and guffawed at the world, seeing the billions and billions that lived on earth – or ever lived for that matter – as suckers, idiots. I didn't believe in anything, and even when I did I always gave it just enough to get through it. More than that and I was just another rat in a maze, a moron on a treadmill.

Lifting a finger, cheating at my lover's game: that was so like me. Anything serious, deep, possibly meaningful was a joke – a joke on everyone.

A joke on you. Was that me, was that beyond me, was that somewhere to the left of my soul? I didn't move, but I did, inside, dropping through layers of mind and memory. Pieces of myself floating by my consciousness: birthday traumas, schoolyard pain, moments of clarity and what I thought to be understanding. I won't go through them all, not that they're too intimate, but rather that thinking about them now they're just too damned dull.

I wanted to laugh, but not like I had before. I felt the muscles of my face start to pull and stretch me into a grin but I stopped them cold. No movement. None at all. Paralysis. But inside I moved a lot. Looking back at it all, looking down and through myself, I realized that I didn't have anything. I was good at things, but never very good at anything. I moved towards things – work, avocations, even love – but I never got close. I stopped just short of so much, but never stepped beyond. Doing anything with all of me would mean that I'd stepped out beyond my smirking safety zone.

My leg cramped but I tried to ignore it. Pain flared there, a pulsing new kind of discomfort, but I tried to push it away, keeping the tightened muscles from becoming knots. It was important, very important that I not move, not at all, not even a little bit.

My eyes were dry but I didn't want to blink. Blinking was movement and movement would mean losing the game. Then I remembered the game allowed that kind of thing, so I carefully, slowly, blinked. It felt good, but I vowed not to do it again – or at least not often.

What had I done? In my life? I could have done so much more, I realized, but I hadn't. My life suddenly seemed shallow. What had I ever done except laugh a lot? I remember hearing that a friend of mine in college had written a novel, and for some reason that struck me as pathetic: that he'd spent nights and nights working on something that would probably never see the light of day, or if it did it'd vanish from the stands in a week or two. A friend from high school had been all around the world, visiting the Dalai Lama, being there when the wall came down in Berlin and I giggled that she'd spent all that money, used up all that time, and she came away with nothing but memories and some snapshots.

My lower back started to ache. It felt like a slug of heavy metal had been slapped against my spine. I so wanted to sit up tall, stretch, listen to the music of my bones realigning themselves. But I didn't. I didn't move. I was frozen. In bondage. I was in bondage and so couldn't, wouldn't move.

What have you done? What have you accomplished?

I'd had girlfriends, women I thought I might – kinda, sorta – love, but they hadn't lasted. They'd wanted to talk, to think about the future. I'd just wanted to have fun. How many had had there been? One of them, a fun little redhead named Cheryl, had gotten married, and I remember laughing that she was so ridiculous to stand up there in front of the world and say that she was doing it, when – more than likely – she and her husband would be talking to divorce sharks in a year or two.

What have I done? The answer was not hard – not hard in that I didn't want to say it, to think it, because it came up as zero. Nothing. I laughed a lot, and that was all. I wanted to cry. I wanted to cry like I'd never wanted to cry before. Self-pity surged through me, like a hot compress of shame. I wanted Sylvia – who was still looking at me with her deep amber eyes – to hold me, to hold me while my sorrow came out. I wanted her to make it all better, because I realized that she was right there in front of me, filling my vision, and that I loved her.

But I didn't cry. Crying would mean moving, would mean that some part of my body would move and I would have failed. I didn't want to screw this up. I wanted to make this happen, to win this game. I wanted to feel good and, right along with that, I wanted Sylvia to feel good about me. I wanted her to know that I could and would do this small, impossible thing that she had asked. *Because* she had asked.

My body was a knot. Pain rolled up through my muscles, tendons and even – I swear – my bones. My cock was still like a rock. In fact it hadn't changed at all during my inward moving. I thought about it as I sat there in bondage: how I wanted to touch it, to wrap my hand around it and enjoy its very-hardness. I wanted Sylvia to see it, to admire it. I wanted to share it with her – to make love to her as we had before – but I also wanted her to see what had happened to me, for her to see that for the first time in my entire life, I was trying. I was trying my best.

My best. My best. I'm trying my best. I will not move. I will not move. I will do this. I want to feel that I've done something special here today, I want to feel pride in this accomplishment, and I want Sylvia to understand that.

She was still sitting quietly, her eyes moving over my unmoving body. I could feel her gaze like a physical touch, a warm caress that soothed, for a moment, the pains in my cramped limbs. There was a question in her eyes, and though I couldn't quite put it into words, I knew the answer. Yes. Yes, Sylvia, yes my love, whatever you require of me, whatever you desire, I'll do my best to give that to you. To give my self to you.

Did she feel me? Did she hear my silent answer? Her thoughtful half-smile never wavered, but once again I felt a ghost of her touch. My cock throbbed in time with my heart. But I didn't allow it to move.

My legs ached. My back ached. My hand felt like it would never move again. Minutes? No, it felt like hours of immobility. I wanted to blink again, but didn't. My eyes were dry; they burned. I held my breath, because breathing was movement. It was OK, according to the rules, but not according to my rules. I didn't want to win by the rules, I wanted to do better than the rules. For her.

My head started to swim and for a heart-pounding minute I thought I'd moved, that my head had tipped forward and I felt a surge of panic and shame. But then I realized that I was still where I'd been. Still frozen in place.

My cheeks felt strange. Had I moved? I had I failed? I didn't want to – I wanted to rise up, to move beyond what and where I'd been before. My cheeks felt strange. I hoped I hadn't moved. I hoped, prayed that I hadn't moved.

Sylvia got up, walked towards me, the expression on her face new, unusual. I hadn't seen her like this before. I'd seen her laugh, cry, orgasm, sigh, be angry, but this was new. Was this disappointment? Deep sorrow that I'd failed her. I hoped not. I really, honestly hoped not.

I didn't move.

Her hand went up to my face, my cheek. The touch of her fingers on my skin was like an electric shock and I felt like my whole body would jump at the contact. But I didn't. I felt the come boiling up into my dick, ready to explode. I didn't move. Not an inch, not a little bit, not at all. I didn't move.

"Sweetheart," she said, bending down to look at my eyes. "Sweetheart," she said again. "Thank you, thank you so much. You've done what I wanted and more."

That look on her face, and there in her eyes. Something new, something I wanted more and more of. Something I'd been missing for all those years, something I'd given up. Respect.

It was more than I'd ever hoped for, better than any orgasm. I slipped off the bench and into her arms, trembling all over.

"Thank you, Mistress," I said, the tears now pouring down my cheeks. "Thank you."

The Mattress

Kay Jaybee

The way the two women sniggered as they spotted me lying on the ground, made me sure they hadn't expected their walk to produce such a convenient opportunity to fuck.

From the scent of them, I'd say they'd been drinking cocktails. The mildly sickly scent of boozy peach and mango fruit clung to them, suggesting they'd partaken of enough alcohol to be without inhibition, but not enough to be without decision-making abilities.

The minute they saw me, cast aside, damaged and unwanted amongst a pile of autumn leaves at the edge of a wood, they knew what they wanted to do, and their giggling became laced with purpose.

Somehow, during the periods of inaction between eventful episodes of accidental discovery by passers-by, I've almost blended into the landscape, forming a hinterland of sexual promise between the woods to my right, and a farmer's field to my left. However, like so many of my opportune visitors, these young ladies didn't care that a number of my springs were poking out of my sides, or that nights and days of rainfall had given me the musty aroma of the trees that surround me.

You could see the need for sex burn in the women's matching green eyes. I'd know that look anywhere. I used to see it in the old days when I'd been working as half of a partnership. "Mattress and bed!" What a team we'd formed when we'd resided together in a cheap hotel in town. Couple after couple would visit me and my divan support back then, in a "rent me by the hour" sort of a way. I miss that life. I miss making people happy. I miss fulfilling my purpose properly.

I think my latest visitors must have been together for a while. The way they regarded each other spoke volumes. I could read many nights of tender love etched across their faces; but the way their hands attacked each other's clothes made me wonder if it was their very first time in the great outdoors.

I relished the weight of their bodies as they climbed aboard me, kicking off their shoes. I sighed beneath them as they dropped to their knees; emerald gaze locked into jade gaze; turquoise painted fingernails eager at oversized jumpers. Despite the November chill, in their keenness to reach the bare skin hidden beneath the necessary winter layers, they removed their tops, recklessly laying them on the leaf crack-lingly frosty ground.

The taller of the girls had sleek long brunette hair, and as her bottle red-headed companion murmured gently against her neck, I learnt her name was Yasmin.

Yasmin's body radiated desire as her nameless girlfriend brought ruby lips to her right breast, making her squeal and chuckle, as her buttocks clenched within her denims upon my aged buckled surface.

As the more forceful redhead's hand shot down the front of her now open jeans, clenching her lover's pussy in a deli-ciously repetitive opening and closing palm, Yasmin's light breathing became laboured and short, until suddenly she became completely silent.

I could feel the brunette's bent knees go rigid, her whole being centred on the twin sensations at her crotch and chest. Nothing else mattered. Not the damp evening sky. Nor the possibility that other strolling lovers might have escaped into the woods and witness their coupling. Absolutely nothing. The whole world revolved around the immediate giving and receiving of a mind-blowing finger-fuck.

Too cold to linger, as soon as Yasmin had got her rocks off, the women wrapped themselves in each other's arms.

Snogging until they could stand the chill of late evening no longer, they left me as quickly as they'd come. The last thing I heard, as they disappeared between the shadows of the trees, was Yasmin's promise to return the favour to her partner as soon as they got to the warmth of home.

I smiled to myself; content to have been of service, and convinced that they would visit me again someday. Probably when the sun was shining.

The first time I'd been used alfresco was in circumstances a million miles from my new semi-neglected life.

My old home, the pseudo hotel, boarding house, knocking shop (whatever you'd like to call it), had a large scheduled walled garden. That day, many years ago, the summer sky had been blindingly blue and stickily humid. I, along with two of my neighbouring rooms' double mattresses, had been lugged from our beds, and placed side by side on the grass next to a yellow paved patio and a mini hot tub.

Tiny silver star-shaped glitter had been sprinkled across the crisp white sheets that our owner had stretched over us as we waited for the players in the game to arrive. I could only imagine how the shimmering stars might irritate if they became wedged in the wrong places! Yet, after appearing in such productions before, I appreciated how eye-catching they'd look as they caught the light, and twinkled against the sexually perspiring skin that was soon to roll over them.

Despite the glare of the intense sunshine, a lighting rig had been set up all around us, and there were cameras at all angles. Excitement suspended in the air as my fellow mattresses and I imagined what the humans who'd soon be rebounding off us would do to each other, as the ever mute film crew watched, keeping their own lust in check until the show was captured. Then they could dispel their own physical requirements by booking a hotel room for that very purpose . . . which they often did with wild abandon.

Water had sprayed over me that day. Not the dull persistent drizzle of the rain I am frequently subjected to now, but a pleasantly warm happy splashing from the hot tub. Naked males and females engaged in extreme foreplay within its depths, before climbing gracefully out and, sprawling and dripping, fell across our makeshift alfresco bed.

Only seconds later, cocks were sucked, caressed and sunk within juice-sodden channels. Arses were spanked and invaded. Breasts were manhandled and bitten, and mouths were used as receptacles of insertion for everything from lollipops to dildos, from fingers, dicks and tits.

When I was so unceremoniously dumped in this field some weeks ago, I'd assumed I was here for another outside session at first; that some film company had paid the landlord for my services. I never dreamt I'd ever be replaced; that my days of sexual adventure were over; that my purpose had been lost. But as the day fell to night, and no one but rabbits passed me by, despondency hit me. *Never again*, I thought as I lay against the grass-stubbled ground, *will my springs creak in time to the rutting of my beloved, ever lustful, humans.*

I need not have worried. Humans will always find a place to ease their appetites, and I will always be one of those places. It took less than twenty-four hours from the time when the uncaring driver of a removal van had thrown me from his Transit, over a fence into a field, for me to be discovered.

Tutting and cursing fly-tippers for dumping their rubbish on his property, a farmer had spotted me from the cab of his tractor, jumped free of his vehicle, dragged me the length of the cornfield, and left me languishing on the hinterland between the arable land and the wood that bordered its top side. I'd felt sad at first when he'd left me there. The touch of his rough hands had been very welcome against my worn edges as I'd been bumped and scraped across the muddy earth. He'd only gone three paces however, before he returned.

His face was thoughtful as he keenly scanned the landscape around him, as if inspecting the area for fellow labourers or lunchtime walkers. Acting on an impulse he'd been unsure whether to obey or not, he knelt upon me, his fly yanked open, his shaft free, his hand pumping back and forth, his wide blue eyes narrowed in forehead-furrowing concentration.

I swear I could almost see the pictures whirling through his imagination. Two women busy before him perhaps? Their mouths working at each other's mound, lapping and kissing each other to climax in the fashion of so many a man's wank fantasies. Or was he into something more extreme? Did the recesses of this labourer's mind visualize a magnificent dark-skinned woman tethered to the post of a wooden four poster bed. Her slender neck secured in a dog collar, her master whispering his dirtiest wishes in her ear, while another filled her with his length, moving so slowly that she had no choice but to beg him to go faster . . .

Sagging and re-forming, I moved with the farmer as his knees pushed harder and deeper against me. I could feel his pulse quicken through the veins in his legs, and shuddered with him as his wrist moved so fast it became barely visible until, with a teeth-clenching shout, he shot his come across me, fertilizing the field with his own seed.

That was when I knew I wasn't going to be alone for long at a time after all.

The man and woman had come prepared. This was an affair – no question about it. You could feel the danger in the atmosphere. Their furtive looks spoke volumes. Had they been followed? Did they have time to do what they planned to do? What they desperately *needed* to do?

The declining late-afternoon temperature was not an issue for them. I could sense their super-heated lust-soaked skin above me as the heavily set man, his arms thick with muscles, his calves bedecked with tattoos, wrenched the clothes from his mistress's body. Without giving himself time to savour the effect of the sexy lingerie she had undoubtedly spent ages selecting to wear, he grunted his pleasure at the sight of her flawless form.

Goosebumps didn't even have the chance to prickle across her plentiful curves as he pulled her feet out from under her.

The woman's porcelain skin crushed me, her dyed golden hair cascading over where once a pillow would have sat. As my greying surface cushioned her spine, the man fell upon her. He was a blur. A haze of hunger as his mouth, arms, hands and legs travelled every inch of her blissfully moaning being. Every pore of his body simply oozed masculinity.

They didn't waste their time on words as pussy liquid trickled across my surface. The murmurs and cries of want escaping from the woman's throat however, as her illicit counterpart took both her wrists, straightened them out above her head, and clamped them still under one of his huge hands, vocally intensified with each passing second. The almost animal groan she gave at her abrupt inability to move was not one of protest, but an echo of dark contentment, which drove her lover on.

Ordering her to roll over, keep her arms still and shut her eyes, he delved a hand into the carrier bag they'd brought with them, the crackling of the plastic telling me he'd reached inside. The subsequent screech of anguished surprise from the woman told me he'd produced either a paddle or a whip. From the noise it made as it hit his willing victim's arse, I would say it was a paddle – there was more of a thwack than a swish as the tool arched the air. Its scent told me it was leather – expensive leather.

With each crack of his weapon, the man barked at her, calling her "a whore" and "a bitch". Over and over again, he told her how "dirty" she was, and what a "bad girl" she'd become since she'd started cheating on her husband with him.

When he ordered her to turn over again, I was reminded of a film that had been shot in my old hotel about a year ago. The actors had spoken lines that resembled almost every utterance that came out of his mouth. This guy was unquestionably a connoisseur of the porn movie.

Rather than be offended, his lover gloried in every second. As the smacks continued across her breasts, her master massaged his left hand over her snatch and nub in two strong firm strokes and, with a prolonged wolf-like yowl, she bucked

and screamed her release like a thing possessed. Her beautifully manicured fingernails clawed into me as her smooth
palms and bare knees clasped my sides. She was like a bull in
a rodeo, a wild creature of passion trying to dislodge her
cowboy.

The second his submissive had finished convulsing, desperate for his own climax, the tattooed man dropped his weapon.
Flipping her over, he bounced his borrowed woman against
me, impaling his urgent cock inside her so hard that I am sure
my few remaining springs must have dug into her, bruising
her flesh in a way that would have been awkward to explain
away to her husband later.

Proving that he cared for the blonde as much as he hankered
after her body (well, almost as much), the spent man speedily
dressed his mistress, who was now quivering more with expo-
sure than desire. Wrapping his arms around her, he met her
lips gently, telling her, with a tenderness in complete contrast
to the abuse he'd hurled at her only moments go, that she was
unbelievable.

I remember everyone who comes here, just as I recall the
shape and feel of all those who came to me when I had the
comfort of a roof over my head.

Usually my visitors come alone or in couples, but not
always . . .

I hadn't seen this man before. He was new, but he'd obviously
been told where to find me, for his stride as he approached
was purposeful, his long paces aimed straight for me. His
heavy mud-covered boots, his worn-thin denims, and his
thick-weave jumper, combined with the essence of hard work
that enveloped him, despite the fact it was only about eight
o'clock in the morning, made me think that this was another
farmer. Possibly, from the possessive way he looked about
him, the owner of the land himself.

He walked around me, examining my king-sized shape as if
I was something suspicious, before using his hefty right boot

to kick my side. There was something about his expression, however, that made me think he was weighing me up for future possibilities rather than simply dismissing me as a piece of unwanted and inconvenient rubbish.

I had thought he was going to indulge in some solo gratification just as his colleague had done when I'd first been discovered, but instead he thrust his hands into his pockets, nodded as if satisfied, and simply strode away.

Excitement rose inside me. My springs positively bristled with expectation. I'd seen expressions like his before. This man would be back, and he wouldn't be coming alone.

As the day wore on, rather than hope for someone else to find me nestled on the crisp autumn ground, I longed for him to come back and do whatever it was he planned to do. I knew he'd do something. I just hoped it would be soon.

My patience was wearing nearly as thin as my fabric when the sound of approaching footsteps dragged me from the increasingly lurid musings of my memories. It was his stride; there was no question about that. And he was not alone. Nor was he in the company of only one other. There were four sets of feet heading my way. I braced my springs, and yearned for them to walk faster.

The group chattered in low whispers, but even at a subdued level their tones were heavy with erotic expectation. The voice of the man I'd assumed to be the farmer was husky, and hinted of a smoker's habit. I could smell no lingering aroma of nicotine though, so I would guess he'd given up, but not before the years of tobacco had left their mark upon his vocal cords.

He was plainly in charge of this party, who I could now see was made up of two couples, one of which contained the wanking man who'd first found me dumped in the field some weeks ago. So I had been right, he must have told his colleague about where to find me.

I realized I'd been wrong about one thing, however. It was not the farmer who was calling the shots here.

With a simultaneous flick of their wrists the two women, standing side by side, indicated that their male companions should drop to their knees, their weight supported in the very centre of my back.

Acting as if they'd rehearsed every move, the females, their hands on their hips, instructed the men to remove their jumpers and shirts, so they were naked to the waist.

If I'd had lips I would have licked them. The two hard torsos instantly reacted to the cold, their nipples hardening as the air caressed them and the women's devilish eyes bored into them.

Although they moved as one, the women could not have been more different. One tall and slim with jet-black hair, the other pale fleshed and fair, with a cushion soft curviness that would make anyone's mouth water.

Lipsticked mouths came to the men's chests; smudges of red make-up marking the trail of kisses from their necklines to the waistbands of their jeans. Somehow the farmers didn't respond, but kept their arms limp at their sides. Their breathing gave them away though. The sound of the blood in their veins screamed out to me, telling me how badly they wanted to touch their partners, but that they understood that not touching their girls yet would be far more rewarding in the end.

Wrapped up in the orgy about to commence, I didn't register which of the women spoke, but the order for the men to put their hands on their heads came in a tone that would brook no argument.

Then, with the men's gaze barely even blinking, so they didn't miss a single second of the forthcoming show, the mistresses acted. My mind was subconsciously filled with the music from *The Stripper*, as in total silence the females removed their tops and skirts, standing provocatively before their subjects in sensibly warm thigh-length fur-lined boots, stockings, and basques as raven black as the taller dominatrix's hair.

I half expected a whip to appear out of each boot, but pain was not the agenda here. Patience and self-control was. Seemingly unaffected by the first fingers of the evening's frost, heated to some extent by their scanty garments and their physical proximity, the women smiled at their partners, before twisting to face each other, lust darting between them like gamma rays.

A spark of happiness shot through my padding. It had been a long time since I'd hosted this particular brand of controlled kink.

As the women's lips met, their fingers linked briefly, before separating again and lazily cupping breasts, teasing each other's hips and knicker lines with the lightest of touches.

The men remained still. Mesmerized by the spectacle before them, their digits gripped together, scrunching through almost identical spiked haircuts into their own scalps, continuing to deny themselves the option of lunging forward to join the coupling women.

I thought the females would stop soon. That they would dive upon their men, using them to work off the craving they'd engendered against each other, but they kept going. Long fallen leaves crunched beneath their heeled boots as they shuffled apart a little, giving each room to slip delving fingertips inside the other's panties. Their throaty gasps spoke volumes as they locked eyes. Each woman had one hand busy in the other's knickers, and another buffing a nipple, or squeezing a tit through the thin satin of their opposite's bra.

The scent of pussy cream was sharp and sweet on the wind as the men observed. How long? I wondered. How long before they'd snap and reach for their women?

The taller woman was panting louder now, her legs were stretched further apart, and her more shapely companion was muttering to her encouragingly, telling her she was going to make her come any second.

A whimper of yearning escaped from the smudged crimson lips as, with a sudden smack of the right globe, which coincided with a deliberate tap of the hidden clit, the taller woman began to judder. Her friend repeated the move, the spank of the dark-skinned woman's breasts becoming harder with each well-aimed strike.

Every fibre of my being, every spring and every segment of

poorly stitched fabric felt taut as I watched and waited. Surely the men would move now. Even if they'd seen this scenario a thousand times before, their time must surely have come?

Sagging for a fraction of a second against the blonde, the taller woman gathered herself as fast as she could, before twirling her partner around, and pointing her towards the men. Buffering her nipples against the shorter girl's lightly freckled back, passing her hands around so she could grab the lusciously full breasts in her hands, the spent woman kneaded the silky bust with her palms. Rubbing the soaked satin of her own knickers against the apple-shaped bottom before her, the taller woman dropped one hand to the shaved mound on display to the men, and began to apply the same sensual magic she'd just enjoyed herself.

That was when they snapped. That was when the men could wait no longer.

It was the farmer who broke the masculine silence, gruffly asking, "May we?"

That was all he said.

The women inclined their heads at the same time, too intent on continuing their own pleasure to deny their comrades.

I was only marginally surprised when it was not the women the men reached for, but each other. As large calloused hands gripped denim-clad waists, the male mouths kissed furiously, and the appreciation of the view from the women, as the shorter one was thrown into a frame-shaking orgasm, was undeniable.

The rustling from the tree above, as the evening breeze began to stir the denuded branches, was almost drowned out by the combined murmurings of relief that were coming from the quartet of lust. As all four bodies fell upon me, my sound-less voice shouted a "Yes!" of contentment as the limbs of the men and women abruptly became interchangeable. I had no doubt that the climaxes of the women had already been forgotten, discarded as two moments of fun on the way to the main event.

The breeze was beginning to be accompanied by a thin drizzle, but the spots of water that found gaps between the writhing figures on my back went unnoticed as they continued unheeding.

I could hear the rip of condom packets as the men, their jeans and boxers dispensed with at great speed, prepared for more ultimately satisfying action.

No one was in charge now. The rules, if indeed they'd made any, were forgotten in a tangle of mouths and skin, as man kissed woman, man and fondled man and woman alike, in a desperate tangle of deep breathing and hungry desire.

As the trickles of rainwater became more persistent and began to stream across their backs and chests, I could hear tongues lap them up, as if the rain was just another sensation to be enjoyed in the bacchanal tumble.

Then, as abruptly as the random formation of body parts had fallen on me, there was a gruff grunt from the farmer, and two sets of male hands were manoeuvring the women into a new position.

A joy like I haven't known since my days indoors swept through me as, face to face, their mouths already passionately glued together, the women were placed on their hands and knees.

With a nod of mutual approval, the farmers stood behind their women and, in one well-timed motion, plunged within them. Leaning over the pliant females, the men's mouths met, their hands holding each other's face, as their hips frantically pummelled the happily mewling women's backsides.

As the foursome moved and mewled together, they looked like some exotically obscene mystical sixteen-limbed creature. Soaked in sweat and rainwater, they were oblivious to everything around them, as they vocalized the sounds of their sexy journey from four ravenous mouths in a crescendo of climatic shock.

They left almost as soon as the last person had stopped shaking from their combined coming, uncaring that they had to put rain-soaked clothes on top of rain-soaked flesh.

The euphoria that I feel whenever I am used for my proper purpose is usually quickly lost. As I see one couple go, I am already eagerly awaiting the next person willing to go alfresco on my spacious back. This time though, it had been like the old days, and I continued to feel the essence of their group sex flow through me for hours after they'd gone.

I longed for them to come back.

I knew they'd come back.

Everyone comes back.

If humans are this wanton in the autumn, what will they do upon me come the spring?

The Naughty Chair

Donna George Storey

The naughty chair was one of the most unremarkable pieces of furniture Jillian had ever seen. It was made of oak, square and squat with two wooden slats across the back and a worn upholstered seat of a blue material that resembled burlap. Zach had inherited his dining set from the apartment's last tenant. Three of the chairs were of a matching black plastic minimalist design from IKEA, making the naughty chair, despite its homeliness, the most comfortable of the lot. This is why Zach insisted she enjoy its comforts when he hosted her for meals. And this is why she was sitting on the chair the very day it earned its name.

Zach was fully dressed because he'd just run down to the corner café for bagels and lattes. Jillian was naked under his terrycloth bathrobe, which she'd purposely tied to show some cleavage. Fresh from Sunday morning wake-up sex, their glowing eyes and knowing smiles suggested round two was soon to follow. Jillian turned her chair toward Zach and lounged back, extending one bare foot to rest on his blue-jeaned thigh. He squeezed her toes in his large, warm hand, but she couldn't help but notice how uncomfortable he looked in that rigid, straight-backed Scandinavian chair.

"Do you want to finish eating in bed?" she suggested.

"Well, I was planning to finish by eating *you* in bed." Zach wiggled his eyebrows.

"Why wait?" Jillian replied. She envisioned an immediate shift from the dining room to a picnic on his futon, but Zach interpreted her words differently. He nudged her foot from his leg and fell to his knees before her. Looping his hands under her thighs, he opened her legs, tugged at her belt and let the robe fall open around her.

Giggling in surprise, Jillian glanced guiltily toward the dining room window. The faded lace curtains would probably hide them from all but the most prying eyes, but the very *thought* that someone might see made her blush.

"Not here, Zach."

Smiling mischievously, he bent over and planted a kiss on her brown curls, right above her clit.

She let out a squeal and tried to get up off the chair. While the idea of someone watching made her belly clench with dark pleasure, she'd never been as bold in her actions as in her fantasies.

"Give me two minutes, Jillian. If you don't want me to continue after that, I'll stop."

She nodded, not wanting to seem prudish so early on in a promising relationship. Yet no sooner had he lavished one long, slow lick along her cleft, than she instinctively put her hands on his shoulders and pushed him away. Zach sat back on his heels and narrowed his eyes.

"Naughty girl. This time I want you to hold on to the edges of the chair. Tightly. So you won't sabotage my efforts."

To her own surprise, Jillian obeyed, curling her fingers around the cool, oaken edges of the chair seat. Oddly, the sensation of the sturdy wood soothed her, making her feel grounded and safe.

Zach made no move to continue. He seemed to be enjoying the view. *If he only has two minutes, why is he just staring?* Then it struck her that there was no clock in the room, nor were either of them wearing a watch.

"Look, you're so excited, you've already made my robe damp," he murmured.

She let out a soft "oh" of embarrassment as her right hand reflexively moved to cover herself.

Clicking his tongue, Zach grabbed her wrist and moved her

hand back to the edge of the chair. "One more slip-up and I'm going out to my car to get some rope to tie your hands to this damned chair."

Jillian's body jerked as if she'd been slapped. Yet the image of Zach marching back into the apartment with a coil of golden rope made her cheeks flame and her vagina flutter.

"But you won't make me do that, will you, Jillian? You're going to be a very good girl and cooperate. Because you know you want this."

Jillian squirmed, but she dutifully kept her hands clenched around the edges of the chair. She wasn't quite sure how he got the idea she wanted him to eat her pussy in front of the window, but his game was arousing her intensely. Her breasts were flushed, her belly churned with lust, and her clit was impossibly stiff, as if it were preening before his gaze like a tiny cock.

"You do want it, don't you, Jillian?"

She whimpered and bit her lip.

"Tell me you want me to lick your tasty twat right here on my dining room chair until you come so hard you scream."

Zach had whispered dirty things to her in bed before, but this was different. His bold words seemed to slither up inside her, hot and hard and nasty.

"Say it, darling. Say you want this." His voice was softer now, almost pleading.

He was right, she *did* want it. She opened her mouth to speak. "I . . ." She tried again. "I want . . ." Her throat closed up around the shameful confession.

"I understand," Zach said. "It's hard for a woman to admit these desires out loud. But as long as you hold on tight to the chair, I'll know I should keep going. As soon as you let go, I'll stop. The power is in your hands."

Her fingers clutched the chair tighter. She closed her eyes. It was as if she were at the crest of a roller coaster, waiting for the bottom to drop out.

Hot breath tickled her thighs. Then a gentle hiss of air caressed her vulva.

"Good girl. You're showing them you want it. All the people looking in at us through the window with their binoculars. Now if I did tie you to the chair, they might think I was forcing you. But this is voluntary bondage. One woman's struggle between her desire and her inhibition. It's really something to watch. I wonder which side will win?"

His low, insinuating voice made sweat rise all over Jillian's body. Strange how these words alone could inflame her desire, creating an obscene picture of voyeuristic neighbors across the alley – a grey-templed man in a Hawaiian shirt, a housewife still glowing from her weekend morning yoga class – studying her wanton sexual display through big, sporty binoculars, their own hands creeping between their legs.

Zach started in again, flicking her clit with lazy, cat-like motions. At first, she was still able to worry – faintly – that someone could actually see them. As he picked up the tempo, pleasure overtook caution. The pressure on her hands set her arms tingling with the strain. Gradually, the sensation moved into her chest, her torso, swirling down to meet the thrumming pleasure of his mouth on her sweet spot. With each breath the feeling grew, until her whole body was like a buzzing clit. She felt the telltale pressure of an orgasm deep in her core, but she didn't want to come yet. This taut, raw feeling was too delicious.

Still, it took all the willpower she had to pry her hand from the chair and touch his shoulder.

He pulled back, smacking his lips. "Had enough?"

"No, I didn't mean stop . . ." she faltered.

"But you just asked me to stop. Those were the rules."

She opened her eyes and gazed straight into his. Then she deliberately curled her fingers around the edge of the chair again.

"Ho, ho, it's not as easy as that. You have to pay a forfeit." He wasn't smiling, but his eyes danced with amusement.

"What kind of forfeit?"

He paused. "Tell me you want it, Jillian."

Why was this so difficult? After all it was just a few simple words. She'd already *done* worse, exposing herself to any stranger with a view of the window. "I want it," she said softly.

"Even with the whole neighborhood watching?" he teased.

Jillian's throat tightened. This was still the shame for her – and the thrill. "I . . . want them to see me come," she choked out.

"Right then. Let's give them a good show."

His tongue slipped into the magic groove to the right of her clitoral hood, while his hands slid up over her belly to take her nipples between his fingers. Using the chair as an anchor, Jillian pushed her breasts forward provocatively as if she were a stripper performing the headliner show. She closed her eyes again.

There behind her eyelids she could see *them*. Her audience. Watching her. Watching her body twist and tremble with their desperate, hungry stares. She pressed her fingers into the chair with such force, she was sure she would leave a permanent mark on the wood.

Just then Zach pinched her nipples hard, tipping her over the edge.

She bellowed as she came, her thighs jerking, her hands milking the edge of the chair in time with her contractions.

Zach pulled her to the carpet and wrapped her in his arms. "Oh, my God, you are so hot. I'm taking you to bed right now to make you come again on my cock."

"Why not here?" she asked with a playful frown. "Don't *you* have the nerve to perform for your neighbors?"

He grinned back. "The couple in the next house over are on vacation. I saw them get into an airport van yesterday."

She had to laugh as he led her back to the bedroom. He might have told her a little lie for fun, but he did keep his promise to make her come again – twice – before the afternoon was over.

Jillian didn't visit Zach's apartment again for several days. He stayed over at her condo a few times that week instead. Although her place was more upscale – Zach worked at a new-age pharmacy and was studying for his acupuncture license – Jillian actually preferred the bohemian charm of his Noe Valley fourplex. On Friday night, they finally went back to his apartment after hanging out at a club downtown. Zach retreated to his galley kitchen to get them both glasses of cold water to take the edge off of the martinis.

This left Jillian alone in the darkened dining room with the chair.

There it is – the naughty chair.

A pang of lust shot through her. She and Zach had already decided to sleep off the liquor and make love in the morning, but suddenly Jillian wanted it *now*. On that chair. She crossed her arms over her tingling nipples. Of course, she was being ridiculous. It was just a chair. A perfectly plain, old, boring chair. Not in the least naughty – why had she just given it that name? If it were fitted out with black leather straps and fixtures to attach self-twirling dildos and vibrating butt plugs, maybe her arousal would be justified. She must be drunker than she thought to react so strongly. Giving the chair a dismissive scowl, she followed Zach to bed.

The next morning Jillian awoke to the smell of coffee and fresh oranges.

"You were sleeping so soundly, I thought I'd make us breakfast first to fuel up," Zach said cheerfully. Another advantage of staying over with him was that he always insisted on playing the proper host.

Rubbing her eyes, Jillian wandered into the dining room to find a place set out for her in front of the naughty chair. Her pulse leaped. *This is absolutely ridiculous. A chair can't make me do anything I don't want to do.* Defiantly, she settled herself on the burlap seat. It felt oddly warm against her buttocks, and softer than she remembered – as if she were sitting on a cushion of flesh.

Over Zach's eggs and toast and fruit salad, Jillian managed to fake her way through a discussion of the jazz combo they'd heard the night before. But she still couldn't stop thinking about the chair. The way she screamed and thrashed as she climaxed on Zach's mouth. Her own wrists, bound with a rope that snaked under the chair to keep her in place, so that she was forced to endure more indignities at his pleasure. Then she pictured Zach kneeling between her legs, this time to slide his cock in and out of her until his pubic hair was frothy with her juices.

The seat of the chair began to pulse beneath her.

"Something the matter?" Zach asked with concern.

"Ah, well, I was just remembering our breakfast last Sunday."

He smiled.

"It's weird though. It's like this chair remembers it, too."

Zach didn't laugh as she feared he might. "Maybe it does. It was pretty memorable."

"Speaking of last week . . ."

"Yes?"

Jillian swallowed. Then again, Zach did say he liked it when she talked about sex. "Do you really have rope in your car?"

The flicker in his eyes made her stomach do a little flip.

"No, I made that up. It felt right at the time. I hope you don't mind."

"Oh, no. I was just wondering if . . . if you'd ever tied anyone up for real."

To her surprise, he blushed. "I've dabbled in it. Pantyhose, scarves. Once I buckled my belt around a woman's knees, and then I . . . Well, as I said, I messed around a bit, but I'm no expert."

"Oh, that's fine," she said, a bit too quickly. Silence settled over the table. She shifted in her seat. "OK, Zach, I have to ask you something else."

"Shoot."

"Will *you* sit on this chair for a while? I swear there's some energy happening here. Or else I'm still messed up from last night and totally hallucinating."

"Sure, let's switch. I'll give you my professional opinion. Energy flow is my specialty."

This was yet another advantage of dating a new-age guy

– you got the inside scoop on auras and meridians and things like that. Yet when the exchange of chairs was done, she felt a bit silly sitting in his rigid, unexpressive chair while he sat in hers, his head tilted and lips pursed as if he really were making a diagnosis.

"I don't feel anything yet," he said, "but let's give it some time. Since we're on the topic, may I ask you if you've had experience with bondage?"

"Just pictures and a couple of articles. And, well, last week with you, although that might not count. You didn't actually tie me up."

"Oh, that definitely counts. Bondage is more about the head space than the actual ropes." He took a sip of coffee, as if they were discussing the weather.

His nonchalance made her bold. "Have you ever been . . . tied up by a woman?"

Zach shrugged. "Officially, yes, but there wasn't much psychological punch. It's not easy to top, especially for beginners."

"Maybe that's why it's a profession? I read in a magazine that lots of powerful men pay a dominatrix to tie them up and 'torture' them because they're tired of bossing everyone around and want a rest."

He frowned. "That strikes me as a little too easy an explanation. Masters of the universe are as trapped by their positions in society as the little guy. I worked on a fair number when I was a masseur at an overpriced spa a few years ago – their bodies are a wreck."

"Because of all those sessions in dungeons?"

He snorted. "They'd be more relaxed if they were having that much fun. I have a different theory. I think BDSM isn't only about reversing roles. Sometimes it intensifies conflicts that are already there. Being rich and powerful is a kind of prison, but they can't admit that, even to themselves. It's the pure honesty of the scene that gets them off."

"But why was it so effective for me? I'm not a powerful man."

"You're pretty important at work, aren't you?" Zach lifted an eyebrow. "Actually I have another theory about you."

"Do you now, doctor?"

"Women are told they're sluts if they express sexual desire outside of marriage and the missionary position. Only a total slut would give a cunnilingus show to the neighbors, right? I pushed you a little – to enjoy yourself. Apparently you did."

She couldn't exactly argue with him there. "And what about you?"

Zach glanced down at his lap. Jillian recognized his "I'm getting a boner" smirk. "Well, I think you might be right about this chair."

"Good, it's not just me," she said.

"Or it could be that talking about bondage and domination with a smart, beautiful woman is simply a total turn-on for me."

"It's the chair, I'm telling you. I never came so hard in my life. Maybe just sitting on it isn't enough? Maybe you have to have an orgasm there to feel a real connection?"

Zach's broad grin suggested he agreed.

Jillian eyes wandered down to the oaken edge of the chair seat, peeping coyly out around his thighs. Taunting her. Challenging her.

Without a word, she rose, closed the curtains and went to get her pantyhose from the bedroom.

"May I tie your hands to the chair?" she asked, keeping her tone as even as she could.

He nodded, a cool smile playing over his lips. "All right."

"Hold the edges tight."

Zach did as he was told. Jillian wrapped one leg of the pantyhose around his thick wrist and tied it in a square knot. "Not too tight?"

"Oh, no." He still seemed perfectly at ease.

She pulled the pantyhose underneath the seat of the chair and secured his other wrist using the other leg.

"Let's pull down your pants," she said. "I want to watch your cock get hard."

Only then did a flush creep over his cheeks. Jillian was surprised at the surge of pleasure in her belly. Maybe she *could* be as wild in her actions as in her fantasies? Before she could lose her nerve, she knelt before him and loosened the tie of his pajama pants. He obligingly lifted his hips and she pulled them down to his ankles. He was already erect, of course, but she knew he could get harder. Indeed, before her eyes, his penis twitched higher, like a gentleman rising in the presence of a lady.

She stood and gave him a leisurely once-over. She was enjoying this side of it more than she expected. She fixed her eyes on his cock.

"We both know it's hard for a woman to express her sexuality honestly, but I can see it's sometimes so very, very hard to be a man, too."

Zach glanced down at his hard-on with amusement, but seemed to know it was not his place to reply.

"You poor men. You're surrounded by attractive women, strangers you'll never touch, but oh how they taunt you with their pretty faces and their full breasts straining against their blouses and sweaters. As if they're just begging to be cupped and caressed and kissed by your hungry lips. These women look so innocent, so unaware, but they know what they're doing. They plan it out in their bedrooms – the low-cut tops that show off the shadowy valley between their tits, the tight skirts that hug their full, round, fuckable asses. They do it all on purpose to see the helpless look of longing in your eyes. They do it just to make you hard."

Zach sighed and shifted in the chair. The veins in his cock seemed to throb, and the head was now swollen to a shiny, purplish-red hue.

"Am I right, Zach? Do you get turned on by attractive women? Do you imagine them naked and get stiff in your pants?"

He nodded and looked away.

"Don't you want to see me naked?"

His eyes darted back to her face. The eagerness in his

expression was answer enough. Jillian inched the collar of the bathrobe down over her shoulders. Her breasts tumbled free. She cradled them and flicked the nipples with her thumbs.

His face was deeply flushed now, and his fingers tightened around the chair.

"Girls aren't supposed to touch themselves, but they do," she cooed. "I'm a very naughty girl. After our first date, remember? You were so *respectful* that you didn't even kiss me goodnight. But I was bad. I was so hot for you, I went to bed and masturbated. I said your name over and over when I came."

"Oh, God, Jillian."

"Do you want to see what I did that night? Should I re-enact the scene right here in front of you? You know how much I like to be watched."

Zach made a funny sound in his throat.

She smiled and let the robe fall to the floor. His eyes glinted with a silvery light as they traveled up and down her body.

"How am I doing for my first time? Is there enough *punch*?"

"Actually, you're doing very well," he whispered.

"Thanks. But maybe I'll save the self-love exhibition for next time. Because today I want to make you come in the naughty chair. I could give you a blow job, but I'm a selfish girl. I want to come, too."

Jillian stepped in front of the chair and turned her back to him. Straddling his thighs, she took his shaft in her hand and guided the knob to her entrance. Then she lowered herself onto him as if she were merely sitting in his lap.

Zach let out a groan.

"Don't have too much fun yet. You aren't allowed to come until I'm satisfied. That's what a gentleman does, right? So just hold tight to the chair and let it happen. Feel the energy."

She rested her left elbow on the table to support herself, then dipped her right hand between her legs.

"I'm using you for my pleasure, just like a horny, sex-crazed man uses a woman. I'm *using* your body," she chanted.

"Yes," he whispered. "*Use* me."

"Remember, all you can do is sit there and stay hard."

"I will," he breathed.

Jillian tweaked her nipple with her free hand and strummed her clit faster, rocking back and forth on Zach's lap. He was part of the chair now, a tool for her pleasure. His cock felt harder and thicker than ever, pushing into soft, new places inside her, like her own custom-ordered sex toy. She tightened her walls around him, raising herself up, then sliding back down again and again.

Soon she felt the orgasm rising, up from the fleshy seat of his thighs, fanning out through her belly. She grunted and cupped her mons as her body shuddered around his cock. He grunted, too, and began thrusting into her, his hands still firmly riveted to the chair. She braced herself against the table, letting him use her in return. She smiled as he came with a long, low howl.

They rested there together for a moment, enjoying the glow.

"OK, I definitely felt something," he said lazily.

"See, isn't the naughty chair amazing?" she asked over her shoulder, still perched on top of him.

He planted a kiss on her back. "I can't deny it, but I have to point out this was just a plain old chair until you came along. I think there's something special going on between you two."

"Are you jealous?"

"A little, but I'm glad you're bringing out the best in each other. Just don't do anything too wild without me."

A few months later, when his lease came up, Jillian invited Zach to move in with her. The very first thing he unloaded from his hatchback was the naughty chair.

It didn't exactly fit with her Mission dining room suite, but she immediately placed it at the head of the table.

Homely as it is, it's still her favorite place to sit to this day.

Endangered

Michael Crawley

The world population of Three-toed Tasmanian Tree Mice was down to seventeen. I imported some trees that weren't indigenous to the area and infected them with a rather repulsive and malodorous fungus. The mice soon learned to use the gills of the fungus as safe havens. It benefited from their droppings, so it was a symbiotic relationship. Now, the population of those mice is over two hundred. That's still "endangered" but less so.

These rodents aren't cute little bundles of fur. They have grotesque overbites with which they dig lice from the cracks in bark. They are mainly hairless. The rodents smear themselves with their own excrement to make themselves less palatable to predators.

I helped them because they were at risk, as a species, not because they were cute.

Two years ago, I paddled a dugout canoe three hundred miles up the Amazon to transplant some tiny poisonous toads from a habitat that was threatened by development.

I don't always work alone. I own just under two hundred acres in the Himalayas – most of them vertical. A family of Sherpas in my employ leaves hay, carrots and pork sausages on a particular flat rock once a week. The family thinks I'm crazy and doesn't question where the provisions disappear to.

With all the traveling that my work entails, it's good to get back home to England once in a while. Last October I visited the little Dorset village of Suthercombe Abbey. The abbey itself had been destroyed by Oliver Cromwell, in 1656. All that remains is a single mossy stone wall, a few cracked flagstones and some vague tales about a deep crypt that no one knows how to get into. It's a National Trust property so excavation is prohibited.

I was on my way down to breakfast at the Abbey Inn when I was waylaid by a young woman of about twenty-something. We were passing in a narrow seventeenth-century passageway but it wasn't so tight that she was forced to stop with the peaks of her pretty little breasts poking at my diaphragm, though she did. Who was I to object?

"Excuse me," she husked, "my brother and I would like to buy you breakfast, if you don't mind."

I'm large, and my mother once remarked that my face was ugly but rugged. Even so, I've been accosted by young women before, particularly those one might describe as "effete". Different strokes, I guess.

I accepted the invitation. She was slight and barely came up to my shoulder, but my bulk didn't seem to intimidate her. That, and the way her stretch jersey clung, intrigued me. Even that early, she was wearing far too much eyeliner, which added a hint of decadence to her pixie features.

The girl, Alexis, introduced me to her brother, Alex. Both had pale oval faces and longish black floppy hair, making their family relationship obvious. Their emotional one was more obscure.

We found a booth. Alexis squished in beside me. I ordered the "working man's special" – baked beans, three eggs, four meaty rashers of bacon and as many thick slices of fried bread as I could eat.

I ate. They tried not to watch.

"Ever since we overheard you talking in the bar last night, we've been arguing about where you're from," Alexis told me. "Alex says Australia but I insist on South Africa."

"Sorry. Nothing so exotic. I was born in London, within the sound of Bow Bells, so that makes me a true Cockney."

"You don't sound . . ." Alex began.

"I've traveled a fair bit. Some of the rough edges have worn off."

"Traveled?" Alexis asked. "May we ask, doing what?"

"Various. Soldiering, sometimes."

They exchanged satisfied looks.

"Soldier of Fortune," Alexis guessed, with emphasized capitals. Her foot touched mine under the table.

"Mercenary," her brother added.

Alexis's calf pressed against mine. Her hand squeezed my thigh. Subtle, she wasn't, but I didn't complain.

I grunted and let them interpret it however they liked.

"Are you, may we ask, 'employed' at the moment?" Alexis asked as she massaged me.

"Not this week. I'm taking a break."

"Would you be open to a job offer, for a single day's work? A thousand pounds? For one day? That's got to be good money, no?"

"As I said, I'm on a break. Thanks, but no thanks."

Both made puppy-dog eyes.

Alexis said, "Please?" and laid a finger of her free hand on my wrist.

"Sorry." I dabbed my lips with a napkin, swallowed the last of my coffee, excused myself and left them to sulk.

I woke in my room at three in the morning. A slender figure was silhouetted against the light of a full moon that streamed through the window. My eyes adjusted. Alexis was wearing something long and black but very diaphanous. It fastened at her throat and V-ed wide open down from there to her ankles. One naked thigh gleamed palely. Alexis had chosen her pose well. My body reacted instantly.

"I thought I'd try to persuade you to change your mind," she whispered. "I can be very persuasive." Her left thigh rubbed against her right. She caught her breath as if from a sudden and unexpected but very welcome caress.

I said nothing. That can be an effective negotiating tactic, I've found.

"If you'd prefer, my brother could take my place, or would having both of us at once please you?"

"I'm boringly heterosexual," I told her.

She took two steps closer, sweeping her negligée behind her and part turning to let the moon kiss a small but shapely breast. In that light, her skin was as white as talcum but her nipple looked sooty black. I think "chiaroscuro" is the artistic term for the effect.

"Let me see what I can do to persuade you, no strings. If you still refuse to help us, come morning, I'll accept that decision. Fair?"

"Fair," I allowed.

"One thing first – I'm a virgin."

I inched back on my bed. I don't do virgins, even decadent ones. Being a girl's first brings ethical obligations that I'm not willing to take on. "Oh?" I said. "Perhaps you should save yourself for a man who means more to you than to serve as a pack mule that you rent by the day."

"It's not like that. I've had sex before, lots of it. It's just that I have a phobia against vaginal penetration of any sort. I promise you that you won't go unsatisfied." She scooped her chiffon over one arm and held it before her face. In a very bad imitation of Bela Lugosi, she said, "I want to suck your . . ." In her own voice, she continued, awkwardly, ". . .cock."

I gave her more silence.

"Really. I mean it. I get off on it. Will you indulge me?"

Well, I'm an indulgent man when it comes to the ladies. I swept my bedclothes aside to let her see my reaction.

"No vaginal penetration? I can trust you on that?" Her hips swayed. Her thighs rubbed together sensuously. Either she was an excellent actress or she was *very* turned on already.

I told her, "On that, no penetration, yes, you can, absolutely. Come over here, Alexis."

She headed for halfway down the bed but I forestalled that. I might be easy but even I am entitled to some foreplay. I drew her full length on top of me. With her being so slight and me being quite large, there was lots of room for her to lay on my chest. My left hand took the back of her head and turned her mouth up towards mine.

When our lips were just an inch apart, she resisted, holding back. I allowed that. It was too soon for me to assume that she liked to be forced. If she did, that'd become apparent soon enough.

She whispered, "Tongue?"

I took that as a request and extended mine. She pressed hers against it, forcing it to turn down so that we were rubbing the flats of our tongues on each other. She sipped and licked and sucked, all without her lips meeting mine. It was a different sort of kissing – pleasant enough, but different. She certainly seemed to like it. She played that way for what seemed like an age before closing that inch and lapping into my mouth. Her tongue explored behind my lower lip, then my upper. She nibbled on my lips with hers, then used her sharp little teeth, but very gently. I never felt that I was in any danger of being bitten.

From my mouth, her lips mumbled across my cheek and down my neck, which she nipped from time to time, though not painfully, although she did pause to suck hard. I hadn't been given hickeys since my teens so I found it quite nostalgic and sweet, in a strange way. From my neck, she trailed to my left nipple. Mine aren't very sensitive so it did little for me to have one sucked. She, however, made little moaning noises between sucks, so I guessed she enjoyed that form of play.

Nor was her body still. She writhed and twisted on top of me. Her thighs clamped around my erection and slid together like snakes mating.

Alexis twisted down. Her hand found my shaft. She started to curl towards my cock but I forestalled her once again. I'm old school. In my book, "Ladies come first." She couldn't have weighed a hundred pounds. I cupped her delicate ribcage between my palms and lifted her up high. She obliged by spreading her thighs wide as I lowered her onto my face. Her sex was cool but quite wet already. I burrowed for a while, showing off the length, strength and flexibility of my tongue, before raising my aim and working, slowly and gently, on her clitoris. Alexis panted and gasped in a satisfying way, screwing up my pillow in her tiny hands and jerking her hips at me. When she climaxed, she reared up and slammed her fists down, one to either side of my head, but she didn't cry out. A little of her essence trickled onto my tongue. She was sweet, with a subtle hint of pineapple. I believe diet affects the flavor of people's intimate juices. I wondered what it was that she ate to give herself that particular savor. Perhaps she was a vegetarian?

She collapsed onto me with one breast close enough to my face that I could give its nipple some oral attention. Some women can't bear to be touched erotically right after an orgasm but not Alexis. She began to shiver and to push her breast into my mouth. I tested her with a gentle nibble. She shivered and groaned, so I bit down harder.

"Yes! Make it hurt, please?"

That gave me a plain indication of her erotic preferences. I worried at one nipple, then the other, gave her bottom a few good hard spanks and then worked a finger up between her clenched buttocks. She pushed it back at me. I took a moment to wet that finger in her juices before rimming her tight little ring with its pad.

"It's going to penetrate you," I warned.

"It's so thick!" she exclaimed. "It—it's the other way I don't allow. Finger-fuck my bum hole, please?"

"Beg for it."

"I'm begging. Please? Stretch me open with your fingers. Force it in deep, no matter how tight I am. Make me feel it! Make it hurt!"

I shrugged her off my body onto her side. One hand cupped her bottom, with a wet finger squirming into the dry rubbery heat of her rectum. The fingers of my other hand strummed her clit, being very careful not to do more than part her lips in doing so. Whichever hand did the trick, she climaxed again, writhing and twisting into a fœtal position, but in silence, apart from her panting.

"That was good," she finally told me.

"I'm glad you enjoyed it."

"Now it's your turn."

I flopped onto my back. "Help yourself. Would it bother you if I caressed you a little while you – er – do it?"

"I'd rather concentrate."

"Then be my guest." I laced my hands behind my neck so they wouldn't be tempted. It would have been nice to have the light on so I could watch but I didn't think it the right time to interrupt her.

Alexis had been truthful. Virgin or not, she'd had lots of practice at fellatio. She took her time and I'm self-controlled enough that I didn't rush her. She used the tip of her tongue, tantalizing me from below my scrotum to the eye of my cock's head, over and over, slowly increasing her pressure, no hands, followed by soft warm panting breaths on my glans, no contact, until she drooled a little spit into my cock's eye and scooped it out with her tongue. That was followed by a subtle wet fingertip ringing my rectum, zero penetration, as she mumbled on my cock's head with soft and mobile lips.

She must have been playing those little games for half an hour at least before I felt her lips close over me and her head start to bob, very slowly, gradually accelerating and deepening. The flat of her tongue pressed the head of my cock against the roof of her mouth. I held back for a long time before I finally released.

"You're very persuasive," I told her.

"You'll do it?"

"We'll talk it over at breakfast."

She snuggled close and took my limp cock in one tiny hand. "After we return from a successful mission, I plan a little celebratory party, just you, me, and a bottle of champagne."

"I prefer Scotch."

"All the more champagne for me."

I asked, "How about your brother? Doesn't he get to celebrate?"

"Alex prefers to party on his own."

"But you offered him to me?"

"He'd have enjoyed that, if you'd taken me up on it, but he likes to party solo best."

"I'm confused," I confessed.

"He has his own rituals and games, his absinthe, his toys and his *other* things."

I tried not to think about what the "other" things might be or how they might contribute to a one-man party.

Alexis's hand worked gently on my shaft. "I was talking about *our* party."

"Sorry."

"I want you to tie me up with ropes." Her hand tightened.

"I could do that."

"Then I want you to bugger me, hard and rough."

"That wouldn't break your rules?"

"I told you, it's vaginal I don't allow."

My cock was rising again, whether from her words or her caresses, I didn't know. I remarked, "My finger was a tight fit. Do you think you could take my cock?"

Alexis continued, "That's the whole point. It'll hurt, even if you lubricate. I'll scream and beg for mercy, but you must ignore that. Just force it in, no matter what. Call me names, 'bitch' and 'slut' and 'whore'. I want to see bruises when you're done."

"How about spanking?"

"That'd be good." Her hand was pumping me in earnest.

I'm not made of stone. She had me erect and hard. I asked, "Would you like a rehearsal, tonight, right now?"

"The point is that it'd be a celebration of our success, that's if you agree to help us."

"A bonus?"

"For us both, I promise. I'll enjoy it at least as much as you will. Rough sex is my favorite."

"And as an incentive to take the job?"

"Of course, that as well." She turned her head toward where a bean of moonlight illuminated the way her hand was working furiously on my shaft. "You could fuck my mouth though, if you like? You've been too gentle with me, so far."

I almost apologized, but that wouldn't have been fitting, under the circumstances. Instead, I rolled onto my side and pushed her head down toward my cock.

Alexis sobbed out an insincere, "No!" before parting her lips.

My fist knotted in her hair and twisted hard enough to tug on her hair's roots.

She just managed to get out an eager, "Yes," before I made it impossible for her to speak.

At nine the next morning, I had the fried black pudding with scrambled eggs and broiled lamb kidneys. They both ordered muesli with skimmed milk but hardly touched it.

I asked, "Is this job legal?"

They grinned in unison. "That's open to interpretation," Alexis said.

"Intriguing. What'd I have to do?"

Alex explained, "We want to make a vertical descent, about a hundred or maybe a hundred and fifty feet. To get to it we'll have to cross some rough country."

"You're going underground?" I offered.

Alex leaned forward. "How did you know?"

"There are no cliffs near here, not even decent hills. There's no 'up' to climb so you'd have to be going somewhere subterranean."

The young man sat back. His sister stroked my thigh and leaned her head against my biceps.

I said, "I'd need to get some spelunking gear, at your expense. I could be back early this afternoon, ready to move out."

"That'd be fine."

I met them in the saloon bar. Both wore jeans and carried heavy backpacks. I was pretty well laden down with ropes and tools. Alexis drove us in an old Land Rover as far as

Suthercombe Fields, the conservation area the remains of the abbey are in. From there we set off on foot, guided by Alex's hand-held GPS. About three miles in, we came to an area where the spaces between the trees were choked by old brambles and dead ferns. I whacked away with my machete, working in a cloud of black dust from decayed vegetation. My employers didn't complain, though they coughed a lot and, like me, ended up wearing blackface.

The trail I hacked out ended in a tiny clearing with an abandoned lidless well in the center. The light from one of the lanterns I'd brought didn't reach the bottom.

"I'll go down first and see what we're up against," I told them.

"Be careful!" Alexis sounded genuinely concerned for my welfare.

That was touching. I told her, "I've done this sort of thing before – caving."

"And rappelling," she guessed. "In the military?"

I secured a line around the trunk of the nearest sturdy tree and went over the edge. It was an easy and fast descent. About eighty-five feet down I came to the entrance to a tunnel. The lantern I set down ten feet in didn't show much more than that the flagstone floor sloped up gently.

The brother and sister were making enquiring noises from up above. I yelled to reassure them, dumped my pack and tools, and went back up the rope pretty well at a run.

"Easiest and safest way," I explained, "is piggyback." I squatted. "You first, Alex. Hop on."

"Could you take our packs down first, please?" he asked.

"Sure." Something in their faces told me that they were really concerned about being below and separated from their gear.

Their packs came to maybe a hundred and fifty pounds, combined. Neither of the siblings weighed more than two-thirds of that. I barely broke a sweat, and I sweat easily. At Alex's insistence, we carried four powerful lanterns, me two and them one each.

Alexis explained, "Rats. I don't like them."

I didn't point out that this deep down there'd be nothing for a rodent to live on. We strode ahead at a good pace, despite the slope and the loads. My employers were small but not weak. The walls of the tunnel were slimy but free of cobwebs. With us carrying four powerful lanterns between us, the dust we kicked up sparkled like silver. Ghosts of shadows danced, appearing and disappearing, across the ceiling, walls and floor.

I asked, "Do you know how far we're going?"

Alex checked his GPS, which told him nothing. "Not much further, I don't think."

"And what do we expect to find?"

Alexis told me, "You'll soon see." She giggled. It wasn't a nice sound. "Mister 'Well-traveled', you might just get a surprise when we get where we're going."

"I've been surprised before, so that's nothing new."

They'd changed subtly, these two. To someone with my years and experience, they'd come across as young and naive, but now there was something predatory and far from innocent about them.

The tunnel opened into what had to be the long-lost crypt of Suthercombe Abbey. The granite walls were dry and unworn. In the center stood a crude sarcophagus, about eight feet by four by four, with an overlapping lid that looked to me to weigh around four hundred pounds. It'd been carved from the traditional limestone that gave sarcophagi their name. It's Greek for "flesh eater".

"A tomb," I remarked, stating the obvious.

"Could you get the lid off?" Alexis asked me.

"Sure." I clunked my pack to the floor and took out a collapsible pry-bar.

"You come well equipped," Alex observed.

"That's why you pay me the big bucks." It wasn't difficult to slide the lid aside. The hard part came in lowering it to the floor. It'd have been a shame to break it.

Alexis set her lantern on the side of the box to illuminate its interior. "There," she said. "Surprised?"

The inside wasn't as deep as the outside suggested. The figure within was no more than three feet from the top. She was naked, perfectly preserved, and had been no more than a girl when she'd ceased living. I'd like to tell you that she was a raving beauty but in fact, she was anorexic thin, but had a pretty face. Her kind is almost always attractive. It must be natural selection. If I was to pick a companion for the next thousand or so years, I'd want her to be good to look at, at least, when fed.

Alexis handed Alex a wooden stake and a heavy mallet. He bent over the edge and presented the point of his stake just to the left of the girl's breastbone.

I said, "That's enough, Alex."

Alexis told him, "Do it! Be quick about it."

I waved my revolver to draw their attention to it. It's a US Navy Colt forty-four, so it's quite impressive.

"Can't you see?" Alex demanded of me. "It's a vampire. We've already put seven of the monsters to rest. It's our mission in life."

Before I could respond, the vampire jerked into life and grabbed Alex's wrist.

I told her, as I had Alex, "That's enough!"

She glared at me. "Fool! Do you think a pistol can harm me?"

"As a matter of fact, I think this one can. It's called a revolver and can fire six times quite quickly."

She shrugged.

I continued, "I make the ammunition myself. The bullets are made from hardened nylon and filled with liquid Teflon. Suspended in the Teflon of each one are three slivers of wood, three tiny capsules of garlic and three pellets of sodium. Sodium ignites on contact with water and burns very hot. Even if none of those are deadly to you, this ammunition is designed for impact, not range. If I shot someone in the hip, it'd take their leg off. With you, if you made me, I'd aim for your neck. Even the undead find decapitation somewhat disconcerting, I imagine."

Alexis snarled, "What do you think you're doing? This *thing* is a monster, an *abomination*."

I ignored her and asked the vampire, "What is it you call it when you turn a human into one of your kind? Embracing?"

"Elevating."

I chuckled at that. "Well, whatever you call it, I want you to do it, right now, to these two."

She said, "My pleasure," and sank her fangs into Alex's wrist.

Alexis screamed at me and would have attacked me, I'm sure, if my revolver hadn't been pointed at her. "What sort of man *are* you?" she demanded.

"You've told me that you and your brother have already destroyed seven vampires. By my research, that means there are only eleven of the undead still in existence, worldwide. If you continue your 'work', soon there'll be none left. What sort of man am I, you ask? I'm the sort of man who protects endangered species, even the ugliest ones."

The Bondage Pig

Kristina Lloyd

Ralph brought the pig home when I was out, whether by accident or design, I couldn't say. I got back from the community
garden, dumped a bag of veg on the kitchen table, and immediately sensed a presence, a dark anticipation lurking in the
house. Dread is too strong a word for what I felt. It was more
akin to the unease experienced before a thunderstorm, that
time of waiting when you long for release but the imminent
violence bothers you.

"What?" I asked.

Ralph was rinsing a pan of pearl barley in the sink. "What's
what?"

"Dunno. Something's up."

Ralph shrugged. "Nothing's up. You OK?"

"Sure."

Ralph put the pan on the hob, paid too much attention to
the dial, then straightened. He smiled, thumbs in the pockets of his jeans, looking guilty. "I have to work tonight,
sorry."

"No worries. What is it?"

"A repair," he said. "Looks a bit of a bastard. Not sure how
I'm going to tackle it."

"Repair of what?"

Ralph shrugged. "Just a, um, Victorian curiosity. Anyway,
sorry, Sim. I need to . . ."

"Honestly, it's fine. But try not to be too late coming to bed,
eh? It's been ages."

"Yeah, sorry."
Ralph's always sorry.

I took a bath later that evening. I could hear Ralph clattering above me in his attic workshop. I was aching and dirty from an afternoon's gardening followed by two hours of squashing sodden newspaper into a press to make bricks for the fire. The gardening I enjoy, the brick-making's a chore, but Ralph and I are committed to ethical, green living. The bathwater around me was grey, its surface filmy with soap, and the subaquatic shadow of my pubes was a lonely, ominous rock on a seabed of flesh, my nipples cresting in two coral peaks.

Bath-time makes me dreamy. The room was smudged with mist, a great cloud lit from within by the diffuse glow of a shaving light. Outside, the sky was black and, on the window-sill, a large fern glittered with sequins of peeping moonlight, its green fronds veiled by the room's haze. My body became mysterious and charmed, a powerful primeval thing in a land of carboniferous forests, swamps, stars and lumbering, long-necked monsters.

I listened to Ralph pacing to and fro as he does when there's a problem to solve. I fancied it would be the repair troubling him rather than the real problem: us, grown dull and old too fast, doing the same thing week in, week out. I heard him sawing and hammering, pictured his lanky frame hunched over his workbench, straggly blond hair tucked behind his ears. I hung on to silences until my thoughts wandered off, a thump or a scrape returning me to the moment. I drained away water, topped up with hot. Steam curled lazily in the half-light. I was hoping to emerge from the bath when Ralph had finished work then lie down on the bed, pink and clean, and have him sully me with scents of sawdust, sweat and leather, his fingertips rough from labor. Unfortunately, he appeared to be in no rush to leave the attic.

I pinched my nose and sank my head underwater, wondering what the repair was. I wanted to stay submerged a long time, enveloped by fluid, not breathing. It was peaceful and warm. When I came up for air, I thought I heard a faint cry of pleasure from upstairs. I held still, listening. A few seconds later, I caught the noise again. Then again, louder this time and almost pained. Was he . . . ? Yes, he was! Ralph was jerking off!

I was angry, embarrassed and humiliated: angry because he should be saving that for me; embarrassed because we had a lodger, Jack, who was probably home by now and could well be within earshot; and humiliated because if Jack heard, he would know Ralph no longer desired me and I'd rather those mortifying, domestic intimacies were kept private, thanks very much.

A series of long, guttural groans shivered through the house, each cry stretched thin with torment and incredulity. I remembered, with the anguish of loss, how it used to be when Ralph would grab me by the hair and bang me six ways till Sunday.

Despite my resentment, the noise from the attic, so strangely and horribly potent, snagged at my cunt. As Ralph's cries rose to a pitch of near-bestial abandonment, I hooked my fingers inside myself, thrashing my clit in a frenzy of tiny splashes. I kept my moans as soft as I could. When I came, someone paused the universe. I shattered into a million little pieces and was blasted across time, at one with the dinosaurs and space travel and everything in between. Angels danced in my thighs, their revelry light, perfect and joyous.

When the clutches subsided, my thighs grew heavy. I rested my head against the slope of the bath, panting and confused. The sick taint of shame stole over me as it used to when I was a teenager. Ralph's weird cries echoed in my ears and I lay in the cringing regret of my post-orgasmic stupor.

I didn't know why I felt so bad when it had just felt so good. I simply knew I couldn't stay in that space any longer. I needed to distance myself from whatever had just happened. Quickly, I wrapped myself in a towel, bundled my hair in a turban and pulled the plug, leaving the scene of the crime with steam billowing around me like dry ice. Jack, our lodger, was sat opposite the bathroom door, slumped, cool and rebellious. His knees were raised and open, his back to the wall, a cigarette in one hand, a saucer of ash on the floor.

I pulled up short, heat rising in my already-hot cheeks. Jack stood but it was more like he bloomed in fast-motion, a surly, stubborn bud unfurling and swelling to become a glorious tropical flower whose nectar was poison. Tribal tattoos swirled on one big bicep and his short hair wasn't merely red. It was a tantalizingly decadent russet, reminiscent of ruthless Tudor kings, forest hunts and witchcraft. He smelled of beer and cigarettes.

I gripped my towel. "We don't allow smoking in the house."

Jack swaggered past me into the bathroom and tossed the butt into the toilet. A small hiss extinguished the cigarette. "I forgot," he said flatly. He stood before the toilet, looking at me as he unzipped.

I wrapped my towel tighter, hurrying away.

I didn't get a chance to investigate the attic until Saturday morning when Ralph was holding his weekly whittling workshop at the community center in town. I hadn't asked about the repair. Something told me not to. The closest I came to mentioning anything was when I complained Jack had been smoking in the house while Ralph had been busy upstairs. I tried to make the word "busy" sound as loaded as possible.

Ralph shrugged. "Ah, he'd probably been down the pub, that's all."

"Well, aren't you going to call him on it?" I said. "He's more your friend than mine."

"It'll be a one-off, don't fret."

But I wasn't convinced and I did fret. I was disappointed, too, that Ralph had sided with Jack. We didn't even know him very well. He was a friend of a friend of Ralph's, in need of somewhere to stay so we'd offered him our spare room for a nominal rent. The deal was supposed to last a couple of weeks but he'd already been with us a month. Some people, you give them an inch and they take a mile. Sure, the extra money was useful, but we should have been charging more for a long-term let. However, we aim to be good and kind, and Jack was out of work. Mind you, he always managed to find beer money, didn't he? But, on the plus side, he slept late and, since Ralph and I have our morning routines, I was grateful for that.

And if I'm being honest, I rather liked how Jack's presence disrupted the normality of me and Ralph. The mild threat, while often irritating, was secretly welcome.

It was a bright autumn day of low temperatures and crisp sunshine. I heaped the fireplace in the living room with dried newspaper bricks and pine cones while Ralph stirred porridge in the kitchen. I gazed into the leaping, blood-orange flames, entranced. At the fire's heart, the pine cones were charred, malevolent flowers. When Ralph left for his class, he pecked me on the forehead and, even though he'd recently showered, I caught a hint of the smell that had been hanging around him for days. It wasn't his smell. This was feral and musky, on the edge of repellent. To my shame, I found its nastiness arousing.

Ralph hadn't cleaned the pan he'd used for the porridge nor had he returned the milk to the fridge. This was unusual. He's a tidy man. Jack was in bed. This wasn't unusual. He rarely emerged before noon on a weekend. I made for the attic, intrigued but also drawn by an inexplicable pull. It seemed to me discovering what was up there would satisfy my mind and a whole lot more.

Crazy, I know, but ever since Ralph had brought his Victorian curiosity home, I'd been twisted up with vast, unfathomable cravings. It was a yearning for nicotine, sugar, sex and heroin; for ecstasy, annihilation and for flinging myself off a cliff and embracing airy, exhilarating transcendence. It was all those things and none of them.

The door was ajar and that smell seeped out as I pushed, an ancient, earthy scent riding the regular aromatic wave of fresh wood and leather. My hands were shaking. Sunlight slanted in through two large, sloping windows, pale angles hanging like a ghostly representation of the attic's pine beams. A dusty haze fuzzed the center of the workshop and I switched on a random selection of lights, sending shadows scuttling out of the corners.

Ralph's work surfaces were strewn with chaos, while sawdust, leather, chunks of wood and mess littered the floor. The corrugated tube of a dust extractor snaked among the debris. Saws bared their teeth. Tools and knives, dangling from hooks and poking from pots, glinted with medieval menace. From a high beam, a wooden African mask gazed down with blank, black eye sockets.

But I was used to the mask's face. It was always there. The face that troubled me was a new one, a dark, burnished face with beady, glass eyes and a broad snout pierced by a ring. It belonged to a life-sized, stuffed leather pig, deeply upholstered like a Chesterfield sofa. "Grotesque" is the word that sprang to mind. I stared at the inert beast, my heart quickening. I couldn't say if I was excited or afraid. I knew only that I was reacting strongly to the pig's presence.

Leaving the attic door open so I could listen out for Jack or the phone, I drew hesitantly closer. The pig was unlike anything I'd ever seen. It stood on metal trotters, sunlight glossing its quilted bulk. The leather was a dark oxblood, its pouches and pits so taut the skin gleamed with the hard polish of wood. On the pig's back was a brown wooden saddle, a fine crack running vertically down its center.

I might have guessed at the pig being a plaything from a nineteenth-century nursery if it hadn't been for the huge, ruddy phallus protruding below its hindquarters. The penis wasn't corkscrew-shaped as on a living, breathing pig, but realism obviously wasn't the aim here. If I'd been looking for confirmation the Victorians were an odd bunch, it was jutting out in front of me, larger than life, and then some.

I glanced around the attic, wondering what Ralph made of this bizarre artefact. I recalled hearing him jerk off on the night he'd supposedly been working on the repair. Christ, our problems were bigger than I feared if my love rival was a leather pig, hung like a horse.

But no, this was something else. The attic possessed an

unsettling atmosphere, a brooding eroticism hanging in the air, oppressive and enticing. Objectively speaking, the pig wasn't attractive, I could see that. But somehow, it created an attraction, almost as if it had charisma. I know this sounds loopy but I sensed an intangible danger lying in wait for me. In my head, one voice urged me to leave and get a breath of air while another voice begged me to stay. The latter was not the voice of reason; it was fueled by lust and, even though I've been a committed atheist since the age of fifteen, I felt as if the devil himself had a hand in it. And I couldn't turn away.

On one of Ralph's workbenches, a number of carved, miniature pigs, all with spread wings, were scattered about the surface. Flying pigs, I mused, as I rolled one in my hand. It was unvarnished, still slightly rough in its execution and, at a guess, made from beech. Other pigs were well shaped and finely crafted, while some had been abandoned at an early stage. I set the pig down, feeling as if I no longer knew or understood Ralph. Is this, I wondered, how marriages disintegrate? You find flying pigs in your attic and can't discuss it with your husband?

The attic was warm although it shouldn't have been. I wondered if Jack had surfaced yet. I hoped when he did, he would add more bricks to the fire to keep the living room heated. I imagined he wouldn't; too much of a layabout to care. He'll start to care when it gets colder, I thought. I slung my cardigan over a chair, comfortable enough in one of Ralph's old shirts and a pair of stripy legwarmers I'd knitted for myself two winters ago.

I knew what I wanted to do. I wanted to sit astride the pig. I'd wanted to do so ever since I'd first entered the attic. And I might have done that, might have kept it nice and simple if, on approaching the pig, I hadn't been struck by an overwhelming urge to handle its big, shiny phallus. I suddenly wanted to feel it in my fingers, hard, polished and lewd. My hunger to touch the pig was also, inexplicably, driven by a desire to give pleasure to a lover. I had to remind myself this was an unpleasant object whose heart was sawdust, whose cock was wood.

I dropped to the floor alongside the pig, reaching below to fondle its phallus like some sick milkmaid. My fingers couldn't encircle the pig's girth so I ran my hand, cupped like a C, up and down its length. The wood was as smooth as glass and marble! That irresistible tactility practically powered my caress. I stroked greedily, slipping along the swinish shaft then molding my palm to its blunt, rounded end. My groin tingled as I imagined a thick, hard cock sliding inside me, and I remembered, with a tug of nostalgia, the wooden dildo Ralph had once carved for me. It was curved to hit my G-spot. We'd named it Nessie after the Loch Ness Monster. I didn't know where it was any more. I needed to rectify that.

An overenthusiastic caress on my part caused the pig's stout member to creak and shift. For one terrible moment, I thought the beast was alive, its porcine arousal swelling in my hand. I tested again, eliciting another grunt from the wood. Then, terrifyingly, the shaft dipped a fraction as if it were coming loose in my hand.

Oh hell. I held my breath, fearing I might have broken the monster. How on earth would I explain that to Ralph? But no, not broken. This cock, I realized, was much more than a cock. I repeated the action, pulling the shaft backwards. The entire pig shuddered and squeaked. With a groan, the wooden saddle split open down the center and began to rise and separate. I pulled harder on the phallus, now understanding it functioned as a lever. I leaned backwards as the saddle separated further, a compartment emerging from the pig's center, three tiers of drawers opening out beneath each saddle-half, staggered like those of a cantilever sewing box.

I shuffled backwards on my knees, gawping in astonishment. The drawers resembled wings. Ralph's miniature, flying-pig carvings immediately made sense. Or at least, I saw a connection between them and this. There was no sense anywhere in the attic. It was a madman's playroom.

I couldn't deny my excitement. My heart was thumping, my stomach fluttering. Our attic had the weirdest treasure. I was about to peer forward to inspect the contents of the drawers, when I glimpsed a figure in the corner of my eye. I shrieked. I had company. My heart stalled. I felt woozy, hot.

Standing in the attic doorway was Jack, wearing nothing but a pair of faded, black jogging bottoms, ragged at the hem. He was propped against the door jamb, arms folded, smirking. His biceps curved into the broad bulk of his shoulders, black tattoos licking at his contours. The hair on his creamily pale chest glinted red-gold in the mellow, autumn light and further down, a neat coppery line ran from his navel, down his flat belly, and disappeared into the waistband of his joggers.

I pressed my hand to my chest as if to keep my heart from leaping out. "How long have you been there?"

"Long enough," he replied smoothly.

I blushed, saying nothing. There was no point.

"Stunning, isn't it?" Jack strode into the room, hands in his baggy pockets. His outline smudged when he walked through a wedge of dusty sunlight. He looked mythic, other-worldly. Sensation pulsed in my groin, and I quickly grew tender and wet.

"You shouldn't smoke in the house," I said.

"I'm not smoking."

"But sometimes you do. Ralph and I don't smoke and we don't want people smoking in our house either. You have to go outside. I can smell it from your room too. It's not on, I don't like it, this is our house, mine and Ralph's. You can't just—"

"OK, OK. I've got the message."

"What are you doing up here?"

"Same as you," he said. He stood a few feet from me, looking down and smiling. His cock was lifting inside his joggers, pushing obscenely at the fabric. I wished I wasn't on my knees, wished my cunt wasn't tingling so insistently.

"No, this is my house," I said, sounding bolder than I felt. "This is my husband's workshop. I have every right to be here. You don't. You've overstepped the mark, Jack. You're arrogant and presumptuous. And nosey. You have no damn—"

"Quit with the attack!" He jerked his chin at me, eyes flinty with anger. "I saw you. I stood here and watched you work that shiny pig-dick. Saw how you loved it." He took a step closer, deliberately intimidating. "And you know what? I did exactly the same thing when you and Ralph were sleeping. Yeah, that's right. Crept up here one night and wound up making out with . . . with that." He flipped a dismissive hand toward the pig. "Because I had no choice, see? I had no fucking choice."

He gave me a long, hard stare as if, with the force if his eyes, he could make his words sink in.

I looked at the ground. "I know. I'm sorry."

"And Ralph had no choice. None of us do."

I nodded. "It's the smell."

"I don't know what it is," he replied. "But it's here, that crazy, fucked-up . . . bondage pig. And it's got to us. We have no choice."

I nodded again.

"Take a look." His voice was gentler, but his words still felt like an order. "It's worth exploring."

I have to confess, at first I thought he was referring to his cock. His directness thrilled me and I imagined dipping a hand into his joggers to free him. One tug of the drawstring and he'd be mine. An urge to betray Ralph swept over me. I wanted to be reckless and greedy, wanted to have another man all over me, inside me, everywhere. When I caught Jack's intended meaning, I mentally backtracked and kneeled up to examine the contents of the pig's trays as politely as I could. Jack moved to stand behind me, his bare feet astride my legs. He swept my hair back over my shoulders, his gesture tenderly proprietorial. My cunt throbbed with need.

Spread before me, the six shallow drawers were cluttered with bondage gear and strange-looking implements. Tentatively, I rummaged among the tangle of brown leather and brass, growing more confident and curious by the second. Jack continued to lightly stroke and lift my hair, making me nervous although I liked it. I selected a slim, wooden paddle, unvarnished and crudely fashioned, and ran a thumb along its chipped, rough edges. I was glad Jack couldn't see my face.

"Spanking," he said as I set the piece on the ground. He wasn't informing me. He knew I wasn't naive. He was itemizing the things we would do together. Or at any rate, that's how it sounded to me. We hear what we want to hear.

When I set aside another paddle, this one in dark, brittle leather and patterned with a grid of holes, Jack said, "More spanking."

I swallowed and noted my hand was trembling when I reached into the trays again. Arousal swam between my thighs. *Stop this*, I told myself, *stop this!* Another voice said, *Hey, you're doing nothing wrong, just inspecting a freaky antique with your lodger.* Yeah, right, Simone. A lodger with a boner who's stroking your hair while your husband's at work.

My fingertips skimmed over rough and smooth, soft and hard. Objects clinked together, some pieces too entangled to budge. I took care to choose something interesting.

"Pinwheel," said Jack.

I held a small brass roller, its wide, leather-coated wheel spiked with four rows of metal spines.

"What's it for?" I asked.

Jack reached out a hand from behind me. I passed back the roller. With one hand, he unfastened the top buttons of my shirt. He slipped my clothes down from my shoulders and swept my hair aside, baring my neck and back. I clutched my shirt by my breasts, covering myself because I was naked beneath, not yet dressed for the day. I caught a waft of Jack's sweat as he leaned close. His murmured words were warm against my ear.

"Say again?" he taunted.

My voice creaked with lust. "What's it for?"

A pause. "It's for punishing sluts who ask stupid fucking questions."

The spikes stabbed my skin and he rolled the wheel across my shoulders, slow and hard. I groaned loudly, his insults and the pain sparking a surge of fierce, dark lust. "Again," I whispered. I seemed to speak the words before I'd even thought them. I dipped my head like a supplicant, offering him my naked back. "Again."

"Like this?" He rolled another track across my shoulders then stopped.

"More! Please."

He gave a soft, satisfied laugh then rolled the barbed wheel up and down, round and round, fast and slow until I couldn't tell one track from another. I felt as if a thousand hot, tiny spears were raining down on my skin, a monsoon of cruel sensation. I writhed, swayed, hunched and gasped, and whenever Ralph popped into my head, I told myself I couldn't help it, none of us could, we weren't to blame. We were in the grip of a power that defied comprehension. This wasn't me asking for it; nor was Jack doling it out. This was the bondage pig, who'd come to corrupt us, to drag us down a path of chaos and depravity. We weren't to blame.

"Please!" My heart and hands racing, I tugged open several more buttons and shucked off my shirt, arching back to present him with my breasts, my nipples hard and high. Jack rolled the wheel over one shoulder, down between the valley of my breasts, below the underswell, up, around, down, and oh, oh, fire stabbed my nipple and I was dizzy with longing, crying out for something and not knowing if I wanted more of this or less.

Then a voice cut into my consciousness, cold as ice.

"We should use the collar on her. You can attach wrist cuffs to it, front or back. Take away her hands then we can use her how we want."

"Ralph!"

From behind, Jack cupped my chin firmly in his hand, tipping my head back against his crotch. His erection pressed against me. "Sounds like a plan."

He held me fast, and I felt so deeply ashamed, sluttish, aroused. This near-stranger had me in his hands, fixing me on my knees so my bared, adulterous body was being offered to my husband. I closed my eyes, the after-image of Ralph in the attic doorway stamped on my mind. Wide-shouldered and athletically lean, he stood much as Jack had done earlier, arms folded and coolly observing. Where Jack was red-haired, Ralph was fair, but both men scared me: Jack because he was trouble; Ralph because he'd caught me *in flagrante* with Trouble and I feared he might be angry. He had every right to be.

Ralph strolled toward us. My heart thumped and, when Ralph passed through the dusty shaft of sunlight, something peculiar happened. He was transformed to me. Briefly, he appeared to be a magnificent, celestial vision, but the real change must have been in my perception. My earnest, reliable and slightly dull husband became the man I fell in love with all those years ago: passionate, idealistic, driven; a man determined to get what he wants. And I knew that what Ralph wanted right then was me; and for me, him and Jack to surrender to wild, primal lust and destroy all limits of seemliness and order.

Quick and efficient, Ralph selected a couple of brown leather items from the pig's deepest drawers and tossed a handful of brass clips in his palm. Jack stepped aside with a chuckle of approval.

"Hands behind your back," said Ralph. "Not like that. Higher."

Deftly, he cuffed and buckled my wrists between my shoulder blades, his bossiness making my horniness soar.

"And just so we know who you belong to . . ." With those words, he fastened a matching leather collar around my neck, slipping his long fingers inside to check it wasn't too tight. Metal clinked as he linked my cuffed wrists to my collar. When I let the collar take the strain of my arms, it pulled against my throat so I had to keep my hands high. I found the position uncomfortable but, in spite of that or perhaps because of it, intensely arousing.

Jack bobbed down in front of me and lifted my breasts in turn as if testing their weight. He grinned at me, looking me dead in the eye. I glanced away, ashamed, because I didn't want to like this but couldn't hide how much it was turning me on. Jack tapped harder, slapping upwards, his hand skimming off me as I bounced. I groaned and Ralph dropped to his knees at my other side, wrapping an arm around my waist. Jack stepped back as Ralph tilted me forward to deliver a series of hard, merciless blows to my ass. "You like that, do you, Sim?" he hissed. Slap. Slap. Slap. "Like it when some other guy plays with your tits."

I yelped and squealed, heat blossoming under my husband's hand. "Yes," I gasped. "Yes, I like it." Ralph was rough, messy and energetic in the way he spanked me, his breath huffing fast, his arm clasping me tight. I flinched and jerked, writhing to escape and wobbling awkwardly in his grip.

"Put your dick in her mouth," Ralph urged Jack, but Jack was about to do precisely that so the request was redundant. I figured it wasn't actually a request, more a granting of permission, not that Jack was asking. His joggers were off, his cock was hard, and he was aiming himself at my mouth. Ralph pinched my jaw, raising my head to Jack's level. I opened to take him, spluttering crudely around his length as I drew back and forth, still unsteady on my knees.

"Go on, Simone," encouraged Ralph, his voice by my ear. "Show him what you can do."

Jack held my head still, fists in my hair, and moved according to his pace, hips rolling with languid ease. My breathing steadied and I lashed my tongue around his shaft. When he let me, I slurped hard on his end, making little popping noises because that's how Ralph likes it. Jack seemed to like it too. Pleasure rumbled in his throat and he clutched my hair tighter, my scalp stinging.

"That's my girl," said Ralph, hooking his arm around my back. Keeping me upright and balanced, he reached his free hand between my thighs and plunged his fingers into me, hard and fast. "Let's see what we have here."

He curled his fingers into me, pressing and shunting until my head was spinning and I had to break off from Jack to gasp and whimper.

"She's so wet," Ralph said to Jack. "Go on, try her."

Jack fell to one knee and did what Ralph had just done, his thrusts equally vigorous. Ralph stood behind me, tucked his hand into my armpits and eased me backwards. At that angle, with my knees spread for Jack, my hands locked in cuffs, I felt defenseless and exposed, a thing to be used by these two eager men.

Jack's hand pumped between my thighs and, as my cries hurried to a peak, he ducked down to taste me. With his tongue flat and generous, he rubbed at my clit. I felt so loose, so wet, and then, in the dizzying midst of that, Jack's tongue began darting over my bud in sharp, intentional patterns. Ralph propped me against his chest and massaged my breasts, his calloused fingers scuffing my nipples. My pleasure tightened, I panted with nearness, and Jack's tongue was pure, unadulterated magic.

"She's going to come," Ralph said. "Just a little more. Keep going."

I focused on the bondage pig, on its cantilever trays and stout, buttoned haunches. The color of the leather seeped into my mind. Such a beautiful color, red-black, like blood and ink. Jack slid a bunch of fingers into me, screwing left–right–left when my swollen tightness resisted him. I wailed to feel the fullness of him. His tongue skittered on my point and then, oh, I was gone, lost, tumbling through crimson skies as my orgasm pulsed and clenched. Over and over I fell, six distinct waves of pleasure coursing through my body.

"Good girl," said Ralph.

Jack knelt up, his mouth shining with my juices. "Fuck," he breathed. "I felt that." I stared at him through my post-orgasmic daze. He wiped the back of his hand across his mouth. His lips still gleamed and his eyes were heavy and serious, altered by lust.

Ralph unclipped me. I let my hands fall, each wrist still wrapped in a tatty, brown cuff, my neck still collared. I wondered about all the people who'd worn these cuffs, all the scenes the pig had witnessed. I was weak, as floppy as a rag doll, and when Ralph indicated I should kneel on all fours, I tipped forwards onto my elbows, unable to bear my weight on my arms.

I hardly knew what was happening to me. And then I knew Jack was fucking me because Ralph said, "Be my guest," and a cock was pushing into me and it wasn't Ralph's. Inside, I was pink and sensitive. Jack's hard, fat shaft pried me open until I was snug and pulpy around him, the contact so hot I fancied I must be melting.

"Oh, jeez, that's good," he sighed. "Such a sweet, little pussy."

He was slow to start, every lunge and retreat making me moan for more. I was hazily aware of Ralph undressing and then I was acutely aware of him lifting my shoulders. His cock reared up before me, his head glossy and blood-flushed, his length surging high, a network of blue veins spread beneath his velvet-smooth skin. I found strength in my arms and took him in my mouth, clamping my lips below the rim of his tip and fondling his warm, weighty balls. As I bobbed on Ralph's end, Jack began to fuck with more urgency, his fingers digging into my hips. I slid to the root of Ralph and he gave a low, appreciative growl, holding my head to keep me there.

When I withdrew and swallowed him down again, he said, "We've got you skewered, Sim."

"Spit-roasting you," gasped Jack.

I moaned around Ralph's cock as Jack powered with increasing savagery, his fingertips on my hips creating dents of pain. Exhausted and half delirious, I was being buffeted between the two men, unable to do anything much except take them. Then, with a harsh, rasping cry, Jack pulled out of me and, seconds later, his climax pattered on my back in several hot splashes.

Ralph cried out in response, sounding agonized and shocked. I knew that sound so well. So close, so close. Moments before he came, I felt him swell to a peak of rigidity in my mouth. He held still, thighs shuddering as his liquid jetted at my throat and I was drinking him down, fresh, thin and salty. When I released him, he was quick to kiss me, seeking out his own taste as he held my face, light, affectionate and almost proud.

After catching his breath, he said, "You're amazing."

I could hardly speak. "So are you," I managed. "Both of you." I reached for Jack. "Dirty bastards. But amazing with it."

Jack flopped onto the wooden floor, an arm flung above his head, copper hair glinting like filaments in his armpit. "I blame the pig," he said.

"Likewise," I said. "Don't you dare get rid of it, Ralph."

We laughed tiredly, united in post-coital cosiness.

"Man, I need a cigarette," said Jack, idly strumming his chest.

"Smoke away," I said. "I don't care."

Jack turned to Ralph who shrugged, saying, "I don't give a fuck either. Don't give a fuck about anything right now. I hope the house isn't on fire. Don't think I could move."

Jack grunted in amusement. I thought about the fire I'd made that morning. It seemed silly now to think how concerned I'd been about Jack keeping it alight. Nothing mattered. We could stay in the attic all day if we wanted, pausing to fetch food and fucking till we ran out of energy. Yes, I thought, we could do that quite easily. To hell with responsibility. And so that's what we did, as if the hands on the clock had stopped and the world had fallen away, leaving only the three of us.

Jack moved out after five weeks, saying, "Three's a crowd." We were sad to see him go, but our parting was entirely amicable. He tempered our disappointment with a promise to stop by occasionally for some "attic-time" – as we'd begun to refer to sex, even when it didn't take place in the attic.

A week later, Ralph got rid of the pig. By that point, we were practically stupefied with horniness and fatigue, yet the impulse to continue never wavered. We'd tried every kinky object stored inside the beast several times over, and our house was a disaster zone, domestic duties falling by the wayside as the hunger to fuck took over. We tested friendships and family relationships by neglecting social events, emails and phone calls, preferring sex to anything else. We were insatiable. And sore too, especially in the first week with Jack.

The pig's original owner no longer wanted his possession back, claiming life was more manageable without "that thing" to feed. I could understand. Ralph sold the pig at auction for a tidy sum and we dusted ourselves down, still happily horny but not crazily so. Now, every day on a chain around my neck, I wear one of Ralph's tiny, flying pigs, a hand-carved reminder of the glorious times we shared. I often wonder where the bondage pig is, and whether others see its influence as a blessing or a curse.

Sometimes, I swear pockets of that weird, feral scent are still lingering in the attic. When I catch a hint of the aroma, I breathe in its darkness, convinced the spirit of the beast is still with us, keeping our fires burning bright.

Slowhand

Isabella Johns

I

As I lie in my king-size bed late at night, my husband dozing by my side after a glorious round of lovemaking, I really do remember it as if it were yesterday . . . *my first orgasm.*

It was the summer just after my college graduation and I was hired as a swim counselor at a water sports camp on the Caribbean island of St Lucia. My boyfriend Art was the water-ski director. He didn't have the muscle-bound fullness and hard-bodied abs of a romance cover hottie. There was a tight firmness to his chest and stomach, coupled with broad shoulders and a narrow waist. His dark hair cascaded down to his back in thick curls, eyes a deep brown, his skin perpetually shaded to a lovely auburn from the bright Caribbean sun. All feminine eyes gravitated toward him – whether a teen camper or adult staff member – as he strolled the beach in his tight skimpy Speedos and thick ski vest that seemed to accentuate his perfectly proportioned body and helped cast the confident, manly aura of a lean, shirtless, eighties rocker performing onstage.

Whether slaloming, barefooting, one-skiing, or jumping, he looked as natural on the water as he did on land. And, indeed, he also played a mean guitar and regaled the camp once a week with his reggae style and raspy voice. He was one of those men who had a stately handsomeness, not just because of his physicality, frame and features, but because of how good he was at everything he did.

The water sports camp was at a resort leased exclusively for the summer. It was right on the beach against a backdrop of soothing sounds from the never-ending waves lapping onto the shore. The Caribbean Sea was a clear aqua blue, the sand soft and white, the many palm trees heavy with coconuts. The nights were exquisite, especially when the moon was full, reflecting off the water with light nearly as bold as sunshine. This beautiful romantic atmosphere, along with the visual stimulation of everyone nearly naked and wet throughout the day, helped make St Lucia an erotic paradise.

The teenaged campers found ways to sneak out. The staff greedily welcomed time off to attend to their own needs. And somehow Art took an interest in me ... which was surprising, considering I spent most of the day in a bikini that I filled out so poorly it was painfully obvious I could've gone topless.

The first time Art and I made love, he took me to the ski shack, where they stored the vests, skis, and tow ropes. It was always a challenge to find a comfortable place to do it. The resort rooms could not be locked, everyone had two room-mates, the property was fenced in, and there was nothing but dusty fields and a run-down village waiting beyond the gates. It was expensive to rent a room somewhere else on a night off, so everyone had to be creative. The ski shack was dingy, with barely room to lie down on an uneven cushion of ski vests, and it smelled of gasoline. But it did have a door that could be locked from the inside.

He kissed as well as he played guitar. During the year he tried to eke out a living with his own rock band, but it was a series of part-time jobs that paid the rent. This was my first summer, but as the story goes, there was a night off the previous summer when Art jammed at a local bar and when he finished a man in baseball cap and sunglasses approached from the shadows in the back, took Art's hand as if to shake, but instead kissed it then receded into the night. Several patrons identified the figure as Eric Clapton, a lover of the Caribbean as well as great guitar playing.

To be touched by the fingers that were kissed by Mr Slow-hand himself was quite a thrill. Even more thrilling was the seductive way Art removed my tank top, skirt, and panties, as if he were lovingly tuning his guitar. He stroked his fingers through my long blonde hair, which made me ache to feel his hands everywhere. We had talked about getting together the last few days – the anticipation moistening my bikini bottom as we flirted at lunch – and we finally made it happen. His deep kisses and tender tongue created songs in my mouth. His taut frame was luxurious and I couldn't help trailing my hands along it, caresses that started at his shoulders then glided easily all the way to his legs. But when his soft lips made their way down my neck and his tongue began circling my nipples laying limply against my *flat* chest, my body suddenly tightened, full anxiousness rising in my throat.

It wasn't that I was a late bloomer. I just never blossomed.

As a pre-teen I waited patiently for my breasts to grow. As a teen I became impatient, then frenetic, then downright obsessed. My pediatrician told me I was perfectly healthy, the breasts might develop, that some women are just flat-chested and don't get anything until they have children, and I should be thankful I wouldn't have to deal with sagging.

Thankful? *Flat-chested* was an understatement. If I lay on my back there would be only nipples resting like compressed dots against my chest. If I stood . . . nothing. I even tried examinations in my bedroom mirror while on all fours: a little *hang* in the nipples, but not one tit-like curve or bump, not even a slight arc rising. No change in college.

I tried to even out my breaths as Art kissed the tips of my nipples. He saw me in a bikini all day. He had to know he wasn't getting a swimsuit model.

It was not the deep breaths, but the loving way Art licked and sucked that eased my anxieties. His tongue was gentle as he lapped and circled my yielding flesh, causing my nipples to swell to lengths I did not think possible. I ran my hand through his hair and turned him so our eyes met. I kissed him deeply with extreme gratefulness. He could not *pretend* such interest and it made me even more comfortable to lie naked with this extraordinary man.

As with his guitar, he was an artist with oral pleasure: his tongue the pick, my body his strings. He bathed me with its length and thickness, painting swirls and wet portraits along my belly, down the sides of my hips, inside the delicate flesh of my thighs, behind my knees, a final undulation through my toes. He tuned, primed, prepared, unwrapped me, until finally he positioned his face between my thighs, his long legs sprawled somewhere behind him amid a pile of more vests, my pussy totally ready for the completion of his opening act.

His foreplay had been eminently patient, applying a grace that I had not been exposed to previously. It was as if my body were a fully occupied apartment building and he had traveled to every room to alert the inhabitants that a fire was about to start on the middle floor.

He kissed my pussy gently, seemingly already in love with it. I couldn't help reaching down and stroking his thick curly hair, careful not to guide him anywhere, cautious not to lead this artist off track, because it was obvious he was familiar with every note.

The kisses turned to slow licks and nibbles all along the sides of my outer lips. He seemed eager to know, with great intimacy, every part of my pussy, which greeted him as a cherished confidant.

Following the kisses and licks was a deep penetration. His tongue seemed as large as the cocks of several former lovers, though size certainly never mattered to me. I've always been sympathetic, perhaps bonding more closely with those not well endowed. He made his tongue stiff and began a slow rhythmic thrusting. His hands slid over my belly and came to rest at my nipples, playing with them once again, teasing them, lightly twisting as if they were knobs dotted on the body of his electric guitar.

He made me so damn open and wet. True to his name, he

*art*fully laid out a foundation for multiple feelings, then layered and built the sensations, constructing his own pyramid of pleasure. His strong, long fingers delicately spread the lips of my pussy, exposing my swollen clitoris. He circled it slowly with his tongue, as he had done with my nipples, making it throb and ache for more touch, pressure, friction. Then he greeted it fully, first with kisses, then with delightful tongue swirls.

"You're magic," I told him.

He remained focused, at work, his tongue latching onto my clit as if embracing a dance partner then leading her through a series of tantalizing moves. I could fall in love with this man . . . someone who took so much care, who unwrapped my body with his wizardry and made me feel brand new.

As he sucked my clit into his mouth, held it there lightly with his teeth, flicked with a dedicated, steady rhythm, it was clear the foreplay was over and he wanted me to come.

As a teenager – in addition to being a serial bra-stuffer – I took a lot of grief from boys because of my prudishness. My anxiety on dates had to do with the knowledge that when the boy's attempt to make second base turned into a full strikeout, I would be the laughing stock of my high school. So I never let it get that far.

My social life at home was no better. Alone in my bedroom, while reading YA romances, later much dirtier books, or looking through magazines at the actors or rock stars I wanted to fuck, I felt some arousal, and tried my best at fingering, teasing, rubbing, finger-fucking, and voracious pillow humping to complete some sort of orgasmic bond to my fantasies, to find that satisfied release. It all added up to a lot of reddish soreness and extreme frustration.

Either I was too pissed at my body to make the kind of warm connection I needed, or my body wasn't satisfied with marking me for life as a pre-pubescent and was intent on dooming me to an existence of downtrodden frigidity.

On my back in the ski shack, legs spread, Art's face buried deep inside my pussy, his tongue casting a variety of spells, I felt many wonderful sensations, ones that inspired the whistle and hum of intense gratification. But somehow, as usual, there was no sense of finality waiting for me. I was as wet as the sea just yards from the shack. And sure there were jolts. It was immensely pleasant. But when it came to constructing a climax, each thrust of his tongue, each fine-tuning by his fingers was like a flint fruitlessly chipping at a stone. Over and over he repeated his movements, finally shifting into a flurry that included the full repeated sucking of my clit while his tongue continued to dance over it, trying to give me the first of what he probably anticipated as many glorious climaxes . . . but only the incessant sparks without a flame.

All of this caused that familiar anxiety to rise again from my chest, this time so thick, so palpable, that his continual flicks threatened to siphon the air from my lungs. I had no choice but to scramble out from under him, quickly reverse our positions, and hide my angst behind my great and true desire to suck his cock.

A tasty cock it was. No matter how hard we scrubbed in the shower, neither of us could lose the flavor of the Caribbean Sea on and within our bodies. He was delicious. Certainly a hint of salt, but more of an organic taste, one familiar to my mouth. It held the scent of the outdoors, an aroma that perfumed the stale stuffiness of this storage shack like a soft breeze floating in from the sea-moistened air.

I kissed his cock with great tenderness, grateful for the chance to savor him. It stood firm in my hand and I licked the underside of his shaft, near the base, over and over, while my hands caressed his thighs. It was thrilling to hear his moans, to feel him grow underneath the tip of my tongue. He became fully erect as I caressed his manhood with my wet lips. His long thin cock seemed to be a mini-version of the man himself. At the base was the same dark curly hair and the circumcised head seemed to angle a bit, just the way his neck arced side-ways when he patiently encouraged his students.

I wished I could see his face, which was lost in the shadows of this room, the outside spotlight seeping unevenly through the narrow spaces between the wall boards. But the squirming of his body, and the arching of his hips that caused his cock to greet my open mouth, revealed his full pleasure, and I welcomed him warmly by relaxing my throat muscles and taking all of him down for a blissful penetration. I sucked him gently, lovingly, recalling the great affection he had already shown me. Both his hands tugged lightly on the long strands of my hair.

And finally, as I increased my rhythm, my head bobbing up and down on him while I held his cock firmly at the base, I felt the round head begin to swell even larger in my mouth. I eagerly prepared to receive the full splash of his semen. Though I longed to have him deep inside me, his wet surge and taste would provide more than enough pleasure and would certainly postpone the intense uneasiness I usually felt during any first time with a man (and the times after that) when his best efforts came up short.

But Art would have none of it. All at once he pulled out and guided my mouth toward his.

We lay on our sides, opposite the other. He held my face in his long-fingered hands and kissed me sweetly. I reached down, found his cock, and gently guided him inside my plentiful wetness.

We made love. As passionate lovers do. We rotated our hips in unison as we continued to kiss. It was difficult in this position, on top of ski vests, for him to go deep into me, but it was a delightful joining of our bodies.

He took his turn on top. I received him with complete openness. I wanted this man. I wanted him from the day we met at the first staff meeting. His good humor, easy smile, quiet confidence made it difficult to concentrate on what the director had to say and had me squirming in my chair as I crossed and uncrossed my legs.

He was able to go deeper now and I welcomed this forceful penetration. My arms went around his back, and his chest rested against mine as he licked my neck and my nipples while I squeezed him even closer, enjoying every bit of this tight joining of our bodies.

And then it was my turn to ride.

I managed to roll him first to his side then onto his back without that delectable manhood ever leaving my pussy. My hands rested on his firm belly while I ground his cock deep inside me, rotating my hips with the carefree, frenetic flow of a samba dancer.

"Fuck me with that pussy," he urged, which caused me to gallop even faster.

I felt much elation from receiving this man I had lusted after, intense satisfaction from giving him pleasure, feeling him grow and press forward into me. My hands explored his chest, pinching his nipples firmly and he moaned his approval. While still managing to keep him inside, I leaned down and kissed him deeply, the bridge to our chorus always our lips pressed together, our tongues slip-sliding in each other's mouth.

When I pulled back I was able to see that his eyes were open, watching me. I tried to meet his gaze, but the intensity of my pounding caused my lids to squeeze tight as I sprinted to the finish line . . . well, his finish line. I wanted to give him a grand release, something he would remember, something that inspired further desire to be with me all summer. I felt another final swelling, but that was it. I sensed him holding back. I opened my eyes now, stared down at him. I could tell he was watching my movements closely, listening to my sounds, trying to glean whether I was close to orgasming, trying to time his release with mine.

How do I tell him just to go with his own flow and not worry about me?

How do I explain that I don't come and I've learned where to find my own pleasure and I'm grateful for every nuance I feel?

These worried thoughts caused a dryness within me and I fretted that something so beautiful, once again, had the potential to turn awkward.

Undaunted, he slid out from under me, went down on my pussy one more time to relubricate, releasing a steady flow of moisture from his mouth, then turned me onto my stomach, then up onto my knees, and entered me from behind.

This position allowed for the deepest penetration yet, one I suspect he felt would do the trick.

He thrust into me with full force. No longer the soulful musician, he attacked my pussy as if grasping the tow rope hard from behind the ski boat while bouncing fiercely on rough waters. He grazed his nails along my shoulder blades and I arched my back and purred like a jungle cat. Then his hands grabbed my hips and he was able to lift me slightly back toward him, my knees off the ground, forcing my body to meet the explosiveness of his ramming. This feeling of being possessed inspired even more titillation. He reached around, rubbed my clit, and I swooned. The calloused nub on his finger stimulated my clit with grace, with force, but not too hard. He found the perfect music of thrusting and fingering; his cock strummed me deep, while his fingers manipulated a complete array of sensual sounds.

There was only so long anyone could keep up this tempo and the impending dread from not being able to give him all he wanted threatened to rid me again of inner lubrication. I was sure it felt equally as rough, as dryly frictioned, for him. This man had taken so much care with me and my body. I so wanted to give him the complete satisfaction he craved and have him reach his fulfillment while fully satisfying me. Not only this moment, but the entire summer seemed to be rapidly slipping away. The only moistness forming now was in my eyes as I fought off, once again, the dark familiar heartbreak caused by a body that refuses to cooperate.

Against my better judgment, I began making slow, deep orgasmic sounds, ones that never came naturally to me, but were copied from the ladies of porn. I was careful not to overdo it, starting off lightly, then building, latching onto the rhythms of his thrusts. I was rewarded with the deep harmony of masculine grunts that fashioned an explosive beat in my ears, vibrated along his hands and cock, and buzzed delightfully through my body. There was a final expansive growth in his head and shaft that created contact at a deep uncharted spot and a thickness against my inner walls. All of it was followed by the pleasant gush of his semen and his satisfied cry of, "You're such a hot sweet fuck!" At the same time I released a final, majestic, extended moan that was genuine, not from the feeling at my clit, but from the true joy of making love with this man.

He withdrew, condom-less, I on the pill, both copulating in an era just before sex could mean a fatal health tragedy, and we collapsed side by side again in each other's arms, embracing tightly.

I felt wonderful. My complete vision returned: the two of us hand in hand, boyfriend and girlfriend, many weeks ahead to explore the beauty of each other amid the glory of this tropical paradise.

We both breathed heavily, a long time before it was easy to talk, but then my heart plummeted when he said, "You faked it, didn't you?"

I'd tried so hard when I got to college not to let my boob-lessness define my existence. I started swimming competitively, just daring someone to comment on how my *streamlined* figure gave me an advantage. My body toned in delightful ways, arms curved and lean, shoulders strong, legs long and sturdy, belly as flat as, well, you know. Competing gave me confidence. Blessed with good skin and a pretty smile, I did have boyfriends. Some of them gave it the old college try, forever patient with manual stimulation, with oral, with slow to frenzied lovemaking, but still no orgasm. Some, either because of my chest or my frigidity, quickly became frustrated. Some accepted me for who I was. And others, the ones I really liked and was most keen on keeping, the ones I didn't want to risk losing because of the uncomfortable no-can-do talk coupled with my brief but frustrating sexual history, were treated to faked orgasms that could've gotten me a gig in any porno. I was able to garner significant pleasure from being held, kissed, touched, caressed and penetrated. I enjoyed making a man come with my hand, body and mouth. There were other things in life aside from hitching a ride on a mind-blowing orgasm. Though I wondered if there were many that allowed a woman to feel completely in touch with her body, to experience such myriad sensations, to know all there was to know about one's potential for pleasure.

Art already seemed to know so much about me. I took some pleasure in that. But despite how gently he had posed his question, he got me during the wide open vulnerability of the *moment after*, that time when every emotion is of monumental importance and one's ability to pretend or hide is at its lowest.

I burst into tears.

He held me close, kissing the top of my head, whispering, "No problem. Really. Totally cool. I just want you to know that you don't need to do that. I love getting it on with you."

Once again he was quite patient, allowing me time to regroup. Finally, eyes dried, breath even, I was able to whisper back, "Please believe me. It's not you. I've never been able to come. It's my cross to bear, but it doesn't mean I didn't have an awesome time. You're incredible!"

"You've never got off?" he echoed, trying to hide his surprise. "Even alone?"

"Even alone," I repeated. I kissed him gently on the mouth. "Believe me I've tried everything, from tantric breathing to a vibrator. It's a road that always leads to a dead end."

"Really," he said. The faint light filtering through the wall cracks allowed me to make out his playful smile, one that seemed to welcome challenges with great confidence. "We'll have to see about that . . ."

II

Art was smart enough not to let my frigidity become too big a deal. We made love every night – always in search of new discreet places to be alone – in mostly the same fashion as our first night in the ski shack. Art didn't go out of his way to make me come, though he always did to make me feel good. I was more than happy with what we shared. But every Wednesday, in more ways than one, was hump day. We both had this night off, and he approached each mid-week encounter as if attempting to write a song with a whole new approach, an entirely fresh style.

He tied my wrists, had me call him Master, and dominated me late at night under the tennis bleachers.

Another Wednesday he took me to the end of the boat dock, laid me out on a towel, and massaged me from head to toe with warm coconut oil.

During one hump day lunch break, he had me swim with him to the far end of the resort's cove where a group of local women congregated on shore, weaving baskets for the next batch of tourists. We stopped, stood in the shallow sea, the water up to my shoulders and his chest. He waved at the ladies; they waved back and stared at us curiously. He slipped off my bikini bottom and made love to me from behind, our lower halves hidden underwater, while telling me what a dirty, naughty girl I was, letting everyone watch my sexual *baptism* in the Caribbean Sea.

All of it did seem dirty, naughty, sweet, and thrilling, but I still couldn't orgasm. On these days he would refuse to come if I didn't, dedicating the encounters entirely to me and his quest for complete pleasure for both of us. No more tears, sometimes laughter. I became incredibly comfortable with this man, who made me feel sexier than anyone ever had. His patience, his creativity, his devotion to opening new worlds for me made it impossible for me not to fall in love with him.

On the last Wednesday of the summer, it was my twenty-second birthday. Art had the resort chef make a special cake and the camp sang "Happy Birthday". Later, while the campers and counselors prepared for a team quiz bowl event, Art and I sat on a bench in an elevated gazebo and watched the sun set – all of it made extra special because Art strummed his acoustic and sang for me: sweet songs, ballads, verses full of love. When it got dark, we held hands and walked back to the rooms. He stored his guitar in his closet and we walked along the beach toward the end of the resort's property. A cliff blocked further passage, one that rose up about eighty feet and was topped by a large white house where the owner lived. I was ready to turn around, but he motioned for me to wade with him around the bend. Knee deep in water, some quick hopping and stepping on rocks, we soon came to an elevated patch of sand, hidden from the beach, from the house above, and protected from the water by jutting rocks.

And there standing, smiling right at us, to my great surprise, was the dive boat captain, a local, a man in his early thirties, gloriously handsome.

I didn't know if the captain even owned any shirts, because he was mostly seen in a pair of cut-off khakis and nothing more. When steering the boat, or helping to haul equipment, the beautiful blackness of his skin shone with a glittering sheen of sweat reflected by the sun. His chest was sculpted as fine as any bronze god. His powerful legs kept him perfectly balanced no matter how rough the seas, no matter how harsh the bounce, his large feet gripping tightly any slick surface. His brown eyes were piercing, alert, intelligent, as if he could size up anyone in an instant. He would be completely intimidating if it wasn't for the brilliant flash of teeth he displayed with the warmest of smiles.

Art grinned and I remained flabbergasted. The two men grabbed each other in a bro' shake, hands clasped, arms tucked in, chests briefly bumping.

"Wassup, brother mon?" asked the captain.

"Easy," returned Art. So many years in the Caribbean, playing with local reggae artists, he flowed into local slang with natural ease, the accent near perfect.

Then the captain greeted me with a warm hug and a very delicate kiss on my cheek. I didn't know why I was so shocked the captain was here; Art was a very determined man.

We sat on the sand in a small circle and the captain presented a cigar-sized spliff of marijuana and Art produced a lighter.

We passed the joint among us and the deep sucks of potent uncut ganja streamed through our bodies and mellowed our minds. Already this birthday was unforgettable: being sung to while watching a blazing Caribbean sunset melt into the blue horizon, then welcoming a star-filled night with the intoxicating inhalations of local home-grown, something that rounded out everything, leaving no edges in sight.

The fact was not lost that this private, secluded, tropical spot soon gifted me with the illusion of our bodies floating on water.

Nor that I was with my slender rock star and the muscular captain, two sex gods of mammoth proportions, so tightly entwined in our circle that everyone's thighs touched.

The captain kissed me first. His thick short tongue was completely unfamiliar, which titillated me greatly, the newness of it, the exotic flavor. There was a rustle of bodies, soon all of us were naked, and I was laid gently onto my back, the captain resting over me as he continued to kiss me with his forceful lips. Instinctively, my hands went behind him, my fingers following the distinct firm lines of his compact curves and rippling back muscles.

The captain's body seemed especially bulky and massive after the long slenderness of Art. I brought a hand around and touched a powerful, erect nipple. His muscular breast, the full hardness of it dwarfing my palm, had far more volume and curve than both my breasts put together.

I didn't dwell on this, perhaps because the captain – his mouth still at mine – slid his body off to my left side and Art pressed his full length against my right. The captain nibbled along my neck, which allowed my first deep kiss of the night with Art. He had never verbally declared his love, but what we shared was so full of tender feeling it was surely as if his mouth and tongue communicated this precise emotion. I touched his face with gratitude.

When we had approached our spot I had wondered, with both anticipation and anxiety, what he had in mind for this special hump day. At this moment, perhaps because of the marijuana, I managed to will myself to stop thinking, to fall short of a full evaluation of whether something like this would work. It was Art's voice in my head mouthing, *Easy.*

It was. The feeling of two mouths, two tongues, four hands exploring my body, while I was lost in the haze of an earthy high, was truly spiritual. I closed my eyes and allowed them to touch, lick and kiss me everywhere. There was a strong temptation to reciprocate, to touch a nipple, to kiss a neck, caress a cock, but what they did was so passionate and overwhelming that I could only lie back and experience.

The captain was the first one at my pussy, his thick tongue spreading me in a new way. He didn't have the patience of Art, but the muscular strength of his approach was quite gratifying. Art positioned himself over me, facing toward my feet. He lowered his cock and balls onto my face, smothering me with his stiff shaft, soft sac, and curly pubic hair. The feel of him rubbing all over my features, marking me with his delicious scent, presenting me the prize of his hardness – while another man ate out my pussy – aroused me into a moist fever, my moans vibrating on Art's full length.

The captain probed deep inside me with his tongue, his finger playing with my clit, another teasing my ass. Art rose up enough so that my mouth instinctively opened and his cock was able to slide easily down my throat.

Truly penetrated, in multiple ways, possessed. Both men intent on pleasing me.

I was relaxed, but not without inhibition. The focus on me always brought on some tension of expectation. I was used to not coming around Art.

But what about the captain and his expectations?

Some unseen signal seemed to pass from Art to the captain and they suddenly reversed positions. Art's delicate tongue explored my pussy, while the sweet thickness of the captain's cock probed my mouth.

Art remained patient, but the captain picked up his pace. The expectation of feeling him explode semen down my throat certainly enhanced my buzz. But he wasn't coming. He, too, was focused on me and how aroused I must be to have this new cock in my mouth.

"Relax, baby girl," he whispered, "and full pleasure will be yours."

The captain seemed determined to fulfill his expectations with his vigorous penetration of my mouth, and I tightened my lips to create some fluid resistance, which inspired a groan of approval. Art tried to remain steady, but increased his tongue tempo to match the rhythm of the captain's sway. I wanted to get lost in these feelings, and I almost did, but the tightness in my chest was still there.

Art pulled out first, clearly sensing my anxiety, then touched the captain on his shoulder, who responded by removing his cock from my mouth.

Words shaped at my lips, some sort of mumbling that threatened to fashion itself into a sorrowful explanation or apology, but they didn't have time to fully form. To my great astonishment, Art slid up from my body and kissed the captain hard on the mouth.

I could only gasp.

I wondered if there would now be tension between them, if Art had overstepped this evening's boundaries.

I needn't have worried. The captain embraced Art strongly, pulling his narrow torso toward the width of his defined chest as he opened his mouth and slipped his tongue deep inside my lover's mouth.

I remained stretched out on the sand, staring. The two men went at each other with a fierceness, as if this sort of pleasure had been tightly locked then suddenly freed.

Art sucked the captain's nipples, one at a time, roughly, inspiring the familiar feel of his mouth on my nipples as well.

The captain stroked Art's cock with his thick hand and Art responded with expanded length and width.

It was deeply arousing to see two men kiss, with such enjoyment, with so much passion.

Instinctively, as not a word was spoken, the captain lay on his back and Art reclined in the reverse direction so they could sixty-nine. The sight of two vigorous cocks going inside the strong lips of two men was also a wonder to behold.

They each seemed so lost in the heated sensations produced by the other it was as if I had melted into the sand.

How delightful. And so kinky. Just to watch. While these two men sought their pleasure. A front row seat for an exclusive performance.

They pumped each other's mouth, they licked each other's shaft, they kissed each other's balls. They grunted and moaned their man sounds, their hands exploring the hard unfamiliar shapes of their bodies with zest.

It was Art who eventually pulled his cock away. He spun around so his face was still between the captain's legs, but now his own legs shot out behind him and he could look straight up the other man's belly. Art placed his hands on each of the captain's lower thighs and pushed up so the knees bent and the feet lay flat, supporting the legs. Art's long thin fingers, the ones that made both his guitar and me sing so sweetly, began teasing along the captain's hindquarters, making him release a startled sound of arousal. Art pressed his face forward, his long tongue darting out, and began to lick all of the delicate places his fingers had touched. The captain squirmed. Art's tongue circles got smaller and smaller, closer and closer, now tantalizing the tender opening ... until finally, after some articulate pleading from the captain, Art entered the ass deep with his thick moistness.

The captain moaned loudly, a sound that surely went up the sheer wall of the cliff to the veranda of the owner's house, who usually sat there and drank himself to sleep each night.

Art tongue-fucked the captain's ass, one that most of the female staff usually stared at intently through his form-fitting wet khakis as he loaded equipment onto the dive boat. The absence of underwear had further highlighted its muscularity, defining a crack so deep and powerful it was as if each cheek was its own mountain. It was an ass that could not be denied, a beautifully shaped globular vision that was complete perfection.

There was a temptation to crawl forward and give the captain an extra treat by sucking his cock while Art's tongue

penetrated his ass. And I so did want to revisit that tasty goodness. But I liked remaining in the background, a fly on the
wall. My hand crept down to my pussy and began a sensual
rubbing.

Seemingly unaware of me now, Art withdrew his tongue,
and gave a push at the side of the captain's left hip, directing
him to turn over on all fours. The captain's opening was
soaked by Art's lathering. And Art was hard enough to rest his
curved cock, heavily, on the captain's ass cheeks, the moonlight shimmering off the rivulets of sweat trailing down the
darkness of the man's back. With a feminine gentleness and a
masculine boldness, Art pulled back then pressed slowly
forward, expanding both the captain's most delicate entrance
and his mind with the capacity to feel pleasure. Soon Art was
deep inside, paused, letting the captain get used to his size.
Perhaps there was an urge, at this moment, for Art to look
over at me and smile. For Art was claiming (for both of us?)
the captain's magnificent, hard, muscular pussy, one that
engulfed a penis in such a complete masculine way.

But Art never looked at me, perhaps wary of bringing me
into the scene, instinctively understanding how much I liked
watching. He fucked the captain. At first easy, then hard, with
force. The captain supported himself with his knees and
elbows, mostly looking down at the sand, or through his legs
at Art's hard cock thrusting into him, occasionally looking up,
allowing me to see the tight pleasure in his eyes, this sensation
so opposite to what he usually experienced.

My pussy was soaked. I was invisible. And loved it. I rubbed
even harder, focusing on my swollen clit that was becoming
overwhelmed with unfamiliar sensations, ones that flowed and
escalated now at the pace of Art on his knees, ramming the
captain's ass.

When the captain reached through his legs to stroke his
own cock, I elevated even farther into completely new territory. The sight of him grabbing his engorged member,
moaning rhythmically with each parry of my lover's cock, was
indeed glorious. Art's head leaned back and his eyes closed;

his familiar posture just before coming. But it was not me who was making him come. It was not me thinking about him and hoping it was good even though I couldn't do the same. I was simply an observer, someone scrutinizing one man pleasuring another, watching one man receive Art's cock the way I had so often this summer, that man fisting his shaft with vigorous strokes while my hand attacked my pussy with delicious frenzy. All of us were at the same tempo, with the same manic speed. All of us moaned together in perfect pitch. All of us neared orgasm in full synchronized harmony.

I cannoned a long deep howl from within, a sound of joy, a reverberation of monumental release. Shivers ran all through my body, from my hair follicles to the tip of my red-glazed toenails. It was shattering. It was a righteous liberation from so many years of denial, the countless failed attempts. It was an explosive gush of fluid, like the tide now rapidly rising against the rocks. It was a palm pounding on some pleasure spot that was finally roused from its deep slumber and sent thunder to my brain that twitched my eyes and caused me to bite down on my lower lip until it bled.

Art screamed with triumph as well while he made his final thrusts.

The captain groaned with ecstasy as he pumped out his last strokes.

We all joined in this purging of pleasure, this epiphany of satisfaction – the captain's semen spilling onto the sand, leaking down his hand, Art's ejaculation shooting deep into the captain's ass, my pussy all soaked and tender from such a wonderful, complete release.

My eyes, literally, rolled back into my head.

Done, I found myself breathing rapidly, as if I was a novice swimmer who had just been pulled from the water. The Caribbean Sea beat even harder against the rocks.

It was a moment that much more sensational because although I came by myself, I was not alone.

These two athletic, powerful male specimens were soon lying next to me, one on each side. They took turns kissing me. They caressed me simultaneously. They made me feel loved, wanted, cared for. They completed this heart-opening *moment after.*

They brushed along my neck with their soft lips. Their fingers touched me with strength and confidence. Their cocks remained stiff against each of my hips, perhaps because of the continuous pleasure of what they were doing, or perhaps because the arousal from their fucking had not disappeared. I was tightly sandwiched by my two male lovers, my white body Oreoed between the coal darkness of the captain, and the bronze Semitic swarthiness of my lover, not caring that from the waist up we probably looked like two men and a boy embracing. I became even more aroused by how much they both wanted to share me, which seemed to please the other as well.

Art turned me on my side so I faced him. He looked deeply into my eyes and I stared back with love. He kissed me. His stiff cock pressed against the moistness of my pussy. I turned my head the other way and kissed the captain with extreme gratitude. His swollen manhood was soaked from his own semen and from rubbing the length of it through my legs, along the bottom edges of my pussy. Art scooped some water into his hand and washed his cock with the rising Caribbean Sea. The captain worked his way down to my ass, lubed me with his tongue, then straightened his frame along the back of my body.

The two men entered me at the same time.

Still on my side, Art was able to slide in deeply from the front, through my velvet-slick vaginal canal. The captain took his time, slowly entering my ass halfway from behind, knowing exactly how this must feel. The pair soon began a rhythmic fucking, penetrating me fully, two cocks entering my body simultaneously, with no real pain thanks to the ganja's relaxing effects, only total fullness, conjuring the most complete possession I ever felt.

They took turns kissing me. They leaned across me and kissed each other as I watched.

Then, with the tide encroaching even higher, smacking hard now against the rocks, spraying us, we found our perfect rhythm. They ducked their necks so Art was able to take my right nipple into his mouth and suck firmly, while the captain nibbled along the left side of my chest.

The two men fucked me.

The two men fucked straight through me.

They worshipped at my breasts, honored them with their complete satisfied attention, showered them with masculine love.

It was the captain who had the most comfortable access to my clit and he took advantage by rubbing with the tip of his wide index finger.

My breasts came alive in an astonishing way.

My body sang in exquisite fashion.

They were hard enough to fuck, but not so swollen as to signal another orgasm for either of them.

It was simply about pleasure. Their pleasure. My pleasure.

I never felt so tranquil, so fulfilled, so love-wrapped, penetrated, adored by such beautiful men.

The second orgasm of my life started not because I was watching, but because I was so *engaged*. It began as a slow rumble, then started to soar, to rise, as if a giant hammer was landing on the base of a carnival game and each strike rose the heavy block up closer to ringing the bell. Until finally, with a huge deep thrust into my pussy by Art, with a final fathomless penetration up my ass by the captain – their cocks seemingly touching somewhere deep inside me, making me whole – the bell tolled again. My mouth flew open, theirs clasped shut on my flesh. Out of me came a sound that was unearthly in its delight, mythic in its proportion.

I screamed.

With joy.

With pleasure.

With unparalleled orgasmic release and satisfaction that seemingly went on for several minutes and doubled its intensity when Art whispered, "I love you, sweetheart."

When my sound stopped, two pairs of lips released me, my mouth closed, their cocks withdrew, and the sea finally began to flood our paradise. As we frantically scrambled to our feet – our clothes already swept away – we heard the gruff, drunken voice of the resort owner booming down from the house above:

"WHAT THE FUCK IS GOING ON DOWN THERE?"

We scurried over rocks, swam through the deluge of incoming water, laughing uproariously as we finally hopped safely to dry land and scooted naked down the beach, Art to my left, the captain to my right, each holding one of my hands.

What answer could I give the resort owner? This priceless gift from my lover was not something that could ever be fully explained.

III

I can't help breaking into a broad smile now as I lie in my king-size bed, my husband at my right, my body still tingling from tonight's lovemaking, and remember that special evening. What a wonderful twenty-second birthday it was! What an amazing unwrapped present I received! I long ago lost touch with Art, a true free spirit, and can only hope that he, as he did for me that summer, fulfilled his wildest dream.

I make an abrupt turn onto my left side, trying to find a comfortable position that will finally bring me some late night sleep. This sudden movement awakens my husband.

"You still up?" he asks sleepily.

"Yes, sorry," I whisper. "Still glowing from what we shared tonight and all of the sweet memories it inspired."

"Lovely," he mumbles. "Now it's time to sleep."

I imagine his smile.

"Yes, let's all try to get some sleep," mutters the tired voice from the other side of the bed, our boyfriend, who reaches a long arm across our bodies and hugs us both tight.

The Nude, Stripped Naked

Jeremy Edwards

He wished everyone had indicator lights, akin to a taxi's roof-mounted mechanism for inviting or warding off a stranger's attention. Patrick would have loved to know, without a shred of doubt, when his gaze on the ass of an attractive individual was or was not welcome.

I shouldn't stare at a strange woman's ass, but it's OK to "notice" it, right? He constantly struggled with the lines that divided *noticing, looking* and *staring*. And this applied to faces as well as asses. He wished he could mount a podium some-day and officially apologize to every stranger, past and future, who might have felt the scrape of his eyes when they lingered too long in a crosswalk or pub or museum.

Patrick wanted to be distant, where appropriate, and daring, where appropriate. He wished his libido and his conscience could sit down in a conference room, mark out the boundaries, then fax him a memo and a map.

"The buttocks lack definition," said Margie.

He started, his ruminations interrupted. "I didn't want to stare," he explained.

"Patrick," said the teacher, with emphasis. "This is figure-drawing class. She's your model."

The problem was that the nude model, a dark-haired vision of about thirty, was the most beautiful woman he'd ever seen, with or without clothes on. Beautiful, not simply in a "Wow, you should be an artist's model" sense (though she was exactly that), but in a flesh-sizzling, chemistry-sparking, all-he-wanted-to-do-was-fuck-her sense. Which wasn't even accurate – because fucking her wasn't *all* Patrick wanted to do. There was also nibbling her thighs, licking her pussy, slapping her ass, tickling her armpits . . .

But these were not things one did to a nude model. These were things one did to a naked woman.

And that was why looking at her at all felt like a transgression – because Patrick was unable to look at her without it being sexual, rather than artistic. His assessment of her shoulder was drenched in a lascivious appreciation for how admirably its shape would satisfy his mouth. His appraisal of her waist, though it drew on the clinical eye for proportion that Margie had helped her students develop, was wired to a groin-deep desire to clutch her in that perfect concavity with one hand while boisterously, reverently exploring her cunt with the other. And to look at his model's derrière with anything but jeans-straining want – to look, especially, at the base of the cheek where it winked into the crack, hinting at the deeper, richer crevice nestled within – was an impossibility.

And yet – though her face blended a soft serenity with an angular brightness; and her petite breasts looked ripe and full presiding over her small swell of tummy; and the triangle of fur at the juncture of her legs had a luxurious sheen – it was the whole, more than the parts, that forbade Patrick to remain detached. She embodied something that he could not name but which he desired to know, hold and feast upon.

Objectively, he could see that the bland lighting of the classroom had a tendency to make flesh mimic marble, that to the other students, the model probably looked timeless rather than present, immortal rather than alive. Just as she was supposed to. Objectively, Patrick recognized that it should have been challenging to imagine her face broken up by laughter . . . her fingertips drumming restlessly on a tabletop . . . her warm, gaping pussy greeting the morning with fresh pee. Nonetheless, he could imagine all this – indeed could not help but imagine it.

And after he'd been sketching another quarter-hour under

Margie's distant but firm supervision, he began to get the impression that his gaze was affecting his model, despite the fact that she couldn't see him watching her. As he drew, her skin seemed to morph from vanilla to the palest pink champagne; and though the studio lights were no more or less hot than they'd been all session, he now discovered a sparkle of perspiration on her shoulder blades. At one point, when she shifted her position minutely, almost imperceptibly, Patrick felt that it meant the difference between repose and auto-erotica . . . that her thighs were now conscious of each other, and of what they enclosed.

"Margie?" He practically whispered it, lest he disturb the exquisite figure.

The instructor walked to Patrick's station, cocking an eyebrow to ask what he needed.

"What's the model's name?" This time he did whisper.

"Why?"

He shrugged, squirming inside with the awkwardness of the situation – but determined. "I feel I'll be able to capture her better if I know her name," he said slyly. Ridiculously.

"A minute ago, you were afraid to look at her."

He stared optimistically at his unfinished drawing.

"Her name is Nicola."

It was hard to tell, with Nicola's face turned three-quarters away from the class, but Patrick thought she smiled.

He realized, in the days that followed, that he was obsessed with her. *Obsessed*, he told himself, almost proudly. It was something more elemental and profound than the usual infatuation, and it made him feel pathetic and grand all at once.

In the yearning throes of masturbation, he felt as if he wanted to be her – as well as himself – while pounding into her: to experience both halves, to get a privileged glimpse into the state of mind of a nude who was being fucked – by him. He felt greedy, narcissistic, and yet generous – he wanted to share it all with her, make her blazingly wet between her naked legs, make her scream shrilly with pleasure, proving to all the world that her throat was raw, sensuous velvet, and not marble.

*   *   *

There was no mistaking that the woman in the high-necked button-down sweater, standing by one of the campus statues with her coffee, was Nicola.

Patrick stopped, a short but safe distance away, to say a good-morning, articulating her name for the umpteenth time that day, but the first time aloud. "You might recognize me from art class," he added tactfully.

"Of course. You're Perry – no, sorry … um, *Patrick*. Patrick?"

Her misstep and her unsureness soothed his jitters, as did the anarchic motion of her stray hairs in the wind. *She looks more like twenty-nine now than thirty*, he said to himself. He knew this was a stupid way to think about it; but at twenty-one, he was a little frightened of women who had attained the presumed perfection of their thirties and beyond.

He nodded. "Yeah, it's Patrick. You must be waiting for somebody."

"No," said Nicola. Then she grinned. "My date is already here."

She put her arm around the waist of Isaac Danton, LLD, a college founder who had been immortalized in concrete, and whose obligatory stiffness further accented Nicola's vitality. Patrick observed that even in the midst of a spontaneous, comical gesture, with a cardboard cup in hand, Nicola's poise was heavenly.

He laughed gratefully at her friendly antics.

"But seriously," she said. "I'm just taking a break. I like standing here with my coffee – it's the crossroads of our little world, isn't it?"

He glanced around. "I see what you mean." Then he looked straight at Professor Danton, avoiding Nicola's eye. "I wish I had a coffee, so I could stand here."

She beckoned him over. "Please. You've already proved yourself better company than Danton. And the coffee is optional."

Encouraged, Patrick became bold. He joined her, at ease now with himself and his actions.

"Can I ask you something?" he said, after a beat.

"Sure."

"What was it like the first time you got . . . nude . . . in front of an artist?" He wanted to know how a flesh-and-blood human beauty transformed herself into pure, bare art.

She blushed. "Wow, when you ask me something, you really ask me something."

"I'm sorry."

"No, it's OK. It's an interesting question." She took a sip of coffee. "I guess—I guess it was sort of strange. Not because I was nervous – I wasn't, really – but because it thrilled me a bit. In just the way the philistines always like to imagine nude models get . . . amorous. To use a genteel word."

She raised her eyebrows. Patrick's fingers sweated in the pockets of his denim jacket, though not from anxiety, now.

Nicola continued. "I worried that this meant I had an 'unprofessional attitude', but I couldn't help it. It wasn't even a question of being attracted to the artist I was modeling for. It was just the fact of exposing myself in such a . . . formal manner. It was different from all the other ways I'd been naked before. So – ta-da! – you're speaking to a card-carrying exhibitionist."

Patrick was tingling all over, feverishly visualizing "all the ways" Nicola had been naked. "Wow. When you answer me something, you really answer."

"Exhibitionists are good at that."

He met her gaze. "I have the same problem. I get, uh, *unprofessional* inside, in art class. Well, lately I do."

Her eyes flickered with the fire of interest. "I know."

Despite his burgeoning confidence, the tension paralysed him here. But Nicola cut through it by kissing him, right there at the elbow of Professor Danton. And just as he was getting used to her warm lips, so curious for his responses, he felt the grope of a small, frisky tongue. A tongue that uttered, non-verbally, the word *more*.

"I've finished my coffee," she said, prying his fingers out of his left pocket.

"Where are we going?" She'd begun walking, without relinquishing her light grip on his hand.

"I don't know. Where were you going before you saw me by the statue?"

"I don't know. I hadn't decided."

She laughed.

"How about you? You said you were taking a break," he recalled. "From what?"

"I don't know. I hadn't decided." She broke into a frivolous run, looking back to make sure he was chasing along behind her.

He caught up easily and grabbed her, daring to let her bottom feel his hardness. "You were much more subdued in the art studio."

"Rambunctious models are not in high demand. And giggling models risk getting ejected."

He squeezed her harder and spoke directly to the teases of ear that were visible through her hair. "I'm glad you weren't ejected." He tickled her midriff, turning her, briefly, into a giggling model.

They ambled on, until Nicola paused in front of the music library. "Do you mind if we stop in here for a second?"

He followed her as she found her way to the bound sheet-music collections she needed. Her hips, lovely but unassuming in her indigo denim, conveyed a subtle rhythmic liveliness as she navigated the aisles.

"People assume that because I model, I'm in the art program," she explained when they were back outside. "But I'm a PhD candidate in music, who's merely posing as an art person. Literally."

"So there's no point trying to seduce you into painting me."

"Nope. You'll have to think of something else to seduce me into."

"You mean like composing a sonata about me?"

"No way. You couldn't possibly sit still that long."

Not with her around, he couldn't.

*   *   *

"Are we going to have another kiss?" She had invited him into her apartment.

He held her shoulders while he did it, letting his tongue fondle her contours as hers had his. "Yes," he said afterward, in belated reply to her query.

"I know you've seen me nude," Nicola said with a pretty quaver in her voice. "But would you like to see me naked?"

The sunlight in her kitchen was a lewd shade of yellow, so different from the academic fluorescence under which he'd previously observed her skin and her shape. And whereas Nicola the model had undressed behind a screen, to emerge in a robe that she shed impersonally upon posing, Nicola the private woman let Patrick see every intimate detail of the process – the way the third button of her jersey clung to the fabric lips that suckled it; the way her jeans required an extra yank to get past the luscious flare of her bottom; the way the elastic of her panties – her moist panties – was digging in on one side, because of having worked themselves slightly off center in the course of the morning. The interplay of the living, bending, wriggling body with the garments appeared to Patrick as a sexual interaction in and of itself, an expression of carnal kineticism that was such a far cry from the isolated idealism of her form as presented to the art students.

He noticed that she had faint freckles on her chest, and he was sure they'd been invisible in the studio. So much had been bleached out there, he now realized, even to his transgressive gaze.

And now the naked woman did something else that the nude model had not: she touched herself. It was the same bare flesh that Patrick had seen in art class, but now Nicola's hands sculpted the weight of her breasts and stroked the pout of her pussy. Now Nicola's body told him that she wanted to be, not studied and sketched, but fingered, fondled and fucked.

She brought a pussy-dipped finger to his mouth. He was so dizzy with excitement that he couldn't really taste the flavor. He could only taste the electricity.

"I'm going to go out on a limb – or at least a thigh – and suggest we visit my bedroom," said Nicola.

He tried to undress himself for her, but her precise, quiet touch was all over him. His shirt was history, then his pants. She covered his torso with kisses, and pulled his briefs to his trembling knees. His cock licked the palm of her hand.

In the hush of the late morning, Nicola sat on Patrick's face, and he nurtured her wiggling succulence until she slathered him, and slathered him again. Her sex-pink ass cheeks, muffin-sweet on his own cheeks, pressed down on him with animal lust, while her fingers made promises to his arching hips, his bouncing balls and his teetering rod.

As if paddling out to sea on a surfboard, she shimmied down his body from face to lap, mounting his cock with a grunt and a singing moan. The pleasure was so intense that he couldn't think, almost couldn't hear or see. He was barely aware of the mechanics by which Nicola was dragging and scraping herself up and down – how she milked him with slow meticulousness, inching her way, both literally and figuratively, toward a consummate tautness that would snap into a cloud of ecstasy.

When it snapped, and Nicola shrieked, he trained his eyes on the molten marble of her back, focusing on the arc of her spine until focus eluded him.

"I always wanted to make love to art." He kissed a nipple.

"*I* am not art, Patrick. A model is only food for thought."

"Mm . . . food." He settled his teeth around her elbow.

"You're the one who makes the art. You're the artist."

"Well, it's just a two-credit elective."

She cracked up into her pillow, her naked ass jiggling in the humble glow of the bedside lamp.

He was so glad it was OK to stare at it.

Cancer

Anna Lidia Vega Serova

Translated by Lawrence Schimel

Obsessions make us rot from within . . . perhaps they drink us from within like those holes in space, and everything that occurs to us falls into them and comes to form part of the whirlwind of the obsession . . . a sort of cancer in the soul.

Jesús Ferrero

1

Hopes, false appearances, slanders, manipulations, myths and chimeras. Searching for the limit, breathing abysses. An amalgam of the virtual and the real, dreams and fictions that lead to the committing of crimes and/or great achievements and everything loses importance before the mere awareness of death.

To delve within the mind, to excavate among the detritus, memories and fantasies, one dream or another, to write another story or achieve another orgasm, which deep down come to be the same thing, at least they both provide a similar purifying effect.

Then it's necessary to find some trash receptacle: an attentive ear or a dazed reader or some prying eyes that will in turn process the shit later to then spew it forth in any other place, upon any other mind.

What's certain is that once someone takes on the role of a latrine, they can't be used for any other purpose. Take note of this: don't mix friendships, don't mistake ties, don't confuse confidences.

The horror of the error. To go too far and not know how to stop or to go back. Then the logical reaction of destruction, like tearing up a written page in vain. Or, better, self-destruction: throwing yourself into the abyss. Torture yourself: do you want me to tell you? From the beginning, not sparing any details?

2

A woman screaming, a woman screaming at all hours, shouting insults, begging for help. Window to window (I opened mine only the day I moved in, to find the shutters of the house across from mine so close I could smell the stench of that nasty dwelling and I closed it immediately); those shouts surprised me whatever I was doing, at any moment, always unexpected, making me tremble, waking me in the night to steal my sleep, leaving me with my face sunk into the mattress, imagining all sorts of atrocities, or excesses. I came to visualize, in Technicolor detail, a young woman bathed in blood, tied to the bed by her wrists and ankles with leather bonds, begging for mercy, while a nefarious-looking man perfunctorily performed some routine torture. I didn't dare to ask anyone, I didn't have anything to do with the neighbors, I avoided contact with strangers, intruders into my world, my intimacy.

Perhaps I mentioned something to some friend, not giving any importance to the matter, hiding my dread of course, perhaps it was one of them who suggested to me with a malicious little smile that it wasn't a case of a victim of abuse, or sickness or madness; or it's possible that I myself, in a moment of inspiration, thought to look for an erotic interpretation, suddenly substituting horror for pleasure, discovering delicious notes in the tone of those howls, an intemperate sex, a savage passion.

Just like certain smells, particular images, specific very obscene words, the shouts of a woman became, for me, an irresistible erotic stimulus. On hearing them, I had to abandon what I was doing, whatever it was, and start to masturbate in that very moment, place and position. Sometimes, among the incomprehensible words of that clamor, I thought I heard my own name and that excited me even more; I'd accelerate the dancing of my fingers against my clitoris, bite my tongue so I didn't start to howl in unison with that unknown woman, murmuring words that were directed to her, turbulent, violent words.

"My *loca*," that's how I called her. For me she was a young nymphomaniac, insatiable and promiscuous, a sexual *loca*. I would have liked to be just as kinky, to search for heated amorous encounters, to act out the tableaus I created in my imagination on hearing those cries, to repeat the eagerness I felt on hearing them, the exact wanting of that woman's wanting; but I didn't dare to, I was full of fears, fearful of feeling pain, of provoking it, afraid of vice, of scandal, and also of prejudices.

I was going out with this guy, a very tame relationship, without any spark, without desire, we made love in an automatic fashion, in his house, which was much more comfortable than my own, more welcoming and clean, once a week, or twice, depending, then we talked for a bit, always the same things, pure routine. I didn't talk to him about myself or about my *loca*, I thought that all that would seem repulsive to him, that he could be horrified by it and say humiliating things to me, look at me in some unbearable way and then kick me out; not that I cared so much as to fear losing him, but I couldn't stand the idea of being abandoned like someone repulsive.

I had lived for more than a year with that double life – an invented life, pulsing and secret, and a public one, impeccable

– when in a conversation between two neighbors who were coming down the stairs while I was going up, I learned from them that my *loca* was a senile and very sick old woman. She had cancer, she was on her deathbed, almost decomposed.

Trembling, I opened the door to my house, ran straight to the bathroom, vomited. I felt an overwhelming disgust, a frustration and a fury like nothing I'd ever experienced before. Just at that moment the old woman began to shout, to beg for help, to call for someone who could alleviate her suffering. I bit my lip, a prisoner of panic, and imagining a monstrous, foul-smelling and bald old woman, I began to masturbate again.

3

It was a large dog, skinny and ugly. It had just one ear and its skin was almost raw with mange. It was wandering between the park benches, when someone threw a stone at it and the dog howled in pain, high enough to make me, as I crossed the park, begin to tremble. I looked at it for a moment. The dog was sick and whining; I am no particular lover of dogs, but this one moved me to the point of immediately bringing it home with me.

Van Gogh, the dog with one ear, lived with me just the exact length of time it took for him to get better, to plump up a bit and improve his temper. I gave him my best care; with a mix of disgust and compassion, I tended him and bathed him, and every time my hands brushed his skin I felt that subtle inner trembling that precedes an amorous act. I masturbated, of course, I had to masturbate while thinking of the wounds of that unhappy dog, imagining its pain, its suffering, reconstructing in my mind its whines, which mixed with the image of my madwoman shouting, her body plagued with sores and ulcers, her suffering.

But Van Gogh recovered completely, turning into a common pet, a happy and fastidious animal, something unbearable; I threw him out, he returned, I threw him out again, he came back again, and I gave him two or three kicks, he left, whining once again, like a farewell gift, and I masturbated thinking of him for the last time, like a farewell gift.

4

I learned that my friend had a cycling accident, nothing serious, but he was in the hospital, under observation.

The smell of hospitals, the smell of medication and disinfectant, the tiled hallways and the iron beds, the sight of people wearing identical pajamas, always a size or two too large, the look of the sick, many pale patients crowded into cubicles, all those patients with their illnesses, their aches and pains, had such an effect on me that it took me a while to recover, I went outside with a headache, dizziness, nausea, completely done in.

But my friend was admitted and I had to visit him, although lately we hardly ever slept together, although increasingly I cared less about him, although I hated hospitals, I needed to visit him, I felt a morbid curiosity to see him helpless, to know that he suffered, that he was vulnerable.

He was pale, his head bandaged, some scratches, but in general he didn't look bad. I was disappointed, but that I understood later, once I was home, remembering the hospital and the episode with the patient in a neighboring room, when I was recovering from the hospital and from that episode, in my bed, with my hands between legs, my fingers on my clitoris, again and again.

I heard shouts, as I was talking with my friend about nothing in particular, I heard these tremendous shouts, I interrupted our conversation, I felt unwell, I said, I'll be right back . . . I couldn't help it, like a rat led by the trill of the flute I moved down the hallway in search of the source of those cries, and two or three doors later I found it. A young man with iron bars sticking out of his thigh and all sorts of apparatus, doctors all around him, nurses injecting him with liquids, and he shouting unendingly. I looked, I looked and sweated, I think I felt ill, very ill, but I couldn't move, it was so sweet, desperately sweet.

5

I returned to the hospital, looked for him, he no longer shouted, I didn't hear him shout again, but I had sex with him nonetheless, it was pathetic and beautiful, I caressed everything, I licked him, licked his penis, a few centimeters from the bars stuck in his flesh, I licked and sucked while looking at his wounds and the iron rods sticking out from his flesh, and I imagined his pain, remembering his shouts, the shouts of my *loca*, Van Gogh, life itself.

I came back often, I had sex often, with him and with others, always risking being discovered; I walked down the hallways and there was always someone very sick, shouting, or at least complaining, someone who could stimulate me. I was thought to be someone charitable, someone very altruistic and generous. I knew that it was something else, that strong commotions were erotic for me, that in my mind suffering, degradation, anguish and disgust were inseparably tied to sex, that the more unpleasant an image or an impression was for me, the more it turned me on. The hospital was therefore the perfect place, my obsession, my habit, my second skin.

6

It wasn't difficult for me to find a position as a hospital cleaner; it was a horrible job that no one wanted to do: dirty, exhausting and poorly paid. But for me it was glorious.

I could channel my pursuit of pleasure with complete propriety, I could recreate fantasies that had been unimaginable until then, although it was impossible to share my sexuality, as if I possessed a secret and therefore useless fortune.

Emptying the trashcan into a garbage bag, in an uncontrollable impulse I grabbed some of the used bandages and held them to my nose. I had to lean against the wall, the smell of blood and piss turned my stomach, I felt cold sweats, dizziness, horror. I felt the anguish of the woman who they had torn these bandages from, there was no doubt that it was a woman, an old woman, I felt her pain, her panic, her delirium, her cries. I discovered that there was someone beside me, I couldn't separate the gauze from my face, but I knew that there was someone smelling the same bandage, breathing, moaning in time with me. Hands sought out my body, a mouth banged against mine, a tongue licked my lips and the blood and the fluids of the old woman on my lips and my tongue responded, my mouth gave itself to them, my hands, my legs, my body giving themselves up to the ecstasy of a shared passion.

We didn't speak. On recovering from her climax, Doctor Esperanza fastened her immaculate white robe and walked away down the hallway without even looking at me. I didn't look at her either nor did I speak to her nor did I seek out more encounters with Doctor Esperanza. I don't like healthy people.

Nonetheless, it doesn't bother me to have an experience like that, or the others that took place from time to time: with Doctor Bernardo, with Bilma the nurse, Ramón the aide, the anesthesiologist Juárez, the morgue attendant, the birthing room cleaner, two or three medical students, how could I recall them all?

It was a benediction to discover that I was wrong in pretending to be unique; I was part of a guild, of a clandestine society, of an exquisite and mind-blowing sect. We are many and every day we are growing in number.

7

I knew it could happen, that it would happen at some point, I often saw how it happened to others, but no one is ever prepared for the cataclysm, no matter how much they prepare themselves, what they are waiting for always takes them by surprise; it took me by surprise. But it didn't destroy me, I tried to see things as if from outside, as if it weren't me that they find in the hallway with a terrible fever and on whom they make all sorts of tests; as if it were some other woman who was delirious on the narrow iron bed, dressed in a pajama that was two sizes larger than what she normally wore, another woman who shouted in pain and panic when they gave her injections and serums and then carried her to the operating room and opened her abdomen and dug in her entrails in search of growths that they'll never extract, so that these will multiply and expand through her entire body and provoke more and more pain.

I try to see it from outside myself to enjoy it more, and I shout and I revel in my shouts more than those of anyone else, I bleed and I revel infinitely in my blood, I suffer and I enjoy my own suffering as if it were the deepest pleasure in the world.

I see them touch themselves, I see them rub their sexes with their hands and kiss one another without taking their eyes off of me, I see them take delight in my delight; I know that deep down they envy me, that each of them would want to be in my place or at least to be the next to fall ill, to be everywhere like me, to propagate like a plague, to contaminate the world with their suppurating seed, to be the most sublime expression of divinity, the most absolute face of love.

The Beautiful Boy

Shaun Levin

And so we all began to walk behind the beautiful boy, some of us more confidently than others; we didn't care what people thought, or how we appeared to those who saw us. So what if we were old and fat and ugly? We lived in hope. You can never know when a beautiful boy will say "yes". It's hard to tell what the young and beautiful want until you've heard a "no" or "no, thank you" or had your hand eased away from a knee. Some of us have heard "no" so many times that one more "no" isn't a big deal, not if there's the slightest possibility – and in every situation there is a possibility – that the beautiful boy will say "yes". He might let us touch, or stroke, or watch him. He might let us kiss his back or his shoulder, the nape of his neck, turning his head, just a fraction, away from us. He might let us kneel before him to accept what he has to offer.

We are happy to follow a boy like this, knowing that we might get a furtive touch, a glance. We have known boys who are happy to be watched, and for some of us that is enough. We don't care that this boy's beauty is clichéd – tall and lean and smooth, though we've noticed he trims his chest and can tell there'd be a substantial covering if he'd let it grow, which a few of us like very much, and for that reason, for the echo and ghost of his manly chest, we like him even more than we would have liked him had he been as smooth as he appears to be, and as he appears to be is how the rest of us like our men. But on the whole, none of us is that picky.

We follow him along the labyrinths of this place, its walls painted black, bits of brickwork exposed, the lights opaque, some a murky yellow, others a dim green or red, too feint to cast shadows, yet bright enough to cloud our vision, especially that green light at the end of the passage, so that when you walk towards it others become silhouettes, and for a moment you fear you'll collide with the man walking towards you or the one leaning against the wall as he waits for the right man to come along.

We aren't sure what kind of man the beautiful man is after, for we've seen men like him – some even *more* beautiful – who've been intimate, even *very* intimate, with men much older or fatter or uglier than we are. And so we keep walking in hope. Some of us fear the beautiful boy might stop in his tracks at any moment and cause a pile-up of lecherous bodies on the dark linoleum floor, like a traffic accident, or like those beached whales on a shore, washed up for some unknown reason, stuck on the wet sand as the waves dab water onto them to keep them alive, then slowly recede as the tide goes out and the fat creatures are left to die.

This place is not a beach, though we are always naked under our towels, and there is somewhere to swim, and we have all escaped from our day-to-day existence.

The beautiful boy leads us along the corridors, past open cabins where men sit and wait to be approached. One or two of us stop to try our luck with a man there; the rest of us keep walking, following the beautiful boy, his back sculpted into a V-shape, the cleft of his spine like a furrow from neck to that clean white towel wrapped tightly across his buttocks. We follow him down the stairs, and up another flight to where the Jacuzzi is, and the steam room and the swimming pool that is big enough for four or five strokes of crawl, just the right size to manage two whole laps underwater. Some of us have done that before, maybe not lately, but we remember having done it, holding our breaths as we swam from one end of the pool to the other, then back again, partly to impress, and partly for the exhilaration of being naked in public and weightless in water.

As if he read our minds, the beautiful boy stands by the chrome ladder that slopes into the water, moves closer to dart his toe across the surface. And so, for the water temperature is pleasing to him, he unfurls his towel and drapes it across the railings while we all stare, even those of us who are not at an angle to see the front of him, though most of us crane our necks to catch a glimpse. He pauses for a moment at the edge of the pool, as if to offer us one last glimpse, then lowers himself into the water.

No matter how many times we experience it, beauty is unfathomable. It delights and surprises. Each witnessing is like the first. Every discovery as if we've chanced upon it for the first time, every encounter a re-encountering of that first boy we were awed by, silenced by, whom we shadowed in the playground, whose marbles we fetched, for whom we took swimming lessons because he did. We wore the same clothes, went to his house to play, invented reasons to sleep over, and at night we dreamed of being him, or so like him that no one could tell us apart, until we were told . . . by whom? The knowledge filtered into us through the air, through the gaze of history, telling us we were not worthy of one so beautiful, not worthy of this kind of proximity. This has always been part of our inner mechanism, even if the exact point in our youths when the seed of this belief was planted is now lost, it's a view that has shaped us, especially when we come this close to beauty.

We watch the boy swim short laps, his body clear and gleaming, his skin shining whenever his back and shoulders rise above the surface. Those of us who've waded in after him, make conversation as if conversation was all we wanted. The boy is kind and gracious, unfazed by the advances we make, but never reciprocating. We hope he might be Brazilian; most of us have met Brazilians who like older men, so different to the rude young men who grow up in the West, haunted by youth even when they are young. Perhaps he is Greek or Romanian, but we can't be sure, nor can we be sure how exactly men from those parts of the world feel about men who are old and fat and ugly.

While the boy showers, we peer at him like boys spying through a hole in the wall at an adult undressing. Some of us guess him to be twenty-five, though it is hard to tell; he could be younger, or older. We don't care. Beauty is the great equalizer of the beautiful. We are happy just to watch the water fall onto his skin, the soap froth and drain from his chest and middle, the quiet way he returns to his towel hanging on its hook as if waiting to have life breathed back into it. By now there are more of us, and we follow the beautiful boy into the steam room; it is small and we have to stand close together. Some of us don't like this. We don't want the man next to us to think we are brushing against him out of desire.

We are an audience to the boy and his beauty, following him with our eyes as he approaches the beautiful man who'd been sitting on the ledge when we all walked in, the lot of us, an entourage to the beautiful boy. The boy sat down as if to rest; he'd worked the hardest, led us through narrow corridors, across a pond, through the showers to finally reach this point where he has found someone else to come to the fore, this man who he turns to now with a look in his eyes that says: You *lead now*. You *call the navigational shots*.

The beautiful man's chest is covered in dark wet hair, his manhood soft and thick between his legs, the hair above it – abundant. Some of us, seeing how desiring the boy is of the beautiful man, feel a pang of reassurance; there was a time when we looked like the beautiful man, and he really is splendid. Graceful and handsome. The word "virile" comes to mind. We have all been virile. The beautiful man looks at us, smiles as if he can tell who we've been and who we really are and that pleases him. Then he rises from his ledge and walks towards us and his breath is warm and his hands are warm and his touch is gentle, his mouth – soft, his embrace – strong, and his voice confident as he whispers the question one asks a man one is in pursuit of: *Are you alone?*

And we nod our heads yes. Yes, we are alone. And he kisses us, every single one of us, from the tall man with the belly to the short Spaniard whose bald patch is as round and shining as a mirror. The rest of us press against the beautiful man and he hugs us and we hug him and feel our soft middles against his firm stomach, and kiss him passionately, the way he kisses us. Our eyes flit around the room, moving from man to man, taking in our faces and our beards, our chins and our hair, the sturdiness of our backs, the strength of our arms, the distances we've covered and how we've survived. Occasionally, we catch glimpses of the beautiful boy perched on the ledge watching us as we touch the beautiful man, but mostly we touch each other, as if discovering something new, or something we'd forgotten, and we hold and stroke and kiss each other as if we've wanted this for a long time, and in that time have dreamt of each other, and now we are together again.

We can't all remember when we saw the beautiful boy go. Some of us believe he left only because we've heard the story told over and over about how he stepped off his perch and hovered amongst us, moved through us, his body sleek with sweat, glowing, his cheeks reddened by the heat, and we felt his skin against ours, the curve of his back and buttocks, the leanness of his abdomen, the heft of his manhood. Then he was at the door and he turned to watch us – that's what some of us saw – but it was as if, by then, we'd changed direction mid-flight, and no one could be sure whether the boy had left, and perhaps he is still with us, swooping and gliding through the sky, moving to some invisible rhythm, beyond words or reason. And us, we are all lighter and younger and more beautiful than we've ever been, and the beautiful boy is amongst us, sometimes in front, and sometimes moving alongside us, with ease, his body held up by the vortex of our wings.

Eighty Days of Christmas

Vina Jackson

"I have a very special request," I asked Viggo. "But it has to remain a secret, all the way to Christmas."

He smiled, his face lighting up with unabashed mischief.

We were sitting in a cavernous Chinatown restaurant, dim sum trolleys and black and white clad diminutive Chinese waitresses circling around us like busy bees in a cloud of honey. Lauralynn was due to join us after her orchestra rehearsals and Dominik was on his way from a meeting with his publishers in Upper St Martin's Lane.

I hadn't much time to explain the plot to Viggo as the waitress poured the complimentary green tea and I expected our respective partners to arrive at any moment.

"Tell me, love," he said. He leaned forward complicitly.

It had been just over nine months since the four of us had all found ourselves together in Dublin for the melodramatic adventures that had led to Luba and Chey's escape. It had been an exhilarating if fraught few days, which had brought us all closer together as we had faced adversity. I was now living with Dominik and bar the occasional spat, we had settled down in a state of blissful domesticity. And the curious relationship between Viggo and Lauralynn appeared to be flourishing.

Nine months. Long enough to conceive and give birth to a child. Not that Dominik or I had ever given any thought to it.

I hurriedly explained to Viggo what I had in mind.

Just the week before, an online retailer that I often used to order my lingerie and other paraphernalia had begun their onslaught of emails reminding me that now was the time to begin planning my Christmas shopping in earnest. I clicked open the link to find a bevy of scantily clad elves and a variety of cheap polyester Mrs Claus outfits on sale and with a sigh of exasperation I had immediately deleted the message, but the looming ghost of Christmas-to-come kept on assaulting my senses repeatedly for the following few days: an advertisement in a newspaper here, a window display in a shop on Hampstead High Street there, a call from my booking agent asking me whether I was planning to take time off around the end of December or wanted to perform anywhere with a seasonal repertoire. This is ridiculous, I thought, looking closely at the calendar, there are still eighty days to Christmas! Had a tree or wreath of holly been present, I would have happily kicked or trampled it underfoot out of spite.

I had always hated Christmas in New Zealand. Somehow Decembers by the beach with hot weather and the sort of blue summer sky that's so bright and sharp it could slice all of the clouds in the world in two just didn't gel with fir trees and mulled wine. My family had made a habit of ignoring the day altogether and instead of cooking a pork roast in lieu of turkey and unwrapping presents we headed to the sea to throw a Frisbee and run in the sand followed by fish and chips and an ice cream cone for lunch. Ironically, Christmas had drawn us close together, if only by virtue of our mutual distaste for it.

I knew that Dominik shared my contrary views.

New Year's Eve was by far my preferred holiday, when my violin teacher Mr van der Vliet always made Oliebollen, the traditional Dutch sweets made from spiced currant filled batter fried in hot oil and served covered in powdered sugar.

Dominik had once taken me to New Orleans to celebrate the New Year, I remembered. That night he had asked me to dance for him on a public stage, and I had done so, as a way to demonstrate how eager I was to please him, but also because I took such pleasure from following his instructions. That had also been the night that we had first come across Luba, the

Russian dancer, who, unknown to us, was suffering her own turmoils in love which would culminate in the Dublin adventure on New Year's Eve years later.

I was running along the South Bank one evening in late November when I realized that like so many other things about England, the thought of Christmas here had finally wormed its way into my heart. I still hated all the cheap gifts and the forced frivolity, but I truly loved the cold dark afternoons and the heavy scents that swept across the streets from the carts of roast chestnuts and mulled-wine sellers, and the sounds from the street performers and musicians who came out in full force to sing their hymns and carols.

Christmas was beautiful in London in a way that I had never found it to be before. And now that Dominik and I were finally evolving into a proper couple maybe I should take the celebration a bit more seriously and begin thinking of what to get him for the occasion. And it struck me that I should make it memorable. After all this was the man, my man, the one who had accepted me for who I truly was and who had awakened so much inside me, things that were buried deep within my nature but which I would never have even thought of before he had come on the scene and I was just happy in my own way, busking in the Underground and treading water in indifferent relationships.

A gift.

Something memorable.

That no else but me could offer him.

And I felt that familiar warmth that had characterized the very particular dynamic of our relationship. I knew that I was going to do something for him that would make him want to do things to me and immediately my blood heated up and my senses rose in unison again in that way that made me feel oh so alive . . .

Dominik was the man who had everything. He owned a beautiful house in a sought-after part of town, he was comfortably off twice over thanks to his past inheritance and the success of his books, but most of all he had modest tastes, which was yet another thing that attracted me to him. He was not ostentatious or prodigal or spendthrift, had no need for exterior signs of wealth, expensive clothes or cars or yachts or helipads (not that a helipad would have fitted onto any Hampstead roof anyway . . .). Whenever he came across something he wanted, he just acquired it, whether a brand-new computer or piece of hardware, a recently published book or CD or DVD, a rare book, a visit to an upmarket restaurant, travel to exotic places. He had it all. We had it all.

Which made the choice of a present a difficult one.

But I knew he collected books with a passion so it made sense that for Christmas this year I should present him with a book.

The most unforgettable book of all.

A limited edition of one.

"So tell me, Viggo, you once said that your stage crew could come up with anything?"

"Masters of magic, that's us," he said, showman to the last. "And I like a challenge, Summer," he added. "Try me."

By the time Lauralynn and I had entered our third store together, I began to think that she had suggested a shopping trip to satisfy her own perverse amusement rather than out of any desire to help me find a costume to go with the gift that I planned to present to Dominik.

"The light in here is terrible," she moaned, "come out front where I can see you properly."

"But I've got practically nothing on!" I hissed, carefully trying to arrange the thin length of satin that the shop assistant had promised was all the rage for women wanting to wrap themselves up for their men.

"Then I'm sure that everyone in the shop is looking forward to giving their assessment as much as I am," she replied wickedly.

When I had complained that tying myself in a red bow was surely the biggest cliché under the sun, Lauralynn had sent me into the fitting room with a leopard-print version instead.

I had finally managed to wrap myself up in it and was pleased with the result, but could only imagine the look on Dominik's face when he saw me clad like this. He despised anything that had even a hint of vulgarity or tackiness.

"I meant come out now, not next week, and I won't ask you again," Lauralynn called over the curtain in her haughtiest voice. Finally I revealed myself, if only to get her to shut up. She was using her domme tone of voice and I felt as though everyone on Oxford Street must by now be wondering what the two of us got up to when in private, if this was the way that we behaved in public.

"Hmmm, lovely," she said, giving my rump a gentle smack as she adjusted the fabric to reveal even more of my skin.

"They're going to throw us out," I warned her, as I saw the shop assistant averting her eyes.

"Oh well," Lauralynn replied cheerily. "Plenty more shops to come. Selfridges has some nice lingerie."

"I'm not going anywhere *near* Mayfair with you in this mood!"

"Oh calm down, darling. You're a terrible submissive, has anyone ever told you that?"

"Many times," I replied, before rushing back into the fitting room and pulling off the length of slippery fabric. I cursed under my breath as I fiddled with the simple knot I had tied to keep the thing together. I was a captive to my desires even at the most impractical times and Lauralynn was one of the few women in the world who had that effect on me.

Even dressed casually for a shopping trip she looked every inch the domme, with her long legs encased in a pair of black wet-look leggings and a white vest overtop that was so thin her skin was visible through the fabric. Lauralynn hated to wear a bra ("shake what your mother gave you" she always said) and she had donned one only at my insistence, but I had noticed when she removed her jacket once we were on the Tube that instead of a normal bra she was wearing a black halter-neck crop top instead. Her curtain of blonde hair was lifted into a high ponytail, exposing the nape of her neck and also the word "Mistress" clearly printed in white on the rubber strap of her top.

"Christ, Lauralynn, did you have to?"

"You did tell me to wear a bra. And you should have learned by now never to tell a dominatrix what to do."

I huffed.

"Besides," she added, "some of us aren't ashamed of our natures."

I was no longer ashamed of the desires that drove my some-times left of centre behaviour, but over time those desires had become more focused on Dominik and exhibitionism didn't hold quite the same thrill for me unless he was responsible for it, as he had been the night that I'd danced for him at The Place, the glamorous club in New Orleans where Luba had once worked.

By the end of the day, my feet were aching and we must have visited almost every shop in London. I had tried on sexy costume after costume, and found all of them to be too frilly, too flouncy, too Christmassy, too tacky, or just the wrong wretched size.

Tired and downhearted, we ended up strolling all the way to Covent Garden where Lauralynn bought us both chilli-flavoured hot chocolates from the Brazilian-themed café in Neal's Yard. Despite the cold, we sat outside on the wooden picnic benches and sipped the burning hot liquid from the paper mugs.

"There's one more store I know of," Lauralynn said, "just around the corner. And I reckon their stuff is much more up your street. And mine. Classy, and fetishistic. Not all this girly lace or Sexy Santa rubbish."

"One more can't hurt, I suppose," I sighed. The whole thing was beginning to feel like a fool's errand and I wondered if I should have just asked Dominik what he wanted and then bought it for him online. But that would have been so unro-mantic. I still had no idea what he was planning to get for me, but based on his previous gifts I felt it was likely to be exotic and surprising.

The mannequin in the shop's window was naked but for a leather waist-cincher covered in spikes.

"Well, I can see why you like the place," I said to Lauralynn as we stepped inside. An image of her naked but for the thick spiked belt flashed into my mind and again I felt that familiar rush of warmth tingling from my groin all the way up my spine and finally scattering all of the thoughts in my mind.

A selection of lingerie hung on racks along the red-painted walls, but it was the glass display shelves near the back that caught my attention. Laid out on lengths of crushed red velvet were a variety of implements. Fur-lined paddles, crops made from a soft leather that looked so gentle but that I knew were not gentle in the slightest when wielded by a firm hand, beautiful glass butt plugs with long tails made from horse's hair.

I wandered over to the counter where a petite, dark-haired young woman was standing on her tiptoes, reaching overhead to hook a garment onto a display rack. As she stretched, the bottom of her blouse rolled up to display a tattoo across the small of her back in dark gothic letters. "A spy in the house of love," it read.

Here was a woman who would understand what I wanted, I thought.

"Can I help you?" she asked, in a thick Italian accent.

I explained the situation and she did not bat an eyelid either at the unusual nature of my gift or at the obvious undertones of my relationship with Dominik that it revealed.

"I think I have just the thing," she replied with a smile.

It was Christmas day in Belsize Park, and the outside facade of Viggo's impressive mansion showed few signs of it. It could have been any day of the year. Which pleased Dominik as he rang the buzzer at the front door of this house he had once broken into some time back on a fool's errand that could have ended so badly but had finally reunited him with Summer.

They had been invited for a festive round of drinks by Viggo and Lauralynn, but Summer had been called out of the blue to a brief meeting in town in the morning with some foreign conductor passing through London, with whom her US-based manager Susan was trying to convince her to work with on some concerts in the New Year, after her current recordings had been completed. She had promised him she wouldn't be long and had agreed to meet up with him directly at Viggo's.

Lauralynn opened the door and greeted him with a kiss on the lips. They had lived together for a long time and shared many perverse adventures, although they had, technically, never been actual lovers. She was her Amazonian self, tall, blonde and imposing, in skintight jeans and white T-shirt, her hair held back by a red elastic band.

"Lovely to see you."

"I hope I'm not late," Dominik said. "I thought I'd just walk down the hill and leave the car at home. Has Summer arrived?"

"Not yet." Lauralynn led him through to the large kitchen where Viggo was sitting at the counter, sipping from a carton of orange juice. Summer was late for everything, no matter how many times Dominik had promised, in jest, to spank it out of her.

"Hello, mate."

"Hi, Viggo."

"Merry Christmas."

Dominik smiled. There was a glint in Viggo's eyes that he recognized from all their other adventures. Something was up. He turned to Lauralynn who avoided his gaze.

Before he could say something or ask any questions, Viggo broke in. "So, are you and Summer making any plans?"

"Actually, I have something of a surprise for her," Dominik remarked.

Both Viggo and Lauralynn raised their eyebrows in unison. "Have you?"

"I've checked she has nothing in her diary and in a couple of days I'm whisking her off to the Caribbean for New Year's Eve in the sun. We're going to the Dominican Republic, a place called La Caleta. I think she'll like it."

"That's nice," Lauralynn said. "Viggo are I are off to New

Orleans, and while we're there we'll include sidetrips to Memphis and Nashville, visit Graceland. Believe it or not, our big rock star here has never been there."

"Oh, I was never really a true Elvis fan, you know. I much preferred Gene Vincent," Viggo pointed out. "But we'll make the pilgrimage. Should be fun."

Dominik looked at his watch. Surely, Summer wouldn't be long now. Or he really would spank it out of her. For a moment he wished that they hadn't agreed to have drinks with friends and had just spent the evening at home alone instead.

"Anyway, let's get started on those drinks, shall we?" Viggo suggested, moving to the nearby lounge where a well-stocked drinks cabinet stood. "We could wait forever before Father Christmas makes an appearance."

He was pouring himself and Lauralynn a tall glass of bourbon, as Dominik buried himself in one of the deep, soft leather sofas scattered across the large room, when the doorbell rang. Dominik noticed one of Viggo's guitars standing by the main sofa alongside Lauralynn's tall, imposing cello. He wondered why, as the instruments were seldom kept in the room.

"That could be her," Dominik suggested.

"Maybe not," Lauralynn corrected him. "I'm expecting a delivery. I was told it would arrive today of all days. Dominik, would you give me a hand and help me bring it in?"

Dominik rose and followed her to the front door.

A UPS van was parked outside Viggo's mansion and a uniformed attendant was wheeling a large rectangular box towards the house. It was enormous, over six and a half feet in height and three feet across, with "UP" and "DOWN" clearly marked on the thick cardboard box's exterior. A bunch of "FRAGILE" stickers were also scattered across its perimeter.

The three of them carefully carried the box from the cart and set it down in the hall. It was surprisingly heavy.

"It's huge," Dominik pointed out, as Lauralynn signed a receipt for the outsized parcel. "A present for Viggo?"

Lauralynn didn't answer.

As the driver walked back to his brown van, Dominik

noticed the man looking back at them with an enigmatic smile. For a few seconds, he got the feeling he'd briefly seen the man before, but couldn't quite recall where this might have been.

"You take one end, I'll take the other," Lauralynn suggested, bending down to take hold of the large parcel. Dominik followed her instructions and helped her carry it to the lounge where Viggo was now sitting.

Lauralynn steadied the parcel vertically against one of the leather sofas.

"That looks truly spectacular," Dominik said. "So, who's going to open their big present?" he asked.

Viggo and Lauralynn nodded at him "It's for you."

"Really?"

He warily approached the tall standing box, examined the small label situated, like a stamp, in its top right-hand corner. Indeed, his name was listed there.

His eyes wandered across the contours of the box until a tab, marked, "Pull open here", finally caught his attention.

"Do it carefully, mate," Viggo said, calmly sipping his drink a few steps away from Dominik.

He proceeded slowly, gradually pulling the packaging apart. It peeled away like a banana skin and fell to the floor, unveiling a life-sized book.

Dominik chuckled.

The outsized book's cover was a blown-up reproduction of his Paris book, his first novel, and whoever had put the artwork together had photoshopped a photograph of Summer's face at the centre of the violin which had been used to illustrate the cover.

What a wonderful joke, he thought. He was beginning to enjoy Viggo's sense of humour. Although he also suspected a heavy involvement on Lauralynn's part.

"Nice but it won't fit on my shelves, you know," he pointed out.

Just as he said this, the large book burst open.

I caught sight of Dominik's shocked expression as I leapt out naked from between the covers. Viggo and Lauralynn seized their instruments as we had rehearsed and the music began.

Lauralynn had agreed to sing along as both Viggo and she also played on guitar and cello, "I Love You (Me Either)", in the version by Cat Power and Karen Elson and Lauralynn's husky untrained voice counterpointed Viggo's throaty rock 'n' roll growl perfectly.

"I go and I come . . ." they harmonized together, as I swayed in time as best as I could, knowing that Dominik's eyes must be locked on the simple outfit I had selected with the help of the young Italian woman who ran the lingerie store near Neal's Yard.

The nipple clamps, with their copper-red jewels, stung a little as I moved and the metal clips bit against the weight of my breasts. I had heavily rouged my nipples and my nether lips, although the thin layer of dust was no protection against the sharp bite of the clamps.

I heard a hiss as Domink inhaled sharply and I knew, from our lovemaking sessions too numerous to count, that he would be holding his breath, transfixed, watching me, caught between his voyeur's desire to stand still and gaze and his longing to pounce on me there and then.

With pronounced coquettishness I turned and waggled my backside burlesque-style, then bent forward slowly to display the matching jewelled plug that was clasped deep within my arse.

When the short song came to an end, Viggo and Lauralynn remained absolutely silent as I had instructed them.

Dominik stepped forward and took me into his arms. "How did you . . . ?"

"These?" I asked, cupping my breasts in my hands and pointing towards the nipple clamps.

He examined them closer, and then spun me around and dropped to his knees to stare at the plug that decorated my arse.

I gasped as Dominik pushed my legs apart and ran his hand between my thighs. He withdrew as quickly as he had approached, teasing me with just a light stroke of his fingers. A promise of things to come.

"You didn't go all the way to New Orleans to buy these? I looked online myself since then but could never find any just the right colour . . ."

The nipple clamps and the butt plug were exactly the same as the ones that Madame Denoux, the woman who ran The Place had instructed me to wear when I had danced for Dominik in New Orleans. Even the box that the small Italian girl had presented to me was just the same as the one I had seen them in that night.

"The woman who sold them to me knew Luba – perhaps they worked together."

"Coincidence does seem to follow you around, Summer."

He raised my chin and held me in place as he met my lips with his.

"Now," he said. "Let's go and celebrate Christmas in private."

He took my hand and pulled me downstairs towards Viggo's underground grotto close to the room where Dominik had once broken in to rescue my precious violin.

"That was the best present I've ever been given," Dominik remarked, as their limbs reluctantly disentangled.

"Worth a rare violin?" Summer asked.

"A thousand times over," he agreed, his hand lingering vicariously over her humid buttocks.

They were both bathing in sweat.

Dominik eyed the emerald waters of the subterranean pool. "I think we both need to cool down," he said, "and I'm sure Viggo won't mind."

"I'm sure he won't," Summer remarked, taking him by the hand as they both dived into the water.

They had been lounging quietly in the warm water for ages, savouring the proximity of their bare, tired, loved-out bodies and the weight of their silence, when they finally heard Lauralynn's voice from the room's threshold.

"Hey, guys, can we join you?"

"Of course," Summer cried out, her wet red hair draped like a curtain of fire across her whiter than white shoulders.

"Good," Viggo remarked. "I just hope you're as thoroughly indecent as we are." Lauralynn and Viggo stepped into the room and stopped briefly at the far end of the pool. They were both totally naked.

"It's Christmas," Dominik said. "'Tis the season to be indecent."

Viggo and Lauralynn jumped into the pool in one bound and joined them.

Fluffed

Mathew Klickstein

I'm pinching her tiny, button-nose nostrils shut, ensuring – with stone-hard erection lodged firmly down her warm and moist, most-welcoming gullet – my vitriolic ejaculation will ruthlessly gag her just as I prefer.

See . . . I don't want her to merely *swallow* the full messy load I hear tell tastes of sweaty cookie dough. I want this little angel-dove to choke on it, to hack and cough it up (with nowhere for it to go). The real deal, full-throttle chest cold inflicted by yours truly and his penis fulminating with the strongest of swimming semen launching from my body and into hers.

Or maybe that's much too much.

Maybe just a *bit* of the choking on my soppy goop of stringy sperm pummeling the slimy cavity of her throat, mouth, possibly sinuses depending on where it all goes courtesy her nose being clamped shut.

Playful, but real.

Right now, she's *my* property, *my* fuck toy, and I'll do with her what I want.

Looking down onto her splendid, perfect Snow White face topped by a shock of shoulder-length stark black silken hair in which a light-lavender ribbon is nearly lost, I marvel at her wide-eyed azure oceans of irises peering longingly back up at me squatting like a ninja-monkey over her body.

The lack of air (my cock forcefully thrust down her throat, my fingers vice-ing her nose shut) is effectively blood-shotting those same eyes slightly, steadily. An almost imperceptible light-lavender vein appears across her powdery, sweat-droplet-lined forehead, which is even now slowly turning purplish along with the rest of her face. I've seen it before with girls in this same spectacular mine-mine-mine position.

As with her predecessors, I know this coquettish darling rendered feeble, sucking me dry – outright *nursing* on my salubrious penis teeming with thousands of microscopic, life-affirming wiggling and wily spermatozoa about to explosively propel themselves into her pint-sized body resting back on her legs (painfully) folded inward as support – *needs* it, *wants* it, *must have it*.

Here. Now. Christ, *forever*.

And you know something? In a few more heavenly protracted seconds, she shall have it!

Those coruscated jewels of blue eyes moistening ever-more, reddening ever-more, goading me on ever-more, imploring me with her strident soul muted by my manhood haughtily spearing her vocal cords; and I'm flashing on the fantastic notion that the girl beneath me is a whopping ten years younger than I!

This randy revelation popping into my head before I flash too on how – oh! – how amazing it will feel when I finally do blast in her throat.

I turn briefly to the other girl in the corner of the damp and cramped bathroom; she's scrunched herself nicely into the cleavage that is the two beige intersecting walls, her already too-short tattered denim skirt pulled up to the top of her thighs, revealing she wears no underwear, slender honey-baked legs opened wide with knees pulled up against her bleachy tan-lined chest as she maniacally manhandles her left perky pointy tit standing out as shockingly white in stark contrast to her burnt-sienna hand (I don't know where her shirt went) while feverishly strumming her meticulously shaved rose-pink vagina like a stony jazzman lost in closed-eyed, mouth-gaping blissed-out euphoria with fingers blurringly attacking his upright bass.

And all I can think about before erupting into this girl's mouth beneath me is a silent echo of the titanically iconic lyric from that Talking Heads song: *How did I get here?*

The answer was a simple one: *I didn't really care.*

But, there I was three or four hours earlier on my way to a party at Mike's place in Bushwick.

The subways are a reliable problem on the weekends, of course, but not having enough money (as usual) for a cab, not having a job at the moment (as usual) to *get* the money to get a cab, and being more or less scared shitless to get in a cab during the wild, mad crush of a Friday night on the hopelessly dangerous by ways of our New York City streets, the subways – as notoriously flawed as they might be – were my only choice for nocturnal transport.

"Why go out at all?" you may be asking.

My fair-weather girlfriend had yet again pissed me off something awful, and we needed a little time apart. I needed time alone. By myself.

Which of course means that I needed to find a party bulging to the rim with sweaty young people raging the night away. Particularly those sweaty young people with hot baby bums and midriffs scandalously showing off pierced bellybuttons. (No "outties" need apply, thank you. Just go away.)

After a quick popping into my local liquor purveyor (still a might bit miffed you can't grab a medium-sized bottle of Wild Turkey at a grocery store the way you can back in California), I stole a few guzzles of warm whiskey that had been nicely heating up on display by the sun-blitzed window from its black plastic bag and bounded down the subway stairs, clutching the bagged Turkey in one hand and a copy of something-or-other by Schopenhauer in the other, with a full stop at the turnstile where I pulled out my yellow MetroCard, swiping the fucker in the slick-smooth slot as a hopeful portent of things to come.

This made me chortle in a way that led the leathery, sinewy old anorexic lady next to me to furrow her brow as I realized the alcohol had already – likely thanks to the oppressive summer heat – taken its pleasantly anaesthetizing effects on me.

I caught the train right as it arrived at the platform, and as always had a quick mindful blip of leaping in front of the mobile mechanical monster – just as always again – before deciding against it at the terminal millisecond, surviving yet another night in the ever-alluring NYC transit subway system.

Hopping onto the train, I found – success! – an empty seat. Reveling in the welcomed embrace of the AC that is the one component of the subway that alone might make the mode of conveyance worthwhile, I snuck another swig of my black-bagged Turkey and continued reading my Schopenhauer from where I had previously stopped.

I'd read maybe the third line of the first page when I noticed that across from me sat the most darling lone waif, who couldn't have been more than eighteen and showed it by her adorable lack of sophistication in not remembering to stop opening and closing her legs, ever-so-slightly revealing (courtesy of her diaphanous, white flower-girl dress and signaling to all the ravenous world the utmost of purity and innocence) her magnificently tempting, totally taboo inner-workings.

Schopenhauer tells us men's relations are based on indifference, whereas women's are based on antagonism.

I'm thinking about this in some modicum of correlation with a buddy of mine's sage adage likely glommed from someone not *too* dissimilar from Schopenhauer (Kierkegaard?): *Men use love to get sex; women use sex to get love.*

Whatever the case, I'm certainly not the least bit indifferent to the lovely creature across from me languorously opening and closing the door to her womanly wonders encased by girlishly white underwear spotted with multicolored but otherwise identical butterflies.

A Lisa Frank monkey Band-Aid on her scuffed, faintly grass-stained right knee.

Odiously peeking over my Schopenhauer, I'm all but justifying my voyeuristic eye-raping here, finding it to be *her* fault I'm staring at her appearing-disappearing-and-then-reappearing butterfly-peppered undergarments.

The girl-child before me lying back in dispassionate repose, still obviously feeling the brutality of the tyrannical heat outside in the world beyond us two here together in our isolated subway car bubble.

She taking in the chilled invigoration of the AC, as am I. She twirling her blonde Alice in Wonderland strand of hair with one bright-pink fingernailed index finger and looking away to no one in particular with those shimmering emerald eyes of hers, sparkling with the sprightly spirit of untainted, unfathomable, unremitting youth.

Her mouth falls open and through impossibly pencil-thin wide lips (the same cartoonishly pink hue as her nails) she sighs loudly and I catch a glint of her silver braces reflecting the harsh ceiling light of the subway car. The blinding radiance of the braces is enhanced by the puffy roseate redness of her flushed, peach-colored chubby chipmunk cheeks, pathetically sunburned, and I know I must have this quasi-pixie but never, ever will.

This is the exact specimen of girl who – fairly reeking of virginity (a scent not unlike baby powder and peppermint, as accurately assessed by F. Scott Fitzgerald) – evil, selfish, red-meat-devouring beasts such as myself can only *fantasize* about in horribly debauched prurient visions: me not *wanting* her to consent; me slurping and sucking at that peach, sunburned face of hers, desperately lapping up her irredeemably salty, glittery streaks of tears streaming down her velutinous baby face . . .

. . . The accusatory DING of the subway car – "LORIMER STREET," the imperious, disembodied voice does declare – and I'm at once unceremoniously ejected from my sexually sociopathetic flight of fancy, squeezing my book, gripping my black bag of Turkey and leaving through the automatically closing rush of the door after passing the girl I'll never penetrate; and as the door whooshes shut on me, on her, on us forevermore, I hear her burp and I take another slug of my whiskey before saluting her and the fast-moving, bombastic train rocketing away from me, emancipating me from her bewitching spell, permitting me to somehow end up at Mike's party in an apartment building whose name and number I'll never be able to fully recall.

Mike is one of at least five Mikes I know (including my dad and step-dad) and maybe another six that I don't. I myself get mistaken for a "Mike" sometimes (if not the occasional "Mark" or even less frequent "Marc").

But that's not important right now.

What *is* important right now, what's *essential* right now is that, after ingesting nearly half the bottle of scalding-hot whiskey by this point in my adventure, I was about to bust a ball (or maybe both) and shambled my wobbly way down a narrow, faded-vintage-store-art-covered corridor with shadowy people standing and sitting on either side so that it almost made it impossible to juggernaut my way through to the bathroom, beyond which lay the light at the end of the tunnel (in the kitchen so many spiraling miles away).

There was one girl dressed as a slutty Tinker Bell for some reason, complete with translucent, feathery wings I had to shove past to get to the fucking toilet so I could immediately relieve myself of the veritable poison coursing through me and my burning shaft pulsing painfully with hot magma.

Tinker Bell at least had the good grace to kiss me drunkenly on the cheek (*why?*), cackling to herself or maybe to (what one could only hope were) her dude-ish friends holding red plastic cups before she clownishly collapsed to the floor in a heap of almost no clothes at all aside from those wings, which was fine by me, especially as I was able to now more easily walk *over* the mess of laughing girl and make it at long last to the bathroom so I could take a much-needed victorious piss.

Date rape wasn't my problem right now, though: pissing my pants *was*, so I left the supremely vulnerable girl behind and shouldered my way through the brown plywood door that – thanks probably to the expansive heat and just the general

shoddiness of shitty bohemian pre-WWII Brooklyn apart-
ments – I almost couldn't get through, but then did with a
loud grunt and a pain to the side of my arm that I fortunately
wouldn't feel until my sober morning thereafter.

I think I may have also shoved some snooty little bitch with
a surprisingly large forest-green handbag aside before going
through the door, too ... but I can't really be sure and it
doesn't much matter anyway, because, as previously
mentioned, *I really had to go to the bathroom BAD.* Whatever
that chick had been calling out to me while I was closing the
door in her fat fucking face didn't much matter either, as
everything had that serene flatness one hears of the surface
world while under a few shallow inches of water.

Thus, no harm done.

This was, by the by, how I was hearing everything by now,
thanks to the halcyon inebriation that made even the petard
crash of routine party cacophony through the closed/locked
door sound as though played off of a Lo-Fi record from the
eighties.

So, I'm finishing that truly triumphant piss of mine, right
there into the scum-lined porcelain toilet bowl, when the door
blasts open – right through the shittily shoddy lock that had
hardly put up a fight – and two giggly girls (the twee, raven-
haired Snow White: face beaming with those saucer-sized
blue eyes and topped by the childish, light-lavender bow in
her French New Wave bobbed hair; and her lusciously tanned,
honey-glazed svelte friend with denim skirt so short that when
she turned to the side, one could see the paradisal rondure of
her sepia-colored left buttock just barely nosing out as though
it were about to play Peek-A-Boo but quickly thought better
of it) bungled inside, and loudly slammed the door shut before
they toppled to the wet, mildewy and cracked tiled floor.

They were clinging to one another as though conjoined at
the chests, and while continuing to cackle like two parts of a
coven of witches (I couldn't tell if they were serious in their
laughter or not), the ribboned, alabaster-skinned Snow White

turns to me – who's now turned to her, to both of them, with my dripping dick in my hand – and she says to Honeyglazed with her long, straight golden hair (staring either at me or my cock; it's hard to tell for sure from my angle): "Oh my God! That guy looks *pissed!*"

The bathetic joke of course elicits in them a thunderous peal of uproarious laughter something awful. Both of the girls there on the moldy tile that is scum-lined almost as heartily as the inside of the toilet bowl over which I'm hovering.

Honeyglazed leans into her Snow White friend conspiratorially and, holding her delicate, petite head tightly between her hands (for a second, I think they're going to touch lips to lips; but no such luck – not *yet* anyway), Honeyglazed *does* whisper something tacitly lascivious into Snow White's double-pierced china doll ear.

"Lascivious" I say because upon hearing the whispered susurrus, Snow White's blood-red lips purse and she stops laughing. All has gone almost somber, as her characteristically wide eyes do now narrow with drastic determination.

"Mmm," she agreeably coos, as Honeyglazed stealthily stretches her bare slink of a burnished arm up to the dust-crusted doorknob above her straw-haired head and relocks it without looking (she must, of course, fumble with it a bit, as it's now somewhat broken, breaking with the fantasy slightly, but then, there we are: locked in the room, we three).

—CLICK—

I'm about to put myself away while watching the somewhat amusing impromptu show here when Snow White asks me, "Hey, you got any coke?"

When I tell her no, zipping up, she responds that I needn't worry: They've *"of course"* got some and if I unzip my pants again, they'll maybe possibly probably likely OK whatever sure share a bump or two with me.

I'm a little confused and now *very* drunk, and ask why they would want me to unzip my pants.

Honeyglazed chortles loudly but Snow White tilts her chin down with her eyes pointing upward from the floor impishly and with deeply stoned oculars, she says almost caustically, "'Cause there's no one else here."

We're on our knees on the ground, snorting neatly laid-out lines on the tiled floor (*meh, why not?*) and I'm *not* thinking about the grime and flecks of dirt the floor is absolutely caked in and that I'm obviously vacuuming up into my brain along with the crystalline granules of cocaine.

I *am*, however, thinking about how delightfully pleasant it feels that my hand is being pulled toward Honeyglazed on the ground there next to me, sun-baked feminine legs strewn out messily before her, as she's unzipping the front of her too-short jean skirt, slowly unbuttoning the top brass button and revealing her immaculately clean-shaven slit below her belly-button.

There's a barely perceptible rose tattoo – a bit faded and very small but definitely there – beneath her lovely bellybutton and, after she guides my fingers down to lightly caress it with slow, steady swivels, I loudly snort up half of a line, she guffaws mannishly, Snow White falls back against a nearby wall, and Honeyglazed at once jams my index and middle fingers into her warm, milky maw before disgorging them with a loud, disgusting spitting sound before she shoves the lubricated digits deeply into her awaiting, warm-oven pussy that feels as equally creamy as her luscious mouth.

Honeyglazed moans softly.

The rest of the dim, amber suffusion of light in this box of a bathroom, illuminated only by a bulb dangling perilously from a DIY twisty circuit of some sort from the low ceiling just above our heads, consigns us to otherwise near-silence but for the underwater throb-throbbing of the ongoing party outside hardly muted by the locked door and my own deepening effects of bacchic torpor, which continues to make me hear all of this as though from underwater.

The gooshing, squishing sounds of my finger burrowing farther and deeper into the honey-glazed girl's gooey cream of twat breaks through that silence, though, and I bend over to my left and (with my left hand, despite being a righty) self-ishly huff up one more line of ice-stingy snow.

Perhaps Time does flit in Dorothy Parker's estimation or perhaps it does not, but whatever the case, I'm there on my fourth or seventh line of coke, torrents of blazing sweat streaking down my temple, my eyes on fire, concrete erection nonetheless swelling in the tiny doll hands of the Snow White girl in front of me, fingers of my hand *not* holding the rolled-up twenty probing ever deeper into the belly of the honey-glazed girl making out with her friend now, all silent but for the wet pops and juicy slurps that traditionally punctuate such scenarios . . .

. . . when Snow White recoils at once and proclaims, "Wait."

I stop in place, anxiously (*"Anxiety is the dizziness of freedom,"* *Kierkegaard definitely DID say*).

Honeyglazed appears equally pensive, as though she was just caught in the act but isn't sure exactly which one.

My fingers remain up inside her but no longer gyrating and shifting about as they had been before this strange cessation. My fingers are now merely hibernating in the warm, marly enclosure of her most womanly part.

Snow White snorts laughingly and rocks backward on the floor, at once bounding back at me like one of those inflatable boxing clowns and is suddenly so close to my face . . . Closer . . . And closer still. I can feel my face is so flushed, so overheated and showing how sweatily rapt in hot-hot anticipation I so sincerely am. (*God, I want to just get this thing PREG-NANT, and I don't think it's simply the coke. It can't be. Can it be?*)

She sniffs hard and fast, pulling back a rivulet of toxic snot infused with coke particles into her button nose, closes her eyes and opens them again to pronounce, "Before you do another bump, you *gotta* let me give you a blow job."

Is she serious?

"Seriously," she says.

For the briefest of moments, I think she's clearly kidding. I mean, I don't even *know* these crazy bitches. Fingering and making out and my cock in her hand and free coke on the bathroom floor is one thing, but sucking me off? That's a whole other ball game, and I'm *terrible* at sports.

But my already painfully hard erection is thickening still in her soft satiny pillows of pussy-cat paws, and Snow White's friend lets out one of their characteristic cackles, followed by, "Oh my *God*, Julie! You really are *suhhhhhhhch* a *slut!*"

There's a quick moment of shoe-gaze contemplation where I realize: *Gee, maybe I'm not so special after all* along with: *Gosh, I wonder how disease-ridden this bitch's mouth might be*.

Thankfully, the coke and whiskey sportively drown out that part of my brain, as the anima takes over and I realize, far more importantly, that I'm about to have my dick in this chick's mouth and she looks *exactly* like a hipster Snow White, as I've said, so who the fuck wouldn't want *that*?

In the approximately .5 seconds all this goes through my mind (*Thanks again, cocaine!*), Honeyglazed has fallen over with rumbling laughter at her friend's demand, hitting her head against the tile but not really caring (that was one loud *CRACK*, I can tell you) and Snow White ("Julie"? Had I heard correctly?) points a finger with the entitled authority of a spoiled toddler princess wanting more birthday presents at her lustful gal pal, demanding in the most alluringly youthful helium voice, "You: Over there and watch. In the corner. Right now. *Go!*"

Honeyglazed's blonde rabbit-fuzz eyebrows bolt up comically, as though she's as befuddled as I, but this doesn't stop her from scooting across the tile backwards with her well-exposed, bony butt cheeks that squeak with intermittent high-pitch sounds along with the scratchy shimmying noise of her not-quite-yet-all-the-way-off denim skirt until she collides with the wall and finds her designated place where the two walls meet.

Snow White/Julie turns back to me, gazely gazing penetratingly into my eyes – gravely serious now despite the moppet composure of her adorably neotenous disposition that just makes you want to pinch her cheek and shake it like an avuncular grandfather – and says to her friend while looking so profoundly into, I swear, my fucking soul: "You do whatever you want over there, but—" and she takes a deep, deep breath into her importunate little lungs "—this cock is *mine*."

And that is when she swallows me whole.

There's that all-consuming jolly joy of *SHE'S LETTING ME IN* that comes with the bodily penetration of any girl on that first journey inward and then I'm reverting back to my primal, evil self . . . The bursting *jouissance* literally throbbing through my urethra hot as Tabasco sauce enflaming my tip and tubular shaft alike, absolutely *needing* to fire a long and hot load into her gaping maw wrapped around my entire penis like a gooey, gushing condom filled to the brim with lukewarm spittle. My (what I've been told by more than one girl) mutantly massive balls squashing up against her beautiful little button nose.

I lean my head back and close my eyes, wanting to shout something silly like *Open wider, bitch!*, but I'm not a frat gay or some overprivileged white kid who's listened to too many New School hip-hop lyrics (one in the same?). I'm no longer *that* drunk.

Snow White's violently, desperately, ferociously slurping, sucking, drinking, licking, lapping me all up.

That sound. That marvelously mellifluous sound of swishing around an overwhelming amount of rancid mouthwash. Her mouth is way too small for my man-sized member, but she takes it anyway, first poking at the inside of her right cherubic cheek, then the left . . . and that sound underpins the equally rancid smell of heat-battered cock, that not-too-distinct cheese variety that far too many young girls and clearly a healthy amount of gay men must more than *tolerate*: they patently can't get enough of it.

Me, myself? I'm smelling the cheese stink and listening to the goop-glop of the girl I don't even friggin' *know* aside from her resemblance to a supremely salacious Snow White (I only *now* notice the sparkling pink ruby stud embedded in her left nostril) and I lean forward again, holding her fucking head in the grip of my – of course – sweat-lined, red and calloused palms.

In so doing, in so encaging her twee basketball of a head (I'm all but trying to crush like a super-slimy grape), I'm mashing her entire face now into my hot-ass fenny swamp of a wet-furry crotch and doing my damndest to choke this little slut so she'll never, ever forget me (though it's more obvious still that she's been in this position many a time before, as I flash too on the little young one on the subway train without rejecting the influx of foggy visions of her fluttering her legs – open/shut/open/shut like the wings of a smoke-lined moth) and Snow White's not pushing me away or pulling her head back – she *wants* me to do this to her, goddamn it! – and she's sublimating herself, subjugating herself, giving herself over to me entirely like the good little girl she should be and is even now, yes, rising up on her knees, her folded legs beneath and behind her expanding upward like a construction site's cherry-picker, while she unclamps her delicate hands from the back of my denim-enveloped pants before reaching down to her 1950s-ish black-and-white polka dotted dress to slowly, furtively pull down her stretchy, long black underwear that must have come from some magnificently unholy combination of Hot Topic and Victoria's Secret, and once they're down to her reddened and road-rashed knobby knees, she commences with fingering herself, squishing, squashing, squooshing, gooshing and grappling with her swelling bubble of a cream-covered clit I'll never see and don't need to see because, well, across the room, hunkered there in the corner is Honeyglazed with legs spread wide open as though at the gyno (clearly a psychotic one who needs pussy the way an astronaut needs oxygen) and *oop!* there's *her* clit.

Yes, I can actually see it from over here and maybe there's something wrong with these chicks, but who really gives a fiddler's fuck as Snow White is sucking me while fingering herself, and Honeyglazed is over there in that jazz-man closed-eyed bliss of hers, working at her own oyster's pearl.

I realize at once I've been holding my breath, as though

waiting to hear the results of a pregnancy/AIDS test, and with that sound of super-suckling for nature's perfect goodness in the thick, humid air, I flash once more on (don't blame me, I'm just a man) the butterfly underwear of that nearly-too-young damsel on the subway, moistened by the New York summer's balmy heat, and BOOM:

It comes, I come, I squeeze the nose of the Snow White Julie girl so tight I almost worry I'm going to make that shit bleed, what with the roseate ruby stud in there (but I of course pinch harder anyway – FUCK IT) and it's all going up and down into her as I gaze below on the majesty of the lavender ribbon embowered in her murder-of-crows hair and she's desperately sucking back, fiendishly pulling it into her tiny little body and robbing me of all my essence so powerfully that it actually pierces the tip of my burning penis.

Guttural, soggy hacking sounds emit from her overfilled mouth so that she cannot say no but only grab hold of my buttocks once more, squeezing them, her fingers digging into my pants as I'm still choking her here with my cock, slimy slobber foaming down the sides of her cheeks as my load continues pumping into her, into her mouth, her throat, her stomach, her intestines, flushing its way through her entire body, into her fucking *lungs* no doubt, flooding her entire system with me, me, me – a complete stranger . . .

. . . I turn my attention from the girl I'm squatting over to the girl fingering herself to a final climaxing squirt in the corner – *I've never seen that in real life before; she's really squirting and massaging it into the tan-lined tits (one of which I now see has a round, skin-colored Band-Aid on it, which yet again reminds me of the girl-child on the subway) and cleavage that weirdly matches up to that crevice of the two converging walls behind her (the squirting looks like clear urine, but who knows)* – and her eyes bolt open, as she bangs her head against the wall behind her, seizing like a spastic while quivering with a stentorian release of unintelligible girl-noise . . .

. . . I pull away from Snow White, she tumbles backward over her folded legs, laughing and coughing, hacking away, and wiping her mouth of her spit and my semen, and rolls over to her stomach.

I spank her up-turned ass for no reason at all (*hard*, I say), and she baby-crawls over to her friend, they begin cackling again like the two witches they are, with Honeyglazed saying, "Oh, my *God*! What does he *taste* like?" and to show her, so she can know first hand, Snow White pounces at her friend, tackling her mouth-to-mouth and they're sharing what I've pumped into her frigging doe-faced *punim* and one of them (I forget which) reaches for the door from the floor, unlocks it and they both shamble out of the room – "Oh, my God, it's all *lemony*!" – and out of my life forevermore.

BREATHE. JUST BREATHE.

I am standing there, pants down, the bathroom door wide open, the sounds of the party loud and true now (no more underwater sounds; I am suddenly sober), and someone comes in (thankfully a dude, and he's obviously totally wasted) and he asks me if I'm done, without even acknowledging I'm half-naked.

I swallow, inhale deeply, turn to see myself in the fogged-up small mirror next to the toilet, and tell him it's all his.

I pull my pants up, zip up and am about to leave, about to let him take over from here, when I stop him at once. "Wait," I say, and I bound over before he has a chance to use the toilet, scooping up my nearly forgotten Schopenhauer off the floor before revealing:

"I forgot to flush."

Beating the Gothic Out of Her

Amanda Earl

*"My love for Heathcliff resembles the eternal rocks beneath:
a source of little visible delight, but necessary. Nelly, I AM
Heathcliff! He's always, always in my mind: not as a pleasure, any more than I am always a pleasure to myself, but as
my own being."*

Catherine Earnshaw, *Wuthering Heights*

"Repeat after me, 'Heathcliff was a fucked-up character.'"

Silence.

"Annabelle. Repeat after me, 'Heathcliff was a fucked-up
character.'"

She could tell by the tone of Roman's voice that the punishment was going to be severe but she couldn't say it, wouldn't
say it. *Wuthering Heights* was her favourite book of all time.
She understood it had been a mistake to constantly seek men
with Heathcliff's dark and brooding temperament throughout
her adult life. But she had this longing for intense, passionate
men. Not just a longing, more like an addiction. She wanted
divine intoxication, to lose herself in the depths of a man's
desire for her, his need.

As a child, Annabelle devoured gothic novels. It wasn't just
the remote castles by the sea, the underground passages, or
the sudden and untimely appearances of ghosts, serving staff
or the discovery of skeletons of dead wives in attics, it was the

sexual tension created by the vulnerability of the young governesses in the throes of passion over the impossibly beautiful but darkly malevolent anti-heroes, who pursued the innocent maidens with uncontrollable fervour. Annabelle romanticized these men and fantasized about them, most especially Heathcliff.

She had read the book so many times, she'd had to replace each dog-eared, tattered copy with a new one. She even rubbed its spine over her clit when she was too desperate to find her vibrator. She imagined herself as Catherine being chased over the misty Yorkshire moors by the dark anti-hero, caught in the rain during a storm, being forced to accept his kiss. She had masturbated more than once to the fantasy of herself as Catherine confronting Heathcliff in all his trembling fury, trying to comfort him . . . having that comfort turn into a good hard fuck on the floor of Thrushcross Grange.

After she had confessed her Heathcliff fantasies and told Roman about her history with real life anti-heroes – an insecure rock star wannabe who took his assertiveness issues out on Annabelle by thumping her with his guitar; an ageing, tattoo-covered glam rocker with an addiction to painkillers; and a rich moody manchild with mommy issues and a sophisticated sense of fashion, who preyed on naive young women willing to act as doormats to his domineering personality – Roman suggested to her that she had wounded bird syndrome, the need to repair damaged men. Some men were simply incapable of redemption, he told her. Subjecting oneself to their mercurial will was self-destructive and dangerous.

Annabelle had tried various schemes to satisfy her desires. Finally, a friend had suggested BDSM. Perhaps there she would find a strong man capable of sharing her intensity but without the fucked-up personality. She wasn't naive, she knew about bondage and domination. She loved the film, *Secretary*, had imagined herself under E. Edward Grey's hand, lying on the desk with her bare bottom reddened. So it wasn't a stretch to think she might be attracted to some form of sadomasochism or even able to surrender to a strong man's will. She decided to attend a munch, a gathering for BDSM lifestylers and enthusiasts.

She was turned off. The dominants at the munch seemed like poseurs. Annabelle's brief impression of the group was that the doms expected their submissives to bow down to them, keep their eyes cast down and wear their collars or act as their servants. It was useless to her. She was a spirited, intelligent woman with a backbone, not some spongy door-mat whose sole role was to soak up some guy's power trip. Annabelle wasn't unlike many who had a tendency to rush to judgment about BDSM or any other activity that made them uncomfortable. She didn't question why she was uncomfortable.

She bumped into Roman when he was on his way in and she was on her way out. Her face was red as she flounced out of the restaurant. Avoiding a collision, Roman put his hand on her shoulder; she looked into his deep brown eyes, and her anger dissipated.

They ended up at a nearby café where she told him her life story. To Annabelle, Roman seemed to be the kind of man who she could say anything to. He looked to be in his late forties. His hair was already beginning to silver. He recounted tales from his own life too. He was an antiquarian book dealer, selling books on the internet from his home. He seemed steady, intelligent and rational.

So when he told her she had the wrong idea about BDSM, while her first reaction was to tell him he was crazy, she listened. Yes, there were some poseurs, some people more interested in the drama than establishing and maintaining a power relationship, but not everyone was like that. He took her hand in his. Her pulse quickened as his fingers circled her wrist.

Over email, he suggested books she should read, a local support group for submissives, and other resources. The idea of submission held increasing appeal for Annabelle. Roman loaned her erotic BDSM fiction that sent her into a frenzy of self-pleasure.

He'd made one condition when he loaned her the books. He asked that she email him to tell him about her reactions, what turned her on, what turned her off. The heat between them built over email and on the telephone. She asked if she could meet him again in person.

They met in a bookstore. Annabelle was wearing the outfit he'd asked for. At this point she felt a reasonable amount of trust towards Roman. He wasn't asking her to do anything dangerous, just wear a loose skirt with a slit in it and a blouse with buttons that could be easily undone.

The thought had made her wet. She felt desired. She found Roman in the erotica section, juggling a pile of smut in his hands. He smiled when she arrived.

"Maybe you could help me with these?"

Annabelle chortled a bit as she picked up a book that was threatening to topple to the floor. Its cover depicted a cartoon-ish picture of a wide-eyed blonde with a man's hand around her neck. She found herself bristling right away and yet she felt aroused at the same time. She raised her eyebrows at Roman.

"I know it looks cheesy, but the stories inside may just ring your bell, Annie Bell," Roman said. He'd taken to calling her a nickname that she had never been fond of, but for some reason with him it seemed fun, made her feel girlish. She wasn't some shy young virgin, she was a grown woman in her mid-thirties who'd seen her fair share of life. She'd made some bad decisions about men, but her eyes were wide open the whole time.

As they waited in line at the cash register, he put his hand between the parting made by the slit of her skirt and gently caressed her leg. Annabelle trembled. She liked the way that hand felt on her skin. The wait was interminable. There were many people buying books on a rainy night in October. A woman behind them glanced at the books she and Roman were carrying and gave them a look of disdain. Roman gave Annabelle a saucy wink. Annabelle looked him straight in the eye and winked right back. She had no idea what Roman planned for them that night but she wanted to give it a try, was excited about the possibilities.

She thought again of their recent telephone conversation about Georges Bataille's *The Story of the Eye*.

"Did the thought of the girl's humiliation titillate you, Annabelle?"

"Yes . . . I have to say—" she cleared her throat "—I was excited." Annabelle was wet just listening to the sound of Roman's voice. The story had made her squirm in a confusing way. She knew she wasn't supposed to be turned on by the idea of a young man and his girlfriend taking advantage of another young girl. She wanted to be clear. "But . . . I wouldn't want that sort of thing in real life . . . you know . . . I wouldn't want some jerk to take advantage of me. I've had enough of that."

"Real life is a different matter, isn't it, Annie Bell? You do understand the difference between fiction and reality, don't you, girl?" His voice was low and sexy.

"Yessss. I . . . uh . . . I guess so."

"We'll have to work on that."

She didn't know then what he meant. In the bookstore the line-up continued its slow and inevitable pace to the checkout.

"Honestly Roman, why don't you just buy eBooks?" Annabelle was being feisty and she knew it. An antiquarian bookseller wouldn't have much use for eBooks, she realized. He'd want to smell the old paper, enjoy its texture, appreciate the beauty of letterpress type set into the paper, he'd want to touch it, run his fingers along the binding. She thought of his fingers trailing their way along the heavy paper, and it made her wet.

Roman laughed. "You'll see, my girl, you'll see. It's hot in here, don't you think? Why don't you unbutton the top two buttons of your blouse?"

Annabelle looked around at the crowd, especially the disdaining old woman. Well, why not, she thought, why not let this man lead her into temptation. Perhaps he had a devilish streak . . . just like Heathcliff. She met his eyes and nodded.

Her body responded to the mischievous twinkle in his eyes and the persuasive tone in his voice.

She unbuttoned the blouse as he asked. He gave her a leer. She felt sexy all over. Her stomach muscles coiled with desire and anticipation. She wondered if Roman was finding the wait a strain. She turned towards him and dropped one of the books she was holding. As she rose, her hand briefly glanced over his crotch. Yes, there was a slight bulge. As she got to her feet, her eyes met his. He raised his eyebrows and whispered in her ear. "I'm going to deal with you soon, Annie Bell. Brazen, forward Annie Bell."

That night she saw Roman's house for the first time. It wasn't fancy. He didn't make a lot of money as an antiquarian bookseller. His kitchen was a mess, with dishes stacked all over the place. The living room was cluttered with books everywhere: on the couch, on the stuffed armchairs, on the fireplace mantle. Clearly he had no servants as her previous suitor Chris had. It had been unnerving to visit the manchild's penthouse only to find he had a few minders to cook and clean up after him.

Roman lived alone. His home reflected his worldliness and his sophisticated tastes. She imagined he'd make a good old man. The thought of sitting on the old man's lap made her libido come to life once more.

Roman apologized for the mess and ushered her into his library. In this room all the books were in their places on floor-to-ceiling shelves. A black leather chair was placed in front of a formidable oak desk that was empty of objects except for a wooden yardstick, a pipe, some matches and a cake of tobacco.

"One of my vices," Roman said. He took the cake of tobacco, rubbed it between his fingers to make it loose enough to pack into his pipe, pressed it into the bowl of the pipe with his thumb, lit a match and waited briefly for the sulphur to burn away from the tip, then moved the match clockwise over the bowl to light the tobacco. Annabelle realized she was dealing with a very methodical man and she liked that.

"Why don't you hop up on the desk, Annie Bell, let me get a closer look."

Annabelle placed her posterior, which she knew to be generous enough for a good ride by any gentleman, on top of the desk. Her partially undone blouse revealed more cleavage as she sat. Roman fingered the buttons, causing them to undo. He put his hand in her hair, which had been tied neatly in a bun. Roman undid the ribbon and her heavy brown locks tumbled to her shoulders.

"You should wear your hair down more often, Annie Bell. You look like a siren ready to seduce a sailor."

"I hope we don't crash on the rocks," said Annabelle, causing Roman to laugh.

"You have a delightful sense of humour," he said, as he took slow, deliberate puffs on his pipe.

Annabelle thought about the places that pipe could go, how warm it would feel on her naked skin and shuddered.

"Where'd you get that pipe? It looks expensive."

Roman's eyes darkened as he looked down at her. Annabelle wondered if he could read her thoughts and blushed.

"It is. It's a calabash, Sherlock Holmes's favourite pipe. I inherited it from my father and that was the only thing I got from him. I left home at sixteen and never looked back."

Annabelle wondered why the men she chose were always parentless. "You don't have parent issues, do you?"

"Goodness, Annie Bell, I dealt with those years ago. The only issue I have right now is getting you out of that damned skirt and blouse and ravishing you on this desk."

The woodsy aroma of the pipe filled the air. Somewhere a grandfather clock ticked in the background.

Annabelle trembled, tried to get hold of herself.

"No hearts hiding under the floorboards, are there, Roman?" Annabelle said.

"You vixen!" he said. "Are you trying to thwart my attentions, you impossible woman? And you don't know how pleased I am to know that you're a Poe enthusiast."

"Not at all." Annabelle leaned in for a kiss.

Roman didn't hesitate, he put out the pipe and moved towards her, pressing his lips against hers while reaching in to take her breasts out of her bra. Annabelle sighed as she felt the tugging of his fingers on her nipple.

"One day we'll have to clamp these, you know," Roman whispered.

The effect was like a hum over Annabelle's flesh, causing it to tingle. Her nipples hardened between his fingers as he stroked them.

He pulled the blouse off her body so that it formed a prison of her arms.

"Now you're trussed up, Annie Bell, what are you going to do about it?"

She thought she must have made a fetching picture with her shirt open and binding her arms, her breasts overflowing from her bra and her nipples stiff as pencil rubbers. The thought of the tiny teeth on the clamps biting down on her needy little teats. She squirmed on top of the desk to accommodate her tingling cunt.

"Trying to lure me, are you, Annie Bell, with those seductive thrusts?" Roman said, as he yanked the skirt and blouse off her. "Stand up," he said quietly. This time he didn't use the nickname.

His voice sent shivers skyrocketing through her body, onto her clit, on each tiny pinpoint of her nipples, releasing a heady shock of adrenaline to her system, causing her legs to tremble as she struggled to obey the dark-eyed man in front of her. Annabelle took a sharp intake of breath and rose.

She started to move towards him.

"Be still."

Annabelle shut her eyes against the onslaught of need that washed over her.

"Now turn around, lean over the desk, Annie Bell, bend over. Let me see that fine rump of yours."

Annabelle felt sexy as hell as she did what he asked. She saw him reach over for the yardstick. He was going to spank her ass with it. Chris had tried something similar and it was a complete disaster. She'd ended up running out of his red room of whatever.

She started to rise, but Roman put his hand on her back.

"Relax, Annie Bell, you have to pay for being a minx, you know," he said and lightly slapped her with the yardstick. It sounded loud, but the yardstick itself didn't cause much heat on her ass, just made her cunt quake with desire as it rubbed against the desk. He insinuated a finger into her cunt and let her hump against it for a few minutes.

"Not yet, Annie Bell, not yet."

Roman turned her to face him and proceeded to touch every part of her body. He caressed her hair, rubbed his thumb over her forehead, her cheeks, her lips, parted them and put his thumb into her mouth.

"Suck," he ordered.

Annabelle took the thumb gently into her mouth and licked it for a few seconds. Roman nodded. He stroked her brows with one hand while his other hand roved down her body, into the little divot made by her protruding collarbone. He dipped his head down and tongued the space.

Annabelle moaned as she felt the heat of his breath over her body, on her breasts.

"Spread your legs," he told her and she did, letting herself open for him as she leaned against the desk. She imagined she looked like a strumpet, some back alley whore waiting to be used and the thought excited her.

He removed his shirt and carefully folded it, placing it on the chair. She marvelled at his bare chest with its small amount of fine grey hairs. She would have loved to press her lips against his chest, but she was letting Roman guide her and it felt wonderful to do so. He undid his leather belt and held it up to her nose. The scent of leather overcame her. She opened her lips and licked along the belt, letting the dark taste enter her mouth.

Roman removed his trousers and briefs. His cock was fully erect, pointed towards her. She wanted it inside her. Roman pushed her onto the desk and pressed his naked body against

Amanda Earl

her own, breast to breast, belly to belly, cock to cunt. He put his finger on the nub of her cunt, stroking her clit, sliding the finger down into the valley of her cunt.

She writhed against his finger as his cock pressed hard into her thigh. She reached down to stroke him, his cockslit already spilling pre-come. He moved above her, pressed himself down onto her and into her cunt. They groaned as they fucked each other raw, their bodies covered in sweat, their tongues tasting each other's tongue.

She made a map of his body with her lips, lingering on the strong jawline of his face, his full lush lips, stroking his dark brows with her fingers. She stopped at his chest, pressing her hands against his strong shoulders, moving down to his still firm abs and then lower, lingering on his cock, opening her mouth and taking it down her tight warm throat, then sliding down further to lick his firm thighs, his inner thighs, his calves, his shins, to press a kiss onto the instep of each foot, to worship each toe, to throw herself at the ground before him as his slave.

And that was only the first night.

Over time, Annabelle discovered that Roman was a stable man with an even temperament, a well-endowed library and a fiendish imagination, as witnessed by the scene they were currently playing out in said library.

Slap. Annabelle felt the thud of the heavy tome on her naked derrière.

"No, Master, please stop."

"Then say it, Annie Bell, or I bring out the cane. Heathcliff was a fucked-up character."

She felt the cold book hit her ass once again. Her lover was going to destroy her prized rare edition. How dare he? It had been a gift from Chris, who was, she'd finally admitted to herself, the epitome of fuck-uppery. She contemplated using her safe word, something she'd not done yet. But the thought of the dastardly cane to come made her silent.

"You're being very bratty, Annie Bell." There it was, that

nickname again, the one Roman used when he was in no rush, when he wanted to tease her, to subject her to sexual torture so tantalizing it was more insistent, more frustrating than a tickle.

She heard the drawer slide open. The cane made a whistling sound as Roman sliced it through the air. Annabelle shivered in dread and anticipation.

"One last chance, Annabelle, say it or I decorate your ass. One . . ."

Annabelle squirmed, pressing her cunt and breasts hard against the red vinyl bench in the middle of the library.

"Two . . ." Roman drew a line down Annabelle's back with the cane.

Annabelle tensed her body, took a deep, cleansing breath, as they'd talked about, and let herself relax.

"Three!"

The cane struck her tender bottom. Annabelle felt a red burst of pain across her ass.

Again it hit. She tensed again, then breathed out and in. Focused on the feeling of the cane. Yielded as it hit her again and again. Her cunt grew wet, her nipples tightened against the hot vinyl.

"Now hump for me, Annabelle, fuck the bench."

As Roman continued to strike her ass with the cane, Annabelle had a brief flash of Heathcliff with his stormy eyes, standing over her and punishing her for ridiculing him. She rubbed her swollen clit against the sweaty bench. She felt Roman's hot breath against her face as he leaned down and whispered in her ear.

"Heathcliff was a fucked-up character," he said. "Keep fucking."

He dropped the cane and came to the front of the bench. She looked up to see his naked form looming above her, his cock hard and waiting for service.

"Open your mouth, Annabelle."

She warmed his cock with her mouth. He groaned as she licked and stroked him with her tongue, taking his cock deeper, letting it rest in her throat briefly. She resumed licking, tasting the first salt of his pre-come. She felt his hands around her neck, then sliding down her back as he leaned forward, tracing the marks of his cane on her ass, soothing it. Then he turned her over, spread her legs and fucked her raw.

Afterwards, over a cup of tea, they talked about the scene.

"I still can't forgive you for ruining that book, Roman."

"Annabelle, my dear, it was just a cheap copy. Your Heathcliff is safely stored behind the glass cabinet along with O, Justine, Simone, Marcelle and all the other deviant fictional characters you love so much. And you still have to be punished for not admitting how fucked up Heathcliff is."

"You're such a mind-fuck, Roman," Annabelle said as she poured another cup of English breakfast tea from the chipped Brown Betty.

He stuck his tongue out at her and returned to puffing on his calabash, as he read the newspaper. Annabelle wondered what their next scene would be. She hoped she would be assigned the role of O again as she arrived with her lover at Roissy. She loved the scene where O was blindfolded, covered only by a red cloak that revealed her naked breasts and shaved cunt. Loved it when O is being told the rules by the severe gentlemen. Perhaps Roman would even bring over other men to put a gloved hand inside her and enter her back passage.

They returned to their day. Roman to the library to catalogue rare books to send to customers, her to her preparation for the day's lesson. Because Annabelle really was a governess.

Madame Chocolat

Vanessa Clark

Have you ever tasted the chocolate from Madame Chocolat? In Paris 1952, on the Butte Montmartre, Madame Chocolat was the place where men, women, and children alike got their chocolate fix. No other *confiserie* in the entire city of Paris compared or matched the pure heavenly delight and ecstasy of biting into a Madame Chocolat truffle, bonbon, éclair, bar, tarte, or *canelé*. The craftsmanship and the art of the chocolate, its many shapes and designs, from the classic and simple to the whimsical and complex, were as admirable to the human eye as those who have seen the artwork of Vincent van Gogh and Théophile Steinlen. The delightful complexity of the flavors ranging from coconut, cinnamon, honey, cherry, raspberry, and rum, from the buttery high notes and the sour and sugary undertones, was as if it were steeped in all the flavors and textures of the trade. Who was responsible for all this? A woman. A woman whose real name not many actually knew; they only called her by the name of her popular *confiserie*, Madame Chocolat. She became a local celebrity, often on the cover of magazines and headlined in the newspaper. Not only for her famous chocolate creations, but because she was quite a beauty, who innocently but purposely used sex to sell her brand. Coming from both a French and Irish background, she was a buxom redhead with jaw-dropping curves, an infectious red-lipped smile, big green eyes, freckles on her cheek, and wore glasses that somehow added more to her already electrifying sex appeal. Looking part innocent housewife, part fiery burlesque dancer in one single image. She wore loud and colorful dresses that were as bright and flavorful as the decor of her shop, dresses that showcased every curve of her waist, hips and buttocks with the same tenderness and care as her chocolates were displayed in boxes and glass platforms. Cleavage and lips as supple as the finest of her chocolate-covered strawberries and cherries. Her walk, the sway of her hips, and the wink of her eye, luscious and captivating. A smile so sweet and charming that it made her proud display of sexual prowess seem not as manipulative or intimidating to the mothers who brought their children to see her and buy her chocolate. A smile that as innocent as it was could still bring about dirty thoughts to one's mind.

Perverted men and love-struck gay women came far and wide not just for her chocolate, but for *her*, to get a chance to catch a glimpse of her, to perhaps strike a conversation with her, and woo her, if they were lucky. Not many were so. Not because she was cold or distant, but because she was the one who liked to pursue, wished to conquer, not to be pursued and conquered. I, too, was deeply attracted to this successful and intriguing businesswoman, but just like many others, was unlucky enough not to attract her attention. Somehow, my roommate, friend and lover, Danielle, who preferred to be called by her drag persona Danny, was one of the lucky few who caught her eye. Danny did not usually divulge details of her erotic affairs with other women, since she knew that I was prone to jealousy (I did love her, I really did!), but when it came to Madame Chocolat (I later learned that her real name was Annette), I wanted to hear about every saucy escapade that the two shared. Though I still experienced a pang of jealousy and envy hearing about it, how aroused and wet I became when she told me of their countless passionate nights together. Making love underneath the stars, of taking promenades in the nude through the Père Lachaise cemetery, performing cunnilingus in the bathroom stalls of the Moulin Rouge, finger-fucking one another inside Notre Dame while mass was in session, and other erotic obscenities that made my jaw drop and my body shiver. Admittedly, as she would retell her sexcapades to me, I often fantasized of Annette and all the naughty things I could do to her and what she might do to me.

This fantasy was my secret, one that I kept to myself and did not dare act out in person. Especially when what was first only lust became a deep romance between her and Danny. A romance that I saw invade every fiber of Danny's soul. All she ever talked about was Annette. Most of her evenings were spent with Annette. It seemed as if every breath she took was so she could live for Annette. It turned into something even deeper than love; it was an obsession. I admired and was very much intrigued by this obsession, and to a small extent, very happy for her, but at the same time, I worried that her undying love was consuming her.

Gradually, I observed how Danny's habits had changed. She turned to smoking, drugs, and drinking in such a way that became unsavory and cringing. Her personality became more confrontational, irritable and boisterous, away from the fun, laid-back, and likeable Danny I used to know. The more I saw her change, the more I often wondered what it was about Annette that made her such a bad influence on my beloved friend. Every time I was with them, I closely observed her ways: how she had Danny wrapped around her finger, had control over her with every wink, pout and jiggle of her body, and how with those eyes and those eyes alone, she was more powerful than God and Danny had become her devout saint. How at times the seemingly harmless and gentle Annette had quite a temper and lashed out at Danny leaving bruises on her arms and shoulders and scratches on her face. How forgivable Danny was of her, how, despite Annette's controlling and devious behavior, she remained still in love with her, perhaps more than ever before. It sickened me to see Danny become such a weakling and a *pion*.

I only once confronted Danny about her sudden change of character and habits since dating Annette. She did not take it too well; she cursed and scolded me for being nosey and rude. It pained me to see Danny on the verge of tears for me speaking so negatively of Annette, so with that, I apologized, we cuddled and lavished an abundance of passionate kisses underneath the bed sheets like old times, and from there, I moved on, at least for the time being.

I focused my attention on a particular case that quickly became headline news. Some Parisian citizens (four to be precise) had died from a "stomach ailment" with no cause as to why or how it happened. All within a two-week period. I found this quite intriguing because these victims all happened to be masculine women not unlike Danny. Was it a coincidence that they all met with the same fate? I did not think so. It became the talk of the city. Every time the radio mentioned what they were calling *Les Morts Mystérieuses*, Danny would turn it off. Even the slightest mention of it by me made her tense, cold, nervous and defensive. It made me ponder if since these female victims so closely resembled her, a *gouine*, and in the way they dressed as men, that she was afraid that she may turn into the next unfortunate soul in the obituary column?

I found it quite odd and troubling how Danny changed even more after the news broke out. Her loud, vibrant, humorous personality became increasingly dull, jaded and worn. Her hair that was once short and healthy became matted, greasy and unkempt. She was more pale and skinnier with each passing day and night. In her face alone, I could sense a heavy darkness in her eyes, this burden on her shoulders, this weight pulling her down to the depths of sorrow and madness. I sensed that it all had to do with Annette and their rocky relationship that was taking a turn for the worse. I tried to keep all my thoughts, concerns and worry all to myself for her sake, but one fateful night, I had to speak. I had had enough.

Raindrops were falling on our heads as we were crossing the Place de la Concorde. My hand reached out to hers, gripping onto it tight.

"What is that for?" She smirked.

"I miss the way we held hands when we were lovers."

She didn't say anything; she gripped my hand as well in response.

"Talk to me, Danny. Like the way we used to, about everything. Lately you've seemed so . . . dejected. Is there something wrong?"

Silence was still her friend and my worst enemy. The only other thing I could say was a phrase I hadn't told her in quite a long time: "*Je t'aime.*"

"*Je t'aime aussi, ma chérie* . . ." she whispered.

She was silent again, but this time, I knew she was trying to sort out what else to say. We stopped at the Jardin des Tuileries, standing underneath a tree to partially shield ourselves from the rain. She embraced me in a way that she hadn't done since dating Annette. Tight. As if holding on for dear life to the strength of our love. Then she kissed me. A kiss that only dreams are made of, with hope and longing. When our lips parted, she whispered into my ear, "Annette and I are going through some problems. I can't tell you why because . . ."

She began to cry. The tears fell heavily down her cheeks; and she laid her head deep into my shoulder as she shivered uncontrollably.

"Annette will kill me if I utter a word."

The tone of her voice gave me chills. She had never sounded so serious and urgent. Her fear and her paranoia were tightly coiled by the strength of her words, causing me to find it hard to breathe, suffocating in the emotion.

"You don't really mean that, do you?" I responded.

"I mean every word."

I held her desperately, saying "Nobody is going to harm you, not while I'm here."

Later that evening, I advised her that perhaps she should leave Paris for a holiday, to take a break from Annette and from the burden she was carrying of Annette's secret. How relieved I was that she was not angered by my suggestion. Instead, she took it as sincere advice from a dear friend. A couple of days later, she left for Calais. She would remain there for a couple of months to free herself from her demons and troubles.

Since her leaving, the *Morts Mystérieuses* had slowly

dissipated in the press. Yet, I felt driven to continue doing my research on the case for it still left me with an intense curiosity that I couldn't shake off. Whenever I looked back on how Danny had reacted to every mention of it, it further drove me to read more about it. I perused every article I could find. There was one that described in detail the state of one of the victims: cold as ice and stiff as a board on her bed with an empty box of chocolates from Madame Chocolat on the floor. I felt almost sick to my stomach at just seeing the name of Annette's *confiserie*. Wondering to myself what secret Annette wanted Danny to keep, and just how dark and deep it was to cause Danny such fear and for Annette to create such a threat to her.

Nothing about Annette had changed since Danny's departure. She was still the centerpiece of many culinary magazines, the muse for many artists in the streets of Paris, and an object of lust and desire, the forbidden fruit that one yearned to take a bite from. I would be lying to myself if I said I didn't still have unforgivable feelings for Annette. I went to her *confiserie* more often, wearing black pants, a white blouse and a black tie, with my hair cut shorter an inch above my shoulders, admiring her from afar. To my surprise, she did take notice of me, and we crossed paths more often: in the park, at the bar, along the Champs-Élysées. Exchanging "*bonjours*" and "*au revoirs*" to one another, until one day, she invited me to join her for lunch, just her and me. From that *déjeuner* onwards, we met further for coffee, for a drink and for walks in the park, talking for hours. We weren't becoming lovers, but, at times, I imagined that we were. We playfully flirted with one another, never kissing, never holding hands, but often being cheek to cheek, hip to hip, and shoulder to shoulder. It all seemed so innocent, fun, and comforting, until that one fateful day when she invited me to her apartment for me to sample her newest chocolate creation before it made its debut at Madame Chocolat.

I had only ever dreamed of Annette appearing before me in her natural goddess-like splendor. A dream that in a matter of only half an hour came true before my eyes. After a conversation over a glass of whiskey about mundane affairs, I sat on the couch in her tiny but cosy living room as I waited for her to showcase her new chocolate cordials. When she walked in, blood rushed immediately to my clitoris, causing it to swell, while the rest of my body buzzed with an indescribable pleasure that I had never felt before until that moment. Annette was completely nude. I was hypnotized by the bounce of her gorgeous breasts and the sway of her hips as she moved towards me, holding a tray of four gorgeous, delectable bite-sized cordials on a silver platter. My mouth gaped as she lay on her back on the long coffee table that was in front of me; immediately I realized that she was the table, and I was to dine on her new chocolates over her bare naked flesh. She placed each chocolate cordial on the most delicious areas of her body: one on each breast, one on her belly button, and one between her legs.

"*Bon appétit,*" she cooed, her devilish eyes staring straight into mine.

"Annette." I trembled. "You can't be serious . . . how can I eat with you . . . like this."

"Don't be shy." She winked. "How can one resist a home-made cordial?"

My hands slightly shook as I sat on my knees before her, and took a bite out of the cordial. With one bite the hazelnut-flavored syrup spilled on her perky nipple.

"I'm sorry!" I gasped. "Already making a mess!"

"You silly girl," she laughed. "Lick it off me. Make me clean."

Her eyes, that smile, seemed more devious by each second. In the back of my head I thought of Danny, and what she would think if she knew what I was doing right now. I wanted to stop, I wanted to get up and walk out, but I could not, the syrup glistening on her breast and nipple looked so divine . . . too irresistible. I did as I was told and sucked it off, making her clean. I bit into the other cordial; the same mess occurred and, without being told the second time, I hungrily sucked the raspberry-flavored syrup off her nipple, sucking on it harder, long after I licked and slurped every drop. The cordial that I ate above her belly button created an even more glorious mess; her entire belly was dripping with *jus de cordial*. It was not the whiskey that made me drunk and mad, but it was that body, my tongue dancing along every curve of her, chasing after the syrup, sucking her flesh into my mouth so I could taste it, bite it, moan and growl against it, until she too moaned, growled and panted for more. When it came time for me to sample the last cordial that was placed between her legs . . .I no longer had a desire to eat it. Instead, I wanted to eat *her*. Without needing to ask, and as if she read my mind, her long legs wrapped around my neck like a serpent ready to make me its prey, as my tongue dived into her wet and glistening cunt. It tasted sweeter than the cordial, more delicious than any chocolate of hers that I ever had the pleasure of eating, more sinful than gluttony. My tongue swam and drowned in the depths of her, as well as my four fingers, swirling and twirling and churning into her, creating a smooth creamy white butter that was her come.

At a later point in the evening, she had me use her monstrous dildo on her, and I fucked her in such a way that I had never fucked a woman before. With a powerful thrust that was so hard and wicked it even caught me by surprise. How I made her scream, cry and come for me all night until the sun came up. Until our nude bodies became too exhausted to move, and, even then, my mouth and my fingers still had the strength to zap her back into erotic oblivion. Her scream, her cry, and the display of ecstasy that we shared echoed for days and nights onward, becoming a sweet lullaby that lulled me to sleep in pure heavenly delight, but also became a nightmare that kept me awake in a cold sweat.

The guilt drove me crazy. Yet, I was still crazy for her and afraid of her, but I had to do what was right. I told Annette that me coming to her apartment was a mistake and that I no longer wanted us to carry on the way things were. She thought it funny that I suddenly had a change of heart, but I sensed her anger and humility at being rejected by me. It was then that I truly felt the fear . . . a fear of the uncertainty of what she was capable of.

Days following our first and only night of debauchery, I got a letter from Danny. A frightening letter that revealed Annette's secret, a secret that Danny could no longer keep, and that she could only tell to me and me alone so to relieve herself from the burden. The chocolates that Annette had built her entire career and livelihood out of were also what she would use to kill for pleasure as well as for profit. For any woman who she used to love, a love that would turn into hate and revenge, she would make a single chocolate filled with poison. A poison that was hardly noticeable because the recipe she included it in was extra sweet and rich. She would send it to her ex-lover as a token of forgiveness, as a souvenir of her love. Any close friend of hers who was as wicked and evil as she was would also pay her a hefty fee to create a killer-chocolate so they could use it to steal the life of any person they wished to be gone. The *Morts Mystérieuses* were all her doing. Neither for pleasure, nor for profit. Just for fun. Taking the lives of women that she dated, courted, or slept with. I could not believe it, that she not only did it but had got away with it, with no conscience and no remorse. Now I understood it all. Danny's downward spiral into despair and hopelessness. Danny loved Annette, but how could one love a killer? And now there I was, becoming like Danny. Carrying the guilt of me sleeping with my best friend's lover, the shame of me falling for Annette's trap of seduction and infidelity, and now the burden of her secret that I was sworn to keep as well, was eating me alive. Did Annette notice? Did she care? Could she care? Did she have a heart at all? A woman like that noticed with watchful eyes as sharp and agile as a hawk, but a woman like that would never have a care for the innocent. There was only one mission: *créer pour destruire*, to conquer and to destroy.

A week later, I received another letter from Danny. She wrote: *Now I know why you wanted me to leave for Calais! Annette told me. You wanted me away so you could take her as your own, to replace me as hers! Dressing like me, acting as me, and seducing her and making love to her as if you were me. You are as evil as she is. I want nothing to do with you, ever again. This pain I feel is worse than death, it's pure hell. ALL BECAUSE OF YOU AND HER!*

I screamed as I read her writing. In an indescribable rage, I went to Annette's apartment, and from the moment she opened the door, I pushed her to the floor and began strangling her, wrapping my hands around her neck. She laughed wickedly, as if she enjoyed my choking her. I let her go, and could do nothing else but cry and ask, "Why?" She stood up, looked down at me, and smiled.

"Because I want her dead," she snarled. "And the only way she'll die is if she knew that her precious Lynn tried to take me from her. And I want you to suffer too for rejecting me."

She was mad. How could she want to kill a woman she loved? A woman that I loved?

I knew that Annette had the power to kill through chocolate, but never did I think that she could kill with words and words alone. I wrote a letter back to Danny explaining my faults, explaining the error of my ways, and confirming that my intention in wanting her to leave for Calais was only to save herself from Annette. I only wished what was best for her. I told her that I loved her more than she'd ever know or realize. I never heard back from her. Instead, I heard back from her brother. I received the news from him in a letter that she had committed suicide by hanging.

The next day, I received a package. A bright pink box wrapped with a golden ribbon. On the ribbon the words "Madame Chocolat" were stitched. I opened it, and knew exactly what it was. Death disguised in the form of one single chocolate shaped as a heart. Underneath the chocolate was a note, in Annette's writing. She wrote:

Chère Lynn,
My condolences for the death of Danny . . . I send to you this chocolate as a token of my love. All it takes is one to take away the pain. My thoughts and prayers are with you. Until we meet again . . .
Sincerely,
Madame Chocolat

Federico

Michèle Larue

Translated by Noel Burch

The first time I rang his bell, Federico opened the door stark naked. His tanned body seemed very much at ease in its suit of skin. He had a dancer's long muscles and loose blond curls. His laughing brown eyes perpetually sought to seduce, all the while conveying an enigmatic aloofness which intrigued me no end.

"I love doing things with my hands, how would you like a massage, Wendy?"

"Well . . . uh . . . sure, why not?"

I was one of those women who are keen to flaunt their sexual liberation, but are also quite timid: a half-dozen occasional lovers were always greeted by the sight of my body in a dim light and fragmented by lingerie. After a few text messages between us, I had no problem accepting a date at Federico's place. I was turned on knowing he sculpted human figures and posed in the nude at L'École des Beaux-Arts. At least that was what he'd told modest little me, sitting zipped to the neck in the rowing machine next to his at that fitness club where we both worked out . . . Federico wanted to know what was under my full body-suit . . . My long, Nordic locks seemed to fascinate him . . .

Maybe he'd run out of models, I thought to myself, as I undressed, hidden in a recess in his studio wall, not a little disturbed (excited?) by the idea of his seeing me naked and running his hands over my skin.

Cloaked in a kimono that was waiting for me, I followed him across his studio, climbed after him onto a bed that took up a whole alcove. I had to remove my kimono and lie on my back in broad daylight! I wished I could bury my face in the pillow. He sat cross-legged between my thighs. I felt embarrassed and avoided his gaze for fear of blushing. All the while he was massaging me, I stared at his hairless chest. He asked me to turn over. The new position made me imagine he couldn't see me any more. I offered him my buttocks and his hands lingered there for a while.

Each time we had a date in his studio on the heights of Ménilmontant, I trembled as I disrobed, thrilling to the anticipated feel of his hands on my skin. Federico was a superb masseur. He knew where and how to touch me. Inside and out. I paid him with a thousand tremors, abandoning myself to the whims of his fingers on my skin, achieving a kind of ecstasy. Time stood still. His touch was unique, sensual, inimitable. Back in the street, I said to myself I had "discovered" the god of caresses.

Federico was a *plasticien*, he worked with clay and plaster. His high reliefs all represented female bodies, their mouths open, heads thrown back. Women's bodies were his soul source of inspiration. After a massage one day, I thought I recognized myself in one of those white plaster portraits, lit by the sun streaming through the glass roof, and so realistic it might have been cast from life. It had my hair, my mouth . . .

"It looks like me, doesn't it?" I said to Federico, transfixed by the image.

"My sculptures of women all look alike," he replied airily. The first time we met at the gym, I'd been taken aback by his casual manner. I thought he might be working there as a coach since he seemed to know everybody, exchanging a few words with this person or that, always with that same superior smile. Our own relationship was confined to those moments of intimacy in his alcove after a couple of text messages if we hadn't run into each other at the gym.

Then one day he invited me to a soirée. At last I was going

to meet the art-school mates he'd told me about: they were organising a party in his studio. One afternoon, we had just finished an erotic massage in the alcove when his friend Renato popped in, another Italian, a distinguished-looking, delicate-featured dandy. Renato had a sister, Eva, whom Federico had referred to as a sex bomb. She too posed in the nude for art students.

"Eva is going to give a performance at the party. She has amazing breasts."

"A striptease, I suppose?"

"I'm not allowed to talk about it, it's a surprise."

I arrived at ten sharp, wearing a skirt as requested by Federico. The three front rows of chairs and sagging sofas lent by neighbours for the occasion were entirely occupied by women. All of them quite pretty. All of them wearing dresses or skirts. Federico had given us all the same instruction: no slacks! I recognized a dozen women from the gym; I felt a twinge of jealousy thinking they too will have had their massages in Federico's alcove. Some forty spectators were seated facing an empty set – an armchair, a pedestal table and a vintage telephone – when Eva arrived, a yellow PVC handbag on her arm.

A tall brunette with voluptuous hips, wearing high-heeled mules in red patent leather and a white see-through blouse with rolled-up sleeves. Her bra was visible and could scarcely contain her breasts. Federico had not been exaggerating. She was a hot number. Enticing in the manner of a sixties pin-up. She sat down next to the phone and gazed at it languorously, running a nonchalant hand through her dark hair. The performance consisted of a monologue, a one-woman show. Screwing up a bright red mouth with too much lipstick, Eva started telling us about the married man she was expecting to ring any minute now, pouring out an account of the dates cut short and the hours spent waiting, the usual routine for a married man's mistress. She droned on about how hot she was for this man, whom she was prepared to marry as soon as he got a divorce for her sake. These amorous illusions recited by a telephone reminded me of Cocteau's play, *La Voix Humaine*. The summer holidays had just begun, and Eva's lover was with his family in Brittany. While she was waiting, Eva explained, she made daily use of her sex toys. Matching her action to her words, she opened the yellow handbag and took out a mother-of-pearl vibrator and began to stroke it with a lewd gaze, all the while painting a cynical portrait of other men, the gullible womanizers who promise the moon and never keep their word. The audience was suspended on her fleshy lips, waiting for her to demonstrate the sex toy she was using now to stroke her breasts through the thin fabric of her blouse. Was she about to slowly roll up the flowered skirt that lay in pleats around her naked legs and slip the sex toy between her thighs? During the pauses between sentences, Eva sighed deeply and ran her tongue over her lips. With this woman, anything seemed possible.

Suddenly, female screeches could be heard coming from the front row and two guests were waving their hands wildly: the woman with them had fainted. The heat, no doubt. All these people crowded into this studio in the middle of July. Federico went to the woman who'd collapsed on floor. He applied a damp handkerchief to her forehead, he gave her the kiss of life. When she failed to regain consciousness, he asked Renato to call the firemen.* Bent over the woman again, Federico was slapping her lightly on the cheeks when the lights went out. Renato exhorted the audience to keep calm. It was just a power failure. Torch strapped to his forehead, he vanished into the hallway looking for the fuse box.

The stricken woman lay stretched on the concrete floor in the beam of the head-torch Federico was now wearing as well. Her face appeared in a pallid blue halo, her arms and legs gracefully splayed like a broken doll's on either side of a mini-skirt, which had ridden up to reveal the tops of her thighs.

A few minutes later, helmeted and dark as winter shadows,

---

* In France, as perhaps nowhere else, it is customary to call upon the fire department to deal with an emergency of this kind.

the firemen arrived hard on Renato's heels in a thunder of boots. They bent over the ailing woman. One of them applied the kiss of life, kneeling beside her in the halo of blue light. The woman opened her eyes, gripped the fireman's leather jacket, began detaching his belt. The fireman assisted her, sliding his trousers down around his thighs. His hard-on was plainly visible, in the centre of the beam of light. The woman opened her mouth and swallowed the stiff dick. We looked on in amazement, as the fellatio went on and on. Commentaries came thick and fast. "A plucky lot, these firemen," a woman remarked to a slovenly chap who'd sidled up to her and laid a hand on her knee. "Sometimes they wake me up at night, because you see I live near the firehouse and when there's an alarm—" The man silenced her with a kiss.

The torchlight wandered away from the stricken woman and made a beeline for Eva where she sat by her vintage phone, skirt wrapped around her waist, sucking the cock that a fireman with his trousers down was holding in his hand over the armrest of her chair, while another firefighter stood behind her vigorously masturbating her with the sex toy, while his other hand held out his glistening cock like an offering in the torchlight, tugging ostentatiously at the foreskin. Two women crawled to his feet and vied for his cock, both licking it simultaneously in the circle of light. Firemen were copulating with women from the front row, all of whom appeared to be having a whale of a time, with their skirts up. One was lying on the floor, another squatting on a fireman's belly, with the bright beam sweeping over them from time to time like a watchtower searchlight. One of the men pulled my head back and kissed me full on the mouth. On her knees beside me a busy woman was noisily sucking him off. He released my mouth and withdrew from the woman's to come on the floor. The firemen left the studio as they had arrived in a thunder of boots.

The lights were still out and Eva lazily resumed her one-woman show. Her chair was bathed in the beam of an industrial spotlight powered by a humming battery. An empty silence pervaded the room, interspersed with moans and sighs. One could hear the rustle of clothing being rearranged.

Renato's perverse instincts, however, did not stop there. A few minutes had gone by when a stealthy herd of four-footed animals entered the studio. I felt rough hair on my legs. Sheep and goats were nuzzling between the women's thighs, bleating in the darkness.

Terrified at the idea of what might come next, I took to my heels without asking for my due. When I returned one afternoon to enjoy the skill of his hands in the alcove, Federico refused to tell me what happened after I left.

The Corruption of
the Innocent Pornographer

Destiny Moon

When asked what she wanted for Christmas, my lover told me she wanted an *experience*. She didn't need any *things*, she emphasized. It's true. She is a minimalist. She has that perfect butch bathroom equipped with a bar of soap, a toothbrush, natural toothpaste and unscented lotion. She is still using the same bottle of shampoo she was using when we first started dating almost one year ago.

Even though my own bathroom is full of products and scented delights, I never want to change anything about her. She's the yin to my yang.

It only took a couple of clicks online to find an experience I was quite sure she would treasure: a stay at a bed and breakfast called The Chocolate Suite, run by a couple of passionate chocolatiers who make organic chocolate from scratch. In addition to their chocolate shop storefront, they created the ultimate lesbian fantasy – a private resort where the decor is chocolate brown and the shelves are lined with chocolate-themed movies and books. Guests also get a complimentary box of chocolates. I was sold. I booked it and then I proudly announced – in the first week of December – that my Christmas shopping was officially done.

That was not entirely true because I still needed to buy beeswax candles, new lingerie, massage oil and wrist restraints. All month, she was tortured and wanted to know what treat I was preparing for her. I told her she was in control and if she really wanted to know, all she had to do was ask and I'd tell her. The traditionalist in her couldn't stand the thought of finding out before Christmas morning so, like a good bottom, she waited patiently.

Meanwhile, I plotted. I planned. I turned myself on thinking about everything I was going to surprise her with. Semi-frustrated, I masturbated. No amount of solo climaxes equaled the pleasure that I craved. Throughout December, we maintained our scheduled dates. We had the same stellar sex we always have. But secretly, I longed to take us in a new direction.

But before I go on, I need to back up. To fully appreciate the events that took place at The Chocolate Suite, it is important to understand a few things about my lover. The first thing is that she is a pornographer. She documents lesbian sex and, as a natural spin-off of filming lesbian sex as a business, she also starred in a number of lesbian porn movies, some of her own design and some directed by others. In other words, she knows lesbian sex. She has seen a lot and had a lot. She has a massive circle of fans. She's one of those people who make regular appearances on lists of hot lesbians.

When that was all I knew about her, I wasn't that interested in dating her. I didn't want to be with a "hot lesbian" if she had the ego of one so I spent a long time ignoring her advances. In fact, for half a year, I only saw her to work out. We'd walk or go to the gym and whenever she suggested that something beyond that, I said no.

I had yet to learn the other things about her, the things that make her who she is – the woman I love. She grew up in a small prairie town. Her mother is a minister. She went to Bible camp throughout her youth and she's still deeply spiritual. In addition to being a lesbian sex symbol, she is also painfully shy. She is more of a voyeur than an exhibitionist.

One day, while we were out for a walk, a couple of months before we started dating, she confessed something to me. She told me she is vanilla. I paused. I looked at her. I shook my head. She had just come back from a play party she helped to organize in a different city.

"People don't believe me," she pleaded.

"Of course they don't." I said.

After that, we processed the stuff she had witnessed at the party, things she said she didn't understand. Poor dear.

"My business is lesbian sex. I'm in those circles. People just assume I'm kinky and that I've tried everything but I'm not and I haven't."

I didn't know why she was divulging this to me, but I found it fascinating and encouraged her to tell me more. As workout partners, I found out about her previous relationships and her favorite and least favorite sexual memories. We talked in ways that only workout partners can – panting and sweating up and down hills and pathways without any sexual stimulation. At the time, I was celibate and single and consciously so. I had ended several overlapping poly relationships that called for a pause. I was in a time of self-reflection. I was more than happy to listen to other people's sex stories, especially hers.

She became a curious oddity to me, like Bettie Page. Even though Bettie Page became the poster girl of early kink portraiture, she maintained a certain naive quality, like she never really knew why others found her sexually attractive. In her later years, she gave it all up and went back to the church to live a quiet, humble life of worship and fellowship. Though I and her many fans miss her, I respect her ability to walk away and recreate herself.

Time passed and, eventually, I said yes when my lover asked me on an official date. By then, I already felt like I knew her, respected her, understood her in ways that I hadn't before. That was just before Christmas 2010.

This is Christmas 2011. A year of dating turned out to be a year of bliss and, now that I understood all of these various aspects of my lover, I had also come to understand how delightfully shy she really was.

Once she had identified herself as vanilla to me, it took her a long time to convince me she could be otherwise. It wasn't that I didn't believe her – I spotted the inner Bottom in her a mile away – I just loved teasing her. I loved torturing her. I loved the way she'd blush and become tongue-tied whenever I asked about her fantasies. Pushed to talk about what she wanted, she'd admit that she wanted to be taken, that she fantasized about being dominated and that she really wanted me to have my way with her. This was all music to my ears and I did have my way. A lot.

So, when she asked for *an experience* and when I then came up with the idea of going to a cosy chocolatey retreat on an island, I also had something else in mind.

Only two days after I told her what the present was, we were off. We each carried a backpack. Hers had her clothes and a waterproof jacket so we could hike, even in the rain. Mine was mostly filled with sex toys. We got on the ferry and forgot all about our lives back home. Everything blurred as we crossed the channel in the typical misty, rainy west coast weather.

From the ferry terminal, we hiked along a winding path up the side of a mountain to the village where we met one of the chocolatiers. He showed us to our room, gave us the key and told us he'd bring us Americanos and biscotti in the morning.

"Perfect," I said, locking the door as soon as he left.

"It's gorgeous," my lover said, looking around. She started exploring the pamphlets left out on the dresser about the area, but I was more interested in exploring her.

"Let's check out the shower," I said.

"Mmm," she moaned, "Sounds fantastic."

We opened the door to the bathroom and immediately she commented on the craftsmanship of the shower tiles, how nicely they'd been laid. I appreciate a knowledgeable butch and her eye for detail. I unbuttoned the top button of her shirt and she did the rest. Our clothes were on the floor almost immediately and she adjusted the knobs in the shower to get the temperature just right.

Underneath the steamy steady flow of water, we held each other and exhaled.

"I don't know how my breasts got so dirty," I said. "You'd better lather them up. You wouldn't want to be stuck out here in the woods with a filthy girl, would you?"

"Maybe I would," she said, taking the orange-scented soap in her hands and lathering. Once she had a nice mass of bubbles, she took my breasts in her hands and smeared the frothy soap all over them. My nipples responded to her touch and I could feel my clit doing the same. After some delicious kissing in the wetness of the shower, I needed to get her on the bed.

We toweled off in the bathroom and she got dressed in her new pajamas, my stocking present to her. They fit perfectly and she looked adorable. Sometimes all I want is to cosy up to her and cuddle with her. I love the way our bodies feel next to each other and I love the way she looks in pajamas, but it wasn't what I wanted in that moment. I let her try out the bed while I stayed in the bathroom and changed into my new lingerie, a lacy lavender camisole that barely touched my thighs.

"Wow," she said when I came out, "you look beautiful."

"Really?" I smiled, ever so delighted.

"Yes," she said. "You're so pretty. You're so sexy. I'm so lucky."

"I'm the lucky one," I said. I went into my backpack and pulled out a locked black box containing all of the goodies I'd brought. I carried it over to the side table and set it down. Her eyes widened. I clicked the box open and pulled out the restraints.

"Oooh," she gasped.

Then I pulled out the candles.

"Oh, my," she said.

Finally, I pulled out a bottle of massage oil.

"Take your shirt off," I said, "I want to rub you."

She took it off. I climbed on top of her, straddling her the way I do when I want to orgasm. She still had her pajama bottoms on. I gave her hips a squeeze with my inner thighs and then I rubbed my breasts in her face because I couldn't help myself. I can never help myself.

I held the bottle of oil up and, from several feet above her, I let a couple of drops fall. Then a couple more. I started to rub her chest with the oil and then I leaned down and whispered in her ear. "I have something special planned for you."

"I can't wait," she said.

"You'll have to," I replied. "It's for tomorrow."

"Oh?"

She gave me her best sad puppy eyes so I told her that tonight was just a prelude. As I rubbed her shoulders and chest with oil, I told her what tomorrow would bring.

"I want to restrain you," I said, taking hold of her wrists with my hands. I leaned down on them. "I want to take away your ability to move."

"Mm hmm," she moaned.

"And then I want to slather you with oil," I continued, as I went back to massaging her chest. I concentrated on her breasts, squeezing her nipples between my forefinger and thumb. "Then I want to take this candle . . ."

I reached into the box and pulled out the dark red beeswax candle. "And I want to drop melted wax on you."

She didn't say anything but only because she was nervous. Her smile told me everything I needed to know.

"You see, this weekend, we're corrupting you. You may have been an innocent pornographer up until this point but you're about to be hardcore."

"Oooh," she moaned. "I want you to pop my kink cherry."

"Oh, I know you do."

"I want you to do anything you want with me."

"Oh really," I said.

"Yes."

"You dirty slut," I said.

"Oh yeah." She nodded.

"You're not vanilla at all, are you?"

She shook her head.

"Yeah," I said, "I didn't think so."

I took off her pajama bottoms and pulled out the oil again.

This time I held it up over her pussy and, like before, squeezed out a couple of drops.

"This is what it'll be like when I drop wax onto you," I explained, "only it'll be hot."

"This *is* hot."

"It sure is." I nodded. I massaged her pussy from her belly downwards and from her inner thighs inwards. Finally, I arrived at the wetness. I ran my fingers over her and gasped in delight.

"You are so kinky, my love. Just look at how wet you are, thinking all your dirty, dirty thoughts about tomorrow."

"I know. I am."

"You're a pervert."

"I am! I am a pervert."

"And I'm so glad," I whispered. Then I reached behind her for a pillow and propped her hips on it. "I want to lick your pussy for a while before I let you strap on your cock and fuck me."

She nodded eagerly and moaned beneath my tongue. She let her hips relax into the moment, let me slide my tongue up and down her delectable opening. When we both became too eager, too aroused to stand it any longer, she reached for the vibrator. She buzzed herself into a blissful cloud of ecstasy. My own pussy, meanwhile, throbbed and ached in desperation.

She went to the bathroom and came back adorning her sexy cock. When she lay back down, I straddled her again. I rode her cock up and down as she squeezed my nipples and watched me writhe in delight. She grabbed on to my breasts and took my nipples in her mouth one by one, alternating back and forth in precisely the way she knows that I love. I moaned and writhed and then bucked on top of her as a massive orgasm built within me and exploded all over her. Deflated, I sighed and exhaled and rested on her chest, her cock still inside of me. My muscles pulsated around her and she held me tight as I experienced the overwhelming relief I needed.

When I finally flipped over on my back, she slipped out of her leather strap-on and sat up.

"Oh," she said, almost ladylike, "what's over here?"

She reached for the box of organic chocolates.

"Oh, yeah," I moaned. "Let's open it."

"It'll be like an after-sex cigarette only way better," she joked. She has never been a smoker.

The box contained twelve filled truffle chocolates in various shapes and with various outer dips. We each selected one. She put hers in her mouth and began moaning again, this time even louder than when she climaxed.

"Oh my God," she said. "It's sea salt and caramel and dark chocolate ganache."

I took a bite of mine and immediately related to her sounds. I could feel them coming out of me as well.

"Oh my God," I exclaimed, "this one is kind of spicy and cinnamony with a creamy center."

The chocolate coated my tongue with a rich velvety layer of perfection. We discovered heaven. Over the course of the evening, we became so acquainted with heaven that all twelve divine morsels disappeared. We even invented a new term: mouth-gasm.

The following day, we woke up to Americanos and biscotti at our door. We kissed each other, sipped our espresso beverages and relived the memories of the night before. We made arrangements for another box of chocolates and then, like good lesbians, we went for a hike in the surrounding woods. For two hours, we clambered up and down forest terrain, making our way around a beautiful lake. We talked about resolutions, feelings, and everything that came to mind.

Part of what I treasure so much about my lover is that we can have the most amazing mind-blowing sex and we can also revert to our days of being walking buddies. We can talk about anything. Or nothing. Sometimes it's nice to just walk together in silence.

But once we neared our room, I confessed to her that I'd

been thinking of nothing but this adventure ever since the first week of December and I couldn't wait to get her back to bed so I could play with her.

Back in our room, I showered first. Then I sent her in. While she was in the shower, I went into my backpack and pulled out a sheet I'd brought from home. The main hazard of wax play (that is, if proper safety procedures are followed) is ruined sheets. I also affixed the wrist restraints to the bed. I put the candles on the table, got a lighter out, and clicked open the bottle of massage oil.

I folded up my lover's pajamas and put them on her side table. She came out of the bathroom with a chocolate-brown towel wrapped around her. She saw the arranged bed and immediately her shyness came out. Instinctively, she went for her pajamas.

"Not so fast," I said. "You won't be needing them."

She gulped. "Somehow I thought you might say that."

"I have something else for you to do instead."

"What's that?"

"Come here."

She came over. I sat her down on the bed.

"Your task is to sit here," I said, patting the middle of the bed where I'd propped up some pillows. "I want you to come here and find a position you'll be comfortable in."

She complied but I could tell she was nervous so I kissed her, long and slow and, as our tongues found each other, I could feel her tension disappear.

"I'm not going to do anything you won't like," I said. But then I thought about it for a moment and added, "At least, if I do, it'll be an accident and I'll stop immediately if you say you don't like it."

"I trust you," she said.

"Good," I said, "I never want to do anything to jeopardize that. I love you."

"I love you, too."

"Now come here and give me your wrists."

"OK." She smiled.

"You're so willing to do whatever I say," I observed. "No resistance whatsoever. You must be more of a pervert than I thought, my little Bottom."

She giggled. "I am."

In seconds, her wrists were behind her head, interlocked with each other and attached to the frame of the solid wood bed.

"How's that?" I asked.

"It feels great."

"Try to get loose."

She wriggled and struggled.

"It's no fun if you're not truly rendered helpless."

"I can't move," she said.

"Oh, good."

I straddled her, like I'd done the day before. This time, our pussies touched and I was well aware that she could feel just how wet I was.

I held the oil above her and teased her a little with it before I squirted some out. It splashed on her naked helpless chest and began to dribble down her. I squeezed the bottle some more and watched carefully as the drops fell. Then I slathered the oil all over her, taking special care to squeeze her nipples each time I passed over them.

I excused myself, went to the bathroom and came back with scissors.

"What are these for?" I asked. "Nervous?"

She shook her head. "Maybe a little."

Then I held up the hand-dipped beeswax candles and snipped the wick between them. I put the scissors down along with one of the candles. She looked relieved.

I caressed her with the candle, passing it over her chest like it was a wand that would create a new kind of magic for her.

Then I lit the candle and held it upright for a while to let her get used to the idea.

"Does this make you nervous?" I asked.

"I used to be a firefighter, remember?" she replied. "I used to have to run into burning buildings."

"Yes, but you weren't tied up and helpless, were you?"

"No."

"And you weren't being straddled by a kinky pervert who enjoys inflicting pain."

"Unfortunately, I was not."

I nodded. Then I whispered, "Good answer."

Holding the candle with my right hand, I put my left palm over her chest. "I think you're ready."

I moved my left hand.

Ever so slowly, I tilted the candle. It dripped. Smack. A drop of hot wax hit her chest and she gasped. It hardened immediately. So did her nipples. I moved my hand a little and another drop of wax fell on her. She flinched.

"It hurts more than I thought it would," she said.

"Too much?"

"No. I like it."

"I thought you might."

We found a beautiful rhythm. My dripping, her wincing and flinching and squirming and resisting her natural desire to resist. Moment by moment, we were intensely present, hyper aware of any and all changes.

I let the wax drip over her, inching closer and closer to her left nipple and finally right on it. She held her breath. When I thought she'd had enough, I let her have one more drop and then I stopped. I blew out the candle and put it down.

"That was really intense," she said.

"That was just half the fun. It's also fun when it comes off."

I got a plastic card out and began to scrape the wax off, drop by drop. She moaned.

"That feels good," she said.

I nodded.

I held her and told her I was proud of her, that she was a great bottom and that I loved her.

"And now I'm going to lick your pussy and I want you to direct me because, you see, I want to make you come that way."

"I don't want to direct you."

"Too bad. You have to."

"Um, OK." She gulped. "I guess it's all about endurance. Oh, and up and down motion, but not too heavy."

"Oh, now see? There you go. That's good direction."

My tongue made its way to her wetness and I did just as she said, feeling so privileged to be there with her, honored that she was letting me have my way with her. I really wanted nothing more than to let her body release all of the tension that I could feel she had built up. All of that anticipation. All of those heightened nerves. The intensity of surrendering to someone else's whims and giving up control so that I could take it. I appreciated her so much in that moment. Up and down, my tongue explored the landscape of her labia, made its way over the summit of her clit. Up and down. I could have kept going forever and ever. This was better than chocolate, even organic handcrafted chocolate. And then, she began to writhe and pulsate and moan. I kept my movements as steady as I could. She gasped.

"Oh my God. Oh my God," I heard her say.

Moments later, released from her restraints, I held her in my arms.

"You're a bone fide kinky pervert," I said. "You can hold your head up high at any play party from now on, my sweet sexy bottom."

She smiled. I cradled her in my arms.

"And now for a mouth-gasm," I said, reaching for the box of chocolates. She chose one of the filled chocolates and took a bite. Then she moaned and I watched the tip of her tongue slowly disappear into the creamy center of the truffle.

"Oh my God. Oh my God!" she cried out.

A look of peaceful ecstasy came over her as she savored every sweet moment of the chocolate. I stroked her skin, as her body found returned to its characteristically calm equilibrium. I held her close, absorbing the bliss of our connection.

Then I had my way with her again. And again.

MAN OF MARBLE

N. J. Streitberger

Viola stepped down from the carriage after it had finished rocking. She looked up at the studded wooden doors of the great house and wondered why her uncle hadn't emerged to greet her.

Lord Rookwood was, after all, her last living relative.

She had come at his invitation. In truth, she had had little choice in the matter. At sixteen, she was an orphan, having lost both her parents in a fire caused by a careless maid. Having found temporary accommodation with friends of her parents, she was moved and much relieved to receive a letter from her uncle some weeks after the tragedy, insisting that she place herself in his care. It was a kind offer and she accepted by return of post.

Now she began to have doubts. The house loomed above her, part castellated and part fortified, though in a dreadful state of disrepair. The gardens were unkempt, the trees and shrubbery were wild and untrimmed and there was more moss than stone on the steps. Having retrieved her bag of meagre belongings she watched as the coachman whipped his horses back along the drive with unseemly haste.

Turning back, she started in shock as a huge, grotesque man in a dusty black suit walked stiffly down the steps to greet her and took her bag with a surly nod.

"This way."

She followed him into the house. It was dark and lit fitfully with candles and lamps. It reeked of decay and old smoke, cooked fats and something else, something indefinable.

"His Lordship will see you in his room."

She walked in the direction she was pointed and pushed open the door.

Lord Rookwood sat in a large leather studded Spanish armchair, twirling a glass in his hand. His cadaverous features were accentuated by long, unruly hair and the shadows that filled the room.

"Ah, niece Viola. My pretty niece. Welcome to my humble abode. I hope Dirk didn't alarm you. He is damnably ugly but my one loyal remaining servant. Sit, please."

She sat. Fear rippled through her like a wave. Although she had heard stories about her uncle she had never laid eyes on him until this moment. There was no doubt about it. He was a reservoir of decadence, a repository of evil and sin. His face, sunken cheeks and deep-set eyes shadowed by dark rings, was a map of his dissipation. He was strangely attractive, but even in her wildest fantasies she had never quite imagined herself in the company of such a creature.

"I welcome you to my, uh, family," said Rookwood. "I assume you're the last one of your line. You and I are the only ones left." He paused, seeming to savour the thought.

"Allow me to show you around your new home."

He stood and offered his hand. After a moment's hesitation, she took it and allowed herself to be led through the house. As her uncle showed her the place from top to bottom, her agitation and despair increased with every mouldering chamber, every cracked and creaking staircase. It was a house of nightmares.

Finally, they descended a flight of stone steps into the crypt. Here the family vault contained the tombs and effigies of Rookwoods dating back to the fourteenth century.

"Look here," said her uncle, pausing at a marble tomb whose surface was etched with Latin. "My last wife. Ah, she was a beauty." He grinned. "I doubt very much if she is quite so beautiful now."

A shudder went through Viola at his words, which seemed peculiarly inappropriate and callous. He drifted around the enormous vault, casting the glow of his torch on a variety of dead aristocrats and minor clerics, few of who had distinguished themselves in life. The last tomb, however, was different. It was the oldest in the vault and Rookwood almost spat upon the effigy that lay atop it.

"DeVere Ambrosius Rookwood," he sneered. "A 'verray parfit, gentil knight'."

Viola looked down at the carved marble effigy of her uncle's ancestor. Unusually, he was depicted with his left hand over his heart while his other gripped the hilt of his sword that lay alongside his leg. He appeared, thought Viola, ready to spring into action at a moment's notice.

Upstairs in the salon, Rookwood invited his niece to sit down in front of the poor excuse for a fire. Dirk had entered with a tarnished silver tray containing a dusty bottle and two glasses.

"Well, let us drink to a new beginning," said her uncle. "A new family."

He poured a glass of thick red wine and handed it to Viola. She had rarely drunk anything stronger than hock and seltzer and was conspicuously hesitant.

"Oh pish!" he exclaimed with a frown. "Drink with me now. Don't insult me."

She drank. It was warm and luscious, like sweet blood. Her head swam, her vision fogged. Rookwood smiled revealing vicious, sharp canines and blackened teeth.

"It has been a long time, my dear, since I enjoyed the company of anyone other than my dead ancestors and my disgusting servants."

Her head seemed too heavy for her neck. It drooped towards her chest. She tried to reply and say something but her tongue had grown thick in her mouth.

The flames of the fire seemed to die down and the darkness closed in around her.

In a moment, she knew no more.

Viola awoke in darkness. She tried to open her eyes, but something seemed to be constricting them, holding her eyelids closed. She shifted and tried to move her limbs. They were tied. Her arms were stretched above her and her legs tied at the ankles. She couldn't move. She cried out but it came out as a whimper. As she shifted her body against the cruel bonds her bare skin felt cool stone. She realized with horror that she was entirely naked.

In the crypt beneath the house, Rookwood stood over his niece, bound and helpless before him on the great carved tomb that Lipari Fillippo had hewn from marble and which he had brought over from Italy after the Grand Tour. That was before he had discovered the hellish joys of opiates and strange potions and the searing pleasures of the flesh that he now sought with increasing desperation. Most of his retinue had abandoned him, preferring to take their chances with the world outside than endure his depravities any longer. Servant girls had either run away or been disposed of by Dirk, his last remaining servant, a man whose tastes were almost as hideous and primeval as his own. A man who dined on the raw flesh of just about any creature that walked or ran on four legs. Or two.

He gazed upon the white skin of the immaculate body stretched out before him. He watched as her movements undulated deliciously, sending ripples along her thighs and across her rounded belly. He salivated at the firm round breasts and the pink up-tilted nipples, erect in the cool air of the crypt. He licked his lips as he gazed on the secret heaven between her legs, at the apex of her thighs, shrouded in reddish curly hair and moving with delicious eagerness as she struggled with her bonds.

He was ready now. He drew a shining steel blade from the scabbard along his thigh and kissed the blade. He lowered it between her legs.

Viola shuddered when she felt the chill steel touch the soft skin of her thigh. She had no idea what it might be, but it sent a curious sensation through her, from her toes up through the centre of her being into the roots of her hair. Fear, certainly. But something else. Something strangely delicious and thrilling. Something that leaked through her vitals and made her slick and wet between her legs. It was unlike anything she had ever experienced. As the blade stroked her thigh upwards towards her secret private place, she gasped and sobbed. Oh God. Help me in my hour of need. What is to become of me?

The blade shifted until the point lay between her breasts. Rookwood traced a line from her throat between her precious bright breasts and slid the flat of the blade over each nipple, watching with cruel pleasure as they hardened under the kiss of the steel.

He knew this was his last, his last remaining manner of excitement. Steeped in decadence, he could no longer function as a man under normal sexual congress. New pleasures, obscure stimulations and dark desires now drove him to ever more fathomless depths, to ever more dangerous passions, to ever more sadistic entertainments. This was to be his ultimate, his crowning achievement – the sacrifice of a virgin relative. He would eviscerate her untainted beauty and drive himself into her blood and entrails.

Viola prayed. She felt the steel blade trace itself all over her body and she shifted and shrank away from the lethal point. She knew her end was nigh. She prayed that it wouldn't be too painful, that he would be merciful in her swift despatch. She prayed that he would not torment her with sadistic pleasure. The blade lifted from her soft yielding vulnerable flesh and she waited for the thrust, the coup de grace that she knew was coming. Where would it be? Her heart? Oh God, let it be swift.

A strange calm swept through her then. Having made her peace with her Maker, she found the strength to endure and quell the fear that had been coursing through her. Silence slid through the vault, enveloping her in its comforting embrace.

A creaking sound brought her back to her senses. It was the sound of an old door, long unopened, complaining against its unaccustomed movement. She heard her tormentor mutter something just before a hideous scream pierced the darkness. It was an inhuman sound, as if dragged from the depths of a soul in hell.

There was a crunching, bony thump as an object struck the stone floor. Something hot and wet jetted onto her naked flesh from her stomach to her breasts. She shuddered. It ran and dripped from her ivory skin with a delicious warmth. There was a further thump and then silence. She froze, wondering what was coming next. The creaking sound came closer and she felt something stretch the bonds of her wrists. It sliced through them, liberating her arm. She instinctively drew it down, covering herself and felt something warm and sticky. The other arm was freed with a snick. Then her legs. She lay there, almost as terrified at being free as she had been at being tied and helpless. There was silence. After a while, she reached up and pulled the blindfold roughly from her eyes. She looked around. She looked down at herself. Her body was splashed with scarlet.

Blood.

Shaking, she slid off the stone altar and stood up. The flag-stones of the crypt were strangely comforting beneath her bare feet. She walked round and stopped with a gasp.

Rookwood's body lay stretched out on the floor, still and lifeless. At least most of it was. His head had disappeared, having been struck from his body by a single blow. She stepped over the body, a strange feeling rising in her: confidence, hope. Something else. Something other. She slipped around the room, avoiding the pool of blood that continued to leak from her uncle's severed neck.

She backed against a tomb and turned. It was DeVere, the ancient knight. The last Good Rookwood. Trembling, she ran her hands over the smooth marble of his effigy. She looked at the mighty sword by his side and noticed a dark brown stain along its length. A trick of the light, perhaps. Or maybe an imperfection in the marble.

She touched the figure, the cold marble warming to her

touch, at once alien and familiar. As she slid her hands along his surcoat, she felt something move and shift beneath it.

A mistake, surely. The product of her mind, disordered by her ordeal. Just heightened imagination. She raised her hand involuntarily. Then gently replaced it. No. There was something there. A low throb, a movement as of something rising beneath the surface. Yet it was still marble, still stone. How could it be soft and warm and yielding and hard and cold and solid at the same time?

Her skin undulated as she felt the cooling blood drip down her body and between her legs, sliding into the triangular tuft of hair and into the sweet soft channel beneath before dripping down her thigh. She touched herself there. Ran her fingers along the sweet oyster cleft and gasped. Oh God. Such a feeling! Her knees turned watery and she almost sank to the floor. But she supported herself by holding on to the tomb and the marble effigy of DeVere. She gazed in rapt fascination as the carved marble folds of his surcoat rose and parted, revealing a slim, white member, which turned and came to rest at the hour of two like the hand of a great clock. Driven by a deep atavistic desire, she reached out and tenderly caressed the great marble staff, which seemed to throb and twitch beneath her tender ministrations.

Unschooled as she was in the intimate affairs of men and women, she was nonetheless driven by the instinct of her sex to pursue her course. Before she knew what she was about, she climbed up onto the tomb and straddled the knight's member rampant, just positioning the lips of her sweet and unsullied cunt over the round head of the marble phallus. Oh, exquisite sensation! Her back arched and she shuddered and twisted with pleasure and anticipation of what greater delights it might herald. Gently, she lowered herself onto the shaft, wincing and crying out as it pierced her gossamer virgin barrier, before sliding down to seat herself upon the cool marble with him fully immersed inside her. She rested, drawing great gulps of air through her nose and mouth. She had ceased to wonder, to think. Now she surrendered to the visceral, carnal being that had awakened deep within her. No thought, just sensation. She rose slightly and sank again, sending ripples of pleasure running through her from the walls of her deep insides, carried by her blood around her body and outward to her skin's surface. Moving up and down now, she found a rhythm that pleased her without pain and looked down at the impassive marble hewn features of her saviour. The solid white marble member, oiled by her own juices, delivered wave upon wave of pleasure into her as she moved more rapidly along its length, plunging from the tip down to the base in an ecstasy beyond imagining.

"Oh, my Lord! My Saviour!" she cried, as she reached her peak and the tempest broke within her, carrying her hither and thither through thickets of passion and ecstasy and pleasure that she had never known before. Eventually, she fell forward, and collapsed sobbing with joy and release upon the cold hard effigy beneath her. Darkness came upon her and she was lost.

Seven years passed. As the only traceable relative of Lord Rookwood, Viola inherited his entire estate and proceeded to put matters in order from the moment she signed the deeds. Her uncle's profligacy and fecklessness had reduced his fortune somewhat, though by the time his affairs were settled Viola found herself in the enviable position of being a young independent woman of modest means and a large ancestral house. By judicious leasing of some of the lands attached to the estate to the local farmers she was thus able to secure a not inconsiderable income. Enough, at least, for her to live comfortably and to maintain the house and its immediate surroundings as she wished.

Following the death of his master, Dirk had disappeared. Within a year, his remains were found in the forest, having provided an unexpected feast for the creatures who dwelt there.

Viola's first husband, a handsome officer who courted her after a propitious encounter at a local house party, was killed in the Napoleonic campaigns and she found herself a widow at the tender age of twenty-six. Her second husband was a solid, respectable and very kind gentleman whose income derived from his interests in sugar plantations in the West Indies. After four years of happy if unexciting marriage she was widowed for the second time when he was murdered during a revolt of the local slaves who killed their masters and burnt the plantation to the ground, thereby ensuring that the few who escaped capture and execution would never be able to work again.

Even during her marriages, which were fulfilling up to a point, she assuaged her physical needs from time to time by making her way down into the crypt and communing with her ancestor. DeVere, her saviour, never failed to rise to the occasion and she always emerged from her secret assignations with the man of marble with a smile on her face and a lightness of step for which neither of her husbands could ever account.

Atrocity Ballet

Remittance Girl

From the darkened cool, quiet luxury of the Conrad Hotel, the walk south through the winding Bangkok alleyways is a descent into chaos and heat. At 6.20 p.m. the sun is being devoured by the ragged horizon of the buildings in a burnt-orange conflagration. Bundles of electrical wires, like dusty, lazy anacondas, drape heavily across the alleys. The food vendors around the stadium are gearing up for their evening traffic; the sweet, acrid smoke of grilling meat lies heavy on the stifling, humid air, mixing with the stench of urine and the cloying smell of durian.

My hand has grown slick with sweat in yours. We weave like water snakes through the tide of humanity, converging on the old hexagonal stadium. You tower, a foot taller than the people milling around you, and although we're not Thai, we puzzle them as we pass. Neither beet red with heat flush nor sodden with perspiration the way most tourists would be, they don't quite know what to make of us.

After buying tickets, we walk beneath the high gates and into the huge, gloomy tin can of Lumpini Stadium. Inside, it's a riot; perhaps a thousand people perched on rickety chairs on the concrete stands that surround the small shabby ring. High on the ceiling, fans whir furiously to move the dead air. It reeks of sweat, tobacco, incense: of greed and pain and hope, as well. All that is human.

I've wanted to bring you here for so long, but now I worry that you won't see what I see. It's hard to escape the gravity well of the West and see with other eyes. I'm afraid to look up at your face, so I squeeze your hand instead, pulling you up the rough, broad concrete steps. We could have seats ringside, but that's where the foreigners on holiday sit – not the real world of this place.

From the stands, you can see the little band of old men in shabby blue uniforms who, picking up their alien instruments, begin to play music that, at any other time, in any other place, would be a brand of torture. The horns are high and crazy, weaving in and out of each other's trance-inducing melodies. The gongs, the chimes, the great hollow drum, they're like snake charmers on a collision course. The music slithers into my brain and makes my heart race.

Standing in front of you, your arms drape casually over my shoulders despite the heat. The people around don't notice us; their eyes are on the bright ring where the slight, lithe boxers are receiving the blessings of their stable masters. They *wai* deeply to their trainers, and then to the judges, before setting off, festooned in their coloured head ropes and garlanded necks to perform their formal, individual *wai khru* – fight prayer dances. Their small bodies gleam with sweat and oil, their shoulders and hips roll like young panthers as they step, knee, step, knee their way around the ring.

Each chooses their own way to show their loyalty to their fight stables through their bodies, stopping here and there to pose in the form of mythical creatures. One bows to one knee, arms rising into the air as the demon bird Garuda. The other winds side to side, and then expands his chest and arms wide like the River Naga. All the while, the music screeches on, piercing through the rumble of the crowd.

As they start to fight, the crowd roars, and still the sharp, sinuous music cuts through. It's faster and more frantic now, designed to raise the ire of the boxers, to spur on their aggression, but it doesn't just affect the boys in the ring. The muscles in your forearms, crossed over my chest, twitch almost imperceptibly. But I've been waiting years to feel your physical presence. Now that I have it, I notice everything.

A fat droplet of sweat begins a slow journey down the valley of my spine. In the ring, the first of the quick, vicious shin strikes begin. Then they clinch and tug at each other's neck, trying to force their opponent's head lower. Sharp knees jab upward to connect with kidneys and ribs. Torso muscles flex and protect just before impact. In Muay Thai, it's part of the battle and within the rules; the ref doesn't separate them. He waits until one has failed to tense enough and lets the other go in a cloud of breath-robbed pain.

I'm ashamed of my addiction to this atrocity ballet. The brutality of it should sicken me, and in some sane corner of my mind, it does. But my skin, despite the heat, crawls with goosebumps. My nipples peak and stiffen into barbs that catch and chafe against my cotton shirt when I breathe.

Every muscle poised; every strike of elbow, of hand, of shin, of knee; each place the blow lands and leaves its ruddy mark: I see them all. Sucking in air and holding it through each fast, jagged attack, I cannot look away until the bell rings and the round is over. Only then do I turn in your arms and press my face in your damp shirt.

Behind me, the music has slowed. Behind me, the roar of the crowd has died away into countless hushed arguments over who won the bout. Behind me, your palms rest on the small of my back, pressing the sweat back into my skin. A terrible swell of lust, blinding and feral, tears away every shred of rationalism. The solidity of your cock, snugged tight against my belly, offers me no comfort, grants me no forgiveness. It only amplifies things.

I want to ask you what you think, but worry that my voice will betray the essence of my unnatural arousal. Better to let you think that it's your proximity alone that has me in this state. That is more than a half-truth anyway. Your pores have opened in the swelter and surrendered a veritable sea of unique chemical messengers. Back at the hotel, in the restrained politeness of our first meeting, you were, scent-wise, a cipher. Now, having met you at the molecular level, my cortex is instantly addicted.

You turn me back to face the luminous ring as the second round begins. It opens with speed and savagery; the boxers maintain enough distance to deliver quicksilver shin blows to the arms and chests. I hallucinate the sound of thick bone meeting muscled flesh. And, as your flattened palms slide down over the swell of my breasts, I twitch and press backwards into the hollow of your body. Part of me suspects that you've figured out my secret.

Knowing your mind works constantly, knowing that your revulsions are almost instant, I stand grottoed in the great cave of your body, twitching, my breath catching on the blows, and await some signal, some physical indication that you are repulsed by my attraction.

When the dreaded evidence of revulsion doesn't materialize, a choked sigh of relief worms its way free of my throat and I am plunged into a universe of flesh and impact and the heat and scent of you. I reach back, instinctive and unthinking, to clutch your hip, to pull you closer, to feel the desire swelling, pressing at my spine. In that moment, it feels like you will never, ever be close enough; that my skin is in the way and I would suffer flaying just to gain that extra quarter-inch of proximity. My desire is enormous, rearing up inside me like an impending cataclysm.

And you must read it somehow. Because, when you tug the hem of my skirt up at the side and slide your hand beneath it, over my bare and trembling thigh, to cup my cunt, it only takes the momentarily sustained pressure of the heel of your palm to trip my synapses.

Maybe it's the violence, or the smell of your sweat, or the banal thrill of having your hands on my privates in public, but I don't think so. I orgasm against your cupped hand, rising on tiptoes, my head turning, spine arching until my cheek is pressed hard against your shoulder, until the fluids I've released have soaked through to your fingertips. In that moment, perhaps for only that one adamantine moment, I feel the most complete and unqualified acceptance of the flawed and twisted thing that I am.

As the crowd roars, it draws from me a harsh, broken cry that is absorbed and lost the cacophony of bloodlust and sliced apart by the piercing wail of the music. If you don't put an arm around my waist, I will slither down onto the dirty concrete floor. But you do, and I don't. I feel like I should apologize, but my voice won't work.

Now, in the interior calm that descends, the whole world funnels down to two things: the continuing brutality in the ring, and your erection. My tenuous hold on the passage of time is slipping; I don't know if we are into round three or not. One of the sinewy boxers is bleeding heavily from a cut above his left eye – the result of an encounter with his opponent's elbow. Behind me, you twitch against my spine. I'm not sure if it's deliberate or a reaction to the blood. Absently, you stroke my neck with your fingers, leaving a trail of my wetness in their wake.

You lower your head before you speak. I think of all the things I want you to say and know you will say none of them.

"I'm hungry."

Out on the street, down the broad boulevard of Rama V, there is at least a breeze. It dries the sweat on my back, but does almost nothing for the stickiness between my legs. You walk beside me, sedate, engaged in the surroundings, as if nothing happened. I always knew you would be this way, brilliant at not letting anything show. It's only the subtle tension in the grip of your hand that tells me anything has changed.

I do my best to slide down a shutter on all the rawness I feel boiling inside. I try to be like you, and fail. The food stalls around the entrance to Lumpini Park are crowded with carnivores. Selecting the most popular, I squirm my way through, in an Asian fashion I know you, as an American, will find rude. But if we wait politely in line, we will never get served; someone is always hungrier, pushier, more determined.

Returning with a brace of saté sticks and two glass bottles of Coke, we sit at a tiny plastic table on tiny plastic stools and eat, ripping bits of sweet, grilled pork off sticks. I don't have much of an appetite, but the hum of baseline lust has turned subtly cruel and, somehow, tearing at pieces of meat feels appropriate. We don't say much and perhaps, after years of having to speak – and only speak – this is how it should be. The high-pitched whine of the fight music is still crowding my brain, the muscles just beneath my skin still twitch now and then.

I want you with an intensity that defies language, clichéd as this is, true as it is; it's fossilized my tongue. So, instead of saying what I mean, what I want to say, I resort, between long swathes of silence, to inane questions: Is it too spicy? Is the Coke cold enough? How was the food on your flight?

Later, much later, I'll remember the way you ate, the way you sucked saté sauce from your fingertips, the way your Adam's apple moved as you tilted back your head to drink. I'll possess a fixed image of your dark, dark eyes, and the way you held your shoulders and the ring of your accent.

Every so often, your opaque gaze settles on me and turns the earth sideways. And I can sustain it only for a moment, before the vertigo forces me to look away. I've forgiven you your physical beauty, but the abyss of your attention is something I cannot bear for long. Right now it is all I can do not to touch you constantly, or put down my food and devour your mouth. What I want, more than anything else in the world, is for you to fuck me to a pulp.

The park is eerily peaceful, as if a whole city has agreed to behave with the utmost propriety there. When you kiss me, under the halo of a stark light, the chilli oil on your lips burns mine. You kiss the way I imagined you would; as if you were teasing the end of a thread that, when pulled, would turn me inside out. You suck and bite and push your spicy tongue into me until I'm nothing but mouth. The fingers that spread and dig into my ass say that I'm that, too, and hips and belly, as you grind yourself against me. If you kiss me any harder, my back will snap.

Then we're off, walking fast, my hand clutching yours with the shameful desperation of a junkie who believes she'll die unless she gets a fix. The park is formal and open and affords no privacy.

We plunge back into the alley and I, more than a foot shorter, am struggling to keep up. No longer the guide in this alien city, it's you who are leading, scanning as we weave between slow-moving cars, strolling pedestrians, cart-pushing fruit-sellers, begging monks and working girls. You stop so suddenly I sail past you for a few steps until I come to a halt at the end of the long tether of your arm.

The tiny alley is stacked with heat exchanges, sucking air into the adjacent buildings. The fans, like the whooshing wings of huge metal birds, push a windstorm through the narrow tunnel. Against a clear space of concrete, gritty against my back, my blind fingers fight ineptly with the buttons of your shirt.

Why your shirt? Because as I press my open mouth to the centre of your chest and lap at the trickle of sweat rivering down it, then I'll fight with your trousers. Your face is in my hair, your hands pulling up my skirt, by the time I've gotten you undone and wrapped my shaking hand around your cock. I can't hear your breath, but I can feel it hot against the side of my face. The sound you make when you roll your hips, pushing your erection into my grasp . . . this I can hear. Raising my face to yours, I hit the reality wall of what it means to be physical with you. Because I'm too small to simply hook my thigh around your hip. So, with my free hand, I fumble with my panties, tugging them down until they slither down my legs, and I step out of them awkwardly, and kick them away.

It's the first time I've heard you laugh. It starts in your chest, rises upwards, and slides downwards. Your cock twitches in my hand.

"You're shorter than I thought you'd be," you say, above the whirlwind that whisks away any nuance.

I can't allow myself to wonder if you're disappointed. Rising on tiptoes, my free hand clutching your shoulder, I give you a crooked, uncertain smile. "Lift me."

And you do. My legs wrap around your waist, my back hits the wall and I gasp, guiding you to the entrance of my warm, wet cunt.

For one strangely poignant moment, we just hover there – not gazing into each other's eyes, not whispering gooey inanities, not panting obscenities – before you thrust up, and up again, until you're deep inside my tight, slick space, until there's nowhere left to go. The impact leaves me enough breath to choke out a shocked sob.

My thighs, my arms tighten just before the next glorious, killing thrust. And the dormant snake that has coiled for so long at the base of my spine is awake. For all the times I have imagined what you'd feel like inside me, I never thought it would feel like this: that, as my hips tilt towards you, and the bright red flush of lust rises and burns over my chest and up my neck, as I feel the thin fabric of my shirt tearing against the concrete, as all my nerves fire at once and my body closes down around you, like my soul is jarred free of its moorings.

'Muscles coil tight, squeezing until your cock feels enormous and the thrusts turn into a jagged ache. When you push in and sit engulfed for a moment, the contractions feed me your pulse and the pleasure you are feeling. Then, with a sharp, scorching violence, you come.

Here, in this oddly industrial alley, with my legs around your hips and your cock still buried, still twitching, and my cunt still clenched around you, it starts to rain.

All the river water stolen by an angry sun is suddenly plummeting down in a torrent of warm wetness. You lower your head onto my shoulder, let out a long, deep breath, and laugh. I tilt my head upwards, close my eyes, still panting, and grin stupidly up into the apocalyptic deluge.

If the world had to end, right here and now, it really wouldn't be so bad. And if a story has to end anywhere, this seems like a good place: with you still inside me, under a rain that's hard enough to wash all our sins away.

Pity Fuck

Lawrence Schimel

It was late Sunday morning, which meant that of course we were at Le Caprice for brunch: Trevor, Boris, Jeremy and me. Sylvain, the sexy maître d', had put us in a prime spot at the front windows, which were wide open to let in the spring air, which also allowed us to both see and be seen by all and sundry, whether fellow patrons or passers-by. Which also meant that we were acting up even more than usual, being in the spotlight as we were.

"Look at that utter dog over there," Jeremy said, taking a sip of his Bloody Mary and rolling his eyes at the far corner of the street.

I tried to remember if "dog" was complimentary or not this week in Jeremy-speak as I glanced discreetly at the corner in question, where three young men were sitting on the steps of a brick brownstone. I was seated next to Jeremy, so I could see the guys in question with ease, just by lifting my gaze. Both Trevor and Boris had to twist around to see them, something they both shamelessly did, simultaneously, in a twist as grace-ful and as swift as a pair of synchronized swimmers.

"Oh them," Boris said, turning back to his egg-white omelet with goat cheese and sun-dried tomatoes. Just like that, all three of them were dismissed as being beneath his interest. Which was saying something, since the three specimens were all quite different from one another and ran from one end of the spectrum of male beauty to its polar opposite.

From where I sat, there was the young man on the left, who

I imagined was between twenty-one and twenty-three; a base-ball cap covering his blond hair; he was dressed in sports sweatpants and a white tank top, which revealed a section of a colorful tattoo that covered his lean, muscled torso.

In the middle was a guy who was a little younger, maybe nineteen to twenty-one, Latino or Arabic, with dark hair, dark eyes and dark skin and a huge dose of animal magnetism. All eyes were repeatedly drawn to him, although each time it was a different detail: those plump lips, the curve of a bicep, his large hands as he gesticulated to illustrate a point to the other two, who sat at his feet like disciples, listening to him raptly. I was tempted to prostrate myself at his feet myself, which is why I was surprised Boris had dismissed the entire group so summarily and quickly.

Although when it came to the third guy . . . it was easy to see why. Anyone would suffer in comparison to the Adonis in the middle, but even on his own, this poor fellow was unques-tionably ugly. There just wasn't any softer way to put it. He had beady eyes that weren't even hidden behind glasses, jug-handle ears and an overbite. But more than any individual feature that made him look ugly, it was the overall effect: there was something about his features that made them not fit together right. And he was all awkward and gangly when he moved. I guessed he was between the other two, in terms of age: twenty, twenty-one. And unlike either of them, he wasn't fibrous or muscled. He wasn't fat either; if anything, that might've given him some distinguishing quality or made him attractive – even if only to chubby chasers. Instead, he had an unpleasantness about him, as if he were typecast to play an undertaker in a horror film or something, someone to give you the creeps without any possible morbid sensuality or goth sexiness. Not only was this boy not attractive, something about him provoked an active rejection the longer one stared at him.

Which explained Jeremy's comment. "Dog" meant "ugly as a dog" this week, and not "I want him to hump my leg" or "woof, he's hot!" or something like that.

Lawrence Schimel

Trevor was still watching the three of them with the morbid fascination of someone who couldn't look away from the scene of a car crash on the highway, even while it turned their stomach. I followed Boris's lead and turned my attention back to my food: buttermilk pancakes spread with lingonberry jam and rolled into logs which had been sliced slant-wise to create what looked like a mini fortress of spiked towers crowned with tasty, colored spirals.

"Really," continued Jeremy, never willing to let a snide comment stand when he could beat it to death with further hyperbolic repetition, "there isn't enough money in the world that you could pay me to make me have sex with him."

"It works the other way with those three," Boris said, not bothering to look up from his omelet, his way of signaling his utter disdain for this entire thread of conversation.

"They're hustlers?" I asked him. My voice squeaked from incredulity.

Boris did look up at me then. "You are so naive, Eric."

"All three of them?" I asked.

"All three of them," Boris answered. "You're looking at a dying breed: the street hustler. Nowadays everything is done online, on rentboy.com or with some app that uses your GPS to locate who is available in your adjacent area. Even these three will all have profiles if you open Grindr right now. I think the blond kid was using the handle 'Blue Eye$' last time I saw him online."

I looked up again at Blue Eye$ and Latin Lover and the Ugly Hustler.

"I guess there's a market for everything," I said. "But I just can't imagine . . . you know, how he makes a living, I mean." There was no doubt as to which of the three I was talking about.

"Maybe he has a really big dick," Boris said.

You could tell that all of us contemplated this suggestion in silence for some time.

"Even so, not going there. Not enough money in the world," Jeremy repeated.

"I'd pay to do the one in the middle," Trevor said, still staring dreamily at the man across the street. "Not that I need to pay to have sex," he added immediately, turning his attention back to us at last. "But he looks like he'd be worth it, you know?"

I still couldn't get over the idea of that third guy being a hustler, too. I could easily see how the first two could make a living, with the guy in the middle probably being able to get rich given how in demand he would be among the sugar daddies, or maybe just the right one who'd pay to take him off the market . . . But who would pay that third guy for sex? I couldn't even imagine anyone being desperate enough to take money from him, as Jeremy had joked, to make it worthwhile.

"Have any of you ever paid someone for sex?" I asked.

All three of them stared at me, open-mouthed, although I wasn't sure whether they were affronted that I could even ask or that I thought they'd ever admit it if they had. Jeremy had been chewing a slice of Canadian bacon and seeing him with his mouth open was not a pretty sight.

"Or been paid for sex?" I added, trying to save face.

One by one, my friends shook their heads.

"Someone at a bathhouse once paid me $20 to let him suck me off," I confessed. "I would've let him do me anyway, but of course I took the money."

I had liked the idea of being paid for sex, even more than the actual encounter; the guy who'd paid me was not especially adept with his mouth. But being considered worth paying for really turned me on, and flattered my ego.

I couldn't help wondering if that was why the third guy across the street tried to be a hustler; that rush I'd felt, even from my modest incursion into the exchange of sex for cash. Although I imagined his life must be an unending stream of frustration, watching his two buddies pull client after client while he waited, alone, on their corner, for them to come back after each job. I imagined he must have some other source of income, in order to keep a roof above his head and continue to eat and all that, although his two friends were good-looking enough that they could no doubt earn enough from hustling to make a living. Especially if they were not just young, but horny enough to be able to do multiple tricks a day. Of course, I imagined that while it was important for the john to come, maybe they didn't need to come with each of them, unless that was specified in the transaction and maybe paid for as an extra.

None of which was any help for the ugly hustler, though.

And while my mind was absorbed with these thoughts, my friends grew bored with this thread of conversation and took it elsewhere.

"So it takes twenty bucks to make a whore out of Eric," Jeremy said. "For me, just give me a cocktail and let me loose in the backroom at The Hole. I went there on Friday with Kenny and you would not believe how many men I sucked off . . ."

Once I get an idea in my head, it takes root there, like a tenacious seed, and seems to grow of its own accord, flourishing and growing no matter what I try to do to the contrary. I've learned over the years that it's no use to try to change things, so eventually I had to face the harsh truth:

I had become fascinated with the Ugly Hustler.

It's not as if I did nothing but look for him, or at least think about him. I went to work every morning, went to the gym, occasionally had sex with strangers I met online, met up with friends for drinks or a film or both.

But I kept coming back to the Ugly Hustler. He was like a constant worry, like that feeling that you left the gas on even when you know you've shut it off. Or, given how unattractive he was, maybe a better metaphor might be a sore inside your mouth: your tongue keeps going back to it, time and time, even though it hurts every time your tongue makes contact, but you can't stop yourself from seeking it out again and again.

Sometimes even when I was jerking off, he would invade

my fantasies; not that I fantasized about having sex with him, my thinking about him was anything but sexual, but I might suddenly get sidetracked from a fantasy, wondering what it was like for him, if he got sex in both his work life and his personal life, how he managed to make a living, things like that.

I can honestly say that I never expected to be thinking of the Ugly Hustler while holding my erect cock in my hand, yet exactly that happened more than once.

I will confess to losing my erection quite promptly on such occasions, not something that happens to me often. Although to be honest, this might have happened not just from visualizing him but also from having lost the thread of the fantasy I'd been jerking off to. I began to worry about my virility, not to mention my mental health. What was happening to me that my mind would rather think about this hideous-looking man than engage in erotic fantasies?

And every weekend, when we had brunch at Le Caprice, no matter what table we wound up at (although sweet Sylvain usually put us in the front windows whenever he could) I was sure to seat myself where I could have a clear view of their corner, so I could keep an eye on them during our meal, and especially to see if the Ugly Hustler ever managed to even talk to anyone, let alone snare an actual john.

After Boris's comment, I'd obsessively logged far too many hours online until I'd hunted down all three of them and their profiles. But I never did more than just mark them as "favorites" so I could find them again.

I never IM'd any of them, or sent them messages.

Once, I saw Blue Eye$ at the supermarket, but he never even glanced at me, although I of course recognized him right away. It gave me a thrill, like seeing a movie actor or something, secretly watching them go about the mundane events of their lives, knowing things about them that they didn't know we knew . . . in this case, what he did for a living.

Even though I knew their online handles, I only ever used them for Blue Eye$. I'd already gotten so used to thinking of the three of them as Blue Eye$, Latin Lover and the Ugly Hustler, it was too difficult to try to change their identities now.

The seed was already planted, and it grew and grew, too large now to weed out – no way to even try to pull it up by the roots at this point.

For all that I thought about the Ugly Hustler, it wasn't at all sexual for me.

I had certainly fantasized about Latin Lover. Even to the point of offering money in my fantasies, to do the things to me that I wanted him to do. I will admit (although never to my friends) to contemplating contacting him and offering money in real life to do those same things to me.

But I never contacted any of them.

I figured that when the time was right, I'd run into him. And that when it happened, I'd know what to do.

What I always imagined myself doing, on meeting up with the Ugly Hustler in my mind, was opening my wallet and giving him a crisp hundred-dollar bill. And he was always so grateful. He always offered to do me, of course, but I waved him away, acting as if it were simply my will to offer largesse toward him and not any physical revulsion I felt on looking at him.

I was fantasizing about myself as the noble philanthrope, a role I'd never really envisaged myself in before.

But, of course, when our paths did finally cross, the encounter went nothing like I'd imagined.

Our encounter didn't take place on his corner, or someplace innocently mundane like the supermarket where I saw Blue Eye$. We met late one evening, out on the green (four square blocks that were covered with grass and dotted with trees) when I was out cruising, and he was sitting on a park bench, smoking a cigarette and waiting for someone just like me. He recognized my aimless prowling for sex right away, there was no way to hide or disguise it. He stared at me, invitingly.

And my physical reaction to him was the same as it ever was; the very idea of sex with him made my balls shrivel up, as with fear or cold.

I walked past him. My heart was racing. I didn't know what to do.

But this seemed to be the moment I'd been waiting for these past weeks. The perfect moment to finally go through with it and thereby, hopefully, be able to move on, to forget about him.

I had some money on me, but I hurried to an ATM a few blocks over and withdrew two hundred dollars. Even as I was going through these actions, I knew that they were only partly my following through on instinct, of trying to act out what I'd imagined so often these past weeks; the rest of me was procrastinating, buying myself time with the walk to the ATM, and then the walk back.

He was still seated on the park bench, still smoking the same cigarette, or another one.

I felt a surge of adrenaline when I saw him; it wasn't a fear of any danger from him, that he might rob me or something, more a general fear of finally going through with something I'd only imagined until then.

He watched me, and I was aware again that he knew I'd come to the park looking for sex. Looking in that outdated way of the hunter and the hunted, fallen out of fashion with the fast-food convenience of ordering online whatever you wanted from the nearest source.

He was the one who broke the ice.

"You go stock up for tonight?" he asked, with a smile that might have been meant to be a leer but which looked anything but sexy.

Nor was it menacing. But I blurted out, "I can give you money."

"I'm not holding you up, man," he replied, holding his hands out in the classic open-palmed gesture of peace and goodwill.

"I know," I said, "I didn't say you were, I just meant, like, in case you needed some or something. If you, like, didn't have enough customers or something."

So now it was out in the open between us, the fact that I knew he was a hustler.

"I'm not a charity case or something," he said, his dignity injured.

"No, I didn't mean that," I rambled, "it's just . . ."

It's just that's exactly how I'd been thinking of him. Like he were a beggar. Like he needed me, somehow.

"Look, if you don't want to fuck, that's fine, but go away, you're blocking any other customers."

I was shocked.

Not only was it bad enough that I could be seen in public, trying to make time with such an ugly guy, but even worse, I was getting blown off! I wasn't sure my reputation or my ego could survive such a blow.

"How much?" I asked, thinking I could still give him a hundred bucks or something without having to actually go through having sex with him. I couldn't look at him while I waited for his reply, but nervously scanned up and down the block, checking out whether anyone I knew (or might ever want to know) could see me.

"Two fifty an hour," he answered.

At first, I was relieved, thinking he'd meant $2.50 for an hour. So a hundred bucks would cover quite a lot.

But then I realized he meant $250.

I couldn't believe he had the nerve to ask for so much!

I thought back to the twenty bucks I'd been paid to let some guy suck me off in that bathhouse.

Suddenly, I wasn't just a whore, I was a cheap one!

"How much do your friends charge?" I asked, before I could stop myself. It was rude, to say the least, to compare them like that. Or to doubt his own quoted price. Would I ask a dentist or a surgeon how much his colleagues charge? Of course not.

And it also revealed how long I'd been circling around him, as if I'd been stalking him.

"Two fifty an hour, it's the going rate, do you want a fuck or not?"

I felt trapped. Suddenly my mission of mercy was turning out to be much more expensive than I'd planned. But it was as if I were stuck on a highway with no exits, with no choice but to keep driving and hope that eventually there'd be a turn-off somewhere. While I might've just said, "No thanks," I couldn't make myself say it, couldn't be the one to reject him another time. I didn't see a way of getting out of going through with the whole shebang. With an ugly hustler who insisted on giving bang for his buck. And they say today's youth has no work ethic!

"Fine. Two fifty."

I wondered whether to assure him I had the cash on me. But then I worried that that might be an invitation to rob me or something.

Although I immediately felt ridiculous for worrying about that. Hadn't this all started because I wanted give this guy money, out of pity? And wouldn't I only feel relieved if he got the money that way, without my having to have sex with him?

He stood up. "Your place or a hotel?" he asked.

I hadn't thought this far.

While the green was where many men came to hook up, it was too open for much to actually happen here. Usually guys did it in a car, or took a car somewhere more remote and secluded.

Both of us were on foot.

I wasn't bringing him home with me. Absolutely not. Not only was there a danger that any of my neighbors might see me bringing home such an ugly trick, I didn't feel comfortable with the idea. It's not like I didn't bring other strangers home all the time, people I met over the internet or at a bar, who I didn't know from Adam. But a professional hustler was different, there was an element of . . . unsavoriness there, of threat, that I didn't usually feel with those other pick-ups.

And my mission of mercy suddenly got even more expensive.

"Hotel," I answered.

Let him think what he wanted, that maybe I lived with someone. Or even let him imagine the truth, that I was too scared to bring him home, for whatever reason. Maybe he'd get a thrill out of that.

As I walked beside him, I realized that reality was nothing like I'd imagined it. For one thing, I was starting to wonder how he thought and felt. In my fantasies, I'd only been aware of how grateful he'd felt toward me, and how I'd felt, generously offering him charity.

What a condescending shit I'd been all this time!

Before we got to the next corner, he stopped and turned to me. "Which hotel are we going to?"

And I realized that he knew I had no idea where I was going, that I was in way over my head.

"Why don't you pick one," I said.

And he stared at me for a moment, no doubt asking himself what the hell was going on, if I was actually going to go through with this or not, if I was wasting his time. I forced myself to look back at him, to stare back at his ugly face.

And then he reached out, one hand cradling my head, and pulled me toward him, to kiss me, there on the street, in public.

I forced myself to hold still, to not pull away. As his face drew closer to mine I closed my eyes. I held my breath.

And suddenly his lips met mine. His tongue pushed into my mouth.

And I stopped remembering how ugly he looked. Stopped thinking of him as the recipient of my largesse, as the object of my pity.

Our breaths mingled, his tasting slightly of a cinnamon gum he must've chewed earlier, and the recent cigarette, and I realized I was kissing another human being – even if he made his living offering his body to men in exchange for cash.

Even if I'd constantly underestimated him, despising him without my realizing it, with my attitude toward him, based on his looks.

He was a very good kisser.

It was as if all his attention were focused in that one kiss, which made it one of the most exceptional kisses I'd ever had.

So often, a kiss is a prelude to something else, and both of you are already thinking of that instead of enjoying the kiss for what it was.

But the Ugly Hustler kissed me as if our kiss were the only important thing in the entire world.

Our kiss was so important that I lost track of all my worries and concerns and focused on just kissing him back.

Until he broke our kiss and pulled away.

I opened my eyes again and looked at him. His face was still ugly. The kiss had not magically changed that.

But I saw him now for what he was: a professional, offering a service I wanted, at a price I now realized I was willing to pay.

After holding my gaze for a long moment, he nodded, and said, "OK," and started walking again.

I watched him walk away for a step or two, and realized I was hard.

And I started following after him, to the hotel.

Layover

Lisabet Sarai

"You look good down there."

That's how it started. An accident, a bit of clumsiness on my part. I'd been bringing a couple of Cokes up to the cockpit. A stray breeze from a vent whisked the straws onto the floor. I was crouching, scrambling to pick them up with my right hand while gripping the tray with my left, when the door opened.

Captain Marsden's barely five foot three while I top six feet, but in that situation she towered over me. I froze, immobilized by embarrassment and sudden, inexplicable excitement. Sweat broke out on my forehead and inside my regulation trousers, my cock grew to distinctly uncomfortable proportions. I gazed up at her plain, even features, the reddish brown hair wound into a knot and tucked under her cap, the familiar blue uniform, as though I'd never seen her before.

Her thin lips curled into a tight, knowing smile. Was the bulge in my crotch obvious? I struggled to rise. The cans of soda tumbled off the tray and rolled backward down the aisle. The captain laughed, a clear, bright sound that sent shivers up my spine.

"Not exactly the level of professionalism we expect from our Shambala Air crew members."

I wondered whether I should go retrieve the errant cans. Trapped by her gaze, I simply couldn't. "No, Captain. I'm sorry. The straws . . ."

"I don't like excuses, Andrew. You'll learn soon enough to

take responsibility for your errors." She gave me a frank once-over, a good deal less circumspect than the stewardesses who mooned over my blond hair and athlete's build. My pants grew unbearably tight. "I do think your intentions are good, however. You want to be of service."

"That's my job, ma'am." I felt ridiculous, stranded there on one knee, crumpled straws in one hand, empty tray in the other. Something kept me nailed to the cabin floor. I didn't dare move without her permission.

"But I think its part of your nature, too, to serve. Perhaps that's why you sought out this occupation." Actually, I'd applied to be an air steward because I loved traveling and figured I'd get a lot of pussy. I wasn't about to disagree with her, though.

"Hand me the sodas. I've got to get back to the controls." Despite her command, her gaze held me fast. I groped behind me for the cans. The chill metal burned my palms as I passed them up to her.

"Thank you. I have something for you, also." She pulled a black fabric bag from her uniform pocket, similar in size and shape to the toiletries kits we distributed in first class. "If you're serious about serving, put this on, and leave it on until we land. I'll give you further instructions then."

She disappeared back into the cockpit. The metal door clicked shut. It was easily thirty seconds before I was together enough to stand. I headed for the toilet, thinking I'd give myself some relief before returning to work. What I found inside the bag made that impossible.

I'd never seen a cock cage before, but the purpose of the leather and rubber device was pretty obvious. The largest strap buckled under my balls. The smaller loops encased my shaft in progressively tighter circles. A longitudinal leather strip ran up from the base, along the top of my rod, branching near the bulb into two strips intended to be fastened around my waist. This belt-like component pulled my raging erection tight against my belly. I worried the fluid leaking from my slit would make dark spots on my uniform, but what could I do?

Perhaps Captain Marsden deliberately wanted to add embarrassment to my uncomfortable arousal.

Why did I follow her instructions? To be honest, I never considered refusing. Emma Marsden turned out to be right about me.

The remainder of the fourteen-hour flight was a kind of lustful hell. The ache in my balls became my only reality. I worked to focus on the needs of our passengers, but my mind kept straying to the captain's comments about further instructions. I sat across the aisle from her on the shuttle to the hotel, desperate for some acknowledgement. She never looked in my direction. In the crush at the reception counter, though, she slipped a keycard into my hand. "Four oh three. Be there at midnight," she whispered. "And don't be late, Andrew."

That was the beginning. Now all I have to do is see her name on the duty roster and I'm instantly hard. She doesn't use me on every flight, though. Weeks can pass without her summoning me. That only makes me want her more.

When she plans to play with me, she'll greet me as "Andrew" rather than "Mr Sentosa". And usually, she'll find a way to deliver some devilish item of sexual torture for me to wear throughout the flight: nipple clamps, cock rings, a tight latex jock. Once, on a LAX–Changi run, she gave me a pair of woman's panties, red silk trimmed with black lace. The smooth fabric slithering over my distended prick was just too much. When she handed me her key, I disgraced myself by coming in my pants. She used the come-drenched garment as a gag while she whipped me.

I couldn't sit down for a week.

Tonight we're en route to Bangkok, and the plug embedded in my ass makes every movement delicious agony. Bending over to place dinner trays on the passengers' tables is particularly tough. Lara, our purser, must have noticed my grimace. She asks if I am ill. I grin and make some joke about the hazards of foreign food.

It's one in the morning Thai time, 10 a.m. in Los Angeles, by the time we check in. I'm exhausted yet wired. The narrow streets around the Montien Hotel are bright with neon and crowded with sweaty, scantily dressed bodies – both tourists and natives. My teak-floored room is shadowed, cool and smells of jasmine. I'd love to lie down, but the captain expects me at her door in half an hour. I'd never disappoint her.

I take a quick shower, avoiding my swollen dick except as necessary to get it clean. I leave the plug in place. I'd given myself an enema before boarding, as Emma had taught me, on the chance that she'd want me on this flight. My balls ache when I remember that night in KL, when she first demonstrated her preferred technique. I'd never voided my bowels while someone watched. I wanted to curl up and die of shame. Still, later, when she thrust her latex-sheathed fingers into my raw hole, I came so hard I practically passed out.

I'm at her door one minute before the prescribed time. I wait the required sixty seconds before inserting the key card. The captain cares about punctuality. The delay gives me an opportunity to ponder what she'll do to me tonight. My mind dredges up images so nasty they make me cringe. My erection twitches inside my loose pants. I've been swollen for so long, I can't remember what it feels like not to be hard.

Why am I here? Why do I want this? All-American superstud Andy Sentosa, fraternity president, star quarterback, dream lover and heartbreaker? Why have I placed myself under the thumb of a plain spinster fifteen years older than I am, when I could have a dozen girls, younger and prettier? Why don't I just laugh in her face when she hands me one of her little black bags and tell her to find some other boy to torture?

Because . . . well, I don't understand why. It has something to do with the authority of her position, the only female pilot flying jumbos for Shambala. It's all tied up with the way she looks right through me, knowing what I fear – and want – before I do myself. For some weird reason, I want to prove to her I can take whatever she'll dish out. I want to please her, to coax out that tight, slightly mocking smile that tells me she's aroused, too.

It's time. The card slides soundlessly into the slot. The LED turns green as the lock clicks. My heart's beating loud enough for me to hear it in my ears. I push the door open and step into her presence.

"Good evening, Andrew." She's seated across the room, in an armchair by the window. I note her position with a quick glance, before dropping my eyes to the lush carpet as she likes.

"Good evening, ma'am." By now I know what's required. I strip off my shirt and pants, fold them – the captain has a thing about neatness – and place them on the desk near the door. Then I sink to my hands and knees, as gracefully as a gangly six-footer can, and crawl to her across the rug.

When I reach her bare feet, I press a reverent kiss onto each instep. Her skin is baby soft beneath my lips. Her toenails, a natural pink, draw me. I have the urge to lick between her toes, to suck them into my mouth and bathe them in my saliva. I know better, though, than to make that kind of move without being told to do so.

"Good boy," she murmurs. "You may look at me." She's wearing a teal silk robe I've never seen before, belted around the waist and flowing to her ankles. Her unbound hair floats on her shoulders in russet waves. Her face glows with power. I catch a whiff of lilac cologne, and faintly, the low-tide scent of pussy. New blood surges into my already straining cock.

How could I have thought she was plain? Tonight she's a goddess, and I'm privileged to worship her.

"Time for confession, Andrew. It's been nearly two weeks. Who have you screwed since I had you last?"

"No one, ma'am." It's true. Since Emma Marsden turned her eye in my direction, I haven't really been interested in other women.

"Really? I saw Jennie giving you a look of pure lust when we stopped at Narita. You could have her just by crooking your little finger. You're sure you haven't taken advantage?"

"No, honestly – I've been very good."

Her laughter is like a river dancing over stone. "What about jacking off?"

"Only three times, ma'am. I'm sorry. I really couldn't help it."

"Three times in two weeks! You must be exceptionally horny."

Hot blood climbs into my cheeks. "Yes, Captain. I am."

"Stand up. Let me see." Leaning forward, she traces delicate fingers over my rigid dick, then clasps me in her palm. I clamp down, staring at her small hands and struggling for control. "Mmm. Very hard indeed. We'll have to see what we can do about that. But punishment first. You know my rules. You're still wearing the plug?"

"Of course, ma'am." I try not to whine. Does she really think I would disobey her at this point?

"Excellent. Turn around, Andrew. Nam, come over and help me, please."

My heart nearly leaps out my chest. I'd thought we were alone. Emma has never invited anyone else to participate in our scenes. But now a tall, willowy Thai beauty rises from the shadowed corner chair where she's been watching the proceedings.

Ebony hair flows almost to the girl's waist. Silver bangles decorate her brown wrists; matching loops shine in her ears. She wears a lot of make-up, gleaming purple eye shadow and dense, probably fake eyelashes. Her purple miniskirt just clears the bottom of her bum and a white, sequin-crusted tank top shows off her dusky cleavage. She smells like the incense the Thais burn in their shrines.

"Suck him, Nam, while I give him his strapping." The exotic creature sinks to her knees with palpable grace and takes me in her slender fingers. My balls tighten; I hang on the edge, knowing that if I come, I'm in for far more severe correction. I'm tempted to let go anyway, to give in and damn the consequences. But that would displease my mistress.

Emma's moving behind me. Something cool and smooth slithers up my back. "My belt," she confirms. "Five strokes for each unauthorized orgasm, or fifteen in all. Count them, Andrew."

Swat! The leather strap lands squarely on my butt, nudging the plug, leaving a dull burn in its wake. At the same moment, the Thai woman swallows my cock. Pleasure streaks to my brain, muddling the hurt.

"One," I manage to croak, as Nam turns on the suction. "Two." This stroke catches the back of my thigh like a lick of flame. Nam's tongue is rough as a cat's, swirling over my knob. Fluid climbs into my shaft, though I try to force it down.

Snap! The belt slashes my shoulder, with yet a different flavor of pain. I arch instinctively, driving down Nam's throat. "Three." How will I survive another twelve lashes? Balanced between ecstasy and agony, only the counting saves me from flying apart. "Four. Five. Six."

Emma pauses to knead my bruised ass and twist the plug. "You're doing well. Hold on now." Another four strokes, biting into my back, my legs, my buttocks. Nam fondles my balls while sliding her tongue up and down my length. I'm OK now, or so I think, above it all, letting the sensations wash through me without trying to sort them out. "Five more, Andrew," my mistress intones and I count them automatically, determined not to disappoint the captain no matter what she asks of me.

It's over at last. Nam pulls away as the captain's belt sizzles across my butt cheeks for the last time. I think I'll collapse, but Emma steps up behind me, the cool silk of her garment soothing my abraded skin. She wraps her arms around my waist. Contentment blooms in my chest. It's all worth it – all the pain, the humiliation, the doubts that attack me when we're apart. This is where I belong.

"Good boy," she murmurs, rubbing her body against my back. She lays her cheek in the hollow between my shoulder blades and licks at one of my stripes. She's so tiny, and yet so powerful . . .

Then something hard emerges from all her softness, prodding the gap between my thighs. My body stiffens – I know what that poking means. She chuckles and steps away, leaving me bereft.

"Of course I brought my harness. Why do you think I wanted you to wear the plug? I need you nice and loose. I plan to fuck you until you scream for mercy. If that's all right with you, that is."

She's already fiddling with the plug. I bow my head in silent assent as she pulls it from my bowels. It emerges with an obscene pop that sends new blood to my prick. I'm ready to explode. I clench my sphincter, gaping after hours of impalement.

"Kneel on the bed, Andrew." She positions me crosswise near the foot, my hands near one edge. "Nam – over here." The Thai woman circles to stand in front of me. Her breasts sparkle under her jeweled shirt. Sweat mingled with sandalwood pricks my nostrils.

Emma sweeps her arm around the girl's shoulder and pulls her into a passionate kiss. Nam has to bend to reach my mistress's mouth. My loins ache, watching – the captain has never kissed me, in all these months. Just as I'm thinking this, she releases the Thai and leans over to brush her lips across mine. It's the briefest of caresses, but I almost moan with joy.

She has discarded her robe. Black straps encircle her waist and thighs, a stark contrast to her pale skin. Her favorite dildo, eight inches long and wreathed with veins, juts from her pubis. She has pulled her hair back from her face. She wears the barest of smiles as she smears lube along the length of her artificial cock.

"Now, Andrew. I'm going to fuck you, as I promised. Meanwhile, I want you to suck Nam. Make her come, and you can come too."

The silent Thai steps forward, to within inches of my face, and raises the hem of her tiny skirt. She wears nothing underneath. Her pubis is completely hairless. And protruding from that smooth triangle at the top of her tawny thighs is a small but definitely erect penis.

"No!" I scream. The captain's behind me, kneeling on the bed. She holds my hips with impossible strength. "No, please – I can't."

"Can't, Andrew? Or won't?"

I twist around, away from the freakish sight in front of me, to plead with my mistress. "I'm not gay – don't make me suck his – her – cock. Please, I'll do anything you want . . ."

"*This* is what I want, Andrew. I thought you liked making me happy. That you enjoyed obeying me." She shrugs and releases her grip. "Very well. Go back to your room then."

Climbing off the bed with an audible sigh, she goes to pick up my clothing from the desk. Nam and I both watch her. I'm entranced by the confident power I see in her neat, muscular body. In a uniform, a silk robe or naked, she was born to command.

Emma tosses my clothes on the bed. "Get dressed. Get out." The coldness in her voice makes me shudder.

"No . . . wait . . . I don't want to go."

"Either you obey me, or you leave. I don't have time or patience for this sort of game."

I stare at her stern beauty. How can I leave? I turn back to the miniature erection bobbing obscenely in the Thai's crotch. How can I?

I swallow the disgust that rises in my throat. "OK, OK. I'll do it."

"Don't do me any favors, boy."

"Please, ma'am. Forgive me. Let me suck Nam's cock while you fuck me. I'll do anything – anything to make you happy."

The ghost of a smile crosses Emma's face, like sun peaking out behind thunderclouds. "You're sure, boy?"

I nod.

"Well, then . . ." She resumes her position behind me, her fingers digging into my hips. The slippery tip of her artificial cock presses against my sphincter. "Do it, boy."

I close my eyes and open my mouth. Nam's cock slides between my lips as Emma's drives into my ass.

The dildo's not as thick as the plug – not quite – but considerably longer. The captain wields it, without mercy, plunging deep into my bowels with each fierce thrust. Her hips bang against my leather-scarred butt cheeks, adding bright sparks of pain to the richer, darker sensations of being buggered.

The cock in my mouth swells larger as I lap and suck as best I can. Nam's flesh tastes salty and slightly bitter. The musk rising from her groin is nothing like a woman's. Nevertheless, it excites me when she sinks her fingers into my hair and works my mouth up and down over her hardness. My nose bangs against her bare pubis as she strains for release. Saliva streams down my chin until she's soaked. My lips feel bruised and swollen, but she doesn't let up, and neither does the captain.

They fuck me for a long time. I hang in a weird limbo, drunk with the pleasure of being so thoroughly used. *This is who I am*, I realize. *I was born to serve and to obey.* The thought makes me ridiculously happy.

Nam's penis twitches. She moans, the first sound she's uttered all night. A spurt of fluid erupts on my tongue. I force myself to swallow, though my gorge rises in disgust, knowing without being told that this is what my captain requires. More come floods my mouth. I'm sputtering, choking, drowning in spunk.

Emma rams into me, grinding her pelvis against my ass. A shudder shakes her body and transmits itself to mine. She jerks against me, uttering little cries that I know mean she's reached her peak. I'm so proud, so glad I've done what she asked. I arch back, offering my ass, wanting to give her everything.

She slumps forward, her small breasts mashed against my kidneys. God, she feels good! I'm on the verge of climax myself, but I've been there forever. I can wait, if she wants me to.

But she reaches beneath me to grasp my swollen rod and whispers her permission. I explode at last, spilling my come all over her small, strong fingers.

We lie on the bed for a sweet space, her body draped across mine. I don't know what's happened to the transsexual. I drift on the edge of dreams, wanting nothing but to remain there forever. After a while, though, she elbows me in the ribs.

"Get up, Andrew. Time to go back to your room."

Regret stabs at my chest. "Please, ma'am, let me stay . . ." She's never allowed me to sleep with her before, but after tonight, perhaps things will change.

"No. Back to your room, right now." She's sitting up beside me, rolling me off the bed and onto the floor.

"OK, OK. You're the boss." Stiff, my battered flesh protesting, I try to don my pants.

She gives me a satisfied grin. "That's right. I'm glad you haven't forgotten." Her voice mellows. "We have a two day layover here in Bangkok, you know. I'm shopping tomorrow, and having dinner with friends in the evening, but perhaps after that you'll join me."

"I'd like that, ma'am." I'm sure she hears the raw need in my voice. I don't care.

"Perhaps I'll have Nam back, have her fuck you. Or have you fuck her. Get you over your little homophobic qualms."

A sickish thrill runs through me. My cock starts to harden.

"Whatever you say, Captain."

Does Immortality come with a Pension?

Robert Buckley

The young nun's hips swayed so sweetly Locan half expected her to glance back at him over her shoulder and wink. She did smile as she gestured to him to follow her into the bishop's study.

Bishop Galway hunkered over his desk scowling at newspaper clippings.

"Sister Sonja's skirt looks shorter," Locan said.

Galway raised his gaze, but not a muscle in his face relaxed.

"Cut the shit, Locan. Where the hell is your partner?"

"She had a late night."

"What?"

"She had a date . . . she hasn't come home yet."

"A date? But . . . I thought you two . . . well, what the hell is with you two anyway?"

"Sorry, Bishop, I don't get your meaning."

"Hmm, I suppose I've made certain assumptions; I ought to know better. Well, how *modern* of you to countenance Miss McDaniel sharing her charms with other men. She doesn't eat them, does she?"

"She hasn't been that hungry lately. And as far as making faulty assumptions, her date was with a woman."

Galway's visage soured again. "For the love of God. And that doesn't bother you?"

"What . . . that she likely woke up with a girl today, or that she woke up with somebody else – period?"

"I suppose you think I have no basis to be making . . . *assumptions* . . . faulty or otherwise."

"Well, Colonel, it isn't like you're running along the same track."

"I wasn't born celibate, you know. When I was a young Marine—"

"Did you really want to see me and her to tell us war stories?"

"Careful, Locan . . . I give you plenty of leeway, but cross the line and . . ."

"Hard to tell where the line is, Bishop."

"You crossed it when you disrupted Cardinal Lex's eightieth birthday party."

"I did no such thing."

"Oh? And every newspaper in Italy got it wrong, I suppose. You were arrested, weren't you?"

"Hell, no. I knew the cop in charge; he gave us a slide. Anyway, I didn't start it."

"I know your opinion of Cardinal Lex."

"That he ought to be doing time in a state pen back home? Yeah, that's right. But I had no idea that shitbum was involved until the swill hit the fan."

"His people claim you accosted several of his party . . ."

"Look, Rachel and I were having dinner in this restaurant she's been talking about for months. We were the only two people in the place when these two pig-faced nuns burst in and started trying to roust us."

"What?"

"Yeah, they said they'd reserved the room we were in. One of them grabbed Rachel by the arm like she was some poor little kid in a parochial school. The one who grabbed my arm got pushed back. Then the other clowns came in with the owner insisting we had to leave. I told them we'd leave after we'd finished dinner. Then some twerp of a monsignor poked me in the chest."

"That 'twerp of a monsignor' says you knocked his bridgework loose."

"He was lucky."

"And you had no idea they were with Cardinal Lex?"

"Not until the cops showed up. I saw him outside, the smug prick, sitting in the back of a limo."

"Locan . . . this unit is supposed to be super-secret, need-to-know only, and you end up getting your picture taken during a brawl at a cardinal's birthday celebration and all sorts of the wrong questions are being asked."

"I told you, we didn't start it."

"Uh-huh, well, I'll try to explain that to the boss, but in the meantime, you and Miss McDaniel are going away for a while."

"Together?"

"Yeah, just the two of you. No girlfriends in tow."

Locan glared.

"Sorry, that was uncalled for . . . but so what. I just wonder . . ."

"What?"

"Never mind."

"Bishop Galway, that girl's going to live longer than you and me combined. Hell, we'll be dust and she'll still look like she hasn't cracked thirty. I can't put any claim on her. The time'll come when she'll have to move on and leave me behind."

Galway's features softened. He nodded. "Well . . . um . . . you're being sent to Connemara."

"Eh? Ireland?"

"Don't know of any place else that has a Connemara."

"But . . . there's nothing there except sheep and people who only speak Irish and not even many of them."

"Better brush up on your Gaelic then – something beyond *'pog ma thoin'.*"

"What in hell is there in Connemara that you're sending us there?"

"A private school for girls. I'm talking about the cream of Europe; they send their daughters there for safekeeping."

"Safekeeping?"

"They're the daughters of ultra-wealthy financiers, industrialists – the kind of people you never hear about in the news, but who pretty much run the world."

"What's the story on this school?"

"It's run by the Sisters of the Society of St Barbara. It's what they used to call a 'finishing school'. The girls are slightly older than high school age, eighteen to twenty. It's smack in the middle of nowhere, and there are no boys around – for miles."

"Safekeeping you said – you mean safekeeping their cherries."

Galway grimaced. "Locan, the super-rich are just like us when it comes to their children, especially daughters. Especially young ladies whom they might suspect are predisposed to give in to their hormonal urges."

"So they lock them away in some . . . convent? A lesbian boot camp, I'd say."

"The tuition, as you might expect, is quite substantial."

"And I suppose quite a bit of that money gets funneled to Rome."

"That's not our concern."

"OK, so why is the Vatican dispatching two Paladins to Ireland's version of East Bumfuck?"

"The mother superior, Abbess Marie, informed us a month ago that Monsignor Padraigh O'Callaghan had arrived to take over the administration of the school."

"So? The old bat resents giving up the top slot to a priest . . . a man?"

"Obedience is not an issue with the sisters."

"Really?"

"The problem is, Monsignor O'Callaghan, while expected at the school, arrived a bit later than scheduled."

"When was he supposed to get there?"

"He left from Dublin in October . . . 1873."

"Hmmm."

"Yeah."

"Imposter?"

"Obviously. But there's something else."

"Huh?"

"Some of the students' families have contacted various cardinals at the Vatican. They are concerned because their daughters have tried to dissuade them from visiting."

"Hmm."

"Yeah, usually the kids are begging for a visit, or to be taken away entirely. Instead they write – and they have to write because there's no internet out there – about what a lovely time they are having, and enjoying their lessons, that sort of thing."

"Teenaged girls? Yeah, something's fucked up. Has anyone tried to contact the abbess, or this O'Callaghan?"

"Yes, they say all is well. I myself spoke to O'Callaghan – charming fellow, a real gift of the blarney."

"Why not have the Garda check things out?"

"We did. No suspicions raised."

"We didn't tell them he was impersonating a priest from the nineteenth century?"

"We left that bit of information out. We just wanted them to give us a read on the guy."

"Why us? Why Paladins?"

"Just a feeling, a hunch. There's something off about the guy, besides the fact he was supposed to arrive a hundred and forty years ago."

"OK."

"You'll fly to Shannon, stay overnight in Limerick. The Garda will take you to the school."

"OK."

"Locan, the boss is very concerned about this."

Locan chuckled. "Well, then I guess we'll have to solve this mystery. Maybe there'll be a red hat in it for you."

"Not likely. This new guy seems to have no use for cardinals."

"Hmm."

A young Garda greeted them at the diplomatic gate at Shannon Airport.

"*Fáilte go dtí Éire.*"

"Huh?" A pair of heavy-lidded eyes peered back at the young man.

"Um . . . welcome to Ireland. I thought you'd be apt to brush up on your Irish. People won't reply in English where we're going."

"Uh-huh." Locan nodded, his voice gravelly. "Well, most of the people I'll be talking to won't be so hindered."

The young Garda nodded. "Sorry, you must be tired from the flight, but there's been a change in plans. I'm to take you right on to Galway and thence to Connemara. Sorry, it's a bit of a ride."

"How much of a bit?"

"Six hours . . . maybe."

"Can't we stop to freshen up, at least," Rachel pleaded.

"We can make a quick stop in Galway, miss."

She looked toward Locan. "What's the freaking hurry? Tell me again: why are we being sent here exactly?"

Locan shrugged, lowered his voice, "A guy arrived a hundred and forty years late for work. You'd think they could stand to let us put off interviewing him a day more."

"And a night."

"OK, officer. Let's hit the road."

They stopped at a small inn on the outskirts of Galway where they were invited to refresh themselves. The hostess showed Rachel to a room with a shower. Locan waited in a small bar with the young Garda.

"So, you work for the Vatican, do you?" the young man asked.

"We do."

"Interesting work, is it?"

"It has its moments."

"Hmm, have you met the pope?"

"No."

"Never?"

"Not one, not yet."

"Ah, that's a shame."

"Oh, I don't know."

"Miss McDaniel – if you don't mind my saying – she doesn't look like the type of woman who would work for the Vatican."

"Oh? What should a woman who works for the Vatican look like."

"Well, like a nun, I'd imagine."

"Who's to say she isn't a nun?"

"You don't say? She's awfully pretty."

At that moment Rachel entered the bar. Conversation stopped as every eye traced the tight, cable-knit white sweater that clung to her curves and continued to the black wool mini that generously exposed her pale thighs an inch or two above her knees. Black boots clad her lower legs and made her seem taller than she was. Locan smiled. She'd acquired a fine fashion sense since the first time he'd met her.

"A nun, you say?" the young Garda gasped.

Locan chuckled and gestured to her to join them.

"We'd better be one and done," their guide said. "It'll be dark before we reach the school if we don't set out."

"No rest for the weary." Locan nodded.

They left Galway behind. Traffic was scant save for a pair of tourist buses.

"There are more houses here than I remember," Locan said.

"You've been here before?" Rachel asked.

"Long, long time ago. It seemed more remote then."

"Just wait a bit," the Garda said.

Before long they cruised between high green peaks streaked with pink-purple slashes of heather, as if a giant had taken a paintbrush to the hills.

"What are those white dots way up on the mountains," Rachel said, pointing out the window.

"Sheep," Locan said.

"There are hundreds of them, but only one or two together."

"Lots of room to roam."

Mountains rose to their right at the rim of a great bowl-shaped valley.

"Those peaks are some hundred miles distant," the Garda said.

Altogether the place exuded a profound sense of emptiness.

"It's beautiful," Rachel said. "But I'd hate to be a young girl and having to spend any time here. I'd feel like I was marooned on the moon."

There was more of the same landscape ahead, beautiful but depressing somehow, as if the craggy valleys harbored lost souls.

They continued on for another hour.

"You haven't asked me about Gina?" Rachel said. The break in silence made Locan start.

"Huh?"

"The girl you insisted I go out with the other night."

"I didn't insist. You said she was cute. I just said go for it."

"Hmm. Well, don't you want to know?"

"Know what?"

"How things went."

Locan shrugged. "None of my business."

"You make me crazy."

"Huh?"

"You goad me to go out with a girl and then you pretend not to care what happened next."

"Goad you? C'mon. We agreed I wouldn't . . . that is, if you wanted . . . anyway, you seemed to like this Gina chick. Besides, when you were still MIA in the morning I figured you must have had a good time."

"She's nice. She's also Sicilian. A little pushy, possessive. I won't be seeing her again."

Locan shrugged once more.

Rachel hissed an exasperated sigh. "You make me nuts."

After a few more hours Locan leaned forward to ask the Garda if they were lost, but in an instant the school appeared as a castle hugging the side of a mountain. The Garda steered the car along a drive to a parking area. A tourist bus began to pull away as they came to a stop.

A group of young girls in jackets and tartan skirts eyed them with undisguised curiosity. Rachel stepped out and stretched. She noticed the girls exchange whispers. One of the girls stepped in front of her companions and smiled.

But Rachel's gaze was drawn to the front of the girl's skirt. Locan stepped around her. "We better find O'Callaghan."

"Locan, look at that girl's skirt."

"Huh? What about it?"

"Look at it!"

Locan rubbed his eyes. The girl boldly gazed back at them. "Her skirt? Why . . . what . . . what the fuck?"

The girl turned back to her companions as her skirt swirled and lifted, allowing a glimpse of her thighs. The group giggled and started back toward the school.

"Did you see?" Rachel pressed.

"I think so." He shrugged.

A nun and the Garda exchanged some words, then he gestured to Locan and Rachel.

"The sister will take you to the monsignor. Call me when you're ready to leave. Uh, your phones are satellite-based?"

"Yes."

"Good. It's a big dead zone here, and the landline isn't always reliable. I'll leave your luggage here. Someone will come for it, the sister says."

"A little chat in the Irish?"

"No. She's Romanian, but we both speak a bit of French."

"Hmm."

The nun curled her finger and turned. They followed her toward the castle.

She led them into a hall with long tables and a low dais toward the front. The nun left them without a word.

Locan and Rachel assessed the crystal chandeliers and elegant wallpapers depicting rustic scenes. The tables were polished, a deep, dark wood. The dark wooden floor gleamed.

"Quite a dump," Locan said.

"Lavish, isn't it? Lovely place to retire to . . . it is that."

Locan and Rachel turned toward the dais where an elderly priest smiled and stepped down. His white hair piled atop his scalp like a wave about to break over his forehead. His face was craggy, and there was a mischievous glint to his pale-blue eyes.

"Monsignor O'Callaghan?"

"I am," he said, and effected a slight bow. "And you'd be the visitors from Rome. Glad to have you, but mightily curious about your visit."

"Well, we can discuss that."

"No time like the present." The priest nodded; his grin widened. "Get the business out of the way at once. Now, Gary, me boy, it's lovely to see you, but why are you here?"

Rachel looked at Locan and mouthed, *Gary?* He shrugged in reply.

"Well, monsignor, the Church is concerned that—"

"Your mother called you Gary, did she? When she told you stories of the faery folk, when you were just a wee bit of a lad."

Locan's mouth hung open at his interruption. "I . . . no, my mother never called me Gary."

"Hmm, and how is your mum?"

"My mother died . . . about fourteen years ago."

"Aw, and don't we miss her."

"Monsignor . . ."

But the cleric had turned his gaze to Rachel. "Darlin', lovely that you've come to visit. There's always room for another *cailín deas* – that is, another pretty lass here."

"Uh, thank you, but—"

"Did you notice the faery hounds lurking about?"

"Huh . . . hounds?"

"Did ya not? Great white shaggy beasts, except of course for their ears all fiery red, and their eyes . . . red as demon's eyes they are."

The cleric turned again to Locan. "Surely your mum told you of the faery hounds." He grinned.

His gaze snapped toward Rachel again. "I would have thought *you'd* have espied them. Never to mind, then. They'll not be far away. Pests they make of themselves."

Rachel leaned toward Locan and whispered, "What the hell is he talking about?"

A capsule of memory burst in Locan's mind. Could he have been even four years old? His mother held him in her lap and told him the stories. The faery hounds . . . chief antagonists of the . . .

"Aw, shit! Fuck me . . . fuck us!"

"Now, now, there, Gary boy, mind your talk. There are young ladies about and the sisters."

"Fuck you! Son of a bitch bastard!"

"Now, we can't have you going on like that."

Rachel's eyes went wide as her glance darted between Locan and the cleric. "Locan! What's wrong?"

"Aw, shit! He's a fucking pooka!"

Blue electricity danced up Rachel's arms and around her head.

"No, Racey, don't shift!" But Locan's warning came too late; he averted his eyes at the brilliant flash of blue.

"Ah, now there's a bit of ephemera I've not seen for ages," the cleric said, his voice pleasant, even. "I think I may have known her great-great-great-grandfather. You know, the one who paid his respects to grow inside her great-great-great-grandmum's belly. Passed the gift along the generations, I see."

Locan's eyes adjusted. His gaze darted about the room. Rachel was nowhere in sight.

He yanked his Sig 9 from its shoulder holster.

"Uh-uh, put away your fusee! You know it can do you no good, and we don't want innocent bystanders getting hurt now; do we Gary, me boy?"

"Stop calling me Gary, you prick! What have you done with her?"

"Eh? Oh, the darlin' Rachel. She's right there, and well enough." He pointed with his finger to a place on the floor where a squalling puppy awkwardly tried to gain her footing on the high-polished surface. "Adorable," O'Callaghan said. "Do you not think so?"

"Bring her back, or I swear, pooka or not, I'll find a way to—"

"No need for ultimatums and such. She can right herself." He knelt over the puppy. "Come now, darlin'. Bring yourself back to us." He glanced at Locan. "Better to shield your eyes, boyo."

Locan turned away just as the room shone again in intense blue light. "Oh, no!"

Rachel stood as a cascade of blue fireflies fell off her shoulders and evaporated. She shielded herself in the classic stance of a young woman caught naked.

"Well, aren't you a wonderment, young lady? I take it your clothes don't survive that big bright thing you do?"

"No!" she snapped.

"Dear, dear, I beg your pardon. Not to worry, we'll respect your modesty." He called out and a nun and four girls came into the room. The girls giggled at Rachel's predicament.

"Our guest, Miss McDaniel, seems to have lost her clothes. Would one of you ladies lend her your jacket, just for the nonce, until she can retrieve her baggage?"

The bold girl from the parking lot slipped her school jacket off her shoulders and held it out to Rachel, just enough to make her drop her arms from her bosom and snatch it. The girl grinned.

It was then that Locan noticed the girl's skirt and the prominent tent in front.

"Would you come with us, please," the girl asked, perhaps a bit too sweetly.

Rachel glanced at Locan.

"Go ahead. I'll be OK."

"You'll be more than OK, Gary, and so will the lovely Rachel. Run along with the girls, darlin', we'll see you soon enough."

Rachel followed the giggling girls. The hem of the jacket didn't quite cover her behind.

"You'll be having dinner with us, will ya?"

"Listen, O'Callaghan, or whatever your name is . . ."

"You couldn't pronounce it, boyo."

"Whatever. Just so you understand, I'll do whatever I can to keep you from abusing these girls and these sisters. Twisted mother—"

"Uh-uh, no need for nasty talk. We're all friends here."

"You're a damned pooka, you don't have friends."

Locan wasn't prepared for the shadow of melancholy that darkened the pooka's visage.

"Ah, true enough. But, we're turning over a new leaf, as it were. Have a seat, young Paladin."

"You knew."

"Oh, Gary, saw you coming leagues away. The young lady too; although, it took me a moment to realize she carried the gift."

"Gift?"

O'Callaghan shrugged. "Affliction, if you will. Depends on how you look at it on any particular day. Now there's something I have in common with your lass: a lot of days – in my case, stretching on into that place they call forever."

"What are you doing here? What happened to the real Monsignor O'Callaghan?"

"Well, now, that good father suffered gravely from a wounded spirit. He sought ease by taking an occasional dram or two . . . or more, much more. Something about the emptiness of the country wore on his heart. He died near an abandoned hovel – one of hundreds that lie between here and Dublin. I'd been his shadow for a part of his journey – I couldn't tell you why. I felt . . . well, you'd call it pity for the old man."

"You – a pooka – felt pity?"

"Bucko, it came as a surprise to me too. Anyway, I sat at his wake, kept the goblins and the faery hounds at bay till his soul took flight to wherever souls fly to. And then I had meself a good long think."

"Did you?"

"I did that. And I thought I'd continue his journey for him. Take up his burden."

"That was almost a century and a half ago."

"Is that so?" He shrugged. "I tend not to notice such things."

"So, you're here now."

"I am."

"And exactly what the hell do you suppose you're doing here?"

"Making things better."

"You're shitting me."

"Why would I . . . Sorry, I don't get your meaning."

"You're a pooka. You don't make things better. You screw things up. You screw with people's heads."

"Ah, well. That's all behind me now. I've retired, don't you see?"

"Retired? Now I've heard everything."

"No, you haven't, Gary. But you will; I promise."

Locan shook his head, a long sigh of exasperation escaped his lips.

"Now then, boyo, will you take a bit of a walk with me. It'll build your appetite. The young ladies and the sisters love to cook for guests. We have them so infrequently. I expect they'll prepare a grand repast."

"Yeah, sure. Cripes."

They ambled through the woods, along the shore of the mountain lake, as O'Callaghan's narrative meandered off on a series of tangents and into a dozen tales. His soft, gravelly brogue was disarming, and Locan had to concentrate on suppressing a nascent affection for the being he knew could bring no good to the world.

"Well, now, Gary. Are you hungry?"

"I guess I could eat something."

"Come along, then."

They returned to the castle. Locan followed as O'Callaghan led him inside back to the hall, where they had first encountered him. About forty girls were seated at the tables as a crew of younger girls brought bowls and dishes and served.

"Aren't they lovely?" O'Callaghan said. "Ah, and here's Rachel, all dressed and decent."

Locan's jaw fell when he spied her. She was dressed in a schoolgirl's uniform, right down to the knee stockings and flat patent leather shoes.

"Don't you dare say a thing," she warned. "They claim they misplaced my bag."

"Sorry, for a second I thought you had enrolled."

"Locan. I warned you."

"Sorry," he said as he tried to suppress a grin. "You look like an extra in a movie I saw once. *Schoolgirl Lust,* I think the title was."

"Locan!"

"OK, OK. I'll lay off . . . promise. Jesus, you're cute."

"Shut up!"

He nodded, took her arm and led her to their seats.

After they were settled, Rachel leaned and whispered to Locan.

"That girl – she has a dick."

"Huh?"

"The girl from the parking lot, the one who lent me her jacket."

"You mean she's not a girl?"

"No. She's a girl, but she has a dick."

"I don't get it. What, she's wearing a strap-on? Is that what was poking up from under her—"

"Locan, listen to what I'm saying. She's a girl . . . and she has a dick . . . and a pair of balls too. She showed me; she said I gave her a hard-on. Jesus!"

Locan remained gape-mouthed for a moment. "Damn, I might have known. Fucking pooka. Jesus, these girls must be traumatized."

"You mean O'Callaghan gave her a dick?"

"Not really. It's all in their heads . . . our heads. That's how the fuckers amuse themselves. They love to humiliate human beings. Jesus, these poor kids are going to need therapy once we get this bastard out of here."

"How do we do that?"

He shook his head. "About all you can do is wait him out, wait until he gets bored. Maybe we can divert his attention elsewhere."

O'Callaghan sat opposite Locan and Rachel. "Lovely combination: goose and trout. Fins and feathers."

"So, you think you're making things right around here?"

"I do, and why are you taking that tone with me?"

"What you've done to these girls isn't just immoral, it's sick perversion."

"Whatever do you mean, Gary? Oh, Rachel must have glimpsed their alterations."

"Alterations?"

"Look about you, all you see are happy young women. Do you detect even the slightest bit of unease, anxiety? All confident, smiling faces. The sisters too."

"Horseshit!"

"Do you know who these girls are?"

"They're from the wealthiest families in Europe."

"They are that. Families with such wealth, and such power. Did ya know, things haven't much changed since the feudal days. Women . . . girls are still used as a medium of exchange. These girls are . . . how shall we put it? Deal sealers. Just like back in the Dark Ages – ah, there was a time – they are expected to marry a selected mate. And just like in the Dark Ages, they are expected to be virginal."

"It's the twenty-first century, pooka."

"It is that. So what? I have always chuckled at the premium human beings set on a female's virginity. I've come to hate the concept meself. Poor virgins, they're martyred, sacrificed, fed to dragons and such."

"Dragons?"

"Oh, not like in the faery tales either. You've not read of the likes of these dragons."

"Uh-huh."

"These girls have been sheltered their entire lives. One day they'll be given to a man and be expected to know what the hell to do. Incubators, that's all they are, expected to carry the genes of an unbroken line. Can you imagine the terror a girl experiences on her wedding night, benighted and encumbered as she is by ignorance of her own body?"

"But," Rachel said, "what does that have to do with *altering* a girl, giving her a penis?"

O'Callaghan's face brightened. "Now, that was a stroke of genius, even if I do say so meself. These girls share rooms with others who will be their best friends for life. So, after a bit of a think, it came to me. Who else to explore their bodies' mysteries with than with their best friend, someone they trust, someone they love perhaps more than a sister?"

"So you . . . ?"

He grinned. "I gave one of them a cock. Just for a week at a time. They alternate. This way they explore, experiment, and an added benefit, they express their masculine nature, as well as their feminine. They're as well adjusted and balanced as any child ought to be. Now, I ask you again, do you see a distressed face among any of the young ladies here?"

Rachel and Locan looked about the hall. Everywhere girls laughed, giggled, hugged their companions. Everywhere there was mirth. Even the nuns smiled.

"This could be a picture you are planting in our heads," Locan replied. "And by the way, where is the abbess?"

"Oh, Mother Marie is enjoying a tryst with St Sebastian."

"Huh?"

"The poor dear. She's dedicated her life to God and his church, and her young charges. All the while she's entertained an erotic connection to St Sebastian. Something about a beefy young man with arrows sticking out of his armpits stokes her fires. Well, I arranged for her to fulfill her yearnings. She's tending to the young man now."

"In her mind?"

"And does that really make it any less real?"

"You . . . are so fucked up. Giving girls dicks, setting up an elderly nun with a canonized pincushion. Only a goofy fuck-ing pooka could come up with something like that."

Rachel raised a finger to her lip as if to silently admonish Locan. "What's in it for you?" she asked the pooka.

Again his smile did not fade entirely, but a shadow of melancholy came over his visage. "Have you ever seen a man drown in a bog?" he asked.

"Huh? Um, no. I've managed to avoid that."

He nodded. "At first, it's almost a lark. He's sure he'll extri-cate himself. But the more he moves, and then struggles, the quicker it sucks him down into the muck. After a bit he can't make any headway, can't even struggle as he tries to slog through that heavy, spongy stuff that is neither water nor earth.

"Time is like that," the pooka continued. "A few thousand years go by and it's all fun and games. But then you feel the tug of the centuries, weighing you down as you slog toward forever."

Rachel's eyes began to pool with tears.

"Now, there darlin'. I know. But, be at ease. Your time is finite."

"It . . . it is? But—"

"I cannot tell you when. I cannot even tell you if it will be a long ways away. I'm afraid I have a faulty grasp of what is lengthy in regard to time. But I can tell you, I'm tired, I want to stop someplace and take a bit of ease. I've decided this is the place, for now. And I'll do some good as long as I'm here, so long as the faery hounds keep their peace and distance."

No one said a word. Finally, O'Callaghan smiled.

"You'll be wanting to take your rest. I'll have a young lady show you to your room. Have a good night, now. We'll talk in the morning."

Rachel and Locan stood and followed a girl out of the hall. Rachel walked ahead of Locan who watched her hips sway and her tartan skirt swirl.

Damn, she looks cute, he mused.

Their room contained lush furnishings and a puffy feather bed.

"What do you think?" Rachel said.

"A feather bed. Been a long time since I slept in one of those. You'll go right out."

"I mean, what do you think of O'Callaghan?"

"I know he seems like a nice old guy, but he's a pooka. We can't trust him. They were created just to fuck with human minds."

Rachel let her jacket slip off her shoulders, then unbuttoned the white blouse. She let it fall and turned, standing topless in her tartan skirt and knee socks. Her gaze locked on Locan.

"What?" he said.

"My God, does this really turn you on?"

He shrugged. "Well, it is a different look for you."

"Cripes, you're leaking so much you've stained your pants. Can you at least wait until I get undressed, or maybe you want me to wear this thing to bed too."

"Huh?" He looked down at his crotch. His pants were indeed darkened by a large wet spot. Could he have exuded so much pre-come? Damn if it didn't look like he'd pissed himself.

Rachel walked past him to the bathroom as Locan continued to puzzle at his wet crotch. Then he heard Rachel shriek.

He turned to bolt toward the bathroom, but she stepped through the door, naked.

"Oh, my God, Locan, look!"

He shut his eyes tight and opened them again. He couldn't be seeing what he was seeing. Of course, he wasn't; the damned pooka was playing with his head.

"My God, Locan. He's given me a dick!" Rachel's chin trembled.

"Hold on there, kid. He hasn't . . . that is . . . it's not really there. It's just in your head . . . our heads."

"Well, it goddamned feels like it's there," she cried. She reached down and delicately lifted the penis in her fingers. She slid her fingertips along its length. "Whoo!"

"What?"

"My God, that felt ..." She gingerly slid her fingertips along the underside again. It came to life and bobbed out of her grasp. "Locan ... holy shit! It's getting hard. I'm having a hard on!"

"Well, it will do that if you keep rubbing it like that."

"Oh, my God." She began to stroke it. "I can feel it getting hard. Ooo! It feels ... it feels ..."

Rachel's cock stood out like the prow of a ship. Locan could only stare dumbstruck, mesmerized.

It occurred to him that it was a pretty dick, the most feminine-looking dick he'd ever seen. If a girl had to have a dick, especially a girl like Rachel, she couldn't have hoped for a prettier, more girlish dick than the one she stroked with increasing desperation.

It was pale as porcelain, and tapered, hairless. Then he noticed the pair of balls that hung between her thighs, contained in a pale, smooth, hairless sac.

"Locan, what am I supposed to do? I need to do something. Help me, Locan! You're a guy, what am I supposed to do with it?"

Should he tell her to jerk herself off?

"Um, look, it's not really there. What you're feeling, it's just in your head."

"I don't care. I'm ... Oh, Locan."

"All right, stop stroking it. Get into bed and try to relax. Maybe it will disappear."

"But, Locan, I can't help ..."

"Yes you can! Get into bed."

Rachel reluctantly let go of her hard-on and waddled toward the bed. "How the hell do you guys walk with all this junk between your legs?"

"Never mind, just get into bed. Look, I'll rub your back or something to get your mind off it. Go ahead, I'm right behind you."

Rachel mumbled, "How am I supposed to lie on it?" She climbed into the feather bed and sank into valleys formed by the bedclothes.

Locan dropped his pants as she watched.

"Locan! You . . . you're . . . you have a pussy!"

"What?" He looked down. "Aw, fuck. You're shitting me."

Rachel began to laugh.

"What's so fucking funny?"

"You're soaked. My God, I've never seen a pussy so sopping wet."

"I . . . never mind. That prick, immortal my ass, I'll find a way to kill him." His ears burned as he sidled into bed, all the while attempting to shield his crotch.

Rachel giggled like she was being tickled mercilessly. "Oh, Locan, you should have seen your face."

"Right, like you were looking at my face."

"Locan, please, I'm still hard. Look, it's making a tent in the bedclothes."

"Racey, you're just going to have to—"

"Give me a blow job," she pleaded.

"What!"

"Please. I just want to know what it feels like."

"Look, whatever it feels like you can't trust it. It's all in your head."

"Locan, please. It's so hard, I need some relief. Please?"

"I can't."

"If you really cared about me you wouldn't leave me in such misery."

"Huh? Are you kidding? Look, I don't suck cock."

"But it's not just any cock; it's my cock. It's a pretty cock, isn't it?" She lifted the bedclothes displaying her newly acquired phallus, curving delicately like a fleshy scimitar, reaching, yearning.

"I . . . But . . ."

"Please, please, Locan. I don't think I can take much more."

It was her eyes, those wide, liquid puppy-dog pleading eyes.

"Jesus . . . if you ever tell anyone . . ."

"I won't, ever, cross my heart. Please, Locan, hurry."

He began to lean under the covers, but she tossed them off.

"Do it like you like me to do it," she said.

"Jesus."

He took her cock between his thumb and forefinger. It was truly a girl's cock, creamy smooth to the touch.

Rachel moaned.

"OK," Locan said. He extended his tongue and licked the underside.

"Oooo! Whoa! Oh-my-God! Locan, Jesus, no wonder you guys plead and beg and whine and cry like little girls for us to do that to you."

"What?"

"Don't stop, stupid! C'mon, lick me some more. Take me in your mouth. Ohhh, gawwwd!"

He had taken her penis into his mouth, lapping its length from base to tip, then re-engulfing it. Rachel was past intelligent speech, and communicated in squeaks, shrieks and high-pitched sighs.

He felt the cock expand and withdrew it from his mouth.

"Owww, no! Why'd you stop?"

"Listen, when you feel like you have to . . . uh . . . let loose, give me a warning."

"What? Aw, shit, OK, OK, I promise I won't come in your mouth . . . OK? Please, don't stop again."

"Jesus, OK, OK."

He resumed sucking her lovely cock and after some moments found himself suppressing a chuckle. She was so vocal while her fists grabbed handfuls of sheets, or pounded the mattress. He was driving her crazy and he was enjoying every second of her exquisite agony.

He fondled her balls as he sucked her, eliciting even more shrieks, sighs and the occasional nasty word.

He felt an almost imperceptible contraction of her ball sac and the tip of her cock knocked up against the back of his throat. He tried to expel her, but she held his head fast and thrust against his face, fucking his throat.

When her cock jerked he resigned himself to what was coming. It flowed into his throat as his tongue tried to divert it out the side of his mouth. Then his mouth tasted like an entire peppermint patty had melted inside it.

As her shrunken cock slipped past his lips, he mumbled, "Fucking crazy pooka."

Rachel lay like a helpless rag doll. "Oh, Locan, I had no idea. That was so . . . fantastic. I'll never make fun of anyone for begging for a blow job again."

Suddenly, she lifted herself into a sit, took his head in her hands and kissed him. "You taste nice." She grinned. "Like peppermint. I'm sorry for not telling you I was going to come . . . I just . . ."

"Yeah, I know. It's okay."

"Locan, that was beautiful. Such sensations. The urge to come . . . like I wanted to explode."

"Glad you enjoyed yourself."

"Let me do something for you."

"Huh?"

"Let me lick your pussy. I know how to make you crazy."

"Uh . . . that's okay."

"Don't be embarrassed; I promise you'll like it."

"Aw, jeez."

In an instant, she was kneeling between his thighs. Her hair fell over his crotch and then her tongue's tip slid along his vulva lips.

"Whoa!"

His exclamation spurred her to accelerate her attentions. Her tongue dodging about his clit, pulling at his lips with her own. Locan couldn't move; he could barely breathe. Rachel's tongue tapped out a tattoo on his clit and his eyes rolled back and his toes curled.

It was an orgasm like he'd never experienced before, a zing of electricity followed by a series of pulses that spread like ripples in a pond under his belly and chest.

His eyes opened, glazed, lazy. Rachel grinned above him, licking her lips.

"Locan, you taste like cinnamon syrup."

"Uh . . . huh."

She molded her body to his. "You really liked it, didn't you? I did it just the way I like it done to me, you know, when I have a pussy."

"It was . . . incredible."

"Locan, this isn't so bad. I mean, I hope we turn back to normal, but maybe this isn't such a bad thing."

"Racey, I can't think right now."

"Yeah . . . okay." She smiled and kissed him.

They lay together, dozing from time to time. Rachel awoke and brushed her lips against Locan's ears and whispered, "Hey, I guess you're a cocksucker."

Locan bolted up into a sit.

Rachel giggled. "Oh, don't be mad. I'm just being a bitch."

"You . . . you little . . ."

"I'm hard again."

"What?"

"Let me fuck you, Locan."

"Ah, no, I don't think . . ."

"C'mon. I'll never get a chance to feel what it's like."

"Racey, Jesus, no. I don't think . . ."

"Oh, don't be shy." She straddled him, grinned and demanded, "Spread them."

"Haven't you ever heard 'no means no'?"

"You say no, but you really mean yes."

"God, Racey."

"You're sopping again. Ya slut!"

"Hey!"

She thrust her cock into him and all at once he experienced a sense of being filled; his insides clenched her cock as she withdrew and thrust again until she had achieved a regular, if accelerating rhythm.

Locan surrendered and clasped his hands over her hips, guiding her as she corkscrewed her pelvis, penetrating him ever deeper.

"Oh, baby," he whimpered.

She shuddered, and he felt her fluids splash inside him. He wondered what flavor they were this time, not that it mattered.

As she slid out of him, he felt a low yield charge explode in his belly. "Oh, wow," he sighed.

Rachel bent down and kissed him.

"I love you, Locan."

She'd never said that before; they'd avoided saying it to each other.

He closed his hands around her hips and slid them up to her ribs. "I love you too, Rachel."

A tear splashed on his cheek.

"What?" he said.

"It's just . . . you only call me Rachel when you're serious."

They molded their bodies together in a tight embrace.

"I never knew," she said. "It was like I was taking possession of you, Locan. And, then, like I was becoming you, melding with you."

"I know . . . I know."

Their room filled with bright sunshine, drawing them from sleep. Rachel snuck a peek under their bedclothes.

"Aw, gee."

Locan tossed the bedclothes aside. "Back to our old selves, I guess. Disappointed?"

"I would have liked to have done you doggie."

"Hmm."

"Locan?"

"Huh?"

"This wasn't a bad thing – there's no evil going on here, is there?"

A soft knock at the door diverted their attention and caused them to snatch up the bedclothes to cover themselves. A girl peeked inside.

"Excuse me, ma'am, sir. We found the lady's luggage."

She left Rachel's bag and quietly closed the door.

They showered together then dressed in sweaters and jeans.

"So, what are we going to do?" Rachel asked. "Pooka he may be, but, damn it, I think he's on to something."

"I don't know. How'd you react when you found you'd suddenly acquired a penis?"

"I know – I screamed my head off."

"You think these girls aren't similarly traumatized?"

"I think their girlfriends probably prepare them. At least now anyway."

"I suppose. OK, let's go see him."

They found O'Callaghan sitting alone at a table lifting a spoonful of oatmeal to his lips.

"Good mornin' to you, darlins. Sleep well, did ya?"

"What do you think?" Locan scowled.

O'Callaghan grinned as Rachel rolled her eyes.

"All right, me boy. What are we going to do? Set me out onto the world to resume me old tricks? Or let me be at ease at this school, here amongst the mountains of the moon, as it were. Aw, Gary, you know in your heart I'm doing no wrong."

"How can I trust you?"

"Aye, you're taking a chance, I'll give you that."

A gaggle of students happened by, laughing, chatting. One hugged O'Callaghan and wished him good morning.

"Did I really see a group of happy girls walk by, or did you make me think I did?"

"Gary, Rachel, do you think you only imagined making love last night?"

"No," Rachel replied. "I didn't imagine anything."

O'Callaghan brushed back his breaker of grey hair and smiled.

Just before dusk, their young Garda drove them past the gate and out onto the road to Limerick.

Rachel asked Locan, "What are you going to tell Bishop Galway?"

"That the school is in good hands, and we'd be wise not to fuck with it, or its new administrator."

Rachel suddenly sat up and leaned out the window of the SUV.

"What?" Locan asked.

"Don't you see them, all shaggy and white with red fiery ears?"

Locan followed her line of sight.

"Faery hounds. Look at them all. Well, I guess they'll be keeping an eye on him for us."

The young Garda looked quizzically at Locan and Rachel and shrugged.

Subbing

Rachel Kramer Bussel

"It's just for a day," Jesse wheedled, begging her best friend, Taylor, to fill in for her on the job. "And you're already kinky," she added, like that sealed the deal, like Taylor would want to spend her Saturday bending over to get spanked and pretending to drool over some guy she wasn't interested in. It was true, she was kinky, not to mention single, but even though they were best friends, Jesse didn't know everything that Taylor was into. She didn't know how much Taylor had loved it when her ex, Brian, choked her – his big meaty hand wrapped around her slender neck while one leg pinned her down and his fingers pressed deep inside her. Jesse definitely didn't know how much Taylor liked it when Brian had called her a slut and "threatened" to bring his friends over to fill all her holes and cover her in come. The dirtier the talk, the harder she'd come. But that was with Brian, not some stranger, even though, she had to admit, when Brian had teased her with the idea of being his whore, getting paid to service his friends, she'd practically crushed the fingers he'd been fucking her with.

In the end, it wasn't the excitement that made Taylor say yes, but the fact that, even more than she was a bad girl, she was a good girl. She knew Jesse would've done anything for her, and she couldn't refuse this rare favor. If she'd fill in for a friend working a cash register or serving as a teaching assistant, her other closest friends' current jobs, she couldn't refuse to get fucked for cash. Well, not fucked, Jesse clarified. "No sex," she said, either ignoring or not seeing Taylor's slight slump of disappointment. Wasn't getting fucked the best part, the icing on the kinky cake?

"OK, you just let them order you around, spank you, tie you up, stuff like that. Some of them want to see you do things to yourself, like suck your own nipple or put a butt plug in. But they can't take photos of you and they can only touch you if you let them. You get a flat fee and you get to keep whatever tips they give you. And dinner wherever you want is on me."

"What should I wear?" Taylor asked. Fashion first was always her motto.

Jesse laughed. "Whatever you want. They're probably going to want you naked anyway. Some of them bring in clothes for you to try on. It's a job, Taylor; you don't have to love it, you just have to pretend to." Jesse gave her all the details, along with a hug and a smile, then left her alone. Taylor plopped down in front of her TV, but all she could think about was the fact that tomorrow at this time, she could be doing anything, with anyone. Well, not anything, but almost; the thought made her wet and, before she knew it, the TV was off and her electric vibrator was in her hand, making her come, as she envisioned two men toying with her, one pressing her down onto her knees to suck the other's cock while he beat her with a riding crop. She knew as her orgasm hit she wouldn't have to fake anything; even a guy she wasn't into was a guy paying for her services, paying for her to show him what a slut she really was. She would be subbing, but she wouldn't be acting, she didn't think.

Taylor showed up for the gig in what she thought was appropriate attire: a simple yet relatively see-through white T-shirt, her nipples jutting forward just enough to make it clear she didn't have on a bra, and a pleated black and red schoolgirl skirt, along with knee-high white socks and shiny black loafers she'd borrowed from her roommate. When in doubt, go for the schoolgirl look, she'd figured. She'd debated until the very last minute – panties or no panties – but had decided on plain white cotton; she could always take them off.

She'd packed a toy bag just in case the dungeon didn't have exactly what her clients requested, although how she could predict what they'd want, she wasn't sure.

"Hello," she told the woman at the dungeon's front desk, who explained that most of the women working there were dommes, and most of their clients usually filled the role she was going to play today. Some of the men were switches, but the ones who mainly wanted a professional sub, which cost more, were usually rich and had limited time on their hands to find a girl willing to do the things he wanted them to do. Plus there were plenty of civilian women who actually wanted to get spanked and strung up, so the rich types didn't have to look too far for girls willing to take orders. The ones who wanted to pay for it had a reason and usually wanted something beyond the average kinky girl's regular repertoire, and Taylor was grateful for that, since she didn't consider herself an "average" anything. She read over the rules, which mentioned the company safeword that all clients were required to agree to, and waited, wondering if it was a faux pas, a mark of an amateur, that she was wet as could be. She was definitely glad she'd worn the panties.

She spied the men coming in, but couldn't discern a pattern. Most were at least in their thirties, many in their fifties, mostly white. Some were hot and hunky, but most were average; it was like a Wall Street parade, no hint of the business about to happen inside from these men's attire. And then she was called on. "Tina," said the clerk, using the name she'd picked, a simple one she would surely remember, one she was sometimes called by vague acquaintances who saw her rarely and couldn't quite recall her more manly moniker. She smiled to herself, knowing that if Jesse hadn't asked her to sub as a sub, she'd be sitting at her favorite coffee shop right now, hunched over some tedious manuscript she was copyediting. This was sure to be far more fun, not to mention lucrative.

She entered the room and wondered where to sit: on one of the chairs? On the floor? Should she stand? They said that the sub was truly the one in control of any kinky scene, but she wasn't so sure about that. Suddenly Taylor had butterflies in her stomach; she wanted to do a good job, on principle, and she wanted it to hurt, in a good way. She needed that rush of endorphins that only submission could give her and, as she took a deep breath in through her nose and slowly let it out through her mouth, she smiled to herself. Yes, she was woman enough to own that she wanted this, that she wasn't really in a chilly dungeon for the money, but for the rush, the thrill, the wetness. She was there because whether cash was involved or not, this was where she belonged.

Taylor decided to kneel, and kept her hands behind her back as she waited for the door to open. She'd been given a buzzer she could press to get security if she needed it, but when the door opened and an older man, one surely at least twice her own twenty-four years, entered, she knew she wasn't going to need it. He wasn't her usual type; he was a little more distinguished yet country, no hint of hipster about him; his aura was stern without trying. There was something old-fashioned about him, like he would be as happy handling a worn leather belt as he might using an implement found in one of her favorite sex toy stores. This man could beat her all over and she'd probably just ask for more. The trick, she'd learned early on, was in holding off on letting them know just how much you liked it. That wouldn't be hard, because Taylor – *Tina*, she reminded herself – liked struggling, even if it meant the internal struggling of keeping her deepest fantasies hidden.

"Hello, Tina, sweetheart," he said, his smile both sweet and sadistic at once. She glanced immediately at his crotch, a bad habit she'd picked up somewhere along the way with guys she was hot for. She could see the outline of his cock against his jeans. "Daddy wants to have a word with you." He took the chair and ragged it across the room, resting his hand on his cock. She looked up at him, grateful he wasn't overly polite, wasn't polluting their time with niceties that would do nothing for her pussy. He knew what he wanted, and so did she. "I have your allowance right here," he said, holding up what she could see was at least a hundred dollars more than her fee.

"Crawl to me, pretty girl," he said, "crawl to Daddy." She did, wondering if he could tell how wet she was, wondering if he knew this was her first time, wondering if any of that mattered.

He kept talking as she reached him, seamlessly sliding the bills into the waistband of her skirt. "I know it was really Janet who stole the car, but since you told me you did it, you're going to get punished for it. You understand, don't you?" Somehow, his voice was soothing, deep and sexy, like he was trying to seduce her, yet the power behind his words vibrated through the air. "Janet will get punished even worse," he said, "but you need to learn not to cover for her. You never lie to your Daddy again, do you hear me?" He didn't yell, but it was the quiet roar in his voice that cued her in. She knew she could back away if she wanted to, but she had no desire to escape; instead, she was irresistibly drawn to that cruel yet sweet voice, its roughness promising pain as well as tender understanding. "Now get me my whip," he said, pointing to a riding crop sticking up out of his briefcase. "Bring it to me between those pretty lips."

She shuddered as she did it, realizing it had been three months since she'd last been beaten, and two more since she'd had someone talk to her like this. Well, not like this, exactly; she'd only played at being a "bad girl", but never Daddy's bad girl. This was different, doubly, even triply hot for all the taboos they were breaking. "You're to keep your panties on, but I want you to show me how wet you are, Tina, show me how much you need to be punished." She pulled down her panties and bent over with the crop between her teeth, her ass in the air. Taylor spread her legs just enough to show the stranger, her new insta-Daddy, how slick her sex was. She started to inch backward, and stopped. Her punishment wasn't going to be a beating there, nor would there be a reward of his fingers or tongue or cock, as she was used to. Her real punishment was that she'd have to wait until later to touch herself there, where she most wanted it.

"I'm going to have to punish you even more for looking so good and teasing your old man, aren't I?" he asked, almost to himself, as he turned her around and grabbed the crop. He stood then used the crop to push her against the wall. "Hands up," he said, and she reached above her, holding on to the metal hooks fitted just for girls like her. He lifted her T-shirt and shoved it between her lips. "Keep that there or I'll rip it off; I bought it for you for your birthday, so technically it's mine – just like you are," he said.

She was aching, dripping, frantic before the crop even touched her. The first touch wasn't a strike but a tease, as it brushed against her hard right nipple like a feather would, except this feather was made of leather, and she knew it wasn't always going to feel so gentle. The man ran the crop all along her front, under each breast, along her gently sloping belly, up her neck. He let it rest gently against her cheek and meandered it along her underarm until she almost sighed in frustration. It was *on*; he tapped it against one nipple then hit the other one. Each nipple rose to attention and, after only a few slaps of the crop, Taylor was gritting her teeth, torn between watching the leather tip strike her tender nubs and closing her eyes to try to deal with the pain, the heat, the glorious rush she got each time the toy landed on her.

Just when her nipples felt like they were on fire, the man once again moved the crop down her body, this time to her inner thighs. He lifted her skirt and nudged her legs apart with his knee, then whapped her inner thighs. Taylor clutched the metal tightly, lest she sink down to the ground or be tempted to grab the crop and rub it against her wetness. The tender, padded flesh leading up to her sex had never been given quite so much attention, and Taylor bit her lip, aching with the sharp, pointed heat he managed to convey so expertly, like he was born to beat girls like her. She could almost forget they were actually playing a game, one in which she got paid for this, and simply be a girl who liked pain, craved it, needed it. It wasn't until that exact moment that Taylor – as Tina – fully owned her innate submissiveness, her masochism, which made even the hint of pain, like when the head of the crop teased her by merely resting against her skin, cause her to feel like she wanted to writhe in ecstasy.

Taylor mashed her lips together, suddenly longing for something between them, something to suck on or simply fill her up, and the look she gave the stranger was one of pure desire, one she was sure he could read just as clearly as the tears that sprouted to her eyes when he let the crop dangle and brushed a thumb lightly over her trembling lower lip. He moved closer, pressing her tight to the wall for a few seconds, then withdrew and raised his hand to her cheek. She shuddered so hard she thought she might come. "There's so much I'd love to do to you, sweet girl," he said softly, an equally fervent need crashing right through his voice. Taylor knew they were sharing a moment, a real one, despite its trappings, and her pussy actually hurt as it clenched around nothing. He'd landed one slap across her tender face and brushed away the tear that trickled down, when a buzzer sounded, signaling they only had five minutes left. Taylor twitched, wondering if the sub could request more time.

Get a hold of yourself, she thought. *This is a job, a favor, not your life. But it is,* another voice inside her said. Not this dungeon, but this – the pain, the submission, the fierceness they both inspired in her – was her life, and it was as real as her wet pussy and hard nipples, as real as the crisp dollars the man had given her.

"Be a good girl for Daddy, Tina," he said, then lifted her up, carried her back to the chair, spread her across his lap and spanked her extremely hard, over and over again. She could tell he was spanking her faster than he ordinarily might have, and she let the tears flow, let herself be a good girl and a bad girl, a woman doing a friend a favor and a misbehaving daughter, a woman who loved pain the way some women loved shoes and a brat who'd misbehaved and needed punishing.

When he lifted her off his lap and placed her on the ground, he kissed his fingers and pressed them to her lips. "Goodbye, beautiful," he said, then reached into his pocket and pressed some more bills into her hand. It wasn't until she got home that she saw he'd also included a slip of paper with his phone number and one word: *Daddy*.

Taylor just shrugged as she sipped her iced coffee while Jesse asked her about her day. There'd been other men, but they'd seemed like children compared to him. "Oh, you saw Dylan, huh? He's a charmer. Hot, if you're into silver foxes." Jesse's voice was light, teasing, with no hint of the intensity Taylor had experienced. Taylor sipped her drink and smiled just as lightly. There was no reason to tell Jesse she had already called him and told him that Tina had crashed his sports car and needed him to pick her up at the mechanic's. He'd told her he'd meet her later, and that she was such a bad girl, he was going to focus on improving her behavior exclusively and let Janet fend for herself. Apparently, there were some things you couldn't find a substitute for, and Taylor didn't mind one bit.

Burned

Alison Tyler

Jenny was the type of girl who stole things. Small things, like
the few bucks remaining in your billfold if you inadvertently
left your wallet on the counter. Important things, like the
carnelian beads your mother had given you for your sixteenth
birthday. Irreplaceable things, like your husband. I've known
her type of women before. In fact, I've gotten good at spotting
them over the years. Why? Because when you're married to a
man like Rick, you have to expect ladies will worm their way
out of the holes in the headboard in order to try to steal him
away.

What makes Rick so fucking special?

Well, there's the fact that he's handsome. And by handsome, I mean turn-your-head, wolf-whistle, cat-call,
panties-wet-when-he-meets-your-eyes, dreamboat, movie-
star handsome.

How did I hook up with a man like that?

Fuck you.

No, really. How many times have I been out to dinner with
my husband and had a waitress pull me aside and ask me that
insensitive question. "So how did you two land together?
What's your secret?" As if a troll like me must have performed
a magic trick by the light of the full moon to woo my man.
Sacrificed a goat. Bathed in pig blood.

I'm not ugly. Don't set yourself on the wrong path there.
But I didn't win the gene pool Olympics the way Rick did. My
man's tall – six feet four inches in bare feet. He's the type of

hunk I grew up gazing at in posters on my wall. Magnum, P.I. The Six Million Dollar Man. Broad-shouldered, barrel-chested, gorgeous from tip to toe, and that tip includes the most beautiful cock I've ever seen.

And me?

I'm barely five feet, and I've got what my grandmother always used to call "character". That means that my lips might be a little fuller than your average runway model. My hair is kinky curly. My nose wrinkles when I smile. My eyes are dark, and I always have those purplish smudges beneath them – part Hungarian bloodline, part insomniac's curse.

Why does Rick love me? Not because I could take on a Victoria's Secret angel. That's for sure. At least, not without playing dirty, sucker punching her when she flapped her white-feathered wings on the catwalk. He loves me because one day two years ago he wandered into my studio while looking for a friend of his who'd just moved out – that was his line, anyway. I was hanging paintings on the wall, organizing oils, stretching drop cloths. The door was open and he stepped in, glanced around, and said, "I like that one."

I turned to see who was talking. I had my black hair scraped back with a red bandana, battered overalls on over a white wife-beater T, kick-ass Docs splattered with teal paint. "Which one?" I asked, turning to look where the stranger was pointing.

"The girl on the bed."

"Oh, her," I said. She was my former. Ex. Lover. Capital on the Ex. I should have taken a knife to the canvas based on what Jenny had done to my heart, but I was too proud of the work to destroy the piece. My goal was to sell the painting for a hefty price tag, and then splurge on a trip to Paris. I thought that selling her ass would give me pleasure. The painting, you see, was a nude.

Rick walked through the studio as if he had a reason to be there. "I'm Lola," I told him, offering a hand. He actually ignored me as he continued to look at the pictures, but he was so intent, I forgave him the rudeness. "You're good," he said.

"I know."

"Really good."

"I *really* know."

I took the time to look him over. Part of me did so automatically. As an artist, I'm always assessing the lines and the angles, the way people's features fit. The way I might paint them if I had a shot. The other part of me looked at him in a less clinical way. I hadn't had a cock in a while. I wondered if he was all show, or if he might be able to do the deed in a manner that would work for me.

"My friend used to live here," he said, finally explaining. "I was in the neighborhood and thought I'd see if he was still around."

"By *friend*, you mean drug dealer?" I asked. I'd found remnants that could mean nothing else. And people had come by at odd hours, other needy folk like Rick, searching for their savior in a dime bag.

He looked at me.

"No judgment," I added.

"In that case . . ."

That's how we found ourselves getting stoned in my studio. I didn't have the bed in yet. We sat on the drop-cloth-strewn floor and smoked the little bit of marijuana I had left in my coffee can. Do all druggies keep their stash in Foldger's, or is it just me?

He told me he was going through a rough break-up. That he hadn't gotten high in forever. That he'd driven to his dealer's place on a whim. I told him that I had moved in here when my ex and I had flamed out. Told him that I painted more when I was unhappy than when I was happy. Rick proved me wrong on that one, let me tell you. He turned all my used-to-be's into so much nonsense. Back then, we were new. We were raw. We were fucking on the floor like animals before the afternoon had ended. The pot? Maybe marijuana helped – we were relaxed, and there was none of the weirdness about going on a date first, wondering if you'd get a kiss on the cheek or a grope on the ass. He had his knees bent, and he touched my foot with his foot.

He put one hand on my leg. We were fondling each other as the late afternoon sun hit the opposite wall.

There was music in the clink of my overall buckles when he undid each one. There was a gentlemanly quality in the way he helped undo the knots on my Docs, the way he pulled off every scrap of my clothing before spreading me out on the floor. But there was brutality in the way he fucked me, and I thought, *I could get used to this.*

I wonder if it's the fact that I didn't act as if I wasn't good enough that turned him on. I mean, since that afternoon I've witnessed the power of Rick's appearance on other people. He makes them stammer. Stutter. Forget their own goddamn names. But I've been painting pretty people all my life. I am not wired in that way. I mean, I wasn't. Yeah, Rick made my panties wet. But maybe it had something more to do with the way he touched me, the way he seemed to understand how my thoughts clicked together, more than the fact that he could have bench-pressed three of me if he tried.

OK, so where does Jenny come into all this?

Well, not at the start. There were two years at the beginning when Rick and I ate and drank and devoured each other. When my man came home for lunch simply to fuck me against the wall, foregoing food in favor of my pussy, or for the flavor of my pussy.

And then one day Jenny showed up. A girl with a black heart. Rick had never been too concerned with the fact that I was bi. He knew I wasn't going to cheat on him, or leave him for another woman or another man. We were rock solid like that. He worked at his job all day while I painted. He fucked me every free second he had. He knew I wouldn't leave him just because he didn't have a pussy. "Bi" in my world simply means that I've been with men and I've been with women. Before Rick there was Jenny. Before Jenny was Max. I go with my heart. I don't care what parts you have as long as they connect with my own.

Jenny showed up the way she always showed up. She came slithering under the doorjamb, appearing in a puff of smoke.

Firebreathers have all sorts of tricks like that. When I returned from a run, Jenny was there on my sofa, curled up in the corner as if she'd been there all along, as if she'd never left. Except we hadn't lived here together. She'd had to look long and hard to find me.

"Lola," she said, as I unlocked the door, startling me enough so that I dropped the keys. While bending to retrieve them, I tried to make sense of the situation. Jenny had left me for a girl in her entourage. She'd literally run away with her to join the circus. I'd had dreams of her burning up, of her getting too drunk to do her trick correctly and incinerating herself until all that remained were ashes. But she looked solid and whole on my sofa, her skin still that translucent shell, nearly iridescent, her lips parted into a smile, her green eyes wide and filled with hope.

Stray kitten, ma'am, won't you take me in?

"You can't stay," I said.

"Nice fucking greeting." Those big green eyes went dark. Her voice held razor blades and whiskey. That's what Jenny hid right beneath the surface: metal shards and Kentucky bourbon. She could take you to a faraway place, a dreamscape you'd never been, build the pleasure until your eyes rolled up and your heart tried to escape from your chest. And then somehow, when you awoke from the bliss, she'd have burned through your credit rating, cremated all your closest relationships, and left even the clothes in your closet soot-stained, singed and smelling of smoke.

"My husband will be home soon," I said. It wasn't a lie. "You have to leave."

"No drink for the road? No kiss for old time's sake? No fuck with your hands over your head and your eyes shut tight?"

I could remember being fucked by Jenny. I could remember the ways she could make me come, her small hand curled into a fist and working inside me. Pleasure, always, tainted with a little bit of pain. That's what you get when you fuck a dragon.

"You can't," I started, "you have to . . ." But she was up, moving quickly toward me, her hands around my waist, her lips on my lips. I remained frozen. Her heat would not melt me. Not any more. I had Rick. I had my sanity. I had money in the bank. All sorts of things I'd had none of with Jenny. But her hand was insinuating down the front of my sweats, and her fingers were searching out my clit in that rough, gaudy way they always did. Dime-store trick, carny whore.

I pushed hard. She fell back on the sofa. "You've changed," she snarled, top lip raised.

"I got *married*," I told her. I didn't care if she could put her fingers up inside of me and make me come like nobody else ever had. I didn't care if Rick and I hadn't gotten to the true kink yet. We were still young. We'd get there.

"Let me meet your man. I'll leave after. I swear. I just need to know that you're truly happy."

"I'm truly happy."

"I saw your work. You only paint like that when something's wrong in your world."

"You'd know," I said softly. "You put me in that state so many times. But it's different now. Rick makes me happy. And I paint better."

"You sound like a fucking Hallmark card."

"I sound like a normal person."

She laughed, but she stood. I was relieved. She wasn't going to hang around. "There's no such thing as normal," she said, and I saw her fan her fingers out, magically showing me five crisp twenties. I knew she'd taken them from my underwear drawer. It's where I always kept a bit of extra. Pot in the coffee can. Cash with the knickers. In case you ever need a quick favor and I'm not there to let you in.

"See ya, Lola," she said as she left. I didn't move until the door clicked shut. Then I went to my bed and masturbated like a fiend.

"I smell smoke," Rick announced when he came home. "Did you light up without me, babe?"

I was still tangled in the white cotton sheets. Since I paint all day, I love surrounding myself in pure whiteness when I dream. Only imaginary colors stain my sheets. "You could say that," I said. "Jenny stopped by."

I hadn't told him everything there was to know about my ex, but I'd spilled as much as I dared. He'd been consumed by her portrait, wanting to own the very last dirty detail of how we'd behaved together. Emotionally, physically, sexually. I knew he was turned on by what I'd told him, but I still hadn't come entirely clean about our bondage-drenched nights. What if he balked? What if he turned away? I loved him, and I didn't want to scare him. So I'd told him most, but not everything there was to know.

"Did you fuck her?"

"Come on, Rick. I'd never cheat on you. You know that."

"But *would* you fuck her?"

That was a different question. Canvases Rick had never seen flickered through my mind. I had never told him about the time she cuffed me to the shower rod and used her leather belt on me. Never told him about the time she splayed me on the kitchen floor and licked my pussy for hours without letting me come, a candle in her hand, drip-dripping wax all over my body whenever I got too close to climax.

"She's dangerous," I said. "You heard what she's like."

"For me?"

I stared at him. What was he asking?

"I mean, if I was there, if I were watching, you wouldn't be cheating. It would be three of us together. I don't care how I participate. I could play with you, or I could sit in a chair across the room and never even move. You could even tie me down."

He was on the mattress. He had my right hand in his. He brought my fingertips to his lips.

"You touched yourself and thought of her," he said.

"I thought of you," I lied.

He started kissing me. My neck. My breasts. He pushed the sheets away and went for the split between my legs. "I can't do for you what she did."

"Thank fucking God," I said, arching my hips.

"No, I mean, I can't be a girl."

"Ditto to what I just said," I murmured. "I don't want a girl." I was moving on the mattress, reaching for his cock.

"Lola." He threw me back on the bed and held me there. I looked into his eyes. We had not done this yet. We had fucked like animals fuck. He had taken me against the wall. He had driven his cock hard into my ass, a drizzle of lube making the ride sublime. But we had done no power play. Not the kind where you might need a safeword. The term bondage hadn't even rippled between us. Until now. "You stay," he said. He had his fingertips pressed against my clit. He alternated between licking that hard bud and rubbing his thumb directly across the top. Giving me too much pressure, too much pleasure, all at once.

"Let me watch," he whispered, and he let his thumb side into my pussy.

"I don't even know where she went." But as I said the words, I knew I wasn't telling the whole truth. Sure she'd disappeared, as she always did, leaving only a vapor trail behind. But the look on her face as she'd walked out of the house told me that she'd be back.

I was wrong.

Jenny didn't come to our house. She went after Rick, all by himself.

Rick's a used car salesman. Before you make up your mind what that means, you have to know him. In his real life, in the garage, he is the type of brilliant mechanic who can take apart the most complicated engine and put the pieces back together. I believe he could do this blindfolded. He operates on touch and sense. He loves cars, the smooth clean lines, the purr of a good motor, the way I love the smell of my paints, the feel of my favorite brushes in my hands.

Rick spent years under cars, getting paid for doing what he loves. And then he was wooed away by the owner of a car dealership – a high-end retro vintage spot where Rick's good looks and the cars' sleek styles come together in happy harmony. Rick makes you want to drive off the lot in a cherry '55 Chevy, and he makes you almost believe that when you do, the whole world will tip on its axis, and you will slide back in time to when the car was new and the world was simpler.

How'd Jenny find him? She has her ways. Thank God, Rick had seen her picture. He recognized her right off, even with all her clothes on. He told me later how she appeared behind him, coming up quick and quiet. She's like that. That whole, morning fog on cat's feet, suddenly all around you in a haze of silver. He turned, and she was there, acting as if she had never seen anything prettier than the car on the showroom floor – and yet wanting, he said, wanting him to tell her that the car did not compare with her own fire-brand of beauty.

She chose a car with flames. Of course, she did. Scarlet flames licking up from the grille. She wanted a test drive, but she didn't have ID, wouldn't cough up her name. He passed, and she tried harder. I remember Jenny when she used to turn up the heat so the flames licked you from every angle.

What was she thinking? That she'd get Rick in the car, drive him off to the Hollywood Hills, and fuck him? And then what? She wasn't into any long haul. Would she come back and gloat to me, or simply move on down the road with another bite mark out of her belt.

Doesn't matter. Rick didn't fall. But he came home that night and told me everything, from the way her red patent leather shoes buckled at the ankles. The way her seamed stockings were perfectly in place.

I sat on the edge of the bed and I looked in his eyes.

"She's going to come here next," I told him. "I know her. She got a whiff of you, a scent of me, and she'll be trying her best to get between us."

"She wants you back?"

I shook my head. "She's not wired like that. But if she can't have me, then she wants me to be as miserably unhappy as she is every day of her life."

"I want to see her fuck you," Rick said.

"Even if it means burning up what we've got?"

"It won't," he promised. "I swear."

When she showed up again, it was nothing like I expected. Never is. She was there all in white on the doorstep, bottle of champagne in one hand, scarlet blooms in the other. I smelled rat even above the roses.

"Just a late wedding gift," she said, "since I didn't get an invite."

"You left no forwarding address."

Rick came up behind me and waited for the introductions. I let Jenny in, reluctantly, and she strode forward as if I'd given her the pass key to my soul.

"Lovely place you have here," she said, sneering at the fact that our pad was clean. There were no piles of ashes anywhere to be seen. Dinner was makeshift, unplanned, awkward. Champagne gave way to whiskey, which gave way to Rick kissing me in front of Jenny and then looking at her straight in the eye. "Do you think you do better than I do?"

"I know it for a fact."

"Show me."

I started to understand this wasn't about Rick getting off on seeing two girls together. He wanted to know what hold Jenny had over me, what she could do that he could not.

Jenny gripped my hair in her hand and pulled me back for a kiss. I grimaced, but I did not flinch. She bit my bottom lip hard, hard enough to leave marks, to draw blood, and then she slapped my face, so that I put a hand up to the sting and stared at her. "You like that?"

I nodded. I couldn't help myself. I refused to look at Rick

She tightened her fist in my hair and then she led me like that to the bedroom. Rick followed.

"Do you have cuffs?"

Rick shook his head, while I motioned to my bottom drawer. Rick looked surprised as Jenny lifted the sterling handcuffs from amidst the tangle of my stockings. "You sure you have the key?" I pointed to my jewelry box. Jenny had my wrists over my head in seconds, had my clothes cut off me and my body smack in the center of the bed.

"Roll over," she said. "Show me your ass."

I obeyed, on autopilot. Rick had said he wanted this. Be careful what you wish for.

"See how wet she is?" Jenny asked him. "Part her legs and touch for yourself."

Rick's fingers felt my wet, slicked-up pussy lips.

"Now, watch this," Jenny said. I saw her undo his belt buckle and pull the leather free. I saw the look on Rick's face as she snapped the leather in the air and then landed the first stripe on my ass. "She's tough," Jenny said. "She can take more than you think she can. And she likes it rough."

Jenny striped me with the belt. This was my penance for moving on, my payment for leaving her, my punishment for being happy now that she was gone. I accepted every stinging stripe, every fiery blow. What was Rick thinking? I couldn't waste a second on that. But Jenny could. She grabbed his hand again and thrust it into my pussy. "See? She's so fucking wet, isn't she? Taste her."

She pushed on him, and Rick climbed between the V of my legs and pressed his face to the split of my body. His tongue against my clit had me crooning under my breath. I didn't care if Jenny saw this. I didn't care about anything except pain and pleasure – melting together – filling me up.

"Move back," she said, and she started to stripe me again, that belt like fire on my skin. "I like to make her earn the climax. I like to make her cry out, beg for release."

She knew exactly how much I could take, and only when my ass felt hot and throbbing, swollen from the punishment, did she drop the belt next to me on the mattress.

"You do it like this," she said, and she shoved me over and sealed her face to my pussy, sucking on my clit as if she'd never stop. My hands were cuffed. I couldn't push her away, but Rick could have, and he didn't. He sat next to her and watched – learned everything he could in a few short minutes. When I came, I saw angels, I swear, wings beating in front of me. I saw fire, white hot plumes of smoke, and then I saw Jenny's face, that sneer, grinning down at me.

"You like it," she said. "You'll always like it like that, won't you, slut?"

Then she kissed Rick – my taste clearly on her lips – and patted him on the cheek.

"You keep her satisfied, won't you, stud? The way she needs. The way she craves. I won't bother you any more, if you promise me that."

He nodded, but he seemed too shocked to speak. Jenny was up then, in motion, fumbling around in my jewelry drawer, reaching for the key. "I ought to leave you like that," she said with wet steel in her voice, but she tossed the key to Rick. Her hand darted into my dresser drawer, and I knew she was palming the few twenties that remained.

"Don't make me come back," she said, smiling at us as she left the room. I heard her heels, heard the front door close.

Rick looked at me. I didn't know what he'd say, what he'd do. He moved forward, as if he was going to unlock the cuffs, and then he set the key down on the edge of the mattress where I could see it and reached for the belt. I felt my stomach tighten as he rolled me over onto my stomach once more.

"So that's how you like it?" he asked, his voice harsh.

I nodded.

"Why didn't you say?"

"I thought we'd get there . . ."

"We're there," he said, and he snapped the belt, making it sing just like Jenny had. "Oh, baby, we're there now."

And we were – we are – in that place where pain and pleasure meet, where they war to top each other. Rick takes care of me in all the dirty ways I so desperately crave. He makes sure I go to sleep with my ass hot from his palm or his belt. He collars me, cuffs me, works me the way I need. So I have Jenny to thank for that, I guess. My dragon girlfriend, my lover from hell.

But I'll tell you one thing. I never did sell the painting. I took it out to the backyard the next morning. Rick doused the edges with gasoline. Together we watched the canvas burn.

The Saturday Pet

N. T. Morley

As they left Bonne Femme, Luis said something to Tera that
made her heart stop.

"Let's go to the pet store."

Neither Tera nor Luis had a pet.

Well, it could be said in one sense, that Luis *did* have a pet.
It was not a canine or feline beast, however; his pet was Tera.
He kept her and groomed her, dressed her when he saw fit
and left her undressed when he saw fit to do that instead. For
their trip to the mall, he had done something in between; she
wore a bit of a dress, but not much else. Although Luis had
just dropped hundreds of dollars on lingerie, none of what
Tera already owned had made it onto her body before they
left the house for the mall.

She had asked to wear a bra, but Luis wasn't having it.
She'd even tried to get him to let her wear panties, which she
usually didn't – certainly never on a Saturday, and never when
the weather was so warm.

But Luis had said, no, just the dress and the heels, and not
much to the former. The dress was quite a slutty little
sundress, pale yellow and almost see-through, low cut and
short. Tera's body was revealed quite plainly at several key
places – her pert little butt, her cleavage, her nipples. Between
the way the dress plunged and the way the thin yellow cotton
hung to her flesh, Tera felt almost more naked than if she'd
been naked. She felt almost more revealed walking through
the concourse at the mall than she had when she'd stripped

down in the changing room and cycled through numerous skimpy lace outfits for Luis. By insisting that Tera wear a dress so thoroughly revealing to go to the mall to try on slutty lingerie, Luis had reminded her – as if she could ever forget! – that her body was his to show off, and that she need not worry about whether others wanted to look. If it pleased Luis to *let* them look, they would look. It was as simple as that.

And this was only one of the many ways in which Luis controlled her life – deliciously so. He decided when she would eat, when she would sleep. He told her when and in what way she would shower, and whether she would use the shower massager to bring herself off, or, much more commonly, to bring herself right to the edge and then back off. He decided when she would touch herself elsewhere, too. She did so in bed while he was at work, sometimes, when he gave her permission by phone – always with the proviso that she would have him on speakerphone when she did, and that she would ask permission before she came. Sometimes he gave it. Other times he did not. If permission was granted, Luis insisted that Tera come very loud for him. She never, ever failed him; Tera loved being a "screamer".

Tera was trained, and usually obedient. Sometimes she did not obey her owner – and then she was punished.

How else could a pet be defined?

She might kid herself and identify as his "girlfriend", but she was a girlfriend who did exactly what he told her, when he told her. All that was required for her to be utterly subject to Luis's whim was for Tera to be in "that place" – meaning "sub space", as he called it. But the fact was that Tera was there in sub space with increasing frequency lately. And when she was not, she was ever aware that Luis could put her there with a stern look, a caress at her neck or a single harsh word. She almost never talked back to him any more; she almost never needed to. She always wanted to do as he said.

More and more, Tera found herself her boyfriend's plaything.

And so Tera said, with only the slightest embarrassed quaver to her voice:

"Yes, darling . . . I think that would be lovely."

It was a glorious day and the mall through which they walked was a vast suburban structure, its skylights open to the outside and sunbeams streaming beautifully down. Tera felt largely neutral toward the existence of this mall, though very positive toward the fact that it was the only place around to shop for lingerie. She liked the fact that Bonne Femme, the expensive "intimates boutique", had a big enough and private enough dressing room that Luis could be admitted to sit with her while she tried on lingerie for him.

Tera knew from experience – she often slipped away and went there in the middle of the day when Luis was at work – that for most women, the companions who came into the fitting room to give opinions were more often girlfriends. Perhaps it was a little scandalous in this drab suburb that Luis was often there with her as she tried on a whole parade of sweet nothings. But the store clerks did not know that Luis insisted on snapping photos of each outfit on his cell phone as Tera tried it on. "So I can recall what worked and what didn't," he said. "For when I'm deciding what you'll wear to bed."

Luis *always* decided what she'd wear at night. It aroused Tera intensely to put on exactly the lingerie he specified, in exactly the way he ordered. Almost as much as it turned her on to try it on for him.

In the end, he'd bought her several new garter belts, a cute little bustier, a white rhinestone-studded merry widow, a corset and three cute see-through nighties. They were all very slutty – extremely suggestive. Tera had very much enjoyed looking at herself in the full-length mirror while Luis sat there, wearing his suit even though it was Saturday – the son of a bitch always wore a suit.

Occasionally, when Tera was "between outfits" – meaning she was stark naked except for her high-heeled shoes – Luis would finger her a little, just to keep things interesting.

If the ladies who worked at the shop thought something dirty was going on in the fitting room, they didn't say a word.

At least, not to the couple. Perhaps the clerks knew they could count on a very large sale. Or perhaps they wished to save their gossipy comments for each other, after Tera and Luis had left. Regardless, they left with their arms full of packages – hundreds of dollars' worth of petwear for Luis's favorite pet. Only one thing remained.

"Let's buy you a collar," purred Luis softly as he guided his excited girlfriend toward Pet Parade.

Tera had been in enough pet stores throughout her life. She and her family had both cats and dogs growing up, and her older sister had a parakeet and her younger sister had hamsters. She knew all too well the strange mélange of scent that spelled "pet store" to anyone who'd ever visited one. It was a mix of cat food, dog food, birdseed, cat litter, rabbit shavings, plastic, leather . . .

It had never aroused her before. Now it did; it turned her on intensely. The great wall of collars loomed at the far end of the shop, and her heart pounded as she thought about one of those going around her throat.

Though the location of the collars was obvious from where they both stood at the front of the store, Luis saw fit to engage the pretty clerk – packed into a tight yellow polo shirt and snug jeans – in their charade.

He asked as soon as they walked in: "Where would I find the collars?"

He looked Tera up and down before he added, "For a dog about one-oh-five.

Tera's thighs felt like rubber. She reddened. Luis made a soft sharp clicking sound as he walked with his walking stick behind the helpful female clerk, making no attempt to camouflage the open interest he felt toward her butt as she walked. Tera had to admit it was a very nice butt. She wondered if the clerk had ever worn a collar.

Luis thanked the clerk, who told them to summon her if

they had any further questions. If she knew why the collar was being bought, she played it reasonably cool – but that was more than just a typical flirty smile Tera glimpsed on the clerk's face as she flitted away back to the counter.

Luis reached up and withdrew the first collar from the wall. It was big and black leather and had shiny metal studs on it.

He set their lingerie bags aside, leaned his walking stick up against a shelf, and held the collar up to Tera's throat.

Tera recoiled. "You're not going to put that thing on me, are you?" she hissed. "In public?"

Luis answered: "Of course I am."

"Right here in the store?" whimpered Tera.

"How else," Luis asked, "do you propose I ensure a proper fitting for my pet?"

"But people are watching!" said Tera, her face now very red. She felt a fierce and powerful arousal as humiliation washed through her. "Perhaps we could just . . . um . . . estimate?" she asked weakly.

Tera gulped and said, "But it's not *supposed* to fit *me*!"

"Says who?" Luis smiled, his voice a soothing purr. "It's for a *pet*. And as you'll recall, it's my decision who knows you're my pet. Isn't that what I told you when I made you lift your skirt for that trucker last weekend?"

Tera blushed very red; her nipples stood out painfully through the thin cotton dress. She'd forgotten all about that. Her clit throbbed. Her pussy felt wet; her thighs seemed slick, and it wasn't just from sweat. The air conditioning of the pet store chilled her flesh. She goosebumped all over; she shivered.

"Yes, Sir," she said.

"And he liked it quite a bit, didn't he?"

"Yes, Sir," she said.

"But I think you liked it more."

Tera nodded. "Yes, Sir."

"Then come here," said Luis firmly, "and let me fit my pet for its collar."

Tera felt dizzy. *It*. She was "it".

When Tera shied away again as he went to put the collar on her, he spoke very sharply to her.

"Tera, I won't ask you again. If I have to tell you again, that skirt is coming up, and that clerk who's been watching us so intently is going to see you get your ass reddened."

The second he mentioned spanking her, Tera was helpless to resist. She already knew she could expect to be spanked when they got home – just for questioning Luis's order to her. But she was positively destroyed by the thought of having it happen right here in the pet store. She knew she'd be revisiting that hopefully never-to-happen moment in her fantasies the next time Luis gave her permission to masturbate.

Tera stepped forward; Luis buckled the collar around her throat.

If the clerk at the counter had not known before what – or whom – the collar was for, she certainly knew now. She was watching them like a hawk.

And from the look on her face, she certainly seemed to approve. The pretty young woman could not have been much older than twenty, but she clearly knew her way in the world.

Luis tugged at the heavy D-ring of the black leather collar. Its weight sent a ripple through Tera's body.

"This one will do for when you're at home, fighting my authority . . . like you just did. But I think you need a prettier one for when you're out in public. One that matches that rhinestone merry widow I just bought you, don't you think?"

Tera's eyes went wide. Her jaw dropped. Her pretty mouth twisted in an expression of horror. "In . . . in public?" she whimpered.

Luis planted his mouth on hers and kissed her deeply.

As he kissed her, he tugged at the D-ring of the heavy leather collar. The pressure on the back of Tera's neck sent a spasm of pleasure through her.

Luis took the black leather collar off her and set it aside.

He took down at a far more slender collar – one of white leather, with rhinestones circling it. It had a delicate little buckle. There was no D-ring on it; it was clearly not made for a leash. And it was made for a female dog – one about Tera's size. It must have been made for a very large dog who *always* followed its Master's commands.

Tera felt the snug embrace of the smaller collar as Luis buckled it around her throat.

Tera saw his eyes widen. He seemed to catch his breath.

"What a shame," he said, "that they don't have mirrors in pet stores. You look quite stunning in it. Once I get you in that rhinestone number . . ."

Tera frowned. The white rhinestone-studded merry widow that Luis had just purchased for her had been bought over Tera's objections. She felt it made her look tacky, slutty and cheap. "I look like a stripper," she'd said. "I don't want to look like a stripper!"

"But that's not for you to decide," Luis had told her.

"This one doesn't have a D-ring for a leash," he said breathlessly. "It's only for when you're very, very good. For when I know you'll do exactly as I say. When no leash is neces-sary. Can you promise me you'll try to earn this collar, Tera? Otherwise . . ."

With a smile, Luis reached up and seized a leash from the wall – a huge one, long and leather, with a big leather loop and a chain at the end; the clip that hooked to a beast's collar was clearly made to resist the pull of a very strong dog.

He held up the black leather leash and the black leather collar together, and said firmly, "Try to earn the pretty little one, will you? Try to be a good pet for me?"

Tera nodded emphatically. Her voice rich with arousal, she whimpered, "Yes, Sir. I'll try."

He took the rhinestone collar off of her. They gathered the Bonne Femme bags, the leash and the two collars.

They took them up to the clerk, who rang them up.

Her pretty eyes lingered lushly in a slow circuit from Luis to Tera, then to the collars.

She named their price.

Luis winked at her.

The young pretty clerk blushed. She was forced, by the pet

store chain, to wear a uniform polo shirt that was not very flattering to her figure. She chose, however, to wear it two sizes too small. The strained fabric tented slightly more as her nipples stiffened.

Both Luis and Tera could see it as the clerk ran Luis's credit card, and he signed.

Tera and Luis left the pet store.

Outside the pet store, right where the clerk could see them . . . right where *anybody* could see them, Luis stopped and opened the bag from the pet store.

"I think we know what kind of a collar you need for tonight, don't we?"

Tera didn't, but she answered, "Yes, of course, Sir." She hoped he would tell her, not ask her, because she didn't know if tonight Luis expected that she would be his obedient pet, pretty and perfect and cuddly, or a ravenous beast that needed to be collared and chained. Right now, she felt more like a beast. Her pussy ached to be filled. With Luis deliciously humiliating her in public like this, Tera didn't entirely trust herself not to throw herself on him in the car, or, worse, to try to wrestle him onto one of the mall's many benches and ride him like a pony before he could stop her. She was so turned on she feared she could not control herself.

She felt very much like an animal, and wanted to be collared.

To her relief, however, Luis had more faith in Tera than she had in herself. He believed her to be a very safe pet.

He said: "You've been very good, even with all those people watching."

"They're still watching, Sir," gulped Tera nervously, shifting her body and wriggling from side to side as her deep sense of humiliated arousal only grew with her anticipation.

Luis smiled. "Yes, there are quite a few people around, aren't there? Perhaps they'll know why a boyfriend would collar his girlfriend like this. Perhaps they'll know what this means."

He reached into the bag and took out the white rhinestone collar. He held it up. He fished his penknife out of the pocket of his suit pants and sliced the tag off the collar.

Tera made surreptitious glances all up and down the mall. There were people standing nearby and a few were surreptitiously watching them – a group of college girls, a trio of food court employees who seemed to have just gotten off work. Tera felt very aroused and very embarrassed.

Luis held up the collar for her.

He said, "I won't need a leash tonight, will I? Will you do everything I say tonight, Tera? Will you be my very good pet?"

Tera nodded, and she stepped forward into the embrace of the white rhinestone collar.

She felt Luis buckling it around her throat. She never looked away as he did so, and neither did he; they locked eyes until the white rhinestone collar was secure around her throat.

"Yes," she told him. "Everything."

His arms went around her. He held her close. His body felt warm as his hands came to rest on her ass.

He turned her around and steered her toward the parking lot.

Stolen Hours

Madeline Moore

"How long have you been fucking my husband?" Her voice is husky. I can hear the Mediterranean influence in her accent; all that hot blood heating up the phone line.

Mitchell warned me that she might call. He wants to get call screen so we can block her number (*their* number, until recently) but we haven't got around to setting it up. Too busy fucking.

"I beg your pardon?" This little stall is a trick of Mitchell's. Until very recently I'd automatically answered any question asked of me, no matter how rhetorical or rude. Mitchell helped me fix that.

"Are you deaf?"

"No." Damn! Except when I'm nervous.

"I beg your pardon?" She's mimicking me and mocking me. Reminding me that he's taught her all his little communication tricks, too.

"Please sign the papers." I've rehearsed this line. It's important to both of us that the separation and divorce be speedy. Mitchell and me, I mean.

"Not until you tell me how long this has been going on."

"What difference does it make?"

"I want to know for how long I was sleeping beside my husband and his hands were sticky from your cunt." She hisses like a reptile. I visualize a Komodo dragon, then hastily revise, picturing something smaller and less dangerous. A chameleon? Or is that me?

A shriek catches in my throat as Mitchell's ancient cat twitches her rat-tail at my calf in passing. I'm not used to her, yet. For a moment I regard her stop-start progress across the kitchen floor. Step, stop, cough, shudder, step. God she's fucking *ancient*, that cat. His wife hates the cat which means I don't, I mean, which means I love that cat. Or will soon.

I hang up. My hands are shaking.

This business of stealing another woman's man is unnerving. I don't know anyone who's managed to pull it off. My friends who've fucked married men were all, eventually, jilted. *He always goes back to the wife.* Any woman old enough to read an advice column or a glossy women's magazine knows *that*.

I drop into a chair at my kitchen table (ours, now). It's a wood farm table from a second-hand store. I stripped it and varnished the legs, then painted the top white and added a découpage border of vine leaves. The four wooden chairs, none of them a match for another, are painted the same vibrant green as the vine. Découpage is what I do. Not as a hobby, as a career. I do OK.

My legs are shaking, too.

I know the answer to her question, of course; eight months to the day we met he moved out, and he's been living with me for two days, so I've been fucking him eight months and two days. That is, if you include finger-fucking.

We'd arranged to meet at a little restaurant. He was there when I arrived, seated at the back in a banquette, facing the door so we couldn't miss each other. Clean shaven, expectant, silver hair and hazel eyes as bright as wet pebbles. He was wearing a suit and tie, which I found reassuring. He looked like a gentleman.

I propelled myself forward. A lot of thought had gone into my outfit, of course, and I was wearing heels, so I walked slowly. He already knew I had lousy peripheral vision. He already knew a lot about me. A whole lot. I faltered. We met, as they say, online. We connected.

"Evelyn." He was quick to his feet, to touch my elbow,

discreetly steadying me. "Hello, Mitchell." I sank onto the padded bench of the banquette and he sat beside me.

By the time the main course was served, he was finger-fucking me.

My pussy was so wet I would've been embarrassed if he hadn't been so pleased to find it so. I was favoured with his grin. It melted what was left of my molten heart. I was a puddle, so no surprise that I was wet as one.

I get wet thinking about it. We knew we had something special, right from the start.

The anticipation never dulled. Every meeting was another amorous adventure. No matter how many hours we stole to be together they were never enough. I came on his hand, right there in the restaurant, before our first meeting was half over. How could I not? He was discreet but unconcerned. I was horrified but thrilled.

He made me come again in the alleyway en route to his car, and again in the passenger seat while he distractedly drove. Parked on a side street near my apartment, I finally got my chance to reciprocate.

His cock strained against his fly, the tip level with his belt. I jerked his belt open, unzipped him, and showered his erection with adoration, using my lips and tongue to convey what I was still too shy to say.

It didn't take long. He came in my mouth in a full body shudder. His hand twisted in my hair and he pulled my head free of him and we kissed for the first time.

Then I got out of the car and he went home. It might not count as fucking, but that would've been the first night his fingers were sticky with my cunt. Eight months and two days ago.

I get back to work. An upscale little shop awaits; six ring boxes and I have to varnish them a hundred times apiece before they're done.

We've agreed not to have any secrets but when Mitchell gets home from work I don't tell him the calls have started. I wait for him to ask and he doesn't, so I don't volunteer the information. This is just lying by omission, but, according to our lofty ideals, it counts as lying.

Mitchell makes dinner and I set the table and put some dinner music on. I crank it up loud enough to cover the sound of the cat.

Sure enough the cat hacks and kacks throughout the meal. I'd say "on cue" but the cat kacks constantly. Still, I glance in her direction every time. She puts me off my food, which is one way, I guess, to lose a few pounds.

Her name is Mieu. She finishes shuddering and resumes her motionless position. She's Siamese. Sitting like that, she resembles a statue. No, not true. She resembles a moth-eaten mounted and taxidermied critter, the kind you come across in curio shops, so startling you examine it longer than you should, maybe even consider it as a joke gift for someone, then hastily move on, dusting your hands in case you inadvertently touched it. She looks like the bag the cat was in before someone let it out.

"Evelyn?"

"Sorry. I was thinking."

"Save it for when I'm not home," he says. His eyes twinkle. I laugh. He thinks I think too much. I know I do.

He pushes back his chair and pats his lap. "Come here, I'll feed you."

I scamper into his lap. Can't help it, that's just how he makes me feel. Eager and appealing and adoring and ready to be adored. I try to steal a kiss.

"None of that. You look peaked; I think you need more iron. Eat more of this delicious asparagus." He spears a spear with his fork and raises it high.

I stick out my tongue to catch the creamy drippings off the tip. "Mmmm, yummy," I announce, like a kid with a sweet. Like I say, can't help it. He loves it, anyway, so why *should* I help it?

He dances the tip on my tongue, once, then feeds it to me nicely. He tips his glass of wine to my lips and I take a sip. He sets the glass down, deliberately. The air is charged. That's the way it is with us. It used to be that way all the time, when we didn't live together. Now he makes it that way whenever he wants. I'm not sure exactly *how*. It's something I can feel. It always makes my knees weak and my skin hot and my juices flow and this is no exception.

Mitchell kisses me hard on the mouth. He's wearing cotton pyjama pants and through the thin material I feel his cock stiffen along the crack of my bum. His left arm is around my waist. It tightens, his hand closing firmly over my hipbone. That's because his other hand is sliding up my legs, pushing them apart so he can cup my cotton-covered pussy. Sure enough, as he starts to scratch at the gusset with his thumbnail, I go limp. If he weren't holding me tight I'd fall to the floor and flop about like a fish out of water. That's the way it is, with us.

"What do you like?" he'd typed in Private Messenger.

"I like to be fingered," I typed. I didn't even hesitate. So easy, isn't it, when you're alone and not even speaking the words?

"I think you like to be accepted," he said, when we'd progressed to the telephone. "Accepted and admired by all." His voice was a silken quilt that covered me and made me feel safe.

"Sort of," I answered. "Accepted and admired by one."

He chuckled. "This is going to be fun," he said.

I chuckled, too. "Fun" was exactly what I was after. "Will you always talk so sweet to me?"

"Of course," he said.

His fingers are busy, pushing aside the cotton to get to my crotch. He's not impatient, that's not why he doesn't strip me of my panties first. Mitchell is incredibly patient. This is because, he says, "I waited a lifetime for you." No, the reason my panties stay on is because that's the way I like it.

"Ahhh," he sighs when at last his middle finger slips inside me. His cock twitches underneath my bum.

Used to be I could take a lot of this sort of action, it being my favourite and all. I'd press my face into my lover's shoulder and curl up, my knees at his elbow, the hair on his arm tickling my calves, his hand and his fingers trapped between my thighs.

But with Mitchell my secret need is as quick and obvious as the punchline to a silly joke. A fierce ache to have him inside me turns my eagerness to aggression, so there's no time to hide my face or try to trap his arm between my legs.

I swivel in his lap. "Fuck me," I say. No doubt about it, no rising inflection at the end to even suggest a request.

Mitchell laughs. "A tigress, tonight, are we?"

Our hands fumble at separate tasks as he frees his cock from his pyjamas and I press the crotch of my panties to one side. He thrusts up into me in one smooth stroke that forces a grunt from my mouth. Doesn't matter. We don't care what sounds we make as long as we're having a good time. I hope the elastic doesn't hurt him, but I don't care enough to take the panties off. If it hurts he'll say so, or just cut them off me with a knife or his teeth. Anyway goddammit I'm already coming.

"That's a girl," he murmurs. He's got a grip on my hips so I can hump him with abandon, but he shifts one hand, now, to my bum. He toys with the delicate, pleated skin at the entrance of my ass, using the thick pad of his finger to press against its natural resistance.

"So good," I moan. Usually, when I come I stop moving, but this time I just keep going, as if my orgasm is in his cock and my pussy is drawing it out of him and deep into me with every thrust.

I have to let go of the elastic and now a part of me knows for sure that it's got to be scraping the length of him with every thrust. "Fuck it," I mutter. I want to finger my clit so I can squeeze another spasm out of him and into me. There's no time to change anything, I'm coming as if I haven't come in a month, my need as desperate as ever, as though our hours together are still stolen.

The next time she calls I'm a little more poised.

"Did you tell him I called?"

"No,"

"Why?"

"I don't want him to get upset."

"Nothing upsets him. Don't you know that?"

I do, actually. He's like a rock, half submerged. I'm the little fish that takes shelter in the nooks and crannies of him. He's like a massive tree, roots deep in the ground and branches thick, solid. I hide inside him, figuratively anyway. If I could, I would literally crawl inside him so I could see what it's like to be big and steadfast and sturdy.

"Hello?"

"We'd like those papers signed."

"There is no *we* for you. I'm his wife. He is part of *my* we, not yours."

I think of the suburban house he left behind. It must be empty without his big presence. He didn't bring much with him, just two carloads, the first, mostly books. Then I drove him back to his house so we could leave the car in the driveway for her and fetch the cat. He invited me in but I said no. I probably should've gone in and grabbed some art or at least a few towels (he uses a lot of them) but I was too terrified to move. His wife was at work, so it wasn't the possibility of seeing her that scared me. I think I was just frightened by the enormity of what we were doing. In stark contrast to me, he was one cool dude, whistling, talking in rhyme, a cowboy hat from the time he went to the Calgary Stampede jaunty on his head. I'd never seen him so high-spirited. It was, he told me that night, the happiest day of his life.

All the way home he talked about his plans for our future and I listened to Mieu's futile cough. *God*, I wondered. *What have I done?*

"Hello?"

"I'm here," I say. I look around the apartment. His books have yet to be put away. I've offered to alphabetize the collection for him, once we get shelves. The kitchen table, my customary workplace, is littered with his stuff, so I have half the space I'm used to to work on my latest project. Well, I have half the space I'm used to to do anything, actually. Even sleep.

"I bought some spray shellac," she says in a conversational tone. "And some gourds. I'm going to stick decals on the gourds and then shellac them and sell them at the Art Fair."

At first I don't get where she's going with this and, so help me, I open my mouth to offer a few hints that'll guarantee a superior finished product.

"That's what you do, correct? Cut up little bits of paper and paste them on old things and then shellac them. That's what you do for a living, correct?" She cackles.

"Découpage," I say automatically. My cheeks burn. My grandpa used to offer to give me "a good shellacking" and that's what she's doing now. Mitchell warned me she can be vicious, although in truth she's not the only one to find my occupation amusing.

"So you will live on, what? Love?" She's hissing again. Lizard lips. "He's lost his job, you know. I made sure of that."

Once, when I was a kid, I almost drowned in the deep end of a community swimming pool. That's what it feels like now, like I'm drowning, only back when it really happened the pool was full of moving adult bodies I could grab on to. This time I'm alone. I hang up.

So, every day when he heads off to work he is lying by omission. Breaking the rules. Of course, so am I, but I always thought he was better than me. Plus, we've confessed our abiding contempt for liars. What does this mean?

The project I'm working on is fantastic. The box is as deep and wide as a shoebox. The wood is pine, nothing special, but the joints are tongue and groove and the hinges are brass. No nails anywhere. I don't even know what its original use once was, but I know exactly what's going inside it once I'm done.

So I get the box out, along with my supplies, and set up shop on a corner of the table. There are dishes to be done, the bed to be made, and all those towels in the bathroom to be collected and washed, but none of these chores will help my present mood. This will, because the box is a thing of beauty, now.

The wood has been lovingly sanded to smooth perfection, by me, of course. I kept the paper appliqués to a minimum. One medium sized deco-like black silhouette of a nude, reclining woman, smack dab in the middle of the top. Four bits of paper, each one no bigger than my thumbnail, decorate the corners of the box in the form of tiny blocks of intense green and blue and yellow and red, tumbling like dice without dots down its sides.

I found them on an old shopping bag that was used to hold the items I bought at a garage sale. The best score of the day was free! And now I have used an old shopping bag and an old empty wooden box and yeah, paper and glue and I have made art.

My fingers twitch. I wanted to add some gold gilt, free hand, and I still do. But it's too late now because I've varnished the whole thing five hundred times, give or take a few hundred. The brass hinges gleam like gold, anyway, and that's enough shiny stuff for this piece.

Nothing left to do but line the inside. I used cuticle scissors to cut out the appliqués but for this, the cutting of handmade paper, I use a pair of sturdy, sharp shears. I've chosen a beautiful sheet of acid-free Japanese paper, grey with gold threads. My brown paper pattern is already taped in place but, as I raise my scissors to commence cutting, I hit a wall.

The Japanese paper isn't right. Damn.

Ordinarily, I'd light up a smoke and think, but I quit smoking when Mitchell moved in so that's not an option.

It's like a fashion crisis, where you're dressed to the nines and as you screw your earrings into place you realize, no, they aren't right, but you still need one perfect accessory to complete your look. Should it be a necklace? A belt? A scarf? Before you know it your *coiffe* is undone and there are wrinkles in your dress because you're down on your knees, digging through some battered box of junk trying to find something, a chain belt? A bit of lace? Something that will complete an outfit that has plummeted from divine to crappy in the blink of an eye.

That's what I do now; dig through my trunk of carefully sorted and stacked lining materials. The big bright squares of felt go flying. They aren't what I want right now, so they don't matter one bit. Paper, cotton, velvet, silk – wrong wrong wrong.

Mieu totters into the room and I know she'll try to puke on my stuff if I don't get it all back into the trunk, but I don't care. Goddam I need a smoke.

"I can be a real bitch," I warned him when he unveiled his plan to leave his wife and come live with me.

"I doubt that," he said with a smile.

"You shouldn't." It's one thing to dress up and adore each other and have great sex a few hours every week. It's quite another to try and pull it off on a daily basis. I wasn't sure it could even be done. "I've been called one enough times."

"The only time I'll ever call you a bitch you can be sure it will be prefaced with an adjective. Like 'sexy' or maybe 'silly'. Anyway," he concluded, "I've decided."

The cat starts to kack. I force myself to smarten up and repack the box. The rest of the day is spent doing chores and trying not to run to the corner store for smokes.

So I'm particularly bugged when the phone rings and it's her, again.

"You are going to regret what you've done!" She's screaming, and it's late afternoon. Probably in a bar, hopefully not one close to my place. For the first time I wonder if I'm safe. "He won't get anything from me."

"He'll get half the money from the sale of the house," I say. I'm getting used to her interruptions, same as I'm getting used to Mieu trying to puke on my stuff. "It's the law." Honestly, we human beings can get used to anything. Even ruining someone else's life.

"I'll never sell."

"Sign the papers."

"How long? How long have you been fucking my husband?"

"If sex was so unimportant in the marriage, why is it such a big deal outside the marriage?" I've been wondering this for a while but I never thought I'd actually say it. Only, it's getting late now and I want to finish, or at least put everything away, before Mitchell comes home.

"Fuck off! How long have you been fucking my husband, you fucking piece of shit? How long?"

"Eight inches, I'd say." I hang up.

Mieu chokes and shudders and I turn on her in a fury. "You fucking piece of shit," I say. The cat gives me a rheumy look, clearly unperturbed, but I feel marginally better.

"You think too much," says Mitchell.

I've been grooming him since we finished dinner, using all my creams and lotions to soothe his face, the creases of his thighs, and his hands and feet.

"I know," I say.

"Would you like me to still the windmills of your mind?"

"I need a break tonight,' I confess.

"Weary of me already?"

"Are you kidding?" I tickle his wide, short foot in the centre of his unusually high arch. He yanks his foot from my lap, setting it on his other knee. "Not now that you're such a hot metrosexual."

He laughs. "My hooves have never been happier," he says. He admires his foot.

"All the girls will want you," I say.

"Makes no difference to me," he replies.

"Why?"

"Without you I have no cock."

I rest my right leg on my left and press the bottom of my foot to his. "Sole mates," I say.

Mitchell guffaws. His pleasure makes me giddy. Mitchell thinks I'm funny. I think Mitchell's dreamy. We're living on love.

I stroke the sole of his foot with my big toe.

"Mieu is suffering," I begin.

Naturally, when we both give the cat our undivided attention, she curls up tighter into a cute little ball. She's maybe a couple of pounds from the tip of her black nose to the tip of her black tail.

"She looks OK to me," he says.

"My work is suffering too," I say.

Finally, the fucking cat kicks into action. She staggers to her feet, kacks a few times, and commences shuddering.

"She's stroking out, Mitchell. A dozen times a day."

He watches in silence. "Let's go to bed," he says.

It's the first night we've ever spent together where we don't have sex. I cuddle close and gently stroke his back until he falls asleep.

When I get up he's already gone and so is Mieu. I hurry to gather up her bowls and her litter box so he won't have to do it later, but they're gone too. It had to be and I'm glad it's come to pass, glad for her as well as myself, but I'm not happy for my man.

This morning I woke up with the answer to the problem of the lining. Simple as sunshine, easy as a stream, rippling from the unconscious to the conscious mind.

The fabric is lustrous, heavy velvet, the colour of the French drink, *chocolat*. I'd dismissed the idea of velvet off the top, which was why it took so long to come to mind. Too luxe, I'd thought at the time. But now that the box is finished it cries out for velvet, and finally I've heard the call.

It'll be tricky. My fingers twitch with anticipation. Hours pass in blessed silence. I don't stop until the box is lined and full and hidden in my closet.

Whenever I complete a special project I like to smoke and drink a beer on my balcony and that's exactly what I want to do now. When I fetch a cold one from the fridge I'm reminded of a half-pack of cigs, not my brand, which I stuck in there after my last get-together with my girlfriends.

Never has a long, skinny extra lite looked so good. I take my beer and my smokes onto the balcony and kick back. The beer slides down my throat, making the harshness of the smoke easier to take. It's time to touch base with Anne. I'm lucky enough to have a brilliant best friend. She's been giving Mitchell and me "space", but I'm ready to talk.

The phone rings and I pick up right away, sure that it's her. "Hey, girlfriend!" My voice is giddy. I slug my beer.

"You're fat," she says.

"Plump," I correct her. "He says my belly is 'a wave on a sea of milk'." I chug the last of my beer and stifle the impulse to send the bottle crashing to the sidewalk below. Instead, I saunter to the kitchen, smoke between my lips, and grab a fresh one.

"He likes slender women, like me," she rasps.

"He says you remind him of Gandhi," I shoot back. "And you know how he hates Gandhi." The latter is true, but the former I've made up on the spot.

Mitchell thinks it was wrong of Gandhi to use the decency of the British Empire against it. "If the Nazis had been driving that train when Gandhi and his followers lay across the tracks, what do you think would have happened?" His cheeks were pink when he said this so I knew he meant it.

"I don't like Oprah," I'd confessed. "Too full of herself."

"Evil Evelyn," he said. He was grinning. "Beautiful, evil Eve-after-the-fall."

"Not so sweet after all?" I pouted.

"You, my pet, are so sweet I might have to give you a bottle of milk."

She's sputtering, which I find I quite enjoy. "You're going to the poorhouse," she says.

"Not straight to hell?" I eyeball the amber bottle in my hand. So pretty in the sunlight. I think about the poorhouse, which is another thing my grandpa used to talk about when he was fussing about funds. "Straight to the poorhouse," he'd mutter. How old is this broad?

"You think this is funny? You've ruined me, for what?"

"For love."

She sputters some more.

I light another cig. My mind is clicking at a thousand rpm.

"He'll tire of you," she hisses.

"Never," I shoot back.

"I guarantee it."

"Impossible. Without me he has no cock."

She snorts. "You'll get sick of him and his disgusting cat. *You'll* tire of him, mark my words."

Mark my words? But Grandpa, what does it mean?

"He's a messy, grey-haired old man with a flat ass and ugly feet," she says.

"That tears it," I say. This is also something Grandpa used to say but that's OK because it's just about time I spoke to her in a language she can understand. I slug my beer, crush out my smoke and swing my feet down, planting them, as Mitchell would say, so my gravity is perfectly centred.

"His hair is silver and his ass is perfect," I shout. "His feet are beautiful and so is he." I lower my voice. "You're right about the poorhouse, though. We'll meet you there."

"I'm not – I have a job, a career."

"But he doesn't, not any more. You made sure of that. There's not a lot of money in découpage, as you can well imagine. You're on your own with the mortgage on that big house."

Too bad I crushed out my smoke because there's plenty of time to finish it. I give her time to think, but then I jump in to fill the silence. "You don't want him," I say. "You don't love him. You don't even take care of him."

"I do – I—"

"Sign the papers. Let's get that house up for sale as soon as possible."

"I'm not ready."

"We're going on a long holiday. He's taking me to Disney World. You know how much he loves Disney World." The latter, again, is true. The former, again, is false. "Let's get it done before we leave."

"How can you go on a holiday when you have no money?"

"I told you, we live on love."

"You fucking husband-stealing hussy whore—"

I'm ready, willing and able. "He was ripe for the plucking, you dried up old bat. It was like taking candy from a baby. Easy as pie."

"You cunt. Cunt. Cunt."

"Sticks and stones . . ."

"Cunt."

"Sign the papers."

She starts to cry. "OK."

This is, I realize, the first time I've heard her cry. It's not from grief, of that I'm sure. She's lost and she likes to win. Tough titty. Still . . .

"You can get a new man, younger, neater. And just think, no more Mieu hacking all over your stuff." (I could add "for either of us" but I don't.)

"I hate you."

"I can live with it."

"Cunt." She hangs up.

Score one for the home team.

I'm still in the shower when Mitchell comes home. He calls out to me, loud, and knocks on the bathroom door. He does this because he knows I scare easily and I'm not used to living with him yet. He doesn't want to give me a heart attack.

Mitchell likes to unwrap me so I slip on my terry robe before emerging from the bathroom. There are grocery bags on the kitchen counter. Before I can start unpacking them, he summons me into the bedroom.

He's busy arranging my full-length mirror to stand opposite another full-length mirror. Both are on wooden platforms that swivel. Mine is an antique. The new one is unfinished pine.

"We already have a mirror, Mitchell." Visions of the poorhouse dance in my head.

"We need two."

"Why?"

"You'll see." The mirrors are about three feet apart. He stands back. "Perfect." He focuses all his formidable attention on me. "Hi, Fabby," he says.

"Hi, Marv," I reply. I can't help but smile. Fabby and Marv are the nicknames I made up for us. Our surname is Ulous.

"I have a new job." He grabs me by the lapels of my robe, tough-guy style, and plants a fat, sloppy kiss on my mouth. "No job security working for friends of the ex, know what I mean?"

"Yup." (Do I ever.)

He opens my robe and slides it off my body. "Come." Mitchell arranges me between the two mirrors, arms and legs wide open, feet planted and palms out. When he's satisfied with my pose, he circles me and the mirrors.

I keep still except for my eyes, like I'm in REM. Mitchell's surprised me, and not just with his gift. I'd imagined he'd need consoling on the passing of Mieu.

Then there's *my* gift, a pair of navy-blue Triple EEE size 7 men's slippers with a roomy arch. In my mind's eye he'd been comforted by my thoughtfulness (the slippers) and delighted by my talent (the box).

I'd imagined telling him about his ex-wife's phone calls and trying to get him to admit he'd lost his job. Suddenly, it seems as if, in my mind's eye, I'd just imagined a whole lot of *conversation*.

I close my mind's eyelid.

"What a wonderful tableau you make, my dear," he says. He's standing in front of me again and now he rubs his hands with glee.

"Thank you," I whisper. Sometimes I'm embarrassed by how much he adores me. Never mind my maniacal nature, which he's yet to fully experience. I'm not even all that special physically, in my opinion, but it's not my opinion that counts.

"Turn your head to the left," he says, and I do. I see me, naked, reflected in a mirror, and so on.

"Now to the right." I do as I am bid.

"What do you see?"

I meet his eyes with mine. His are brighter than ever. Wet, in fact.

"I see me." My body starts to tremble as fresh lust travels

from my heart to my arteries to my veins and capillaries and clit. I'd envisioned, maybe, a long slow healing lovemaking session but again, still, urgency has roared to life and devastated all in its path.

"Know what I see?" His voice is as gentle as dew.

I shake my head.

"I see an infinite number of Evelyns to love."

Mitchell kneels before me. He puts his hands on my hips and leans in, inhaling my aroma. His tongue flicks out to taste me. I'm wet, wet as his eyes, and he purrs his pleasure at finding me so.

There's going to be time for us, after all. Lots of time to get the house sold and lots of time to find out what his new job is and lots of time to give him my gift and lots of time, even, to go to Disney World. I get that now, but it doesn't slake my need.

How can it, when his lips are parting my pussy lips and he's pressing his tongue flat against my slit?

I need, I need, I need his tongue to dance and his fingers to explore. I need him to make me come. I need him.

I press my fingertips to his shoulders to help me keep my balance. I glance to the left, to the right. Yes, an infinite number of Evelyns.

He's out of range of the mirrors so there's only one of him, but that's OK.

One Mitchell is all I want.

In Control

M. Christian

We met in the dark corner of an internet chatroom. SLUT-SLAVE, a nubile profile full of in-the-know vernacular with damned good typing skills; and MASTER017, my digital persona. We didn't really meet there, of course, but that's where we first started to talk. The dance was slow, at first. I've heard other doms say that they don't like it slow, sedate, careful – they'd rather snap their fingers and have them drop to their knees. Me? I like the dance, the approach, the "chat" in "chatroom". Besides, I've had a few of my own snaps, the eager young slaves with sparkles in their eyes, and not a clue between the ears. Give me someone who knows what they're getting into. It's better, after all, to be wanted by someone who wants the best, as opposed to someone who just wants.

So we danced, we chatted, SLUTSLAVE and I – or at least that cyberspace mask I wore. Finally, after many a midnight typing, she complained with a sideways smile – ;-) – that she was looking for something where more than just her wrists got a workout.

Like I said: step one, two, three, turn, step one, two, three. Careful moves in this courtship dance. No snap from me. I made her sing for her supper, pushing her along, not making it easy for her. "Do you know what you're asking for, Slave?" I asked, clicking and clacking on my keyboard.

She did the same, and the dance changed its tempo: "Yes, Master. I do."

We made a date to get together the next weekend.

A knock on the door. Normally, even when it's expected, it can be jarring. Fist on wood. Bang, bang, bang! But not that night. I opened it. "Welcome."

I had a picture, of course, and the flesh was just like it, though filled out in three-dimensional reality. Unlike the door, seeing her jarred me, but not unpleasantly.

"Thanks," she said with a smile, walking in. I closed the door behind her. Full bodied, curved, somewhere between too young and too old, tight and firm from exercise. Eyes gleaming with sharpness, mouth parted just *so* with anticipation. Curly dark hair, her skin a Mediterranean patina.

We didn't have to say much, most of our negotiations having been done in emails back and forth. I knew she couldn't stay on her feet for too long (*plantar fasciitis*), didn't like metal restraints or canes – all of it. But her list of *yes* was longer than her list of *no*.

"Stand there," I said, pointing to the center of my wool rug. My room looked odd, with all the furniture pushed back, piled up: spare chairs on my big oak table, ottoman tucked underneath. The room was just the rug, a coarse wool bullseye, and my favorite plush wing-back.

"Yes, sir," she said, the grin never leaving her lips, as she walked to the center.

"Stop." She did, turning slowly to face me. Her breasts were big, wide. Not a girl's, a woman's. Twin peaks on cotton fabric. I reached out to one of the points, circled it slowly with a stiff finger. The smiled stayed, but her breathing deepened, sped up. "Did I tell you what to call me?"

"No," she hissed, trying to swallow a scream, as I pinched her nipple, hard. One of my *no's* concerned sound. My apartment had thin walls.

"Call me, 'Master'," I said, low and mean, grumbling and growling, as I pinched even more.

"Yes ... M-Master," she said, with a delightful stammer against the pain.

I released the pressure. "Pain is your punishment. It will be frequent. Pleasure is your reward. It will be rare. I'm not going to ask you if you understand. If you didn't you wouldn't be here. Undress."

She did, sensually but efficiently. The white cotton dress went next. Under was an everyday bra, pearl and white, and a pair of everyday panties, just white. No hose, only socks and shoes. As I had requested. Lingerie doesn't interest me. Bodies don't even interest me. She didn't interest me. But what I could do to her – that was what interested me.

She was naked. Her body was good. Not ideal, but with a warmth and reality to her. Big, full tits with just enough sag to mean reality and not silicone or somesuch. A plump little tummy. A plump mons with a gentle tuft of dark hair. It wasn't a body that you'd hang on your wall, but it was a body you'd want to fuck. But that was on her *no* list, which was fine by me. I definitely wanted to fuck with her, just not with her body.

Her hands kept drifting up, a force of will keeping them from hiding her breasts, covering her nipples. I smiled. SLUT-SLAVE had a modest streak. Priceless.

I got out my toolbag, my own kind of wry smile on my face. Other tops went on and on about their toys, pissing on each other about the quality of the leather, the weight, the evilness of certain objects. I sat back and watched them: wry grin then, wry grin now. If I had a headboard, I'd have it carved: *A workman is as good as his tools*, it would say. *A great one doesn't need them at all.*

I added it up once. Fifty dollars was as high as I got. Show me any other hobby that could give as much pleasure as my little bag of toys – or as much wonderful discomfort to SLUT-SLAVE.

I laid them out on the rug in front of her. I felt like a surgeon – or a priest. "We're going to play a game," I said. "The rules are very simple. I ask a question. If you tell me the truth you get a reward, if you don't you get punished. Again, I won't ask if you understand."

I picked up a favorite – though to tell my own truth I like

them all. This one was just the favorite of the moment. I squeezed, and the clothespin yawned open. I held it out to her nipple, which – I noticed – was nicely wrinkled, erect. "Are you wet?"

"Yes," she said in a breathy whisper. I could tell, her musk was thick in the room. I was hard. Hell, I was hard when I opened the front door, but hearing that, knowing that, my jeans grew that much tighter.

"First lesson. It's an important one. Sometimes even the truth can mean pain," I said, in my best of voices, as I released the spring on the clothespin, letting it bite down sharp and quick on her thickening nipple.

Her sigh was a lovely musical tone, a bass rumble of pain that peaked towards pleasure. Oh, yes, that was it. The first note of a long musical composition. Her knees buckled because of it, and I put a hand on her shoulder to steady her.

I kept it on for a mental beat of ten. Not long, but long enough. I released it, keeping my hand on her shoulder. It always hurts so much worse coming off than it does going on. Sure enough, her knees buckled even more and she slipped, dropped down to my rug.

Still on her knees, breathing much more regularly, she looked up at me, chin level with my crotch. I knew if I said to, she'd unzip my fly, undo my belt, reach in with eager, strong fingers to fish out my dick, stick it into her hot mouth. She'd do it, I knew, but like the clothespin, it's so much better if you wait. So I did.

I stepped back, grinning at the flicker of disappointment on her face. You'll have to wait too, I thought. I retrieved my bag, and sat down in my chair, facing her. The clothespin was still in my hand and I found myself absently opening and closing it. A dom's worry bead, I guess. "Stand up. Right now."

She did. Her knees seemed a bit weak. "Come closer." She did, her gait slow and controlled. I reached down to my bag at my feet, picked up something new. "You're mine. You belong to me," I said, looking into her face. Her eyes shone, gleamed. "I won't ask if you understand."

When I was a kid, I used to play with dolls. Well, maybe not "dolls", not exactly. No Raggedy Anns, no Barbies – not like that. I liked that they were mine; they belonged to me. I could make them do anything, at any time, and they didn't say a word. They just did it, forever smiling.

It was a new toy, another deceivingly simple thing. I saw it in some import/export place down in the city. Elegant and simple, black and glossy. Seeing it, I knew I had to have it. Having it, I couldn't wait to use it.

"Lean back," I said. I was tapping it against my palm, a lacquer metronome. Tilted back, her breasts swayed gently apart, just beginning to make that armpit migration – she was younger than I thought.

I ran the tip of the chopstick around her right nipple, feeling it skip and slide over her areola, the contours traveling down the length of it into my fingertips. She sighed, softly.

Way back when, just after I outgrew those plastic dolls, I wondered if I had a dead thing – you know, preferring girls stiff and cold rather than warm and breathing. But that wasn't it. It wasn't them being immobile, plastic, it was me being in control, making them do what I wanted. Right then, she was my doll, my plaything, and I was completely in control.

I started tapping, steadily, almost softly at first. A smooth double-time. But after a dozen or so beats I moved it up to a harder, more insistent tempo. Her breathing quickened, started to grow close, to almost, maybe match my beats with the lacquered stick. I watched her stomach rise and fall, a background accompaniment, echo to her hisses and signs.

I moved, circled her breast and nipple with my stick, painting her with the beats. Tap, tap, tap, sigh, sigh, moan, sigh. Then the other breast, but a little harder this time. She started to glow, shine with gentle sweat. I could smell her, a thick rutting musk. Now she really was wet.

Now just, only her nipples. Each impact steady, sure, quick and hard. She started to unconsciously twist her body, a little this way then the opposite, to get away from the beats. For a moment, I thought about stopping. Make her stand up, make her get dressed, kick her out for such a show of life and independence, but that would mean throwing away, stop using this lovely new toy. The stick as well as SLUTSLAVE.

Then I did stop. Time for the next movement. She lifted her head, looking long at me, breathing heavy and hard. Her eyes flicked with a bit of fear but more than anything, a kind of plead: *More.*

Back into the bag. Simple. When you have control, you don't need gadgets, gizmos, fine leathers. Fifty dollars in the right hands, with the right toy, and you have all you need. I came up with a pair matching the first clip. Her eyes grew even wider, breathing deeper and quicker. She knew what was coming next. I didn't have to say anything.

The right one first. Instead, I leaned down and held it there, open, threatening around her so-hard nipple. She looked at it, then looked at me. Again, fear, but more than anything a desire for me to let go.

So I did. Her guttural bellow peaked threateningly towards a scream but didn't as she swallowed and swallowed, hissed and hissed it back down into herself. I was impressed.

I kept the clip on. It was wonderful to watch it bob up and down with her steady, deep breaths. I could have watched it all day, thinking: *This is mine. This is mine. This is mine.* I could have, but I had another tit to play with.

During all this, my cock had been confined, trapped in my pants. Turning to the other tit, I felt how very, very hard I'd gotten. But that would wait. I was in control here. Not my dick.

The other one. Again, I held it there, looming over a tight little point of nipple. Again, I let go.

This time a short, quick, honest scream blew past her lips. Sound was a concern, but frankly I didn't care. This was good – damned good. She was a good toy, a good plaything. She was mine to do with as I wanted.

I watched her, making sure the pain of the clips wasn't too much for her. She whistled her breaths, in and out, belly rising falling as she tried to accept, flow with, use, and enjoy what was happening to her nipples, breasts and body. I liked to watch her, knowing that I was the cause of all this. Yes, my cock was hard – steel, stone, rigid – in my pants, but this was almost better. The bliss painting her body in shimmering sweat, making her pant and moan, making her clit twitch, wasn't something of mine that could ever go soft, ever come too quick. I could make her come and come and come again and never take off my pants.

Time for the next step. Both pins were in place, both nodded, dipped and rose from their grips on her nipples as she squirmed against the pain. I picked up the chow stick again. "See this?" I said. She pulled herself up from her blurry rapture. Her eyes took a long time to focus. She looked, she nodded.

I tapped one clothespin, hard, sending serious shocks down through it into her already aching nipple. She squealed in shock, in endorphin delight. I did the same to the other, then back again. Back and forth. She was a wonderful plaything, a fun little toy. I enjoyed playing with her very much. Oh, the things we could do.

I glanced up at the clock. A qualifier of our time together rang in my mind. Just a few hours, she had said, to start. Time had flown.

"Listen to me," I said. Her vision was almost lost against the waves of sensation, but she managed to finally see me. "We're almost finished – for tonight that is. But before we do, I'm going to fuck you."

She frowned past what was happening to her nipples, her tits, her body, her cunt. My words reached through it all and created a worry.

Not good to have my plaything in such a state. Time to demonstrate that I am in control, that for her, I'm the boss, I'm the Master – and she is just a toy, and toys have nothing, not even a worry.

I reached into my bag at my feet, pulled it out, tossed it at her feet. "I said I'm going to fuck you. My dick – right there in front of you – is going in your cunt. Do you have a problem with that?"

She didn't. The smell of her, the grin that flashed on her gleaming face told me that. Her legs were already gently parted, the kind of reckless, unselfconscious display that only a plaything in the middle of a high-flying pleasure/pain/endorphin rush could have. She may have had a worry, but she was more a hungry cunt. A wet and ready cunt. A wet and very ready cunt with a rubber dick on the floor in front of her.

"Pick it up," I said, though I didn't have to, not really, "and fuck yourself with it."

She bent forward, picked it up. Parting her thighs just a bit more, she showed me her pink wetness. The bare thatch of hair that descended from her mons was matted and gleaming with juice. Her lips were already gently apart, swollen and ready for my store-bought dick.

I knew I could probably have fucked her with my own cock, or simply unzipped my fly and stuck myself into her hot, wet mouth. But that would mean I was flesh and blood, a man, and not the Master I really was. A Master is cold, a Master knows what to do with a plaything, a toy, a doll. I knew what to do. That's what I lived for: that dominance, that autthority, that control.

She slipped the dildo into herself, just an inch to start. Then out, then in deeper, with a slow twist. She bit her lip in concentration; she closed her eyes in bliss – lost to the pain in her tits, the cock in her cunt.

Kneeling on my rug, legs very wide, she fucked herself. The gentle part ended quickly. She was now really, strongly fucking herself. A soft foam rimmed her cunt where the plastic slicked in and out. Some of her pubic hairs streaked along the length on the outstroke, curled in on the return. The hiss that had been only from the clips on her nipples was joined by the deeper sounds of a rolling, approaching come.

I didn't know her that well, but a good Master knows the sounds, no matter the toy, and I could tell that she could see it coming, could smell, taste it coming. Her breathing broke, became shorter, panting. Now, right now, I thought, as I bent forward and put thumbs and fingers on the pins. I pulled.

Her eyes snapped open, fear lighting her irises. This time she didn't say, without words, *More* but rather *Oh my God*.

I pulled. Not hard, just enough to drag her orgasm out, draw it farther out. Her fucking had slowed, eased, but she was too far along to stop. She couldn't if she wanted to.

I didn't want her to. So she didn't. I didn't need to say it, she understood it: the language of Master to SLUTSLAVE. Her fucking increased, pushing herself back up to the precipice. It didn't take long for her to be looking down the fast slope to her come. This time she said, without words, *Now*.

Yes, SLUTSLAVE: *Now*. The pins came off. Screw noise concerns. Her scream came from her nipples, her tits, but also from her spasming, quivering, quaking cunt. Her come rattled her, making her shake, her head bob back and forth. Her legs, already tensed from holding her forward, collapsed, spilling her backward on my old scratchy rug.

I watched her. Her breathing, after a long while, eased to a regular, resting rhythm. Then I went to my bathroom, got a big fluffy towel and draped it over her. She didn't say anything, not even thanks.

I got her a glass of water from my kitchen, even put a little slice of lemon in it. She took it with gently quivering fingers. Drank all of it, handed it back. Then she said, "Thanks," but for the glass or the evening I didn't know.

Slowly, she got up, started hunting for her panties, her bra. I helped her, handing them over to her. She seemed to be happy.

Finally, she was dressed, though she looked funny with her hair messed. "Are you OK to go home?" I asked her, my hand on her arm. "Should I call you a cab?"

"I'm—whooo," she breathed, laughing for second with a shivering after-feeling. "I'm OK. Really. Thank you," she finally said. "That was a blast."

"I'm glad. I'd love to do it again sometime – soon."

"So would I. Really." Her hand was on the doorknob.

"Write me," I said, holding it open for her. "Send me a message and we'll pick a date."

"That'd be fun. Sure." She walked down the hall. When she got to the end, she turned, waved to me. I waved back.

I checked my messages an hour or so later. Nothing. I watched some television, something I barely remember. Cops, I think. Or doctors. Something like that. Before I went to bed, I checked again. Nothing. I sent her a message: "Hope you had a good time. Write when you get a chance."

In the morning, nothing. I browsed some of the chatrooms, even though I'd never known her to be there that early. Nothing of course.

When I got home from work I checked again. Spam. A few messages from some friends. Nothing. She's just busy. Things happen, I told myself, not believing my own thoughts.

Before I went to bed I wrote another message. But I didn't send it. Maybe in a few days, I thought.

I checked again the instant I walked in after work. Nothing. Nothing at all. I wrote her, against my better judgement. Simple, direct: "Concerned about how you're feeling. Please write."

That will do it, I thought. That'll reach her. Was it too much to ask? I thought she had fun. I thought she did.

But when I went to bed there was nothing but more spam, a few other messages. Nothing from her.

Around midnight, late for me, I went to bed. Nothing at all. I tried to masturbate but it didn't work out.

Eventually, I fell asleep.

In the morning I checked again, first thing. Nothing. Nothing at all.

I never used the handle MASTER017 again.

Of Canes and Men

Sacha Lasalle

He leaned over and whispered in my ear, "She's quite exqui-site."

I simply nodded.

"Is—"

Silencing him with my finger, I stood, motioning for him to follow me out of the room. Waiting until he was through the doorway, I closed the door quietly behind him.

"I'm sorry. No, she's not."

He put his hand in his pocket and nodded. "I see. That's a shame. I could make it worth your while."

We both laughed. Even if I desperately needed the money, my answer would still be the same.

"Where did you find her? It's not like you to hide some-thing so beautiful. Although we all know your habit of sharing . . . you're not usually interested unless you're ready to let them go."

I shrugged. For some reason I was reluctant to discuss it. "It's only early days."

He nodded again and I opened the door. We re-entered, taking our seats. She hadn't moved. I watched as he admired her form. Finishing the last of his drink in a gulp, he stood up. Following suit, I walked him to the front door. He collected his coat and we shook hands.

"Well, if you should ever change your mind, I'd like you to call me."

I raised a brow. "I see. Not at the club?"

He cocked his head slightly and looked at me. "Yes. But for some reason, I don't think I'll be hearing from you."

Offering him a measured smile, I tried not to give anything away.

After he left, I returned to the den. Leaning against the door frame I observed her silently before removing the tumblers and gently lifting the glass tabletop from her back. After putting it away I walked back in, circling her naked body slowly. She still hadn't moved. I was pleased.

"You may sit, pet."

Eyes shut, she sat back on her heels. Watching her face, I noticed her bottom lip quivering. A tear ran down her cheek.

"What is wrong, pet?"

Opening her eyes, her dark irises focused on mine. "Please . . . please . . . I don't want . . ."

I sighed and shook my head. "You did not ask and I did not give permission to speak freely. I thought we would have been clear by now."

Stiffening, she pursed her lips tightly, trying not to cry. I sighed again. Disobedience after such good behaviour.

I spoke quietly, "Now, what did you do wrong?"

She sucked in a deep breath, struggling for control. "I'm sorry, Sir. I spoke freely without permission and I allowed my emotions to get in the way. I am not here to serve my needs. I am here to serve yours."

Her husky voice did not miss a beat. I would have been proud – it had almost been a perfect night. Pressing my lips together, I contemplated her punishment. To be honest, I wasn't really in the mood, but I could not let this go unpunished.

Reluctantly, I opened the cupboard and surveyed my collection. It seemed that I had developed quite the cane fetish over the years as it rapidly dominated all my other tools. Eventually, I packed away what little I had left, just in case.

Several years ago, I was put onto a man who had spent decades making canes. His was an interesting story. He had become so obsessed with making them, it had taken over his life. Word had it that the closest he seemed to get to any sort of gratification these days, was watching his partner stroke specific canes with her slender fingers, which then drove him into a frenzy.

Of course I never did ask. Seeing him was by appointment only. In fact, you could only meet him by referral and even then, he decided whether he would allow you to purchase, or make your custom request. Thankfully his reaction to me was a positive one.

I wasn't sure what he saw in me, but he'd taken a liking, often asking me down to his place of creation and bantering with me to try out his prototypes. Though I suspected he had me figured from the first moment he met me. He also seemed to be able to predict with uncanny accuracy how long I would keep the partners that I had.

The canes were mounted vertically in the cabinet. I was primarily a single shaft man, with only one multi-strand cane in the closet. My eyes stopped on the whangee that I no longer used.

I doubted it was an uncommon story among the men I knew, but once was enough for me. For a while I was acquainted with an alluring redhead. Very Jessica Rabbit-like. Quick witted and highly intelligent. Corporate ball-buster by day and pain addict during the downtime. She was an interesting creature, with perfect, creamy, unblemished skin.

At first – and even occasionally afterwards – it seemed to me that it was almost a terrible thing to mark her flesh. She was a dangerous woman, too. After all, we were only men. I should have known the moment I looked into her eyes, as she was bent over on all fours. Her derrière was irresistible, and out of her mouth came everything you wanted to hear, but it was her eyes that told another story. Continuous pale-green ice; goading, challenging and almost contemptuous. That look could drive a man to lose control.

Sometimes it concerned me that she was possibly vicariously administering self-punishment. For what reason, I didn't know, but it eventually came to a head. After numerous sessions, it was clear that beyond anything the pain had become first and foremost. It was bigger than the both of us and driving us down a hazardous path. On the final night, I had severely bruised her skin and broken the flesh in two places, as I teetered on the edge, and then regained my senses and pulled back.

Her fiery red hair was matted around her forehead and cheeks in a combination of perspiration and tears that covered her face. With serene eyes she looked at me, whispered, "Thank you," and promptly passed out. After checking her pulse, I cleaned her wounds, applied ice, and then a salve for the bruising, very aware of how painful it was going to be. I attempted several times to discuss our last session, but she remained mute on the subject.

Afterwards, everything changed. I lost whatever desire I had for her, and she – for lack of a better word – had been broken in. Her demeanour had changed. She became completely acquiescent with a hint of desperation, and no longer the defiant woman I once knew. She also wanted to continue, and whether she wanted more or less as result of what happened, I didn't have the heart to discover.

I recommended her to a gentleman I knew. She didn't need an extremely hard Master. She needed someone who was experienced enough to be able to understand what was going on. It was possible I could've read it wrong, but an absolute pain slut was not what I was particularly interested in.

It was difficult to say whether what happened was any sort of achievement, triumph or dismal failure. Either way, it was something I'd never forget. Perhaps it explained why the whangee was mounted at the very top of the case. I knew I'd never use it again.

I often thought about whether it was significant, but to me it was. When it no longer mattered who was administering the cane – like a flaccid cock – I lost interest. It seemed that maybe over the years I'd become too apt with the cane and that was the phallus they fell in love with.

Still, despite it all – and a period of hiatus where I wanted to see if I could survive without my dark affliction – here I was. And there she was. The dark-haired woman kneeling in my den. I didn't mention it, but I'd ordered a cane especially for her. It had never bothered me before. I'd used all my canes on several bottoms, but I didn't want that for her. I wanted her to have her own, regardless of what happened.

Somehow yet again, the custom cane maker knew something I didn't. When I arrived to pick up the cane I'd ordered, he unwrapped a cloth and handed it to me.

"What's this?" I frowned.

"Your cane."

"I didn't order this."

"I know." He grinned. "Go on, pick it up."

I shied away from fancy or adorned canes. Some of the designs I found far too garish, although others no doubt would have found them beautiful. All my canes were undecorated, right down to the handle. This one was embellished – a simple black handle, with what appeared to be an onyx embedded on the top. The wood was not rattan, only betrayed by its reddish colour.

I held it in my hand. It felt perfect. I'd never thought of that before and it struck me as odd. Letting the cane bounce downward between my palm and thumb, I then gripped the handle and rotated my wrist, flicking it back.

He'd lost his grin, giving me a serious knowing look. I felt that he wanted to tell me it was the one, but restrained himself.

"It's certainly beautiful."

He nodded. "That it is."

"What is it?"

"Padauk." He shrugged. "I've had it for a while. It just didn't come to me how to fashion it, until recently."

I nodded. "I see. What do I owe you?"

He waved his hand in the air as if to dismiss my question.

I shook my head. "I can't."

"You can and you will. You know what to do with it." He

smiled kindly at me. "Take it as a thank you for being a friend."

I didn't know what to say. I rapped it against my palm, feeling the sting. "Thank you. I'm honoured."

He smiled again. "While a gentleman never tells, should you ever feel inclined . . ."

I smiled back. Perhaps I would offer him something more descriptive to go with his visual fetish.

I did have a looped cane which sat unused. The thought of adorning flesh with petals or butterfly wings appeared to appeal to me, but when it came to deciding I seemed to always reach for my trusted rods. Picking up her black-handled cane, I closed the cabinet and turned to her.

Fear flashed in her eyes before she tried to replace it with resolve, and I paused. This would be her first time and I considered giving her a choice.

"My pet, do you wish for an alternative punishment?"

She looked down at the floor. "No, Sir. I will accept my reprimand, however you choose to deliver it."

I didn't realize I'd held my breath. The anticipation stirred in me instantly and I wondered where it had been before this moment. Touching the tip of the cane with the pad of my finger, I slowly ran the shaft back and forth over my palm.

Sometimes it didn't matter how well practised or controlled I was, occasionally I still had the urge to go against common sense. To let my lust distract me from my sense of responsibility. The thought of caning her backside without mercy, and the visualization of the angry red marks on her flesh made my cock excruciatingly hard.

Gripping the cane tightly, my knuckles whitened at the imagery. I almost lost it when I envisaged pushing through her tight sphincter, as it resisted my forceful entry. For a split second the line blurred. Carnal lust almost overtook me. I hadn't moved, but it was as though I'd reached for her.

Looking back, I was grateful that she hadn't looked up, or tried to. If the appearance of the cane instilled fear into her, no doubt my moment of inability to keep my desires from my face would have inspired tenfold. Silently, I took slow deep breaths to regain focus.

I pointed to the lounger with the cane. "Pet."

Obediently she got up and kneeled on the lounger, proffering her unmarked ass in the air. Gently, I ran the back of my fingers along her flesh, noting it was a little cool to the touch. The temperature had dropped a couple of degrees and while I hadn't looked outside, it was obvious that evening had fallen. She would be warm soon enough.

Tapping the cane gently, I watched it bounce against her skin. Although it barely carried any force, her initial reaction was to flinch. Stopping, I looked over her body. What dark hair didn't cover her shoulder blades, hung down past her neck. I traced the curve of her spine to where it met the small of her back, and then curved over yet again, into the crevice that hid her lips from view. Despite the curves, her body was rigid. This would not do.

"Relax."

I watched as she battled to control herself and stop from tensing. Somehow she managed something in between. I knew she wouldn't stop from flinching. At least not this time.

"Breathe."

I heard her breathe out shakily. She didn't realize she'd been holding her breath. I tapped her again with the cane, and this time – although she flinched – she recovered quickly and tried in earnest to relax. This time I did not stop.

Applying the cane against her skin in short rapid strokes, I worked it against both cheeks firmly, but not enough to cause significant pain. Her flesh turned a pretty shade of pink under the wood. It was akin to quickly flicking paint with a long-handled brush.

I noted she'd stayed silent throughout when I finally stopped and inspected her arse. I liked to keep the area confined specifically to the cheeks and, while I still enjoyed administering the occasional spanking, I was specific with that too. I disliked it when the colour travelled down past the top of the thighs.

Gently pressing my palm against her pink skin, I felt the warmth as I gave both cheeks a rub. Pressing the cane between her thighs, I motioned for her to spread her legs, contemplating sliding the cane against her sex. Pain before pleasure. *Eight*. I would give her eight.

The cane whirred beautifully, complemented by the scream that ripped from her mouth. My lower gut tightened and I felt a small satisfied smile tug at the corner of my lips. I was controlled, but no doubt the tip would still feel as though it was slicing flesh.

By the third she was sobbing and I executed the fourth, listening to her cry out. I almost wanted to stop, slide my throbbing cock into her mouth and feel her quivering lips around me. By the sixth stroke she was shaking, unable to control her spasming body. I was harder and more coiled than I could recall.

There were two moments that often fought for supremacy, and it was merely a difference between standing and falling. Sometimes it was a twisted cycle between the satisfaction and pleasure of control. Occasionally when they broke and begged me to stop, it was both thrilling and disappointing, in the same way as when they withstood.

This time, however, the pleasure and pride were overwhelming. I resisted the urge to make the last two strikes harder. Her screams didn't change and neither did her sobbing. It probably didn't help that I hadn't told her how many she would receive.

I stopped and she flinched hard, feeling my palms against her burning skin. Rubbing gently over the eight welts, they looked like eight perfect fingers splayed over her cheeks. I relished the feeling of the raised flesh underneath my hands, until I could almost take no more. I slid my fingers between her legs, and to my sheer delight found her incredibly wet. After flipping her over, I quickly freed my cock and plunged into her.

She looked at me wide-eyed, her lips forming an "o", fresh tears sliding down the edges of her eyes. Her cheeks were scarlet – almost matching her backside – and she grunted hard as I squeezed her ass tightly. More tears fell as I fucked her. I could feel the rise as she was coming apart under me. Gripping her hips painfully I continued to thrust, losing myself in the lustful high that fogged my brain.

"Permission to be free," I ground out, as she gripped my cock. My head tipped back from the pleasure.

Her groans chimed in with the sounds of our wet flesh. "Sir. I'm. Sorry." She spoke haltingly.

I simply nodded. She'd already apologized. I'd accepted and reprimanded her. There was no need to apologize again.

"No, Sir, I'm really sorry. I—I—"

I didn't stop, but I frowned at her as I increased my speed, thrusting harder between her legs. I slid one of my hands between her breasts, and up around her throat, as she looked me in the eye. The sharp rise clawed within, caught up in the vortex that was pulling us both down, amplifying every thrust.

"Don't share me."

I blinked. She'd said it so quickly that I wasn't sure of what I heard, her words drowned out by the rush as I came. Her legs shook around me as I slowly rocked inside her, running my fingers over her insistent welts. I groaned. No matter how many times I touched the raised flesh of my own doing, it was like a never-ending aphrodisiac. She tugged my wrist and brought my hand to her mouth, gently kissing my palm. I stopped, almost taken by surprise as what she'd said slowly registered.

She looked at me with not a pleading, but what seemed like determination. I couldn't suppress the short, sharp swell of my heart. It seemed that my one deeply buried desire had just been resurrected, and suddenly I wasn't sure how I was supposed to feel.

"I see." Withdrawing, I pressed against her sphincter. My lids drew down as she pushed against me, forcing my head into her tightness. Our groans reached my ears as I slid in slowly, nearly driven out of my mind. I thumbed over her clit and she bucked, the grip breathtaking as I started to stroke.

"Ohhh." A long animalistic groan rolled slowly from her lips.

Grunting in unison, I pushed my full weight on her, pressing her legs back against her body and thrusting madly like a man possessed.

"Beat me if you must. Punish me. Cane me, or whip my cunt, but don't share me." Her words were punctuated by gasping breaths.

Whipping wasn't usually my thing, but the sudden image of whipping between her legs made me stop sharply and squeeze her hips tighter. She grimaced, her face contorting. I watched in fascination before realizing how hard I had pinned my fingers to her flesh. Slowly I released them.

"Do you know what you are asking?" *Of me*, I thought. The words sounded strange to my ears.

Suspended, she looked at me, eventually nodding. With a rush of violent possession I took her until she screamed.

Escape

Mitzi Szereto

Night after night, day after day, I wait. I wait for what I cannot avoid: *the inevitable*.

I do not wish to marry him. He is old, and he is ugly. The flesh hangs from his neck and upper arms in mottled rolls; I dare not think of the rest of him! His teeth are the shade of rotting timber with holes riddled through by worms. His eyes rake over me with a familiarity that causes my body to flush with shame. It's as if he has already tasted my flesh, smelled my scent. When I see him I want to curl up into a tight ball and hide. But hide I cannot. For Father has other plans.

It is considered acceptable for pretty young women whose bodies retain the flush of youth to marry ancient trolls, but this is a fate I'm unwilling to bear. Of course, I realize I am not as young as most of the others; my choices are not those that can be made with any great degree of pickiness. Were it not for the circumstances, it should be unlikely I'd secure a husband at all, since the men of my land seek out those that are as fruit on the bough rather than those ready to drop to the ground. Indeed, some of us are old enough to remember such rarities as fruit before the evil of our leaders caused the gods to forsake us.

Having managed to avoid my fate for this many changes of season is a miracle in itself. Yet even with my seniority of years, I have something that allows me to be worthy of considera-tion: I bleed every month. Well, that and the fact that I'm still comely in appearance. A bleeding womb, prized though it may be, is increased in value by the package in which it's contained. I wonder if it is the same in other lands? Though I have never been to other lands. I have only been *here*.

Many years ago a terrible disease ravaged our already barren landscape, taking with it the majority of female children and girls and leaving yet more barrenness behind. Perhaps it was further punishment for the greed and wickedness of our rulers as they sought to acquire more and more of the territory surrounding us, annexing anything and everyone in their wake. The blood that has been spilled could fill rivers and probably has.

The lesson has not been learned, however, and the greed and wickedness continue to flourish. Our men grow worse with each passing day, becoming as cruel and ugly as the land upon which we live. The young ones learn from the old, since it is the old that seek out new wives after their current ones are no longer of use as bed or breeding partners. The discarded wives are either buried beneath stones in the town center or cast out of the kingdom, where they're left to wander toward the horizon until the elements accomplish the same thing as the stones. Our arid land is littered with the corpses of these women, whose bodies could no longer provide their husbands with fruit.

There are no young men in our kingdom in possession of a wife. Rather they are forced to wait until the old have taken their pick of what little remains to be taken – and by then the young too have grown old. And so the cycle begins anew when the female results of these unions attain womanhood and can produce future brood mares. I think it should be better if our race died out than to continue a life in this wretched place. But my opinion matters not.

Our women are kept imprisoned under lock and key from the onset of their menses until marriage; it's the only way to guarantee they remain pure for the men to whom they've been promised. The pedigree of the children they bear their husbands must not be in any way suspect. Even servants attending to the needs of these prisoners – for we are, indeed, *prisoners* – are female. It is not unusual for couplings to take place between prisoner and servant, and a blind eye is turned to such transgressions. The men do not care what transpires in the stone cells of our bedchambers as long as no seed has reached our fertile wombs. The touch of another can be as valuable as gold to a body hungering for it. Women locked away until such time as they are to be married off to husbands that will only maul and misuse them are starved for tenderness and affection. Me? Hah! I am no different from my sisters-in-misery.

It is past nightfall when my servant comes to me. The sky turns black the tiny window of the cell that constitutes my bedchamber. Even the stars refuse to twinkle over our land, choosing instead to shine on the verdant horizon most of us covet and dream of. A shaft of light from a lantern cuts a wedge in the floor as the door opens carefully; despite our nocturnal activities being common knowledge, the women and their servants are discreet. I lie in my small bed, my heart pounding in expectation of the pleasure I know I'm to be given on this night – the pleasure that assures me I'm still alive. At first I feel a caress of lips against my cheek so light it's barely discernible. A whisper of sweet breath against my ear follows, and it holds my name: Gwendolen.

Hearing my name spoken by my caller summons the moisture from my loins and my pelvis rises in answer. The voice is nearly enough to send me over into the oblivion of bliss. My limbs pull taut as the strings on a lyre when plucked by the miniature hands of the King's musicians when they perform in the public square. Like the women of childbearing age, the Small Ones are also imprisoned by their designated roles in society, their only function being to entertain just as ours is to procreate.

Gwendolen.

A hand reaches beneath my sleeping-dress and locates the core of moisture. A subtle shift of movement and I feel something sliding gently into me as warm lips close over mine. My thighs fall open as I sigh a name that I'd never dare to speak aloud. Despite the common bonds we share, even secrets cannot be shared in this place of women. The weight of another body is full upon me now, pressing me down into the straw mattress. The sound of my wetness fills the room as I'm penetrated with greater speed. A finger lays claim to that most responsive part of me, manipulating it with less gentleness than might be required. As my breath quickens, along with the beating of my heart, I find I don't mind the roughness. The swiftness with which events take place below my waist is dizzying, and suddenly my body bucks and writhes against that of my pleasure-giver's, my cry of delight hushed by a tongue as its muted response joins mine.

And so we spend our nights, taking what joys there are to be found in the arms of a servant before being dispatched to the arms of an aged brute. Such is the destiny of women.

The man I'm to marry is rich and powerful. He is a man who, with a casual flip of his hand, can have heads lopped off – and *has*. One of these heads shall be Father's should our union not take place. I would not shed a tear if this came to pass. Indeed, I would cheer the loudest, for Father is no better than the filthy troll who seeks to penetrate and impregnate me. Yet I cannot curse my betrothed and wish he'd never lived, because without his life, my heart would be as barren as this land.

For it is his son I desire.

It is Evrain whom I love.

It is his name I sigh when I am given pleasure.

He is young and beautiful, his flesh smooth and unmarred by battle or the relentless sun that bakes dry everything beneath our feet. His eyes are as brilliant and multifaceted as the jewels in the King's crown, and each time he looks at me, I experience a melting in the place where my thighs meet and a corresponding ache in my womb that I desire only to have filled by his sweet seed. How he can be the progeny of his father I cannot imagine, and I often wonder if his mother had secretly managed to offer a home inside her to the seed of another, rejecting the foul offering dispatched by her husband,

Houdain. Oh, I can only wish it were so! For I could not love anything that originated from so repellent a creature as Houdain.

Evrain is being groomed for battle and, despite his youth, has already proved a formidable swordsman. Soon it will be time for him to be sent into the hinterland, where he will be successful and acquire more land for our miserable kingdom, or be killed by foreign soldiers. Alas, his taste for blood is not as highly developed as those of his peers; he has no appetite for battle and death; to kill or be killed are not fates he seeks. But time is running out for him.

And for me.

To flee is what the women of our kingdom seek, though there are few among us who would survive the journey across the dead landscape to the rich green mists beyond – mists that hold the promise of a better life for those cursed to have been born female. It's impossible to know if any of us has been successful; a woman's disappearance can either signify that she's gone to her death or, if she's extremely fortunate, escaped from the land that dooms her. Not surprisingly, the men take every opportunity to regale us with tales of horror, featuring great scaly creatures that exhale fire through their mouths and nostrils, turning everything in their path to cinders, especially foolish young women who think they can escape their destiny. And if one is so fortunate as to sneak past them, packs of red-eyed beasts with fangs sharper than the King's finest sword lie in wait to make of her a meal. Whether these creatures exist I do not know, but they reportedly guard the borders of our land (as if anyone should wish to come here!), also making certain that no one passes through to the green sanctuary that lies beyond.

As for whether I choose to believe in their existence, well . . . I am not as ignorant and silly as most of my fellow females; however, I'm also not willing to risk finding out for myself. Life is not easy for a woman without the guardianship of a man. Had I the protection and love of the one to whom I've given my heart, I might risk having my flesh scorched by these fire-breathing creatures or torn to shreds by their comrades if it meant I could be free. In fact, I might risk anything!

And so we plot our escape, for Evrain does not desire to remain here any more than I do.

My caller comes to me again in the night, full of quiet whispers and soft touches. But this time it's different. The day of my wedding draws near and with each tender kiss upon my breast and each impassioned lick of my sex, we know that our stolen moments will soon be at an end. This bedchamber that is naught more than a prison cell may seem like a lovers' paradise when compared with what awaits should my beloved Evrain and I fail in our escape. Yet as the heat of luxurious sensation builds in my loins, I muse upon a life far away from here – a simple and pure life with Evrain and myself living off the treasures the rich earth will offer us. We will build our home from the scented boughs of trees and walk barefoot on a blanket of cool green rather than being showered with grey dust, the smell of death perpetually in our nostrils. We will eat what is fresh and new and succulent rather than gnawing on what is gristly and old and dry.

The tongue between my thighs continues to lave and probe and circle, and my body tenses. The wave is near and, as I feel it rising, I keep my breath deep in my chest, knowing that tonight this wave will crash down upon me with greater force than ever. I feel something slipping inside me, though I'm so wet it barely registers. Only when it moves around to make love to my other opening do I finally realize it's a finger – and that is when I lose myself. My pelvis hoists itself up in a maddened thrust, my hands clawing at the hair on the head moving between my thighs. "Evrain!" I sob into the night.

Evrain and I conspire in the darkness. We cannot let many more days go past, as Houdain awaits me in his bed and has made it clear to Father that his patience has its limits. It matters not that our wedding day has already been set; Houdain has indicated that he wishes to consummate the marriage before it has even taken place!

And there are few in our kingdom that would deny him what he wants, least of all Father, who shits himself at the mere sound of the man's voice.

Though my beloved does not share the bloodlust of others of his sex, Evrain is primed for the task at hand. We have discussed it in depth, and I believe in my heart that he'll not suffer a moment's guilt. Not only will it eliminate one problem, but it will serve as a cloak for our escape, a way of directing attention elsewhere. This is what we require for our plan to succeed. The fact that it involves murder does negligible damage to our consciences. Evrain would not mourn the loss of his father any more than I would the loss of mine. One is evil, the other a coward. Both are equal in deserving our hatred.

It's arranged for me to be ready when the moon is at its smallest in the night sky. There will be no time for lovemaking, yet nevertheless we do so, for we are unable to be in each other's presence without the need to touch. The fact that Evrain has come to me with blood on his hands matters not. As always, he slips into my room in the guise of the female servant who has been slipping in all these many nights, the darkness and servant's garb sufficient to avoid raising suspicion. I wonder if any of the others are clever enough to have conceived of such a ploy. Surely there must be more than one inside this stone prison that has loved.

Evrain shucks off his servant's garments, allowing them to fall to the floor, and climbs into my bed. I can feel his desire for me pressing against my mound before our lips even meet. The wet tip of him nuzzles me as he rubs it against my sensitive place, each movement as maddening as it is exhilarating. I want to shout out my joy, but we are so close to realizing our plan that I dare not. Instead I bite back all sound as he continues his movements, urging me toward release. His breath grows quicker and I wonder if he's going to spill his seed before he manages to slide inside me. I feel he is close, as am

I. And then it happens, and I'm soaring up toward the stone ceiling, his name catching like a hook in my throat. The pleasure is sweeter for knowing it may be the last.

Evrain shifts position, yet before he can enter me, I too shift position and bend low to take him into my mouth. His shocked intake of breath is loud and reverberates off the walls. I have never tasted him or thought to do so, but this night has made me daring – the danger of death has made me daring. He is tangy sweet and musky all at the same time and my tongue licks hungrily of the moisture he gives me. "Gwendolen!" My name joins the echoes of his sighs and my heart swells with love as he swells in my mouth. I feel him pulse against my tongue and he pulls out quickly, placing himself between my thighs and entering me with one hard thrust.

Our moment is short, for Evrain cannot hold back from his finish. His limbs tense and he collapses onto me with his full weight, his cry of pleasure smothering itself against my lips. It is at this moment that I know he has planted a child inside me. Now we have still more to lose if our plan does not succeed.

We are as two shadows as we make our way out of the town. I'm wearing the coarse dark cloak Evrain brought for me, and it covers me from head to toe. There are still a few hours remaining before daylight and the discovery of Houdain, who was driven to take his own life for reasons known only to him. Though he did not leave behind a letter explaining his motives or instructing his family of his final wishes, his death was neat and quick and dispatched by his own hand and his favorite jeweled dagger. The fact that his hand received some assistance from the hand of his youngest son is unlikely to become known. Nor is it likely that anyone in the family should seek to question his end. Houdain was despised in equal measure by all, particularly Evrain's eldest brother, who will now take control of the family's fortune.

Evrain holds tight to my hand, leading me farther and farther away from the town center and everything I've ever known since I first arrived screaming into this world. I've never ventured beyond these confines, and it's exciting, yet terrifying as well. But with Evrain I am safe; he won't let anything happen to me. Although it's too dark to see each other, I know we're both covered in a coating of grey dust. It's impossible to step outside into the open without the dead soil of our land covering our skin and garments and getting into our eyes and nostrils. I wonder how many corpses I've inhaled in my lifetime, for our land is littered with their dust.

Our last stolen moments of love return to me in a flash and suddenly I fear I'm experiencing the end of my life. They say you can see images pass through your mind when you're near to death. If it is to be so, then I'm grateful I'll die with Evrain's seed inside me.

I stumble over some rubble and cry out. Evrain's hand moves quickly to close over my lips, though it's already too late – the sound has been heard.

"Who goes there?" comes the gruff shout of a man from somewhere in the blackness behind us.

Evrain and I stop, our chests heaving with fear. We're so close to the edge of the town that we can almost touch the hinterland. To be found out now would be cruel irony, indeed. We remain still, waiting for a second shout. When it doesn't come, we continue on our way, our bodies stiff with unease.

We know we have left the town behind us when we feel the cold biting through our garments like sharp teeth. There are no stone walls here to protect us, nothing to hide behind. We're out in the open now and the dusty wind hits us at full force, the grit catching in our teeth so that we don't dare try to speak for fear of it choking us. Evrain draws my hood down farther over my face in an attempt to shield my eyes; I can barely see now and I must cling to his arm like the unsighted beggars that take up residence in the town square whenever there's a burial beneath stones, as if a discarded wife being put to her death is a festive occasion and worthy of inspiring the locals to be charitable toward the unfortunate.

It feels as if we've walked for hours, though it's possibly only minutes. The wind lashes at us and pushes us back toward where we came from, but we forge forward to the border. We will either leave this place forever or die; there's no other option. I'm sick with fright as I recall the tales of fire-spitting creatures and beasts with fangs that can rip the flesh from my bones, and with every step we take I await their appearance, certain not even Evrain can save us from them.

Yet as the night begins to give way to day, they do not come. And when at last we step away from the dead grey earth and into the misty green land beyond, I know they never will.

I wake to music, the melody sweet and cheerful in my ears. Suddenly I fear I'm back in the town and it is the Small Ones playing their instruments in the square that I'm hearing. I nearly shriek in horror until I see the brilliant blue of the wide-open sky and the jewel-dappled green of the leaves that partially shade me from the sun. My breath flies out of me in a cloud of relief when I realize that I'm lying on a soft bed of green with my beloved by my side. The music is coming from the tiny feathered and winged creatures that roost on the boughs of the trees surrounding us. It's birdsong. We didn't have birdsong in our town. We didn't have birds.

Evrain takes me into his arms. I am home.

Business Managing

Teresa Noelle Roberts

"How many times do I have to tell you that a scribbled note on a stained napkin isn't a receipt?" The strained patience in Ms Bridges' voice stroked Dan's cock.

He shrugged, acting like the slightly flaky entrepreneur that he sometimes was, talking to his long-suffering business manager. "I'm sorry. I forgot to get one when we ordered and by the time I stopped back, the truck had moved."

Dan's business was fair-trade, organic specialty products: coffee, chocolate, spices, sauces. Ms Bridges' business was keeping Dan organized so he could focus on the parts of the job he loved: travelling to exotic places, working directly with farmers and artisanal producers, helping them get better lives for their families at the same time he got delicious products for his customers.

At least that was what he'd hired Ms Bridges to do. At the final interview, he'd explained he needed someone tough-minded and detail-oriented to keep him in line. "I'm creative and very passionate," he'd explained, "but I need someone to keep me disciplined." He'd meant he needed someone who'd keep him on track about the myriad details of running a small business, which he tended to neglect in favor of the fun parts. As soon as he said the words, though, he realized he'd been looking at the tall, lean blonde in a suit too severe for his casual office and fantasizing about needing her discipline in areas other than keeping tax paperwork organized. He felt his face blaze, hoping it was hidden under the tan of his recent trip to

Central America. Maybe, he hoped, he hadn't made a complete ass of himself and offended the best candidate for a business manager he'd interviewed yet.

Somehow the Devil had been on his side that day. She'd smiled in a way that lit her somewhat austere face and said, "I think that would be a pleasure, in every sense of the word."

Dan might own the company, but the business manager was the real boss – especially after hours, when they were alone in the office. And right now, the business manager had some pointed questions.

"Why in the world are you taking a supermarket buyer to lunch at a taco truck anyway?" This time he read amusement under the cool facade. Good. It wouldn't do to actually piss off Ms Bridges – her name was Melanie, but she insisted on being called Ms Bridges, like a much older woman might. Annoyed, she'd just keep up the dealing-with-the-idiot-boss routine. That would be no fun for either of them. If he amused and aggravated her in equal measure, though, things would be different, and much, much better.

Dan broke into a grin. "If he didn't appreciate Juan's Tacos, there was no way he'd appreciate what we're doing here. People have to see more than the bottom line, because our products cost a bit more than mass-produced crap. They have to understand flavor, and get that handmade with love *should* cost a little more, and that flavor matters more than glossy packaging. Juan makes the best tacos in town."

"Point." Ms Bridges stood and leaned forward over the big executive desk. He'd bought it for himself originally, but found a battered nineteenth-century kitchen table, scarred by generations of long-dead cooks, suited his style much better – and the classic executive desk suited Ms Bridges. The stretch across the expanse of cool steel accented the long, slender lines of her body and suggested a cleavage view that her serious, round-necked knit top didn't allow. "But take people for tacos *after* you've sealed the deal, and get a receipt when you do – in English, and not on a napkin."

Dan's cock jumped at the vehemence in her voice. She was

controlled, but there was fire under the control, and he'd learned to trace its flickerings in the most mundane moments. There was a hint of a smile in her eyes, not echoed in the stern set of her lips.

Perfect.

Now would be the time to tell her. "I sealed the deal. He said his mind was made up, while he was still here, tasting the coffee and the new chocolate line, and seeing how well you had the business side of things under control."

Ms Bridges smiled at him in that special way that let him know under the cool facade she was just excited as he was. "Congratulations. You worked hard on that deal and listened to me when I had to rein you in and keep you focused on it instead of tilting at fifty-seven windmills. I'm proud of you, Dan. That deserves a reward." She half crawled onto the desk to kiss him, looking like some great, predatory cat. His head swam at the taste of her lipstick, at the hint of orange chocolate on her breath – on the simple closeness after a few long days when they were too busy with work to acknowledge the other side of their relationship.

She pulled back long before Dan wanted, but he knew better than to hold her when she was ready to go. "On the other hand, there was the matter of the receipt, and the fact you still haven't returned a potentially important call from Monday – I know because she called again today – so there will be punishment as well as reward."

Ms Bridges settled back in her chair as if nothing unusual had been said or done.

He shivered with anticipation. Her rare rewards were extremely motivational. Then again, her punishments were at least as delicious.

But this one could be bad. The receipt was nothing and they both knew it, the kind of thing he'd do deliberately just to give her a reason to spank him. But not returning that particular call was another story. "I'd been putting off calling the woman from Whole Foods back until I was done with the Hannaford meeting. Truth is, we can work with a regional supermarket chain like Hannaford now, but we're not ready to go national. We don't have the supply chain in place yet, and I can only build that chain one village co-op at a time. And I was afraid . . ."

"You were afraid you'd get too excited and make a commitment you couldn't meet if you didn't take the time to think it through. That makes sense, but, Dan, you should have had me call back and set up a call later in the week when you could focus, not leave her hanging."

Dan nodded, his excitement and his cock both sinking. Ms Bridges was right, of course. The Whole Foods buyer would understand if he set up a call for a mutually convenient time but wouldn't understand being blown off. He might not be ready to work with Whole Foods yet, but he'd hate to burn any bridges.

"Do you think she'd believe me if I said I'd been in Columbia or something?"

Ms Bridges smiled rather evilly. "I said Indonesia, since you were there last week, in case she asked questions. I figured the time difference was enough you'd have an excuse for not calling on your cell. But you owe me."

"Extra vacation day?" he said hopefully, knowing that while she might take him up on it, it wouldn't save him.

"I was thinking more like ten stripes, and lines. Definitely lines."

He knew he shouldn't bargain, but damn it, lines were a waste of time. "Twenty stripes and no lines?" He couldn't help himself. He grinned as he said it, although he knew it was probably the last thing he should do.

"Fifteen stripes and lines. I'm not a cocoa producer who expects you to bargain for the best price."

Now he'd done it. He winced, thinking of how sore his ass would be by the time she was done with him, and how much time tonight he'd waste writing lines. At the same time, his cock was stirring, stretching, hardening at the thought. It would hurt. He knew it would hurt.

It would hurt wonderfully.

And he needed to learn to be more organized and responsible if the business was going to succeed, so the lines were a wise idea as well. He hated lines, but they always seemed to work to remind him not to screw up whatever he'd screwed up.

And he needed to learn to obey Ms Bridges without question.

"Position!" Ms Bridges said sharply.

Dan scrambled to his feet and dropped his pants without delay, kicking off his shoes as the pants crumpled around his ankles. Resisting the temptation to simply kick pants and shoes aside, he folded the pants over the arm of his chair and set the shoes neatly next to it, as Ms Bridges would want.

He wasn't wearing underwear. It made life easier if he didn't, with the amount of time he ended up over Ms Bridges' knee, or bent over her desk.

He leaned forward, bracing his hands on the cool edge of the desk. His whole body clenched into a knot of anticipation, half fear and half wicked excitement. It was barely six o'clock and it was possible someone else from their small staff was still in the office. That made the surge of terror and desire stronger, knowing the edge they walked. Ms Bridges usually waited until later, when she was sure they were alone. If she was going to work him over now, he must really deserve it.

And she must really need it, as badly as he did. That thought stiffened his cock as much as anything else. Dan knew he needed her, craved her like coffee and chocolate, but she rarely let him know she needed a sub to torment and mold as much as he needed to be tormented and molded. Part of her game was to pretend it was all in a day's work.

She unlocked the top drawer of the desk and took out a small, slender fiberglass wand, almost like a conductor's baton. There was no room to stash a classic cane in the office, but this little toy more than did the trick.

Dan closed his eyes and followed the sound of her movements: the click of her high heels on the wood floor behind the desk, and the shush of her skirts, astonishingly loud in the quiet. The only thing louder was the rush of his own blood, the pounding of his heart. It was only a few steps around the desk, but it took a lifetime for her to take them.

Her voice came from behind. "Count, Dan," she said, her voice stern but not unkind, like a kindergarten teacher keeping a child in line.

Fire slashed across his ass. "One," he counted, managing not to shriek by sheer force of will. He'd wind up yelling and whimpering, but Ms Bridges liked him to start out tough.

It gave her something to break, and he liked the feeling of being broken.

Sometimes she gave him time between strokes to reach the point that pain seared into pleasure. Not this time. The fierce little baton cracked down again, laying a line parallel to the first one. "Two." Three, four, five and six came in rapid succession, too fast to process. His voice was still steady as he counted, but his cock wasn't steady at all. It fell with the sharp pain of each blow, but started to bounce back in the seconds before she struck again. The pleasurable kind of pain was just out of reach. His cock knew it, even if his brain and his abused butt weren't so sure. He flinched away instinctively, then equally instinctively pushed back to catch the next stroke.

She paused between six and seven, and again between seven and eight, giving him time to catch up, to feel the hot pain transmute to hot joy, spreading out from the tender stripes on his ass and sliding through his whole body.

Eight was harder than the others, jolting him so the number became a cry of pain. At the same time, the shock of pain filled his bones with heat and his cock with blood, while it emptied his brain of fear.

He hadn't known how nervous he'd been about the meeting today, how anxious he still was about the big commitment he'd made on behalf of his little company. Ms. Bridges' caning was taking him away from that place of anxiety to a place where nothing mattered except sensation and need, except pain and lust, except Ms Bridges and pleasing her.

The next few blows were harder yet, cutting through all his

defense. He managed to get the numbers out, but even to his own ears, they seemed less and less intelligible, more like incoherent snarls. He didn't pull away, though every muscle and nerve screamed for him to do so. She trusted him to hold still when she beat him, so he would, dammit.

His brain slipped away. The baton struck again, and he thought it was just as hard as before, but all he could feel was heat, overwhelming his reason and hardening his cock unbearably. "Twelve," he gasped. "No . . . eleven."

"Good boy, Dan." A small, cool hand stroked his hot ass, soothing and enflaming him simultaneously. "Honest even when it would be to your benefit not to be. Do you want me to go easy on you with the last four?"

His muddled mind would have had trouble coming up with an answer to most questions, but this one was easy. "Only if you want to." He wasn't sure if he hoped she'd go easy or she wouldn't.

She didn't, but she murmured, "Good boy, good, brave boy," with each strike and so the pain didn't matter. He soared on it, rode it to a place above his own body where he could gaze at Ms Bridges' terrible beauty, even though in the real world he was facing away from her. Time blurred. He was counting because she'd told him to, but he didn't know what the numbers meant any more; he only knew she wanted them.

The fifteenth blow felt like a knife slicing into his flesh, slicing away everything unnecessary. He sobbed out the number, unashamed of the tears he couldn't control.

Ms Bridges did something then she didn't often do: she helped him stand, turning him slightly as she did, then put her arms around him and drew him close. She never left him alone at the end of a session to put himself back together. She'd stay in contact, one hand on his shoulder or thigh, but she rarely cuddled like this. Through the blur of tears and the bigger blur of endorphins, Dan drank in her smile, her touch. "I'm proud of you, Dan. Proud of how you took that, but also proud of where you're taking the company. We're on the verge of something big."

"Couldn't have done it without you." His words slurred like he was an old drunk. "That's why . . . I'm gonna make you a partner."

She silenced him with a kiss that somehow managed to be both passionate and protective. He hesitated for a second, then dared to kiss her back. Her lips were sweeter and richer and more complex than the chocolate he got from that little village in Mexico, the coarse-textured stone-ground stuff with a touch of chili along with vanilla and dark pilon sugar. He groaned into her mouth. With his last reserves of will, he managed not to pump his straining cock against her – an effort that she subverted by grinding against him.

"I'm serious about the partnership," he continued when she moved away from his mouth. "You deserve it."

"I probably do – and I definitely like the idea. But you have about four brain cells left and they're all saying 'Whee!' so we'll talk about it tomorrow. Right now, I want your cock."

Dan gaped. They'd fucked a few times, always at her whim, but it was such a rarity he'd almost given up yearning for it, hoping for it.

Almost. He was only human.

"I told you that you deserve a reward. Lie down, Dan."

The carpet was thin and the floor was hard, but, drunk on endorphins and anticipation, Dan didn't care. She tossed a condom packet onto his stomach and he scrambled to put it on, watching her undress as he did. He didn't get to do that nearly often enough, but he suspected it would never get old.

Ms Bridges undressed as efficiently as she did everything else, placing her clothes neatly over her chair. Under her sweater and skirt, she wore sheer grey stockings, a red garter belt and a pair of tiny red panties that she slipped off without disturbing the garter belt. A red lacy bra that accented her breasts more than it hid them completed the look. She caught him gaping like a cartoon character, shrugged, and said, "Some things become clichés because they work."

He made a strangled noise of affirmation. He'd intended words to be involved, but at that moment, she crouched down over him and words failed. "I'm going to ride you hard," she whispered, her voice husky with need under a facade of pretend-cool. "But don't you dare come until I say you can."

The authority in her words pushed him closer to the edge, and the feel of her cunt pushed him even closer, hot and tight and slick as she engulfed him. She let out a soft moan, sounding almost surprised by her own pleasure. Dan froze, already hovering near the precipice of orgasm, afraid to move lest he fall over. "Touch me," she snarled and his hands moved to obey while his brain focused desperately on not coming.

He could only think about Central American politics, coffee roasts and the fact they needed to hire someone to deal with social media for so long, though, with Ms Bridges' clit slick under his fingers, Ms Bridges' cunt gripping him, Ms Bridges riding him hard, Ms Bridges' stripes on his ass getting abraded against the carpet from the force of her fucking, the pain adding to the pleasure. Her abs were quivering already – she'd gotten worked up from the beating as much as he had. She leaned forward, pressing herself against his hand, slamming onto his cock. The smell of female desire and his own heat combined deliciously with the ever-present coffee scent from the roasting room downstairs and he had the ridiculous thought that if he could make a specialty flavor of that combination, he'd become a rich man overnight. She was riding him, gripping him, controlling him, only he couldn't control himself much longer. His cock was twitching and bucking, and he wanted to obey, but his damn body had its own ideas and he didn't know if his will would contain his lust much longer.

Ms Bridges laid one hand on his chest. "Breathe," she whispered. "I need you to hold on a little while longer. Just a little while." Her hand was cool and her voice was calm, but her cunt was hot and rippling and her eyes were wild, and it was obvious she was working as hard at containing herself as he was.

That made it easier to hold out. She wanted him to hold on, just a little while longer, so he would let go and follow her will.

Simple as that. He breathed deeply, concentrated on her face rather than the movements of her body and the grip of her sex. His cock throbbed as wildly as ever, but he detached himself from it, focusing on the woman who rode him, on her pleasure rather than his own. It wasn't long before her muscles locked and she exclaimed harshly, "Now, Dan."

He let go everything he'd been holding in check, gripping her hips and pumping up into her. She cried out again, convulsing hard around him, then collapsed forward onto his chest. "Come," she said, her voice a little dazed, but still commanding.

He released in a hot explosion that burned away all the residual stresses of the week.

Ms Bridges kissed him on the forehead before she stood and began cleaning herself up. Even if she'd been a snuggly person the office floor wasn't exactly comfortable. Now that his sexual high was subsiding, Dan was noticing just how scratchy the carpet was, especially on his butt, which now probably had rug burns on top of the stripes.

It wasn't until they were both dressed and semi-composed that Ms Bridges said, "About those lines . . ."

Dan's face fell. He knew better than to beg, but damn, he'd hoped the heat of sex had burned the lines right out of her brain – even though he knew all too well that she forgot nothing.

"I'd been thinking about 'I will remember to get receipts,' or 'I will always return phone calls promptly, if only to set up a better time to talk.' But I think, 'I will talk to my business manager if I'm getting overwhelmed and need backup, because that's why I hired her in the first place' will do. One hundred times, best penmanship, on my desk tomorrow."

His hand ached just thinking about it, but he couldn't help grinning. She knew what he needed. "How about business partner? I have my pants on now, so we can talk about it."

She grinned back. "You entrepreneurial types can do what you want, but I don't like to talk business after hours. We'll talk about that in the morning – after you give me the lines."

Pages and Play Things

Haralambi Markov

He ate all kinds of pain.
He ate the pain of losing a limb; he ate the pain of burying
a sin.
He ate the unrequited love over broken hearts; he ate the
lament of long lost art.
                    —excerpt from the book with no title

Proper etiquette mid-group-coitus dictates paying at the very least *partial* attention to who has their penis deep in your rectum, closing your eyes as you suck someone's lips a shade of sore-red, and remembering that it's always polite to swallow. Yet, I'm distracted.

Around nine hundred and seventy-two erotic novels I have read, catalogued and committed to memory flare with yearning in mind. I hear their sighs as the chips in my retinas scan through them in search of the perfect scene which reflects my situation. One by one, scenes of groups caught in sex flare, stream alongside each other and replay to enhance the sensations my teammates inflict on my already-too-often-fucked body.

Being a Reader has its perks, but not when Feeder, my damn team leader, ambushes me with sex every day to lose the bet.

The bet . . . Read the book the old-fashioned way within a

month. That is all I have to do to win. It all seems a bit too easy.

Through the haze, the book materializes. An actual book! With covers and a spine! I look at it, a relic splattered on the floor in the training room, where sweat causes our uniforms to squeak from the friction.

Pages lay open like an orifice I should be pleasuring, rather than copulating with my fellow superheroes. Ink waits to be traced with fingers, paper thirsty to drink the sweat and grease of my skin. I yearn to prick my fingers on the corners of the hard copy, but Tower has pinned my hands above my head with one of his oversized paws. The pressure on my bones feels good, and the unnatural heat off his skin feels better.

I can't even construct a pair of hands to lift the book above their heads and read.

That's where the hard part is.

I'm pinned and prodded, licked and kissed, penetrated, rubbed and humped.

Feeder is now deep within me with his thin penis, which goes on and on, but since he can hijack every sensation and emotion in the human body with a touch, his rhythms overshadow all others I have ever had. Even though I can see how his body lacks the muscles to penetrate with the urgency I revel in, and how his narrow hips fail to deliver each thrust with a bang, I'm all his. I need his smell, I need his sweat and saliva. I need him all.

No, there won't be any reading done anytime soon. Not when I'm spread wide-open and have my left leg resting on Tower's massive shoulder and the other in his free hand, which he feeds on. There's the warmth of his mouth as he swallows my foot to the ankle in his maw, and if I could, I would squirm in his mouth in my entirety. His multiple tongues flick between my toes and the sharp points of his teeth prick my skin with a promise of rupture, if I misbehave. I'm tempted to try.

The last member of the team, Shard, has me in her mouth. My orgasm arrives more times in those two hours than in the last month. Laced within my head are the countless climax scenes from the entire catalogue; wet, sloppy and eager to finish along with the reader.

In the back of my mind, I experience another form of screwing – and that is the memory of how the book came to the team's possession.

"Once in a village, he would find an old fat woman, who would give him her house, her water and a palm laced with so many scars it felt like a pelt made of river rocks and nettles."

The darkness remains unmoved even though I have turned the luminescence to maximum. No shadows dance back and forth as I tiptoe through the wreckage. The dark draws back, but it's slow, weighed down by the years and silence of this dead city, which until now has slept under ours. Until the murders, that is.

I'm accompanied by the hiss of my breath through my mask, the soft crunches as I step on dried dust and the annoying beeps my scanners send faster and faster. The readings indicate a location with biological residue, older than the flesh and blood of the victims that Unit Member Tower is in the process of preserving.

"Sculptor, I don't want to treat you like a baby." Unit Member Feeder's voice clips the silence and startles me. "But you are expected to stay within the safety perimeter at all times."

I jump mid-stride, though I try to avoid vocalizing my surprise. I'm a professional. Or at least I will become one, once I repeat it to myself with enough conviction or live through enough missions with my unit.

"And if I can refer you to my initial contract, you'll confirm that among other duties I have to inspect, sample and catalogue all instances of biological material. Do you think I want to be separated in the dark?" I add a bit of attitude. I need a bit of an attitude. Some "oomph" to cover up the goosebumps that creep in patches all over my body.

Unfortunately, my experience calls forth the sections of all horror novels I have ever read to prepare me for the countless ways my venturing alone in the dark could go wrong.

"'Fraid of the dark, rookie? Better cast a barrier to lower your heartbeat. I can hear it loud and clear from here." Unit Member Shard joins the line with a serious case of "I mock you, pitiful newbie" in her voice.

I browse the file with pre-written quips I have stored in my memory chip for situations like this. It takes only milliseconds to find the perfect counter.

"Not as much I am of you, if I have to be honest, but this ranks pretty high, too."

The line erupts into laughter, with Unit Member Tower's thunder-for-a-voice throwing the line into a fuzzy cloud of snorts. Then all is back to normal and I know Feeder's silence is my green light to venture on. The horror novels recoil at my decision, while a choir of psychology textbooks quote all the rationales for me to continue. Of course, I try to resolve the conflict before another war of virtual quotations erupts in my head, but no such luck.

The scanners are the one to stop the search, as their bleeping reaches a tortured crescendo and I find myself in front of the rusty skeleton of a big shelf, a head above my level. Whatever has been stacked on its rafts now seems black under my mask's flashlight. Dust has blurred the lines, but nevertheless I can make out the rows of small, rectangular objects.

The smell of rot is recognizable even through filters, but at the same time it is familiar; as if I had inhaled it in a dream, but then lost it through the constant chatter from data transmissions. Most of the objects have grown together, sewn by the dust and mold. Above the surface, mold hasn't been spotted for more than two decades.

The whole shelf resembles a set of ribs with living tissue. I touch the books to allow for the suit to scrape a sample. The mass gives under my fingers with a squish and I see how my fingers sink. My heart rate spikes, but I don't vocalize it. No screw-ups on this task, or else I'll have to serve another course in re-education for my incompetence. In the back of my mind, seventy-one horror novels concerning bacteria feeding on humans replay the passages where characters die as food for unstoppable, squishy matter.

Quiet, quiet. All is quiet.

The scanner doesn't sound off an alert for radioactivity and the mass doesn't attack me – which is always a good sign. No, I am not a cast member of *Pride and Damnation* and I will not have to combat ancient, virulent nanotechnology.

I dislodge from the mass and wait for the suit to process the data, when the electronics fizzle and another disturbance shocks the whole frame. The flashlight dies, the signal cuts off and I'm in the dark.

No line.

No light.

My heart spikes again.

"Guys, are we dead?" I scream through the darkness.

Hey, I just cracked.

My mind flexes and I construct the thickest barrier I can muster, until the intensity of it causes my temples to pulsate.

"If we're dead, then you're pretty vocal." I hear Feeder's voice and I realize how utterly unprofessional I've been.

I wish I could convey this to my body.

Not professional. Definitely not professional.

"Maintain your position. I'll come get you."

I don't dare to move. The darkness feels so heavy I think it wants to bury me.

The barrier tints the shelf in violet light, but I see nothing else. It's as if I'm staring through a window, where the world has forgotten how to exist.

Now a noise creeps and stalks through the dark. I wish I could blame it on the headache, but it's too corporeal. Too real to be something else.

I remember the blood splatter and the possibility that maybe the killer hasn't escaped, but has instead hidden. More violet lights form around my body as I think of the sharpest, meanest knives, all of whose handles hover an inch away from my skin. The immediate perimeter reveals nothing and I do my best to rotate my body, ears swiveling with the noise. A thousand scenarios cross my mind, all evoked by this emotion, all from one book or another stacked in my memory, then downloaded to haunt me. In these moments, I hate being a Reader. I loathe how my mind breeds a corpse-nest of fears and anxieties.

Then I see it: a shape in bright blue ahead of me.

"Stand down and let me in." I register Feeder's voice, but don't know. Thirty-four novel scenes confirm this to be a hologram, eighty-two to be a possession, twelve that he will kill me and a hundred and fifty-seven that it's a shape-shifter.

All novels concur that doing as he says will end things badly.

"How do I know you're not going to kill me? You're all glowing on me."

"This is your fear, Hideaki. I'm glowing blue, because you're projecting fear left and right. Now, allow me to come inside and help you."

The headache has grown heavy and pounds within my temples, so I'm tempted to give him free pass, but then again 541 novels agree that it's a strategic mistake to trust a potential predator in time of personal danger. Nothing good comes from lowering your guard.

"Don't listen to everything you've read, Hideaki. Those are stories that have happened to other people. This is happening to you. Now. I won't order you to do it. I'm asking you as your teammate, as your friend, as your partner in bed, to let me in and help you. This happens to all Readers in time, but I can help you."

Unfortunately for me and the 541 novels and reports, I enjoy the good dramatic romance and, with each word, I let go of my barrier and my headache. I take off my mask, as does he.

Feeder steps to me and kisses me. The blue in his skin spikes as he eats my fear with his tongue. I lap at his lips, suck on his tongue and dance with mine on his teeth. The cold and the panic all dissolve under the sensory quakes of pleasure he launches, as his thin fingerprints press all the right spots on my body. The pressure of his fingertips causes my muscles to twitch and jump in all-encompassing anticipation.

It is when I feel how I have pinched Feeder's bony leg between my thighs and grind at his hip, that the kiss ends and Feeder glows brighter than any of my constructs. The hue is a cool neon blue that reminds me of permafrost on top of skyscrapers and dead kisses. Every line on his face seems all the sharper, as if cut from diamond.

"I'm sorry," I mutter, even though I know *sorry* has been banned from the operatives' dictionary. No place for regret and apologies in the field.

"I know," he says and kisses me on the forehead. "All Readers get through these stages, especially the talented ones. Now what did you find?"

He shakes off his leg from my grip and points at the shelves. I follow his gaze and prepare my answer, but then I see that all shelves have been cleared of the moldy material. Instead, there is one, solid object made from fresh biological material.

Without the moss, I recognize it.

It's a book.

Funny thing is that books haven't been printed in almost a century.

"The boy doesn't know when the hunger came and told him how to truly eat. What he remembers clearly is the old hunger, the cruel hunger, which liked to tease and wear the finest garments. The old hunger would settle for nothing, but the thinnest skin and weakest limbs."

The book gives birth to the desire to read it. Its pages speak of hunger, and now the hunger has spread through every room of our HQ.

It doesn't matter that the book could very well be planted evidence from the Naturalists. Working with antiques as reminders of the Old Era is their trademark. I had space only for the desire in my head. It overcomes reason (as in, hide an important piece of evidence), and at this so fine a tipping point, I consent to Feeder's bet (otherwise known as blackmail).

All I have to do is read the book within a month. If I win, I assume control over the team for a month. If Feeder wins, the team will assume control over me for a month. All clear, simple rules, right up to the point where Feeder announces the team is allowed to distract me however they wish.

As a result I find myself with a hand kneading me between my legs.

I'm set on ignoring Tower's fingertips as they glide over my after-training sweat or his inquisitive middle finger teasing my asshole – as much as one can ignore these things. Now all I can do is rewind to the one sentence I've spent ten minutes on.

"You're not making much progress with this book now, are you?" Tower asks me, and as predictable and over the top as he is, his mouth is close enough to my ear for his tongues to lick my ear lobe as he pronounces his words. Boy, does he take his time with the enunciation.

I consider what to say, because it's not easy to admit defeat, especially when it comes to reading a book within a month. My reputation as a Reader weighs heavily, so my answer isn't too quick to come as I'm fighting against an inevitable erection.

"I'm perfectly on my way to the middle."

I chew the words, see if they fit for size, though it's easy to spot how ill fitted they sit, how wrinkled with the trembles of pre-coitus anticipation they appear, how short of conviction they are, but most worrisome, how much of my personal failure they bare to the others.

I'm far from the middle and Tower knows it.

Actually, everybody on the team knows it.

"But do you have enough time to finish it?" he asks and as his intonation heads uphill, his fingertip sinks through me, curls to get a good grip and pulls up.

I grind my buttocks in an attempt to silence the sensation before it makes me whimper or gasp or otherwise reveal how much I enjoy the attention. At this point, Tower has already pressed his monster chest behind my back and I feel as if I have taken a seat on the best throne in the whole world, hot-blooded metahuman muscle and countless applications for fun.

He has me, damn him. I know he does. He knows he does. Fuck, that's the last time I say yes to one of Feeder's insane bets. I'm a superhero, not a sex thing. Not that I mind being the latter, but not being able to read a book for so long does things to a bibliophile.

"Is Sculptor having a go at it again?" I hear Feeder yell from below and that's my reading done for the day.

Tower can make me forget the beginning of a sentence, but when Feeder comes to play, I can forget I had a book to read in the first place.

I flex that muscle which is simultaneously everywhere in my body and nowhere at all, and Tower's finger uncurls and slips out. The resistance sends off additional thrills as he shakes from the strain to keep his hand there, palm still firmly pressed against my dick, and my erection threatens to send the wrong message about my endurance in bed.

"The library is closed, but I hope tomorrow will be a better day," I say and mentally push the rest of Tower's hand off my genitals.

"Ah, isn't that a shame." Feeder comments as if he really shares my frustration. A master spy, he isn't.

"Nobody likes a gloater, Eero." Feeder makes a certain face at the mention of his name that convinces me I'm playing toe to toe with him.

The book snaps shut with the dramatic rustle of its pages and floats weightless ahead. I flex the muscle again, conscious of the act, and follow the book to the center of our gym. When I use my powers, all else draws back into my mind, even erections, and that is precisely what I need at the moment (along with a cold, cold shower).

"You think you will win the bet through sex, right?"

The ground feels clammy underneath my feet and gravity rushes in as I release my body. I try not to tumble, but I nevertheless do and Feeder is already there to steady me as he does in the field.

No matter.

I will not give in to his charm. I construct a cocoon around my body and pass him as I watch the intent and energy in his eyes. Fingers dance, eager to touch my skin and inflict the pleasure. With each progress reached, every single one of my teammates acts sharper, feels eager devotion to detract me. Hungry to distract.

Eyes linger on my fingers and stalk. They wait for the thin sliver of naked paper exposed for my sight. Every page changes the dynamics in our group, alters the reality inside our pod, and soon it has grown enough to concern me.

"The pain of the men of faith always crawls to their lips, which are swollen, but still hard and shriveled. Every day the Father cuts his lips and his tongue on the words of death, agony and torture. These words bruise and secrete the holy pain on over until it forms a crystal and you have to suck at it for hours, these words of pain."

No one understands the letters and the words.

To an extent neither do I. Not really. Individually, all is well. I've taken classes in what it is now known as classical reading, but the words, they trickle. They trail into a snake, which circles out of my understanding.

The reading days grow shorter as every attempt to open the book ends with an attempt on my genitalia. For a week I forget about the purpose behind opening the covers and part them with a conspiratorial gentleness. My fingers plot a coup as they trail after a sentence and I'm all ears for the shadows of footsteps behind my back, a hand on my hip or passion emblazoned with a colorful insignia.

I love the power. Drink it in as much as I can before it all dries up. Readers don't issue the orders or lead the teams.

We're too consumed within the streams of data to function well in a crisis situation. This is why I couldn't have resisted Feeder's proposal. In a way, I think I have won the bet without reading the book to the end.

"The days pass quickly as the boy is out to feed."

I should have picked the warning signs earlier. The bet is no longer friendly.

However, I suspect the bet should not carry the blame as the book has turned any time off from a mission into an elaborate covert affair mission, which department reports from at least thirty years ago inform me resemble the infamous initiative to weed out any operatives working on the side of the Naturalists.

Nevertheless, I continue with my work. No other Reader has achieved what I intend to.

The most perused quotes from standard, department instructional manuals support my ambition with an intensity I can only visually associate with bold letters, which abound in this book. These words stick on the pages and I continue to read without assimilation, but the book promises a swift epiphany once I complete it. Our pact has been made the moment I've run my nostrils across the compact pages without my mask.

In this connection I sense the superiority of this novel, because what I am reading is a novel but with its plot in hiding. This book will be the novel on top of my collection. A novel of silence, of voiceless messages. A mute king among the needy, who scream at night, steal thoughts and edit the bits that make you, you, in favor of their passages.

"He's ready to leave, when one man appears with great sadness. The boy has never seen such pain. Pain between the legs, which trickles from the man's trousers. Pain as dark as a well in a starless night."

I can't ignore how we co-exist in the pod any more. No matter how many books of how many clashing genres I revive in my memory to battle out in color and sound, I can see her red eyes. Her eyes pierce through the forest of characters and I can't hide behind the stories I have read. I can't soften the heaviness of her gaze with the cacophony of conversation.

Shard's red eyeballs hang in the air above me. They rise as twin crimson moons whenever I separate from the rest of them, and they follow me through the rooms. Watch me when I sleep, when I eat, and especially when I find myself in a room with the book. Counting the hours she has spent in observation has become pointless, and soon I see how her real eyes resemble her red projection: dry, bloodshot and tired. How many days has she gone without sleeping?

I now sleep with the sheets above my head and my retinas set for infrared vision. Shard knows when I read like this and I hear the shuffle of steps behind my door, but no one dares to force it. Explaining why Tower would tear my door would inconvenience their plans. What I have to do now is read all the faster.

Faster, faster.

Faster, faster, faster . . .

"The pain is a cloud. The pain fumes off the blackest skin he has ever seen.
The blacksmith is young and pale, except for his groin. The man allows the boy to map the skin from his belly to his manhood and the far side of his thighs, all black as dried soot in a long-forgotten fire pit."

Haste bears mistakes and my haste has mothered too many mistakes.

I'm on the kitchen table with eyes locked with Shard's. She hasn't slept in what I think is days, and her eyes show it. The white has overtaken the sockets, her eyelids shrunken back in her skull. She remains beautiful even so: mesmerizing.

Exhaustion marks her body with little muscle twitches on

her thighs, but fails to drain her of her beautiful, naked savagery. She rests against the counter with thick, caramel legs crossed and those small breasts of hers in a state of arousal. Red light bleeds from the stumps where her wrists should begin. More red light bleeds from the dozen projections of her hands as they work on my body.

I return to my reading. Let her hands' severed floating clones pinch and rub the curves of my body. Nothing will distract me from the page.

I follow the sentences and pray for thick, heavy passages and centipedes of sentences, not fragments caught in writing punctuation. A coma here and I'm aware some of her fingers are preoccupied with my nipples; a full stop there and I notice a tip of a nail gliding on top of my piss slit, distending the tiny space.

Never mind the building orgasm. All I think about is the book, the story and how my eyes slow down with each letter they identify, scan and store in my brain. The porcelain pieces screech as I grind them to fine dust, in full orbit around my head. Reading, and exerting my power, keep my body in lock-down.

The pages I have yet to read have waned, melted from my greedy, sweaty fingers and the perspiration of sex. It's as if the team has worn the book thin with their gyrations, instead of me.

I've promised myself to read the best book in my life and I have made a promise to myself to read the book to its final page. Give the story a climax of its own.

The page ends and I forget about these grand words, when I feel how Shard has charted the map of all my erogenous zones and I come then and there.

"There, was that so hard?" Shard asks, the first time I have heard her speak inside our HQ in days.

I feel the absence of the hundred or so fingers as she dissolves the clones in thin air.

"You made me work for that ending," she says and rights herself, hands clasped together, her fingers an angry red.

"I'm the guy with the ultimate focus. I plan on living up to the name."

"Dream on. You might be the team leader's pet Reader, but you're selling yourself high on the idea that you're the best."

"As I see it, you and the rest of the team gang-bang me whenever you see me, because you are too afraid that I may actually win. Why wouldn't you do it, if I wasn't the greatest?"

Lies. I know I'm fabricating lies. This, everything here, feels like a story that I've read a long, long time ago and am now in the process of rewriting over my reality.

The emergency alarm rings.

I see the hunger in her eyes turn to vapor.

I think I shiver.

"Summer wanes and soon the people will forget about the house in the forest, so he knows he has time to work. He kneels in front and the blacksmith allows him to remove the trousers, the layers of his clothing and eat."

It is when I reach the blood, two-thirds into the book and on the twenty-fourth day, that I genuinely come to terms with the fact that the book has not been a decoy to steer me off in a different direction. I have considered the book an interesting artefact bound to distract a Reader from doing proper research.

I steal a few lines after I lock myself in the toilet, but still hear Tower's bronco-breathing outside and I have to still my hands on the pages, dried paper licking my palms like the dried tongue of a mutant and shift awkwardly so that he doesn't suspect I take too long.

A page goes by while I compose and file my report for the chief.

I have officially lost the bet three weeks ago, but the book remains in my possession and at this stage I notice how my teammates feel like clones, like a product of the Naturalists. Either clones, or androids that look like them, walk like them and talk like them – but each gesture comes off bloated with exaggeration.

Outside we perform our tasks. Everyone acts as they should, feel as they should, but it is around the book that Feeder's smile slices through his cheeks and Shard's body grows tense as if in readiness to launch at some unsuspecting victim.

Novels (thirteen to be precise) whisper to me of stale breath, pasty skin and the wet cold of stones. There, figures half existing in shadows do things in those corners where the eyes can't see. Things no one will ever know about, because the affections of these shades with nails for fingertips will have taken your voice, your reason, your life.

The pod, where we train and live, has three interconnected levels with stairs and tubes, and through every corner I can see at least one of the team clock me: brooding, restless. Starving.

Some days, when I check three or four pages, they remain clothed with the uniform after a mission, damages and stains visible. The smell of battle lingers as a cloak on their shoulders.

Their eyes wait for the corners.

"The boy's feast continues for days and nights.
The blacksmith sits and eats on occasion and the bed is now a mural of pots and plates and the smell of stale air.
It is a December morning, when the boy realizes the blacksmith has died and the bed holds nothing else but bones, skin and a flaccid manhood, which lies like a severed umbilical cord."

It's in the corners in my mind, where they find me, though.

Apocalyptic texts have risen from their archives to scream about the end. Not the end of all things. Not the end of cities or scrapers or heroes, but the end of me.

The artificial sky malfunctions. Winds drop onto the city with their writhing weight and a storm soon casts raindrops like needle teeth into the shells of the city's pods. Buildings warn citizens to remain home. Walls tremble for hours on end with the choir of disinterested voices that the city council has installed for any and all emergencies.

This night I have crawled, through months of sore-sex, to the final pages.

I force my mind into the page, thrust my understanding of the text deep into the typed letters. The archives in my mind sound fainter and fainter. If I have paid attention, then I'd have heard the warning, the impending interruption.

I would see the lustful glow Feeder emits. Foresee the pinch on my shoulder and the surge of accumulated lust that jacks my body, which disconnects from my mind, so that I roll off the window seat to a conveyor belt of floating hands, which unhook and strip me.

I lose the book from my grasp, just when the dissected bodies of sentences stir into a being of its own. Mute, blind, wafer thin and made of paper, a starved thing of a story gains hold in my head. It's nothing like the stories I have grown used to tearing through my nerve endings upon downloading.

No. It feeds with slow licks, burrowed deep in the folds of my grey matter, but now it's without a limb, without the smallest part that would reveal the whole.

No one speaks, when I touch the floor with my back, and I all see is Feeder's hairless crotch, glow-tinted with a sunset shade, descend on my face.

I open my mouth and take all of him. The taste is sweet.

What else can I do than surrender and lock my lips on his shaft as he slides deep in me. I feel like a sword-swallower. Just another antique like the book, which has become instinct except in my mind.

The scent of sex rises in my nostrils as his scrotum slaps my nose in the rhythms of the storm and my fingers dig into his narrow hips, against his bones, then crawl between his cheeks and burrow in him the way he has burrowed in me. Feeder spreads my arms and with the help of Shard's compact and muscled palms, his calves move below my shoulders and I'm locked into submission. I grow aware of Tower's tongues forcing themselves in my anus and soon Shard takes her seat on this writhing throne, her sex twisting and pulsing to get a hold.

They take what they need and I'm not sure whether it's the physical they relish, or the fact that I'm dissolved in the acidic knowledge I've but a few pages left.

Our positions switch and it's Feeder's penis instead of Tower's tongue filling me, while I come to lie on Shard and suck on her breasts. It's then that I hear a click of a tongue against teeth and look up to see Tower with his own tower-of-an-organ, bigger than any natural human orifice. And it points at my face.

He guides my chin to the large knob of his glans, which to me seems like a gelatinous full moon, and to its one unseeing eye that drips its own juice. I dart out my tongue and fit it through the tight opening, where his pre-seminal fluid rushes to meet my taste buds. It tastes like he looks: thick, heavy and alien in my mouth.

I thrust deep into Shard, causing Feeder to follow my example. I grunt and smother my face with Tower's liquids. He's not close to coming, though. He'll have to work for his big finish and soon enough he leaves the stage.

I hear the abrupt tearing noise. I haven't heard in real life, but know where it must come from.

"Here's your book," I hear Tower say and feel the pages meet my face with a wet slap. The books scream in their archived graves at the blasphemy and I find myself scream with them.

A headache ruptures through my skull as I shake off Feeder's power and give in to mine. It's time for my hands to play and the room suddenly glows violet with constructed hands and ropes and straightjackets. The three of them fly, and hit the walls, and feel the metal bend behind their shapes.

Something else in me rises as I find footing, wet, loose and pinching everywhere. I peel off the pages from my face, lick their musty surfaces clean of Tower's juices and summon the discarded book. A glowing platter delivers it to me, where I glue the wet final two pages and read.

I reach the end and, as the final words slip into my consciousness, I feel the story in my head has finally nourished itself and now stands in its entirety.

Words crawl together.

Sentences sew themselves into a mass.

The boy, now an old man with a swollen belly, buries the blacksmith and lays himself down in the bed, waiting for spring, when his hunger will be born.

"It has won." All three whisper in one voice and it's then that I feel the book tremble. It leaks heat and light, then pulses in its throes to transcend its paper prison.

The book is alive.

The book has its wants and hungers.

And what it wants is to play.

Thumbelina

Vanessa de Sade

In his dream he was walking along the boardwalk at Coney Island with Ray Bradbury and Lana Turner. Except it wasn't really Coney Island, it was the Coney Island set from *Imitation of Life*. Which was rather disconcerting as it wasn't the first of his dreams to be referencing a Douglas Sirk movie.

Anyway, in this dream Ray Bradbury turns to him and says, "You know, I've always admired you, Stanhope, in fact, I based one of my most famous short stories on you."

"Oh yeah, which?" Stanhope says, all pleased, but Ray just looks at him kinda slyly and laughs.

"Why, *The Dwarf*, of course," he replies with a smirk and Lana Turner giggles, the both of them looking at him sideways like they know something.

And, yes, when he was being honest with himself Stanhope had to admit that he *did* have a thing for small women. Not small as in schoolgirls or young-in-years small or anything like that, but small as in small-in-height, less than five feet tall or smaller, much smaller. And, yes, all right then, dwarves, if you will.

It had all started fairly innocently, of course, as these things often do. He had been standing in the small grocery store in their seaside town, deep in thought, trying to make up his mind between Coca-Cola and Dr Pepper, when this voice behind him said, "Excuse me, would you mind reaching a can of Diet Pepsi for me," and he turned to behold the most beautiful woman he had ever seen. Except she wasn't a proper woman like the ones he masturbated over in his magazines. Well, actually, she *was* a proper woman, and way hotter than any of his magazine girls, in fact, but instead of the leggy versions he normally leered at this beauty was only four foot six tall but with luscious blonde hair, pouty ruby lips and the most fantastic tits he'd ever seen.

"Diet Pepsi?" she said again, barely suppressing the impatience in her tone. "I can't reach it, will you help me?"

"Sure, sure," he'd stammered, reaching for the can, "but don't you want the full sugar version, you don't need to diet, I mean, you're great the way you are." But the woman had just grabbed her drink and stalked off angrily towards the cash register, muttering something uncomplimentary about fucking nerds as she went.

And that should have been that, but Stanhope just couldn't get the image of her out of his head, and, the soft drinks question forgotten, he hurried back home and into his bedroom, yanking down his zipper with one hand as he did so, his cock already like a broom pole and curving upward with arousal as he relived his encounter in the grocer's shop.

At nineteen, Stanhope reckoned that he had been blessed with a pretty good cock and was ready to show it off to the opposite sex and do a little pussy pleasing of his own, but so far the applications for his services were looking pretty thin on the ground. He was slender, pale youth, very thin but not puny, he thought, with profuse body hair on his abdomen and chest, and, of course, a great thicket of it round his cock. And his cock itself was pretty impressive too, long and slim with low-slung balls, and firm and smooth like a young sapling when it was up, which it usually was. And, all in all, he thought he'd be a really good catch if anyone ever took the trouble to find out.

The trouble was that nobody *had* taken the trouble, but there had been this one time – though they'd both agreed never to talk about it, *ever* again – when he and his best mate, Rodney, had jerked off together over a particularly juicy morsel in one of Rodders' dirty mags. They had been up in Rodney's narrow mezzanine bedroom, an architecturally cramped chamber that had somehow been squashed in under the staircase of his mother's house and had only one narrow window that looked out at the struts of the rickety wooden roller coaster in the nearby fairground. Stanhope could remember it clearly. He'd been staring at the woman on the page and was aware of how painfully erect he was, and suddenly realized that Rod was in an equal state of arousal, and, before they knew what was happening, they had both started to masturbate over the magazine woman.

At first they'd just yanked their cocks out through their flies, because that was what guys did when they peed together at a sheet urinal, wasn't it, and it didn't make you a homosexual or anything, did it? But, as they got more and more into it, first one then the other let their jeans drop, and soon everything they had was out there on display.

"Fuck, I'd thought all cocks were the same, but they're not, are they," Rodney had suddenly said, his eyes darting from the magazine woman's cunt to Stanhope's cock and then his own.

Stanhope gulped nervously and moved his eyes from the page, where he had held them fixedly since all this started, and stole a furtive glance at his friend's cock and was amazed. Whereas his own dick was long and thin and curving, Rodney's was thick and stocky, his balls tight and compact, his shaft knobbly with swollen veins, the monster standing out straight in front of him like a monolith.

"We could so fuck women as a twosome, you and me," Rodney went on, yanking hard at his own dick, the head huge and weeping fluids. "We could just fill both their holes, me in front, you behind . . ."

And Stanhope had visualized it, some curvy little fox from *Penthouse* sandwiched between them both, his cock right up her tight little ass while Rodders fucked her up her cunt, their two volatile members roughly grazing each other through the thin membrane of her lower passages. And then he had started to come, in perfect sync with his friend, both of them shooting great jets of scalding white semen all over the magazines and each other, their cocks arching with desire as they thrust futilely into the empty air, bare buttocks pumping in the greenish light of the early-season rain and the rattle of the roller coaster as it trundled by the uncurtained window.

"Whew," Rodney muttered, still milking his big thick cock for fat globules of sperm, "intense, mate . . ." but Stanhope said nothing, still reeling from the shock of what he had just done.

And after that he didn't see so much of Rodders.

However, to get back to the dwarf thing. Stanhope had been pleasuring himself like a milking machine for three whole days now, running through every publication he owned in his quest for the perfect orgasm, but all to no avail. And so, ragged with frustration, he cracked open the clay pot on his window-sill, the money he had earmarked for a new Walkman the next time he went into Manchester, and went down to Mister Ahmed's newsagents on the front and boldly parted the bead curtains at the back of the ordinary magazine rack. Then, feeling like Bluebeard's wife, he took a deep breath and tiptoed quickly into the gleaming incense-scented den beyond.

"No more than ten minutes, Stanhope," Mister Ahmed's voice called after him through a rent in the fabric of the universe, but he couldn't heed the words as he tumbled head-first into wonderland, the back room with its soft Turkish rugs and faded red flock wallpaper calling him home like a lost pilgrim blundering into the garden of Earthly delights.

Here, the air was filled with wanton apparitions, and every possible form of debauchery embraced him and whispered words of seduction through its honeyed lips. There were magazines full of huge-breasted ladies; young honeys with their hair scraped into bunches and mature grannies holding open print frocks, their low-slung bosoms bare and inviting. Lactating mothers beckoned, prim county girls promised unspeakable acts with their gleaming steeds, and mascara-eyed boys in tiny thongs thrust their sizable cocks in his eager direction.

"Have to hurry you, Stanhope." Mister Ahmed's voice floated through the ether, and Stanhope suddenly visualized the shopkeeper dressed in a quiz-master's glittering lurex jacket, thrusting a microphone into his face as he fumbled for the right words for tonight's star prize.

Peaches, Juicy Jugs, Slutty She-Males, Bangkok Lady Boys, Mature Mamas, Nasty Vixens, Bondage Fillies, Pony Girls, Tough Little Twinkies, Studs and Stallions. The titles flew mockingly around his face as he searched vainly for the correct answer, and then, nestled primly on the top shelf, its cover only dimly visible through the thick cellophane bag that enveloped it, was what he sought. "*Midgetina*," he breathed triumphantly to the fantasy Chris Tarrant, "that's my answer, ten tiny Munchkin misses all naked for my debauched delight."

"That's twenty pounds for that one, Stanhope," Mister Ahmed said warningly, "you sure it's what you want?"

And he nodded. After all, there would be plenty of time to save up for another Walkman next summer.

He was hard well before he got home, his long thin cock almost panting with desire and quite visible through his jeans when his parka flapped open in the brisk sea breeze. Girls shivering in fluttering spotted dresses made eyes and catcalled after him as he hurried past them along the prom, clutching his precious cargo to his chest, but he heard them not, so intent was he on his purpose, and, ignoring his mother's greeting, he threw his coat at the hallstand and mounted the stairs two at a time, unzipping himself before he had even shut his bedroom door behind him.

The pink and white wrapping blandly stating, "Ahmed's Seafront Stores, Rock Specialists", peeled off like a stripper's leotard, and he pulled the brittle cellophane to shreds as he ripped it asunder. He desperately jerked at his cock with his left hand as he thumbed the pages, groaning in pleasure as he beheld the miniscule delights within.

The magazine was small and crudely printed, its glossy pages redolent with the smell of cheap printer's ink, but he didn't care. The girls were all that mattered. And, as promised, there were ten of them, the tallest just five feet in height, the smallest barely making three foot ten. Some were in costumes, some disrobed like strippers in their sets, others were just plain naked. And they were all so *different*. There were aggressive young midgets with razor cuts and punkish make-up defiantly spreading their legs and displaying their perfectly formed little cunts. Faded circus dwarves posed more sedately in their old spangled costumes, pulling their sparkling bodices down to reveal ruby-red rouged nipples, while fat insolent little Munchkin grinned cheekily at him as they stuck their dimpled ass cheeks into the photographers' probing lenses.

He had no idea how many times he came or who at, all he knew was that when he woke up in the small hours, he was lying on the floor by his bed, the magazine and his underpants covered in dried semen, which crackled like frost-caressed leaves when he moved, and his dick feeling like it had just been put through a mangle. Twice.

He slept fitfully for a few more hours, but by breakfast time he was up again, literally, and while his mother clattered in the kitchen downstairs, dishing up greasy platters of bacon and eggs for hungry holidaymakers, he eased his way through the whole magazine again, delaying the urge to splash spunk everywhere until he reached the very end of the book.

It was difficult, but he managed it, just, his cock sore and inflamed as he tugged his normally fluid foreskin up and down over his red-raw and aching head, licking his fingers to keep the rhythm moist and smooth, releasing the pressure and caressing his big heavy balls when it got too much and he thought he was going to come. But, finally, he was there, and Princess Carlotta, a buxom middle-aged lady of four foot eight, dressed only in an old pantomime velvet and ermine robe, dropped her last garment and stood naked before him in just her crown and jewels, her tiny breasts perky with sugar-pink nipples, her freshly shaved pussy wet and inviting.

He could feel his orgasm building up inside him like wire rope on a winch that has been wound tighter and tighter until it snaps and lashes out, slicing through the air and slashing at everything in its path with deadly force. His own come shot out of him the same way, zigzagging across the eiderdown and onto the precious pages of the already-stained magazine, his guttural lust for the bare midget cunt quite audible as he pumped more and more fluid out of himself and onto the pictures.

"Oh fuck!" he muttered, seeing the cheap ink starting to run. He grabbed a tissue to dab ineffectually at the stain. And that was when he saw it. Amidst the usual adverts for mail-order marital aids and obedient oriental brides. A small discreet box in an old-fashioned garnet-coloured font that simply stated, "Tom Thumb's Club, You *Will* Be Amazed", and an address on the far end of the prom of his own seaside town.

He spent the rest of the day accruing money from any place he could get it, the penny jar in his wardrobe, an old post office account that he thought he'd closed years ago, the rest of his Walkman fund and even his mother's tips plate in the front vestibule. And all in all he scraped together fifty quid – not a fortune, but enough to do some damage at Tom Thumb's, he thought.

It had been yet another grey and drizzly early summer day in a typically disappointing season. To make matters worse a thick sea fog had crept in at about six that evening, quickly blanking out the red warning lights on the rotten-teeth stumps of the ruined pier and caressing the faces of drunken holiday-makers with cold, dead fingers like a drowned ghost desperately trying to find its lost lover.

Not that Stanhope even saw it, of course. He had waited in as long as he could bear, pacing his small attic room like a caged tiger in a tiny circus cage, and finally struck out for the boulevards at a little before ten. It was dark by now, the coloured lights of the fairground and seafront fast-food stalls blurred and muted by the thick mist, the hiss and steam of hot-dog men blending with the murky night and turning everything into a lurid modern-day Impressionist water colour.

The club was in Sandylands, on the darker side of the promenade, where only the most ambitious of holidaymakers ventured after dark. The strings of coloured lights that had lit his way ended at the tail of Ocean Boulevard, his path now illuminated only by the warm glow of boarding-house windows and the melancholy swish of light from the distant Wanly lighthouse across the dark and brooding water. The road was quiet here, with just the gentle hiss of the ebb tide caressing the smooth pebbles of the beach below him and a few half-discernible snatches of conversation from open windows. He strode onwards by faith alone, his aching cock driving him without respite.

Some fishermen were casting into the dark water from the old concrete balustrade, their busy hands illuminated in chiaroscuro by the little greenish miners' lamps they wore strapped to their heads, and they whispered and nudged each other as they watched him spot the small red neon sign and gravitate to it like a lost ship following a beacon in on a stormy night.

The club was nestled in a seedy basement, almost hidden from the street above by an old wrought iron railing that led down some stone steps to a heavy door, insulated against the night by thick velvet drapes the colour of midnight.

And now he found himself in a cramped vestibule with yet another door leading inwards – locked – and a tiny box office window where an obese midget sat staring coldly at him, her skimpy red satin dress barely covering her huge expanse of rotund white breasts.

"And how old are you, my bonny lad?" she asked, slightly mockingly, her eyes quickly taking in his spindly frame beneath the open parka, the tight drainpipe jeans and the anticipatory bulge in his crotch. "This is a club for adults, y'know."

Stanhope flushed bright scarlet. "I'm nineteen," he stammered, "I have ID."

The woman laughed. "He has ID," she said, not quite pleasantly, to someone behind her, and another voice laughed.

"Let him in if he's got the money for the ticket," a familiar voice laughed. "I knew it wouldn't be too long before this one sniffed us out."

"You know him?"

"Oh yes, we've already met, and he was as stiff then as he is tonight. Quite a compliment really."

The fat woman looked him over dispassionately, sizing up his cock again. "It's twenty and that doesn't include drinks. You don't try to touch a performer and you don't *ever* expose yourself to one. That means you keep Captain Cocky there securely zipped up during the tableau. If you want to book a hostess afterwards, well, that's another matter, but that's at least another twenty. You got all that?"

He nodded, almost creaming on the spot, and fumbled hastily in his wallet for forty pounds which he handed over with an alacrity that was nothing short of embarrassing. The fat woman laughed. "Keen, ain't he!" she said to her unseen companion.

"Oh yes, he is that. Put him down on my tab, I'll be his hostess tonight."

"You're hostessing? And for twenty? Are you feeling horny or what?"

"Call it an introductory discount," the woman laughed, throatily. Then she leaned forward into the tiny, lit window, confirming his certainty that she was, indeed, the lady he had met in the grocery store. "Go and watch the tableau, kid. I'll join you after the show."

He opened his mouth to say something but no words came, and instead he heard the inner door buzz and swing open, and, taking a deep breath, he walked eagerly into the welcoming darkness within.

*　　　　*　　　　*

Inside Tom Thumb's no concession had been made to full-sized people and Stanhope suddenly felt like a giant as he entered its plush red velvet interior. The cramped, low-ceilinged room was fitted out like a tiny Victorian theatre with an ornate gilded proscenium arch at one side and the remainder of the auditorium devoted to seating. He eased himself into a soft chair as the lights in the overhead chandelier dimmed and a spotlight danced tantalizingly across the heavy red drapes of the little stage's front tabs.

All around him the dark shapes of dormant men suddenly came to life and gazed hungrily at that spot of light like a wolf pack scenting a fresh kill, and when the curtains parted there stood the woman who had started it all for him, looking unbelievably delicious in a red sequined décolleté dress that was a scaled down copy of Marilyn Monroe's ensemble in *Gentlemen Prefer Blondes*.

"Hello and welcome to Tom Thumb's famous tableau," she drawled. "I'm your hostess, Lorelei Lee, and we have ten lovelies for you tonight in one of our most popular shows, ever, 'The Naked History of the World', so, without further ado, I give you the Tom Thumb cabaret!"

A groan of barely suppressed desire echoed around the tiny theatre as the red and gold curtains rose with a swish of hidden wheels and a cold draught swept the auditorium as the stage was revealed. At first it seemed all in darkness, but as a pale light began to glow, a backcloth of sky was revealed and Stanhope's eyes made out a crooked apple tree and a tiny woman, naked save for her long blonde wig, standing in the jagged shadow of its papier-mâché branches.

Music swelled sonorously from hidden loudspeakers and the girl began to dance, a slow languorous ballet, where she spun and lifted her dimpled legs high, her cunt cleanly depilated and her long deep slit on show, all pink and glistening in the spotlight.

"I've died and gone to heaven," Stanhope breathed to himself, his cock so hard under his jeans that it was hurting him, but he didn't care.

"The Temptation of Eve," Lorelei's voice boomed over the swirling music, "where our heroine loses her innocence to the evil of the snake. Sound familiar, boys?"

There was cheer as Eve bent over backwards, her legs akimbo and pussy split open like a peach, before she pirouetted off and three more tiny women entered, two naked, the last dressed in an Egyptian costume, the tree set quickly being masked by an old painted backdrop of the Nile that slid down soundlessly from the fly tower.

The music became Eastern in tempo as the two naked girls proceeded to undress the third woman, Lorelei announcing, "The Bath of Cleopatra. Am I wrong, but is there a snake involved here too, boys?"

Some men laughed, but Stanhope only groaned, recognizing the fat older woman from the box office under the Cleopatra wig, and in seventh heavens of delight as the slave girls bared her huge breasts, the nipples rubbery and erect, the areolae huge and swollen like ripe plums. "Please let her be hairy," he breathed silently, and, moments later, his prayers were granted as the last of the costume hit the ground, revealing a thick reddy-blonde pelt on her fat cunt like tiger fur.

And so it went on, fat girls and slim girls, young, old, hairy and shaved, tiny little breasts and huge udder-like tits all bared for his delight in a mockery of the world's history, until the orgy of minuscule pulchritude finally came to its end, the entire cast lined up naked to take their bows and many curtain calls.

But, eventually, it *was* over and the lights came up, and the shadowy figures of full-sized men began to drift towards the exit or to the small numbered doors at the far side of the room.

"Room six, Lorelei's waiting for you," the fat box office woman whispered in his ear, pushing a small golden key into his hand as she brushed past, her huge breasts still bare and her body hot and sweaty, the distinct aroma of arousal mixed with her scent. "Make the most of it, kid, it won't happen twice in this lifetime."

He started to say something but she was already gone,

enveloped into the embrace of a shadowy man in a tall hat and evening cape, who led her through a low door in the wall. Following them, Stanhope counted off the faded gilt numbers until he found the sixth and tentatively placed his key in the lock and turned it.

Inside the room was cramped and seducing, the walls decorated in old velvet flock with thick Persian rugs on the floor, a snowy white polar bear skin draped over the chaise longue and the whole place lit only by tiny oil lamps on diminutive carved-leg tables. Lorelei stood by the chaise, still in her sequined dress, one of the shoulder straps hanging down and exposing the ivory white of her immaculate breast.

"So, no need to ask you if you enjoyed the show," she laughed, looking straight at his cock, which was virtually banging on the walls of his jeans and demanding to be released. "I knew when I met you in that shop that I was in the presence of a connoisseur."

Stanhope flushed and shut the door quietly behind him.

"Lock it," Lorelei whispered, lighting a small brass nursery lamp, which slowly revolved and threw the shadowy silhouettes of men in tall hats onto the walls, making the small room even smaller, "we don't want to be disturbed by anybody. Or anything . . ."

She faltered for a moment and he thought he saw fear in her eyes, but his lust overrode his natural caution and he brushed her hesitancy away. Seconds later the tiny woman had regained her composure. "Well, Mr President," she whispered huskily, "is there something you want to ask me?"

He blushed again, but asked it anyway, the question that had been haunting him ever since he first saw her. "Can, you know, someone, you know, my size . . ."

". . . fuck someone my size?" she finished for him. "Yes, boy, it's your lucky night, so, in answer to your question, yes, yes you can. My cunt is just as big and just as deep as a tall woman's."

He groaned something that she couldn't decipher and she

laughed. "So I take it you want to fuck me, then?" she asked mockingly, playing with the remaining shoulder strap.

He nodded vigorously, like that crazy toy dog that sat on the back shelf of his granddad's old Austin, and Lorelei laughed again.

"Subtlety's not your strong point, is it, kid? Well, let's see what we can do for you . . ."

She deftly slid his ever-present parka off his shoulders and pulled up his T-shirt, running her hands through the dense fur on his chest. "Now that's unexpectedly manly," she purred, her fingers in the thicket and tracing her way downwards. "I hope I'm going to find more like that."

He nodded, quickly unfastening his jeans for her, and she pulled them roughly down in one tug, taking his underpants with them as she went, suddenly hungry for his cock, which bounced up obediently to meet her like a horny dog, the foreskin unable to contain the hugeness of the large sticky head.

"Now that *is* manly," she whispered, wrapping her tiny fingers in his dense pubic hair and tugging so hard that it hurt. "*That* I'm going to enjoy fucking. Come closer, boy, I'm not going to bite you. Well, not too much anyway."

He brought himself closer to her, his long stiff cock pushing between her big breasts, his hands finally daring to reach out and touch her.

"That's it," she encouraged, rubbing her breasts against him, "pull my dress down at the front and feel my tits. I'm not wearing a bra."

He said nothing, the power of speech quite denied him, but reached for the remaining shoulder strap and tugged, her big white breasts tumbling out as the bodice of her dress released them, her puckered nipples sugar pink and erect, tiny blonde hairs encircling the areolae.

"You like?" she whispered, her breathing laboured. "Will you come on them and make them all wet and sticky for me?"

"If you want me to," he managed to groan, "but I really want to fuck you . . ."

She laughed, a little breathlessly. "All in good time, eager beaver," she teased, "I want you up inside me too, but you're far too excited, you'll come in about two seconds flat as soon as you get into my fanny and Mama wants a proper seeing-to. So here, let me have a little fun first, yes, that's a good boy, slowly now, savour it."

Her little hands had wrapped themselves around his shaft as she spoke and she slowly, agonizingly, stretched his foreskin back as far as it would go, hurting him in her eagerness to expose his naked cock-head. She brought her face up close to inhale all his pheromones, then dragged the velvety skin back upwards until he was all covered up, just so she could denude him all over again.

Stanhope was so aroused it was a miracle that he hadn't come yet, his whole body desperate to drench her in his scalding hot spendings, at the same time reluctant for it ever to stop.

"I'm your first, aren't I?" she whispered, breathing heavily. "Mine are the first tits to ever feel the heat of your spunk splashing all over them. That's an honour, that is. Come on, I need you now, come for me, come for me beautifully . . ."

Her words were honeyed, her breasts soft and eager against his cock, as she expertly tugged him up and down, and his orgasm rose up inside him like a storm, a tidal wave of passion that shuddered right through his entire body destroying everything in its path.

"That's it," she whispered, feeling his animal power as his whole body tensed up, "come for me, come for me beautifully, soak me with your hot salty milk, make my tits as wet as the inside of my cunt is looking at you and touching you."

The shadowy shapes of the men in top hats seemed to whirl around the room like dervishes, as she gripped his cock tightly with both little hands, and the whole chamber began to spin as he felt himself tipping over the edge and into ecstasy. His cock convulsed, shooting out what felt like gallon after gallon onto her creamy white orbs, soaking her tits, face and neck with his scalding desire, as he came and came and came.

She pushed him down onto the chaise, tugging at his jeans

to free up his legs, his cock like a carved wooden fertility symbol and still pumping the last of his jism.

"How did you visualize me?" she whispered, clambering onto him, her short curvaceous thighs encircling his naked legs as he lay panting on the snow-white fur of the slain bear.

"Visualize you?"

"Yes, when you saw me that first day and ran home to jerk off. How did you see me? Were my tits like this? Or did you make them bigger?" She cupped her large breasts as she spoke, squeezing them tantalizingly and covering her tiny fingers with his cooling semen.

"No," he whispered, "just that size, but with darker nipples, like garnets or pomegranates, yours are more like sugared almonds."

She groaned, grinding her crotch savagely into his thigh. "And did you come when you thought that? When you played with your long thin cock and thought about my fat little tits?"

He nodded. "Lots of times."

She smiled. A thin, ever-so-sly, wolverine smile. "And what about my cunt? How did you visualize my little Munchkin pussy? All pink and shaved or furry like the beast I am?"

"Furry," he admitted, "and sleek like a cheetah, thick and blonde, with a slit as deep as midnight."

She purred like a cat, no, not like a *real* cat, like Simone Simon being a cat in *Cat People*, and stretched her little arms submissively above her head. "Time to find out," she whispered, rubbing herself against his cock like an animal.

He needed no second invitation and reached for her. He unfastened her dress, then pulled it quickly above her head to gaze at her. She was quite naked, her big breasts full like fleshy little orbs, her hips wide, a rounded stomach and thighs, but the jewel in her crown was perfection itself. Her beautiful cunt was large and heavy with a huge pronounced mound, like the stylized ones he'd once seen in an old book of Victorian erotica, her natural blonde bush thick but translucent, her slit wide open and displaying layer upon layer of moist dark-pink labia, like a confectioner's rose beaded with sticky nectar.

"Ah, you like that," she sighed happily, looking at his cock, which seemed to have grown an extra inch. "Now let's get that monster up inside me where it belongs."

She took him carefully, gingerly, as if he were made of glass, and lowered herself onto him, gasping as his long tusk-like member slid up inside her with ease. "Now, take this very slowly, you're very big and I'm just little. Yes, that's right, push up gently like that, oh yes, that's right. Now give me your hand and I'll show you how to play with my clit. Carefully now, it's very sensitive, that's right, stroke it gently."

She was moving up and down on him like an old lover, like they'd fucked a thousand times before, each knowing the other's rhythms, his cock one being with her cunt, their two organs melded together with the molten solder of their mutual desire.

"Oh, this is so good," she moaned, riding him hard, his surprisingly skilful fingers tracing around her nut-hard clitoris and driving her wild. "This is so much better than jerking off with Rodney, isn't it?'

"How the fuck do you know about that?" he yelled, startled, when he felt her start to come, her cunt convulsing around his cock as she rode him in earnest.

"Fuck me, fuck me hard!" she yelled, her eyes yellow and her teeth bared, the dancing shadows on the wall whirling round so fast they looked like huge pouncing panthers. "Fuck me like there's no tomorrow!"

His own ejaculation imminent, Stanhope thrust savagely upwards and into her. He gripped her round the waist as he thundered up inside her, feeling her pussy grasping his cock every time another orgasm washed over her, the two of them bucking like a mechanical steer in a Texas bar room as they came together again and again and again.

He must have passed out from the strength of it and he awoke to find Lorelei shaking him and slapping his face, her sparkly dress thrown carelessly to one side and her little body clad in jeans and an old combat sweater. "Come on, wake up, they're coming, they've found you out. They know we've selected our chosen one."

"What? What chosen one? And who's coming?"

She slapped him again and threw his clothes at him. "The Guardians, you idiot, they watch over us. They're supposed to look after us, but they only want the secret of Thumbelina's magic. That's why they're after you, they know that we've found the chosen one."

"I don't understand."

"You don't need to understand, just do what I ask you. You will do that, won't you? You'll do it because you love me?"

He nodded, slowly. "But what about—" he searched for the word "—us?"

She smiled sadly. "There can't be an 'us', kid, but we'll always have Morecambe, they can't take that away from us. Now, hurry, take this, carefully, and guard it with your life. Now fuck off out of here before one of them sees you. We'll stall them for as long as we can!"

"But . . ."

"There isn't time. Go!"

He moved to the door, pulling his parka on with one hand, holding the elaborately carved mahogany box she had entrusted to him steady with the other.

"Lorelei . . ." he faltered, standing stooped in the low door-way.

"Yes, I love you," she replied impatiently, "now click your heels together and get the fuck out of here. They're coming!"

The pubs were turning their customers out into the night and the promenade was full of boisterous people with unsteady gaits as he ran home clutching his precious cargo to his chest, the foggy darkness sinister and threatening as he flew along the crowded boulevards. A man in a tall hat lunged at him and he instinctively leapt to one side, shielding the box, but the figure merely blundered past with the rest of his laughing party, all of them wearing outlandish paper millinery from the joke shop.

Unassured, he balked away anyway, and, remembering he still had ten pounds in his pocket, hailed a passing cab, letting the driver speed him home while he cradled the precious cargo to his beating heart, his mind in a whirl.

What *had* Lorelei entrusted to him and just who the fuck were the Guardians, anyway? Who was Thumbelina for that matter? It sounded like something out of some cheesy Walt Disney film. *Donald Duck and the Secret of Thumbelina's Valley*. He shook himself and looked curiously at the box, at its intricate carvings and what appeared to be tiny air holes dotted at regular intervals in its encrusted edges. He put his ear to it, fancying that he could hear breathing from within.

"Are you there?" he whispered, listening intently for signs of life, but all he could perceive was a thick silence, like whatever was inside was holding its breath and waiting him out. Then he suddenly became aware of the driver's eyes, narrow and furtive, watching him in the mirror and he laid the box quickly back down in his lap again, keeping his arms tightly around it until the taxi finally pulled up at his doorway.

His mother was serving hot chocolate to the guests in the TV room when he blundered in, keeping his parka wrapped tightly around himself to conceal the box as he bolted for the stairs and the safety of his room.

"I want a word with you, Stanhope," she called sharply to his back, gesticulating at him with a packet of Rich Tea biscuits. "I need to know what's going on, young man!"

"Later, Mum," he yelled, before slamming his door behind him and locking it shut. He didn't know if the Guardians existed or not, but he wasn't taking any chances. Why, some of those losers downstairs might even be one of them in disguise. It was obvious that he could trust nobody.

Quickly, he drew the curtains and laid the box carefully on his night table, then sat down gingerly on the bed beside it. "Now," he whispered, "let's see what's *really* in here."

There was a simple catch, built into the intricate carvings of twisted tree trunks with crooked protruding roots like ravens' claws. He slid it back and started as the lid rose slowly up of its own volition.

He was even more startled when he saw what it contained.

The box, though just the size of his mother's jewellery casket on the exterior, was deep and roomy inside, divided into elaborately furnished rooms like the interior of a Victorian dolls' house, each chamber lit with small yellow lamps, the floors richly carpeted in intricate miniature Obasan rugs, the furniture perfect rococo replicas, the walls all covered in scaled-down Sanderson.

And there, in the diminutive lounge with its little potted aspidistras and replica paintings, crouching in the shadow of a tiny grand piano, was a minuscule woman in a long grey dress, no bigger than his index finger, more like the size of his thumb.

"Thumbelina?" he asked, incredulously.

"Chosen one," she sighed, relieved, her big china blue eyes glowing with adoration.

He couldn't believe his eyes, and yet, there she was, complete with her little house and all its furniture, a living and breathing little woman, looking up adoringly at him.

"I have waited for you in the darkness for so long, chosen one," she whispered, her voice soft and ethereal, "and my nights have been long and fearful while I dwelt in the realms of the little people."

He couldn't think of any suitable reply so he just nodded.

"But I knew you would come, chosen one, knew that the long night must eventually give way to morning and that you would come and claim me."

"And if I kiss you will you turn into a full-sized girl?" he asked, his voice full of hope.

Thumbelina laughed. "Ah, the dear Brothers Grimm, what nonsense they have planted in human minds since I saw them last. No, chosen one, my magic is not as powerful as all that, but I will bestow upon you a gift far more precious in return for your allegiance and fidelity."

Lost for words he just nodded again.

"I will grant you eternal youth for as long as you pledge your troth to me and keep me safe, for there are many who seek what I can give and will stop at nothing to try to obtain it. Will you guard me with your very life, chosen one?"

He nodded again, but this time he meant it. "I will," he whispered, "with my very life."

"And grant me your absolute fidelity? Even forsake the Munchkin girl that you have so recently adored?"

He faltered for a moment and then nodded again. The sex he had just shared with Lorelei was more mind-blowing than anything he had ever imagined experiencing in his entire life. It was a good exchange for the celibate years that lay ahead, he thought. "I am yours," he said firmly, "I pledge you my troth and my allegiance."

Thumbelina laughed, reading his mind. "Oh, we will not be celibate, chosen one," she whispered, looking up at him from under her long glittering lashes. "Come, lift me up upon your bed and let me dance for you."

"Dance?" he queried, but the fairy creature merely smiled, clapping her hands for music.

Immediately, a haunting melody filled the air and Thumbelina began to sway to its rhythm. He fancied he could just make out the shadowy forms of mice against the skirting boards, clutching Japanese mandolins, as she danced, her body as sinewy as a flame as she gyrated for his pleasure.

"Are you as stiff for me as you were when I watched you with the little Munchkin, chosen one?" she asked, toying with the fastenings on her bodice.

"More," he gasped, still unable to believe that this was even possible.

"Then show me," she whispered, eyes full of promise, lips pouting and sultry.

"You want me to strip for you?"

She nodded, still swaying. "I have watched you naked with the little people and touched myself in the darkness, now I want to appreciate you openly."

He gulped and pulled off his T-shirt for her, then let his

jeans and underpants fall to the floor. His long cock was huge and curving, the foreskin pulled right back and the purple-red bell-head naked and proud, glistening with fresh clear juices.

"Lie down and lift me onto you," she commanded in a low husky tone.

He almost came straight away as she nestled into his pubic hair and wrapped her arms around his cock, like a hippy protester desperately hugging a tree.

The enchanted music was echoing madly in his ears, robbing him of his reason, and his cock felt like it was exploding with pleasure every time her tiny cherry lips planted a kiss upon the soft suede skin of his shaft or the naked and exposed flesh of his head.

"I'm going to draw your seed and bathe in your spendings," she whispered, her arms working him slowly up and down.

"Do it naked," he gasped, "please, be naked for me."

She smiled and nodded, quickly unfastening her gown and stepping out of it, her body completely bare save for a pair of stockings held up with ornate garters. "Like this, or shall I take these off too?"

"Everything," he groaned, eating her up with his eyes – her long auburn hair and tiny pointed little tits, heavy hips and secretive furry pussy, all warm and sleek like a sleeping ginger kitten.

She smiled disarmingly and quickly slipped them off for him, then embraced his cock again, her body warm and electrifying against his tender flesh as she dragged his foreskin up and down the length of his, by now, pulsing shaft.

"Now," she whispered, raining hot kisses onto his naked head each time she exposed it, "now, engulf me, shroud me with your very essence, and seal our union for all eternity."

He could feel her tiny cunt dragging against his flesh and, miraculously, feel its heat and its wetness as she ground it into him.

"Together," he managed to breathe back, "wash me with your spendings as I engulf you in mine."

"Then come now," she hissed. Her body tensed and she

pushed herself hard onto his cock, her tiny teeth biting and her nails like claws, as the tsunami of her orgasm gripped her and threw her hither and thither.

"Oh my God," he gasped, reeling with the pleasure and the pain, as he felt his own climax take over his body, his long thin cock erupting like a volcano and shooting hot cloudy liquid into the air and all over her and himself, drenching them both with his love and desire. Her eager little tongue lapped it up and her minute hands rubbed it into her skin, as she consumed him, body and soul.

"Mine for all time," she whispered with a satisfied smile.

After two days of pounding on his locked bedroom door, his mother sent for the police, who in turn sent for an ambulance and the social services department before breaking it down. It took the combined strength of three officers and a paramedic armed with a hypodermic to finally subdue him, though none of them could prise the battered shoebox with the old doll inside it from his death-like grasp.

They took him to the cottage hospital in Heysham, but they could do nothing for him there, save sedating him and, eventually, a psychiatrist from the NHS interviewed him and pronounced him catatonic, adding that if he showed no improvement in seven days there would be no alternative but to commit him and lock him away in the old Bedlam Asylum on the far side of Manchester.

His mother was distraught but, a seaside landlady of scant means, she found herself in a blind alley, and was about to give her consent, when a man from New York came to visit her, and sat in her private front parlour and talked long into the night about his experimental facility where Stanhope could go with his box and have the care he needed, and, maybe, even be cured.

Papers were signed and custody granted and she watched, relieved, as her only son was taken by kindly nurses and transferred to a plush private facility, his normally placid eyes wild and deranged.

She sat the next morning on the emerald green steps of a pleasant old house in the Lake District and shook the American's hand with tears of gratitude in her eyes.

"I don't know how to thank you," she gushed, "he's such a sweet boy and he wouldn't normally harm a fly."

"Think nothing of it," the big American replied, patting her awkwardly with his huge clam-like hand, "that's what we're here for. After all, they don't call us the Guardians for nothing, you know."

The Love We Make

Kristina Wright

My boyfriend and I have what some people would call a *volatile* relationship. I call it dysfunctional and addictive. Late at night when I can't sleep and I'm replaying our most recent fight, I call it fucked up.

It's not like Paul and I beat each other. Nothing like that. The only bruises he's ever left on me were during sex. But we fight a lot and we have broken up at least five times in as many years, maybe more if you count the times I've thrown him out of my apartment and told him not to come back. But he always comes back and I always let him. It is what it is, you know? It's just hard to say exactly what it is.

My friends who have overheard some of our fighting or heard about it in the aftermath ask me why I don't just dump his ass and find a nice guy who will treat me right. I could, I guess. But that's so boring. I've dated those guys. The ones who won't raise their voices when they're angry, the ones who will take a few days to "cool off" and then act as if nothing happened. I hated it. Those guys are as boring in bed as they are to fight with. Paul is anything but boring.

What I don't tell my friends, what I don't even tell Paul because he'd say I was the one with the problem and I don't need to give him ammunition, is that I like the fighting. It gets me hot. Yeah, I guess that is fucked up, isn't it? But I think he likes it as much as I do and wouldn't admit it, either. He pushes me and I push him and we fight. And after we fight, we make up. And the making up is hot and heavy and sweaty and sexy. That's part of the reason I like the fighting, but not entirely. I'm not kidding when I say that fighting with Paul gets me hot. It gets me wet. Soaked. I have to change my panties after one of our knock-down, drag-out fights. I'm just wired that way, I guess. He pushes my buttons to piss me off and that does something to my other button. My clit stands at attention when we're going nine rounds over who was flirting with whom at the bar or whatever. I hear myself say things I never thought I would ever say to someone I love, with my hands balled into fists at my side, not sure whether I'd rather slap his face or stroke my clit. Maybe both. Yeah, there's something wrong with me. Right?

I've slapped him a few times, pushing him, taunting him. Waiting to see what he'll do, hoping he'll do what a nice guy would never do. When I started dating, while my friends were being told by their mothers that boys didn't hit girls, my mother was practical and told me not to slap a boy unless I'm prepared to be slapped back. The threat of being hit scared me when I was thirteen but it turns me on at thirty-three.

I guess I could just ask Paul to slap me. But that seems a little twisted, I guess. Nice girls don't ask to be hit and I'm a nice girl. Except with Paul. He brings out the bitch in me. With everyone else, I'm this super-controlled, calm, rational, together woman. The female counterpart to the guys I've dated, who keep their voices modulated and never swear during an argument. People who know me wouldn't recognize me when I'm fighting with Paul. The problem is, I think I'm my truest and most honest self with him – when I'm longing for him to call me a slut and slap my face. Why else would I stay with him and fight with him? He brings out the worst in me – and I love him for it.

"You're a bitch, you know that?" he asked me once during a particularly gruesome battle. I don't even remember what we were fighting about – I only remember the fight itself.

Paul is a high school English teacher, so he's always careful with language. He'll say I'm *being* bitchy or I'm *acting* like a bitch, but that was the first time he'd called me a bitch. My head snapped back like he really had hit me. Hot tears pricked my eyes, but I blinked them back. I didn't want him to think he'd gotten to me. If he thought he'd gotten to me, he would stop. And I wanted more. A lot more. So I just smiled. That's something else my mother taught me. No matter what horrible insult someone hurls at you – smile. It makes them crazy.

"Only to you, baby," I purred. "Only to you."

The veiled meaning was that there was some other guy who I treated better. Jealousy twisted Paul's face into something ugly. Only, that primal female part of me that loved the fighting and wanted more thought it was hot as hell. He looked like a brute – and I wanted him to unleash that brutishness on me.

"What are you saying?" His voice quiet, sinister.

I took a step forward, tears long gone, and smiled sweetly. "I know how to treat a real man."

Lightning fast, he was on me, one hand grabbing my arm to push me up against the wall, the other hand coming up in an arc. I thought he was going to slap me. I really did. Even though I wanted it, was ready for it, I flinched a little.

He blinked, as if touching me had shocked him, and let me go so abruptly, I nearly fell. Damn. It was my own fault.

"Go on, do it," I taunted him, though my voice had lost some of its previous heat. "You were going to hit me, you know you were. Go ahead and do it!"

I was screaming the words, like a child throwing a tantrum because she hadn't gotten what she wanted. It sounded like a plea rather than a taunt. Paul just stared at me as if seeing me for the first time.

"You thought I was going to hit you," he said, something different in his voice. "I was going to hit you. Swear to God, I was."

It finally dawned on me why he sounded different. He sounded sad. I took a step toward him, tried to touch him. "Just do it," I begged. "Do it. You want to."

He shook his head. "I'd never hit a woman. I'd never, ever hit you, Jules."

I said what had been hanging in the air between us, the truth that I couldn't hide from any longer, the reality that maybe was starting to dawn on him. "But I wanted you to."

He rocked back on his heels as if I'd punched him in the stomach. "What the hell is wrong with you? Seriously, Jules, who says that? Who wants that?"

My first reaction was shame and embarrassment. I was messed up, something was wrong with me. He'd just said it. My shame was followed by white-hot anger. I said the other truth that was between us, the truth I'd always suspected and was now willing to put into words. "You want to. I know you do. It's why we're still together. It's why you fight with me and push me and let me push you. You want to take it farther, you want to, but you can't."

His hand came up to my face, but too slow to actually be a blow. Instead, he tucked a lock of my dark-brown hair behind my ear and gave me another sad, puppy-dog smile. "Maybe. But I can't do that. I'm done, Jules."

I thought he meant done fighting, but he fished his keys out of his pocket and took my apartment key off his ring. Laying it on the table by the front door, he walked out. The door closed with a finality that echoed inside me. I didn't start crying for another thirty minutes, but once I started, I couldn't stop. Sometime later, it started to rain.

At 2 a.m., after tossing and turning for hours, I finally got up, threw a raincoat over my short gown and headed out into the night. I had only intended to go for a drive, but I found myself driving to Paul's townhouse and parking on the street. I sat there, windshield wipers dashing away the heavy rain, staring up at his darkened windows and wondering if this was wise. I'd already gone this far, I decided, might as well see it to its bitter conclusion.

He'd given me his key back, but he hadn't asked for mine. I let myself in the front door, shushed his friendly Lab Charlie, and made for the stairs. Paul's voice caught me up short.

"I'm in here," he said, calling to me from the living room just off the front entrance. "Figured you might show up."

The room was dark, so it took my eyes a moment to adjust and see that he was lying on the couch, one arm tucked behind his head. He didn't seem like he'd just woken up, nor did he seem surprised to see me. I took a hesitant step toward him, not at all sure how to read his body language or his neutral tone.

"Paul, I—" I stopped, not even sure what to say. "I'm sorry," I finally said, though I wasn't sure what I was apologizing for. "I don't know what's wrong with me."

"You want me to hit you."

It sounded like a question, but I wasn't sure how to respond. Did I? Maybe. Yes. In the right context. How could I explain it to him when I didn't understand it myself?

"Not hit," I whispered, my throat raw from screaming and sobbing. "Not like that."

"Like how, then?" He sat up and clicked the switch on the lamp beside the couch. A warm glow illuminated his face. He looked exhausted, a five o'clock shadow on his high cheekbones, his black hair tousled like he'd been running his fingers through it in frustration.

I raised my hands in a shrug. "I don't know. A slap, I guess."

"Like a spanking?"

"Yeah, sorta." It felt surreal to be talking about this. "But more. More than a spanking, more than my ass."

"Your face?"

I nodded. "Yeah."

"You want me to slap your face when we're fighting – or when we're fucking?"

"Both," I whispered.

"Do you push me to fight so I'll do that, be rough with you?"

I nodded. "Yeah, I think so. I think I do. It's messed up."

He moved to the edge of the couch, resting his arms on his splayed thighs. "Come here."

I went to him without hesitation. I wasn't sure of his mood

or what was happening between us, but I trusted him. Despite the fights, the angry words, the years of feeling like we were never connecting, I still trusted him.

When I was standing in front of him, he looked up at me. "You're not messed up," he said softly, pulling me down in front of him until I was kneeling on the carpet between his legs. "I think I wanted the same stuff – well, wanted to do it to you. But, that's even more fucked up."

I couldn't help myself, I laughed. He was sitting on the couch, I was on my knees in front of him like I was going to go down on him, but instead we were talking about our mutual desire to do the one thing we couldn't do. "Oh, baby, what the hell have we been doing all this time?"

He shook his head. "Hell if I know. The fighting – it's been off the chain, right? I mean, I never, ever fight with anyone like I fight with you. Never. It's weird."

"Dysfunctional," I agreed.

"And I hate myself when I'm saying those things. Hate you when you're screaming at me. But I can't resist it." He stroked my hair absent-mindedly, as if he was petting Charlie. "I try to ignore you when you start pushing me, but I can't resist."

"You crave it," I said, running my hands up and down his thighs to the same rhythm as he stroked my hair. "You need it."

"Yeah," he said starkly, self-loathing in his expression. "What's wrong with me?"

"What's wrong with us?"

We sat there like that for a while, touching each other as if we couldn't help ourselves – and maybe we couldn't. Maybe this was love, even if it was not what we thought love should be.

He looked at me, searched my face as if searching for some elusive answer. "What now?"

I took a deep breath and let it out in a long, ragged sigh. "It's on the table now. Let's see where it goes."

"You're going to have to take the lead here," he said, pushing my hair behind my ears again as he cupped my face. "This is so outside the realm of my experience I don't know what to do. It feels . . . wrong."

"But I want it," I said.

He just shook his head.

"But I want it." I was louder, more forceful. "Slap me. Slap my face."

He went still. "No."

I could feel the familiar anger beginning to rise. He was teasing me now, playing with my emotions. "Slap me, Paul. Stop messing with my head. Slap me."

"Why should I?"

"Because I want you to."

He laughed. "Not good enough. Why should I do what you want, when you've been such a bitch to me?"

"And a slut," I said, putting that taboo word on the table, too.

He blinked at me, his breath catching in his throat. "Yeah? A slut?"

"Yeah."

"What else?" he asked.

It was my turn to taunt. "You tell me."

"A little whore," he said, the word sounding foreign on his tongue. "Whore."

I was wet. I could feel the wetness gathering between my thighs, soaking through the cotton crotch of my panties. "You want me to be a whore."

"Yeah, I do. But that doesn't mean I'm going to slap you just because you want me to, you bitch." There was a note of anger in his voice, as if the resentment of the past five years of frustration and miscommunication was bubbling up in him, too.

"Fine," I said. "Slap me because you want to. You've always wanted to. You want to slap the smile right off my face, don't you? You want it so bad you can taste it like you can taste my pussy on your tongue."

His hand cracked across my face before I even had time to blink. It wasn't hard, less sting than shock, but it shut me up. I gasped, or maybe he did, and we sat there blinking at each other. I instinctively raised my hand to cup my cheek, but he pulled it away and put it on his bulging crotch.

"That's what you want, isn't it?"

I nodded, swallowing hard. "Yes."

"Want me to fuck you, little slut?"

"Oh God, yeah," I groaned. I pulled off my raincoat, stifling under the weight of it. Stripped my short gown over my head, still kneeling in front of him. "Fuck me."

"I'm not done yet," he said.

This time, I was prepared for the slap across my cheek. Same spot as before, so I really felt it this time. Felt the heat in my face, the throb of the sting corresponding with the throb between my thighs. I stared at him, naked except for my soaking wet panties, thinking I didn't even know who he was. Thinking I loved him, wanted him, needed him.

He grabbed me by my hair and pulled me down to the floor with him. "Little bitch," he growled, dragging me across his lap by my hair and smacking my ass hard with his other hand. "You fucking little bitch, driving me crazy all this time."

I whimpered, my ass burning with every hard slap. "I'm sorry," I said. "I didn't know how to tell you!"

He flipped me over on my back and palmed my pussy through my panties. "Your pussy is so fucking wet. You love this."

"Yes," I gasped. "I do."

"Good," he said, stripping me of my panties with one hand while he got his pants undone and his cock out with the other. "So do I."

He was in me with one quick thrust. I gasped at the onslaught, the sudden sensation of fullness. He sat up, taking me with him, so that he was on his knees and I was wrapped around him as he buried himself inside me. He caught my hair in one hand and pulled it back until my neck arched painfully. Then he slapped me again – not my face this time, my breasts. First one, then the other. I gasped at the sensation, my nipples tingling in pain and pleasure, my clit throbbing, his dick hitting just the right spot.

I came, moaning, whimpering, as he slapped my face, then my breasts, then pinched my nipples hard, once, twice, all the while whispering filthy, nasty things to me. Telling me what a whore I was, what a fucking slut, what a nasty, dirty girl. I agreed to all of it. I even gave him a few more words to use, which only made him fuck me harder.

As my orgasm ebbed, he lowered me back to the floor gently – gently, after all he'd said and done to me – and covered my body with his and fucked me. Hard, steady thrusts to get him where he needed to go, to bring him to where I already was. His breath coming in fast pants, his cock swelling inside me, his balls slapping my ass. Paul. Solid, dependable Paul. My boyfriend, my love.

"Fuck your slut, baby." I whispered the words like a love poem again and again. "Fuck your little whore. Fuck me, fuck me, fuck me. Fill my slutty pussy with your come."

He came with a bestial moan, arching up over me, driving into me one last time before putting his full weight on me, our sweat slick bodies pressed together in a way that was so familiar, and yet so new.

He whispered something in my ear, so soft I couldn't hear him.

"What, baby?"

"I said, I love you," he whispered again. "I love you, I'm in love with you, I've never loved anyone more than I love you. Whatever this is, however fucked up we are, I love you. I want you to know that."

I cradled his head against my shoulder, shifting my hips so that I could bear his weight for as long as he needed to lie there. "I know, baby. I know it. I really do. And I have never loved you more than I do right now."

And as I said the words, I realized how true it was. It didn't matter if anyone else thought we were fucked up. I didn't believe that any more and I would make sure he didn't think or believe it, either. He was mine, I was his and whatever "this" was, it was ours and ours alone.

And that was all that mattered.

Soul Naked

C. Sanchez-Garcia

Tablets, I say to her, running my hand over the swell of her bare haunch as she turns over on her back. Her breasts flatten and settle, the nipples as big as toll-house cookies, staring wall eyed in opposite directions like Homer Simpson's eyeballs. Laptops are getting passé. Young kids like tablets or smart phones. Samsung or Apple. They're all made by the same greedy bastards in China anyway.

What about you? she says.

Well, you know me. I don't go for the new stuff so much as most kids.

Yes, I can see that, she says.

I'm not a Facebook kind of guy. I don't want people to know everything about me.

I pass my hand over her belly as she speaks of her grandson in Florida. She wants to retire in Florida. She knows people there. My hand wanders down the modest swell of her belly, past her ancient Cesarean scar pointing like an arrow to the thick rug of salt and pepper shrubbery down there. I'm slowly combing it through my fingers and trying to imagine how she would look with hairy legs. I think that would be interesting. She looks down her chin to see what's going on. The way she talks about the kid, I would imagine I'm only about five years older than her grandson. I wonder if she was thinking of him a couple minutes ago when I was humped over her on my knees, holding her wide open, hoisting her feet up by the ankles over her shoulders and I was giving it to her hard enough to make her wheeze each time it went in. I love that this old brass bed of hers has real bed springs that squeal in rhythm with you when you're going at it righteous. I love the slappy sound of her breasts flying up and down in time with the bed springs. It's like the greatest drum solo in the world. What do women think of when young men are seriously banging them? Enthusiasm? I don't have the courage to ask.

I would never fuck a girl that way. Never. It would shitlessly scare them. Not just cus' its rough, but because it's intimate that way. It's personal. Girls don't always like personal. Maybe that's why they shave their pussies. There is a world of difference between a girl and a woman. When you've had a woman, you can't go back. Not just a woman, but a beautiful woman at the moment in her life when she's gloriously going to seed. Her wild verdure, sawgrass ass and milkweed tits. Wild oats and wild wheat; gloriously gone to seed and my root sunk deep in the raw of her.

The room we lie in is her room; quiet and small, lived in and fragrant. But also with a feeling of the best things having already passed away before I showed up. It's a place where a couple might go to pass the time while waiting for the next act of their lives to begin. This room is at the top of walk up stairs in a two-story house. For me there is always that feeling of anticipation as I climb the cheap wooden planks, hold the wooden railing of nailed-up whitewashed two by fours; knock my booty call on the door wondering what she'll be wearing, or not, when the chain rattles and it spreads solicitously wide. It's become such that the feeling of wooden planks under my feet and wood rail under my hands is enough now to give me a boner just walking the boardwalk at the beach.

After a year of habit, the habit of walking upstairs, the habit of the opened door, disrobing her is as easy as making a sandwich. It's understood. She keeps nothing on but her white gym socks, because her feet get cold easy, but which she also does for me because it gets me hard. She likes to warm the soles of her feet against my thighs under the blanket on cold afternoons. Thick white pure cotton socks with rows of thick cotton ridges;

elastic tops with a thin blue band and a tiny hole in the tip from her horny toenail, and the taut outline of her toes, which she curls tightly when she's diving deep in her pleasure. When I've got my busy tongue down there and she's moving her feet over my ass with those socks it feels so totally choice. When I can feel she's getting there, I grab one of her feet and hold on to her toes through her gym socks because she talks to me with her toes. I don't think she even knows she's doing it. Always the same way, right just one second before she loses it and screams for Jesus, on each foot she lifts up only her big toe like an alarm and a second later she rams her pussy up hard against my mouth and lifts her back and that's when I suck her clit between my lips and thrum it with the tip of my tongue while she totally goes brain dead. If I keep doing it slow I can make that last for her. I don't make noise when I come. I just sort of tense up and sigh. She jumps up and yells the horniest shit. I love her for that. Girls don't know how to do that either, just let it out, thrash and yell crazy shit. They're thinking about themselves and how they look. Only a woman comes the way a woman comes. Period. I want to record that yell with my cell phone. I want that howl for my ringtone.

You know there's naked and then there's soul naked. Taking your clothes off is one kind of naked. Merely naked. But what you see on a woman's face right when she's in the act of coming hardcore is pure naked. That's Soul Naked. Soul Naked is what we're talking about. Helpless. The defenses down. The emotions bare. Stripped down to where you can't hide what's inside you when you're totally open. And that shook-up look on her face while she's coming down, that's buck bare Soul Naked too. I live for that sweet soul naked. If you want to see that for real, you have to fuck a real woman. Full-grown woman. Full-blown woman. Forget girls.

I like her best when she comes back sweat slicked and unshowered from the gym. She waits on the shower for me to join her because I'm strange and gross in that way. I want all of her; I want her smells. Before she turns the water on I shove my nose in her armpit. I shove my nose up her crotch. I lick her sweaty crotch clean. I'm not like other young men. I'm a strange beast at a time in her life when she longs for the strange things.

There was this one time early on I didn't call ahead and she met me at the door with her hair all up in cheap grey plastic curlers held in place by springy brass clips with plastic tips. Like my mom. Just like my mom. I swear to God. I don't know what it was, but sweet Jesus – it just *skinned* me. Skinned me alive. I manhandled her, stumbled her across the room in pink bunny slippers and a ratty old bathrobe of thick soft cotton. I shoved her down on her back across the brass bed with brute selfishness, too urgent to even bother taking my jeans all the way down. All the while the plastic curlers rained off her head like little bombs on the hard wood floor beneath the squealing old bed; plop plop plop. Her head dangled over the edge of the bed, desperately clutching at the rumpled sheet together with my face nuzzled hard behind her ear, trying not to tumble off with me whaling away on top of her. It was over in a minute, I couldn't even try to last. Those hair curlers, they just ate me up. I was ready to marry her and buy her a house, I wanted her so bad. She rolled me off, sat next to me with her robe ripped open and her hair hanging in her face, yelled at me, sulked, lit up a cigarette and lectured me perfunctorily about women's rights and respecting women. But she didn't tell me to leave. I just said yeah yeah yeah, you're right of course because I was feeling scared she'd throw my ass out for good, but an hour later we were back humping in the shower together. She knew I didn't mean anything bad – because she saw my naked soul; we were eyeball to eyeball when I came all rammed up inside her as deep as I could shove and I came stone soul naked so hard my nuts hurt. She looked into my soul. I stole one of those curlers I'd joggled loose. I still have it. I bought her a nice expensive robe for her birthday too. She knows. I'm a really very good boy.

We can't last. What will remain is the oily smell of the room, which will haunt me whenever someone fries up bacon and eggs. The floozy tobacco smell on the cloth of my clothes when I leave. The easy smoke that curls towards the ceiling fan from the rough leafy brown cheroot between those skillful warm hands at rest.

She's been lying beside me right now, looking through me in the late-afternoon blues. She yanks a Kleenex – ppfft! – from the box and stuffs it up between her thighs like a little flag of surrender because my stuff is drooling out of her.

She renews her chatter about her grandson graduating high school next month and wondering what she should get him. What would be a good tablet?

My hand passes over her lolling breast, then wanders down between her sagging thighs, which have the beginnings of wrinkles, and tosses away the wet Kleenex.

The hair between her thighs is mixed with grey. It can't be colored, or at least no one does. The grey down below is like opening an inner sanctum, an expression of trust, a confession of hidden truth. This is who I really am, say the hairs. The hair is shamelessly unwaxed, thick and wiry. I love the rough, beard strands like the weeds of her secret seedy meadow. I love the animal feel of it against my eyebrows when I'm tongue-fucking this big-breasted mammal. This languidness, looseness, this pliant disintegration mixed with a bit of stiffness in the joints, makes my lover so easy to seduce. I offer her a massage, a foot rub, anything will do, and her clothes melt away with an unctuous eagerness contrived to make me feel masterly over her.

I don't know, I say. Anything by Sony is always good. Apple is overrated. Samsung is cheap and pretty solid. It's all the same cheap junk from China anyway. Not Japan or even Korea any more.

China is where Japan was when I was a little girl, she says. Her hand travels down between my naked thighs and makes me jump. She smiles, feeling the unspoken shift of power from me to her.

Her fingers wander over my junk, affectionately more than sensually. This belongs to me, say the hands. What do you mean? I say.

Japan used to make all these cheap tin shit toys you'd get in dime stores like Woolworth's. You'd play with it and cut your finger it was so awful. You've never heard of Woolworth's have you? After WWII Japan was bombed into the ground and just rebuilding. All their stuff was so cheap—

Huh!

Do you like that, darling boy? I'll remember that. Anyway. So if it said "Made in Japan" on the bottom, well, that was a big joke. It meant crap. Made in Japan, that's what you'd say about something crappy.

Japan is the best these days.

Time changes everything, she whispers. Have you been to New York?

No, I say, feeling myself relax into those excellent fingers down there.

I grew up in Manhattan.

Yes, I say. To what I don't know. I've stopped listening.

She curls her fingers into an obliging soft little pipe and I thrust into them until I'm hard again. We know each other's moves like an old vaudeville act. The bed springs make little squeaks that fill the room with rhythm.

The chenille bedspread we lay on is a kind of thin, tightly woven cotton cloth, sloppy dyed red with a couple of drying stains in the middle. Two so far, but the afternoon isn't over. The cloth is very soft and thick like a baby blanket. It has criss-crossed rows of cotton tufts like little caterpillars you can feel when you're changing positions, when your face is being shoved down hard into them, or your ass being rubbed up squeak squeak squeak against them with warm meaty weight squashing on top of you.

Darling menial, she says.

She lets go of my dick and rolls over on her back, looking up at the ceiling. I'm about to climb on-board but she crosses her legs against me. I don't know what she wants.

Huh?

You look like an elevator boy, she says.

What's an elevator boy?

Sometimes you still see them in big hotels in foreign cities. He opens and closes the doors for the people in the elevator. He rides with them to their floor.

It sounds boring.

It is. Except that in an age without service, all the rich women imagine what it would be like to take a handsome menial servant to their room, someone so much lower than themselves. Order him around and then fuck the daylights out of him. And then you toss him back to his wretched little elevator alone, all fucked up.

If I were an elevator boy, would you bring me to your room?

Oh, hell yes. Twice on Sunday.

She holds my stiff sticky dick in her warm fist and uncrosses her legs.

I should have stayed in New York, she says.

Why didn't you?

I was going to marry this man who worked on Broadway, writing plays. He's a big name now. But you wouldn't have heard of him.

She mentions his name and she's right, I've never heard of him.

Why didn't you marry him?

He was a Jew. My parents wouldn't let me marry him.

Because he was a Jew?

Yes.

That's messed up. Seriously.

I'm glad you think so, she says.

She takes her hand away and I feel some of the shine go out of me. Times change, she says, and I feel her going away from me.

She rolls over on her side, giving her back to me. Lost. After a very long time she speaks and her voice is cracked and old.

What are you good for? she says.

Three Nights Before the Wedding

Catherine Paulssen

She hated the sheer idea of it.

She hated the thought of having to feign enthusiasm over some greasy Latin lover stripping on her lap. She hated that she was supposed to be thrilled to touch his oily skin, when all she could really think about was the warm, slightly dry skin of the man she loved. And she hated the drunken cows outside who had brought her into this situation.

The forced fun of bachelorette parties hadn't held any particular appeal for Imogene ever since the first sparsely leather-clad crotch had been shoved into her face at her cousin's party seven years ago.

Then, she had been appalled. Now, she was seething. And somewhat humiliated.

"Get off – damn it!" In another fit of fury, she rattled at the handcuffs that bound her to a stylish wall radiator, its horizontal pipes shimmering in tarnished gold against the dark crimson wall. She stomped her foot and cursed as she tried to no avail to wriggle her wrists out of the metal rings.

It must have been the stupidest idea she had ever heard. But her bachelorette bunch, consisting of two future sisters-in-law and their friends, had insisted.

Imogene sniffed a little. Her own girls would never have done this to her. But they were on the East Coast, and what could you do about your fiancé's kinfolks? She counted herself lucky they had at least enough money to throw her a bachelorette party in a luxurious Las Vegas hotel.

After another apprehensive glance at the door, she took in the room. In its corner stood a plushy antique chair. The walls were adorned with gilt framed pictures of twenties vaudeville girls. In the corner of her eyes, she could spot part of a velveteen curtain that separated the room from a small vestibule.

It was a fancy room. A men's restroom, mind you, but fancy.

Still, the guys trying their luck in the hotel's casino weren't so different from the regular players in any low-grade arcade. A shudder ran down her spine at the thought of whatever drunken jerk might walk in on her, defenseless, abandoned by the party hosts, who were probably enjoying themselves at the blackjack table right now. The men that had been around while the girls had tied her up, cheering and laughing at her protests, weren't the kind of guys she had any desire of encountering again. She wondered how long it would take before they summoned all their wasted friends to have a feast gawking on the little lady chained up in their restroom, dressed in a cheap veil and a shirt that was so slinky her breasts looked ready for the centerfold. To complete her misery, she would have to persuade one of these boozed-up morons to pay her ransom. That was the deal.

For sure the stupidest idea that Michael's family had come up with in the preparations that would lead to their wedding next Saturday.

Imogene froze as the door was flung open and quick steps rushed into the vestibule. A man in a hurry. She closed her eyes and drew a deep breath, wondering if she would have to listen to him peeing before she could ask him to pay whatever ransom he would be willing to spend on her. He entered the room, and she heard him exhale.

Well, she had to give it to him – it wasn't often that you found a sluttishly attired girl chained to the heater in the men's room.

"Excuse me, could you . . . um . . ."

He walked over to her, his steps slowing, and she bent her

head, but her arms restricted her view of the entrance. She peeked down underneath the pit of her arm. The handcuffs bit into her wrists as she tried to turn, and yet the only glimpse she could catch of him was leather boots and the beginning of slender legs in black pants.

"Wow," he said, and his voice made her shudder. It reached something deep inside her and rolled through her veins, aiming directly at her core. "That must be the most wonderful thing I've seen all evening." His boots clicked on the marble floor as he stepped behind her and stopped at the basin stand next to the radiator. "And you can see a lot of pretty things on a night in Vegas," he added in a low, friendly voice.

"Surely not in a men's restroom," Imogene murmured, more to herself than to him.

He chuckled a bit. "Surely not."

She decided to cut right to the chase. "I need someone to ransom me."

"Have you been naughty to deserve this?"

She held her breath. "Are you flirting with me?"

"Maybe."

She heard the rustling of jeans and saw him crossing his feet. She could practically feel his eyes all over her body. His scent was warm and smelled of fresh soap and cardamom. Imogene exhaled. "Don't you think that would be taking advantage of my situation?"

"Maybe."

"Would you pay my ransom if I flirted back?"

"Maybe."

Imogene rested her head against her arm. "Sounds fair."

He circled around and leaned against the wall in front of her. "That's what I think. But even if you didn't consider it fair, the way I see it, you're not in much of a bargaining position."

"That's not a very gentleman-like thing to say."

"I'm not a gentleman then. How fitting that your shirt is too tight to belong to a lady."

She rolled her eyes. "Tell me something I don't know."

He laughed, abandoning the smoldering tone that had thickened his voice until now. "You're pretty cheeky for someone tied to a radiator."

"There must be something about you that makes me trust you."

The guy whistled. "I see. But what would your future husband say?" He threw a quick glance at the short pink veil attached to the rhinestone tiara in her hazel hair.

She matched the look in his dark eyes as they turned to her face again. "He wants to see me walking down the aisle in three days, so I guess he wouldn't mind."

He tilted his head and puckered his lips into the hint of a smile. "With all due respect to the lucky guy, he's not taking good care of you."

She raised her eyebrows. "You think?"

"Uh huh." He reached out his finger and traced it down the line of her arm. Imogene held her breath as her eyes followed the trail of his tease. "If I were him, I'd make sure you'd be tied to . . ." He ran his long finger up her arm again and, in a playful gesture, moved it over the metal ring and drew a circle in her palm. ". . . nothing but my bedpost."

She bit her lip. "He never does things like that."

"Maybe it's time for him to experiment."

Her heart skipped a beat. "Maybe."

Imogene watched him expectantly, the sparkles that glimmered in his stare making the blood rush to her cheeks. She lowered her gaze to his mouth and licked her lips. "Come here, baby," she purred, smiling at him as he obeyed, his face lighting up. He slowly wrapped his arms around her. "Thank you," she breathed before they melted into each other.

"Thank you for what?" he whispered as their lips parted.

"For being my hero and coming to my rescue!" She threw an annoyed glance at the handcuffs binding her.

"I'm sorry. I'm sorry for my crazy family. You didn't cry, did you?" Michael brushed his thumb over a smear of mascara on her cheek.

"A little bit, maybe." She pouted and lowered her head.

He lifted her chin with his thumb and pulled her a bit closer to him. "I'm here now." He placed another small kiss on her lips. Imogene pressed her body against his. Unable to hug him, she wanted to at least show him how thankful she was. His handsome features had been the last she expected to see tonight, and to be bathed in that tender glow of his dark eyes, a shimmer that had been deepened since his proposal six months ago, turned her giddy inside.

"How did you find me?"

"Martin blabbed. He said something about ransom, so I pressured him to tell me where they had gone with you and what games they had made up."

She rubbed her leg against his. "I'm so glad you did."

"I know how much you loathe pranks."

"This one took a surprisingly nice turn."

Michael returned her smile and ran his hands over her curves. "So you'd like me to experiment, huh?" he said softly against her mouth, teasing her by gently prodding her lips.

"You came here especially for me. You can do anything you want."

"Anything?"

"Yes . . ." she breathed against his lips.

His hand brushed along her waistline. "You know that rule you came up with a couple of weeks ago?"

"No sex before getting married?"

"Uh huh." He parted her hair and placed a kiss on her neck. "I never liked it in the first place."

"I just wanted . . ." Imogene craned her neck. "I wanted us to feel like they did in the old days."

"But we already slept together anyways." Michael grinned at her. "With everything we did, you should be ashamed to even *think* about walking down the aisle in virgin white."

She shook her head, smiling a little, amused by the impatience in his voice. "You don't get it, huh?"

"No, as a matter of fact, I don't." He imbibed the smell of her hair and softly blew against her skin. "What's the point of being with the most beautiful girl in the world when you don't get to make love to her?"

Tiny butterflies fluttered through her stomach and, for a moment, she simply enjoyed the freshly fallen-in-love feeling he could evoke inside of her, even after two years of being together. "I figured it would be a thrill. You know, increasing the anticipation."

He smiled and kissed his way up to her ear. "It did."

"So you do get it after all." She sighed and closed her eyes.

"You still want to wait?" he teased her, softly biting her ear's outer shell.

"No," she whispered, turning her head to kiss him.

"Good," he simply replied and circled her bellybutton with his thumb.

"But what if . . . What if someone walks in on us?"

Michael pulled away a bit, and the expression on his face changed. "I'll be back."

Before she could protest, he had stormed out of the room. Moments later, she heard him lock the door. "Everything's settled." He grinned, slightly out of breath.

"How did you—"

"Shhh." He scooped her up in his arms again and kissed her. For a few moments, he entertained himself with making her try to catch his lips in vain, backing away every time she came close enough before finally sealing her raspberry-colored mouth with a kiss. Imogene could feel his cock swelling against her as his fingers wandered down her hips and found the space between the top of her jeans skirt and the bottom of her shirt where her skin was exposed.

"You're beautiful," he whispered and traced her navel.

She pulled a face. "The shirt's tacky, and I feel stupid wearing it."

"But you *are* property of the groom," he said, referring to the phrase printed over her chest in iridescent colors. Mischief glinting in the corner of his eyes, he leaned back a bit to read it all. "Now and forever." He nipped her with his hands clasped around her waist. "I don't see what's wrong with that. The girls got it damn right!"

She rolled her eyes at him and turned around as far as she could.

"Buy me a shot, I'm tying the knot." Michael laughed. "Want me to strip it off?"

Imogene's eyes flashed below her lashes and she bit her bottom lip, her eyes turning to his mouth.

"Do you?" His hands rubbed her back underneath the shirt.

She licked her lips. "Yes."

"Yes?" he breathed, his eyes watching her as his face moved closer to hers.

"Yes, baby," she moaned softly before meeting his lips. Michael let the tip of his tongue dance with hers for a few tantalizing flutters, then took a step back. With one swift movement, he grabbed the shirt's end and ripped it apart, right through the printing in the middle. She wiggled her upper body in his arms and captured his lips again. "Get it off!"

Michael tore apart the sleeves and stripped the shreds off of her. She purred, satisfied, and wrapped one leg around him. He buried his face between her breasts, playfully tugging at the strapless red bra with his teeth. She threw back her head as they skimmed her nipples, but stiffened the next moment when she heard someone at the door. Eyes widened with shock, she pressed her body against him.

"Don't worry," he whispered, softly sucking at her skin. "It's just the barman."

"The barman?"

He grinned and reached into the pocket of his jacket. "I *persuaded* him to put an out-of-order sign on the door." Slowly, he produced a key and let it run down, between her breasts to her navel. She sighed as the cool metal brushed her skin. "And the only other key is with the janitor."

"What about a key for these?" She rattled the handcuffs.

He kissed her neck. "I didn't bother searching for any familiar-looking chicks in pink shirts."

She gyrated her hips against his crotch. "That gives you a nice pretense to experiment."

Michael uttered a muffled affirmation while opening her skirt's button, then bent down to slide it off her legs. His eyes sparkled as they detected the dark red mesh panties underneath. "Did you . . . ?" he gasped. He tugged at them to confirm what he thought he'd discovered below the see-through textile. "You got so much more than just a manicure the other day!" he exclaimed.

Imogene ducked her head. "I wanted to surprise you on our wedding night. It's called 'The Heart'. You like it?" She let out a little squeak as his forefinger traced the new shape of her bush, deliberately brushing her moist pussy while exploring.

He got on his knees and pulled down her panties. "Very much," he muttered, kissing the heart's lines. "It's extremely sexy."

"As is your head down there," she moaned softly.

"I can't believe you did that." His tongue darted at her bare skin. "Did it hurt?"

She leaned against the wall and closed her eyes. "Only a little . . . a little bit," she panted.

He brushed her clit with his thumb while the caress of his mouth turned to her navel. "I'll make up for that."

Imogene spread her legs as far as she could with her arms bound to the radiator. The pressure of his thumb circling her clit increased, but she couldn't give the sensations her full attention. "Michael?"

"Hm?" He looked up.

"I had so many scenarios in mind of how I would reveal this to you." She giggled.

Michael got up and grinned at her. He kissed her lips, then lifted her up. "Wrap your legs around me. Come on." He grabbed her thighs and pulled her close. His hardened cock pressed against her; Imogene sighed as he ground it against her clit, which was now exposed to the rough material of his jeans.

She arched her back a bit to increase the friction. Michael

fixed his eyes on her erect nipples, perked up so close to his face that every brush of his breath against them sent a trace of goosebumps over her breasts. He gave in to their charms and enclosed the left one with his lips. Imogene threw back her head as he softly sucked on it. The more his tongue probed, the more she became aware of how powerless she was. With a frustrated groan, she yanked at the cuffs. Michael interrupted the caress of his mouth and smirked. He let go of her thighs and moved his hands up to her wrists and, from there, down to the pit of her arms. His light touch tickled her, but before she could plead for him to stop, he put an end to this taunting. Her eyes followed the trail of his fingers as it reached her breasts, and the realization that she was in for an even more intense tease sent a shudder down her spine. As if indecisive about what to do, Michael circled the nipple with his finger that he had just spoiled with his mouth.

"You like being cuffed." He watched her face for any reaction.

Imogene licked her dry lips. She closed her eyes and let herself fall into the sensations. His huge hands cupped her breasts. His breath stroked her naked skin. She wanted nothing more than to roam his body with her hands. A tiny flame licked at her clit, and the urgent pulsation raging between her legs every time he withheld a caress betrayed how much the fact of being bound sparked a desire she hadn't been aware of before. She knew she would let him tie her up again anytime he wanted.

"I do," she heard herself saying.

"Mhm." He licked away a bead of sweat that had formed between her breasts. He cupped her butt and pressed her against the radiator. One of his hands wandered between her legs. He started to stroke her wet pussy with two fingers. "I can tell."

Again, she rattled at the handcuffs – a reflex driven by the urge to wrap herself around him completely, press her body so close to his that she could taste his skin, smell his warmth. Desperation rushed through her, a heated, frantic desperation that dissolved into sizzling tingles exploding under the surface of her skin.

Michael kissed the underside of her breast, and she held her breath as his lips wandered up to her right nipple, then stopped, tantalizingly close. They almost touched her; she could feel the heat of them against her skin. And yet, he wouldn't appease her yearning, and with every push she made, he backed his mouth away until the metal rings restrained her from moving any further. Excruciatingly slowly, the tip of his tongue became visible, at first only to lick his own lip. Her eyes pleaded with him, and she quivered when his mouth finally met her swollen nipple and engulfed it tenderly.

"Take off your pants," she breathed against his lips. "I don't want to wait any longer."

Michael moaned. "Say that again."

"I want to have you." She nibbled at his lip. "Inside of me. Now."

He let her down again and got rid of his clothes. Imogene gnawed at her bottom lip as his hardened cock emerged. Everything within her wanted to get her hands on it and spread the thin drop that dripped off the top generously across the glistening head. Michael met her stare with hardened, aroused eyes. He grabbed her naked butt and yanked her against him.

Her eyes rolled to the back of her head as his cock filled her and was slowly withdrawn again. He knew how to make her burn, even now. Just one look into his agitated face and the relieved moan he formed in his throat when her walls clenched his cock told her he was simmering just as much as she was. Imogene writhed against the handcuffs, fiercely channeling all her force into her thighs to unleash the overwhelming ecstasy. Instead of her hands, it was her feet that dug into his flesh, almost kicking his butt to make him push harder.

His thrusts intensified, but she could tell he was holding back. Her fingers clutched one of the radiator's pipes, and she rocked her hips into his strokes.

A short smile flickered over Michael's face. "Don't be that impatient. You waited long enough for this orgasm."

She shook her head. "Don't you dare tease me, Michael. Don't you—" She gulped as he pulled his length away. It glistened with her cream. He splayed her legs even further, enclosed his shaft in his hands and circled her throbbing clit with it. All she could do was watch and whimper.

"Please . . ." She lifted her head, searching for his mouth. He briefly brushed her open lips, his tongue teasing her longer than his mouth kissed her, his breath heavy on her face. As slowly as he had taken it away from her, he plunged his cock inside her again. His fingers curled around hers as he started to rock her, making her forget about the painful rubbing of the handcuffs against her wrists.

"Oh baby, that's—" She didn't finish her sentence, for at that moment, fists banged against the door and she heard her name yelled by upset female voices. "*Now*? You're worried *now*?"

Michael groaned while the noises at the door got louder. "Let them dangle."

"Imogene, are you in there?"

"Oh, Michael, don't stop," she moaned into his mouth. "Don't stop now."

"Please answer! Sweetie, we're—"

"She's coming," Michael yelled. He ran the back of his fingers along her temple. "She's coming," he said softly and intensified his thrusts. "She's coming," he panted as he pushed her to heights that made her forget about the world outside. Heat shot behind Imogene's navel and from there spread through her body, blanketing her in blissful exhaustion.

With a sigh, she eased her body into his, and he held her tight for some minutes after they came down. The banging at the door had stopped, and she enjoyed his kisses on her neck and the assurance of his love whispered into her ear.

"I want to hug you! And I think I can't feel my hands any more," she added, only half joking.

Michael looked around, a bit at a loss. "Wait, maybe . . ." He kissed her hair and let go of her, causing her to shiver as the warmth of his body was taken away from her. "Let's try this," he murmured and applied soap from the dispenser to her wrists, then rubbed the handcuffs against them. "Does it hurt?"

She shook her head. "I barely feel them, really."

Michael regarded the reddened skin with concern. "I'm going to pull a bit harder once, OK? You need to tell me if it hurts too much."

She nodded and bit her teeth.

"Now!" It did hurt. Even through the numbness of her arms, she could feel the pain stinging her.

At last, Michael got her hands out of both metal rings. "You're free." He smiled and took her hands in his. "Poor baby." He inspected the blotchy skin. "Come here."

A rush of tenderness surged through her as she watched him rinsing her wrists in cool water. "I love you so much."

He just smiled, then carefully dried her hands and arms. He reached for the bottle of lotion next to the sink and massaged the soothing cream into her swollen skin.

"I wonder what they'd have said if you had asked them for the key a few minutes ago," Imogene giggled.

Michael's smile became wider. He lowered his gaze to her irritated skin and softly brushed it with his thumbs. "Would you rather have the wedding without them?"

She slid her arms around his neck. "How would we do that?"

He gave her a peck on her mouth. "We'd skip the big party."

Her eyes widened as she understood his idea. "Well, I do have the veil." She grinned.

Michael threw an amused glance at the pink piece of tulle. "You sure do."

She looked at him, intrigued, but wanted a moment to consider his proposal. "Let's sit down here for a while, hm?"

He placed his jacket on the floor for her to sit on, then handed her his black long-sleeved shirt. "Here, put that on."

She buried her nose in the fabric and sighed with pleasure. "This is one shirt I love to wear."

Michael leaned in for a kiss and laced his fingers through hers. "What do you want?"

She smiled lovingly at him. "What can I choose from?"

"Late summer breeze or early autumn rain."

"Early autumn rain."

He gave her a tender glance, then bent over her hand and covered it with small, quick kisses, followed by a soft tickling with the fingers of his other hand.

"Now do the summer breeze."

Michael led her hand to his lips and kissed it, his lips in a pout, his tongue darting at it. He blew on the skin that his mouth had caressed and ended his treat with a tender kiss on her fingers. She gently squeezed his hand. "When you first played that with me, the night after Martin's party, I knew you were the guy I wanted to marry. I knew that if you ever asked me, I'd say yes without hesitation."

"I meant what I said." He was serious now. "You just say the word, and I'll marry you right now in some gaudy white chapel across the Strip."

"You wouldn't miss your family? And all our friends?"

Michael shrugged. "We can still celebrate with them later."

She held his gaze. Her heart already knew the answer, but her head tried to figure out if there was any reason that spoke against it. "I do," she whispered eventually.

Michael's face lit up. He kissed her hand then jumped up, helping her onto her feet. "Do you want me to buy you anything? Something new?"

"I think I'm all good. I even have something borrowed, something blue." She tugged at the shirt and looked down at her skirt. "But I'd like to have a wedding bouquet."

"Of course." He cupped her face with his hands, kissed her tenderly and adjusted the tiara. "My beautiful bride."

An hour later, Mendelssohn's "Wedding March" filled a small sugary chapel next to the MGM Grand. Imogene's gaze took in Michael, beaming at her from an altar covered in garlands of plastic lilies, then she looked down at her own appearance. She hid a bashful smile in the exquisite bouquet of white roses he had given her and shook her head a little. A sparkling chandelier was dimmed above her head, and she thought about how much this get-up differed from the plans they had made for their big reception. The groom was dressed in jeans and a white V-neck shirt; the bride wore a black long-sleeve that almost covered the whole of her miniskirt. Their only guest was a photographer whose service came as part of the wedding package.

But as Elvis walked her down the aisle and she locked eyes with the man her heart loved with every beat and every fiber, the butterflies in her stomach told her for certain that this bachelorette party was the best she had ever attended.

Double-Cross

Salome Wilde

"There's someone here to see you."

That was Samson – a.k.a. Frank Samuelson – the lug I'd been stuck with as a partner since Robinson took a bullet between the eyes from one of Red Callaghan's thugs. Samson was as wide as he was tall, and as thick as the lifts in his shoes he thought nobody noticed. I knew the Chief had put me with him because he blamed me for Robinson's death. It was hooey, but thick suited me fine. Robinson had been too smart for his own good. But there was thick, and then there was *thick*. "Oh, yeah?" I snapped, tossing the wrapper from the hot dog I'd had for lunch into the trash, expecting some weak punchline.

Samson tipped his square, stubbled jaw in the direction of the ladies' room and winked. "Powdering her nose. Real looker."

I rolled my eyes, sat down at my desk, and put my feet up. Probably some floozy wanting me to spring her worthless palooka from the slammer. She'd be all bedroom eyes and quivering mouth, crossing her legs and hiking up her skirt to give me a gander at the gams – and fantasies of the vanishing point between them. I'd seen it all before, and while I liked the view, the dolls were rarely worth the price of admission.

Still, I had to admit I needed diversion from the boredom. Truth was, we hadn't had a good case in weeks. There was only ever the rich kid who'd run away from home, or the poor kid who'd stolen a car. More lessons from the Chief, who kept giving the juicy stuff to the other team, the guys at the next set of desks over. Double A, I called them. Archer and Aikens: two smug jerks who got along so well, they'd even started looking alike, and the sight wasn't pretty. They were off at the mayor's office now, trying to figure out who'd murdered one of his assistants. I could already guess it was an inside job. That office was so corrupt, you'd have a rough time finding an honest stiff among them.

But no point thinking about it. Double A would solve the case and take the credit – shared with the Chief, of course – and they'd probably get a nice "tip" from the mayor for not spilling any of his dirty secrets along the way.

I was just reaching for my Luckies when the jane stepped out of the john. I smirked. I'd pegged her just right: smoldering hazel eyes, full red lips, chestnut hair like silk. She was curvy in all the right places in her tight black dress, with legs that went on forever. I watched her stalk her way over to my desk, heels clacking, quick and steady, across the floor. Samson was practically drooling, but I kept my cool.

Rising, I offered her a seat, but she wanted no part of it. She came around the desk and bent forward to look straight into my eyes. Little silver earrings glinted from her lobes; they were tiny replicas of the Eiffel Tower. "Cocque sent me," she said.

I jerked a nod and brushed my hair back from my face. Hadn't heard that name in a good while. I turned to Samson. "I'll be back later. Tell the Chief I'm on a case."

Samson grinned. "He won't like it, Cal."

"Nuts to him." I pushed aside the stack of papers on my desk. I was tired of office work.

"Cal?" interrupted the babe. "I was told to find Detective Guy." She bit her lip, looking confused – and confused looked good on her.

"That's me, Calvin Guy. Call me Cal."

She released her lip from the prison of her even, white teeth and tossed her hair. "Please, help me, Cal," she said, voice husky, traces of cheap booze in its smoky depths.

I was hooked.

*   *   *

In a back booth at Joe's, I struck a match to light her cigarette and then lit my own. Joe brought my usual – whiskey, neat – and a gin and tonic with lime for the "lady". She insisted on top shelf, and I let it go, figuring I'd get paid back – one way or the other. "What's your name?" I asked, enjoying the cool darkness of the familiar, grubby bar.

"Candy," she said softly, letting the smoke drift from her mouth. "Candy LeBon."

I raised an eyebrow.

She gave a cute little shrug. "Sounds better than Candy Labonski for a hostess at Callaghan's, *n'est ce pas*?" Her little earrings sparkled and there was a twinkle in her eye.

That perked me up. "Much better," I agreed. I slugged back my drink and she sipped prettily from the little black and red straws. Callaghan's, that explained it. Red Callaghan's gambling joint was on the other end of town, small but getting bigger. The owner had ordered my old partner killed; he was Irish mob through and through. I knew he ran his place like an iron fist in a glove of red velvet drapes – with hatchet men behind them. He watered drinks, fixed games and hired pretty babies like Miss Candy LeBon to soften the blow when the chumps lost all their money – and they always did.

"How do you know Cocque?" I asked. Cocque didn't break bread with creeps like Callaghan any more, at least he hadn't last time I seen him. Cocque was a pretty boy from Quebec who'd worked the streets until the precinct had taken him on as a snitch. When Callaghan caught wise, he'd threatened to off the kid. Now Cocque lived in some downtown penthouse with a rich guy who made "art films".

Candy tapped her butt on the edge of the grimy ashtray. "Let's just say we . . . worked together." She took another drag.

So, she'd been a pro. Cocque had told a tale or three about johns who liked jacks and jills together, said it paid well, but he never coughed up the names of his co-workers. I respected him for that, the gaycat. I looked into Candy's eyes, deep, trying to get a fix. Seemed she thought working for Callaghan was a step up. I wasn't so sure. "How's he doing these days?" I asked, pressing to be sure she was on the up-and-up.

She tipped her head and let her hair slide over an eye, and then flipped it back. Nice trick. "Still bunking up with Aloysius," she said, real straight, like she knew what I was looking for. "Making movies." She smiled. I smiled, too. Yeah, *movies*, the blue kind. She sighed and put a well-manicured hand on mine. The scarlet polish looked black in the dimly lit bar. "He said you'd take care of me."

I wasn't the caretaking type, but I was willing to listen. I leaned back, reclaiming my hand, and put it around my glass. She pouted and stubbed out her cigarette as I blew smoke from mine. She ran a fingernail across a groove in the scarred wood of the table. I swirled the remains of the amber poison in my glass. "So, what kinda trouble are you in?"

That was the question she wanted to be asked. She leaned in eagerly. "Callaghan thinks I stole from him. Fifty large." She frowned. "I didn't do it, Cal. Honest." When I didn't react, she sipped from her drink, a long, slow sip. I kept smoking. "Look, even if I was smart enough to figure out how to do something like that, I'm not stupid enough to try it. Not with Callaghan."

I nodded and flicked ash. It made sense. I'd already sized her up as sharp but no risk-taker. You had to be screwy to take a job with Callaghan just to rake him. The Irish had eyes in the back of his head, about six of them. Three big, dumb, heavily armed tanks. Still, I had to keep up the questions. "So who did it?"

"How should I know?" she said, a bit too snappy. I didn't like that. Even though I believed her – why would she stick around if she did have the loot? – I thought she should at least have a guess. Like she was reading my mind, her voice changed, back to that hoarse purr. "Could be anybody. Bitsy, for one. Bitsy Babbs. She used to go with Callaghan, but he grew tired of her and she's back to working the hostess gig, like me. Or maybe one of those buffoons of his – Huey, Dewey and Louie. They give me the creeps, the way they look at me.

Like they want to take a bite." She shuddered daintily and took another drink.

"You want protection," I replied, knowing damn well that wasn't what she wanted. I drank off the dregs and felt the whiskey warming through me. Booze could make me reckless, though, so when Joe came by asking if we wanted seconds, I waved him off. If this little confection turned out to be poison, I wasn't going to get caught with my hand in the cookie jar.

She waited until Joe was out of earshot before she spoke again. "I want you to find out who did it," she said. She reached out to touch me again, and then, thinking better of it, she toyed with her straws.

"And what if Callaghan makes up his mind to rub you out?"

She winced. "He wouldn't – he won't," she said, like she was trying to convince herself. "He wants his money more than revenge or I'd be dead already. He had my place searched, though he acts like he thinks I don't know it." She ran a long fingernail across her lip. "If you find the real thief, he'll lay off me." She batted her long eyelashes like the pro she was . . . or had been. "I need this job. Help me, *s'il vous plaît*?"

I enjoyed the view and her words came out right, especially the way she rolled the French, but that wasn't why I agreed to take on the case. This was a chance to get close to Callaghan and pay him back for Robinson. I needed some danger in my life, a challenge, and the Chief wasn't going to give it to me and that moron Samson anytime soon. "OK, baby, I'll do it."

"*Merci, beaucoup*," she purred.

Turning my collar up against the cold, I waited around the corner from Callaghan's place for Bitsy Babbs to show up. The hostesses' shifts began at 10 p.m. on the dot, Candy told me, ready to keep the customers close company, so the patsies would spend more than they could afford. Loan sharking worked hand in hand with rigged gambling. And Bitsy apparently always stopped at the newsstand before going in, where she'd get a fresh pack of Doublemint to cover the hooch on her breath. Callaghan wouldn't stand for his girls to be drunk on the job, though it didn't stop *him* from swilling it down.

Candy's description made clear I'd have no trouble recognizing Miss Babbs as she passed by. When I'd quipped that there might be a dozen suicide blondes in white fur coats in that particular part of town, she'd flashed me a wide smile and added Bitsy's preference for pink patent-leather shoes.

And that's just what I saw when the bombshell climbed out of her taxi at quarter to ten. She tipped the cabby and then sashayed over to the newsstand, where she picked up her pack and dug for a bill in the cleavage of the shiny pink dress beneath her fur.

"Allow me," I said, stepping into the light, paying for the gum and looping the doll's arm in mine. She was shocked, but I look pretty good when I shine my shoes, and my smile seemed to convince her not to slug me and run for it.

"Who the heck are you?" she squealed, voice as ridiculous as the rest of her. Everything was excessive on the broad. Not unattractive, just overdone. Callaghan's type, I guessed. Maybe it was the voice that made him throw her over. I reminded myself that in addition to Bitsy, I'd have to find out and have a talk with the twist Callaghan had taken up with lately. They both had good motive.

"Nobody special," I said. "Call me an admirer."

She seemed to like that, though of course she didn't trust it. "You can buy me more than a pack of gum, then," she said with a smile, trying to lead me in the direction of Callaghan's while I was shifting us the other way.

"I'd like to have a little talk first, honey," I said.

She looked around, maybe for Callaghan or his goons, maybe to be sure there were witnesses around if I tried anything. There were plenty of lights from clubs and bars and all-night stores. She was in no real danger as I escorted her to a bench at the corner bus stop. This surprised her most of all. "You wanna talk here?" she squeaked.

"Just a few questions," I reassured her. "I'll make it worth your while."

"Questions?" she echoed. "About what?" She scrunched her face and put her hands on her hips, reminding me of this albino chimp I once saw at the zoo. She made as if to get up and I used my grip to make her think otherwise.

"Listen, I just want the scoop about those fifty thousand smackers somebody lifted from your boss."

She sat back and looked me over. There was a glint in her eye that told me she wasn't as stupid as she looked. She pulled her arm free. "You a cop?" Her voice stayed high and grating.

"Off duty," I told her. I expected to have to renew the physical persuasion, but she just made a sound and pulled out a stick of gum. She unwrapped it, folded it, put it into her pink, painted mouth, and began to chew. She held one out for me. "I'm trying to quit," I quipped.

"So somebody really did take Cal for fifty grand, huh?" she said with a smirk.

The name threw me. "Cal?"

"Cal, Callaghan. Ain't that who we're talking about?"

I set my jaw. I didn't like the idea of the guy having the same nickname as me, but mine was for Calvin not Callaghan, and this Bitsy babe didn't even know my name. "Yeah, that's right," I told her, "Callaghan. You know who took it?"

She shrugged and popped her gum. "Maybe I do, and maybe I don't."

I sighed and dug out my wallet. All I had was twenty bucks and a stub for my dry cleaning. Bitsy was watching over my shoulder and gave a high-pitched snort.

"You cops slay me. Think you're gonna get the goods with sweet talk and lies. You're worse than he is." She turned her face to mine and kissed me, hard.

Her tongue was soft and eager, though like everything else about this jane, her kiss was overdone. It was a bit like drowning, with the flavor of Doublemint. When we came up for air, I could feel her gooey lipstick on my mouth. She pointed. It made her giggle. I wiped it with the back of my hand.

She drew a pink-nailed finger across my chin. "You're too soft for a cop," she cooed.

I took her hand and bit gently into the meat of her palm. She yipped. I wasn't a brute like Callaghan, and didn't have Samson's permanent five o'clock shadow, but I was no softie. "I'm hard as I need to be," I answered.

She giggled again and reached her hand to find out. I stopped her. "Listen, baby, there's better times and places for this sort of thing. For now, just be a good girl and tell me who you think stole the dough."

She huffed but nodded. She drew her tongue over her teeth, and then leaned close to whisper in my ear. "Candy LeBon. New girl at work. She acts suspicious, listens at doors and stuff." She licked my ear, and then stuck her tongue in. It made me squirm . . . the whole thing made me itchy.

I took her by the shoulders and held her back, and then softened it like I was going to kiss her. I had two dames, each blaming the other. Nothing new about that. But this one didn't ring true. I backed up. "Anything else, Miss Babbs?"

She liked the "Miss Babbs" thing. "I think she might have something going with Tommy, the bartender."

"Oh, yeah?"

"He's smooth, too smooth. Keeps an eye on things out front. Makes book for Callaghan on the sly."

I liked it. Not the part about him and Candy, but I liked him for snagging the dough. I stood up and brought Bitsy to her feet beside me. "How about you go on in to work and I spend a few minutes at the bar?"

"How about I call in sick and take you back to my place?" she countered.

I didn't mind having this effect on women. Some days, I even liked it. But not this woman and not now. It was fishy, her making a proposition right when she was due at work. "I'll take a rain check," I said, smooth as silk, and drew her arm through mine again. We legged it to Callaghan's, my noodle working overtime, her gum popping.

I knew I didn't have long before the goons caught wise to me. We'd . . . met before. But it had been a while, and if I kept my head down, I figured I could take stock of this Tommy guy quick before I beat it. I lit a Lucky and looked him over while he was serving some mug at the other end of the bar. He was tall and dark, wearing a sharp black suit with a bow tie. Every hair in place, real put-together. I never trusted that type. But when he came over and put a bowl of fancy mixed nuts in front of me, I couldn't help staring. His eyes were caramel brown, a couple of shades lighter than his skin. If he'd been a skirt, I could get lost in those eyes.

"What can I get for you, sir?" he asked, all refined politeness.

I stubbed out my cigarette and ordered a boilermaker. He went to get it, and I munched nuts and took a careful gander around the little club. Bitsy wasn't hard to find when she came out, like pink champagne, all bubbly. She aimed straight at a guy with diamond cufflinks and a head so bald and shiny you could see yourself in it. Candy was making rounds, too, and she gave me a close little nod I wished she hadn't. I didn't need anyone looking in my direction. She lighted on some butter and egg man with a cowboy hat and a blond mustache big as all outdoors. I turned back to find my whiskey and beer waiting for me.

I hoisted the shot and downed it. Good stuff. Real good. Seemed I was wrong about Callaghan watering his drinks. I watched Tommy mixing something fancy in a shaker. It was for another kitten playing hostess, this one small and slender, black hair done up in a pile of little curls and knots fastened with sparkling clips. Maybe the diamonds were real. Her face was powdered and pale, and she'd done up her almond eyes with thick black liner. Her mouth, like Candy's, was red as a traffic light. When she turned my way, every inch of her said stop. She took the drink from Tommy – something frothy topped with a cherry and an orange slice – and sashayed away in a clingy midnight-blue dress. But she didn't stop at a table, she kept going until she disappeared behind a curtain in the back. Callaghan's new moll, probably. Funny how both Candy and Babbs forgot to mention her.

"Another, sir?" Tommy asked, taking up my whiskey glass. I shrugged, and he poured. "How about a few words, if you've got the time," I said, and knocked it back.

He cocked a glance and let the bartender guise slip. "Shoot."

"It's about Callaghan's money," I said, even and low.

"What about it?" His voice was as direct as his gaze.

I scratched my chin. "You want to see Miss LeBon go down for it?"

He looked over at her, and then back at me. He put his hands on the bar and his expression changed again. This one less readable. "She didn't do it."

I snapped back, fast and hard. "Did *you*?"

"Hell no." He said it loud, too loud, and then his bartender mask shifted back into place. "I got a good thing going here," he explained, sounding nervous. "Why would I mess it up for a measly fifty large?"

"I dunno," I said, smiling. "You tell me."

"You don't have nothing on me."

If I hadn't liked him for it before, I sure did now. "I got plenty," I bluffed.

He leaned in. "OK, you want the goods? Meet me at six tomorrow, behind the bowling alley on 27th."

I nodded, but my head felt heavy. Long day and only a hot dog to eat. I grabbed some more peanuts, but my grip was weak.

"You better get out of here now," he said, tipping his head. "They're coming for you."

I knew who he meant – Callaghan's thugs. I turned to get up, but my head was swimming. Something was rotten. When I tried to stand up, my pins wobbled. I gripped the bar; it was blurry. I fell to the floor and everything went black.

I woke with a whole-body headache in a strange motel room. My mouth tasted like lead and my bean was full of cement. I smelled like garbage. I groaned and tried to sit up.

"Easy now," came a feminine voice, followed by the rest of Miss Candy LeBon. She brought a wet washrag, put it across my forehead, and sat down beside me. "You're a lucky stiff," she said with a smile.

"Lucky," I scoffed, holding the cloth to my face and making it upright. I wanted to lie back down and sleep, but I didn't dare. I might never get up again. I kicked off the blanket. I was down to my skivvies. Not good. "What time is it?" I asked, voice thick.

Candy turned toward the window. I could see a hint of light through the crack in the curtains. "Six, maybe seven," she said, and rose. "Let me get you a glass of water, *chéri*."

I pulled her back down. "Stay put, little bon-bon," I said. "And tell me what gives."

She brushed my hair back from my face, and I noticed how fresh she looked. She was wearing a simple dress and most of her make-up was off. The little Eiffel Tower earrings were still in place.

"Your suit's over there," she explained. "Thought you'd be more comfortable like this." I didn't like the idea that she'd stripped me down while I was out, but she didn't act like she'd seen anything she shouldn't have.

"How'd I get here?"

"Marco and Angelino. They wash dishes and clean up the place. I gave them money to bring you here and pay for the room. And to put you to bed."

That didn't thrill me either, but I let it go.

"Marco gave me the room key when he got back, and I ran straight over after work." When I opened my mouth, she put her finger on my lips. "Don't worry, Cal, nobody followed me."

Her smile was like a tonic. I wanted to drink her down. I nodded, but I still didn't know what was what. "So what happened before your pals brought me here? Last thing I remember, that bartender was telling me I'd better get out, quick."

She nodded, pursing her lips. "I figure Callaghan must've told Tommy to slip you a mickey. When you hit the floor, two of his men took you out back, snagged your gun, and threw you in the dumpster."

I forced my brain into gear. This wasn't making sense. Suddenly, I remembered the little number who ordered a fancy drink to take to the back room. If she was Callaghan's girl, wouldn't she have stayed put while somebody fetched for her? "The baby in the dark blue dress with the crazy hairdo, she Callaghan's new trick?"

A light went on behind Candy's big, hazel eyes. "Mimi," she said, like a revelation. "She must've been the go-between. She must've told Tommy to do it."

"Sounds right," I said, trying to force the cotton wool out of my noggin. I didn't like the fact that I was without my rod, that was for sure.

"Hey," Candy said, excited. "Why didn't I think of it before? Maybe Mimi's in it with Tommy. Maybe they stole the money together and put the blame on me."

I put up a hand. "Slow down. I'm dizzy enough as it is." She might be right, but it could be all wrong. I needed to think things through, get more answers, but I needed to clear my head first. I shifted and swung my legs over the bed. "I need a shower and some joe, baby."

Candy nodded, smile back in place. "Sure, Cal. I'll get some and be right back. I could use some myself." She yawned prettily, right on cue, and I realized she'd been up all night. This was probably her bedtime.

"Thanks for taking care of me," I said, drawing a thumb down her cheek. Then I made for the john and turned up the shower taps. I rubbed a kink in my back and sighed, waiting for it to get nice and steamy. I thought about how everything was pointing toward Tommy, and then wondered why he'd offered to meet me.

I'd have to get another beanshooter, and I'd have to be careful.

I stripped out of my boxers and T-shirt and stepped into the stall. The water beat down on me, hot and hard. I stretched a little and winced when I reached too far. I'd probably landed on something hard in the dumpster. Jerks. I shrugged. I'd had worse. After a good, long dousing, I reached for the little bar of soap and washed the grime off. Then I fumbled with the tiny bottle of shampoo. I'd stink like a flowerbed, but I'd be clean. And it felt good. When I'd had enough, I turned off the taps and toweled dry.

At the sink, I found some gifts from Candy: a razor, a toothbrush and toothpaste. You had to go for a gal who thought about the details. I cleaned my teeth and rinsed my mouth, feeling more myself by the minute. Only two things missing: clean clothes, and a fresh pack of Luckies. I frowned at the thought of putting my dirty shirt and shorts back on, but I didn't have a choice. I wasn't going out there in a towel. I made myself presentable and opened the door. The room was heated, but cold. Waiting for me was something a lot more shocking to the system than that.

Candy was lying on the bed, stretched out in the sheerest of negligées. Her hair was spread across the pillow like a chocolate river and her smile was more inviting than ever. I spotted the strong-smelling java on the nightstand, and reached for it. "This how we're gonna talk, baby?" I asked, and took a sip.

"There's plenty of time to talk, *chéri*," she cooed, and patted the bed beside her. "I've got a little surprise for you."

"Oh, yeah?" I said, sitting. I put down the coffee and brushed back my wet hair with my hands. "Maybe we can surprise each other." I took her by the shoulders and kissed her, hard. Our lips crushed together, fiery and hungry. She threw a leg around my hip and pulled me in. I was more than willing. As she thrust her fingers into my hair, I tongued my way down to her neck, catching the scent of lily of the valley behind her ear, my favorite. Seems the babe had found the time to shower before she'd come to the motel, and I was grateful. I liked my women fresh.

She was purring like the kitten she was as I used my teeth to pull down one of the little straps of her lacy gown and brought a hand around to cup one of her small, high breasts. I could feel her smile as I came up with nothing. I leaned back and looked down. Her chest was flat, and for a minute I couldn't make it jive. Her giggle solved the riddle. No wonder she knew Cocque. I pinned her arms overhead, and glared down into her wide eyes.

"Surprise," she said, still smiling but not moving an inch.

I just held her there, deciding what to do. Tricky little coquette, this one. She'd caught me off guard, and that didn't happen often to Cal Guy.

"Trust me," she whispered.

I huffed. Crazy thing was, I did trust her. Even more now than before. I bent forward, took her nipple between my teeth, and bit down. She yelped. I smiled around the nub, and relaxed my jaw. I didn't release her wrists, though. She shuddered. I pulled down the other strap with my teeth, and sucked first one little button, and then the other, licking my way across the smooth, hairless chest. There wasn't even any stubble. Boy or girl, Candy LeBon was a pretty baby, and I wasn't going to give up my prize, no matter how unexpected the package.

I'd give my own exposé, soon enough.

She began to wriggle a little, in pleasure not fear now. I moved so I could push her nightie up from underneath. As I kissed her belly and tongued her navel, she moaned and whispered my name, a sound so sweet I was hard and leaking in a flash.

When I bent lower and let up on her arms so I could dip a hand into her panties, I was shocked again, not by what I expected to find but by what was missing. Candy giggled above me and spread her legs wide. I dug down and tugged until I released the tiger. I'd always wondered how her type managed to keep their secrets. I'd have asked whether it hurt or not, but I was too busy getting my mouth around it.

Candy made to get up a few times as I tortured her with teasing, licking and sucking that lollipop like a kid at the circus. I took what I wanted and enjoyed every minute. She clutched the sheets and whined, bucking her hips into me, wild and untamed. When her groans became shaky and her stick swelled, I pulled off and jerked her until she shot cream all over her soft, smooth belly.

I sat back and sipped my coffee as she shook and quivered, smirking at the mess I'd made of the pretty kitty. Soon, though, she came to and looked herself over with a laugh. When she pulled the sticky negligée over her head, I took in the whole boyish picture. I gave a little whistle as she lay back down and offered herself for a tongue cleaning.

"Sorry, baby, I don't play that way," I said.

She flashed me a juicy pout, and I bent over her to bite that tempting lip. Before I knew it, she had her mitts on me, tugging my shirt over my head. We found ourselves tangled up, and there was nothing for it but to sit back and strip for her.

"You're injured!" she cried, pointing to the thick bandage that wrapped my chest.

I smiled and shook my head. "Your turn for a surprise, toots." I partly unwound myself and gave her a glimpse she'd not soon forget.

Her jaw dropped and she laughed. A little too much.

"Cheese it," I barked, binding myself back up. I felt like I could crack her one, but I wasn't the type to hit a skirt.

She got the message. "I just can't believe it," she said, keeping her smile a respectful size. "Both of us. It's too good, *n'est ce pas?*"

I smiled back. "A hoot and a holler," I said.

A glint of mischief was in her eye but no malice. She wanted to make nice. Licking her lips, she sat up and took hold of my boxers, pulling them down in one neat yank. The rolled sock I had stitched to the inside went down with them, and she saw the me I save for the holidays. "Merry Christmas, baby," I said.

"Oh, Cal," she gushed, clapping her little hands, the perfect pussycat once again. "It's just what I've always wanted."

I chuckled and lay back at the bottom of the bed, knees bent and steering her straight at the bullseye.

Her lips met mine in a whole new way and she lapped me up like honey. I kept my hands in her hair to show her just how to make it flow. Grinding up into that sweet face I found she held back nothing but her breath. "That's it, baby, just like that." I realized it'd been too long since I'd seen to my needs this way. I liked doing the work, being the man. But with Candy, it was different. And good. Real good.

She licked and sucked and I rode her until I was about to pop. I grunted and let go of her just in time to soak her upturned face. She squealed in disbelief. "Happy New Year," I panted.

She took a bathroom break to tidy up a bit and, when she came out, we shared a butt. She didn't smoke my brand, but I made do. I even let her light mine, with a fancy little gold-plated lighter. I took it and looked it over. It had some arch-type monument engraved on it. "The Arc de Triomphe," she said, and blew a smoke ring.

"You go for that French stuff, huh?" I said, passing back the lighter.

She shrugged, put it beside her. "Paris is the city of love, they say."

"Who needs love, baby," I said, and kissed her again.

A sweaty hour later, the festivities were over for the time being, and Candy needed a wash. As for me, I needed clean clothes and a gun. And we could both use some sleep. We left the motel in separate cabs, setting a date for spaghetti at Luigi's at eight. That'd give me time to hit my apartment, the office and the appointment with Tommy. I hadn't told Candy about the last part. She didn't need to know.

It's amazing what a cheese Danish and a few hours of shut-eye will do for a fella. I took a shower, put on my other suit, and headed to the office to pick up a replacement for the heater Callaghan's lackeys had stripped off me. I'd get back to that high-class dive and retrieve the original, but that could wait. Letting redhots like them underestimate me was a sure strategy.

"You look like crap on a cracker," Samson said with his buffoon grin as I came in, heading for my desk to fill out the paperwork I needed for a new gat. I hated paperwork almost as much as Samson's wisecracks. Almost.

I opened my mouth to reply, and then closed it. He was my partner but a dope, and I didn't want him nosing in. I was going to find out who had the dough and get Candy out of this. Then, with her help, maybe take down Callaghan himself. How? I had no idea. But I'd do it.

Samson gawked over my shoulder. "You lose your gun playing poker? Maybe bet it on the ponies?"

"Nah, I gave it to your wife," I snarled and stood up. I could finish the form at the desk. Sally in weapons supply was a good old girl. She'd make sure I filled everything out right and just give me the gun. No questions asked.

"Jeez, I was only joking," Samson said. He leaned back and started making a paper airplane out of an envelope. "You OK, Cal?"

"Fine," I said, wondering if maybe I should tell him. At least about the get-together with Tommy. Just in case. I shrugged. "Only a little run-in with Callaghan's punks."

"Chief says to leave Callaghan alone. You know that. He's got something big planned for the Irishman."

"I got plans of my own," I shot back, and wished I hadn't.

Samson sighed. "Wouldn't wanna see you get in trouble on account of no dame." He creased and folded the envelope.

"I'm fine," I said again, trying to make it stick, and headed out.

"Watch yourself," Samson said, throwing the airplane and hitting me square in the back.

I got the point: I wasn't on official police business and wasn't letting him in on it, so I was on my own.

Traffic was bad and I was edgy by the time the cab let me off in front of the Strike 'n' Spare on 27th. I was armed again, which felt good, but not as good as having my own rod where I could reach it. The whole ride, I tried to put the pieces together. I hadn't talked to the Callaghan's newest dish, Mimi, I didn't know why Bitsy Babbs had tried to get me away from the club once she'd told me about Tommy, and I didn't know why Tommy wanted to meet me. Would he put the finger on someone, or was he going to try to take me out? Whatever the case, I had to know. After I paid the driver, I slipped out my gun and into the alley.

A few steps in, beside a stack of crates, I saw Tommy. He wasn't ready to shoot me, and he didn't want to talk. In fact, he was never going to talk again. He was sprawled on his back, eyes staring at the sky. His black suit was unbuttoned and blood was making a mess of his fancy white shirt. There was a bullet hole right through his heart. I saw something shiny at his hip and bent to check it out. It was a gun. I put the new tool in my coat pocket and picked up the murder weapon. There were nicks on the handle, three of them. It wasn't just any peashooter, it was mine. "Cheese and rice," I spat.

Before I could say another word, a muzzle was jabbed hard into my back. "Well, well, if it ain't Cal Guy of New York's finest," a gravelly voice said. Another lug grabbed the gun out of my hand and turned me around, putting an ape grip on my arms. "Looks like another copper's gone bad."

I struggled, but couldn't free myself. "You no-good lunks! You set me up!"

"Shut your pie-hole, and don't try anything funny," the one holding my arms said, as they pulled me out of the alley and toward a long, black limo. "I plugged your partner, and I'd be glad to plug you, too."

I growled as I was shoved into the back seat along with Robinson's killer. I found myself face to face with Red Callaghan, big as life and twice as ugly. "Nice to finally meet you, Officer Guy," he said. "How about a drink?"

"I could do with one," I answered, sizing things up. If he wanted me unconscious again, I'd already be out.

He poured us both a double, from a bottle of Irish that would've cost me more than a month's pay. "*Go mbeire muid be oar an am seo arís*," he said, hoisting his glass.

We clinked, but I didn't drink. I wasn't superstitious, but I didn't feel like toasting my own death.

He gave a one-note laugh. "It means, 'May we both be alive this time next year'."

Fat chance, I thought, and I bet he was thinking the same in reverse. I downed the drink, wondering if it'd be my last.

The doors locked and the limo took off, just the driver, me, Callaghan, and a gorilla playing dress-up. He had his gun trained on me.

"So," said Callaghan. "Why don't you make this simple and tell me where Tommy hid my money?" His voice was as smooth as his whiskey.

My mind skipped rope, double-time. Callaghan thought I'd killed Tommy after he confessed to stealing the dough and telling me where to find it. What kind of cockamamie nonsense was that? He had to know a little bag of greenbacks wasn't going to make up for rubbing out Robinson. But I had questions of my own. If Tommy had taken the cash, why did he set up a meeting with me? And if Callaghan's boys hadn't offed him, who did? I was suddenly afraid I knew. "Who told you where we were?" I asked.

Callaghan sipped his whiskey, giving me another look. He shrugged, like it couldn't hurt to tell a talking dead man what he wanted to know. "Candy," he said. "Candy LeBon."

I nodded. Once a pro, always a pro. Why did she have to feel so damn good in my arms? "The bitch," I grumbled, shoving my hands into my pockets. And then I felt the gun.

"Temper, temper, Mr Guy. Candy was just being a good employee – and making sure she wasn't blamed for something she didn't do." He grinned and it gave me the willies. Then he sipped again. "She told me all about you and Bitsy, setting up Tommy, may he rest in peace. Best bartender I ever had."

Callaghan's tone hadn't changed and he gave no order, but the thug cocked his gun. Before he could fire, I shot him twice him in the breadbasket through the pocket of my overcoat, and then whipped out my pistola and aimed it between Callaghan's eyes. "Tell the driver to pull over and unlock the door. Now."

My heart beating like bongos, I jumped out of the limo and into the first cab I saw. It was occupied, but when I took out my badge and said "Official business," the fancy-dressed couple vacated, pronto. "The airport, and step on it," I ordered.

As the cab sped off, I looked around, figuring out where we were. We weaved in and out of city traffic while I thought about how easy it would've been to off Callaghan. I bummed a cigarette off the cabby and let pent-up adrenaline flow out of me with the smoke. I knew the Chief wanted Callaghan, and I'd settled the score that mattered to me. That was enough. But there was still Candy. I savvied everything now, the whole scam. Callaghan's flunkies hadn't taken my heater, she had. Or she'd seen where they'd put it and taken it. And when I was getting ready to go meet Tommy, she was killing him with it. The bumpus probably never saw it coming. That frail was ice, in it for no one but herself. I thought about getting my mitts around that pretty throat and squeezing.

"Which airline?" the cabby interrupted.

"Air France," I said, fingering the gun in my pocket, wondering if I could get my piece back by handing both Candy and the cash over to Callaghan. I took a last drag of the gasper and stubbed it out. Having knocked off Huey, Dewey or Louie would make it tough to bargain.

When we pulled over, I gave up my twenty and beat it, pacing the pavement, thinking, wishing I had another smoke. I checked my watch. *Not long now, baby*, I thought, *not long now*.

Time crawled as I waited, hungry for blood, but knowing I was going to take her back in one piece.

"Cal!" Candy called as she stepped out of a taxi. She didn't miss a beat, reaching out like I was her long lost brother. She was all in black, from skintight dress to high heels, hair done up fancy with a little veil over her eyes, and those damned little Eiffel Tower earrings. She had a black leather case in her hand. We both knew what was in it, and it wasn't lingerie. "I knew you'd be here, *chéri*," she said, breathless. "I knew you'd understand."

Oh, she was good. Sure, it was just possible she figured out that I'd found the one-way ticket to Paris in her handbag when she'd gone to wash off some of my . . . enthusiasm at the motel. But I didn't think so. She was winging it, in more ways than one.

"Understand what, baby?" I said, real low, gripping her by the arms and looking her over like the rotten meat she was. "That you were in this with Tommy until he decided to throw you over? That you followed him to the alley where he'd planned to meet me and give up the goods, and plugged him with my gun?" She denied it, shaking her pretty head and trying to pull away, but I kept her pinned and kept up the heat. "That you told Callaghan where and when to find us, and threw Bitsy under the bus just for kicks? Yeah, baby, I understand."

She stopped fighting me, and under the veil her eyes flashed like lightning. "All right, you bastard. It's true. Every word of it. But I'm not sorry. A girl's gotta look after herself in this crummy world." Her face suddenly crumpled like an old newspaper, and then came the waterworks. "Damn it, Cal, I *am* sorry. I've never been so sorry in my life." She dropped her head onto my chest, and I put my arms around her. I had to. "I thought money would make me happy," she whimpered, "and I didn't care who I hurt. But then I met you. I didn't want to admit I could care, but I do. You're different." She looked up, make-up running down her cheeks. "I want to be your girl."

"I know, baby," I said, and let her go while I took out my handkerchief. I dabbed her face with it.

She put her hand over mine and squeezed it, and then picked up the case of dough. "I'll head to Paris and you take the next flight out. I'll be waiting for you." She smiled up at me, so sweet I could almost believe it was real. But it was poison, all poison.

"Not a bad plan, baby," I said, taking her arm and guiding her to a cab that'd run us straight to the precinct. "But that's one too many double-crosses for this guy."

Sudden Showers

Thomas S. Roche

He meets her in the park, on the famous bridge that over-looks the little creek. His eyes cruise up and down her body, which is shrouded in a long black coat with a shimmering shark-skin texture. The coat is cut very close to her body. It gathers at the waist. It's made of a very light material, so it clings to the shape of her body. It's buttoned all the way up to her neck – but not high enough to cover the silver-studded black leather collar she wears. It has been padlocked around her throat.

The man evaluates the woman openly, obviously noting that the close-fitting coat doesn't hide her curves. Her ample breasts are evident. So is the perfect, smooth swell of her ass.

"Nice night," he says.

"Yes," she agrees. "It's very nice."

"It's quite warm," he adds. "Doesn't look like rain."

She looks up. There are clouds overhead, but they're wispy and forlorn. They don't look dark, and they don't look like rainclouds. The moon is bright overhead; it shines through the fine white clouds enough to illuminate the woman's pale skin.

"No," she says. "But there can always be showers." Her voice is smoky, her eyes provocatively haunted as she lowers them from the sky to the face of her new acquaintance. "Anywhere, any time. I hate to get caught in a shower in the park."

The man wears dark slacks, shiny black wingtips and a

button-front shirt of a rich, silky texture, in a burgundy color. It is unbuttoned far enough that the woman can see the bulky power of his chest. A man his age shouldn't wear an open shirt, she thinks – except that he can get away with it, because that chest is really quite impressive. His height doesn't hurt, either; even with the woman's very high heels, he still stands a bit taller than her. Overall, he looks far more powerful than another man would strolling casually through the park at night dressed like he's on his way to a date.

The man rubs the fabric of his shirt between his thumb and forefinger.

"I'm quite a fan of getting wet, actually. When it's warm like this, it's very sexy to be rained on."

"Yes," says the woman. "It can be. If you're with the right person," she adds tartly.

"You're turning red," says the man. "Are you all right?"

"I'm fine," says the woman.

"Am I embarrassing you?"

"Not at all," she says crisply.

"Then you must be hot. I know I am. What with this heavy air . . ." He pauses and peers at her closely. "No, you're turning quite a bit redder, I see. You seem to get pinker the more I look at you." The man grins. "I hope that doesn't mean you can read minds," he says.

"What if I could?" she asks. "I wouldn't care to read yours."

"No, I imagine you wouldn't. You don't need to be psychic to imagine what's going through my head, meeting a beautiful woman like you."

"With talk like that," says the woman, "you're going to scare me off." She does not move to walk away, however.

"Leave if you want," says the man. "But please don't go because I've embarrassed you. I didn't mean anything by it."

"You haven't embarrassed me," says the woman.

The man *tsks*. "You're not much of a liar. Redheads never are. Girls like you, with such bright hair and pale skin. You're blushing so much, you *must* be reading my mind."

"I'm not blushing," says the woman again.

"Then perhaps you'll stay and chat a bit?" asks the man.

The woman's eyes drop to the ground. She frowns. She pouts. She looks very, very angry.

"If you'd like me to," she says, "I'll stay."

"I'd very much like you to stay," says the man. "What is your name? Mine's Gérard."

"My husband doesn't like me to talk to strangers."

Gérard smiles. "I don't think you've got a husband."

"How would you know?" she asks bitterly.

"Because you look more like the type to have a lover."

The woman considers it. "Do I? Then, all right. My lover told me not to talk to strangers."

"I suspect he didn't tell you that at all," says Gérard. "Or else you like to disobey him. Are you a disobedient girl? Tell me your name."

The woman considers it. "I'm Yvonne," she says. "Pleased to meet you." She says it tightly, as if she were *not* pleased to meet him.

"Yvonne," he says. "That's a very pretty name for a very pretty lady. But you're blushing again. Have I embarrassed you by calling you pretty?"

"I'm not blushing," she says. "I'm not embarrassed." She adds, a little sulkily, "I know I'm pretty."

"Yes," says Gérard. "I imagine men make that obvious whenever they get a look at you. And yet I've barely had the pleasure. If you're not embarrassed, then you're obviously hot, Yvonne – your face is noticeably red. It certainly is warm tonight. You should open your coat."

"Yes," Yvonne admits with a sigh. "I'm a little warm."

"Here," says Gérard, reaching. "Let me help you off with your coat, then."

Yvonne shies away, but doesn't try to leave. "Please," she says nervously. "Don't."

But she does not back away far enough to remove herself from the treat of Gérard's grasping hands.

Gérard smiles. "You'd rather take it off yourself?"

Breathless, Yvonne says: "No, Sir. I'd rather leave it on."

"I don't think so," says Gérard. "Take it off." His voice is hard and commanding. "Take off your coat, Madame. Now."

She corrects him, "*Mademoiselle*."

"I see," he says. "Then that collar you're wearing isn't your husband's?"

Yvonne's face now turns *very* red.

"It's my lover's," she says softly.

"The same lover who doesn't want you to talk to strangers in the park, eh? Yet here you are." Gérard chuckles as Yvonne gets flustered. "I don't think so," he says. "A lover makes love. A lover doesn't train a girl to call men *Sir*. I think the man who locked that collar on you is another sort of intimate entirely."

Yvonne blurts, "I'm just being polite when I call you 'Sir'."

"No one's that polite, Yvonne. Not nowadays."

"Perhaps I am," she says. "Perhaps my lover taught me to be that way."

"I think he taught you to be other ways, too," says Gérard with a sneer. "Now take off your coat, *slave*."

Yvonne's body gives a visible shiver as she hears that word. "I don't think so, Sir," she says.

"I *do* think so," Gérard says. "Take it off."

"I can't, Sir," she says. "I'm not wearing much underneath."

Gérard smiles. "If you ask me, that sounds like a reason you *should*, not a reason you can't." Yvonne's breath deepens. "But in any event, there's no need to take it all the way off, is there? Just give me a little look, Mademoiselle. If you're a slave, as I suspect, many men have looked at you, haven't they? Hasn't your Master shown you off quite a bit? To many, many men?"

Gérard's words are having a visible effect on Yvonne. Not only has her face grown pinker than ever, but she's also having some trouble containing her quickening breaths.

"Come, now, slave. It won't do any harm to show yourself off to a stranger, will it?"

She twists one strand of her copper-red hair around one finger. She tosses her hair. "I guess not, Sir," she says.

"Then open your coat up, Mademoiselle. *Now*."

"I can't, Sir," she says. Then, more defiantly, "I won't."

He chuckles. "And yet, you call me 'Sir'. You're quite a provocative little minx. What's going on in your head, my dear?"

"You're a very rude man, Sir."

"And yet, you're not making tracks," he says. "Perhaps you've been ordered to make new friends?"

Yvonne's eyes drop in shame. She bites her lip. Painted red, her mouth is eminently kissable.

Gérard laughs. "Ah," he says. "You're one of those. That's delightful. You're lucky you found a Master strong and cruel enough to send you out to get what you need."

"It isn't what I need, Sir," she says. "What I need is to be left alone."

"But your Master doesn't allow that, does he?"

Breathlessly, Yvonne says, "No, Sir."

"Then you and I shall have some fun together, Mademoiselle Yvonne." His nostrils flare as he creeps closer to her, reaching out for her. He doesn't quite touch her . . . yet.

She does not pull away. Instead, she looks up at him and breathes very hard.

She says, "My lover also told me not to let strange men touch me," she says. "And not to tell them my name."

"Do you mean your lover or your Master?" asks Gérard.

Breathing hard, Yvonne admits, "He's both."

"He's a very lucky man, to have a beauty like you to train. But you're so disobedient. Open up that coat and let me see your body."

Yvonne's voice is small and submissive: "I mustn't, Sir. I mustn't show you."

There's a heat underneath her words – a longing. Her dark eyes rove up and down Gérard's body. She drinks him in. She evaluates him. She sizes up his stance, his power, his attitude. When her eyes meet his again, they're seething with hunger, fear and desperation.

"Mademoiselle, I'm going to tell you one last time – and then I'm going to open it for you. Open that coat!"

Yvonne's slender fingers toy with her top button. She looks at him fearfully.

Gérard chuckles. "Your Master told you not to talk to strangers, did he?"

"Yes, Sir," she says. "Well," she corrects, "he told me I can talk to them, but I mustn't tell my name."

"That's how they remain strangers," says Gérard with pleasure. He snaps his fingers. "Did he also tell you not to show your body to strangers?"

Yvonne's face goes quickly pink. "No, Sir," she admits. "He told me something very different, in that regard."

"Yes, I see," says Gérard. "He told you that you must show yourself off to any man who asks, didn't he?"

"Not just any man, Sir," smirks Yvonne. "Anyone at all."

"He likes you to swing both ways, does he?"

"That's none of your business," says Yvonne prissily.

"But it is my business what you're wearing under there," says Gérard. "And it's my business how your pretty body looks."

Yvonne bites her lip and looks down.

"Isn't it?" says Gérard. "Isn't it any man's business?"

"Any *one*," Yvonne corrects him. "It's everyone's business. But I'm not allowed to *show*, Sir. You must . . . *look*."

Yvonne's back undulates slightly, forming itself into an arch. She thrusts the prominent curves of her breasts toward Gérard. Her full, firm, red-painted lips part as she breathes heavily. For a moment, she toys with her top button again, caressing it almost as if it is her lover's body.

Then she lowers her hands. She lets her arms hang limp at her sides.

"I don't take orders from strangers," she says. "But I also mustn't *give* them orders. I can only . . . *plead*." Her breasts heave as her labored breathing turns to panting. "Plead with you not to . . . *do* things. Things that all men want to do when they see me." Her eyes turn sultry and sensuous, even as they go wide with fear.

"I must protest," she says. "But I cannot stop you."

"That's easy enough," says Gérard with pleasure.

He comes for her.

Gérard reaches up to Yvonne's throat, just beneath the collar. He makes eye contact with her as he unfastens the button of her coat.

He undoes the next button, and the next and the next. His face betrays his growing pleasure as he sees her exposed.

His hand plucks at each button, slowly, savoring each humiliating touch. Yvonne's back remains arched, her tits thrust toward him as, bare, they become exposed.

Gérard unfastens the belt and undoes the last few buttons. Then he pulls her coat open and looks her up and down.

Her earlier comment that she's not wearing much is, at best, an understatement. In fact, she has on only a garter belt and black fishnet stockings. Her pussy is shaved and her clit is pierced, the silver ring glinting in the moonlight. A small dark word rests just above her sex, where her pubic hair would be – if she had any.

Her black boots come almost to her knees. Constructed of buttery leather, the pointy-toed boots have almost impossibly high heels. Even so, she stands steady, with confidence, even as she arches her back as far as she can to thrust her now-bare tits toward her tormentor in a kind of invitation.

Gérard's hands reach out and caress her tits. She does not stop him. Her breathing deepens as his fingers touch her ample orbs. Firm, they're as pale and freckled as the rest of her, but they turn a deeper pink as the night air – and Gérard's fingers – touch them.

Pinching Yvonne's hardening nipples, Gérard says softly, "Your Master is a very lucky man."

"Thank you, Sir."

"And very wicked," Gérard adds. "What a cruel thing to send a girl like you out here, dressed like that and helpless to stop yourself from being ravished."

"Yes, Sir," Yvonne says. "It's very cruel of him. He's a very cruel man to order me to let you touch me." She adds with a soft gasp, "With the way you're touching me, I'm not sure I can obey him."

"Don't be ridiculous!" sneers Gérard, pinching her nipples firmly. "Why would you disobey? You seem to like it!"

"Yes, Sir," says Yvonne. "That's why I feel the urge to disobey him. I like it. That's . . . humiliating, Sir. It's humiliating to be touched by a stranger and like it." She bites her lip. "I guess you're a man. Perhaps you can't understand."

"I can understand that you want to obey your Master, and that it excites you to be humiliated." Gérard grins as he caresses her neck with one hand and her tits with the other. "In itself, that must be humiliating."

"It is, Sir," says Yvonne. "It's very hard for me to let it happen. I want to run away."

"Well," says Gérard, "that would certainly be grounds for punishment. What does your Master do if you do disobey him?"

"He spanks me, Sir," she says. "Spanks me or whips me. Or . . ." Her breath comes close and hot as she struggles for the words. "Or fucks me in the ass, Sir." The last statement carries the heat of deep humiliation, but Gérard detects a little wiggle in the beautiful woman's hindquarters. She was shaking her butt in the same kind of invitation that her breasts offered when she first thrust them toward Gérard.

Gérard thinks: *She's one of those. She likes it back there, but she thinks it's dirty. She's bad for wanting it. No wonder she's been collared. What a treasure!*

"What a beast!" says Gérard.

"Oh, he does far worse," she says. "Sometimes he does *very* nasty things to me when I'm bad." She shudders. "Filthy things that . . . humiliate me."

"What sort of nasty things? And you're not allowed to resist?"

She shakes her head. "No, Sir. But I can beg you to stop. Please stop." Her eyes shimmer with tears in the moonlight. "Please, Sir. Please don't touch me like that. It's too embarrassing. It's too humiliating." There's a little sob in her voice as she finishes: "Please stop!"

Without warning, Gérard's hand slides down her body. He works his finger into her slit.

"No, no, no, no, Sir," she whines, rocking her hips against him as he fingers her. "Please, Sir, take it out."

"Why does your Master make you do this?" asks Gérard pointedly, looking into Yvonne's eyes while his finger explores her sex.

Yvonne says breathlessly, "I'm being punished."

Gérard grins. "Does the punishment fit the crime, Madame?"

"Mademoiselle," she corrects him. "Yes, Sir. In a sense, Sir."

"Did you try to stop the last man he gave you to?"

Yvonne's breasts heave with the humiliation of the revelation.

Gérard pinches her nipples more firmly. "I've guessed correctly, haven't I? Your Master pimped you out, and you resisted? Am I right?"

"Almost, Sir," pants Yvonne. "I'm being punished for resisting, but he gave me to a woman."

"Ah," says Gérard, working Yvonne's nips. "He *does* like you to swing both ways."

"Yes, Sir," she says. "But . . ." Her eyes roll back in her head. "I really like cock."

"I can see that," Gérard tells her, his finger pushing deeper. "You're amazingly wet."

"When he gave me to that leather dyke, I might have struggled a little too excitedly. It's not that I'm not attracted to women, Sir, it's just that I—" Her voice catches in her throat. She takes a deep breath and blurts: "Sometimes I guess I like to struggle. The men my Master gives me to have an easy time overpowering me. He knows my tastes, Sir. I proved a little more difficult than Sasha cared for. I struggled a little too hard."

"Sasha?"

Yvonne's eyes grow big and wet. "She's my best friend, Sir. He gave me to her."

"Wicked!" says Gérard. "Did she have you after all?"

"Yes, Sir," Yvonne says. "But she had to tie me up first. It was quite a lot of work, Sir. I was a handful. Sasha wasn't in the mood for such an epic struggle. She was annoyed with me, and this displeased my Master. He sent me out here to learn that he owns me . . . as does any man he cares to loan me to."

"Have you learned your lesson yet?" asks Gérard, thumbing her sensitive nipples. Her flesh goosebumps around them.

Yvonne shakes her head. "No, Sir, I haven't."

"You can't stop me from touching you without disobeying him, is that right?"

"No, Sir," Yvonne whispers. "Not if you touch me, not if you . . . *fuck* me. I can't resist. I can protest, but I can't resist. Not without being . . . punished again." She moans softly. "If I fail him this time, I fear he'll do something *really* cruel to me."

Her eyes, big and helpless, drink in Gérard's cruel, savage grin.

"Please, Sir," she whimpers. "Please don't fuck me."

Gérard takes her in his arms. Shivering, Yvonne tries to turn away from him. She tries to pull her coat closed.

But she doesn't try to get away.

She does, however, manage to turn her back to him. She ends up with Gérard leaning hard against her, pinning her to the railing.

"You do like to struggle, don't you?" Gérard thrusts his hands in her coat, groping and slapping her tits and her pussy.

"Sir!" she whimpers. "Please!"

Gérard seizes the back of her coat and sweeps it out of the way, exposing the pale half-moons of her ass.

"Let's get a head start on that punishment your Master's going to owe you, shall we?"

"No, Sir, please!" she whines. "Please don't—oh!"

Her plea turns into an inarticulate cry as Gérard's hand falls quickly on her bare ass. He spanks her hard, a dozen times, while Yvonne leans forward. She grips the railing and whimpers, "Please, Sir, please, Sir, please don't spank me any more! I'll be good!"

"Be good by keeping your mouth shut," he says, and spanks her again, harder and faster this time, striking her with the full weight of his palm as well as with his cupped fingers. Yvonne cries out as he alternates sting and thud. He switches strokes unexpectedly with each blow, now pounding his wide, heavy hand firmly against her the fleshy part of her vulnerable ass, now smacking her viciously so a slap echoes over the water.

Gérard stops spanking her. His hands caress her belly, her thighs. He reaches around and touches her tits, pinching her nipples lightly.

He leans up against her firmly and pins her tight against the railing of the bridge and caresses her under her coat. He advances his hand, feels her cunt. She's smooth underneath – smooth and shaved and very wet with arousal. Her full lips have swollen with hunger for sex.

While Gérard fingers her slit with his right hand, he uses his left to explore the smooth flesh of her belly and hips and breasts. Her skin is goosebumped from the air, even though it's quite a warm night.

"Please, Sir, don't," she whimpers.

"Your Master knows that if he dresses you up like this – or *undresses* you – for a walk in the park at night . . . any man can take advantage of you."

"Yes, Sir," she moans as he fingers her slit more firmly, rubbing her pierced clit. Then she corrects herself, and says, "Not any man, though, Sir. Only a scoundrel."

"Of course," he says, kissing the back of her neck while he fingers the hot skin of her punished ass. "But there are many scoundrels."

"He knows that, Sir." She trembles and shivers. Involuntarily, she pushes herself onto his hand. She moans softly. Gérard seizes her hair and tips her head back. In these high heels, she's just tall enough that it's slightly awkward for the very tall Gérard to kiss her. He manages it anyway, thrusting his tongue deep in her mouth.

He kisses her hard, his tongue forcing its way wet inside her mouth. He takes her mouth with rapacious intent. But her full lips part and her own tongue seethes against his as he kisses her deeply.

As he kisses her, Gérard's hands violate her, his fingers seeming to be all over her at once. He pinches her hard nipples. He pries open the lips of her sex and caresses her entrance. He exposes her pierced clit and rubs it. He makes her moan.

Every now and then, he draws his hand back and slaps or spanks her again – now on her barely covered cunt, now on her tits, once or twice on her face when he takes a brief respite from kissing her. The slaps across her face make Yvonne go redder than ever. They make her tremble all over as her arousal builds. Every instant she's exposed like this makes her hotter. Every second someone might happen up the path excites her more.

"You like to have this done to you in public, don't you?" Gérard accuses her. "You like that anyone might happen along. Isn't that right?"

Yvonne undulates slightly, rubbing her half-naked body up against Gérard. She looks into his eyes. "I hate it, Sir. I despise it. That's why my Master makes me do it, Sir."

Gérard caresses her slit. She moans uncontrollably.

"And yet, you're wet as a faucet."

Red-faced, Yvonne bites her lip. She gives him a whimpering nod of shame, admitting what he already knows. "That's why I hate it so much, Sir. It's humiliating to like being such a slut, Sir. It's far worse than doing it and feeling no pleasure. I would never do this if Master didn't make me."

He grabs her long red hair and pulls. "Good thing you've got a very nasty Master, isn't it?"

"Yes, Sir," Yvonne says.

Gérard's fingers force their way into her cunt – two of them, then three. As he finger-fucks her, Yvonne's full lips part. She struggles for air, inhaling flower-scented summer.

Gérard possesses her cruelly with his hands and his mouth. Gérard watches her like a hawk, so that when she glances around nervously every few seconds, he grins and laughs. He knows what she's doing. She's frightened they'll be discovered. She's frightened she'll be exposed for the huge slut she is. It's very late, and it's a weeknight. Traffic in the park is light. But people still go out for clandestine boat rides, sometimes, using a rubber raft or a small wooden skiff as a place to get drunk, get stoned and engage in illicit sex. There are lights overhead, but the shadows below are deep. There's every chance that someone could be looking up at them from a tiny boat on the water even now.

What's more, a cop or another passer-by could come along the bridge and then it would be all over. They'd both get arrested. They'd be taken to the station. The bad, bad cops might even make her take her coat off. She'd end up in jail wearing almost nothing. The very thought makes her heart race.

Knowing she might get caught makes Yvonne's arousal mount more powerfully with every thrust of Gérard's fingers into her. When he takes his fingers out of her sex and slides them into her mouth. She looks into his eyes and slurps them clean, sucking obediently.

"Your Master has trained you well," says Gérard.

"Thank you, Sir," she says. "I'll tell him you said that."

Gérard seizes her hair. He grabs one of her wrists with the hand that's wet with pussy and spittle.

He spins her around and pushes her up against the railing. He grinds his swollen cock against her ass through his pants and her coat.

"On a warm night like this, even the coat seems too much," he says. "Pull it out of the way and let me fuck you."

"No, Sir, I can't," she says. "Please don't make me. Please don't fuck me. Please, Sir, please don't do anything more. I don't want you to."

Gérard does it for her, sweeping her coat to one side again to expose her ass. He bends her over the railing.

He growls in her ear: "Take it out, and put it in."

"No, Sir, don't make me. Please don't make me."

She says it even as she reaches behind him and fumbles with Gérard's belt buckle. She fumbles because her hands are shaking with excitement, but the fumbling doesn't last for very long. Yvonne is the clearly the kind of girl who's had plenty of experience taking out cocks out and putting them inside her.

But her hand comes away quickly.

"I'm not supposed to help you," she says. "I have to protest. I can't resist, but I—"

Gérard seizes her again. He spins her around and shoves her down to her knees. "You have to say no the whole time, is that it?" growls Gérard. "Well, I'm tired of hearing it!"

He forces her mouth open and shoves his cock inside.

Yvonne squeals as he thrusts his cock deep. At first, she merely kneels there, wet mouth open, helpless. She does nothing to stop him, but nothing to help him. Gérard strokes into her savagely, fucking her passive face to the point where he hears gulping sounds. He chokes her a little. Yvonne surges against him as he does that. He pulls her hair and slaps her face and orders her to disobey her Master.

"You're not supposed to help me," he growls. "Is that it? Fine, then. Earn yourself another spanking, Madame. Earn it like the whore you are."

Yvonne puts her hand around the base of Gérard's cock. She starts sucking, eagerly, drooling down onto his balls. She rubs his cock all over her face, making love to it. She leaves lipstick traces up and down the shaft. She looks up at him with wet eyes. She makes sure he's watching her. She wants him to see just how deeply she's taking him. She swallows his cock almost to the hilt, filling up her throat.

Gérard leans forward, meeting the thrusts of her eager mouth with energetic strokes of his hips. Yvonne's lips glide up and down on his shaft. Trickles of spittle travel down his shaft and onto his balls. He sighs as he relaxes and stops thrusting so quickly. He lets her tongue and her sucking lips work magic all up and down his cock. Her tongue swirls around the head. In the shadows of the railing, only her eyes flash. He looks into them as he undulates rhythmically in time with the eager mouth on his cock.

"Enough!" Gérard gasps, suddenly. "Keep doing that and you'll get a mouthful!"

"Maybe that's what I want," she says wickedly.

"No," says Gérard. "Your Master has something else in mind for you, doesn't he?"

Yvonne says, "Yes, Sir."

"Stand up and bend over," says Gérard.

"Please, Sir, don't make me—" begins Yvonne, but Gérard silences her by putting one hand in her hair and seizing her wrist. He lifts her up. She squeals as he turns her around and bends her over the railing. Gérard kicks Yvonne's legs wide open.

This time he doesn't give her the order to pull her coat out of the way. He does it for her. He exposes her legs and her ass, showing her off to anyone who might be watching from the darkness of the nearby trees. More importantly, he exposes her sex for his cock.

Gérard reaches down to Yvonne's cunt and spreads her full, swollen lips with his fingers.

He tells her, "Open wide."

Yvonne gasps as his cockhead finds its way to her open slit. He works it up and down between her lips for a moment, spreading them further with his fingers, exposing her wet and vulnerable entrance.

He teases her only for a few moments. Then he shoves his cock up inside her, roughly, almost as if he means to hurt her.

But he doesn't hurt her. He almost couldn't – that's how wet and ready she is. Even so, Gérard is big enough that she feels herself stretched and opened by his deep, hard thrust.

His cock enters her all the way, his swollen head pressing against her cervix. She moans softly, pushing back onto him.

His arms hold her close. He caresses her nipples. He pinches them. He fondles her throat. He begins to fuck her roughly, thrusting with a vengeance. He grabs her hair and tips her head back and shoves his mouth against hers. He possesses her mouth with the same pleasure he possesses her pussy.

Yvonne fucks herself wildly against him. Sometimes she whimpers out, "No, Sir, you mustn't," always getting a growl and a harder thrust in response. Her hips never stop moving, even when he pins her tight against the railing.

His hand travels down from her tits to her ass. He spreads her cheeks and exposes her hole. He pulls out his cock and works his fingers into her. Then he pulls them out dripping wet and forces a finger into her ass as he shoves his cock inside her again.

"Oh!" she gasps. "Sir, no, that's too filthy! Have mercy! You mustn't! My master hasn't even had me that way!" She says it with a low moaning sound, her pleasure obviously mounting with each cry of protest.

"I doubt that," says Gérard. As he fucks her, Gérard replaces his finger with his thumb. He works it up deep into Yvonne's asshole, using her tight butt as a handhold to stroke his cock deeper and harder inside her pussy.

"Please, Sir," moans Yvonne. "Not my rear hole, Sir. It's too dirty."

"You're a very dirty girl," growls Gérard. He slides his cock out of her pussy. He guides it up to her ass.

Her pussy is so molten that his cock is very wet, but Gérard can feel that her asshole is also slippery – more than the spit on his fingers and thumb would allow for. When this one's Master sends her out to fuck strangers in the park, he makes sure she's ready for every eventuality. It truly must help with "making friends", Gérard thinks.

Yvonne lets out a great shuddering moan of pleasure and fear and sensation and surrender as Gérard fits the thick head of his cock into her pre-lubricated back entrance.

He presses in slowly. Yvonne has to struggle to take it. Her mouth drops open. She gasps and then moans as Gérard pushes into her.

He fucks his cock all the way into her ass. When he's in her to the hilt, she grips the railing tightly and moans in agonized pleasure.

Yvonne lets out a gasp as Gérard starts to fuck her. Impaled and pinned against the rail, she's helpless to stop him. He works his cock in shallow thrusts, unable to move it very far. Her ass is so tight that it grips his cock securely, almost refusing to surrender its hold when Gérard pulls back.

He pulls back harder, thrusts in more firmly. She feels the fingers of his left hand working her clit, while his right hand travels up to her nipples.

"Everyone is watching," he tells her, growling in her ear.

Yvonne moans softly, "Who, Sir? Who's watching?"

"You'll never know, will you?" Gérard says. "It's awfully dark out there."

"Yes, Sir," she whimpers. "I've got terrible night vision."

"Then you'll never know just how many people saw you get ass-fucked in the park, slave, will you? You'll never know how many, or who they were?"

Yvonne can't respond. Pleasure flows through her, turning her words into inarticulate moans.

Gérard fucks her ass harder, his fingers working her pierced clit and pinching her sensitive nipples. Gérard knows how to mindfuck her. He knows how to push Yvonne over the edge. From the way her eyes are roving over the nearby trees, he knows she can see them there, all the silent eyes watching her. Everyone she knows is out there, watching her public humiliation. Everyone, at least, that she finds even a little bit erotic – and there are plenty of those. Her co-workers are out there; her friends, their neighbors, passing acquaintances. They're all there watching her get fucked in the ass up against a bridge railing, by a stranger whose cock fits her perfectly – in both holes.

Yvonne mewls and starts rocking back and forth with a tight, familiar rhythm. She fucks her loosening ass savagely onto Gérard's cock. Gérard shoves his fingers up inside her. He finger-fucks her pussy with two and then three fingers, while she works her asshole up and down on his cock, enjoying its tightness almost more than she enjoys his fingers.

It's an intense feeling for her to be fucked in both holes, while Gérard's tongue savages her mouth. His cock in her ass fills her and makes her pussy even tighter as she fucks herself against him. His fingers work her sex fervently. He forces a fourth finger into her, making her gasp. Then he pulls out and gives her only two, but curves them around so with each thrust his fingers pump against her G-spot.

She can feel how full she's becoming. She can feel the swell inside her. Maybe Gérard knows it, too. Maybe he knows why it's a damn good thing she wore a raincoat. Maybe he understands that he should have worn one, too.

As he pushes his fingers into her, she can feel his fingertips caressing the swell of her G-spot. When he withdraws his fingers and thrusts his cock up her ass, he stimulates her G-spot even more firmly. Alternating the thrusts of his fingers and his cock has made her grow full to overflowing – exactly the way Gérard likes her.

She feels the liquid sensation growing stronger, until it's all but irresistible. She realizes she's going to squirt. She's about to spend all her pleasure, everywhere, all over her and all over her Master.

Her Master loves it when she ejaculates. He likes it because it proves that she really came. But he also likes it because he knows she finds it more than a little embarrassing. Maybe even a little humiliating. Her Master makes her come all the time. But he's never truly satisfied unless he's worked her up to a frenzy and then stimulated her in just the right way to make her squirt.

Yvonne tries to resist. She knows it will please her Master if she squirts, but she can't let herself do it in public . . . can she?

She realizes with fear and excitement and trepidation that she has no choice. The feeling of fullness inside her is too intense. She's going to explode and squirt and spray everywhere. Her pleasure is building to a crescendo. She's going to ejaculate right here in public – up against the railing with a cock deep in her ass.

She can feel the eagerness of his cock as she struggles to subdue her swelling liquid orgasm. He seizes her hair and puts his mouth wet and warm against her neck. He fingers her pussy deep and says, "Shame we don't have another cock to fill this," he says. "Maybe someone will happen along?"

He says it as he fingers her cunt deep, rubbing her swollen G-spot.

Yvonne moans wildly as he torments her with her own pleasure.

She can't resist any longer. She can't hold back. His filthy threat to pimp her to a second stranger turns her on too much. It drives her over the edge.

Yvonne throws back her head, her red hair scattering everywhere. She fucks herself harder onto his cock, lifting her knees till they're propped against the railing. And she's all but suspended in space, impaled on his cock. The weight of her body drives her hard onto Gérard's thrusting prick; he meets her weight with deep strokes that hit her exactly where she needs it.

She's much smaller than Gérard, but it's still a difficult position to hold for long. Yvonne doesn't need long, though. She's right on the edge already.

She shudders all over as Gérard fucks his cock deep into her ass and bounces her whole body up and down. Her orgasm blasts through her body.

She comes everywhere. The first hot squirt floods her thighs, soaks her fishnet stockings. She trembles all over as she pushes herself onto the cock in her ass. Gérard holds her open and exposes her spurting urethra as she spasms again. Great streams of fluid spray from her sex, covering both of their lower bodies as the full weight of her orgasm overtakes her.

Gérard comes a moment later, groaning as he lets himself go deep inside her. She feels the slickness of his release. She moans as he holds her.

Ejaculate runs down her thighs and into her boots. It coats the bridge beneath them.

Still holding her tightly, Gérard touches her wet thighs. He caresses the wet slit of her sex. "Imagine that," pants Gérard, exhausted, "even on a warm night like this, there can be a sudden shower."

"Yes, Sir," she says.

Then Gérard's fingers travel up to touch the slightly raised letters inscribed above her sex. With his middle finger, he traces the path of his own name.

"Your Master should be very, very pleased with you," he says.

Yvonne wiggles out of Gérard's arms and turns, putting her own arms around him. Still dripping, she holds him close.

"Thank you, Sir," she says breathlessly. "I'll tell him you said that."

"You'd best button your coat," says Gérard. "It's a long walk to the car. We need to get you home for a real shower."

"Yes, Sir," she says.

She buttons up, and they walk to the car.

Becoming Alice

Jean Roberta

Prologue
(to be read by the invisible Narrator):

The road of life goes on until it ends,
Straight as a razor's edge until it bends.
The destination is as clear as day,
And strange enough to take our breath away.

Alice lay in the grass by the side of a stream, studying her multiplication tables. She wanted to do well at maths and to be thought as clever as her two older sisters, but the sun was *so* warm and the music of water running over stones was *so* soothing that the numbers blurred before her eyes and the paper fell gently from her hands.

"I'm late, I'm late," muttered a voice as a white rabbit in a waistcoat ran past Alice. "They'll all start without me." The rabbit ran close to Alice without looking at her, but she recognized him as her old friend (or perhaps "acquaintance" would serve better) from Wonderland.

"White Rabbit!" she called. "Excuse me, won't you stop for a moment? It's Alice!"

He glanced at her, and scarcely slowed his pace or showed any expression of pleasure. (Of course, he *was* a rabbit and could not smile as humans can.) "Yes, yes," he muttered. "It's all very well for you."

Alice picked herself up and chased him until she was out of breath. "Mr Rabbit!" She was not willing to be brushed aside by an animal, even one who could speak English.

When the rabbit disappeared down a hole in the ground, Alice followed close on his heels (and very large, conspicuous heels they were). She felt herself falling down, down, down below the earth. "I wonder where Hell is located?" she asked herself aloud, hoping to comfort herself with the sound of her own voice. "Well, I needn't worry. I didn't see any signposts saying 'Infernal Realm 1 mile' when I was here last."

At last she landed with a bump in a field of grass that seemed to stroke her legs as her skirt billowed about her. "Rabbit!" she called, as he paused to pull his pocket watch out of his waistcoat. "Have you been invited to play croquet with the Queen and King?"

He stopped and fixed her with two round, moist eyes. "Croquet!" he repeated. "Oh you are a baby, aren't you? I must get to the Grand Ball without delay. Can't you hear my biological clock ticking?"

A round object like a red cabbage or a soft, sunburnt pumpkin rolled to a stop at the rabbit's feet. "Tick-tock, tick-tock," it said.

Alice felt distinctly uncomfortable in the proximity of a thing that looked so like a rotting vegetable and sounded so like a bomb.

"'Tis not much to do with you," said the rabbit, running his gaze slowly from her stocking-clad legs to her tangled hair and back down. "Your species doesn't set the standard."

Alice felt quite miffed at that. She couldn't be sure which standard the rabbit meant, but she felt sure that human beings set most standards, at least in the world she knew.

A pair of eyelids opened in the round red object, and a pair of bulging eyes like those of the rabbit, but much bigger, stared openly at Alice. The profile of a nose appeared, and then a gap opened and spread, forming an ill-shaped mouth. "Your time is coming, dear," it said to Alice.

"Your *debut*," mocked the rabbit, affecting a nasal drawl. "Your introduction to your raison d'être."

Alice could see the indented shapes of numbers evenly spaced in the face that was looking at her. "Tick-tock," came the sound from within it.

"I don't understand either of you," said Alice very politely. She *had* been taught to be polite, but condescension from a rabbit and a large, ticking vegetable was very hard to bear. "Rabbit, what standard do you mean?"

"Oh dear, I'm dreadfully late, but you clearly need an education. Have you ever heard the phrase 'fucking like a rabbit'?" he asked smugly.

Alice had heard something of the sort, but only from the servants when they thought she wasn't listening. She felt herself turn almost as red as the rabbit's biological clock. "I'm afraid I don't know exactly what it means," she admitted.

"Not know what FUCK means?" yelled a loud, high-pitched voice. A thin, energetic young woman strode to Alice's side. The young woman smelled of pepper and less agreeable things, and she wore a dirty apron and a cap that sat lopsidedly on her headful of disheveled hair. "Good aft'noon, miss," she said. "I don't think we was ever prop'ly introduced. Doris here, but you could call me Cook. Pleased to see ya in more fortunate circumstances."

The persistent smell of pepper reminded Alice of where she had seen Doris before: in the Duchess's kitchen, where Doris had been stirring a large pot while the Duchess shook a screaming baby. Alice shivered at the memory.

"Fuckin's one thing," said Doris, "but tendin' the results – now, that's another kettle of soup, that is. Vinegar on a sponge, that's what I swear by."

Alice was certain that Doris knew quite a few words for swearing with, and some dreadful recipes, but before Alice could try to distract her from cooking anything, the White Rabbit drew himself up to his full height, quivering from nose to tail. "We rabbits fuck with purpose, and we have large, happy families to show for it. We lose enough innocent babies to hunters as it is."

"And very tasty they are," taunted Doris, stepping closer to the rabbit as though daring him to fight her.

"Tick-tock, tick-tock," said the biological clock, as though counting down the seconds to an explosion.

"Please!" said Alice, looking around the circle. "Won't someone tell me what 'fuck' means?" Her question produced laughter all around.

"I'd rather show you, dear," said the rabbit, "if only you were more conveniently proportioned."

And then he showed his tail to the assembled company, and hopped away.

"I can do that," boasted Doris. "I swings both ways and some that's not gen'ly thought of."

She approached Alice from behind, squeezed her about the waist and lifted her into the air, causing Alice to let out an undignified squeak. "Don't you read the papers, girl?" Doris insinuated into Alice's long brown hair.* "There's plenty of fuckin' in court cases."

"Found Under Carnal Knowledge," said the biological clock. "Above ground, it causes a ridiculous amount of fuss, especially when the parties aren't married – to each other, of course. There are many other words for it, of course, but I'm afraid you need more instruction than I can provide gratis." At that, the biological clock rolled away in the direction the rabbit had gone.

The sound of a trumpet blast arrived on a breeze. "'Ave you ever been to the Grand Ball, Alice?" asked Doris, holding Alice fast. "'Ere, don't wiggle so." Alice didn't like to be kept so close to the cook or her aroma.

"Perhaps we ought to hurry," said Alice, slipping away from Doris and rushing to stay at least one pace ahead of her.

In this way, Alice (a well-raised girl, as she was often told, although she was still quite small) and Doris (a cook of

---

* Alice Liddell, for whom Lewis Carroll wrote the "Alice" books, had dark hair. Another little girl was the model for the original illustrations.

Dubious Reputation, to use a term Alice had previously had no use for) went quickly in the direction of the trumpets. They were almost running.

"Halt!" shouted two footmen, who stood guard beside a large iron gate in a stone wall that surrounded the grounds of a castle. One footman looked remarkably like a fish, and the other was almost certainly a frog. "Have you an invitation?" asked the frog-man.

"Come on, guv'nor," said Doris, raising her skirt to give the two footmen a generous view of her thin legs, petticoat and a patch of curly hair between her thighs. "Ain't this invitin'?"

Unfortunately for her, both footmen seemed to be looking at the sky and the horizon in both directions, but then their eyes were not well placed to observe what Doris showed them.

"We have strict instructions," said the frog-man.

"To keep the riff-raff out," continued the fish-man.

Doris opened her mouth to screech a rebuttal, but she was interrupted.

"There is another difficulty," said a womanly voice with an odd hum in it, like a bass line under the melody. "But it can be resolved."

Alice was overjoyed to see her black cat, Dinah, standing on her hind legs, the better to be noticed by those who were larger than she was. "Dinah! You can speak!"

"I always could, dear," answered the cat, "but you could not always hear me."

Beneath her words, Alice could hear a subtle purr like that of a motor. Listening carefully, she could hear "tick-tick-tick".

"You need to be well raised, Alice," said Dinah, "and since I am your biological clock for the time being, I can arrange time accordingly. But first, you need to become acquainted with your own nature."

"That she does," agreed Doris. "Oh, beg pardon, Puss. I'm Doris, but you can call me Cook."

"Enchanted," said Dinah, although she didn't look it. "You may call me Bastet the Most Blessed, but I answer to Dinah. Do you know 'When Your Bosom's Aflame', Doris?"

"Not now it ain't. Oh, the poem, you mean? Why don't you start, and I'll try to keep up."

Looking meaningfully at Alice, Dinah recited: "When your bosom's aflame / With desire beyond shame / To be fondled, embraced and hard-pressed, / When you're mad as a goat / 'Neath a starched petticoat, / And you wish to be wholly undressed, / Then you're simply alive./ You just need a good swive, / And to satisfy others as well. / No need to tut-tut, / The whole world is in rut, / And you'd find no such pleasures in Hell."

The last line made Alice distinctly uneasy, especially because of the odd sensation she felt under her knickers, as though an invisible hand were tickling her there.

She remembered with confusion the tingling she had felt deep between her legs when her old nurse had spanked her bottom for saying she was not sleepy when it was her bedtime. Well, she *hadn't* been sleepy, and Nurse always said that she should always tell the truth because lying is a sin. Alice suspected that enjoying punishment might be a sin also, even though she hadn't completely enjoyed it. The spanking had hurt, and the tingling had only been an after-effect, like an echo.

After the spanking, Alice had held Dinah tightly in her arms in her bed until Dinah grew restless and took her leave, as cats will. Falling into the land of dreams, Alice imagined Dinah whispering, "I must go mouse-hunting, dear. The chase is in my blood and I am nocturnal, you know."

Remembering that night in her childhood, Alice wondered why cats were never chided for naughtiness like children. She wondered what might be in *her* blood, and what she must do to avoid being sentenced to Hell in the afterlife.

"Alice!" The voice pulled her from her reverie. "Would you like to be well raised at once? Wisdom comes first to the body, but you haven't even had your first heat yet."

Most of Dinah's remarks still made no sense to Alice, but the little cat seemed to have Alice's interests at heart, and her words held a thrilling promise that she could rush Alice past the rest of her childhood as though taking her to the other side of the world in an express airship.

"Yes, please," said Alice.

"Then drink the elixir," Dinah commanded briskly, rubbing herself against a vial of something dark. Alice noticed that Doris the Cook was engaged in conversation with a pony, which was shaking its head and neighing – *or naying*, thought Alice.

"It wasn't made by Doris, was it?" asked Alice in a whisper.

"No, dear," purred Dinah. "The formula is only known to a few, and not to her."

Taking a deep breath, Alice lifted the vial and drank the contents, which (to her great relief) did not taste like ink. The elixir had a fairly pleasant aftertaste of almonds, actually . . .

Which lingered in Alice's mouth when she opened her eyes to find herself inside the walled garden to which she had been denied entrance. What a place it was! A band of octopi, squid and lobsters played music with a strong beat and a kind of warbling melody (*as though heard underwater*, thought Alice) while groups of people and animals strolled among the trees and flowerbeds, which all emitted a potpourri of different fragrances.

Alice herself was attracting quite a bit of attention from a circle of bystanders, including the Mad Hatter, the March Hare, the Duchess (once Mistress to Doris), the disgraced Knave of Hearts, and a number of young men in the same livery, with numbers on their foreheads.

"What a fetching Birthday Suit," said the Mad Hatter, looking at Alice with a gleam in his eyes.

Alice was completely naked! "Don't cover your nipples, darling," coaxed the Knave of Hearts. "We all want to see them."

"That triangle of dark curly hair against her creamy thighs would do well as the focal point of her portrait, don't you think?" asked the Duchess. "Such chiaroscuro is worthy of the Italian masters."

"Where is Mr Dodgson the photographer?" asked one of the men in livery.

Alice felt very self-conscious, but the eyes of her admirers all seemed to be stroking her skin. Although she had never felt so exposed in all her life (not as long as it appeared – but then time seemed to pass so strangely here), the sensation was quite delightful, and not as humiliating as one would suppose. (*But then*, thought Alice, *I'm not on display in Bedlam, or in the executioner's cart.*)

Alice felt her long brown hair, as dark and shiny as ripe chestnuts, as a warm curtain over her shoulders and back. Looking down, she saw that her pink nipples were puckered from the breeze that continuously caressed them – but then, tingles in her skin and cunny (as she thought of it) produced the same effect. When she changed position even slightly, her breasts bounced. *That must be why women are supposed to wear corsets*, thought Alice, *to hold our bodies as still as statues*. She much preferred to be *au naturel*.

"I would gladly be condemned for stealing *this* tart!" said the Knave of Hearts. "Not that I ever did such a thing." His comment was greeted with a chorus of laughter.

Dinah brushed against one of Alice's arms, and the young woman became aware that she was reclining on one elbow like an artist's model. "Stand up, dear," murmured the cat, "then turn round slowly. Your admirers wish to see your legs, and your back view will certainly be of interest."

Alice stood up and curtseyed to her audience, feeling very odd to have to pose her arms gracefully, since she had no skirt to hold on to.

When Alice turned her back on her audience, she heard a collective sigh like an audible wish. She couldn't resist shaking her hips ever so slightly as she felt the heat of the general gaze on her buttocks. They felt quite fleshy to her, but then, a lady's derrière is meant to look exuberant.

"That's becoming," said the March Hare. "Why do young women like this ever wear clothes?"

"Of course it's becoming!" snapped the Mad Hatter, who was himself clad only in a loincloth like a Roman gladiator. "She's becoming herself, and that's why she's here. As for her clothes, you might as well ask why windows have shades."

"Well then, why—" began the March Hare, but he was silenced by a short blast on a trumpet played by the White Rabbit to announce the royal presence.

Since Alice had her back to her audience, she didn't see the King and Queen of Hearts approaching.

"She must certainly lose her head!" announced the Queen, in a voice that carried wonderfully throughout the garden, causing many others to pause in their activities and look in her direction.

Alice turned around so quickly that the ends of her hair fluttered like the fringe of a shawl. "I beg your pardon, Your Majesties!" she gasped, covering her breasts with both hands while curtseying.

"Your maidenhead, my dear," explained the King. "You must lose that, but why would you want to keep it while being presented to Us?"

Because I'm afraid, thought Alice, but then she reminded herself that fears are meant to be overcome. And she had always wanted to make a good impression.

"Alice," murmured Dinah, "you're here to become a woman. You don't have to accept the touch of anyone who displeases you, but the more fucking you take, the more prestige you acquire. You could become a favorite at Court."

"May I test her for Your Majesties?" asked the Knave of Hearts.

"You may not," snapped the Queen, closing her fan closed for emphasis. "It's a woman's prerogative, or at least the *droit de la reine*. Such testing is completely unthinkable in the world above, and therefore it cannot be badly thought of. *Honi soit qui mal y pense*," she finished grandly.

Alice guessed that this motto must mean: *The more honey we collect, the more we get paid for it.*

The Knave opened up a portable throne and placed a cushion on the seat.

"I must gird my loins," said the Queen. She removed her skirt and stood in a pair of pantalettes, with a harness around her hips. Set into the harness was a slender *godemiché* or dildo made of bone but covered in white silk, embroidered with the royal monogram.

"Come here, maiden Alice," commanded the Queen.

"Yes, Your Majesty?" asked Alice. She was not sure what was expected of her, but her self-consciousness had formed itself into a burning in her cunny, which now felt as moist as a mouth that expects to be fed.

"Would you like to sit facing me, or back to front?"

Alice was now standing quite close to the Queen, whose features were more handsome than delicate, and whose whole demeanor unnerved Alice, despite her desire to be deflowered and honored for it.

"Back to front, if it please Your Majesty," she answered.

"You please me greatly, my dear," said the Queen, smiling so broadly that she looked almost amiable. She wrapped her arms around Alice's backside and pulled her forward until Alice was standing between the Queen's knees. The Queen then held Alice's left breast and lifted it while bending down to bestow a long, sucking kiss on its hard little nubbin. She then switched sides to give its twin the same treatment.

"I could spend the whole day kissing you, Alice," she said, "but we have more serious business to attend to. You must sit on my lap and lower yourself onto my love-spear until you are fully seated like a general in the saddle. It will hurt you a little the first time, but once the deed is done, you will be glad for it."

Alice climbed onto the Queen's lap, and found that even the royal thighs were hard under their thin covering. Nervously, Alice reached back and positioned the *godemiché* so that it barely penetrated her lower lips. As the Queen held her arms to steady her, Alice began a slow backward descent.

"Go, Alice!" shouted one of the men in livery.

"Be brave, Alice!" urged the Knave.

"Open yourself for me, darling!" added the Mad Hatter.

"Courage, dear!" said Dinah, the throbbing rhythm of a heartbeat faintly audible in her voice.

The group of onlookers began clapping in rhythm as Alice lowered herself, inch by inch, onto the very solid object that forged a path where none had gone before. "Oh!" she said, feeling a burning tear deep inside her. Luckily, the fluid she had produced earlier helped pave the way.

Alice was determined not to give up until the thing was fully lodged inside her. At length, the cheeks of her bottom sat directly on the muscles of the Queen's thighs (*probably from all the riding she does*, thought Alice.)

"Ohh!" sighed Alice. "I can't go any farther."

"Well done, dear!" crowed the Duchess, clapping enthusiastically. All the rest followed suit, as indeed they should, since some of them were playing cards before their own transformation.

"Are you sore, dear?" whispered the Queen.

"Yes, ma'am," whispered Alice. "I do hope this becomes easier."

The Queen laughed in answer, and stroked Alice's hair while holding her about the waist in a way that felt affectionate and possessive.

Lifting her bottom carefully off the Queen's lap, Alice was relieved to feel her cunny already adjusting to its new state. With help from the Queen, she stepped onto the grass, enjoying its familiar caress on the soles of her bare feet.

The Queen stood up and removed the *godemiché*, now streaked with watery blood. She held it aloft while the Duchess picked up the Queen's skirt and fastened it about her waist.

"Hip, hip, hooray!" shouted the Knave, and he was soon joined by all the rest.

"Well done, my dear," said the King. He embraced the Queen and kissed her heartily on the lips while the Knave folded up the portable throne and packed it into a small case, which could be used as a doorstop.

"Now, Alice, you may choose your next partner in the dance," said the Queen.

"Surely we take precedence," the King objected mildly.

The Duchess shook her sharp chin, which rather resembled a shovel. "Oughtn't our dear little slut receive our attentions in order? It would be thoughtless to fuck her before she has had a chance to heal." Everyone else turned to look at the Duchess, who had never been noted for her common sense before.

The King looked thoughtful. "Then our Knave, who is so fond of tasting things, may use his tongue on her and then we will teach her to use her mouth to give us pleasure. Sound educational principles result in a well-rounded pupil."

Everyone present agreed that Alice must be instructed in logical stages, and she was grateful for their thoroughness.

The Knave wrapped Alice in his arms and pressed his lips to hers. She was surprised to taste the sweetness of his, and willingly opened her mouth to let his tongue inside. The warmth of his invading flesh almost made her swoon, but he held her so tightly that she had no fear of falling. Gently withdrawing from her mouth, he looked lovingly into her eyes. "Alice dear," he said, "the best place to be gamahuched is the Rose Bower. Won't you let me convey you there?"

"I love roses," said Alice, "if it please Your Majesties."

"Go enjoy yourselves," said the King. "And we shall await your return."

In a trice, Alice was lying on her back under an archway of rose bushes that had been trained to bend gracefully and to give useful advice. "Spread your legs a little farther apart, dear," said a matronly rose as the Knave crouched over Alice to explore the mysteries of her lower mouth.

"Oh!" exclaimed Alice when the Knave's clever tongue found her little button of pleasure and coaxed it to grow larger. Carefully opening her outermost petals with one hand, he traced her slippery folds with his tongue, and delved as deeply into her as he could. When he gently nibbled her swollen button, she felt as if she could explode.

Alice could feel the Knave humming into her secret center, and then she could hear him . . . purring? Turning her head, Alice saw Dinah stretched beside her, watching the scene with emerald eyes that shone with grave amusement. Beneath the cat's steady purr, Alice could hear "tick-tick-tick".

As the roses filled the air with their scent, so did Alice. The

Knave breathed her essence as though it were the smell of a fresh tart – as indeed it was. And when he sucked on her button with all his strength, Alice cried out. She shivered in a paroxysm of ecstasy, and he thrust his hand into his codpiece to relieve his own bursting member.

Recovering herself somewhat, Alice watched in fascination. "Does it always stick out that way?" she asked the Knave.

"Only when it's inspired," he replied. "Oh Alice, won't you stroke him for me?"

After carefully observing the Knave's vigorous attention to his aroused cock, Alice slid her little hand around the Knave's pride and imitated his movements. Up and down her hand went as she marveled at the velvety smoothness of his skin over the iron hardness beneath. Under the cock she found two bags of flesh covered with hair, and she cautiously squeezed each in turn until she sensed that she was squeezing too tightly. Alice felt as if she were learning to play a musical instrument.

And so she was not surprised when the small opening in the head of the Knave's cock let out a sound like a steam whistle as liquid spilled forth from it. *It must be like a singing kettle*, thought Alice, *except that every man must carry one about all his life. How curious.* All things considered, Alice decided that she preferred being a woman.

Emerging from the Rose Bower, her hand clasped in that of the Knave, Alice looked about at the other revelers. She was enjoying the festivities immensely, but she dreaded seeing Doris the Cook. What if the odorous woman kissed Alice before she could be stopped? Alice was sure she would be sick.

When Alice and the Knave rejoined their party, a panorama of fucking greeted their sight. The Queen was planted on her hands and knees, clothed only in her skin, while the King knelt behind her, pumping his member in her as though trying to win a race. "Yes!" shouted the Queen. "We shall have an heir after all!"

"Here it comes, my love!" he shouted back. His hindquarters thrust with force when he reached his crisis. And the tail that twitched behind him showed that he was a bull, at least when seen from behind. The roar that came from his mouth confirmed that impression.

Queerest of all to Alice was the sight of the Duchess and her former cook, Doris, belly to back like spoons on the grass (*But that's really not so strange for them*, thought Alice), moaning a duet of carnal delight. On closer inspection, Doris could be seen plunging two fingers between the Duchess's legs, parting the matted hair that showed brown and grey in the sunlight. The two women moved together like dancers long accustomed to each other's movements, and Alice could see that neither found the other repulsive in the least.

"Shameless," said the Knave, sniffily.

"And rightly so," Alice replied, feeling as relieved as though she had escaped unharmed from a rubbish tip.

"Darling," sighed the Knave, "you shall only be fertile for thirty years or thereabouts. How many tartlets will you turn out for me?"

Alice looked about for Dinah, and saw her moving up and down beneath a larger cat that seemed to hover in the air as a grinning face, while its body appeared and reappeared in a rhythm like a pulse.

"The Cheshire Cat," said Alice aloud. "I musn't disturb them."

"Your firstborn is forfeit!" shouted the Queen, but Alice could not be sure to whom she was speaking.

Alice knew that the Knave was still under suspicion of theft and awaiting a retrial. "Perhaps we could wait a year or so before we place a dish in the oven," she told him. She knew how easily a baby could change itself into a pig and wondered whether, in such a case, time could be reversed to change the outcome – or the income, as it were.

Lanterns were being lit throughout the garden, like fireflies illuminating the twilight. The music had become discordant, consisting largely of a rhythmical clattering sound. "Alice!" called a hairy-legged faun who trotted toward her from a gap in a hedge.

"Alice!" shouted the King and Queen, together with all their servants.

"Alice!" mewed a chorus of cats.

"Alice!" squealed Doris and her erstwhile Mistress.

Alice opened her eyes, and found herself in bed with her nightgown twisted about her waist. A milk wagon clattered over the stones of the street below her bedroom window.

"Alice!" repeated her sister Mabel, shaking her. "Wake up or you'll be late for church!"

"Or I might be truant altogether," retorted Alice. "There are more things in heaven and earth than we've been told, Mabel." *They still treat me like a child here*, she thought, *although I'm nearly a woman. In a better climate, I would be a woman already.*

Dinah walked into the room, her tail forming a question mark above her back and her eyes glowing with complicity. Alice realized that she was no longer afraid of what she didn't know. She had gone below the surface of things, and found herself.

And she was very likely to learn more on her next visit.

The Too Beautiful Boy

Arthur Chappell

You might not think so to look at me now but I was once fit, rather than fat. In those days I was sceptical of all things paranormal, but that was before my sexual energies were drained like a barrel of fine wine by the worshippers of Lilith. It was a time of lust and unhealthy appetites, when I could eat and eat without putting weight on, and my passion drive was equally relentless.

I was born too beautiful. That may read like an egotistical boast but it is literally true and my beauty was a curse. When I was three, my mother went mad and tried to disfigure me with a razor blade. My father stopped her before she could cut my face open and she was sectioned under the British Mental Health Act. She died in the asylum soon afterwards. My father only told me of this on his deathbed when I was seventeen. Years before, he had told me that she had been killed in a car crash. My hedonism shocked his already breaking heart, but he died admitting that he would have made love to so many women too, had he shared my stamina and my looks.

My mother had been convinced that I would become vain and narcissistic. She had the wrong mythical archetype though. I was not Narcissus reborn, but the new Ganymede. His was the myth of being the most beautiful of male mortals – so much so that he was snatched from the Earth to serve as a plaything to the Olympian gods, and ultimately a sex slave to Zeus.

My destiny and damnation kept me from any arduous physical work. Building sites and warehouses were not for me. My hands were never to grow hardened and calloused through physical graft. At my Manchester University art course I was moved from being a student to being a life model for endless nude studies, mostly in the classical tradition. I was soon modelling for women's magazines and making a few pornographic movies too.

I rarely had to ask girls to go out with me on dates. They threw themselves at me. Many fainted at the merest glimpse of me. The professors dismissed several studies of me from the art classes as more explicit and erotic than aesthetic. I was a magnet for voyeurs, who would stare at me for hours, mesmerized. Many art students forgot to actually draw, paint or sculpt. They just gazed at me, entranced, drooling, and finding excuses to go out of the room to give themselves hand release.

Inevitably, there were girls to whom I just had to say no. Some regrettably took to self-harm, and at least two committed suicide over me. When I learned of that, I was tempted to disfigure myself, as my mother had tried to do to me, but I didn't have the guts.

I had many male admirers too, but after a brief, and far from unpleasant flirtation with homosexuality, I decided that I was more inclined to pursue the female form, or at least allow myself to be caught more easily by the ladies.

Finding bars where I could go for a quiet drink was quite a challenge. I was refused entry to many where I had flirted with the ladies or where those who had desired me had got into jealous catfights with each other. I left a trail of bitter lovesick rivalry everywhere I went.

In my late twenties, my increasingly insatiable lusts led me to a number of unconventional clubs and societies. I got into the swinging scene because its adherents were more sexually mature and aware. Such bars were also often dark, so I thought it would be easy to sit anonymously in the shadows. What I didn't realize was that some women hunt specifically in such shadows. Two such predators soon found me there. They were 'The Lilith', or Janet and Mary, to give them their independent identities. They both had a fixation on the Lilith myth, and competed to be known by that name.

Initially, I took them for twins, but they were not even sisters and not even related in any way. They had absorbed so much personality from each other that telling them apart was a daunting, though not impossible task. Looking closely, I saw Janet to be an inch taller, though she was a year younger than Mary. Janet was a spontaneous chatterbox, while Mary was thoughtful, introspective and reserved. When she spoke, she could make the most commonplace observation sound profound. She had a more commanding tone. Janet clearly obeyed her final wishes in all matters. There were many individual quirks and personality traits that betrayed their efforts to pass for one another's clones. The girls were reflections of one another's souls, if either had a soul, given their gothic fixation on all things Satanic and pagan.

They wore black – no surprises there, and their hair was set in spikes. Janet had a few purple streaks and, sure enough, Mary had set matching ones to her own. The girls wore short black skirts, with dark panties just visible when they sat down or danced fast. They wore torn fishnets and black boots. Each had an inverted Egyptian ankh round her neck, but relatively little mascara or lip gloss, giving them a natural pale look amidst the over-caked emos and goths posing and prancing around us.

I wore a plain black T-shirt and black jeans. I rarely made a special effort to dress up, other than in trying to disguise my looks. I once went to a fancy dress event as Quasimodo, but several Esmeraldas saw through the disguise quickly.

The Lilith and I danced, shared a few margaritas, and then they positively insisted that I should accompany them back to their place. I sensed from the start of our relationship that I was the guinea pig in some kind of scheme concocted by the ladies. I was being probed, assessed and validated. I seemed to pass the secret tests as the girls increased their interest in me as the night progressed. There were too many knowing glances between them, too many whispers and near telepathic exchanges of information. I caught words like "chosen", and "he is definitely the one" over the loud music. I was tempted to ask them bluntly what was going on, but I kept my paranoia to myself. Words like "slaughtered lamb" sprang to mind, but I was too curious to get myself away from them.

The taxi ride to their place saw me sandwiched between the ladies who sat like bodyguards or kidnappers throughout. Occasionally, their hands brushed over my swelling cock and patted it approvingly. "Soon, soon," Mary whispered greedily, as if not wanting the cabbie to hear.

I half expected them to live in a ruined castle in North Manchester, which would have been absurd. They actually owned a terraced house on a semi-cobbled street in the Charlestown district. The door didn't creak. There was no Igor-like manservant to welcome us in. There were no thunderclaps to punctuate my arrival. It was a typical goth-girl house, ornamented with vampire movie figurines, and with walls decorated in posters of various musicians, and with shelves filled with books on the occult and horror literature. One title struck out at me right away, *Victim Mine!* by Mary Trevory. I hadn't thought to ask the girls their professions. Mary was a horror story author. Janet, when I asked her now, proved to be a failed literature student who had undertaken a research paper on the phenomenally successful young author and her overnight commercial fame. I have to confess that I had never heard of Mary until that moment.

Most of the books were modern, though there was one dusty old volume, called something like *The Necromonicon*, which the girls said they had found in a second-hand gift shop. I was about to browse through its pages when Mary snatched it from me and took it out of the room, as Janet French-kissed me in what I took to be something of a deliberate distraction, without knowing why.

Janet had fallen in love with the author while staying with her to get insight into the writer's mind. Her all too emotional proximity to her subject had got her thrown off her course and her project had not been finished. Janet now made her own clothes for the goth culture market. Two old-fashioned sewing machines and several of her garments in preparation dominated the main living room, along with a plasma screen TV and a cluttered heap of horror movie DVDs.

One other thing stood out in the otherwise ordinary environment – among the easily acquired mass-produced commercial posters, was a nineteenth-century Post-Expressionist painting. It depicted an ageing naked man, with wilting penis, surrounded by naked women, who had all turned their backs on him, as if no longer caring for his advances now that he was effectively less desirable or virile.

"Like it?" Janet asked.

"It's different," I said, finding the image rather sad and haunting.

Mary spoke, having returned without making her footsteps audible on the stairs. "It's by Ronald Montroy. It's called *The Castrated Casanova*. I bought it at an auction with my first royalties cheque."

They offered me a drink. I settled on a cold beer, they drank vodka. I asked them when they were going to sacrifice me to Satan or drink my blood. They laughed and offered to share a bath with me instead.

I got naked. They stripped to their underwear. Janet had a black bra with words in red on each nipple cup – "Bitch" on the left; "Witch" on the right. Mary had a red bra with the same words in black on each breast, but with "Bitch" on the right cup and "Witch" on the left. I knew that they had left the bras on deliberately to show off some of Janet's fashion work. I was impressed, and even more impressed when instead of removing the bras, the girls just pulled the cups down to expose their breasts, and invited me to feel them and express my approval.

They had replaced their bathtub with a large Jacuzzi, and we got in. We had considered filling it with water, but we were too turned on by each other to bother turning on the taps. The girls played at vampires around me. They argued over which one was Lilith that night. They decided that they both were in the end. They fought, but I took the blows. I was a pawn between two dominatrix queens. Each time one brought me close to climax, the other pulled me out of her partner to draw me into herself. I was a rag doll and a total slave and I have to admit that I loved every minute of it. They used me as the parcel in a pass-the-parcel game – seeing which one I was going to be inside when I finally came, while they kept me from coming as long as they possibly could.

The girls entwined themselves around each other and me like serpents. Janet's legs wrapped round my waist and half-way round Mary's too. Mary pressed against my back with her hand partly into my anus and partly into her cunt. Janet's thrusts against my dick helped to push Mary deeper into herself and against me too. Mary's posture helped to keep Janet and I from slipping away from each other. It was short and potent sex. No man could avoid coming quickly like this. I erupted quickly into Mary, declaring her the winner of the game and then the girls switched sides, and I was soon doing exactly the same thing for Janet, as a consolation prize.

Behind me, as Janet licked my chest hair, I heard Mary moving some kind of glass container. I half expected that she had reached for her vodka, but a glance in the mirror showed that she had moved a little of the sperm that had spilt onto her thigh into a small pill bottle, preserving my seed as if planning on examining it under a microscope. I was about to turn to ask what was going on, but Janet bit into my shoulder and grinned, as she drew my hands against her breasts. I quickly forgot to challenge their strange behaviour.

I sank back, exhausted and worn down. I felt the water start to fill the tub, and the girls, now out of the Jacuzzi, soothed my shoulders and soaped me down, telling me to relax. I got so relaxed that I couldn't remember going to bed with them naked on either side of me, but at some point I did.

The girls woke and went downstairs early. I was left to sleep in as long as I needed, and somehow, I really did need to. I wasn't working, as it was now Saturday. I lazed and nodded off again, at which point a terrible dream hit me. I saw myself masturbating while thinking of Lilith, the vampire queen who was woman before Eve. She called to me, "Come, Ganymede, do not be afraid." As if on command, my sperm erupted from me in a gushing white torrent that flooded out, submerging the room, Lilith, and I were drowning, drowning, drowning ... I woke in a hot flush, stifling a scream.

I got up and slipped into the bathroom. My dick was relaxed and, stepping into the hot shower, I woke it up, determined to check that I could still masturbate normally. I dreaded the effect of ejaculation imitating my dream, but I gave normal release, weaker than usual if anything for having made love to two amazing women all night. I calmed down; half-confident that it had just been a nightmare after all.

Janet prepared a light breakfast for us all, while Mary offered a proposal for our next date. "We frequently go to a private club," she said. "A very intense fetish and BDSM bar called The Lust Lounge. We loosely model it on the Hellfire Club – Sir Francis Dashwood's notorious eighteenth-century satanic debauchery society. There are lots of other Lilith wannabes there who would love to meet you. Care to come along a week on Saturday?"

I was tempted to find some excuse to say no, but the girls fascinated me. Many recent dates had been with girls who had rushed me to give them orgasm quickly, and had become possessive and clingy. Janet and Mary seemed more relaxed and took their time in savouring my flesh. They had a tantric fascination for keeping men from orgasm for as long as possible. I found myself agreeing to go along despite my apprehension. I was instructed to meet the girls at the gothic singles club where I had first met them, at around about 9.30 p.m., on the Saturday arranged.

I left their house soon after breakfast, with hugs and kisses by both girls and a final squeeze of my balls by Mary. It was a squeeze that seemed to tell me that they belonged to her now, rather than to me.

*   *   *

The long gap before my next meeting with the Lilith girls and what was my date with my truly terrible destiny passed slowly, beginning with a recurrence of the nightmare in which I drowned in my own semen.

My work suffered. I was restless and unable to keep still. Seeing the canvases and statues of me, I noticed that the keen-eyed students picked up a sense of fear and apprehension in my eyes, though I failed to see it in the mirror.

To pass the time, I picked up a copy of Mary Trevory's novel, *Victim Mine!*, which was readily available in the shops. It told of a young novelist selling her soul to Succubae in return for inspiration, before gaining overnight success, and seducing her leading fans into cult-like reverence and imitation of her. She was a cannibal who devoured her fans or sacrificed them to her Succubae.

I expected good to triumph in the end and the narrator to face some Dorian Gray like comeuppance, but she remained triumphantly evil and immoral throughout.

I looked up the publisher's author biography. Mary Trevory had herself risen to fame overnight, with few previous writings to her name. I found myself wondering if her chief follower in the book was modelled on someone like Janet. More interesting was an internet biography's reference to her family history – her maiden name had been Montroy before her short-lived first marriage. I realized that Mary had been dishonest about the origins of *The Castrated Casanova* painting. It was a family heirloom – not an auction purchase. Her husband had left her, claiming that she believed the rubbish she wrote and kept praying to Satan and other demons. He had freaked out and fled. Some months later he had died in a mysterious fire.

I looked up Montroy, the artist online, and found surprisingly few references to him. His shocking and uncompromisingly explicit images of sodomy, emasculation and castration had been seen as highly seditious and the Catholic Church had arrested him for heresy. While languishing in prison, awaiting his trial, he had been attacked by fellow inmates. His testicles and buttocks had been severed and he had been choked to death with them. Copies of his paintings had later been systematically hunted down, and destroyed by order of the Vatican. Few if any were believed to still exist.

The reading and research kept me from sleeping and therefore kept the recurring nightmares away. I had one during a brief involuntary nap caused by sheer exhaustion, in which Janet and Mary tugged and pulled at my dick and snapped off a testicle each, which they then devoured raw.

The night before my fateful visit to the Lust Lounge, I found myself again slipping into sleep. Rashly, I tried to stay awake by watching a horror movie, *The Wicker Man*, which only fuelled my anxieties further. At least I was no virgin sacrifice like the doomed hero in that story.

The dream came as soon as my eyelids closed. Again, the writer and her loyalist supporter were pulling at my dick, and I was about to erupt in torrents once more, when a strange fat naked male figure grasping a wine bottle and a bunch of grapes appeared in their midst. The ladies shrieked and fled, like vampires confronted with a crucifix. He smiled and whispered to me, "The Lilith lie to you as they lie with you. There will still be love in your life after the events at the Lust Lounge. Put your faith in me and do as I say and you will be spared."

I woke before he could tell me who he was or what he planned to say. If there was some clue in his mannerism and words, I had failed to comprehend it.

With hours to go before my trip to BDSM land, I looked up Lilith online. Lilith was, as I vaguely knew, the true first woman created before Adam. The Bible barely refers to or mentions her story at all, but some ancient Hebrew texts preserve the myths. Her independent-mindedness and vitality made her a formidable woman, and Adam was unable to keep up with her needs. He was afraid of her and wanted more control in his relationship. Worse, every one of his sperm impregnated her and she gave birth to millions of children – each cursed by God as she herself was cast down and away to be replaced by Eve at Adam's prayer of request. The Mother of all monsters became an immortal Succubus, draining the seed of men and struggling to feed and nurture her weak, and dying offspring. Hers was the eternal sorrow of mourning as news of her dying children reached her daily. The Old Testament Leviathan and Behemoth were said to be among her children. Despite the revisionist efforts of biblical scholars to eradicate knowledge of her, Lilith was the subject of several powerful cults in the early Roman Catholic era. The Catholics responded to the cult much as the Romans had, treating them with merciless persecution and massacre. Less organized than the Christian Martyrs, the sisters of Lilith were easily crushed or driven underground. They dared not give Lilith her own feast days so they hijacked and tried to revive the feast of Bacchus (the Roman name for Dionysus), trying to make the Bacchanalia their own. Unfortunately, the followers of Bacchus were reluctant to let their feast be taken over by the Mother of Monsters, so the Sisters of Lilith found themselves facing new persecution – and the two fledgling cults seem to have caused their own mutually assured destruction when they ought to have united against their common foe – the Catholic fathers.

Bacchus was the God of wine, and madness – he represents hedonism, Bohemianism and excess, and also the inevitable consequences of such indulgences. I had been enjoying that which he represented for so long without any acknowledgment of his name, and I felt guilty. The websites about him offered links to pictorial art representations of him – somehow I knew before I clicked on them that I would see pictures of the man who had whispered to me in my dream the night before. Worse, his feasts of old were traditionally held on 16 March – the very date on which I was to go to the Lust Lounge.

I was astonished and disturbed by my reading. It was all-fascinating, but I was scared that I found any of this mythology relevant to my own life and predicament, if indeed I had a predicament. When all was said and done, I was only invited to an orgy. I had never been religious, though mythical reference and analogies had followed me all my life. I had been left convinced that my beauty was in some way preordained and that some great monumental event was ahead of me. I sensed strongly that my fate would present itself at the Lust Lounge, and now was the time for me to prepare myself for my journey there.

I got to the singles bar a few minutes before our rendezvous, and calmed my nerves with a gin and tonic. I wore the same dark jeans and black T-shirt I had worn at our first meeting. Unusually, none of the many beautiful girls in the bar seemed to notice me, let alone flirted with me. I would normally have been the centre of attention by now. I thought of the painting of poor castrated Casanova again. I imagined my face taking the place of his.

My disturbing reverie was soon interrupted. Janet walked in, and came straight towards me. She wore a slinky black catsuit. She snatched up my gin and tonic and gulped it down in one. "The taxi awaits. Mary is sitting in the back. Join us now."

It was the tone of a true dominatrix in the making. I shrugged and followed. I hoped regulars in the bar would notice my presence in the company of the sex bomb. It might help the police investigation if my mangled body was found later. Part of me wanted to run like hell, but on the whole I wanted the strange, sinister situation to come to an end. In fact, my adventures were only beginning.

We got into the taxi with me sandwiched between the identically dressed girls who acted like silent arresting officers.

"Shouldn't you blindfold me so I can't divulge the location of your secret base?" I asked half jokingly.

Janet shook her head. "What would be the point?" she asked.

I didn't respond to that. I seriously wondered if my death would follow whatever the ladies intended to do to me.

The déjà vu taxi ride took us close to Mary's house, and then about three miles north of it to an abandoned crumbling church. There were several cars and a few motorbikes parked in the grounds, and on the overgrown cemetery grass.

St Jude's looked like an ancient crumbling Saxon church. And it was named after the patron saint of lost causes. In fact, its history was more modern. Mary told me about it.

"It was raised in the twenties. It was a fine local parish church until the war. In 1940, during an air raid at the height of the Blitz, an ARP warden spotted some lights shining in the church. He rushed in to warn them about the strict blackout rules. He stumbled into a satanic black mass – there were pentagrams, swastikas and two slaughtered goats. He got help and arrests were made. The ringleaders were hanged as Fifth Columnist spies. The church was closed in disgrace over the scandal. It just got left to rot. The grounds slowly encroached and reclaimed much of the stonework as you can see. The grounds remained quite lovely, and many people came here for romantic picnics with their lovers. In the nineties, the church became a place to hold wild rave parties and sell ecstasy tabs. By 2003, the Sisters Of Lilith had taken over. I bought the church and turned it into the Lust Lounge."

She owned the place. Wow! That was a surprise.

We got out of the taxi. I paid the fare, and we walked over the gravel path and inside through the dark arched entrance.

I expected to see a wretched cobweb-strewn crypt, full of dust, detritus, rats and spiders, with a few skeletons on display. Instead, I was presented with a well-lit mock-marble palatial hall. Old pillars had been wrapped in cloth dyed in the colours of Romanesque columns – it was like seeing a ballroom disguised as the venue for a toga party. I had arrived at a pretend Roman villa. Mary and her Lilith cult followers had undoubtedly gone to a lot of trouble to create such an effect. It seemed tacky, but practical. Candles provided much of the lighting.

Two things stood out for inescapable attention. The first was the large painted canvas beside the entrance chamber – and from its similar style to that of *The Castrated Casanova*, I could tell that it was by the same artist and Mary's ancestor, Ronald Montroy.

Mary smiled. "You recognize it. Good. It's called *The Blood*

Of Chronos. An emasculated god, seeping blood from his ruptured genitals across the gulfs of space – as the torrent swept across the canvas, it becomes planets and stars and solar systems. Zeus seems to be swallowing the severed member of his own father, while the other gods look down on the forming universe. An hourglass gives the suggestion that when Chronos's blood finally runs out and he has bled to death, time itself will end."

I gulped. The Lilith were obsessed with castration art. I wondered if I'd be going home with my testicles in a doggy bag, if I was allowed out at all.

The other inescapable sight was the orgy that had already begun well before our arrival. The floor was a sea of writhing, mostly naked human flesh. People rolled over and into each other and many seemed to be covered in baby oil.

By the far walls, many fat balding naked men stood watching, and grinning. My initial thought was of Bacchus, but then I noticed that the men had no genitals. Bacchus was always depicted as spectacularly well endowed. These men simply had smooth pelvic areas, like children's action dolls. They seemed like crude parodies of Bacchus. I suspected that given the rivalry between Lilith and Bacchus, the look was a deliberate crude parody of the wine-god.

"Where the fuck did you get all the eunuchs from?" I asked.

Mary laughed. "You'd be surprised how many men get turned on by voluntarily becoming eunuchs, even in this day and age."

"That's not what you plan to do to me is it?"

Janet giggled. "Oh no! We need your meat and two veg intact."

"Then what exactly are you planning on doing with me?"

My question was ignored. Mary pointed to the orgy. "Take your clothes off and join in if you like."

I was surprised. "May I?"

Janet nodded. "Yes, but don't come. We need you fully charged up for us shortly. Pull away from anyone who brings you close to ejaculation. The antics in my bathroom last weekend were a test to see if you could prolong the time before erupting, so I know you can keep it all in for me. Do that now. Promise us that you can and will."

I promised, and the ladies removed my clothes. Mary took my pants and shoes and socks. Janet drew my shirt over my head.

"Go on in, big boy," Mary said, as they turned to walk off to a side room.

"Aren't you joining me?"

Janet shrugged. "Not yet. We have work to do, preparing the grand finale. You'll be summoned shortly. Meanwhile, relax. Have fun."

"But don't come, remember!" Mary added, with more than a hint of threatening aggression.

I stepped gingerly into the writhing maelstrom of bodies, concerned about stepping on someone if I moved too quickly. I had barely gone a few feet when someone grabbed my ankles and pulled me down beside herself. My first kiss aimed to her lips missed when a buttock hit my shoulder blades, but the girl pulled me closer in towards herself and we got it right.

The girl grabbed for my balls, and I realized for the first time how erect I was – at this rate not coming was going to be impossible. I was wondering what to do. Instinctively, drawing inspiration almost from nowhere, I whispered to her harshly, "Leave those alone. Mary's orders."

The girl quickly let go. "You're him! You're the one! Oh, you lucky bastard!"

"Care to share any clues about what's in store for me?"

"I can't," she said. "Mary's orders."

Someone licked my feet. Hands tweaked the hairs on my chest. Female thighs came down on either shoulder, owned by the woman drawing her cunt close to docking with my tongue, but before we engaged, other admirers pulled her away to join in some entertainment or other in the madding fornicating crowd.

I felt something sliding against and into my backside. A jet of warm liquid erupted into me. I couldn't come, but others could come in and on me. I turned to see who had taken me, but it was impossible to tell with so many people enjoying themselves in close proximity to me.

A girl began to bite hungrily at my nipples, sucking almost as if she expected to milk me. A eunuch aqua-glided over the people around us, swimming effortlessly between the bodies and nudged her aside.

"Easy, tigress – save some for the rest of us."

He took her place in my arms, mumbling something about a gentleman's excuse me.

"You're joining in the orgy?" I asked, incredulous. Most of the eunuchs stayed in the sidelines acting as referees and, in some cases, spraying the baby oil from fire extinguisher canisters, lubricating and cooling down the revellers. I was soaked too, and people slithered over me as if we were all made of soap.

The eunuch grinned. "Why not? My dick has gone but the rest of me still feels."

I looked at the smooth, hair-free, scar-free plain of flesh between his thighs. I even felt compelled to touch him there. I felt the blood pounding against the mound, blood that would normally have filled the penis muscle and given the man one hell of an erection.

"The blood remembers," he said, and then I found myself holding his cock – a cock that hadn't existed seconds before.

I let go, as if it was a poisonous snake. The eunuch laughed. "Don't be afraid," he whispered. "As I told you before, you will love again. Oh, yes. That was me talking to you in your dreams. I am here to protect you."

"Oh fuck!"

"No, don't fuck. The Lilith really do need your sperm."

"So why don't I just empty it all out here? I can't contain myself much longer anyway."

"Don't empty out whatever you do, or you will die."

"They'd really kill me?"

"Yes, they would, and they intend to destroy you, but if you ejaculate now, I'll kill you myself. Obey all their instructions. I will be there to protect you. As another god you may have heard of might say, have a little faith, baby."

"Why me?"

"You are the most beautiful man in the world, David – besides, you were conceived here in this church."

"What?"

"Your mother and father came in here to shelter from a storm that blew up on an apparently clear day. They had no idea that Mary and her minions had cast spells to enchant the spot on which they ended up making love. The storm itself was her doing. Your destiny was established the very second you were created that day."

So many shocking revelations were hitting me at once that I could barely think. I was lost and disorientated in the maelstrom of writhing bodies, buffeted by everyone around me. So Mary was much older than she looked. And she had caused the distress that led to my mum's insanity. I would kill the evil witch if I got the chance.

I questioned the eunuch's claims. "She'd have to be about fifty now."

"Mary is about seven hundred and fifty years old."

"Seven hundred and fifty?"

"Oh yes. Mary wasn't distantly descended from Montroy – she was his immediate daughter. Her mother was a Succubus. And Janet was her earliest convert."

"That's impossible."

"And a eunuch with a cock who talks to you in your dreams is perfectly possible, is it?"

"Jesus Christ!"

"Wrong god, David. Wrong god."

A gong sounded – the sort that announces dinner is served in some country mansions. There were groans and moans and people around us started to stand up.

"The warm-up orgy is over," Bacchus said, helping me to my feet. We stood quietly, virtually at attention, as if awaiting further instructions. Janet now walked into the hall – she was totally naked.

"Bring the Ganymede forward," she said. "The rest of you men may leave us now. I hope you enjoyed yourselves and thank you for coming. "

The men started to head off to find their clothes. The eunuch who was Bacchus stepped forward, beckoning me to follow. All trace of his magnificent genitalia had vanished again. The men and women around us stepped back to allow us an easy path to the side alcove where Janet waited for us. We followed her through a short gloomy corridor to a room with an old oak door. The door slid open and we went inside. It was only now that I realized that most, if not all, of the fifty still naked women who had been at the orgy had silently followed us. The only men were the eunuch and myself.

The door closed behind us. Janet locked it.

After the well-lit orgy room, the darkness of a more basic BDSM chamber was more than a little disturbing.

Candles were lit, and the room brightened enough to allow me to see the nature of my destiny. The floor was polished stone, marked with a wide circle that filled most of the room. Lines radiated out from a central pentagram, on which Mary stood naked. The lines ran to fifty small blood red circles and the women approached these circles to take their places, standing on them. Janet moved last of all, taking a place on a single slightly larger circle.

Mary stood naked and entranced in the centre, like a medium conducting a séance, as the eunuch followed her instructions. Above us, tied to the ceiling by ropes, there was a black leather hammock like a cradle. The eunuch lowered it, almost to the floor, and instructed me to get in, lying face down, with my throbbing cock poking through the hole at its centre.

Getting into the still-swaying rig was tricky, and though every instinct told me to refuse, I did it. I lay flat out, and felt my engorged cock slip through the hole. My head stuck out one end allowing me to see what went on, and my bare feet stuck out of the back. I was barely in when the eunuch winched me up so I was about five feet above the ground.

I wondered what nature my doom would take. I expected Mary to produce a blade, and cut my balls off and bathe in my blood as I died.

The girls remained ominously silent and, for a moment, so did Mary. The eunuch was clearly there merely to assist with apparatus and maintain crowd control if needed. He stood quietly to one side of the circle now, as if his work was done. Mary clearly had no idea that he was Bacchus incarnate. In hiring his caricatures, she had unwittingly allowed him to come along to deal with her personally. I found myself silently praying to him – he was my only hope of safety in all this diabolical madness.

After a moment, Mary began to recite something in what sounded like cod-Latin or gibberish. I knew that I was listening to some kind of ancient witchcraft spell. She knew it by heart. She had no books or papers before her.

The epic prayer to dark forces ended, and the girls collectively yelled, "So must it be." Mary now grabbed my cock and used it to set me swinging like a pendulum out from the inner to the outer circle. I swung out towards a girl standing close to Janet, who reached up and touched my dick gently with her fingertips, before licking her fingers. She sat down, whispering, "I am Lilith," and spread her legs, exposing her cunt to the centre of the circle, where Mary still stood. Pushed back, I came again to the centre, where Mary used my dick to once more push me to the rim of the circle, where another girl touched my dick lightly, and then sat down in the same posture as the first girl. Again, the words, "I am Lilith," were whispered. One by one, the girls did this as I swung back and forward, guided by Mary from the centre. At no stage did I miss my target. No girl failed to catch me. It was as if some supernatural force guided my trajectory – I felt like the glass on an Ouija board.

Soon, the regular touches to my already highly excited dick set my juices flowing and I knew that I would have to come very soon. Resistance was now impossible. There were few girls left standing – in fact, there were only Janet and Mary.

Janet seemed to grab my dick harder and longer than any girl had before her and she finally reluctantly pushed me back towards Mary and sat down with her legs spread out.

Mary began to lie back in the circle now, as I approached. The cradle drew to a halt right above her. My dick was pointing down directly above her open cunt, like a Damoclean sword, and now I could resist no longer. I came.

It was as violent, but not as gushing, as the ejaculations in my dreams. The fluids streamed out of me. By rights, they should have soaked all over Mary alone. Only a modest stream seeped down into her. Most of the semen defied gravity and spread out, following the ley lines of the circle, to penetrate the open cunts of every woman in the circle at once. I felt them all – I felt as if I was actually making love to them rather than sending my semen across such a distance. I was inside each and every girl, and felt their pussies undulating and taking me in. Their reactions were those of women in deep orgasm.

Only Mary and Janet seemed to be in different states of mind – they screamed as if being burnt, or in sheer unadulterated terror. As the women's orgasms abated around them and the girls lay back in tranquillizing bliss, as if they had been partly anaesthetized, I watched the Witch Queen and her High Priestess stand and shake and tremble violently. Something was clearly going hideously wrong for them.

I looked and saw Mary literally disintegrate, and convulse as if she was touching high voltage cables. Her eyes melted. Her torso collapsed, staved in by some unseen force and her head imploded like bubble wrap in the hands of a geek. Within a minute, she was a heap of biomes on the floor. I looked to my left and saw a similar skeleton – Janet had shared her friend's terrible fate. The other girls watched in terror, shrieked and collectively fled from the room.

"What happened?" I asked of Bacchus who watched the whole thing as if it was happening on a movie screen for his entertainment.

"They received the death they planned for you. The Lilith

was impregnated, but I corrupted your sperm. Traces of my sperm were still dripping on the end of your cock. I poisoned them with my seed. Their centuries caught them up quickly."

"What about the other women? Are they safe?"

"Safe and pregnant, all fifty of them, but the children of the Lilith carry a terrible curse."

"What have you done?"

"Lilith hopes to spread more monsters throughout the human race, but her sons will only get to make love once before they die. Think of it like the sting of the bee – once fired, the bee dies along with its prey, though with Lilith's bees, the women impregnated will not be harmed. They will carry another generation of boys doomed to perish after their only chance to make love. I will tell them of that in their dreams before they get sex – they must choose between celibacy and a pleasure that will lead to rapid painful death."

I was angry. I grabbed the eunuch by the throat. "They are my children."

Bacchus laughed and advised me to look at my hand. I did. It was wrinkled and calloused. It was a middle-aged man's hand. I let go of the god's throat and felt my face. It was no longer smooth and unblemished. I even had traces of a beard.

"What have you done to me?"

"You did this to yourself – it is life that takes its toll on us. You were preserved from the ravages of time by Mary's enchantments, but the enchantments are broken. That which killed Mary has aged you."

"I'm old and ugly?"

"No! Don't be so vain. You look like an ordinary middle-aged man who has overindulged in wine, women and song. You will still be loved, as I promised. Here, let me show you a mirror."

Bacchus turned into a large mirror. I saw little of its ornate frame – I was too focused on my reflection. I had a slight beer gut, and a receding hairline. My cock seemed mercifully as strong as ever given the amount of energy I had just released.

The mirror vanished and Bacchus returned. "Did you tell anyone you were coming here?" he asked.

I shook my head.

"Good. I thought not. Find your clothes and leave. Never return. When you have left I will burn this place to the ground. Mary's house will also be destroyed tonight. You will probably never see or hear from me again, but pray to me as you dine, drink and fuck, won't you? "

Before I could answer, he disappeared. In the time it takes to blink, he had simply gone.

I got dressed and found a taxi passing by on the road close to the church grounds. I went home. I spent the weekend in a fit of depression, wondering what to do with my life from now on. I wanked a few times, to check I still could without pouring out several gallons of semen. There was nothing wrong in that sense.

I phoned in sick to the art department and saw my doctor to check that I was OK. He was the first man who knew me to see me since I had aged. He was naturally astonished. I was worried that I might make medical history, and draw attention to myself, but he attributed my change of physique to the ravages of the flu. He advised me to stay off work for a few weeks. I was happy to oblige. I was wondering if I would ever be allowed to work again, given the nature of my job.

Financially, I gained some security by selling *The Blood of Chronos* canvas I had torn from its frame before leaving St Jude's. I was not going to leave that to burn. It went on eBay for thousands. Sadly, the companion painting at Mary's house probably died in the fire there.

I did lose a lot of my freelance modelling and film work jobs due to my radical change of appearance, but the main university assignments kept going. Their code of political correctness prevented them discriminating against a change of appearance that was, technically speaking, a disability.

The artists came to me to ask what had happened. I knew I would never have old friends approaching me with "haven't seen you for a while, but you haven't changed a bit". I told them the influenza story. They were full of genuine commiseration.

The paintings and sculptures made of me now reflected my tragedy – a youth whose looks had faded suddenly. I could see the dreamy look in the eyes of girls who lamented not getting to date me before the rot set in.

I seriously wondered if I would get to date a girl again or ever make love once more. Bacchus had promised me that I would. He spoke the truth. There was a new girl in class, who seemed to like me for who I was, rather than for who I had been. She had raven hair down to her shoulders and her eyes stared at me in intense curiosity and a hint of pity. She knew that something unusual had occurred in my life – something possibly awful – and she seemed to admire me for coming through it OK, and to appreciate the air of mystery that surrounded me.

Shyly, I invited her for a drink after lessons. She accepted. I took her to a quiet bar and we hit it off. Our lovemaking was gentle rather than tempestuous. We are going steady now. Her name is Lillian. Thank you Bacchus.

I should have guessed the significance of that name right away – Lily, Lillian, Lilith. It was only a week or so into our increasingly passionate relationship when she asked me when I was going to start thinking about how to protect my sons that I realized it really was her.

"Were you among the girls in that room that night?"

"No, but I was watching from afar. The cult of Lilith did not have my blessing. There are many sects that act in my name. None but you know the real me."

"But you left it to Bacchus to stop them. Why didn't you intervene?"

"He had the situation under control. I saw no reason to interfere. Now, however, his cruel punishment of my unborn stepchildren is a little harsh. I'll have to make sure the boys grow up wisely. I'll probably need your help, as you are the father. Are you with me?"

"Will Bacchus approve?"

"No. We'll deal with him if we have to. Are you with me?"

I found myself agreeing to help her.

"Good," she said, kissing me full on the lips. "Such support deserves a reward. Look in the mirror."

I went to my bedroom mirror and saw that my good, Ganymede looks had returned. I laughed and cried at the same time.

"Now come to bed and fuck me," Lillian commanded. I didn't need asking twice.

Peek Hour

Adrea Kore

Her favourite time of day.

The escalators sigh downward, spilling forth the tired tides of office workers onto the subway platform. The less room there is, the more excited Roxy becomes. No matter that she is standing, and no seats remain as people wait and pace and stare at the incoming train times on the screens.

Peak hour.

Roxy is an expert at getting a seat on the train. That's where it's essential to be seated. She has developed this into an art form. Sometimes she is a visibly pregnant woman. Other times, she has too many shopping bags and walks with a limp, wincing slightly at each step until someone offers her their seat.

Seven minutes late, the train arrives, sidling almost guiltily into its place beside the platform. Today, Roxy is wearing a summer dress and sandals, and has one ankle bandaged. She hobbles through the open door, looking expectantly left, then right.

She tries not to count the number of businessmen already inside her carriage; tries to ignore the thrill on her skin as two men in suits brush against her. A tall man, seeing her inca-pacitated ankle, stands up and offers her his seat. She smiles her "thank you" and sits down.

Finally. She is eye level with her favourite subject.

She pulls out a newspaper, as the train pulls out of the station. Her mind, however, is not on the news of the day, but rather, the views of the day.

Roxy is a connoisseur of cock.

And here, in this crowded carriage, a panorama of penises surrounds her. Most of them are elegantly zipped away in discreet wool-blend compartments, but Roxy has a very discerning eye. Like an expert gossip, she can fill in a lot of detail from the vaguest of outlines. The more crowded the train, the more thoroughly and diligently can she conduct her surveillance of this magnificent creature in all its fascinating variations.

Her eyes glide subtly from one to the other, noting the differences in volume and shape. Some lie to the left, others to the right. Roxy can deduce who wears what kind of under-wear by the directionality of their compass points – so to speak. Those gravitating southwards are swinging free in breezy boxers. Those curving north-east or north-west suggest the more humid atmosphere of Y-fronts.

She licks her fingertip, turns a page, as her gaze rests on a particularly well-defined specimen. The owner is in head-phones, oblivious to her penetrative stare, moving rhythmically to his own private rock concert.

This is another thing Roxy has observed. Men *rarely* notice her visual forays into the contents of their trousers. They are used to doing the watching. Their assumed power makes them vulnerable. So confident are they, she thinks, in their position as the initiators of the desiring gaze. Which female affectation or curve will temporarily hold their attention, only to be passed over for yet another? Their seeming innocence to her predilections gives Roxy a feeling of overwhelming tender-ness towards the male gender. And a paradoxical sense of power.

Could she call herself a peniologist? She sees the definition in her mind's eye, as if in the pages of a dictionary:

Peniologist: *(n)* pēnˈɒl.ə.dʒɪst/
a person engaged in the study of the male sex organ.

She giggles to herself, deciding this term is far too clinical to encompass her feelings of affection and admiration for the penis. Returning her attention to the man in headphones, she imagines unzipping his pants, and lovingly freeing his cock from its confines. Tantalizing the warm skin with her fingers, she would kiss its head hungrily, relishing how it would rise and thicken in response to her attention. A mutual adulation.

Roxy has read about cultures that openly worship the phallus: fertility festivals in Japan and Greece. Huge statues in upstanding likeness of the erect penis are paraded through streets full of intoxicated revellers. These symbols of male power and potency are showered with flowers, surrounded by dancing devotees. She imagines herself kneeling at the foot of a phallus almost twice her height to show her adoration, placing figs and flowers as an entreaty for fertility and protection. Rising, she wraps her arms around its girth, feeling its hardness not just between her thighs, but along the entire length of her body. In her mind's eye, she is permeated by an ecstatic masculine energy, and begins to dance around the statue, losing herself in the undulations of her hips, hair and skirts flying. Whirling herself into an orgasmic delirium.

Startled, Roxy realizes she has closed her eyes, and flicks them open to take in the graffiti across a window, the scuffed seat opposite. Hers is a quieter worship in more humble surrounds, though none the less devout.

Penephilia: (n) pēn-ə-ˈfi-lē-ə
a strong positive emotional view towards, or positive emotion caused by the penis. [mod. L. penilis *– of or pertaining to the penis + Gk* philia *– love of or enthusiasm for]*

She sighs. The fact that so many of them in contemporary society are hidden away on a daily basis fills her with melancholy. She would like to liberate them all. At least in the days of ancient Rome and Greece, the male member floated free under soft folds of toga. This surely must have facilitated the ease and frequency of clandestine encounters.

As the train pulls into the first inner-city station with jerky stops and starts, Roxy recalls an afternoon only a few months ago. A series of similar brakings had delivered the crotch of a man right into her delighted face. Her cheek and nose had collided with the sensations of coarse wool; through that a supple coiled softness of flesh. A hot bolt of electricity had shot from her head to her sex. Another jerk thrust him backward again just as abruptly, leaving her with a faint aroma of aftershave and a techno-music heartbeat. The unsuspecting man hadn't realized what he'd bumped into – it had all happened so fast.

It had been her wicked little secret.

Another station. More people were pouring into the carriage now, and only a few made their way out. Late trains always seemed more crowded. Smiling in anticipation, she shifts her buttocks just a little closer to the aisle as more passengers fill the standing spaces. There are women too, of course, but Roxy barely notices them. A man in Lycra bike gear gets on and makes his way down the aisle towards her. She notes the firm thighs outlined in black, then all of a sudden his backpack is nudging against her arm. She looks up, catches his eye as she moves to accommodate the bulk of his backpack.

"Sorry," he says, and shifts away from her arm, so his torso is facing her – should she care to turn her head towards him. As the train lurched into movement again, she cares. Oh my. What a deliciously three-dimensional parcel. Roxy's eyelids are fluttering as she tries to take in the details imperceptibly. It's one of those reassuringly solid versions, making up for its length with girth. She's convinced it's circumcised, and ever-so-slightly aroused. Casually, she leans down to adjust the bandage on her ankle, allowing her upper arm to brush along the front of his lower body, caressing him there again when she straightens up. Did it just twitch? Oh my . . . The corner of Roxy's mouth twitches in response as she thinks about what she might do if the carriage was more congested. She'd take her hand and cup his—

Abruptly, he moves away from her, weaving his way down the carriage, waiting at the doors for the next stop. As they hiss open and he exits, Roxy can see how many people are waiting at this station with impatient expressions. A previous train must have been cancelled.

In a flash, she rises (remembering to hobble) and finds herself on a seat flush against the carriage wall – facing directly out into the standing space. Not quite sure why she's done this, she can only trust her intuition has the spark of strategy. An older woman plonks herself down on the seat to her left, wedging a tall upmarket shopping bag in the narrow space between the seats. Roxy can only just see the top of her head over the bag with its effusive bursts of pink tissue paper. More people edge their way into the standing spaces, as there are now no spare seats. A sea of torsos, legs in pants, and skirts wades before her eyes.

Once again in motion, the train lulls her thoughts into an alluring labyrinth of images. A labyrinth with tall moss-lined walls. Dressed in only a transparent muslin tunic, which falls to her ankles, she wanders, awestruck. At each dead end, there stands a phallic deity – first there is the Indian warrior god Shiva. She kneels before his many arms, looking up at his blue outstretched tongue, mirroring the angle of his phallus. Prostrating herself, she utters a mantra in Hindu. Next, she is confronted by Priapus, the Greek protector of flocks and of bees. She is compelled this time to rub the length of his enormous erection, jutting out of his tunic. In another cul-de-sac, the Norse pagan deity Freyr beckons with his magic sword for her to honour his virile tumescence. As she bends to do so, does the marble feel somehow warm against her mouth?

Before she can confirm this, another deeper voice is calling her name, and her bare feet are pulled down a path into another alcove. And here waits Pan – cloven-footed, twisted-horned and dangerous in his decadent worship of the flesh. Roxy is wet, juices moistening her thighs. She knows what He bids. As she parts herself to the stone cockhead, preparing to move its length into her, she hears a deep laugh and watches the marble become livid flesh, like watching a crystal goblet fill with red wine.

Phallophilia: (n) fal-ə-ˈfi-lē-ə
1. *An intense fascination with, or love of, the erect phallus.*
2. *Sexual urges, preferences or fantasies involving an unusually large erect penis. [Gk* phallos *– an image of the erect penis +* Gk philia *– love of, or enthusiasm for]*

Roxy is pulled out of this fantasy by someone bumping her right shoulder. A woman, intent on her iPhone, is facing away from her, unaware of her intrusion into Roxy's personal space. And then the train is rushing through a tunnel. In the momentary darkness, Roxy squirms, throbbing and wet in her seat, realizing that each carriage-full of the object of her desire forms part of this larger phallic symbol. Each carriage a veritable cornucopia of cock. And that she herself sits in the centre of this onward-hurtling phallus. She is dizzied by the enormity of it all.

A peak-hour train has never seemed so crowded. And she has never felt so aroused. Glancing down at the newspaper, Roxy attempts to compose herself a little, as the train arrives at the second station beyond the inner city. She senses the density of bodies increasing even further. It is often at this point of congestion, Roxy has previously observed, that people insulate themselves in headphones and electronic screens, each plugged-in individual creating a tiny island of mental privacy. Roxy dons no such technological armour, preferring to keep herself wide open to sensory input.

It is then that she senses a male presence very close to her. Right in front of her face, should she decide to lift her gaze. She does, and is eye-to-zipper with a lean pair of hips, wearing grey woollen trousers. He must have an arm steadying himself on a nearby rail, as his hips are thrust slightly outward. Directly into her face. She glances left – the shopping-bag partition is still there – and to her right is the woman's skirted backside. She can't even see this man's face, as someone is wedged close to him with a huge bouquet of tiger lilies. What she can see are the tempting outlines of his cock, a mere cigarette-length away from her face. Definitely wearing Y-fronts, tending north-east.

Roxy takes a breath. *Dare she?*

Testing his receptivity, she leans slightly forward, rubbing her cheek firmly back and forth across his groin. She does it again, just so he knows it's not accidental. She senses him freeze for a moment, then he relaxes and rocks himself closer. Roxy takes hold of the zipper seam with her teeth, tugging suggestively as she leans back further in her seat, affording her more of a safety margin of privacy. His hips move with her.

No going back now. She allows herself to cup the firmness of his testicles as she deftly unzips him and eases his sudden erection up and out of the waistband. His flesh has a warm olive hue, and the head has already emerged from the foreskin. She exhales warm breath onto the tip, honing all her senses down into that small yet engrossing landscape, and takes him in her mouth. The head is as succulent as a mouthful of scallop, with that same hint of zinc and salt. She sucks at him, as her tongue descends in lazy spirals, down his shaft and up again. Looping her right hand around the outside of his thigh to hold him close, she insinuates her fingers into the cleft of his buttocks, caressing the base of his testicles with her fingertips through his trousers. He tastes of ocean and sun-warmed rock. He tastes of transgression.

The rocking of the train gives her mouth a rhythm to ride. She is lost in sensation, noting with pleasure the telltale seep of salty fluid from the tip. She tongues him there, then takes as much of him as she can into her mouth again. Her sex is warm, her clitoris an ecstatic tongue of flame. A broken sigh floats down on her from somewhere above. All she can see are orange tiger lily blooms, as her mouth is suddenly full of heat and liquid pollen. Keeping her lips tight around his length, she swallows once, twice. Full of wonder for the trust given to her by this stranger.

Siderodromophiliac: (n) sid-ər-od-rə-mə-ˈfi--lē -ak
term used for a person who finds engaging in sexual activity in trains to be highly arousing.

She is in the act of tenderly returning him to his underwear, when a hand reaches down and fumbles its way to her cheek, traces her lips' outline gently, brushes her hair off her face. He finds her shoulder, moves down her arm to her hand. With his other hand, he presses something into her palm, squeezes it shut.

Then, he is gone.

As if from a distance, Roxy hears the doors open, a station name being announced. She opens her hand to find a business card. His name, in embossed letters, seems to throb in front of her eyes.

Adam Mansgard
Pan-Optic Consultant

Odd coincidence, the presence of the word "Pan". She's never heard of such a job title. Roxy can still feel his fingers against her lips. The tenderness in his brief touch. This has never happened to her before. The pleasure she has found on these train journeys has been for her sole enjoyment, remaining at the impersonal level. Examining the card, she decides she will call the number. Identify herself. Find out why he was compelled to create the possibility of an ongoing connection, when he could easily have left it at an anonymous encounter.

She looks around her at the crammed carriage, the tired, impassive faces. In contrast, Roxy feels exhilarated, the taste of this man still on her tongue, brimful with the forbidden thrill of her *own* secret peak hour experience.

Porn Enough at Last

Jesse Bullington

Life sucks, nowadays, and so do I. The most I can say for myself is that I haven't sat on my glasses yet.

Hair like the starburst of an exploding rocket frames the tiger-girl's face, only an upside-down check-mark of a nose arresting the enormous eyes that burn into my own. A rogue canine tooth edges over the line of her pursed lips. She cups her breasts in her fingers, the flesh oozing around their edges, and from this vantage point her sharp knees rise up to bookend her bosom. She's squatting, lace-edged panties coiled around one thigh, but everything from her navel to the base of the tentacle(s?) she's riding is obscured behind an unsolvable mosaic puzzle.

There are three main ways the censors desecrated the dirty comic books filling the warehouse I raided after the world ended. The cover-ups are all pixel-based. Sometimes they'd magnify the pixels into one vague lump, sometimes they'd rotate the pixels around, and sometimes they'd scramble the color scheme. The result's the same: a blurry mess instead of hardcore fucking. Which, sure, since they mostly applied the mosaic to penetration there's still plenty of tits, ass, etc. – and you can use your imagination for the rest. It isn't the end of the world; that's *outside* my bunker.

Hentai wasn't really my bag before Armageddon; in fact porn in general was only an occasional indulgence once I got old enough to start slobbering on girlfriends and the odd boyfriend. It wasn't some judgey thing on my part – I was just so damn busy getting busy that I rarely made time for solo porn sessions . . . but I've been making up for that now.

I've also grown to appreciate the moon-eyed style of hentai, thanks to the megaload I discovered – by the time I'd carted everything back to my bunker, the hoard filled an entire room. Squeezing fifty thousand imaginary partners into a ten by ten chamber makes up for the diminished floor space, and I'd like to think that even if I hit it off well enough with one of the other survivors to invite them in, they'd be OK with sacrificing square footage for a cartoon harem. Hell, I know they would be, as the few survivors I associate with are my customers, and they're obviously hot on the library.

Any porn is hard to come by. And talkies? Forget it: you're lucky to find juice at all, let alone enough to get your own juices flowing. I heard an entrepreneur in one of the subterranean colonies has a projector/DVD player-combo wired up to some exercise bikes, and if you've got the barter you can peddle yourself to paradise. I guess I can see the appeal, especially if the seats have comfortable enhancements – and industrial-grade sanitizer for those enhancements – but only barely. I'm as masochistic as the next slob who didn't eat rat poison when the world whimpered, but working out while getting off is a touch kinky even for me.

I say that, sure, but minutes later I'm leering over my current work-in-progress. The thought of watching other people get off, even on some jury-rigged porno-fixies, has riled me up big time. I've gotten good at reading one-handed, flipping sharp pages with an adroit thumb. Then I turn the page, and my tiger-eared teenager riding the veiny hard-on of an intersex superhero goes from *Christ-that-cock-looks-good-up-her-ass* to *what-the-hell-was-I-thinking-this*-was-*vaginal*. I slump back, disappointed in myself. I scan the panels, and yeah, it's a pretty great anal scene, but flipping back confirms that I started it off as vaginal and never transitioned. Which looks semi-OK in some panels, but in others the angle is stupid-off. Back to the drawing board.

Evaluating my handiwork, I opt for a cover-up instead of

shelving the book. There weren't a lot of duplicates in the warehouse, which seems to point to it having been a collector's stash rather than a manufacturer's supply, and so the odds of me seeing this particular volume again are slim. I really like that hermaphroditic superhero's character design, too – leggy but not overly stacked, unlike most intersex characters I've found in hentai, and with a cute butch haircut – so it's time to get busy.

I line up a blank swatch over the appropriate section of the first panel in need of work, which has Tiger-girl bending over a table. Her panties are halfway down her thighs and her tail's in the air while our superhero inserts two dripping fingers into her . . . ass? Damn. I'd just assumed the censored penetration was vaginal, but the sloppy angling I'd done confirms my error. Great Overfiend's Ghost, I've denied poor Tiger-girl a taint! No woman, not even a felid mutant, has her junk *that* far back – this scene was supposed to be anal from the get-go.

Soon I have the first panel penciled in. I remove the swatch before inking it, and then move on to the next panel. And the next. And the next. My hand's cramping and my eyes are squinting. Repairing pornography is slow going, even if I can recognize the obvious improvement I've made as an artist, and even though trading the restored hentai to horny survivors from the colonies is what keeps me in chow and bathtub booze. When I'm in the zone it can be great, but I occasionally dread the work.

I only fixed the first hentai as an escape from boredom – foraging is dicey work, so I'd mostly skulk in my bunker masturbating to censored porn written in a language I couldn't read . . . until I hit on the idea of restoring the mosaic-hidden details. I'd already been slinging the as-found volumes in exchange for supplies, but after bartering a crate's worth for a draughtsman's kit, scissors, glue and a ream of paper, I set to covering up the cover-ups.

My first attempts were . . . bad. Awful. Nevertheless, the horn-dogs went nuts for 'em, and as I've gotten better I've been able to demand more for my labors. Hey, it's easier and faster than drawing a comic from scratch. And I'm not really creative enough to think up my own characters and plots, fun as it sounds.

Restoration is monotonous as hell, and despite my long-standing request nobody has yet delivered a kanji or kana dictionary so I can try to translate the text. Especially when I'm on my third or fourth round of the day, I get the hankering to know what's going on in those panels. Beyond all the fucking, I mean.

I take a break, eat, nap, and when I return to my studio the ink and glue have dried – three full pages worth, each with several swatches pasted over my previous cover-ups, so the pixilated portions are now buried under two layers of meticulously cut and illustrated penetration. If you didn't look for it, you wouldn't be able to tell where the original artwork bleeds into mine, where the line of some dead artist becomes my own, where old pole meets new hole.

My hand isn't cramped any more, and looking over Tiger-girl and her spandexed paramour jumping straight to anal puts me in a happy place, one where I can temporarily forget that it's my hours of labor down there in front of me. I rarely wear pants, because duh, and surveying the book, I slip a hand south. Honestly, anal always intimidated me in the Before Time – but nowadays the nastier the action the better.

Just then the doorbell rings and I nearly sweep everything off the table in a reflexive definitely-not-masturbating-in-here motion.

Another buzz and I catch my breath, remind myself that there are two airlocks and a decontamination chamber between me and my visitor – nobody's peeking through the curtains. Besides, I'm an independent adult who managed to survive the apocalypse – why shouldn't I be allowed to beat off in my own bunker?

I head directly to the foyer, since it's probably Park here for his weekly pick-up. I'll be going through the first airlock to drop off the hentai, which means a hazard suit, which means there's no need to put on pants before answering the door – one advantage to the end of the world.

In the foyer, I stub my toe on the quadruple-bagged parcel of repaired hentai awaiting my best customer – outside of my studio, I keep the track lighting dimmed low, conserving my solar-sapped energy for decon, climate control and showers. I eyeball the periscope-style peephole, just to make sure it's Park.

It's him, all right, the Viking horns crowning his bio-helmet unmistakable, but next to Park is another figure in a less conspicuous haz-suit.

"What the fuck?" I ask the empty foyer, since I can't very well ask Park. As if he's heard me, though, he raises a cardboard sign. It reads:

> **Let's talk. Impor-**
> **-tant. Very lucrative.**
> **Let me+partner in?**

"Hells no!" I say, shaking my head in disbelief. "As if I'd trust some grody perv-merchant!"

Again, it's like he's hearing me, because he flips the board over and on the back I see:

> **Please???**
> **It'll be fun!**

"Well, since you asked so nice," I mutter, leaving the peephole and giving him a toot of my outer alarm to acknowledge that I've seen him. Back in the studio, I grab a pen, meaning to substantially revise the missive I'd stuck to the top of his pick-up – over the last dozen transactions the notes we've exchanged have grown into letters, but if he thinks that means I trust him enough to let him inside, especially with some random goon, he's got another thing coming.

Like my mouth on his cock. His buddy's, too. I can count the number of dicks I've sucked on one hand, but right now some oral swashbuckling is sounding tasty.

Where did that come from? I ask myself, looking up from the giant "FUCK YOUUUUU" I've just scrawled over the top page of the letter. I don't know if I can trust Park not to slit my throat and steal my bunker if I let him, and yet I'm fantasizing about him! I don't know what he looks like, if he's even into what I might offer, or any of the other concerns you ought to consider before letting a stranger into your pants or your bomb-shelter. He might not even be a pervert like me; he might not consume the merchandise at all, just sell it; he might have the sex appeal of an orangutan behind his opaque face-plate . . .

But I'm going to find out. I'm shaking as I crumple up the letter-cum-brush-off and return to the foyer. I pop the outer hatch before I lose my nerve. What decided it for me was this: if Park and partner come inside, they'll shed their haz-suits in the decon chamber, and, call me a creep if you must, I know that *I* don't wear much under my suit. I can barely remember what a real person looks like in their underoos, but as I hear the outer hatch close behind them, it really sinks in that I'm about to get reacquainted with the human form.

Eventually. Decon takes forevs, so I busy myself with a rare shower, and almost get dressed before thinking better of it. They're going to be in their skivvies, at most, and I don't want to be overdressed. A tight shirt and clean underwear that shows off my best assets without seeming too obvious. As if it isn't obvious I'm not wearing anything else . . .

After they're finally through the locks and I get the beep that decon's complete, I fidget in the foyer. This is it. There's no backing out now, no way to give them the message through the decon door to put their suits back on before I re-open the airlock . . .

"Please don't kill me," I whisper, and open the door.

Park is a short dude, and his partner's a tallish woman. They're probably ten years older than me – or maybe not, these days I probably look a decade older myself. His skin's almost as black as a freshly dipped crow-quill pen, his head's shaved to the scalp, and his jaggedly handsome features evoke those of a statue some talented-but-inexperienced sculptor rushed to completion. She's less statue and more oil painting, a severe bob and sharp bangs eclipsing her plain-but-pretty-for-it face, with a few intricate freckle constellations highlighting her moonlight-pale skin.

Both are completely naked. I pretend not to notice either her full bush or his shaved package, but probably don't do a good job of it.

"Alex?" says the woman, her American accent sending a lightning bolt from my ears to my crotch. Not that I have a thing for Yanks, but just to hear another human voice . . .

"That's me," I stammer, self-conscious of my half-naked appearance – they can get away with full nude, fit as they are, but I'm pretty slack about exercise down here.

"Awesome," says the man, stepping into the foyer and offering me his hand. "Good to meet you. I'm Sajit. Park's partner."

"Park?" I shake Sajit's hand as I look to the girl. "I thought you were . . . huh."

"It's Korean – hard to put a face with a last name, I know," she says, smiling, and, to my surprise, she pounces forward, throwing her arms around me. "And hey, just going on *Alex*, I didn't know if you were a man or a woman, either – not that I'm complaining."

The hug is more stimulating than most head I've received, and when I catch Sajit smirking at me over her shoulder I blush with the heat of a megaton explosion.

"No?" I say, trying to keep cool. The things I want to do to these naked strangers is scrambling all semblance of rational thought into an incoherent blur of lecherous possibilities, and when Park drops her arms away I feel it like the amputation of a limb.

"Right, let's get down to business," says Sajit, and I nearly swoon. That we're all instantaneously on the same page is like something out of a hentai, but just as I'm about to make my move Sajit adds, "But do you, uh, have anything I can put on? I'm feeling a little exposed!"

"Ah," I say. "Sure, of course, sure."

"We really won't take long," says Park. "But we've hit on something that'll really elevate your business."

"*Our* business," says Sajit. "I mean, we've been trafficking the porn, yeah? So it's kind of all of our business, especially as—"

It's a straightforward proposal. Sex sells, obviously, and we've all done quite well by my repaired pornographies. But sex with a story sells, too, and is a heretofore untapped demographic. Their proposition is that rather than putting my hentai onto the market with just the censored sex redrawn, Park will rewrite the text that goes with it; all those blocks of kanji and kana thought-bubbles, all that unintelligible pillow talk.

"You can read 'em?" I ask, the three of us standing around my studio, Sajit stuffed into a bathrobe I scrounged up, Park wearing a T-shirt and my only other clean pair of underwear. Both are a little baggy on her, the undies riding low enough on her hips to give me a mouth-watering eyeful whether she's coming or going. "The Japanese, I mean?"

"No," she says. "But I can make up new stories. Already have, in fact – I white-out the Japanese characters, and then write new text for them in Chinese, Spanish or Arabic, depending on what settlement they're bound for."

"Oh," is all I've got, irrationally wounded at her altering my books.

"It was the obvious play," says Park, putting a book down and meeting my gaze. Her eyes are filled with more mischief than the entirety of my collection.

"Customers are busting nut and nest egg alike over 'em," Sajit says. "Charging double, triple what we used to. And we're getting special requests, orders that'll pay ten times as much as regular books."

"Oh," I say again and, out of bruising pride, pout. "Well, what do you need me for? If you're improving my crude pornos anyway, why come here and rub my nose in it?"

"Alex," says Park, stepping over and putting her arm

around my shoulder. Holy fuck does it feel good. "Your work's anything but crude. And nobody said anything about *improving*, just . . .adding another layer. There's a techie who'll pay us in pre-war whisky if we deliver a hentai that's got some schoolgirls sucking off a hairy guy we slap his name on. And a colony mayor who's got three flats of cat food for us if we supply her with a comic where a princess with her moniker gets touched on by a tentacle monster . . . so long as the tentacle monster sings Rick Astley to her."

"The Rickroll Ravisher," says Sajit, shaking his head.

"So we three work together – Sajit securing orders, you and me scouring your library here for suitable source materials. You restore the porn and I write new dialogue . . . you see where we're going?" Park squeezes my shoulder, and I nod. The weirdest thing is that I'm just as excited at the prospect of collaborating with Park as I am about the sensation of a strong, feminine arm burning into my back. This could be just the thing to get me amped about the work again, and if it pays in old school booze and tins of Fancy Feast, even better.

"Is that a yes, Alex?" asks Sajit, coming around to my other side. His robe makes it fairly obvious that his flipping through my works-in-progress has aroused more than his entrepreneurial sensibilities.

"That's a big yes," I say, eyeing the semi-erect penis straining against the terrycloth. His bulge makes me light-headed, and I quickly avert my gaze. In doing so, however, I notice Park's stiff nipples jutting slightly upward through her borrowed shirt, which doesn't exactly cool my overheating radiator. And by *radiator* I mean *genitalia*.

"We could even do some of our own, if you wanted," says Park, and for the first time she actually sounds shy, uncertain. "Porn, sure, but regular comics, too. Like, if you . . . if you liked an idea I had, you could draw everything, instead of just filling in the dirty bits in the hentai."

"Unless Alex prefers just filling in the dirty bits," breathes Sajit, his palm settling on the back of the hand Park still has on my shoulder; flesh covering up flesh covering up flesh. There's a moment of tension as I look back and forth between them, and then all three of us are laughing at the cheesiness of the set-up, the triteness of his come-on.

"I'm down," I say when our shared giggling fit wanes. "Rewriting the hentai's smart, but original stuff sounds even better – *Heavy Metal*-style or Comic Code Approved, what-evs. Let's do it all. I'm just happy you two didn't come in here to murder my ass."

Sajit seems offended. "You need to get out more. It's hardly *Fallout*. People help each other."

"Like we're going to help you," says Park, her hand creeping out from under Sajit's, leaving his on my shoulder while hers runs down my back. "He thought I should outline the proposal in my next letter, but I thought if we all met face to face it would go smoother."

"Smoother," I say, my body locking up as Park's fingers run from the base of my spine to the band of my underwear, toying with the elastic. Then she goes lower still. "I . . . are we . . . ?"

"Only if you want to," says Sajit, licking his lips as his part-ner squeezes my ass. "Me. Her. Both, preferably."

"We talked it out," says Park, her hair tickling my ear as she leans closer. "So long as you weren't too hideous. Something about your taste in porn made me think we'd all get along, regardless of whether or not the mysterious 'Alex' was man or woman, fat or skinny, young or old. We're fresh out of decon and disease-free – so, assuming you're also DF, wanna research our first collaboration?"

"So I'm 'not too hideous'?" I dryly ask Sajit. "I'm flat-tered."

"She just likes to give people a hard time," says Sajit, step-ping closer. He almost manages to add "Me too," without cracking up, but not quite, and then we're all laughing again. And, minutes later, we're all in my bedroom, awkwardly clus-tered at the edge of the bed that was always too spacious for just me. We've got a three-way hug-thing going on, taking turns kissing one another as six hands explore three bodies.

Sajit kisses me first, his coquettish tongue stinging with artificial mint. Then I kiss Park, and the unadulterated, slightly sour taste of her is even hotter than her partner's breath-mint sanitized mouth. She's an aggressive kisser, and feeling her grope one of my buttocks while Sajit brushes the other is enough to make me want to choke on her tongue. When she breaks the kiss I'm winded, and watching her turn to Sajit and give him the same treatment does little to help me catch my breath. They both watch me from the corners of their eyes as they kiss, and I swear to all the horny gods of hentai heaven that I'll never bemoan my life again.

I think that, but then everything goes straight to hell – I take off my shirt, then pop my thumbs into the waistband of my underwear, all set to seductively lower them, when I catch sight of the impossible, the unthinkable, the utterly insane state of my nethers. Or rather, I don't catch sight of anything, which is the problem: from my waistline down it's all just a blur of mosaic tiles. As I said, the light isn't great outside of my studio, but that can't account for *this*.

I blink, waiting for what has to be a hallucination to pass, for my traitorous eyes to stop censoring my own junk, but everything remains scrambled. Sajit and Park are watching me – I must look like a lunatic, gawping down into my stretched-open underwear. It's like a waking nightmare, and I enter full-blown panic mode, convinced that this is actually happening, somehow, that this isn't a hallucination . . . and if my guests notice the mosaic cloud hovering between my legs they'll split for sure, not wanting anything to do with my reality-bending genitalia.

"Um, so yeah . . ." I say, letting my underwear snap back in place. My mind races, too horny to think straight, too scared that they'll bounce if they see the censored state of my crotch . . . and then I hit on what I hope is a plausible fib: "This is super embarrassing, but yeah: I've been masturbating *way* too much recently, and, uh, I hope this doesn't gross you guys out, but I'm too sore to fool around right now. Totally out of commission."

They're both really cool about it, but before the mood gets any less sexy in here I hasten to add, "But please, you guys, can I play with you? Right now? Just, like, lay off me, but I swear if you let me help you two get off I'll never, ever ask for another favor. Please?"

"Ow!" says Park. "Stop twisting my arm already, Alex – but really, we're not in any hurry, so if you're just shy about—"

I move in, showing her how shy I am – impossible intrusion of comic-book censorship into the real world or not, I'm desperate to get better acquainted with these two.

I look back and forth between them as the three of us sprawl out on my bed, limbs overlapped, faces so close that the humidity makes my glasses fog. Sajit looks hesitant, says, "I dunno, it doesn't seem fair to—" when Park leans over and kisses me again, softer this time, yet somehow with even more evident need. Her hand snakes across my belly, and I almost tell her to move it down but again balk at what's going on in my underwear – this is a test, I tell myself, and all I need to do is get these two off, and then the horny gods of hentai heaven will lift my mosaic curse. Look, I know how stupid that sounds, but until you've found your gear disappeared just as you're at the very apex of your randiness . . .

Park's fingers leave my skin, and then I feel Sajit's stiff member pulled loose from the robe to rest against my stomach. The sensation of her knuckles rubbing my belly as she slowly tugs on his shaft makes me shudder with delight.

It's my first threesome, and it's clumsy and weird and tough to get the logistics right. After some more of the tumbled, jumbled three-way kissing and touching, though, Park directs us into position, so that I can go down on her while she continues to kiss and fondle Sajit – she stretches out with a pillow boosting her bottom up in the air, I crouch down between her legs, and he wiggles closer to better caress her pert breasts while they make out.

Crawling between her knees is a transcendental experience. I feel like a priestess in one of my comics, bowing at an altar just before the sex-demon seizes her outrageous bosom, or like one of the wet-dreaming teen boys oblivious to the lusty goddess creeping under his blankets to gobble his dick. Park's muscular legs part to welcome me as I lean closer and closer. There she is, every inch shivering in anticipation, and I nuzzle at her inner thigh. This is . . .

Oh no. Anything but *this*.

I've torn my eyes away from the crazy-hot sight of Sajit sucking on Park's breast as his hand massages the wiry copse wreathing her pubic mound, his fingers gently prodding the skin just above my destination . . . but instead of her vulva, with flesh as light as my preliminary graphite shading, or perhaps as dark as India ink cross-hatching, I see only an impossible puzzle of piebald blocks. The familiar mosaic tiles extend from the pillow beneath her all the way up to the top of her pubes. Sajit's an inch or two above where her clitoris must be, but even still his fingertips blur into vagueness as they enter the pixel cloud.

I close my eyes and count to ten, but it doesn't go away, and I wonder just how insane I've gone. Looking up, neither Park nor Sajit seem to have noticed anything amiss; his lips are off her breast and back at her mouth, the abandoned, spit-slickened nipple standing in relief. Are Park and Sajit even here, or am I hallucinating them both, the same as I must be hallucinating the mosaic tiles over her groin, and my own?

To hell with this. Hentai-sterical blindness or not, the one thing I'm good at is restoring those lovely details that censorship has hidden. I go slow, because even the preliminary pencil line should be as tight and straight as humanly possible, and I kiss my way up her left thigh, into the cloud. At first it's maddening, to have entered the nexus of scrambled pixels – it's even worse than not seeing anything, to have everything there but be so mixed-up, but then, through the miasma of jumbled pixels, I see the goose-pimpled skin of her inner thigh coalesce in puckered-lip-shaped patches. I exhale with relief, the current of my breath reverberating off her still-invisible pussy and bringing me her faintly tangy scent. I duck lower, hands finding her thighs, and begin, carefully, patiently, meticulously, to bring her into focus.

I quickly define her perimeter, drawing the tip of my tongue up one side of her outer labia, skirting the ridge of her clitoral hood, and then back down the other side. I trace my initial sketch with growing confidence and pressure. She squirms, and I happily draft out the intricate interior line-work, establishing borders between minora and majora, between crown and queen. It's been a long time, and I have to remind myself to frequently withdraw my tongue to dip it in the inkwell of saliva I keep behind my teeth. After I reapply moisture to the tip of my instrument, I move back in, but this time she bucks forward, and I close my eyes as I press my tongue into her.

When I open my eyes the rest of the mosaic is gone, the pixel cloud replaced with the cumulus of her jet-black pubic hair, stirring in tandem with the thrusts of my tongue and the exhalations escaping my nose. I slip my tongue out and drag it up to her swelling clit, then back down again to overlap the finger – and then fingers – I set to working on her increasingly slippery entrance.

"Fuck yeah," Park groans, inspiring me to redouble my oral efforts.

I'm so focused on my work that I don't notice Sajit slide down the bed next to me, until a hand settles on one cotton-covered buttock, his fingers inching their way beneath my underwear. Then Park says, "Let him lick your ass, Alex – please? Let him lick you while you lick me?"

"I'll be careful." His eager voice reaches the ear that isn't muted by Park's thigh. "Promise I'll stay back here, only use my tongue. Unless you ask for more."

I'm lying flat on my stomach, and by way of answer clumsily wiggle my ass. I'll have a sore neck tomorrow, and won't mind a bit. There's a moment of fear that my censorship cloud extends back between my legs, but at this point it's a risk I'm willing to take – I need *something*, and bad. He pulls my underwear down until the waistband is snared on the base of my cheeks and then his lips warm my tailbone, his fingers kneading and then spreading my ass as he slowly kisses his way down my crack. His breath blasts me, and I can feel every set of muscles in the neighborhood contract as his tongue teases the top of my anus. He's much slower and gentler with me than I've been with Park, who's cursing up a sexy storm as she watches her partner rim me.

"Fuck yes," Park says. "Oh, fuck, I can't wait to fuck you and Sajit and watch you two fuck and fuck, that's good! Less fingers, please, and more clit. I'm close, Alex, close!"

Again, not much real-life experience with anal beyond a few aborted attempts with overzealous boys and the odd girl, but I am *loving* Sajit's attentions. He takes his time, melting me with his strokes, and when his thick tongue actually penetrates me a little, I gasp, the sensation so overpowering I momentarily stall out. Momentarily. I'm self-conscious, of course, it being my butt and all, but then the awesomely rude sensation sets me to licking Park even harder.

"Fuck," Park grunts. "You two got me so fucking good. You like him licking you, Alex? You love it?"

In answer, I plant my free hand on her thigh and rock her backward to get at her ass. Fumbling around until I've got my expert page-turning thumb atop her vulva, I tenderly sweep my digit over her clit as I bring my mouth into position, panting over her perineum. She gasps, but dutifully keeps herself rocked back as I flit my tongue out and begin circling her dark, delicately crenulated button. After making a few laps, I press into her now-twitching asshole, the exhilarating, almost-bitter taste of her bottom driving me to push my own further into Sajit's face. I want to confess everything, to beg Sajit to start playing with my front as well as my back, even at the risk of his being confused by a cloud of pixels . . . but that would mean taking my mouth off of Park. No fucking way.

My tongue goes deep into her, his tongue goes deep into me, and my pelvis reflexively thrusts forward, causing my throbbing crotch to rub against a hummock of sheets that have bunched up between my legs. I grind harder into the neither too-pliable nor too-firm mound of bedding, burying my tongue teeth-deep in Park's ass. Her glistening contours fill my vision, her entrancing scent making my mouth water all the more; her face and everything else are lost to perspective, my thumb a blur over her clit at the top of the panel. This is really happening, I think, and then it is, the event horizon of my own orgasm crossed before I even realized I was close.

"Don't stop!" Park wails, and I realize I've done just that, distracted by my own imminent collapse. I re-moisten my thumb in my mouth and then speed it back into action as I commence tongue-fucking her ass for all I'm worth. I even manage to get my other hand into play, sliding two fingers into her pussy just as our orgasms hit. It would be something to see, I bet, her face scrunched up, hair plastered to her cheek, but that's on the next page and back here I can't see anything beyond the blur of her convulsing lower body as my own conclusion arrives.

It's like the first time I came: a *where-the-fuck-did-that-come-from* supernova. The craziest part is that while my junk played a small role, rubbing against the snarl of sheets, the real source, I'm sure, is Park. I mean, obviously I have Sajit's tongue up my ass, which at least makes some kind of sense as to producing an orgasm, but it's really more like electricity passing from her into me, frying all my wiring, a power surge that effects the circuits of all my overtaxed organs ... but yeah, the tongue up my ass probably helps, too.

It's too much. I moan in protest, rolling away from Sajit and Park, closing my eyes in a vain attempt to restore order to my brain. Everything's been censored again, the whole world a puzzle, and I shudder with satisfaction as well as fear.

The unmistakable sound of sloppy cock-sucking brings me back to reality. Turning over, I see Sajit standing beside the bed, Park kneeling on a pillow at his feet. There's another mosaic cloud obfuscating where his hard-on and her bobbing head meet, and as always, I wonder what the fuck's the point, obvious as it is what they're doing. My strength flows back into me at the promise of cracking that code with my tongue, of unscrambling the cover-up – I just know that Park looks pretty as a picture with a mouthful of Sajit's cock, and I want to see.

"That looks like fun," I say, scrambling off the bed. My loins throb happily as I settle onto the floor beside her. I can hardly wait to solicit their help in getting rid of my own pixel fog, but fair is fair, and right now Park and I are both one up on Sajit.

Park pulls her head back from the cloud, grinning at me with drool-glossy lips. "Bet he'd taste better if he'd stuck it up your ass first. OCD bastard's too clean for his own good."

"That's just great," says Sajit, smiling down at us. "Very nice."

"You're gagging for it, huh Alex?" Park asks me. Tells me. "Show us how bad you want it."

Park grabs a handful of my hair and playfully guides me into the cloud, getting me all steamed up again. The obscuring nature of the mosaic no longer frustrates but entices, now that I know how easily the puzzle is solved. I'm close; I can smell his sweat, her spit, and then she gently tugs my head to the side.

Sajit's still-moist head brushes my ear, his length rapping against my cheek, insistent as a pervy stranger knocking at my airlock, seeking a lewd shelter from an over-sanitized wasteland. I let him in, erasing the cloud, restoring shape to the shapeless, providing porn for the pornless.

Sucking dick, in other words.

The three of us are going to make such sweet smut together.

Turns out, life is pretty good, even at . . .